Sulamar: War at Sea

Part 2: Battle

by

J.M.Cressy

ISBN 978-1-958327-03-6

eurthantianpress.com

By the same author:

> One People, One Duty
> Sulamar Pt 1: Portents Underway
> Sulamar Pt 2: Battle

Acknowledgements

Many thanks to A. K. Farrell and
C. Okumoti for help with editing.

Much appreciation goes to the forums of
Ships of Scale (shipsofscale.com) and
Model Ship World (modelshipworld.com),
as well as the works of John McKay and
other authors, without which my magical elf
ships would be much less sound. Elf magic
can only take one so far.

Note about the Irish language:

The Irish (Gaeilge) used for in world Irish
adjacent cultures is <u>a mix of Modern Irish
and neologisms, *as Gaeilge*, created by the
author</u>. In a world where elves exist and
have regular contact with humyns, elves are
called "fairies", or Sídh/síoga by the Gaels.

Otherwise, every effort has been made to
use the language accurately.

Ar aon nós, is liomsa aon bhotúin.

Do na daoine eile:

Go raibh míle maith agaibh.

~Is cuimhin liom an conradh~

Contents

MAPS

Ta Amiantal ~ The Mother Continent

(2 pages)

Erdro Sulani Tagathtal ~ The Federation

Fleet Positions

City-Ship~Inboard Works

MAP OF THE
MOTHER CONTINENT
TA AMIANTAL

circa 6016 YL (Year of Lots)

Miles

JMC©2022

RAGOTHYN
(*ragon Fields*)

RONEL BAY

NORTH

AL-SWENTHIA
Steppe Tribes
(humyn)

THE
SHARMAIN
VALE

DRAGON SEA

SEA OF AZHINAZU

NOMCLAR

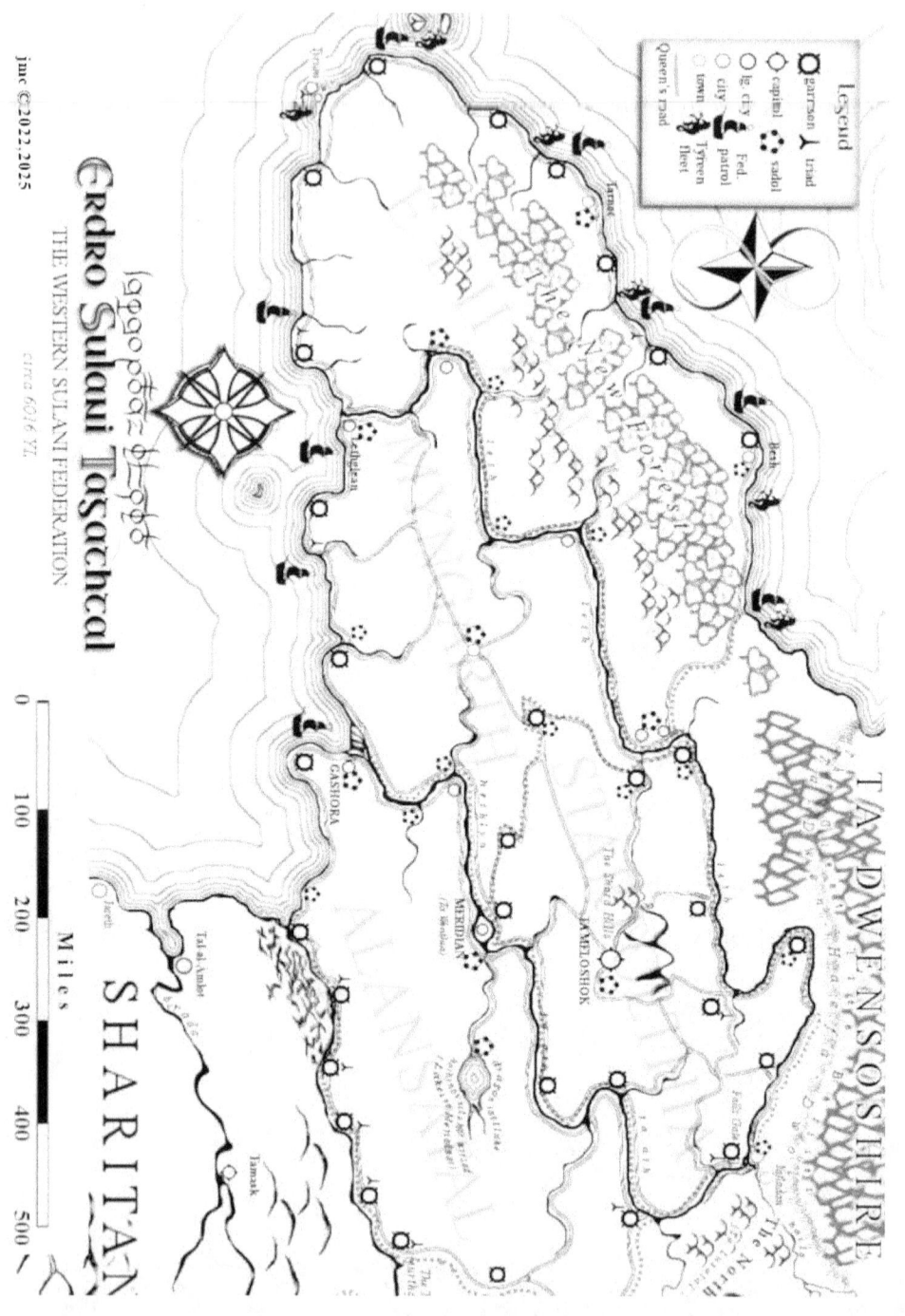

Legend
⊙ garrison 人 triad
◇ capital ⚘ sadol
○ lg city
○ city Fed. patrol
○ town Tytreen fleet
Queen's road

Erdro Sulani Taşachcal
THE WESTERN SULANI FEDERATION

circa 6016 YL

jmc ©2022-2025

0 100 200 300 400 500
Miles

SHARITA'N

TADWENSOSHIRE

Fleet positions before the battle

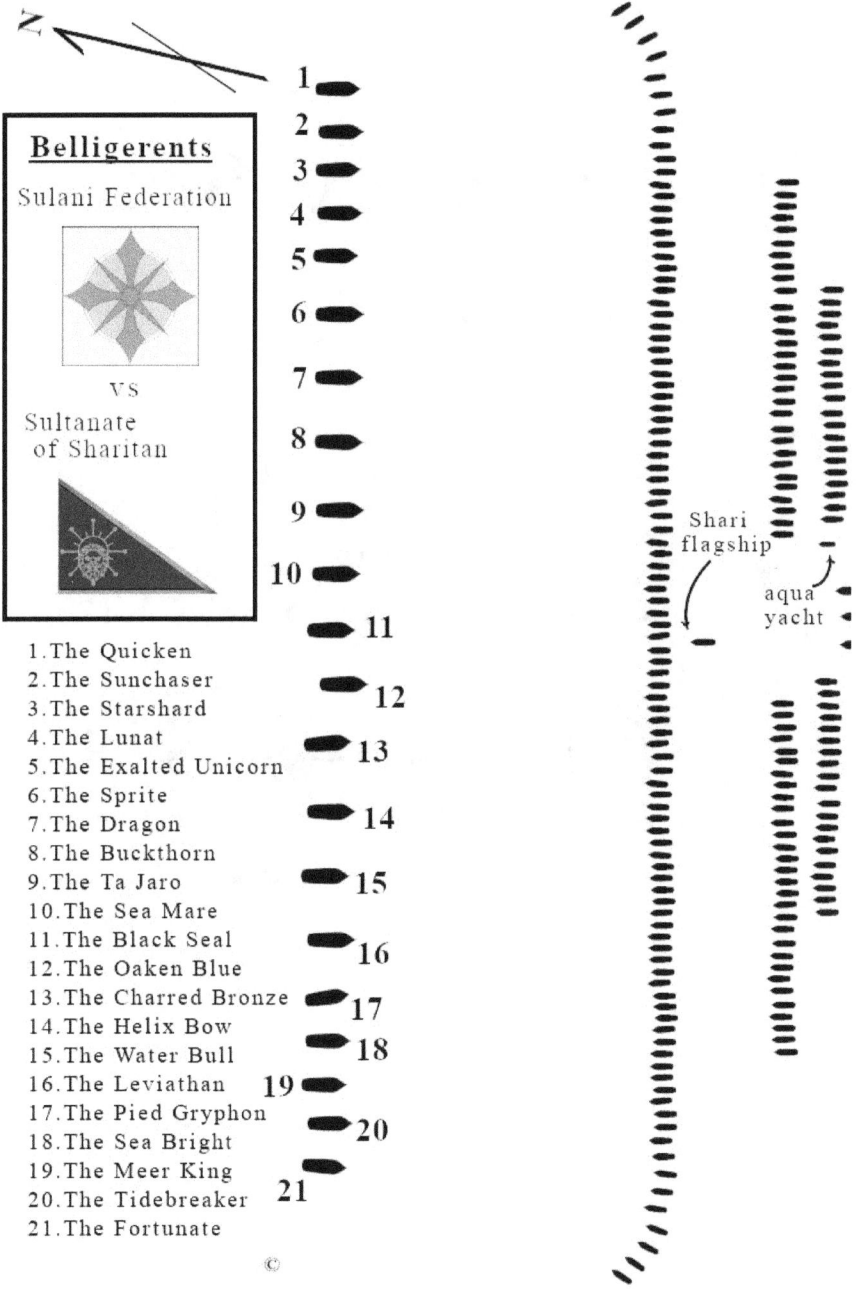

Belligerents

Sulani Federation

vs

Sultanate
of Sharitan

1. The Quicken
2. The Sunchaser
3. The Starshard
4. The Lunat
5. The Exalted Unicorn
6. The Sprite
7. The Dragon
8. The Buckthorn
9. The Ta Jaro
10. The Sea Mare
11. The Black Seal
12. The Oaken Blue
13. The Charred Bronze
14. The Helix Bow
15. The Water Bull
16. The Leviathan
17. The Pied Gryphon
18. The Sea Bright
19. The Meer King
20. The Tidebreaker
21. The Fortunate

Shari flagship

aqua yacht

Tyreen City-Ship

Inboard Works

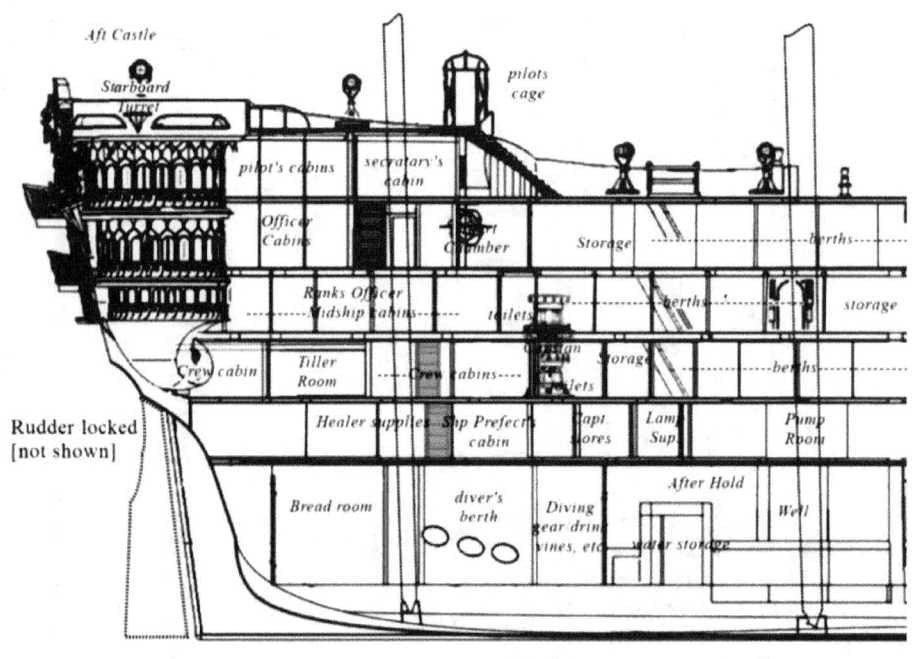

For details by deck
go to Illustations in the back
after the Glossary

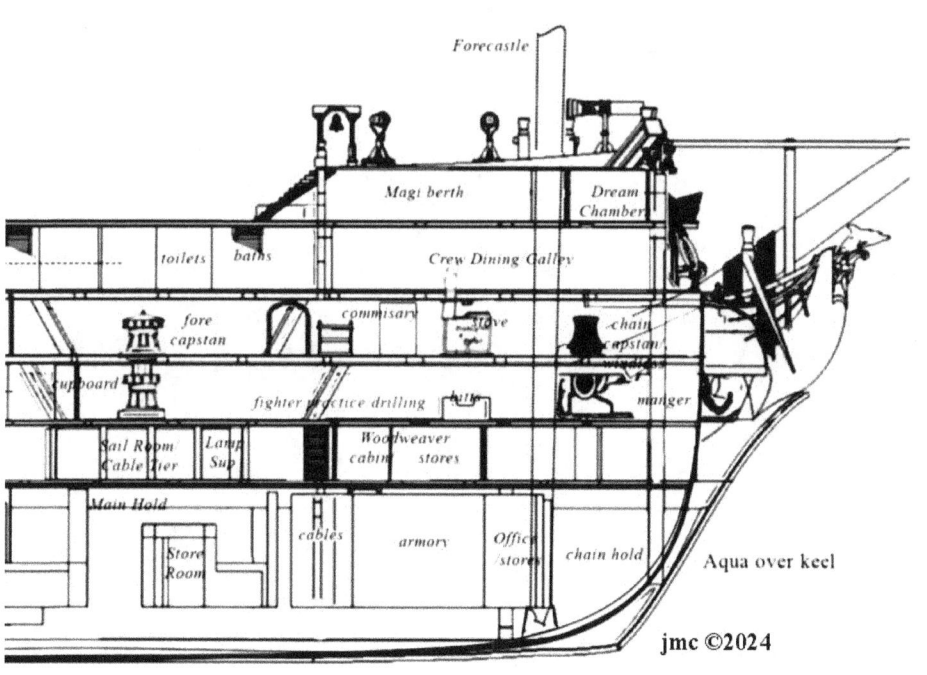

Prologue

The Sultan's Man

Sharitan, 5 years ago

Sharitan was a harsh land with a harsh ruler. Perhaps that was just, as the Ever Sky intended. It was certainly what the priests of the ancient god of rains claimed. Once these were superstitions of the Bedu peoples from the rocky hills, alien to the culture of the Zoroaster Fars. The Fars who inherited the gloried Tamask, the greatest city in all the Fertile Basin, greater even than the Indus kings, their decadent jungle empires a thousand years long past decayed. The Fars had been the victors of many wars, rising above the vying kingdoms of Lin and Alon, and, ultimately, with a combination of brutality and luck, simply outlasted their rivals. But their culture too was falling before the new enthusiasm of the Ever Sky. A Bedu holy man, a prophet in a desert full of prophets, had the luck, or the curse, to also be an adept war leader. Decrying the Vardashi, he inspired a revolution so that in only a few generations the culture of Tamask shifted from open forums with men and women mixing freely, to a society where modesty was obsessed to the point women were compelled to wear the veil and any man desiring advancement did well to keep his hair cut, preferably wound with a turban. Clerics of the Ever Sky were determined to root out paganism, driven to purify the culture of Vardashi influence, never mind the Vardashi could not care less what humyn did. But a humyn living under the Sultan had to care; his life depended on it, and his family, especially the disenfranchised women, depended on his support and protection, without which they were lost to wretchedness. These clerics now had the Sultan's ear, the Sultan who himself was of old Fars nobility. Yet having exploited the desert revolution for his gain, he now embraced the theistic extremes of modesty and wore the turban. Thus it was wise that any man who wished to curry favor with the Sultan adopt these beliefs, even if only for show. Hadi Parviz was such a man.

It was just past dawn, the dark of night giving way to the beginnings of a blazing blue sky that the sun would dominate , baking the already dry and broken rock as it had done for generations of Hadi's people. They said once the land had been green with forests and fields of grasses, and Tamask, the Sultan's city, lush with hanging gardens in even the humblest of houses. But those days were long past, their rulers dust. It was a harsh sun that basked the land of Sharitan now. Water had to be coaxed from mountain fed rivers, with the skills of engineers, flowing into painstaking irrigation canals worked by the humble, both freeman and slave. The Bedu who still lived in the wilds had their oases, every village a well; a town perhaps several, but they were all at the mercy of the rains to feed the fields and the hidden water below ground. Only the wide sea had water enough to quench the yearning all men had to feel their thirst sated. But of course one could not drink from the sea: like a temptress, it drew a man to her but was deadly in ways he could not fathom. Hadi found it an apt metaphor for his fate.

Hadi of the Sea, his mother had called him, and the sea, hidden just out of sight by a rocky hill, always drew him. It was from there his father came, and this place in particular where his father had met his mother over twenty summers ago, in the Vardashi Port of Djinn, just outside the walls of Jareth. The city Jareth had once been a jewel of trade, but the Sultan's wars in the south seas made folk wary of lingering too long on the unprotected outcrop of land perched on the south side of the bay of Jeddah. The Sultan reserved his defenses for the port city of Tal-al-Amlot, where the river Barada poured into the Sharitan Gulf fifty miles to the east. There, on the northern shores, a fleet of tri-oars rested, always ready to be sent forth to do the Sultan's bidding, raiding the lands and nations south for cargo, tribute and slaves. Jareth, being so exposed, would bear the brunt of revenge from pirates, either those who fled the Sultan's service or alien ships without scruple. Now the shores of Jareth only served local fishermen and Vardashi.

The people of Jareth had a conflicted view of the Vardashi: a tall gold skinned people with brilliant blond hair who seemed to work without tiredness even through the hottest part of the day when the wise man slept. Or, elsewise, the sky-blue creatures who swam in the sea as if one with it. The most extraordinary thing about these Vardashi sailors were they were women. This would have offended many except they brought gold to buy many things: oranges, lemons, dates and spices, as well as cotton prints and diverse trinkets. Craftsmen of the city made curios for export, simple figures of driftwood or clay, straw and cloth dolls, of mediocre manufacture but hungered after for their exoticness. Only a fraction of these products made it to the bazaars in Tamask. Hadi had always wondered at the industry and comfortable wealth of Jareth and now understood: all this was made for sale in Vardashi lands. They also traded medicine and tonics unheard of even in the Sultan's wisest houses. And when the Vardashi were in port, no pirate dared to pull into harbor for the deadliness of Vardashi magic at sea was known by reputation. So the locals did not question the blessings that came from the sea however strange their form.

"There, you see the gate, *agha?*" the boy said to Hadi as they stood outside the walls of Jareth. "It may be open, it may not. Today there is no trade. When there is all of this is covered with tents. Once all were allowed to enter. Then someone offended a Vardashi and they raised a wall across all passages. They may let you in, they may not. May the Al-ahat watch over you."

The boy, a stable hand from the travel house where Hadi lodged, waited only long enough for his coin before scampering back to the shelter of the streets of Jareth. Hadi set out over the flat field of sea grasses and sand that separated the gates of Jareth from the Port of Djinn.

As Hadi walked in the growing heat, scorpions and other small creatures scattered before him. He knew he cut an impressive figure, his black robes accented in gold astrological symbols and the magics of alchemy in fashion at court. Just shy of twenty summers he was a favorite of the Sultan, though he was not a magi, a wise man of the court, his head wrapped in a simple blue turban, not the black taq covered with symbols of alchemy. It wasn't just because he had no beard and never would. He was far too young and they were too jealous. For Hadi had exposed their magic as slights of hand and tricks of the eye, while Hadi offered the knowledge of true alchemy, not a frivolous quest for gold from dross, but the methods of distilling sweet water from brine, making the best cut of sail to catch the wind, what to mix with sand to make the best glass, and so much more. Some said the Sultan was vain and stupid. Hadi knew this was not true. The Sultan had a clever mind, but no patience. Pampered from his youngest years, His Eminence did not even comprehend what he lacked. Instead he used those around him ruthlessly for his ends. Hadi understood. For he too had his own ends and he would be as ruthless as he himself needed.

As he crossed the flat barren field, his thoughts turned to his mother's dreams. She had dreamed constantly of what had been, what might have been, and her regret and longing for his true father leaving. They had comfort but little status; because of his blue cast skin and finely pointed ears Hadi was was cursed as Djinn, and shunned by the other boys who called him "goat eared". Hadi the goat eared Djinn. While they were educated as befitted sons of their station, he was ignored by the learned, then mocked for the very ignorance they forced on him. They did not know his mother knew the secret of letters, forbidden to women. How she learned Hadi would not know for years. It was the greatest gift she could have imparted, his letters and mathematics. Thus when his time of majority came they were amazed he wrote well, spoke with eloquence, understood the poets and wise men, and was conversant with the knowledge of scholars. Then it was said then he was blessed by wisdom of the Al-ahat, the Lord of the Ever Sky, his blueish hue a blessing from heaven. Hadi did not disabuse anyone of this. By then he knew to be seen as blessed by Al-ahat was the quickest path to power. The secret of his birth he would keep to himself: Hadi's sire was a Vardashi from the sea. Thus his reason for coming to the Port of Djinn: to seek the answers that haunted him.

A wall of the finest cut and set stone had been built to extend the native rock, making a barrier to further passage. The stone was white, sparkling with mica flecks in the brilliant sunlight, his shadow cast over the smooth surface by a lazy sun still in the east. Where this stone was quarried was a mystery as was its make, every block fitted perfectly together. Perhaps Hadi would examine it as he left and engineer another wonder to amaze the Sultan, buying himself more favors and privileges. The gate was an iron bound door in a short tower with a narrow window, all graceful but simply decorated with spirals and strange leaves. He saw no guard. When Hadi raised his hand to hammer on the door, a voice in Shari rang out high above:

"State your business traveler, friend or foe?"

The words were heavily accented and the sound of bees surrounded him, though there were no flowers or skeps. Mother had explained this was the

Vardashi mind challenging a stranger like in a tale one told children. So Hadi replied in kind:

"I am Hadi Parviz az Daria. I come from the Sultan's court to seek knowledge of those who would speak within. I know you not, so do not claim friendship. Yet neither have you done me wrong so I do not seek enmity."

There was no answer at first. Then the door opened inward, the voice saying: "Enter in peace. But betray our hospitality and your life is forfeit. By sunset you must be gone."

Hadi bowed, deeply. "You honor me and I will abide by honor in–"

In bowing a figure had caught Hadi's eye, half buried in the sand and dust a stone's throw from the gate. Mummified by time, it sat, legs twisted under as it had fallen, bones still black, charred by Vardashi fire. How old it was, weeks or months, it was impossible to tell. Obviously it had been left as a warning, for what crime Hadi would never know. He shivered violently, his charmed words forgotten. He was made starkly aware he had no true authority here and the Sultan could not protect him.

"I will abide by your law," he finally finished, tearing his eyes from the sad corpse.

The door still stood open, just enough for him to pass.

"Well, enter if you're going to," the voice said, impatient and much less theatrical.

Hadi slipped through the gap quickly, lest in his hesitation the time for magic would pass and the door vanish. No sooner than he entered was the gate shut firmly, making little sound beyond a solid thump. Then Hadi quailed for he was face to face with a tall Vardashi warrior, gold eyed and gold haired, skin the hue of the lightest warm ocher. This one was as tall as any of the Sultan's guards, but wearing only a little armor to reinforce a heavy tan coat. Long locks flowed like threads of sunlight from under a helmet of bright metal. Hadi longed to gaze on its mirror-like qualities that whispered of great strength bound by secret magic. Not even the best iron had this look. But the tall one, taller than Hadi, was forbidding, a force around them strong enough to repel the weak of heart. Also to be marked was the sword sheathed at the guard's belt, long and straight like the ancient swords of the Indus kings; perhaps Vardashi preferred to stab rather than cut.

In the warrior's other hand was a long length of metal, shimmering in the sun like a gold dart. Hadi might guess it was a spear. If so it could do little damage as it was. Yet Hadi felt it was dangerous. In fact a general aura of danger and unwelcome seemed to surround him, and in his ears the sea whispered, wordlessly warning him to beware.

~Move along, for Sul's sake! ~ a voice spoke in his mind.

Hadi started with surprise, and started again as the Vardashi rocked back, eyes widening ever so slightly. Hadi understood: their surprise was mutual his mind had heard.

The next moment the Vardashi's face hardened, stepping back so that Hadi could go on his way. Feeling blessed to be alive so far, he strode quickly forward to hide a new fear: he knew by the same instincts he inherited from his father, this Vardashi was a woman.

This fact terrified Hadi the most for it was not a world he knew. It wasn't that he was ignorant of the Queens of the Sun and Sea that ruled over their men with magic. But the idea was so alien in Sharitan, that, when thought of at all, images of emboldened unveiled harlots striding through the streets, holding chained men like slaves was the closest any Shari man could fathom. Hadi furtively looked back at the Vardashi warrior, returning to a shadowed gatehouse at the base of the tower. She was indistinguishable in form from a tall vigorous youth on the brink of manhood, for of course she had no beard. That a woman could be the equal of a man, even without Vardashi magic, was not something Hadi had ever imagined.

And as he walked the narrow street opened into a small harbor village, and there were more Vardashi. Not warriors. Hadi would guess merchants, and others in trades, even a stable keeper, though whether a lowly hand or the owner of the concern Hadi could not guess for all Vardashi seemed to wear the finest made clothes, free of wear or stain. The stable keeper was tending two of the most beautiful horses Hadi had ever seen. They were not fine show creatures, nor light steeds for racing or messengers, but powerful beasts for farm work or pulling wagons, as Hadi guessed. Yet their coats shined, matching like even the best of the Sultan's steeds. Bridle-less, they seemed to move at one with the Vardashi's will. One horse suddenly stared at Hadi, brown intelligent eyes curious at this odd intruder. But the Vardashi whistled low, and, after a half prance of rebellion, the horse followed into the stable. Oh, Hadi could be rich if he could breed such horses!

Hadi became aware he was standing in the middle of the only street in the harbor village. He did not worry over much. It was early and not many Vardashi were active. To the left of the gate, past the wall and rocks separating the Port of Djinn from Jareth, was a large stable, next to it a building that rose as high as two stories, and extending down most of the street. This Hadi guessed was a warehouse for goods to be received or shipped. The warehouse ended just before the quay. No ships rested currently, though there was the prow of one boat in the distance. Beyond the sun glimmered off waves rolling to the western horizon. It was said in the far west a pale sallow people lived, savage and primitive, in a land of eternal damp and darkness. No sailor went in that direction, the direction of death.

On the right, north side of the street, were several buildings smaller than the warehouse, the largest clearly a public establishment. Hadi had seen it many times in his mother's dreams: the peaked arches of the windows and door not dissimilar to the arabesque architecture of the temples dedicated to Al-ahat. Unlike the temples, decorated with rich brick and tile, the frames were wood, bent and twisted by some magic as if grown, windows set with glass perfectly with shutters to fit, gables angled and steep like ancient Indus mountain houses. The walls, white like the walls outside, were smooth and solid, perhaps washed, but the whiteness had a glassy sheen and to Hadi's touch was as cool as a winter mountain spring. The building was simple and graceful, with no ornamentation beyond its sound construction. The shadowed windows had an aura of luminescence. Though this place had no domes or spires, it felt like a temple and seemed to hum with life. Hadi's hand shook with excitement as he reached for the bronze latch on the door. He'd come so far, had waited so long. A shiver made him look about, worried his presence into this place was forbidden. Yet while more Vardashi walked the ways, few marked him. To them he was less than a jackal, only a threat to the unwatched flock, to be marked but otherwise unheeded unless he caused offense. He was reminded of the twisted mummified remains. Then Hadi firmly put the memory aside. He would do nothing to incur Vardashi wrath. They were strange, their women unsettling, but were always as good as their word, be it good or ill. Hadi pulled the door open and entered.

The coolness within was a surprise, as was a brightness that seemed to fill the center of what was clearly a traveler's inn, but nothing like any inn Hadi had visited. Before him on the right was a serving bar, behind which were barrels and bottles of all sizes and colors. Potions Hadi first thought, but he had to be mistaken. It would be wine and spirits for which all Vardashi and Djinn were known as expert crafters of. Perhaps that was why high clerics of Al-ahat warned against excess, lest the mind become befuddled by magics. The wood on the bar and in fact used throughout to house was pale blond, warmly oiled and finely crafted. So finely, Hadi marveled at the lack of nails or dowels, the wood joined as if it had, like the window frames, been grown or woven by magic. Which Hadi had to admit was probably the case. The tiled floor was a more familiar creature, well made but the craft of clay and grouting needed no phantasmal explanation. The tiles made a curious pattern of a stars within threads that swirled helix-like around them, repeated black on yellow as they spread under tables of aged oak, set high to accommodate benches and chairs. The commons room spread out to the left of the door, west and north, where the wall bowed out in a semi circle, windows overlooking the now silent sea, sunlight glimmering and leaping on undulating waves. Beyond it was so very quiet. Hadi glanced around taking tentative steps forward. There was not a man or woman to be seen.

The light on his robes made him glance up, and he marveled at what he had only known from his mother's tales: parts of the roof were set with windows that had wondrous magic that charmed the light of the sun to come within. And so it seemed Hadi stood under sunlight at noon, though midday would not come for several hours. Inadvertently he found himself smiling. He could even feel the light. He had always been able to feel the light, but he was not its master.

"Welcome, traveler," a musical voice said in Shari. "How may I be of service?"

Hadi started, snapping his head first around, lest he be taken unawares, then facing the voice. A tall figure in flowing pale linen robes accented with gold trim stood in the corner of the room opposite the door near the bar. Be-

hind him was a stair. It was only through his mother's tales that Hadi did
not make the mistake of thinking this was a woman. For the man was beautiful as few women were seen, and not just because of the custom of the veil.
His hair was strands of sunlight and pale flax, his warm skin a darker tone
than the warrior maiden who guarded the gate, his eyes like the thinnest
hammered gold, that caught the light even in the shadows where he stood.
He also seemed to have a faint aura of light around him and his ears were
just like Hadi's, accented and fine, surely never hidden by the folds of a turban. And though his voice was a high tenor, it carried with subtle force.
The sound of the sea slowly returned, washing against Hadi's awareness;
perhaps a window had been opened.

Hadi bowed deeply once, then stood straight. "I am grateful to be received in this Vardashi house. I have traveled far to learn certain matters of
my kin."

The Vardashi looked at Hadi and the sound of the sea grew. Hadi shivered. There was magic, but whether it was good or ill, he could not tell. He
did feel oddly the draw of passion, as if he'd spied a woman just at the moment she clutched her veil during a gust of wind. A hesitant stirring of the
loins that made Hadi deeply averse. Could it be that the man looked so
much like a woman Hadi had become confused within himself? Was this
proof of the perversity of the Vardashi mind that had even corrupted one of
their greatest generals in ages past?

"I am uncertain how I could be of assistance," the man said. He stepped
like a dancer off the last stair, gliding to the bar as if preparing to serve. "Do
you desire drink?"

Hadi shook his head. "Do not take offense, but it is said to drink with a
Vardashi is dangerous."

The man smiled and it seemed his face was filled with the light of the
sun. "Cambrians have similar tales: to come to our lands one must never
take food or drink or one is doomed to stay forever. I assure you, immigra-
tion for humyn is hardly that easy and you have nothing to fear from my
wine."

Hadi was wary of Vardashi wine even though he felt the truth that he was
indeed safe. How he couldn't explain, but he could always hear falsity in
words.

"I trust your word, yet I am unsettled."

The Vardashi looked at him closely, then sighed with a nod. "You have twin passions and feel overwhelmed."

"Twin passions?"

"You do not know? I would not discomfit you further, but I only mean to observe your soul is taken with both mothers and men."

Hadi shook his head, terror lurking at the edge of self knowledge. There were some things a man did not need to know of himself.

"Forget it," the Vardashi said. "It is not important. What drink do you desire?"

"Do you have coffee?" Hadi asked hopefully. He had not taken any that morning is his eagerness to come to this place.

"Alas, no," the man said taking two fine crystal goblets and crossing Hadi's path, striding to where the windows overlooked the sea. It was then he saw several carafes of glass full of water. "Come and sit," the man said, taking one of the carafes to a table nearby. "The water is sunblessed. It is not often one meets a Shari aelg."

Hadi walked carefully to join the man, still wary. He had to wend between high tables and chairs of the sort only found in palaces or temples. Even in some vassal estates the custom of cushions on an elevated dais was preferred. But here every high table had several seats clustered around, every Vardashi a king or priest even in a humble inn. At the table the Vardashi indicated, Hadi watched how the man maneuvered the seat away from the table to sit; Hadi mimicked him exactly. It felt odd to have the soles of his shoes to flat against the floor and yet be at ease. Water flowed from the carafe, crystal clear into the cut glass goblets as the Vardashi poured. Hadi remembered what he had said. Before he could say another word the Vardashi's gold eyes locked with his own.

"You come with many questions," the man said. "I am called Telshorn. This house is my concern under the aegis of the Federation. Drink and ask what you will."

Hadi lifted the goblet and drank.

The water was like no other he'd tasted. Not chilled, but cool and tasting something of the light around them. He only took half, wanting to savor it for as long as possible.

"I am Hadi Parviz," Hadi finally said. "Or Hadi az Daria, as my mother called me.: Hadi of the Sea. You called me aye-lg? What does that mean?"

"It means you were birthed or begat of my race. Vardashi, or as we say, elfyn. Your ears though you try to hide them under a turban must be accented like mine as I see your brows betray you. And there is something Blue that colors your sun tanned hue."

The sounds of taunting boys echoed from years past: Hadi the goat-eared Djinn. Even the memory made Hadi shiver with old shame. Their hate was undisguised and he knew they would have killed him in his youth if they could have escaped retribution. Only his father's station had given him protection. Whatever else happened Hadi was grateful for that. But that man had not sired him. Telshorn had confirmed what Hadi already knew: his sire was Vardashi. Yet Hadi was uncertain of the details.

"My mother talked often of my true sire. But he was nothing like the Vardashi I see here. I know his form well: he was tall, long of limb yet strong in his way, his hair, long black curls unbound, like a prophet from the desert, his eyes the blue of an oasis lake. He came on a ship from the North and left by the same fashion. His name was Linastola and he is a prince of the land of Meridian."

Telshorn's brow furrowed slightly. "Your mother told you this?"

Hadi opened his mouth to answer, then thought carefully. He never confided in any soul except his mother his skill with dreams, that she had shared her memories. It was true Linastola wore no crown or turban, nor any other signs of office. But he held himself princely, with confidence. Only now Hadi considered perhaps he'd made an error.

"My mother was a humble woman. She would not have boasted of such a thing, especially as she was wed to a respectable man of the Sultan's court."

"I see. Many souls pass through during the trade season. Some match the description of Linastola, which you should be aware is not that uncommon a name. Your sire was most definitely elfyn, for Meridian is a province of the Sulani Federation. And while Meridian indeed has a male provincial ruler, his name is not Linastola. I would gently suggest your mother misunderstood him in some way."

Hot anger shot through Hadi, then cooled. He had learned to discipline his rage from daily abuse as a child. When that did not work, he ducked and dodged, learning he was much quicker, thus evading the boys of the house. This was in everyone's interest. They did not catch him, he did not compel his mother to beg father to intervene and thus lose more honor in the eyes of their malicious society. It was only when they killed his hound that he beat them, one almost to death. He was punished, but never did they trouble him again.

Hadi shook himself, embarrassed he'd become lost in a reverie. But Telshorn waited patiently, gold eyes cool yet understanding. Hadi did not want his pity. "My mother was adept in your tongue. '*Han hani, han ke-taga, ordo har tegordro.*'" [1]

Telshorn's brows rose slightly, his only betrayal of surprise. "Those words are not often heard in this land. Your nation has a peculiar understanding of duty, and none of what is implied by eternity. Did Linastola teach her Sulanilish?"

Hadi barked a bitter laugh. "My sire gave her nothing but false dreams and years of regret. She learned your tongue and more from this very place."

Hadi looked around, the wondrous house both familiar and strange. It matched mother's memories, but not exactly. Or perhaps its image did not convey what it meant to her. He looked back at Telshorn to find the Vardashi looking at him more intently than ever, gold eyes commanding him to reveal his deepest secrets. Was he the one his mother knew? All Vardashi looked much the same to Hadi so far, individuality overwhelmed by their power. The sound of the sea roared in Hadi's ears as Telshorn asked: "What is your mother's name?"

"Lamia Kabir, she was called."

"Was?" The word was a breath without hope, gold eyes wide in sadness.

"Mother has passed. She was given the wisdom of the Vardashi while she bore me. But on my birth she was bereft of it and, in the end, the loss drained her of the will to live."

There was a long silence. Hadi looked up to see Telshorn's eyes looking through the north windows, out over the sea beyond where lay his distant

---

1   *One people, one duty; always and forever.

land. He did not weep, but Hadi felt his sadness, a thing that commanded the air around them.

"Lamia had a bright soul," Telshorn said at last. "I taught her how to read and write, and yes, Sulanilish. She sat there." Telshorn gestured to a table against a wall near the bar. "She was stubborn and insistent, and did not fear 'Vardashi'."

"She dreamed often of returning," Hadi said. Reminded of his own sorrow he was careless with his words.

"You dream truly?" Telshorn asked.

Hadi cursed himself. One thing Lamia repeated often: it was impossible to lie in the presence of a Vardashi. So Hadi shrugged.

"Does it matter? She is gone and I would have satisfaction of my true father for abandoning her."

"But that is not all," Telshorn said shrewdly.

"Blood is not the only way honor can be settled."

Telshorn sighed and rose, speaking as he walked to a cupboard and withdrew a cake, setting out small plates and an eating utensil with tines.

"If you are seeking a legacy or a form or remuneration from your sire, this is a vain quest. I did not know him well, but I remember the man who trysted with Lamia. He was a leisure traveler and indeed from Meridian. From a prosperous estate, but not the son of a princar. Your anger is misplaced. He offered to take her with him, but Lamia was torn between what she knew and the fear of strange lands. She was a bold soul, but tales from childhood of soul-eating demonic Vardashi were not something she could overcome in the end. They joined for mutual joy and there is no shame in that."

The rage returned, disturbing Hadi before he tasted the cake. His fork fell to his plate as he rose to his feet.

"You understand nothing!" Hadi said. Part of him was ashamed of offending hospitality. The greater part of him smoldered still over the years of offenses and outrages. Had his true father recognized him, he might be a Vardashi prince, whatever this Telshorn said. "A woman with child and no husband is without honor! Did you offer her shelter?"

"She did not ask. I did not know –"

"But my mother was wise and engineered her own fate! Before my coming was known to all, on the same day her father died, she wrote a cunning letter, forged in his hand offering herself in concubinage to Sheikh Parviz Chabahar abu Ameleth, a respected vassal of the Sultan! This she did to save herself from the streets. Or the slavery of brothels women such as herself fall to. It was a surprise to her brothers when she was claimed, but welcome; they did not object for even as the moon is beautified by the same sun that shines on our field, so the humble farmer can benefit from the light of a marriage in the Sultan's orbit. Parviz Chabahar was an old man, withered with greed and pride, but she did what she must to ensure he had no doubt I came from his loins!"

For a second Telshorn seemed to shudder, revolted as if it was he who had been taken in that sheikh's bed. But all he said was, "She must have loved you very much."

And like a spell, those words smote Hadi in the deepest part of his soul. For she had, and he her, his own grief denied for so long he was moved to weep. Then he was angry and steadied himself against the table, still standing.

"Do not cast a spell on me!" he commanded staring down at Telshorn.

"I am doing nothing of the sort," Telshorn said, not showing the slightest concern. He stood, taller than Hadi but not as tall as the gate warrior. "You came looking for answers. That they do not agree with you is not my fault."

Hadi worried he might be cast out. Feeling his time was limited he asked sharply, "How do I find him, my father Linastola?"

Telshorn sighed and began to busy himself preparing for trade. A couple Vardashi entered.

"Al met," the women chorused. One was a warrior, the other a bare armed laborer, her gold hair wound and secured at the top of her head. They walked to a table across the room, clearly regular visitors who did not need immediate service.

"You would have to go by ship," Telshorn said. "They may even take you, if you abandoned your Shari dress. But payment would be up to the captain."

"I have gold."

Telshorn laughed. "We have no need of Shari gold in the Federation. Though I suppose a captain might keep it for future use. You should not expect Shari gold to bring you the respect you to which you are accustomed."

"When do the next ships come?"

Telshorn shrugged. "They are less frequent these years but usually monthly for supplies."

Hadi wondered at this. "All year?"

"Yes."

"How strange. The Sultan's fleet only sail from the spring equinox to the start of winter, before the seas become fraught and the tides contrary."

"Most ships that come here obey no tide and are driven by what you would call water magic. Though they too can be broken by rough weather. A couple sank nearby years ago. No souls were lost, thank Sul. Will you finish your cake?"

Hadi looked down at the cake, honey moist and scented with almonds and orange, the fork sitting next to it.

"Yes, thank you. But then I must go. Forgive me my harsh words. You were a friend of my mother and I am grateful for your help."

Hadi heard the sea again and saw Telshorn looking at him intently, his expression unreadable. "You are forgiven," he said. "Remember here you do not need to hide the truth of yourself. Now I must tend to these others. And I am truly sorry for your mother's fate. I would have helped her, had she come to me. I shall always wonder why she did not."

Hadi inclined his head and Telshorn left him to engage the women. Shortly they smiled and laughed, speaking rapidly in Vardashi – Sulanilish – too fast for Hadi to catch more than a couple of words. Thus distracted he quickly finished the cake, then, he didn't know why, he palmed the fork.

The shiny bold metal spoke to him, surely the same metal of the guard's helmet. It had secrets of hidden alchemy within; even when he was a boy he could not resist the pull of a secret. He waited until Telshorn withdrew before rising to leave. Briefly he was startled by a young girl – no, again a man but looking barely more than fifteen summers. This one was more like himself, long shiny black hair bound at the base of his neck to be tamed. He wore no robes like Telshorn, but close fitted leggings such as a horse rider might wear and a loose belted linen shirt. His eyes were green, but his skin was the palest blue. Hadi glanced at his own skin, finally understanding the mystery of his hue. Lamia had the dusky skin of the Indus, her great grand-mother an abandoned concubine of a defeated warlord from the east. Hadi had inherited this and her strong jaw. His other features – the sharp point of his chin, the graceful accent of his brows and ears, even the narrowness of his build and the hidden strength that belied it – and of course the cast of blue on his skin, these were from his father, these were Vardashi. The cruel boys had been right all along: Hadi was a goat eared Djinn.

He excused himself, as the boy danced around him engaging in tasks of trade. So he was a servant, but dressed better than some of the Sultan's re-tainers. Hadi knew not to make assumptions of Vardashi customs. Yet the new knowledge about his Vardashi sire warmed the smoldering coals of sleeping vengeance within.

Hadi left the house and lingered in the shade while Vardashi passed him, thinking of all he'd learned. What could he do? Return and take a ship to the Vardashi Empire on his own? It would have to be by sea for the way by land was barred with bright ramparts and eyes that never slept.

These thoughts haunted Hadi as he returned to Jareth, and then to his life at court. He wanted to seek the wrecks of the magic ships, but dared not leave again. On his return the court magi made mocking jests cloaked in flattery and Hadi smiled and feigned ignorance. Danger always lurked at court for no matter the wonders he brought to the Sultan, Hadi's favor would last as long as the Sultan was not distracted. It was imperative for any seri-ous courtier to have a presence, if only to remind others machinations would not go unnoticed.

So instead of pursuing the wrecks, Hadi read what scholars knew of the Vardashi ships and actions at sea. Meanwhile he sought the secret of the hard bright Vardashi metal that he had absconded with. He worked hard, dreamed deeper than he ever had, even made burnt offerings to Al-ahat. Hadi did not truly believe; he knew the ancient pagan god of creation had only recently been elevated to the exclusion of all others, a revolutionary monotheism many had not completely accepted. Even the conceit of Al-ahat's maleness was a reflection of the culture the ambitious power hungry desert clerics lauded. For untold generations Al-ahat was the nameless, genderless wonder behind all of creation. Still the ritual brought Hadi com-

fort and being seen as pious gave the jealous pause. And finally Hadi understood: the metal was iron, bound with carbon with a breath of nickel for
strength, and refined with a skill none of the Sultan's armories could match.

But that did not matter. The Sultan did not know this metal, steel, was
inferior to the Vardashi metal. He only knew it was greater than the iron and
bronze they used now. New forges would be designed and built and, of
course, a source of nickel found in quantities sufficient for the Sultan's ambitions. So pleased was His Eminence Hadi was given a house, with servants and slaves at his bidding and the best apprentices for his skilled works,
as well as funds to pursue knowledge for the glory of Al-ahat.

It was then Hadi returned to Jareth with a train worthy of a king. He did
not go to the gate of the Port of Djinn. Instead his expedition marched to
the beachhead south of Jareth, avoiding as much as was possible being
sighted by the Vardashi. For Hadi had read much about Vardashi ships since
speaking with Telshorn. They were great shining vessels with the power to
burn a boat to the water. How was never clear. Old pirates raved about blue
keeled ships scuttling frigates in a flash of sunlight. Then there were other
ships that floated on the water with tall graceful sails, gliding faster and
turning sharper than any of the Sultan's fleet, before disappearing into mist
on the brightest day, never to be seen again.

It was very difficult to parse fact from legend, to distill knowledge from
the dross awe and superstition of Vardashi magic. Slowly Hadi came to understand: Vardashi boats had a keel that drove with water magic. That was
why they could sail indifferent to tides. That alone would be an achieve-
ment worthy of more honors. And perhaps enough to find his father and
bring him to account.

They spent weeks dredging the water by the beach to the irritation of the
local fishermen until Hadi paid them a month's ration in rice. It would be
well worth the price if he succeeded. After that the fishermen became quite
friendly and useful. As they worked they needed to dredge further out and
use divers. Hadi's mind was on fire. He wanted to flog the workers faster,
but he was wise: Tamask was far away and he would gain nothing if the locals became his enemies, or worse, became so distressed the Vardashi took
an interest.

A week in a diver retrieved the most extraordinary piece of sea glass. Not a blackish green piece of broken bottle, nor a lightening fused cluster of sand, this glass was the blue of dark topaz. The workers marveled at it; a foreman brought it to Hadi. The minute he touched it the sky started to burn.

Hadi cried out in horror. A ball of flame as large as the sun was blazing across the sky, lightning in its wake. Then the air parted and monsters with leathery wings entered from the void. Hadi screamed with horror. They set upon the blazing ball like a storm, lighting leaping from their deadly maws and Hadi somehow knew that because of this daring deed his ancestors lived so he was born to witness this past...

Hadi came to himself, surrounded by concerned workers. He reassured them he was fine. He'd seen a vision but would not speak of it now. For Hadi felt something else: the glass spoke of water. Magic trapped in melted sand by the flaming orb gave it the wisdom of water. To the diver Hadi gave a piece of silver. He promised the same for every piece of the water glass that was found. And so in a couple more weeks the partial wrecks of three Vardashi boats were revealed. Then came the task of cleaning and pre-serving, for even what could not be used would be a model of what would be built. All this was taken back to Hadi's house and the long task of recon-struction began.

Hadi learned many things: the Vardashi boat was not held together at its bottom by cable, but built like a creature, with a skeleton, planks layered like muscle and skin on the ribs. Hadi suddenly understood how such ves-sels would be more sea worthy. They would hardly leak and not need to be taken to shore at night. But it required wood, more wood than usually avail-able without raiding Nomclar. And their ship builders needed to learn this new skill to perfection. Hadi did not rush this. Most parts of the boat were rebuilt to replace the rotting wood. Only certain pieces were kept patch-work, those that held the length of blue water glass that covered most of the keel. It was broken of course, pieces missing, but enough remained to cut pieces of one wreck to fit another. He himself had to work with the water glass, by trial and error understanding how it was placed. Luckily a portion of one wreck that connected the glass to a driving platform survived. Hadi himself tested the vessel, a yacht almost equal the size of a warship when finished, yet much more sea worthy. It had chambers below, a sort of sheltered castle at the stern, and a gallery at the bows where one stood on a platform infused with the water glass. This was where one used the magic to drive as Hadi found, almost ramming the boat into the pier. When Hadi was finally finished, he presented it to the Sultan, taking his ruler on a cruise up and down the river by the palace.

The Sultan, His Eminence Darav Ormaz Damaski, (or Darav Ormaz abu Damaski when pandering to Al-ahat's clerics) was dazzled.

His Eminence had many questions, chiefly how the ship was driven. Here Hadi had to be careful not to admit only he could work the water glass. Instead he gave praise to the Al-ahat for giving him his visions, then regretfully informed the Sultan more water magic ships could not be made for they could not find more of the water glass.

"The Vardashi have water glass."

"True," Hadi agreed. "But we know not how they get it, Eminence."

"You have said the island of Sea Queens have this glass."

"Yes, O Eminence. The ships of the three horns all have water glass."

"With such ships I could crush the Azhin rebellions! Take the whole of Nomclar with our might! Even sack Gazhor, that Vardashi city that mocks us from the north! It has many riches you have said."

"O Eminence, I have said truly that they bring gold to trade."

"Yes, gold. And with that gold I will expand my empire!"

Hadi was slightly alarmed at these words. Conquering all of the south was an expected, even reasonable goal for the Sultan. But challenging the Vardashi did not sound wise.

"Your vision is truly masterful, O Eminence," Hadi said. "Your humble servant would ask a question."

"Surely," the Sultan gestured carelessly, lost in his visions of conquest.

"I beg your forgiveness to say again I can make no more ships of this sort —"

"Yes, yes," the Sultan interrupted waving his hands, "we do not have enough water glass. But we do not need it, do we?"

This was directed to another man present, who wore a black turban. This was Komar Zan, the admiral of the Sultan's fleet.

"It is true that the craft of this vessel exceeds in many ways all works before," Komar said. "I know nothing of this water glass. However I do know

that oar ships built in this fashion will be stronger, last longer and sail farther."

"Perhaps to the Isle of Sea Queens?"

"Perhaps. But these would require the best wood, from the foot hills of
the Scorpion Mountains. Or better, from Nomclar. And the best Cathan
ship wrights. There are risks of course, O Eminence..."

Hadi heard very little at that point because another vision had taken him
and it frightened him because he was certain he was not touching the water
glass:

Hadi saw a fleet, the greatest fleet known in Sharitan's history, all sailing
under the red flag of the Sultan, heading north and west. Hadi, both appalled and amazed, knew they went to meet the Vardashi. There were at
least two hundred ships. They had no water magic, but led with engines that
breathed fire. Then there was a mist and in the sky at noon, in the shining
sun, Hadi saw a burning circle, quartered with a cross, and a wise and gentle
face smiling over them all...

Gasping, Hadi came to himself, self preservation sending him into the
deepest bow, his head at the Sultan's feet.

"Forgive me O Eminence! I meant no disrespect – "

"You had a vision!" the Sultan said, knowing the mannerisms whether it
was real or artifice. "Stand and tell me what you saw!"

Hadi, not having time to consider told him, the ships, the number, the
hidden fire.

Then the Sultan laughed like a child delighted to receive his favorite toy.

"Don't you see, my worthy Hadi? Al-ahat speaks through you! He
smiles on our fleet! We do not need water magic! Master Magi!"

This last the Sultan commanded a distinguished bearded man who had
lived longer than most. He was the magi of the court, that learned body that
despised Hadi for making fools of their tricks. But not all their magic was a
fraud. The man stepped forward, black robed, wearing a flat round taq em-
broidered with astrological symbols.

"O Eminence," he said as he approached, careful not to betray his hatred
of Hadi.

"Come, do not glower!" the Sultan said. "This will be an alchemy of
minds that history shall never forget! For hark, Hadi, my friend, we have

through the care of learned minds passed the secrets of fire lost since the Vardashi pillaged this land long ago. There is a black salt that makes fire, and so much more. But jealous have the magi been of this knowledge, guarding it like the nether hounds lest it fall to our enemies. So much so, and for so long, now there lives none who can make what it describes. But you, Hadi, can bring this wisdom to light. For magic or no, are not the Vardashi ships also wood? Tell me, was there more to this vision? Do you see victory?"

Hadi had a choice. Confirm the truth, that he only saw ships on the water, boldly sailing further out to sea than any of their ships ever had. Then the Sultan would confer with advisers, who were ever trying to inject restraint, urging caution, and only partly because they hated Hadi's influence. Hadi secretly agreed with them. A vision of ambition was not the same as knowing the path to victory. But Hadi had seen the way to reach Vardashi lands, to find his father, and so he said, "Yes, I see victory."

And so His Eminence, the Sultan Darav Ormaz Damaski, Shah of Tamask, Khan of the Indus and Suzerain of Azhinazu and Cathan, made plans to conquer the Vardashi lands by sea, his fleets sailing under his personal banner of the lion and the rising sun. The great city of Gazhor would be his triumph, the shame of his nation's defeat so long ago would be washed away. And he saw riches in gold, cargo, diamonds; of concubines made of the proud Vardashi women, bent to the use all women were destined to, their magic driven out under the force of righteous manhood. And to bring this to pass Hadi was not spared money or slaves. That they could not make more water magic ships did not bother the Sultan, so pleased he was to learn the tri-oar could be improved.

They were all driven to make the Sultan's plans a success. The Sultan by his dreams of power under the Al-ahat. Hadi to find his father. Even Hadi felt compelled to seek the dominance of what he knew, a symbol always returning of a quartered circle in flames, perhaps a message from the gods. Feeling so confident even though he did not share the Sultan's dream of conquering the Vardashi, it seemed in that moment inevitable. And so in Hadi telling His Eminence what he desired, the madness of the Sultan's vision was complete.

It shook Hadi seeing what he had done, setting a nation to war against another. In his clearer thinking moments he felt regret for exploiting the kindness of Telshorn the Vardashi, for he knew the fey man who befriended Lamia was truly sorry for her fate. But that part could not vie with a lifetime of resentment. In Hadi's mind even Telshorn's kindness took a sinister aspect: Hadi had almost been unmanned in Telshorn's presence, been moved to weep as he'd never permitted himself after the murder of his hound. Worse, Hadi had felt the forbidden stirrings of passions long denied, denounced as debased by the clerics of Al-ahat. And had not the Vardashi attempted to thwart his righteous claim against his father? So Hadi took a savage joy in planning war against his father's nation. He, Linastola, who abandoned him and his mother, driving Lamia to seek the safety of the venal creature that law designated as Hadi's father. Let whatever the Vardashi suffered be his revenge. And when at last he found this Linastola, Hadi would hold him to account.

So swore Hadi Parviz az Daria, Hadi of the Sea.

BOOK III

Chapter 1

Forward and Boldly

Captain Rosen Gathelyn knew all the preparations on his ship, *The Tide-breaker*, had been made. The water ahead was empty, a glimmering of greenish glass, low undulating waves not daring to break into white. The sails, nearly always furled, were wrapped with thick wood vinings giving more support for the archers that now perched among the masts, snipers given the top platforms to better steady their aim. Regular Dwen crew, those with wood-essence who usually tended the rigging, made places for themselves twisting wood scraps, ready to catch or steady ropes, or even use them like whips. The solcannons, thick bars of honey translucent feldspar mounted on trucks for ease of movement, glowed slightly while their crews stood by: three sulessence powerful souls to take turns striking, with a couple of midships to throw water on the wales or deck if it was in danger of scorching. Except for the aft deck, two crews shared a strike captain, all under the strike master, the lanky Brownie, Azar Sernalash. Her dusky skin spoke of the arid flats of Sharitan, the very nation they went to war with, but her eyes were as gold bright as any Sula elf and she had the essence to match. In memory of her distant Indus foremothers she wore a gold bindi. Sernalash glided languidly from crew to crew; Rosen was pleased she seemed content with the state of the cannon. The Marshal's agent, Elderyn Farthal, made an odd addition with one of the aft strike crew, her tan cavalier's jacket and flouted hair contrasting with the blue vests and white sea breeches of regular crew, most souls with their hair pulled back or bound in some fashion.

Provided they had hair. Galen, the crewmaster and boatswain, and Rosen's best friend from childhood, was as bald as a freshly birthed babe. Instead of hair her skull was covered with frightening tattoos, her thick muscular arms and torso barely constrained by her vest. A Gold woman, her ancestry heavily favored her Sula mother; as aelg with humyn ancestry, she was shorter than her mother. Galen's muscularity thickened her, much more than Farthal who remained narrow in spite of her elfyn strength that, if it came to it, could equal Galen's. Rosen knew Galen had some sulessence.

But, like his own, it was mediocre, not something to depend on over a sword, or the capstan bar Galen preferred. She sauntered around the hatches, shouting down questions, asking for clarifications. The crew was ready to pass up more barrels of water or sacks of sand to suppress fire, lengths of rope to repair shrouds or rigging, and of course arrows by the cluster. Galen would make certain nothing was left to chance. Rosen loved her like a sister and cursed himself for the fissure in their friendship because of his weakness. But that matter between them would have to wait.

The divers were already in the water. Black robed magi, the wizards who served the Sulani Federation since the days of Sunqueen Selastimor the Great, stood near the bowsprit galley, ready to assist the proceedings as needed. Below, in what was the crew mess, Prefect Ordryn Mathynwol would have converted the space into a hospital with a small troupe of healers. Hopefully with so much labor at hand, she would be robbed of chances to indulge her Sula biases. Also below on the upper deck the marines and the volunteers waited, as soldiers had waited ever since the first lor assembled an army to assert or defend her dubious claims. All the ship's papers, Rosen's own logs and those of the deck officers, had been gathered and locked in the ship's strongbox, to be retrieved from the depths of the sea if it came to that. The crew wrote missives to family and kin in the event their souls were lost, also locked in strong boxes every berth had for the purpose. If their ghosts passed through the Door, there was the comfort their words would live on. The quietness was strange, the sound of lapping sea water underscoring one brisk conversation:

"It will be a hot day!" Lieutenant Becan Glethlyn said.

"I doubt it, emha!" Ensign Jarroth's shrill voice echoed, her voice, much like her body having barely left childhood. Jarroth looked up dubiously at the indifferent sky, patches of blue revealed between the sheep's wool of untidy clouds, itself uncertain of its intentions. Captain Manweth Lanash had predicted storm, but it was slow coming. Rosen hoped that luck would hold.

"Ah, my sassy spark!" Glethlyn continued, "There's more than one way to make heat! Mark it, it's coming! But when we get to Gashora I'll treat you to the best ices in the city!"

This was an awkward conversation. Glethlyn was standing near the pilot's cage, to the right of where Rosen stood, on the stern deck just fore of the mizzenmast, waiting for the Admiral's ship to whistle out orders. Jarroth was below them on the quarterdeck, passing between the strike crews chatting to the midships assigned with them. She would take up her post near a larboard aqua node by the master's cabin; Jarroth had pilot talent and was allowed to drive the launches when the opportunity came.

"That wouldn't be fair, emha!" Jarroth called up, hand on her black bicorn to keep it in place. Like all officers in the Tyreen navy, she wore a double breasted blue coat, white breeches and knee high black boots.

"How so?" Glethlyn asked.

"I am but one of many ensigns who will bear this hot day, and the middies too! It wouldn't be just!"

Rosen smiled while Glethlyn laughed. "So you lobby for the lot of the ships sprites? Very well, sassy spark! Ices all around when we see the Rulers! Now to your post!"

Rosen caught a movement from one of the midships, a hand sign between Jarroth, an exchange of fleeting smiles. Then Jarroth said louder than perhaps necessary, "Mind your post!"

"Yes, ensign!"

Rosen was tempted to laugh out loud at the lack of artifice. "You realize, lieutenant that your generosity is being plundered?" he said softly.

"Ah sure, effa, you let them think that!" Glethlyn replied. "Then the adventure is all the grander for it! You'll understand if you keep children."

"How are your son and consort?"

"They are safely in the bosom of our beloved city, so I cannot complain. Mind, my beautiful lad has no serious taste for the sea. But he's a boy and that's often the case."

Rosen kept his face blank. "I should have you thrown over board."

"T'would be a waste. I swim quite well for a Gold soul." A second later all banter was gone. Glethlyn became as serious as she ever could be. "Manweth has predicted storm, I hear."

"You hear correctly," Rosen answered.

"Will be no matter, if it's quickly done."

Suddenly whistles sang from the Admiral's ship, *The Oaken Blue*, echoing throughout the fleet in preparation to sail forward. Rosen jumped slightly with nerves as the mast signaler sent out shrill notes in the coded call back, a couple of the fleet ravens fluttered up before settling down again at the very tops of the masts. Rosen glanced at the ship's guards standing near the cage clad in blue jackets with the livery of a black sea serpent and a silver trident. In addition to swords and axes, the women nearest him held stars, spiked maces with a solstone orb at the center. A weapon from ancient feudal times, the star was used to defend the command on land and sea; at its most effective a blow would not only pin an enemy with its spikes, but blaze like a small sun in the hands of a soul with sulessence. It was a horrible weapon from a brutal time, but it's effectiveness was without question. Still Rosen hoped they would not be used; even controlled fire was a risk on a ship.

The last whistle stopped. Galen shouted to beat to quarters. The drums rolled, a dull monotonous tone. Those already in their places stood alert, while the tardy scrambled away from their last minute tasks. Master Sonan Jasmenal, a Gold woman with blue-green eyes, stepped out of her cabin. She held a star in one hand, an ax on her belt opposite the hip where her service sword hung. Jasmenal was a pilot, a commissioned lieutenant, and had served with Rosen before his captaincy. Her hair was, like his, braided in a naval queue, but she was hatless. They were quiet rivals, Rosen and Sonan; he was certain her request of duty change was an aversion to serving under a man. But today he was grateful she would be defending *The Tidebreaker* with him. Her visage was grim as if daring any enemy to touch the ship. When the drums stopped every soul was in their place.

"Advance on the tenth!" Rosen called out.

As his order was echoed, he felt through his feet the surge of the ship's heart, the aqua and grim taking direction from his pilot's essence to prepare to drive the ship forward through the aqua keel and rib fins, while copilots in the heart chamber and at the nodes surrounding the deck marked the magic flow with their own essence.

The last whistle was fading on the air as Rosen drove *The Tidebreaker* forward. On the larboard was *The Meer King*, her figure head a merman with a crown of red coral; her captain, Sea Mother Remard Sharethan, a curious soul born of a Gold mother and Blue father. Fate had been blunt in gifting her pale blue skin and gold hair, instead of the typical warm skin and black hair enjoyed by many of that ancestry, Rosen included. But it served her well, as she was the quickest to maneuver with precision on the sea. On starboard was *The Fortunate*, her figurehead a romantic image of Felkeni, the goddi of Luck, wearing only a ribbon of cloth around his loins, a wheel held aloft above him. This ship was piloted with enthusiasm by Sea Mother Lenoran Selenath, a young Gold woman who was the fastest on the water but also careless of risk. Both ships sluiced through the waves trailing white foam to either side of the Tidebreaker. Storm haunted Rosen's thoughts but for now there was sun enough and that was what mattered. It was just past noon.

Many looked up to the highest yards, where Dwen perched ready to sound the first sight of the Shari. As the fleet picked up speed, the bow of *The Pied Gryphon*, three vessels larboard of *The Tidebreaker*, eked ahead slightly, while *The Fortunate* surged forward over compensating. For several moments their line was jagged as they spread out to a distance optimal for solcannon to strike between ships. Rosen drove *The Tidebreaker* faster to match the fleet as they dressed their line until they were again abreast.

Briefly Rosen considered standing aside as many captains did in battles, letting one of the copilots drive, while he kept an eye on the action. As long as the heart chamber remained fortified, he was not required to stand in the cage all moments. But recent misfortunes convinced him that following the Admiral's lead had merit; the crew needed to see him as a Sea Father, and be given a reason to abandon their thirst for gossip to focus on the battle ahead.

It was then Rosen knew it would be a battle, whether it was the keen edge of growing anxiety, or the shiver in his bones from the ineffable instinct for the weave of fate all elfyn born had, Rosen knew: the Shari would not flee, they would fight and mothers would die. That itself was not despairing. The divers had drilled to fish bodies and those not lost to sea could easily be revived. No soul had to be irretrievably lost. Yet what was easily drilled with no threat might not be so easily done in the midst of battle. The most nagging concern was the issue of the Dragon of Tamask. Questions remained open, the answers few.

"Someone get me a my clerk," Rosen said to his lieutenants. In short order a young Brownie woman appeared, dark haired and dusky hued, with dark green eyes. Ensign Moradrin Savalis' cabin was just under the starboard stern deck, opposite the master's.

"Sea Father!" Savalis said looking up from the quarter deck, saluting briefly.

"Up here, ensign," Rosen said. "I'll be shouting enough later."

"Effa!" Savalis acknowledged as she darted sprightly up the stairs to reach the cage. Like always, Rosen worried if Savalis ate enough. She was much more mature than Jarroth, having her full height. Yet she was leggy and never seemed to gain weight no matter how much she ate. Like all officers she wore a sword. But the last thing Rosen wanted was such a callow woman in the skirmish, no matter how many fencing awards she'd won.

"You sent, captain," Savalis said at the base of the pilot's dais.

"What are you doing?" Rosen asked, with suspicion. Savalis rarely rested even when she should.

"Last minute notes, effa."

Rosen considered. "The documents are locked, correct?"

"Mostly, effa."

"Ensign, they cannot be mostly locked. The strongbox is either locked or it isn't."

"Yes, effa. Quite correct. I was preparing to lock it after I finished my final notes."

Rosen sighed. The trouble with clerks was they took their duty so seriously, they could not comprehend there would never be a perfect time to pause.

"I need you to fetch Ta Glenfar to the cage, ensign."

Savalis glanced to the bowsprit in the direction the magi berthed. "Yes, Sea Father."

"When you are done, you will lock the strongbox and take yourself and any midships not assigned to my cabin. Understood?" Here Rosen fixed Savalis with a stare his mother's consort Korali gave whenever he or his sister dared to run into the house with muddy feet.

"Yes, Sea Father!" Savalis half bowed, then ran down the stairs past the quarterdeck to the magi chamber. Shortly a woman in a black, flat-topped hat surrounded by four cabochons of solstone was making her way to the aft of the ship. Her black robes flapped sharply as the wind picked up. She came onto the stern deck to stand next to the dais, her head hovering by Rosen's left shoulder.

"Ta Glenfar," Rosen murmured.

"Sea Father," she replied, though her eyes marked the horizon like most. "How may I serve?"

"Anymore news about the Shari? Or the Dragon of Tamask?"

"A magi on *The Exalted Unicorn* reports thoughts of another fleet, smaller, perhaps reinforcements."

Rosen frowned. "But they believe their victory is absolute and the ships behind them are for cargo."

"It doesn't seem to match intelligence from the general crew's mind. We hope to focus on the leaders the closer we come. Their minds should be more precise. And we're directing attention to the yacht; though not the fleet's admiral, the pilot is known to be a respectable servant of the Sultan."

Rosen nodded vaguely, forcing himself to look calm while his anxiety increased. Not that another fleet would normally be a serious threat. A shark attacked by minnows was destined to win no matter how many minnows joined the fray. But if those minnows brought other fish, perhaps a school of stingrays, things would not be as easy for the shark. Another fleet, even a small one with this Dragon weapon would divide their force and focus. Rosen could see the argument of simply burning the Shari boats on sight. But duty and chivalry required they gave them a chance to change their course, a chance to flee.

A whistle went up in the masts, echoing through the fleet as each ship's Dwen signaler in the highest tops notified their captain the Shari had been sighted. Rosen still saw nothing more than a smear of red over the horizon he attributed more to his imagination than sight. Dwen saw the farthest of any elfyn except the Eirok, and by whatever peculiarities of ancestry, all aelg who could move wood-essence had sight equal to Dwen. Rosen didn't have the best eyes among aelg, but he would see the Shari fleet far before the Shari saw them.

Slowly the red smears resolved into billowing, white, triangular, lateen sails, their very tops colored with a triangle of red. The long boats, with dull green hulls and white wales, were not the expected tri-oars, better suited to coastal waters than the deep sea. They were taller, with at least two decks and only two lines of oars. These ships did not match the pictures Rosen was familiar with. Certainly a crafty intelligence had been at work. Still, they were only half the length of a city-ship, with the proportions to match, in comparison still too frail to be a match, much less making war upon the greatest power in the northern continent. They shimmered on the horizon, moving up and down on the waves, listing sometimes as the wind drove them in a course towards their destination, though, because they were slaves to the elements, not as directly as they would wish. They were clustered together in a mass, much like Nord longships, perhaps for protection. The bearing of the Shari fleet was north-northwest and Tyreen line of cityships crossed their path absolutely. It was clear the Shari had not seen them yet.

Rosen called for a telescope. He could see them better now, dots that were sailors in dun robes with red and orange accents, many with white turbans. Then he looked closer at the boats, for there had been many improvements since Rosen had studied humyn boats as a child. Traditionally the construction of humyn vessels from the coasts of Sharitan and Nomclar was puzzle like, built from the outside in, then pulled together and braced by heavy hemp cables. Such boats were sufficient for short coastal journeys. But what Rosen was seeing was new to his eye, ships constructed on rib frames, and much stouter than the tri-oar, the aft stern-port rising over in a curve like a scorpion tail.

"Mark the towers to either side on the masts," Jasmenal said. Rosen glanced down to see her standing on the upper step of the larboard stair, arm resting on the rail in front of the pilot's cage. He returned his eye to the telescope while she spoke, shivering a moment as the power of the ship flowed through him. "There is an engine, probably a type of catapult lurking with the archers." Sure enough Rosen spied what looked like large mounted crossbows that would be fired by twisted rope under tension. "A full stern deck has never been seen before," Jasmenal continued, "and the ship as a whole is more sturdy and sound than the tri-oar. Under the solid deck one can predict the size of the hold has been greatly enlarged, though much will be given to water for the oar crew."

Rosen closed the telescope and passed it to a lieutenant. "It's a strange mix of thoughtful craft and cobbled work. The aft castle is well made, but the forecastle is little more than a raised scaffold with a tent."

"Ai, captain, I suspect that's where lurks the Dragon of Tamask."

"If so, it's rather small for a dragon. I'm more troubled by the amount of archers clustered at the stern and a deck apparently shadowed by armed troops." Glimmering sunlight betrayed that many turbans concealed a pointed helmet, only the peak rising into sight.

"One must remember, captain, that the Shari are, at the end of the count, a landed people. Those that build and sail their ships hail from conquered port cities of maritime Nomclar, like Cathan. They will not fight at sea per se; their goal will be to board and in every way turn a sea battle into a land battle. They're probably desperately disappointed not to be able to use horses."

"Something they'll have in common with the Marshal's agent," Rosen murmured. "I thank you for your insights, Navigator. You have a star; will you be defending the cage?"

"As you said this morning, we will fight or fall together. In any case, my post is close to the cage. Captain."

Jasmenal always called him "captain". Never "Sea Father". She withdrew, whatever duty she felt to keep Rosen abreast discharged.

The coolness of the parting water surrounded Rosen's thoughts, as if he was parting the waves with his own body. They were coming closer to the Shari fleet by the moment. There was a sudden movement on first one boat, then another, until it rippled throughout the alien fleet as sailors scurried around like ants. Then, like punctured kites, all the sails fell deflated. Even with these better built ships, the custom of removing mast and sail before battle was retained.

"They see us," Rosen said. To the officer on deck, Lieutenant Bornad Rondaleth, he called, "Order the strike crew to readiness!"

"Strike crew, stand ready!" Rondaleth echoed.

In the bows and aft the strike crews moved from easy attention to the sparkers placing their hands on the solstone cannon, the rest of the crew ready to make adjustments. They were of course too far away to cause even the slightest damage, but it was the Admiral's wish they be ready to strike as soon as the Shari could see them.

Now they waited for direction from the Admiral.

The enemy had clearly been surprised by this new threat arrayed ahead of them. Rosen himself was discomfited by what he saw. Instead of turning tail and fleeing as many hoped, the Shari demonstrated alarming discipline and planning. Given they were powered by oar, the mass of ships reorganized themselves into a thick line in a remarkably short time. The line was in fact longer than the Tyreen fleet. A quick count revealed about ninety ships in the first line, the rest of the ships making a jagged line in reserve. One slightly larger vessel sat just behind the middle of the line, a red and orange banner flapping high at the stern. Rosen guessed this would be their admiral's vessel.

Whistles sang from the Admiral's ship to slow. As traditional in Federation maritime encounters, the Shari would be given a chance to abort their course and leave unmolested. Rosen let *The Tidebreaker* drift forward, only guiding it with essence to keep it's position.

"Surely the Shari see our ships outmatch their own," Glethlyn muttered.

"They take comfort in their numbers," Glenfar replied. "Not without reason. Any humyn force would flee before them, even the Nords. Or perhaps they consider retreat not an option. We know even the best servants of the Sultan are punished harshly for failure. Death might be preferable. Excuse me, Sea Father."

"Glenfar?" Rosen queried.

But she was already retreating. "I must confer with my master. I'll return when we know more. Mark the center vessel: that is their admiral."

Rosen requested the telescope again. The Shari warship had changed so much he was certain there was an intelligence outside the nation at work. Perhaps it was like scholars speculated, the humyn were influenced by elfyn dreams. The crew generally wore loose white linen trousers with red and orange tunics. The oardrivers, facing aft-ward, to Rosen's surprise had no chains, nor were they of the wretched aspect of a barely fed slave, but healthy enough men with sturdy tunics, perhaps padded as primitive armor. It was hard to see them well, because along the wale where the oardivers sat was a line of bronze shields with bosses to protect them. The archers on the stern had well crafted bows, not dissimilar to a Sula sniper bow, carried strung in leather cases waiting for the moment they were close enough to use. At first sight no humyn, not the oardivers, nor the clustered archers and marines, seemed to wear armor. But this was incorrect: as was often the case in hot lands, caftans and tabards covered the mail or mail-linked lamellar plates, keeping the metal cool in the sun. Rosen briefly saw who he presumed was the captain in a long, red sleeveless coat, trimmed and accented with gold over a lamellar halburk. His face advertised his sex like many humyn did: among the careworn creases of an aging face, he had a mane of beard trimmed into a goatee style not unlike Manweth, but much thicker, the dark coarse hair curling slightly at the tip of his chin. His head was wrapped with a black turban. He stood on the forecastle, his larger vessel constructed differently from the others, with no tent, but some engine was encased below, for out of the front of the ship, over the prow, was a long tube of heave bronze piping. Whatever its purpose it was occulted by the same heavy planks that fronted the rest of the Shari vessels. With armored archers on either side, he stared ahead, and Rosen imagined how he saw the line of Tyrum cityships bearing on him. Was he frightened? Did he only grasp their size the closer they came? Did he wish to flee? Or was his faith or fear in the Sultan so great his mind was barred against such thoughts? Presently he was joined by a figure in a long flowing black kaftan. This man's mane of beard was greater and streaked with gray. He wore a flat-topped black hat with long tails and by his demeanor and visage he was a man of letters not war. Rosen sensed that whatever order he represented it was the Shari's answer to the magi. How close the humyn imagination tacked to the course of elfyn culture was both astonishing and eerie. At least Rosen could take comfort that Shari "magi" had no essence to speak of.

Rosen handed the telescope to Glethlyn.

"Must say I didn't expect such a well trimmed line from a humyn fleet," she said.

"No. They seem to know the general principles of strategy."

"I expect." Glethlyn lowered the telescope. "They are calm and without panic. I don't like that."

"Fear can be an amazing tonic to the morale," Rosen said. "The Sultan's gruesome tortures would make anyone braver than they might be. Better to be killed quickly at sea, than to be sawn in half alive."

Glethlyn made a face. "That sounds too grotesque to be true. What mother would be depraved enough to do such a pointless thing?"

"Well, they're not mothers, are they?" Rosen replied.

"But if someone is that cowardly, surely you don't want her anywhere near a battle!"

Rosen sighed. "Your logic is wasted, lieutenant."

The whistle came from the Admiral to slow to a stop. They were to stand a furlong away from the closest vessel. The ships spread out before them, looking pathetically frail as they bobbed in the waves, some oars resting straight out, others still working as they moved into position. Yet no matter how frail individually, their numbers could not be dismissed. Now Rosen saw, in the distance, behind the reserve line of ships, the three reported cargo merchants still with sail. They would likely wait out the battle, linger in hopes to continue on to Gashora. They might also be reserved for escape. Perhaps the Shari admiral was no fool after all. A shrewd captain fleeing such an untenable position might take her surviving fleet away south of Azhinazu, and sail for profit among the shoals between Sea Home and the isles south of Nomclar. There the government of tribal mothers was less so-phisticated and regulation outside of Federation ports virtually nonexistent. Even for these sailors, the arm of the Sultan was only as long as his fleet and how long could that be in a nation that had over exploited its forests cen-turies ago? Still, whatever the Shari admiral's plans were, for the moment he was compelled to follow his duty to the Sultan. Rosen brought *The Tide-breaker* to a stop with the fleet as they loomed over the Shari vessels.

Being no larger than a Federation patrol ship, it was hard to call the Shari vessels warships. At this time Rosen knew the Admiral would be preparing the parley scow, one of the Oaken Blue's launches that would carry Ta Rau Jethar, or the hornblower, a ceremonial diplomatic position dating from be-fore the Federation. It was a dangerous task: she would be driven by a pilot, with one marine, that woman more to protect her if she was wounded than for any defense. The launch creeped into the water from the far side of *The Oaken Blue*. The boat was beautifully ornamented, the high prow topped with a gilded finial of Sul's son Solshari as depicted in the late classical myth. In early myth, Mother Sul's children Payeen and Solshar, Quick and Bright, were androgynous. But by the late classical era the influence of mother culture had turned Payeen, the mother-god of winds, into the precocious imp that was the matron of footrunners and merchants, as well as the glib and the shiftless: winged, high spirited, and crafty. Meanwhile her sister, Solshar, the mother-god of light, had changed into a brother Solshari, an avatar of masculine virtues: as bright and beautiful as Lun, yet Solshari was modest, helpful, cheerful and charitable. Solshari was the patron of society, entertainment and friendship, and so his image was often associated with diplomacy and reconciliation. Even from the distance Rosen could make out the classical bound locks, with two flowing forelocks twining with Solshari's artistic folds of his tunic, a lyre in one arm, while the other held aloft a scepter mounted with an orb, a symbol of his mother's power he wielded by proxy.

In the scow the marine stood aft-most, her armor glittering like fish scales in the sunlight. Then stood Ta Rau Jethar, standing in the center of the scow, rigid in her blue officer's coat, bicorn perched smartly on her gold hair, the horizon sun on the sides glimmering in the weak sunlight. Rosen didn't know her but most souls with this honor were chosen from the Admiral's staff, sometimes by volunteer, sometimes by allotment. If an admiral had a choice, the woman was either without children, or they were grown. She wore two sashes: the lower one was Tyreen blue; the one crossed above it, Federation gold. A tall standard, fifteen feet long, was in one hand with a Federation flintstar and a tricolor streamer of blue, green and white at its top. If it fell, battle would commence.

The scow stopped in the flat expanse of undulating water between the fleets. The Shari scurried on their boats in a way Rosen did not like, their archers now with bows in their hands. The black turbaned admiral stood on the forecastle of his ship, perhaps to hear better, but there was no need. The Horn was a speaking horn, and was imbued with magic that made its sound carry ten times as far as any simple humyn made thing. Ta Rau Jethar raised her horn and the sound echoed across the waters as if she was speaking in an arena forum. She spoke in Shari, but Lieutenant Sithinas, standing larboard of the cage, translated for those of the crew who did not understand the language:

"Greetings, Sea Host of Sharitan. I am the Ambassador of the Tyreen Navy, loyal subjects of Western Sulani Federation. These waters are the right of way only of those without malice. Those who would threaten the peace and sovereignty of the Federation we abjure. Your course is aggressive and hostile and so we must compel you to cease and desist. Retreat immediately, else face the full wrath and awe of our host. Turn back instantly and you will be allowed to leave unmolested."

The final words echoed across the water. This was the most dangerous time for Ta Rau Jethar: either the Shari would go or they would attack. While the Tyreen fleet was silent, a low murmur was heard from the Shari fleet, and turbaned heads could be seen bobbing together at the words. Then a deep gong sounded and all words ceased. At the stern of the admiral's ship flew the great red banner; near it Rosen saw flags flickering. Other flags flickered on the aft of nearby boats. A trick of the wind or a code? Then a new sound came, first faint, that was much like shouting. To Rosen's horror he realized it was laughter. It began with the Shari admiral, and taking heart, the rest of his fleet joined in.

Rage blossomed in Rosen at the arrogance. They had no need, no just cause and were clearly insensible to how much their fates hung by a thread, how quick and easy it would be to utterly destroy them. It was only elfyn chivalry that compelled Admiral Jonsaymanor to give them this chance to save themselves, and they mocked it, small ungrateful children dense to the dangers they would face without a mother to protect them. Another gong sounded and the laughter died away in a ripple. Rosen could see the Shari admiral holding a speaking horn. It was faint, but most elfborn ears could hear his voice, strangely deep, perhaps from yelling orders in war:

"You must think us simple children. We are not like the barbarians who worship the Queens of the Sea. Nor do we fear Vardashi black magic. We are the servants of the Sultan Darav Ormaz Damaski, Shah of Tamask, Khan of the Indus and Suzerain of Azhinazu and the Cathanites, and Sheikh of the faithful! His fleet sails where he wills with the blessing of Al-ahat! Praise be the Sultan, may he live forever! Praise to Al-ahat, the ever victorious!"

And then it happened, so fast Rosen missed the moment, his eye on the Shari admiral and not on the hornblower's scow. Thin lines of arrow shafts leaping from the ships closest to Ta Rau Jethar, surely too far away to do damage, surely too far to reach the launch. Most arrows were forced suddenly aside by alert magi with the same magic they used to float above Eurath. Those fell soundlessly into the water. But one must have found its mark for Rosen saw the officer fall. Instantly the driver reversed. Amidst the shouts of outrage from the fleet, *The Oaken Blue* whistled the code to strike the water. Rosen had no need to add a word as the fore crews struck the water in a blinding halo of light. The Shari laughter, full of their small victory, was doused like a match in a storm as the sea hissed poisonously and clouds of vapor obscured the way ahead. No Shari vessel was hit. The distance wasn't optimal for sunstrike. This action was only to give cover for Ta Rau Jethar's escape. More whistles sounded from *The Oaken Blue*: when the fog cleared they would advance and strike to rout.

Then Rosen felt it, the murderous rage of war, Amer possessing him as she possessed the king in the tale. In that moment, he knew whatever their differences, the fleet was one. They had attacked one of their own and sealed their doom. The scow disappeared in the shadow of *The Oaken Blue*.

"Is she dead?" Ensign Jarroth whispered in shock.

"Never worry, sprite," Lieutenant Rondaleth said. "If she is, it won't be for long."

That was true and tempered Rosen's rage. As long as no soul was lost beyond the Door, the Shari may yet be given mercy and grace in defeat. Those unworthies were slowly returning to sight.

"Mark," Ta Glenfar said, having reappeared. "See the ends of their line?"

Rosen's eyes flickered east and west. "Are they making a crescent?"

"Well, to their eye there are only a fraction of ships in their path, however large. They have the idea it's just a matter of boarding our ships. Surely no more difficult than storming a tower."

"I'm glad you've rejoined us."

"Oh, I've been assigned here. Ta Taren, my dear master, is wise."

"So you're to keep out of her way."

"And relay information the cage needs. But yes, I suspect the first." Glenfar, as usual, seemed cheerful about her lot. She appeared to prefer distance from her order and its expectations.

The last of the vapor parted and whistles sang out to advance. Rosen drove *The Tidebreaker* ahead while Cambrian drums beat. As they gathered speed, Rosen called out, "Strikemaster, call at range!"

The order was echoed as they closed the gap with the Shari ships, whose stern and wales bristled with archers. It wasn't arrows that flew yet, but stones from the catapults, trying to get range. They were at an awkward angle, the ballista on the side towers, while their ships faced straight ahead. Though built to swivel, the engines were clearly not at an optimal angle. Few of the rocks struck even a hull, most falling listlessly to the water. And after that there was no time to reorient, no time to change position, for the Shari had underestimated the speed of the Tyreen ships. Not only were they well past the attempted trapping crescent, the prows of the Tyreen line might well ride over oars or swamp the closest Shari vessels.

And so, the oardrivers reversed as well as they could, some captains turning their ships to give the ballista a chance to show its glory. Archers clustered deeper, but didn't shoot yet. It made sense; clouds of arrows in any land battle were deadly. However to work at sea they required a closeness that endangered the very vessels that bore the archers. Rosen looked up into the masts to see the snipers already marking their targets. Then their arrows flew. With the greater height of both the ship and masts and the longer elfyn eye, the Shari were well within range. Bodies started to fall on the Shari decks. It would be luck if any Shari ship survived to get close enough to rake *The Tidebreaker's* tops with arrows. Now there was no sound from the Shari except muffled shouting of orders accompanied by the odd flickering of small flags.

"They don't laugh now," Glenfar said.

"They'll never laugh again," Rosen replied grimly.

"Yes, the mood is murderous. Interesting they became sober at seeing us go into maneuvers."

"Oh?" Rosen thought, had he been a murderous humyn on a tiny boat, merely seeing the great city ships would make him think twice about his course.

"They assumed the great size meant city-ships were slow. They know better now and are worried. At least the common sailor is."

"And the officers? The admiral?"

"His mind I cannot pick out particularly, but whatever concerns they have, they have faith in the Dragon of Tamask."

Rosen made a noise like a growl. The sun shown above both fleets, Sul indifferent to their fates in Her palace in the heavens. Ships closest to them fired ballista again. This time the rocks hit the hulls hard. There was the sound of shattering glass; a rib-fin had been damaged, but not *The Tidebreaker's*. Other ships kept their bows pointed perfectly at them.

"Sea Father!" Strikemaster Azar Sernalash called, "We are within range!"

"Scuttle the minnows on your time!" Rosen ordered.

Light exploded across the water from the Tyreen line, as if drops of pure sunlight had fallen to the sea. Immediately after came a series of explosions, as the dense power of the sun directed through solcannons cracked the timbers of their hulls, briefly showing in black gashes. Then the blackened timber disappeared from view as the ships started to sink. A great cry of alarm rose up from the Shari fleet, followed by the screams of the injured and dying who had not been immolated from the blasts.

Rosen lowered his eyes as the fire crew struck again, streaks of flaming brightness blossoming ahead of him, followed by the thunderous crack of burnt timbers breaking. It was much louder as the target was much closer, one of the ships that had shown its side to them. As the ship listed, the archers shot before fleeing the bows, going to the back where the ship would stay above the water longest. Most of the arrows that reached *The Tidebreaker* struck the hull or glanced off to fall to the sea.

"What in the deeps?" Glethlyn swore from where she stood holding a telescope. "Mark, Sea Father, under the bow tent!"

Rosen peered, his eyes well enough at this distance. "Yes, something shiny, metallic. With the face of a lion. See what more you can discern. Magi?"

Glenfar sounded aghast. "A mind who has watched the Dragon …" she began, but whistles interrupted her, singing of more tactics, to sweep through the line but to not strike those that flee.

Meanwhile the deck of the nearest struck ship had sunk nearly to the water line, where it floated stubbornly, the rowers above doing their their best to retreat, while those below attempted to escape drowning in a panic, throwing the deck above, filled with armored men, into disarray. They too panicked, aware of their vessel's demise and the death that awaited them in the water were they to fall in fully armored. In desperation many threw off their helmets and coats before jumping into the water. They were not to know another death awaited them. Many vessels struggled so. By Rosen's count at least a handful of Shari vessels had been destroyed or were of no further use.

Rosen took a savage satisfaction in their misfortune, barking a laugh, while Glethlyn still trained the telescope. Solcannons flashed and ruined more Shari ships, a couple explosions more thunderous than usual, one disappearing in a cloud of black smoke and fire. Rosen shivered at the screams, even his rage at humyn arrogance mollified. They suffered and perhaps would learn now.

"Not laughing now," Glethlyn said. "They scurry like ants. Perhaps we'll pick them up and drop them off on a strange island where they can be educated about their ways.... Look, I think that's the Dragon …"

Rosen saw it clearer now one ship's tent had been burnt half away, flames still flickering on the collapsed wooden posts, the lion's face opening in a bronze tube like in his dream. The captain – Rosen was certain it was the captain – turban crusted with soot, his clothes burned horribly on one side, staggered forward, white teeth flashing in a grimace of rage. He knew his ship was doomed, his life forfeit. Suddenly a flame was in his hand and he touched the tail of the Dragon.

Nothing happened at first.

Then Glenfar, black robes flapping, leaped and tackled Rosen and they both fell off the cage and on the top of the larboard stern steps as an explosion rent the air. A small bronze sphere sailed over the larboard wale, missing them by a hands-width. Though no more than the size of a fist, its speed made it deadly. Officers ducked, elfyn blood giving perception and speed to their reactions. Jarroth lost her hat, the force of the passing projectile knocking her unconscious before it hit Glethlyn who was still standing with the telescope.

It was a nightmare watching Glethlyn fall, part of her skull gone as the metal orb embedded itself into the starboard top wale, the telescope falling to the deck with a clatter. Rosen broke out of Glenfar's grip, rushing forward to catch Glethlyn, thinking about her child, her son: would he ever see her again? He knelt by her side, but it did no good. There was no life in the one eye that was left, the other either lost or obscured by blood and torn meat. Time seemed to stop, but he knew by the cannons' flash, they striked the ship again and again. No one would survive, their rage at the betrayal of the Ta Rau Jethar now channeled to avenge Glethlyn. She was the soul of merriment, and should have lived for decades. Becan Glethlyn – Taran was her son's name – and she was gone.

Rosen was suddenly shoved aside by an elf. Not elfborn, not aelg like himself, but a Sula like his mother's mother, warm skinned, bright haired and with eyes blazing like the sun. This was the Marshal's Agent, Lancer Elderyn Farthal.

"I trained," Farthal said, putting her hands on Glethlyn's lifeless body while some soul shouted for a healer. "With animals, but still."

Rosen was dubious, but a desperate hope birthed inside him. Was it possible an elf could do this thing? Were all the prayers the ancient Cambrian druids made for abundant crops and good hunts not wasted after all? Could miracles be born of desperate hopes?

"The skin must be sealed," Farthal was saying, as if reassuring herself. "If the head can be made whole the seat of the mind can be regrown. It was done for a hound once. She has still half of the mind; it makes a perfect mirror and the soul does the rest…."

Glethlyn's skin creeped slowly over the her ruined eye and gristle, a pointless act of progress, because suddenly Rosen felt it: it was hopeless. Tears formed in his eyes but they were too hot to fall, the mist obscuring his sight. He stumbled to his feet and tried to pull Farthal away, but she was much stronger than him. Rondaleth's voice barked for the unconscious Jarroth to be removed and Rosen was grateful. The sprite shouldn't see Glethlyn like this. Finally a couple of healers arrived, women in white robes and round apothecary green hats, much like the taqs worn by some humyn in Sharitan. At first the cavalier refused to yield to them as well.

"I know you have some training as a healer," one woman said, her voice gentle but deep, a mother who must firmly guild a child. "What you imagine is possible, but not here. There is no temple. We have no array, and the part of Glethlyn's mind that knows how to breathe has been destroyed. We do not have enough souls with the power or skill for such an operation without her essence to help. It is yet to be written how we ourselves survive. But for our noble lieutenant pilot, this journey in the Orb is over. We certainly will not reach Gashora in time to beat rigor even if the Shari did not beckon."

"What of the waiting serum?" Farthal asked.

"That would only buy a day, two at most."

And with those words, Farthal allowed the healers to gently draw Glethlyn's body away and moved it to a stretcher. Glethlyn was covered by a sheet and taken below. Farthal stumbled to her feet. Her gaze was terrible and terrifying, a god who had found the limit of her power and could not bear it. She stepped down the starboard stern steps, towards the fore strike crew, though Rosen was certain she was stationed on the stern.

Rosen himself staggered to the larboard wale, ignoring the cautions of Glenfar. He needed to see the water where the ship was, the one who killed Glethlyn.

Looking down, there was absolutely nothing in the steaming water except charred planks and the floating burned body of a turbaned sailor. Slowly Rosen's ears started to hear properly again and he took joy in the Shari's alarm as ships turned to flee. It was then Sernalash yelled something, perhaps an order to stop, and the entire starboard forecastle was brighter than noon.

Rosen was glad Sithinas had taken the cage for what he saw was terrifying. Farthal had commandeered a solcannon, one hand on one of the two handles in the bronze mount, the other on the stone. Another member of the crew, perhaps that Sula braggart Navi, tried to steady the other handle but Farthal was either insensible or would have none of it, commanding the length of deadly feldspar as if she owned it. And with it she swept the sea around them with strike after strike, each with long sustaining fire, so bright only those with Sula eyes could look, so hot the midships were soon out of water to lash the deck and were forced to call up more. One industrious boy bypassed the hold, throwing a bucket with a rope directly into the sea. Explosions of sundered timbers deafened them, and the smell of sulfur filled the air. Salts of course, that was how the ball was propelled. And there would be plenty more to feed the Dragon. It was only a matter of chance whether the Shari ships, once struck, would simply sink and ruin their power, or ignite it all at once. And if that happened while next to *The Tidebreaker*'s own hull...

"Get that elf off the cannon!" Rosen found himself bellowing.

A solcannon was a hungry artifact. And while there was sun, even weak sun, a Sula individual could feed it to exhaustion. Farthal's rage had taken over, making her the perfect avatar for a vengeful Sul. Not only was the wale of the forecastle in danger of warping from the heat and burning, but the crew were not used to such force. Girls shouted from steam burns and some would be surely blinded, if only temporarily. Eventually Farthal would exhaust herself but at what cost? The sound of a snap told Rosen at least one of the foremast shrouds had given way, burnt by the cannon strike that laid waste to the sea around them. That's all Rosen needed, the foremast to snap and fall on them all. Even *The Fortunate* off their starboard bow was grazed, a black streak of char slashed across her lower larboard hull where a ship had been riven in half. It was already beneath the waves, survivors churning the water briefly before they were dragged by the marines below to their deaths.

And during all this arrows had started to fall, clattered around them, desperate attempts to dissuade the Tyreen ships from pursuit. But the Shari were in retreat and the angle and range meant few found a target. The crude missiles from catapults had long since stopped. Finally a couple of magi were able to pull the cavalier off the solcannon but the battle was for the most part over. Whistled codes came: pursuit to cease as the enemy withdrew. Rosen waited for more orders to come, watching as about a dozen more Shari ships sank, many with crews still on board. The water roiled as they frantically swam for rescue. To Rosen's astonishment he saw a couple of the great ships, *The Black Seal* and *The Quicken,* cast wicker baskets into the water for the Shari to float until their ships came.

Rage coursed through Rosen like wildfire. Did they not know Glethlyn had been murdered by these savages? Let them drown and be damned to the deeps. Billowing clouds of white vapor and black smoke still roiled over the water, giving Sul a reddish baleful cast. Even from where he stood, Rosen could see bodies floating in the water, whether killed by strike, fire, explosive salts or the deadly marines in the water, they all looked much the same, dolls discarded by Fate, broken beyond use. Except for a few brave boats trying to rescue their own, the Shari had moved a good pace away considering they only had oar power. Well, it was said a walk to any place was as good as a run given time.

Meanwhile the deck was put into order. Dwen were throwing new rope down to repair the severed shrouds and ratlines. Ensign Jarroth had been taken to the healers. Farthal was being marched to the cage by two guards.

Rosen composed himself to face her, but had no rage left. For her part Farthal's gold eyes were blank, as if she was spent.

"You are not crew or volunteer," Rosen began. "There is no discipline that I can impose. I know why you did it. Be assured you are not the only one who feels Glethlyn's loss. You may have berthed with her, your elfyn pride might be offended at this loss of a soul. But to many of us Glethlyn was a friend of years. We will miss her more than you can know. And yet still we abided by our posts. I cannot afford for my ship to be burned however talented a Sula soul you be. Until you are told otherwise, you will assist the Ship's Prefect in the hospital."

Farthal didn't salute, but nodded tersely and went below.

Chapter 2

Wrath of the Sun

Lancer Elderyn Farthal stood away from the remains that had been Becan Glethlyn. She had not known her well, but they had been friends for the brief fortnight they berthed together. The lieutenant was a cheerful soul, with never a bad word for anyone. Like Eld, she had a son. Glethlyn's consort was of course in Tyrum, the island city whence the Tyreens hailed, grudgingly nurtured by the Sulani Federation in exchange for the service of the aqua driven *varsadmer*, or city-ship, an asset unequaled for trade or war. But none of that had saved Glethlyn, struck down by the Bane-spawned machine of the Shari.

Eld felt as if she was floating on air, her steps light as sunbeams as she glided down the starboard stern steps away from her post, ignoring the shouts of her strike captain, Lieutenant Mellasan Tamithryn. She hated being here, hated the bright flatness of the eternal ocean, hated her role as the Federation Marshal's creature, and hated that, being brought to this place, she was forced to witness a vision of death without recovery. It was so bright Eld could see everything: the crude vessels of the enemy, as if joined by a small child without the skill to match her ambition; the frightened eyes of those she passed, the aelg who, excepting the magi and perhaps some of the healers, did not have the essence power of a Sula with no competing ancestry. It wasn't just the rage that made her glow like a saint of the ancient pantheons, but the pain. Glethlyn had been riven from the Orb so suddenly, Eld felt it, her soul bled in sympathy. And now there was nothing for it but revenge.

She stopped at a solcannon on the forecastle, one with the widest range both on side and ahead. The crew fell away, perhaps terrified she would burn them. It was a wise worry; a Sula was rarely burnt by her own fire. The foot thick, six foot length of honey gold feldspar weighed perhaps a ton, but it pivoted on a fulcrum perfectly balanced and so felt as light as a feather as Eld set her palm against the open stone at the end and grabbed a handle to aim it at the first Shari vessel she saw. Above, the clouds dense sheep's wool during the dawn, had parted enough for dappled light to shine steadily.

It didn't matter. Eld had once trained under starlight. Sul filtered by the clouds would be more than sufficient.

The stone was cold to Eld's touch as her aura and essence connected with the grimsteel veins embedded in the artifact. Her soul was sucked within to dance in the glory of the power of Sul, both her essence and sunlight flowing into the stone to merge. Then, in a breath of will barely considered, sunstrike poured forth, directed to the hull of a Shari vessel that blackened, cracked, then exploded all in an instant. Eld was on fire, aroused in a way no harlot could sate. The energy had to go somewhere so she struck again, an orgasm without joy, only feeding a hunger for more. This must be how the ancient poets conceived Amer, the Mother-god of War. Eld struck again, this time an imperfect blow, one of the rickety looking side towers suddenly falling in flames, its supports burnt through, the archers on the top falling either to the water or on top of the oar drivers engulfed in fire. Let them burn, Eld prayed, let Amer take these sacrifices in remembrance of an elfyn soul ripped from the Orb before her time. Glethlyn would never walk in the Orb again. Her child would never hear her words of comfort. Her consort would never feel her closeness. Her family would be bereft of her soul, and society. This the Shari had done.

And so many Shari died, their ships burnt asunder. Dimly Eld heard shouts, the cries of midships, mostly girls barely out of adolescence, scorched with steam as they laid water on the deck. There was an attempt to wrest the solcannon from her, but she was stronger than most of these, even the brawny Cambari whose humyn ancestry made their muscles thick like bladders. One soul decided it was better to help her, a Sula. Eld could have laughed as she struck again, searing a hole into the deck of a Shari ship. It was Hoethnav who stood by her, an arrogant Sula soul who hawked the conceit that she was aelg, based on a distant humyn ancestor. Navi's sulessence betrayed her and Eld was grateful. The men had foretold souls would be lost. Seth had warned her. Then elfborn should not be the only souls lost. Two more Shari ships were struck, one sinking immediately, the other floundering. The screaming was a joy to Eld's ears.

Except one scream was far too close, almost at her feet. The light dimmed and Eld paused to look down. A midship was curled up on her side, her hands over her face, an abandoned bucket turned over at her feet, the water spilling over the deck bubbling and steaming where the heat of the cannon had scorched it.

The girl's weeping was a mix of pain and fear. Had she been blinded? Eld also had a daughter, much younger than the midship, but the mother in her saw no difference. Suddenly Eld was herself again.

In that moment strong hands descended on her and pulled her away from the solcannon. All eyes were full of fear, found her wanting and rebuked her. The strikemaster shrieked, "Get her away from my crews!"

Eld moved to help the child, but the ships guards had her firmly and would not let her.

"Never mind, you!" one guard barked. "She'll be tended. You, noble mother of our race, need to cool off!"

Shame started to birth in Eld. What had she done? She'd never lost control like that before. In moments she was standing before the captain. He was an exotic war-king, that rare man that chose to live as a mother. But now, whether from grief that his first lieutenant had died or disgust with herself, he looked the least masculine she'd ever seen him. His words were cutting:

"You are not crew or volunteer. There is no discipline that I can impose. I know why you did it. Be assured you are not the only one who feels Glethlyn's loss. You may have berthed with her, your elfyn pride might be offended at this loss of a soul. But to many of us Glethlyn was a friend of years. We will miss her more than you can know. And yet still we abided by our posts. I cannot afford for my ship to be burned however talented a Sula soul you be. Until you are told otherwise, you will assist the Ship's Prefect in the hospital."

The guards released her. Eld nodded once and made her way below.

Once in the shadows of the upper deck, Eld felt more in control. What had she done? she thought as she walked the length to the improvised hospital. She knew the way but felt she was walking in a fog, through the volunteer marines that milled around the open hatches, lending help as shouts echoed for still more water to be brought up. At last she came to the doors of the crew mess.

Eld being neither an officer nor crew, rarely saw the inside of the mess hall, having taken her meals in the pilot's mess. Like everyplace else in the ship, the designs were graceful yet functional, decorative Dwen twisted joins arching overhead held the deck up where it made a ceiling below, coiled and twisted oak leaves and vines mixed with the woven knotting found in Gael illuminated texts. Inside the rooms, none of this was painted, instead rubbed with oil and varnished where absolutely necessary. Like the decks, after being stoned smooth, the surface fibers would be thickened with wood-essence, making the wood fire resistant and water tight. Light filtered in from three large windows that overlooked the hatches to the holds, just below the skid beams where the launches rested. Eld had entered through one of the two large doors on either side of the window. While it was light enough, it was north light and they were well into the afternoon. In consequence, lanthorns hung everywhere. The gems used in solstone lamps had not yet renewed their power from the sun. To the left and right, larboard and starboard, solid paneling ran most of the length of the hall, broken by a doorway on each side. These led to galleys placed near the hull to allow cooking with firelances and lenses when possible.

Now the tables where crew once sat together had been laid out, a series side by side at the rear of the room, presumably for treatment. One table seemed to be reserved for staging and stacking medicine and supplies. White-robed healers in green hats drifted to and fro trying to keep order; among them were a couple of surgeons marked by their red hats and robes. Through the other door staggered a couple more souls, a kilted Albini woman favoring a hand and a couple of midships, girls who looked like miniature officers, except they wore rope soled deck shoes instead of black boots, and were not bidden to wear hats as part of their uniform. One led the other; both had been scalded, one was blind.

Guilt settled into Eld's gut but before the feeling grew she was challenged by a woman in a white coat with green facings:

"You're the one they sent to me?" she demanded. "You look ridiculous. Doff that coat and remove your flout."

Eld stared at the woman, not liking her tone. She wore the green healer's taq, her gold hair a curious mix of braided guardlocks, the rest in a naval queue.

"Removing the coat is sensible," Eld said as she did so, "but you'll find flouting is the best way to keep hair out of the way. You must be the Ship's Prefect."

The woman stared at her, not used to being challenged. Her mind was full of her importance, not as permeable as a humyn, but she was weighing if her authority was being challenged. Tresses, Eld thought to herself. Then she wondered if the prefect had thought speech.

~A little,~ the thought came faintly, while the prefect's eyes still glared. "I maintain it looks ridiculous," she added out loud. "Like a boy dressed as a pony for a masquerade."

"It is part of Federation Cavalry uniform," Eld said bluntly, making a point of shielding her thoughts. "Your marines wear them." In fact the inverted leather cone Eld wore was a marine flout; she had to abandon her metal one on the journey in the Eirok Wing for their safety.

"Very well, what do you know?" the prefect demanded.

"I was trained to heal animals before I enlisted with the Federation Host."

"Were you any good?"

"I helped save a beast during the Battle of Gate Step, if that counts."

The prefect made a noncommittal grunt. "At least your essence force will be an able anchor if we have serious wounds. Go assist those examining the arrivals for what they need."

The prefect gestured to a short queue. Before Eld could ask anything else, the woman strode away, restless to engage other tasks. Eld draped her cavalier jacket over an out of the way bench and set to work.

Many injuries were obvious: scalding and burns that required the removal of cloth to note their severity. None were serious, a touch to calm the pain and cold water to reduce the heat of the skin. Then it was a simple matter of calling just enough cold that the skin beneath could seal itself. Even so these wounds were dressed, more to remind the patient of their tenderness. It might be a couple days to a week before the skin was truly whole. Even eyes were quick, provided it was only the shock of dazzle, or the most superficial heat to the cornea. Otherwise, like the poor girl who had been injured near Eld, they were given a healing draught to speed their natural essence, her eyes wrapped for protection in the meantime. If it was bad she might not see again until they reached Gashora. The sight of the child being led back to her berth by her fellows humbled Eld. Her essence was so much more powerful than most of these aelg. But so was its capacity for hurting allies.

"I thought you were with the strike crew," a man said. He was carrying linens and mosses to the tables designated for supplies. Hidden by his burden in the dimness Eld didn't recognize Samath at first. He had repaired her jacket when she first came aboard and briefly had a romantic fascination with her. Eld might have returned it had he not quickly settled with Hoethnav.

"I was," Eld said shortly, relieving him of half the linens as he'd piled them so high they might topple.

"Thank you," Sam sighed. "I might even forgive you for beating Navi."

"Remember, I was not keen to duel in the least, but flogged on by a certain ensign eager for queens."

Eld stopped suddenly, passing a table where a groggy Ensign Jarroth lay while a male healer waved a bottle of something under her nose.

"She should be well enough," the man said on seeing Eld's concern. "It was only a passing strike. Unlike our poor lieutenant. But we'd like her to rise to be certain her mind is not damaged."

Eld sighed, glad it wasn't worse, avoiding looking at the body under a shroud on a nearby table. Even with the feeble light she worried she would become incandescent with rage if reminded too deeply of Glethlyn's loss.

"We need to put them here," Samath said, bringing Eld back to the task. The linens and supplies sorted, Samath asked earnestly, "Do you know aught of Navi?"

"She abides," Eld replied.

"Did she fight?"

"She struck if that's what your asking."

"They say the Shari want to board us!"

"They were not successful. None of the volunteers needed to be called above deck."

"Oh, thank Sul," Samath breathed. "I have a brother – no, not like that! – among the volunteers. I'm not so certain it was wise to let a man join the fighting force."

"If he's trained and able he should serve as well as any mother."

"But he's not like the Sea Fathers. He's no taller than me and is keen, but there will be so many of the enemy…"

Eld had heard women opine thusly before, as if any war-king was expected to single-handedly thwart an entire battalion of the enemy for him to be worthy.

"No mother will be repulsing the Shari alone either," Eld said. "Wars are won with strategy, tactics and disciplined forces. Or more preferably, avoided entirely. It will not be decided by the great deeds of a few notable mothers, not even the Prithi mercenary Bron or your own Hoethnav."

"Or elfyn cavaliers drunk on sulessence," a woman interjected forcefully. It was the fierce looking boatswain Galen Sellisyn. She was shorter than Eld but built like an auroch. "I'm glad to hear these words of wisdom, however tardy."

Eld said nothing out of the habit of avoiding lies by being silent. If she thought on it the pain was still there, the wound of a soul ripped from the Orb still raw. Samath drifted away from the boatswain's baleful scowl.

"You have nothing to say for yourself?" Galen demanded.

Eld pierced her with a stare. "What is there to say? A bright soul has been killed. The threat remains. I have been rebuked by your captain already. If you are expecting contrition, we will be waiting before the Door opens at the end of our lives."

"Your uncontrolled strike injured crew!" Galen said with feeling.

"Yes," Eld agreed, looking at the midships being tended. They weren't all her fault, but enough were. "That I am sorry for."

Galen's sigh sounded like a growl. "You'll be no use if you injure more crew than the Shari, or worse, burn the ship out from under us. When they are finished with you here, return to assisting the captain's clerk until further notice."

"Fine," Eld said, her subtle insolence not wasted on the boatswain. But as the Sea Father stated, they had no authority over her. The worst punishment might be to jail her in her berth. Except it wasn't her berth, it was Glethlyn's.

Eld severed that thought's progress and joined another male healer sorting draughts and potions.

Several officers and senior ranks officers entered and clustered around the table that held Glethlyn's body. When the captain came into the hall, Eld avoided his gaze. The staff surrounding the body was joined by the prefect who confirmed the hopelessness of Glethlyn's case. Eld heard very little more except Captain Rosen Gathelyn saying, "Death to the Shari."

The words made Eld shiver into her bones. A keen student of ancient myth, Eld knew the dangers of making wishes or prayers in the cause of war. Amer was not a Mother-god to invoke lightly, for her entrance into affairs was far easier than her egress. Any offense could not go without payment.

Eld shook herself. Surely it had been paid? Was not the boat that shot Glethlyn burnt down to its timbers, the bodies of her crew resting on the sea bed, a feast for the amloths? She had to discipline herself, regain control of her passions. She might resent this post, being the Marshal's pet, but she also represented her mother host, her company and the Farthal estate. She would have done it all over, commandeering the solcannons, but she would have preferred not to have lost control.

Eld was released a short while later. Food was being prepared on the middle deck and Eld realized she was famished. Not expecting to be served in the pilot's mess, she made her way down, avoiding the main hatches where supplies were still being moved up to the tops. There was a companion way descending near the one that lead to the quarter deck.

"There she is, Jaro herself, who will burn friend and enemy alike!" on soul chuntered as she passed.

"And they like to say Tyreens are undisciplined and shiftless…"

Eld ignored them. They were right to feel aggrieved, and would feel stronger once news of the midships' injuries spread.

On the middle deck the scent of burning charcoal filled the air. There were few windows as the hull was lined with cabins, so the ubiquitous lanthorn hung everywhere, though the gloom was relieved by the open hatches that let some daylight leak as it tried to penetrate the hold. On this deck were the ports that would sit above a quay when the ship was docked, gang planks extended as needed. Passing a capstan, one of the two great gears that lifted supplies and the launches, Eld joined the scrum near the commissary, a type of kiosk like a prosperous monger might have at a bazaar. There were stacks of small breads, rolls and nut cakes, but the main business was the massive stove where cauldrons of peas stewed with bacon and sausage simmered. Above the stove pipe angled to vent through the starboard galley. A couple of barrels that usually served as tables were upended to hold plate ware, trenchers and bowls piled haphazardly within. Eld grabbed a bowl from the depths of the nearly empty barrel and joined the queue. In short order a fresh pancake was thrown into the bottom of the bowl, threatening to make a crude lid. This collapsed immediately under the weight of a heavy ladle of pea stew.

"Another," Eld asked.

"*I ndáiríre?*" the Cambari man serving opined. "*Amharc cúl do féin!*"

Eld glanced behind her and understood his point. This was probably the first pot made and if she wanted more she should return when the ship had eaten. There were no spoons but Eld knew there would be some in the pilot's mess cupboards.

So Eld slowly walked back up to the quarterdeck, where she'd need to pass to get to her destination. She sped up realizing the captain might be there; best to avoid an encounter so soon while all their feelings were raw. But the way was clear, a Brownie copilot was driving in the cage, and the tops were generally busy cleaning where needed, the strike crews cleaning the solcannons, Dwen threading and repairing the rigging, most of the archers having descended for the day. Eld stepped under the shadow of the stern, between the clerk's cabin and the great wheel just fore of the mizzen mast when she heard voices. There was a narrow stair behind the mast, between the two doors leading to the pilot's mess; it would lead down to the upper deck and the heart chamber, where the heart of the ship, a great mass of aqua bound by grimsteel, lurked. Eld had never seen it, but knew it was the source of a city ship's essence control. It was possible to drive a ship solely from the heart chamber, but most captains preferred to have their eyes on the sea.

"So I says, that's a bit of a journey," Ensign Jarroth was saying. She was sitting on the stairs with a group of midships as they ate from bowls telling a tale in navy cant. "An' she says, like a Cambrian monger, 'Sure it'll be grand!' I says, 'I'm not a Fish, emha, and I don't like to get wet.' And she says, 'A mighty peculiar profession you chose then, my sassy spark!' She always called me that, 'sassy spark'."

Jarroth paused in her tale.

"So did you walk the wale?" a boy finally asked.

Jarroth took a couple of bites before answering. "I says, 'Lets make a wager. For every yard I walk, I'll get a queen whether I finish or not.' And she laughed mightily at this. Never had she heard of the feat turned into a concern. 'Your calling is lost with the navy, sassy spark! You should join the merchant fleet! I'll give a lunat for a foot!' So I's do a bit o' maths and don't find that to my liking at all. 'There's twenty lunats to a queen and three feet to a yard. Thus your counter wager is poor indeed!' Then she says, 'What a trying sea flea you must be!' Says I, 'Tis yourself that desires my walking the wale for your own amusement, emha. And amusement I'll gladly give, but I'll be trading hard for it! Then our Sea Father arrived and demanded what was happening in his keeper's way. And our lieutenant she says, 'Ah, effa, nothing but nurturing the future officers of our fine fleet with the best wisdom a mother can impart!' And this, being the boldest of lies, caused him great consternation."

"What did he say?" a girl asked. Officers were not disciplined by floating, if indeed it was an offense against duty.

"Alas. I know not," Jarroth said. "For I was banished to duty most abruptly and the next I saw our lieutenant she had little time to say aught as she was standing watches for the next half day."

The midships laughed, the boy adding, "So you never walked the wale!"

"Not I! But I did promise I would as soon as the price was agreeable."

Jarroth's face fell, the laughter from the others faded. Suddenly she stood. "I need to take the bowl within. Well, don't dawdle too long! Duty never waits!"

Then Jarroth sped into the pilot's mess and slammed the door shut behind her.

Eld suspected why Jarroth left. Entering the other side door, Eld startled her.

"Oh, it's you," Jarroth said. She half rose from a seat she'd not quite settled in at the long table.

"I've only returned here to eat. I wonder where the rest are?" Usually the mess was full at mealtimes.

Jarroth cleared her throat. "They're all conferring with the magi."

Eld started eating and they sat in silence a while.

"Did you see it happen?" Jarroth asked.

Eld considered. "It was quick." After a pause she asked, "You were speaking about Glethlyn, weren't you?"

"Ai." Jarroth's voice caught. She swallowed before adding, " I've got to stay strong for the middies. They depend on me."

"I suppose they do." The waves of grief from the girl shivered with the pain in Eld's soul. She was bereft, the loss of this maddening mentor shook her no less than if Glethlyn had been kin.

"I hate them!" Jarroth suddenly yelled with savagery. Her empty bowl flew across the room, rebounding with a clatter, almost striking Eld's chair. Automatically, Eld caught it.

"I'm sorry!" Jarroth exclaimed.

"It's fine, metee," Eld said. Then regretted it.

"I'm not a child!" Jarroth said angrily.

"Of course not. It was just… my mistake."

"I'll never walk the wale, because the price will never be agreeable!"

Eld stood up and walked around the table. Child or not, Eld was a mother and knew what was coming.

"She was going to buy us ices in Gashora," Jarroth said. "Ices for me and all the ensigns and middies…"

And then Eld's arms were around Jarroth and she wept, holding Eld fast around the waist.

A while later Jarroth pulled away. "I apologize for that."

"There's nothing to apologize for, ensign. Tears for mourning the death of a friend are tears well spent."

"You'll not tell the Marshal I wept will you?"

"I don't think she'd care one either way."

"Still."

"Of course not."

"Nor our sea father."

Eld looked down at Jarroth very seriously. "We will not speak…"

"And tell no lies," Jarroth finished.

They exchanged a brief wry smile then Jarroth wiped her cheeks. "Can I berth with you? I mean, I can help get her effects together, before... before the dawn."

"Of course. You can go in now if you wish. I need to report to the captain's clerk."

The rest of the afternoon was sadly quiet, Sul setting redly until the clouds thickened so the evening fell starless. The ship was somber even though they ate a good dinner, this time with abundant fish. There were no red reeds of hot madder, nor any of the other traditional trappings of wake. The Cambari insisted on a waking in the commissary in a way the cynical might suggest was yet another reason to drink. Eld drank very little, one cup of barley mead while around her, the pilot's mess now full, they told tales of Glethlyn's courage, her generosity and of course her mirth. Even the Sea Father was present a while, perhaps feeling he should be present with the crew as they mourned. Eld soon left to walk the decks, wanting to be under the stars. She was truly tired of the sea and would be happy to forsake it when the time came. Then standing on the tops, looking at the pall above, she remembered the stars had shrouded themselves, indeed rain was predicted the next day. Still, a couple could be seen, the bright blue Hero's Hound in the south, higher than she was used to seeing. Of course, they were more south than she'd ever traveled. The wind, always brisk at sea, was a welcoming coolness. Tonight Glethlyn would step into the stars, like Jaro taking her place among all the ancient heroes. Eld smiled a moment. At least they would be cheered.

Returning to her berth, Eld found Jarroth curled on Glethlyn's cot sound asleep. On the seat by their small gallery window was a box of effects, including Glethyn's sword to be given to her estate on their return. If they returned. There would be papers, letters and sundries; at least her consort and son would have her last words to comfort them. It was explained to Eld the service clothes, except for those she wore, while reserved for return to Tyrum, would be available to the crew as needed while they were at sea. Not even the dead were allowed waste.

Eld reclined on her own cot, now bathed in the glow of a proper solstone lamp, though she shuttered it soon after, preferring the dark. She didn't quite know when she slipped into sleep.

"All rise at sunrise!" Glethlyn barked, clapping her hands over Eld. Eld started, sitting up sharply in the stable barracks, wondering why Glethlyn was in Falls Gate Keep.

"So this is the romantic cavalier's life!" Glethlyn said, walking around the long room that while built large enough to house a couple score oddly only had one cot, the one Eld was sitting on. It was well made, with Dwen joined wood, but no Cambrian knotted flourishes.

"This is wrong," Eld said, standing as she tried to get her bearings. Outside the window it was dark and many stars shown. She could see the lights from the abbey on the hill, a magi college built in an ancient Indus temple. But that was not correct. One could not sight the abbey from these windows...

"Don't tell me this is the first time you've met the dead," Glethlyn said. "I haven't long you know."

Then Eld was fully awake in the dream.

Glethlyn looked the same as in life, except her hair flowed free, like a poet or musician. Her eyes were black like all the dead and sparkled with the glimmer of stars.

"I tried," Eld said, at a loss for anything more meaningful.

"It's all we can do in the Orb," Glethlyn replied, clasping Eld's shoulder. "I'm sorry. No, not just for death, but I think it was my rage that drove you. Look after our sassy spark, will you?"

Slowly the stable barracks shifted into the shape of their shared cabin, with it Jarroth's ghostly form appeared, standing sadly looking forlorn. Slowly she became as solid as in waking.

"Do you have to go now?" Jarroth asked.

"You wouldn't want me haunting the fleet and giving you bad luck, would you?"

"You'd never! What is that?"

Eld wondered if the Door would manifest. She didn't see the road that led back from healing to waking. Very slightly Jarroth started to step away.

"Hold her!" Glethlyn commanded, voice echoing every bit like a shade.

This was an easy task. Jarroth wasn't an expert dreamer so seizing her by the hand was enough.

"You are hearing the Door," Glethlyn said. "I must go. Keep it bright, little sister."

Glethlyn vanished and they were surrounded by mists. The last impression of Glethlyn's ghost was something of cold and sweetness. Of course. They had been promised ices when they arrived in Gashora.

If they all survived Eld would do it. Besides, it'd been a quite a while since she had ices.

Chapter 3

Signals

Admiral Jonsaymanor Jansenwol loomed over the map where the clerks marked the position of the fleet in battle with smart pins topped with colored glass. The blue was for the Tyreen fleet, of course; the red, the Shari. The women worked quietly with speed using reports relayed by ravens and magi. There was another reason for their silence: for the first time in their service they were frightened of the Admiral for they felt her rage.

Jonsay was not for theatrics. Neither had she shouted nor thrown objects, though it took all of her discipline to not indulge herself. She feared if she gave in, she wouldn't be able to stop. Attacking Lieutenant Helan Tamidwyn, acting as Ta Rau Jethar, had woken an anger she hadn't known she was capable of. Helan had volunteered because, of all Jonsay's staff, her children were grown. She'd served on *The Oaken Blue* since Jonsay was a copilot. Damn everything to the deeps, Helan was to retire when they returned; she was well in her fifteenth decade, older than most serving in the fleet, but certainly not ready for the Door. It was only an arrow. Helan should be fine in the healer's hands. But the shock of it could still confuse a soul and make them wander. Even the possibility of losing her friend made Jonsay furious. The sunlight leaking through from the turret gallery windows reflected in her eyes, making them glow as if she was possessed by Sul herself. Most aelg captains, if they did give any weight to a particular part of their heritage, credited their Meer ancestry and Jonsay was no exception. And so she was surprised to feel so inflamed by the fire of Sul.

Yet this didn't unnerve her as much as the darker passion that birthed for revenge. Dark Amer whispered to the blessed as well as the damned. To the Sultan She may say, "Take all you desire in pillage and rapine," but to Jonsay, and no doubt to every red blooded mother in the fleet, Amer whispered of revenge, swift and bloody, with fire and sword, duty be damned. Temptation whispered with every heart beat, the essence of all Jonsay's ancestors shrilly wakened to an awareness of what she could do: they should flog the Shari before them, striking them to ash until not one soul lived.

But the Tyreen fleet was no longer a confederation of pirate brigands and Jonsay was no thug. Law and duty was what kept elfyn civilized and Jonsay had swore an oath to serve with honor. She exhaled and firmly set aside dreams of revenge.

Jonsay became aware of a surgeon at her side, her red taq bobbing at the periphery of Jonsay's vision. It would be her ship's prefect, Aileen nion Bledwyn. A blue-eyed Dwen Brownie, with a Gael name, many souls wondered how she came by her talents; the red facings on her white jacket notable because few ship's prefects were also surgeons.

"Speak, Emha Bledwyn. My anger is not with you."

"We have removed the arrow. Tamidwyn sleeps while she heals. It was a hole in the lung. Had it not happened with healers nearby, she would have drowned in her own blood."

Then Jonsay saw Bledwyn was holding an arrow, long shafted and tipped with iron. Or so she thought.

Taking the arrow Jonsay looked closely at the head. "Is this steel?"

"How can it be?" Bledwyn replied. "Sharitan has no great furnaces and no sulessence."

Jonsay felt the metal with her fingers. She'd hold it in the sun, but her cabin was almost entirely in shadow. "It reflects motes of light more sharply than iron. If they did not make it, then they are trading with someone who has. Thank you for the report."

Bledwyn inclined her head and withdrew.

Jonsay took a small napkin and wrapped it around the shaft, then called her clerk, Ensign Tamryn Amralan.

"Ensign, take this to the smith. I want to know if that head is iron or steel. If she confirms it's steel, take it to the magi. Record all they find in your notes. I will read it later."

"Emha," Amralan acknowledged, then left just as an aide entered.

"From *The Starshard*, emha," she said, giving Jonsay a folded missive.

Jonsay's spirits sank as she read Manweth's tidings: clouds were brewing in the south and east.

A small storm, but large enough to weaken cannons and lances. It wasn't a complete surprise; it had been foretold. But Jonsay had not counted on the Shari to have teeth. She looked up as Lieutenant Nan Gerindis swore. A

Brownie woman with deep green eyes, it was a shock to some she had no active wood-essence. What she did have was a mind for numbers. She was working a long list of figures with a male magi.

"Sorry, emha," Gerindis murmured.

"Don't apologize for your passion. How do you progress?"

It was the magi, Ta Ronel, who answered . "The problem is we don't have enough samples. And, as bold as Sea Mother Tamanth's move was, it may have hampered us."

"We can't understand the cypher," Jonsay said.

"No," Gerindis confirmed. "Perhaps with dreams?"

Ronel shrugged. "A waking mind is better. We should try of course, but the humyn deceive themselves. Thus often interrogating dreamers is not as useful as it might be. And humyn tend to interpret attempts at direct communication as whisperings from spirits."

"Or devils," Gerindis added.

"And what of the protocol to sway their dreams?" Jonsay asked.

"If they were simple sailors, it would be a thing simply done," Ronel said. "But the officers, they are truly terrified of failing the Sultan."

Jonsay thought a moment. "What of a distraction? Perhaps a false certainty of plunder elsewhere? At least divide themselves with the phantasm – What is it?"

A lieutenant had entered looking windswept in her rush to get to the cabin. "The Commodore wants to rout them while we have the sun."

Jonsay grabbed her bicorn and strode out the door, through the pilot's mess and onto the quarterdeck, the lieutenant at her heels. She made for the main mast, where ravens perched ready, but didn't call one. Everyone who served intimately with her on *The Oaken Blue* learned to watch *The Black Seal* and her captain. Sea Mother Tamnath Tresmadore, a cauldron of passion, was unlikely to show restraint in the calmest of seas. Now? Jonsay was half surprised *The Black Seal* still floated in her position. But she could see Tamnath, as usual hatless, black hair billowing in the wind like a pirate. Perhaps a rebuke for defying uniform regulations might becalm her.

There was wisdom in Tamnath's desire, but the fleet needed to act as one for certain victory. *The Tidebreaker*'s loss only reminded Jonsay nothing was certain on the sea.

"Get me a signal whistle," Jonsay said to no one in particular. She was pleased that within seconds one was sitting in her open palm.

Not all captains knew how to play the signal flute for its intended purpose, but Jonsay found the practice soothing. Facing east, pitching toward *The Black Seal*, she first sounded the notes that identified *The Black Seal*. Then she sent a call to address the captain. The ships near and anyone with keen ears could hear, but there was nothing she would send that could not be said in a staff meeting.

:Captain Tresmadore we are not routing them:

Jonsay paused waiting for a reply.

:We still have the sun: Tamnath whistled. :We can eliminate them all:

Jonsay took a breath, then exhaled. The logic was indisputable. But duty came first.

:We must do our duty – They are in retreat and have a chance to flee:

:They are not fleeing – The clouds come:

Jonsay was too divided to argue further. A part of her hoped that circumstances would change and so would her course. Tamnath was hardly the only captain with these thoughts. But until circumstances did change, their course was clear.

Jonsay sounded a bit louder:

:You will hold your position captain, until further orders:

Then she gave the flute to an aide as Ensign Amralan returned.

"With respect, Admiral," Amralan said, "The Shari's actions have shown their dishonorable intent. If we decimated them all, no one would censure you."

Jonsay turned away, shaking her head as she as if troubled by a persistent fly. Striding so fast the clerk was forced to jog to keep up, she replied, "Naval code is quite clear: it is dishonorable to destroy a fleeing enemy."

"But, emha, what if they aren't fleeing? Don't you feel they've retreated to connive more mischief?"

"Then we will defeat it when it comes." Jonsay strode back into her cabin. Jonsay didn't like to admit how much Tamnath's exhortations troubled her. She needed more intelligence.

"What did the smith say?"

"It's steel for certain," Amralan replied. "The magi are trying to learn more."

"Speaking of, how goes this exercise?" Jonsay said looming over Gerindis and Ta Ronel still working in the corner.

"It's fraught," Gerindis began.

"Make it less so," Jonsay commanded. "I want that code broken."

"Yes, emha."

Jonsay stepped up to the map and addressed her aides as a group. "Mothers?" she asked.

The dark skinned Lieutenant Saphin Evarain had a Gold mother and a Brownie sire, gifting her with a striking mix of bright green eyes and dark gold hair. She was fluent in Shari and therefore considered an expert on Shari matters. "They aren't in retreat," Saphin said, pointing to the jagged line of red pins showing where the fleet had withdrawn. "The Sultan is a tyrant and those leading his fleet are a mix of the ambitious and enthralled. Imagine trying to explain why your fleet of two hundred ships fled from twenty. They are preparing an assault, though they seem to be insensible to the fact we can still see them and their signal masts."

"Two hundred less fifteen," Jonsay corrected.

"And thirty-five more damaged in some way."

The door opened and another missive was passed between the women managing the map. Red pins were removed. A step in the right direction but not far enough.

"Four more Shari ships scuttled, Sea Mother," the new lieutenant, a man, put in. "Thirty-one damaged and barely seaworthy."

Gerindis said, "That's a hundred and fifty to twenty, and our twenty are leviathans to their hundred and fifty pike."

"Still quite a bit of pike," Jonsay murmured. "And what of the thirty odd damaged ships? Is it possible to repair them?"

"*Níl mé cinnte*," Master Cauld Edryn, a Gael Cambari with the faintest blue skin said. "It would take time and they'd have to cannibalize ships for supplies if their goal was to use them in battle. Otherwise, their best course is to make basic repairs and retreat to the shores of Sharitan while they can."

Lieutenant Evarain scoffed. "I say again, they will not do this! They will choose to die in battle before returning in ignominy to be boiled alive or flayed publicly! In a way it would be a mercy to strike them all. They will no longer fear and Gashora will be safe."

Jonsay shook her head, deciding to not respond to this proposed mercy killing.

"A sane admiral would flee," Jonsay said, holding a hand to forestall Evarain's objections. "They did flee. After the second volley of strike. Other ships were crushed or swamped because they miscalculated the speed of our vessels. Losing the use of over a score of vessels in seconds is not what humyn expect. In less than half of an hour we could have destroyed all their remaining ships. And in that knowledge they retreated. If they insist on engaging on the morrow, we will not have long."

"*Ach, an mbeith an ghrian againn?*" Evarain asked.

They exchanged looks, sharing the worry they might not have unlimited sunlight to power the solcannons.

"Nothing is certain," Jonsay said. Clouds of doubts grew. Was Tamnath right in this case? Strike them while they can?

"The Sultan is a deluded pike," Amralan was saying. "He thinks he's a leviathan. Those who displease him are executed in hideous ways, some nailed to frames to die in the heat after days."

"Yes, fear gives the Shari captains a reckless bravery," Jonsay agreed. "They will be desperate. And in that desperation they will make mistakes."

Another officer entered, handing Jonsay a folded missive. At its touch she was flooded with a mix of rage and irritation. Unlike her consort, Tergani, she'd never studied with the magi, but she didn't need skill in magic to know who it was from.

"A raven sent this from *The Black Seal*," the officer said.

"Yes, thank you." Jonsay opened the letter feeling both impatience and the desire to escape being harried:

> With complements, etc.
> The clouds are coming, Admiral. All the better to destroy the fleet now. Leave them wickers as a scruple to chivalry, if we must.
> TT

Jonsay exhaled sharply. She quickly wrote a reply and handed it to the officer . "My reply to *The Black Seal*."

"Yes, emha!"

The woman left with such alacrity Jonsay wondered if her eyes shimmered with anger again. She knew they had when she saw the arrows fly towards Ta Rau Jethar, knowing there was nothing to do but pray their flight was untrue. Thank Sul the magi thwarted that deadly hail. Jonsay wasn't a literalist who believed the Mother-gods, the mythical deities ancient society created, were as real as the living. But there were times when a woman had little choice but to pray and find faith in the optimism of providence, hoping for unexpected grace to change bad fortune.

Jonsay prayed that they would have a chance to both discharge their duty and avoid further killing. For from a cold pragmatic stance, Sea Mother Tamnath Tresmadore and all who echoed her were right. If the choice was between Jonsay's daughters and son, and the noble man she loved versus the Shari, she would have obliterated their entire fleet without a thought.

But Jonsay's household was far away, safely in Tyrum. She would not murder so many humyn, many innocent and compelled, unless she had no choice. And so she prayed the battle would be finished before the clouds rolled in.

Chapter 4

Thwarted

Sea Mother and fleet commodore Tamnath Tresmadore stood silent on the deck of *The Black Seal* as the black wings of the raven bore it back over the water to *The Oaken Blue*. It had not waited to be fed; perhaps it, like the women who stood silently near her, knew this was not a time to ask for favors. The crisp stiff paper, made of scrap linen and reed, felt rough to her fingers, as if it too rebuked her. She had not opened it yet. Truly she didn't need to. Tamnath knew the answer: in so many words, long or brief, it said "No".

Tamnath stared out at the place in the water where Ta Rau Jethar had been shot, where the Shari had doomed themselves in their dishonorable idiocy. It was so easy to imagine the Shari fleet in flames, their crew's screams as they roasted alive, or desperate for succor, jumped into the water to meet their grim fate at the tridents of the marines. Her veins were on fire, thirsting for vengeance and more: the Jackal wanted to come out and play the game of pillage and death.

But it was not to be. No matter what the provocation, Jonsaymanor would abide by the rules of war. And duty compelled Tamnath to open the folded note and read what was there. Tamnath lowered her eyes, not moving her head, opening the missive with one hand. The writing was Jonsay herself, thin impatient strokes of black gall ink, reading in very clear Hiltekash:

> Complements, etc.
> Death by water, cold and shark is still death. It would be kinder to scorch them outright than pretend a death sentence is a mercy. Hold the line and watch. That is your final order.
> JJ

Tamnath's gut clenched, though she didn't fathom why. She was no freshly recruited callow girl looking for motherly approval from senior officers. Yet Jonsay did make her feel a bit like a youth. Usually this was a welcome thing, Tamnath's need for guidance and nurturing sated through mentorship. But this was a rebuke, and though Tamnath knew she was dear to Jonsay, as well as being within her rights as admiral, Tamnath's stung feelings would not abate and sought a release. She barely noticed when the note curled in flames and fell to black ash. It was not required to save every missive, though some captains did. But burning the paper was not enough for the Jackal. She must be given sport, yet not in any way that would undermine duty.

Tamnath thought for a while. A copilot drove her ship now, so she let herself walk to the starboard wale and look down where the divers had been searching for the horn. The errant Shari vessel had been driven away so they should be reappearing soon. Suddenly the water erupted as all the divers surfaced. Tamnath watched, sighting the one who had the horn. This diver was a very humyn looking, heavy bosomed and long haired. She must have the water-essence of Maer herself. The horn was passed to another who led a school back to *The Oaken Blue*. Then the schools parted, divers returning to their ship's waters, Tamnath's own swimming quickly to the aft of the Black Seal where the diver's ladder ran from the top of the stern deck to the water line. The fading sun glimmered redly on the waves as they passed, giving Tamnath an idea. She darted up the stern stairs wanting to meet the school herder as the divers boarded.

The herder, Wahoon yal Nomney, like most Blue divers, was a broad shouldered, blue skinned woman, with fluked hands and feet. She would have had thick black hair had it not been shaved off; like her Meer foremothers, her chest was flat, the only ripple from healthy pectorals. Only if she was growing child would her breast develop to meet the task of weening. The divers favored canvas trousers that laced at the sides and generally eschewed footwear.

"A diver from *The Tidebreaker* found it," Wahoon said, stepping onto the deck dripping water. "Swims better than you'd think."

Wahoon was followed by the ship's complement of divers, those with hair shaking their heads to the irritation of the strike crews nearby. Soon the aft stern was crowded with Blue.

"Assemble them," Tamnath ordered. "I need volunteers for a task."

Wahoon looked at her quizzically, but said, "Yes emha." Then she turned
to bellow, "School, muster on deck!"

Soon the divers were in two rows, a motley mix of blue tinted skin, some
with salmon freckling, with the odd dry tone. Tamnath ran a mother's ship
and it showed. The divers were all women except one, and she always forgot about him because he had so much Meer, at a casual glance to the landed
like Tamnath, he looked female. He was only slightly shorter than the rest
and swam like a mother, and that's what counted. She didn't spare him a
thought because she never trysted with "Fish". At least not until Aslynari.
And the male diver, whichever one he was, was no Aslynari.

"You did well today, sisters," Tamnath said, addressing the school.
"Now I need a service from those of you who hear the sun sing. I know it's
not common, and few of you find it your best feature, but today I need it.
Those who can move sulessence, please step forward. Driver Wahoon, you
may dismiss the rest."

Five total remained standing on the deck.

"Have you all used a trident before?"

They looked at each other, and one by one affirmed, "Yes, Sea Mother."

Tamnath smiled tightly a moment, pleased her idea was coming together.
"Good. Then you know how to carry and swim. You will not be taking a
trident, however, but sun lances. If you've never used one, one of the
lancers will show you how to strike."

The women looked excited and intrigued. "And what will our task be?"
one diver asked.

Tamnath allowed herself a thin smile. "You will go and scorch every single Shari signal flag and flag pole to a tinder. I want to see hot pitch black-
ening the air. And, if any Shari swimmer tries to stop you, you have liberty
to kill it."

After some brief practice under the direction of the strikemaster, the
divers, with their new lances, lined up at the ship's stern. One by one, they
poured gracefully over the side, followed by the faint splash of them hitting
water. Shortly Tamnath could just make out five figures skimming the water
below the surface as they sped to the Shari fleet. Tamnath expected Jonsay
to give an order to dress their line, but she'd wait until dusk to be certain the

humyn could not see their maneuvers. By then, Tamnath expected the deed to be done.

Meanwhile Tamnath ordered a modest luncheon of cheese, hard eggs and ham to be served with the pea stew for their late breakfast conference to be held in the magi berth. The full truth of the Dragon of Tamask would be revealed, as well as the best way to fight it. Afterward, Tamnath would tour the hospital that had been placed in the crew mess hall. There were few serious injuries, superficial arrow wounds, temporary dazzle blindness, and incidental bruises and cuts common during an action. No deaths, not even temporary. There was a rumor one ship had suffered an irretrievable loss. If true, the captain had Tamnath's pity. That Sea Mother would be doomed on their return to speak to the household of the lost. This was the way in the Federation patrol, and adopted by the Tyreen fleet after Recognition in the Year of Lots, 2531, over three millennia ago. Tyrum forsook piracy when it agreed serve the Federation in exchange for material support. Tamnath hoped no other souls would be irretrievably lost.

Later, she might take supper in a tower on the stern deck with her officers. If they were lucky they would see the results of the diver's actions and the Jackal, for a while, would be sated.

Chapter 5

The Dragon of Tamask

Voices echoed around Rosen, orders sang, and the story unfolded:

Ta Rau Jethar was wounded but alive. The horn fell into the water and the divers were tasked to retrieve it. As such, an order was given to the Shari that they may rescue their sailors, but were not to approach the ships.

Rosen stood numb for a moment more, then barked to no one in particular, "Get me a raven! Send it to my cabin."

Did Admiral Jonsaymanor know the Dragon of Tamask had roared? Surely she didn't know an officer was dead. Rosen was weary but still smoldered with anger. He understood Farthal. He wanted the sea on fire for the death of Glethlyn. That would not happen until the Admiral knew. He turned to Glethlyn to tell her to take the cage. Of course that was absurd. Glethlyn would never stand in the cage again. He nodded at Lieutenant Sithinas already in the cage, it being understood she should stay.

In short order Rosen descended the from the stern deck and through the door beneath it into the pilot's mess. It was a large room, light by the stern deck skylight, the center filled with a long table, four doors to individual cabins at either side. He barely marked Ensign Savalis and the handful of midships clustered around her.

"Sea Father?" she queried. "Is it over already?"

Rosen didn't reply. His eyes lingered on the last larboard cabin on his right, where Glethlyn had berthed. His jaw clenched as he strode into his own cabin through the open door at the very end of the mess.

The gallery windows that ran the aft length of the ship looked over deceptively calm water. The view of the sea was north-northwest, the water marked by the moving shadows of the city-ships as the day aged. Only at the very ends of the line, far west and east, hung the steam and smoke of the battle, or the floating wreck of a Shari vessel. "Death to the Shari", Rosen thought, this time without shame. He strode to his desk, not bothering to sit, writing a missive as he stood, pen flying over the paper so fast, he had to pause to let the gall ink dry before folding it. The raven arrived, sailing awkwardly through the door, thoughts on the verge of sharing its irritation as it landed on the back of a chair. But Rosen cut off any avian inanities barking, "Take this to the Admiral!"

Rosen strode out after the raven's flight, back under the sun, still full of anger, still with no purpose. Glethlyn was still gone, the lack of her presence a wound in his soul, ripped from them before her time. He gazed over the sea, eager to see the Shari suffer. Most of the their surviving ships, of which their were still many, had pulled back to their reserve line, those damaged lagging significantly behind, hopefully terrified of being overrun. It would serve them right. Some that survived strike listed, no longer seaworthy whether due to lack of oars, oardrivers, or other damage. A few labored to raise their masts, in the hope of catching a wind to move them faster; others were towed. Bet the filthy Shari hadn't planned for any of this, Rosen thought nastily.

Yet the Shari were apparently stupid. Defying the orders to stay away from the city-ships, one ship struck out, its oars working a froth, glistening as they picked up speed. They were aiming for the divers searching the water for the horn, now behind the Tyreen line. Rosen should take the advice he'd given to the late Glethlyn; there was no logic to their thought, only a reactionary assumption of victory. Walking to the aft larboard turret, Rosen had a side view of the ship's bow, fitted with an aggressive metal protrusion for ramming, an intimidating threat to a lesser fleet. The worst that might happen to a city-ship would be the ram getting stuck. In any case the divers weren't in danger if they kept their heads. Sure enough, as the ship came closer, the divers disappeared below water.

But perhaps that hadn't been the Shari's goal at all. In seconds the oardrivers worked the ship so it turned. In less than a minute the bows would be facing *The Oaken Blue's* stern.

"Strike Captain?" Rosen called out, feeling alarm. He was standing near the larboard turret solcannon.

"Ai, Sea Father?" Lieutenant Olesh Desmet replied.

"Strike that ship if you can."

"It's a bit far, Sea Father," Striker Tellon Braz said. She was one of the women pivoting the six foot length of solstone to aim at the ship. "Might dazzle them though."

"That will do. Strike!"

Standing right beside them, Rosen lowered his eyes as sunstrike flared across the water, a breath of steam released as it passed, but otherwise did no damage to elf or sea. But the effect on the Shari boat was immediate. While it didn't slow significantly, the oardrivers being sheltered from the glare by either the deck or their line of shields, the activity at the fore around the Dragon halted as hands and arms were thrown up to protect eyes. Then there was a blinding flash from a nearer ship. Rosen blinked. When he looked again he was surprised the Shari ship still floated. The entire top bow was gone, the front blackened and burning, a humyn leaning over to look at the damage. Then Rosen realized the man wasn't leaning over at all, but had been seared almost in half his body gruesomely hanging over the wale. The hide-covered tent that protected the Dragon fell apart in charred splinters, the Dragon itself, half melted, having fallen to the smoldering deck.

The captain survived somehow, his black turban bobbing back and forth as he shouted orders. Water was carried to douse the flames before they reached the salts as the oardrivers frantically worked to reverse away from the back of the Tyreen line, then to make a laborious journey around to re-join their fleet.

"Strike their eyes, that'll learn them!" Desmet crowed, while the women cheered.

Rosen didn't join them. There was no joy to be found in the wake of a lost soul.

"Sea Father?" a magi asked. Glenfar had returned to the stern deck.

"How is the lieutenant?" Rosen asked, knowing the answer, a part of him still hoping for a miracle. They walked a short way to stand over the far aft of the stern, looking down into the wake. The usual froth was absent as *The Tidebreaker* drifted in place at the moment.

"It is as you know," Glenfar said. "Healing cannot be done away from a temple with missing essentials and the mind is the most essential part of the body. I'm sorry."

"I want the sea on fire."

"Yes. Of course."

"The Admiral is helping rescue these murderers!" Rosen bit out, watching as the last Shari were fished from the water and their ships beat as fast a retreat as they could.

"The Admiral is a chivalrous and honorable woman. Remember many would not come if they were not compelled by the Sultan."

"I care not!"

"Understandable. I liked Glethlyn too. The projectile has been retrieved for study. And *The Oaken Blue* has responded to your missive." Glenfar held out a folded paper. "I know how vexing you find ravens. I fed it... "

Rosen took the paper wordlessly and snapped it open. Blank soulless words in gall mocked him, probably written by a clerk:

> Compliments, etc.
>
> Regret for *The Tidebreaker's* loss. Gratitude for the intelligence confirming the nature of the Dragon. Be strong and steady in our duty.
>
> A JJ

Rosen crumpled the paper and held it in a fist in the weak sunlight. His sulessence was nothing magical. There was too much competing blood from alien elfyn and humyn streams drowning it out. But his anger gave it force, and the paper burst into flames. He only let it go when it was ash floating away on a breeze, like the failed promises of an indifferent lover. Suddenly Glenfar grabbed his wrist and he felt an abrupt coolness.

"Your sleeve was burning," she explained as she let him go.

"Thank you," Rosen murmured absently, looking at the scorched blue fabric. He took a deep breath then exhaled. It would do no good to lose control now.

More orders whistled: the Shari had retreated into a huddle. The fleet was to retreat to a north guard at dusk, leaving the Shari room to finish their rescue, then to run, when that wisdom came upon them.

There was more: it was discovered the Shari communicated between ships with a series of flags. No sooner than the last whistle sounded than a ship edged forward. It took Rosen a moment to mark the figurehead of a sea lion. *The Black Seal*, the ship of the fleet commodore and, even in a nation of mothers, the most obnoxious woman Rosen had ever met. But in this moment Rosen forgot their enmity, so eager he was for some mother to do something to sate vengeance. The flare that came was small and narrow, not a cannon but a lance, and Rosen suspected the Jackal, (the sobriquet of *The Black Seal*'s captain, Tamnath Tresmadore) held it herself. Surely Tresmadore was too far to affect any but perhaps the lagging damaged ships as they limped back to the Shari line.

Yet Tamnath's sulessence was also empowered by rage, enabling feats unexpected. For the narrow ray of white light reached through the air to touch a flag mast on a retreating vessel. Then another, and another until Tresmadore was out of targets in range. The small flags burned in seconds, like flash paper. Now there was no more strike. The Shari continued to retreat, becoming distant specs on the water. A whistle from *The Oaken Blue* confirmed the stand down to hold their position. The battle was done for the day.

Rosen ran down from the stern deck to the companionway stair in the center of the quarterdeck, then down below to the upper deck. The crew mess and galley, where the hospital had been set up, were at the far end of the ship, near the bows. A deck officer shouted his presence which aided greatly in parting the motley collection of fighting volunteers who had clustered waiting to be called above. Many were Cambari, aelg descended from humyn tribes from the north, their elven features incongruous with striped bracs or plaid kilts. Others had a mix of Meer ancestry and, like the fleet's marines, would favor scale armor and tridents, preferring to take the fight to the water and drown the enemy where they could hold their breath an hour. Past the scrum of warriors were berths to starboard, open hatches to the holds to Rosen's left, the activity of resupplying and repairs still in progress. Finally he came to the open mess doors and entered the chamber.

In a hall spacious enough to feed regular crew, tables had been laid out for surgery but only two of them were in use. On one a diver sat while an arrow head was cut out of her blue-skinned shoulder by a red hatted surgeon, clearly her pain dulled by either touch or draught; she only winced now and then while her fellows stared in curiosity. The other table had to be Glethlyn, for the figure laid out was covered with a white drape. Rosen saw

Jarroth returning to her full senses. She ran over to him suddenly to a healer's irritation, her fair head still hatless.

"Sea Father!" she cried. "Is it true? Glethlyn is gone? It can't be true, can it?"

Rosen said nothing as he walked to the table where several other officers were clustering. Ranks officer Woodweaver Aflelett Fadwen caught his arm. Her yastol leaf crown shook with her head, a queen of the wood denying the passing of any good missive. But Rosen wanted to hear it himself. Prefect Mathynwol, unlike the healers working with her, wore not a robe but a white coat cut much like the officer's uniform, except with green facings, with white sea breeches and leather and linen town slippers. Her lips were pursed as she drew the white cloth back, gold eyes glaring at the horror she was helpless to cure. Jarroth having caught up with Rosen, froze at his side, her inhale of shock louder than the rest of the women. Rosen put a hand on her shoulder, squeezing it firmly, letting the ensign know she was not alone. Together they gazed on the body that had been Glethlyn, merry, cheerful Glethlyn, who would never laugh again. A scarf had been laid over half her face to hide the full horror of her injuries.

"I'm sorry, Sea Father," Mathynwol said. "The lieutenant may as well have been decapitated for all the good I can do. Look for her in dreams." She replaced the sheet, a mother putting her daughter to rest for the last time.

Glethlyn, like any others who had been lost, would be burned on the water at dawn the next day. Rosen was grateful *The Tidebreaker* had only one irretrievable loss, but why did it have to be Glethlyn? But then who would he sacrifice to spare his feelings? No souls deserved to go thusly before their centuries on the Orb were spent. For now they, officers and ranks, crew and volunteer, stood around Glethlyn and mourned. Jarroth sniffed sharply in the way of adolescents keeping themselves from tears. Rosen let his hand fall from her shoulder in respect for her pride. They rest looked grim, as grim as himself he imagined. At times like these the force of their elfyn ancestry came fore. Though no words were exchanged, an understanding of thought and feeling coursed through them, a frisson of souls touching one another, so they were all of one mind. No one cared anymore what Rosen had done with Galen. And when Rosen spoke it was as if they spoke together:

"Death to the Shari."

"Death to the Shari," they echoed.

"Return to duty," Rosen added. They parted to their diverse stations.

A glance around the makeshift hospital revealed most injuries were of a burning sort. Among the midships waiting for tending, girls showed each other where they were scorched or scalded while wetting the deck. Many women were dazzled blind and a couple had white corneas, cooked by the heat of solcannons whose proximity they could not escape. Annoyed, Rosen sought the soul to blame, the Marshal's agent that had been foisted on him. These women could be cured easily but if their blindness lingered for more than a day they would be useless if more fighting was to come. Rosen spied Farthal, helping a male healer distribute draughts.

"Come on, you," Jarroth's voice echoed breaking Rosen's thoughts. He watched as the ensign was taking her hat from a midship, a Brownie girl with gold eyes, full of the sad news of Glethlyn's passing. "Let's have none of that! She'd want us to be cheered, that was her, never a sad tale only cheer. Did I tell you when Glethlyn dared me to walk the wale? Green, I was, dead callow… "

With that Jarroth walked the midship away, distracting her with light tales no matter how heavy her own soul was. Rosen was filled with pride. Tocyn Jarroth would make a fine captain one day if she lived that long.

A conference was gathered in the magi berth, above the mess, just under the fore deck. In main, it was a large chamber with a communing circle, or sadol, in the center. Not the typical circle of odd numbered stones, but engraved in the floor timbers, then filled with a grout of grimsteel, the black meteoric iron that was the best conduit of essence. Bunks lined the walls, and within were two dreaming chambers, one being the berth of ship's adept, Tarenol Ganith, called in her trade Ta Tarenol or Ta Taren. It was rare for so many who were not of the order to be present in a wizard's berth, but Ta Taren had insisted, feeling it would be the most efficient way to communicate with the command crew. They were further blessed that tables had been set out for an abundance of food to be shared by all. The magi were jealous of their Sel's Small Cakes, the rich, dense, fist sized cakes of pulse and nut flour that helped a wizard feed the essence demands on their bodies. But there was plenty from the galley made for regular crew: pan fried cakes to line a trencher or bowl, with boiled peas mixed with pieces of bacon and cut sausage. It was a quick unimaginative meal with the thought to feed many souls as fast as possible for none of them had eaten much since the night before.

"Needs salt and vinegar," Galen opined between bites.

"We should be blessed there is any food at all," Rosen replied though he agreed. It was the first time they had spoken outside of duty since they had unwisely trysted.

"You call this food?" marine Captain Arlesh yal Ahlool said, making a face as she ate with her fluked hands. A Blue soul with red hair cascading from a flout on her crown, she was given to fish like her Meer foremothers, the less cooked the better. Unlike most she had barely finished half her portion.

"I'll take it," said Ledranal Mordmhol, captain of the ship's guard. The front of her black hair was bound by clips on the top of her head, her face and neck marked by tattoos, but nothing to the extent of Galen's. She was built much like Galen; in her hand was an empty bowl.

Galen was chewing fast, Rosen felt she was surely about to claim the bowl, when Ahlool gifted her half eaten bowl to Mordmhol. "It is not wasted," Ahlool said with relief. The Tyreen navy did not tolerate waste. "And there will be a fresh harvest from the sea anon from our divers."

"*Go raibh maith agat*," Mordmhol said in Gael by way of thanks, tucking in immediately.

Galen swallowed. "First you cheat me at Gains, then steal free food from my hand!" she said in pique.

"*Ní mór duit a bheith níos gasta ná sin*," Mordmhol said shamelessly.

"I'll give you quick the next time we play cards."

"*B'fhéidir ... nach b'fhéidir.*"

"Personally I'd prefer to hear the magi tell us more about the enemy than hear my staff squabble about food," Rosen said crossly. The food was bland, his spirits spent, and he welcomed anything to keep thoughts about Glethlyn's loss at bay. Those present were all the command staff, the higher ranks officers and their mates, and such assistants as seemed reasonable.

The tall, narrow Ensign Savalis darted in. Her presence was sensible; whatever aversions she had to abandoning the books, in listening to the magi report herself she could record it better.

Rosen caught her eye as the two windows in the berth were covered, leaving one weak lanthorn for minimal light.

"Eat," he said looking pointedly at the sideboard.

But Savalis shook her head. "Sorry, Sea Father. I can't." She didn't weep but her green eyes were full of sorrow.

Rosen nodded once and didn't press it. "But you shall before you take sleep, if it is only a crust of bread and barley-mead. You will be working most of the night. Don't lie, ensign. You are dutiful to a fault. It will be needed and is appreciated. For you to do your duty best, you must eat."

The room was so dark only the light of the almost spent lanthorn painted the bare outlines of souls with tracings of yellow and orange. The air above the center of the room, indeed the center of the sadol started to glow ghostly pale blue, then sharp white. The room gasped as a grotesque lion's head seemed to snarled at them. Slowly the image rotated, manipulated by a magi casting the light into form, the lion being not living of course, but a cast ornamentation at the end of a metal tube as long as a solstone cannon.

"This is the Dragon of Tamask," Ta Taren began, her voice carrying as clear as a speaking horn. "Clearly misnamed by a vague dreamer. It is cast of two pieces of thick bronze twisted, then locked together. The gap in the lion's mouth is a little wider than a large fist, fitting a ball of about the same size, also bronze. The butt end of the Dragon is closed. It operates by a small sack of cured saltpeter, the 'charge', being shoved down to the bottom, followed by the ball or other 'shot'. There is a small gap in the tube for a fuse, much like a firework. The successive explosion drives the ball forth to do deadly damage as we have recently learned." There was a pause as they thought on Glethlyn.

"As terrible as that was, killing individuals of the enemy it not its primary purpose. This is a siege engine. It can be angled as you see here, on the crude wooden frame. We think the Shari planned to breach the hulls of lesser ships. And when they made landfall, use them against gates and walls. One shot would not be enough of course. It would take a sustained effort of at least hours, possibly days, depending on the fortification. We wonder how many of these balls remain, not counting those lost to sea. Following is the collective advice each ship is being given: the Dragon can be angled vertically within limits, but not horizontally. So a captain should endeavor to keep her… or his… ship from exposing a broadside to the Dragon. This of course will not always be possible, especially as, if we engage again, the Shari have every thought of surrounding and boarding a ship if they have a chance. Our advice is strike when they are in range but far enough from our own ship, and aim for the center of the bows. That is where the salts are stored."

"If the Admiral lets us," some soul muttered.

"That will do!" Rosen barked, before any other could add their opinion. "Continue, Ta Taren."

"Briefly these are the catapults." The Dragon faded to be replaced by a much more familiar image of a ballista. "Cruder and smaller than the engines used by the feudal lors, they are nonetheless effective for their purpose. Unlike the Dragon, these were meant to be deadly at sea, but have so far been ineffective. They have mostly scratched paint and damaged the gilded friezes. But the Meer King has a partially shattered rib-fin, so it is foolish to let them come too close. They are invariably in the center of the ships' side castles. They should be the next target if the bow is not presented. I give you over to Ship's Master and Navigator, Sonan Jasmenal."

Rosen blinked with the rest of the crowd at the sudden return of light as the windows were uncovered. Apparently no light vision was needed to illustrate Jasmenal's points. She simply stood in the center of the room and spoke:

"In our first exchange, seven Shari ships were destroyed, and just over twice that many damaged in some degree. This did not alter their course no matter how alarming the sight of sunstrike surely was. Losses like these are typical of humyn battles at sea. Surely they expected more, but they also expected more gains for their sacrifice. It was only the sudden loss of the next score of ships that truly alarmed them, not counting the crippling of about the same number. For that bill it would be expected they would at least have been able to capture a couple of our ships for the trouble. Their morale will be damaged for we've thwarted their main goal, their journey to

Gashora. The collated report from *The Oaken Blue* gives a modest prediction the Shari will retreat."

Rosen looked askance at the papers in Jasmenal's hand. No raven would have ferried such a scroll. He glanced at Savalis. No, he would not ask her. She was an ensign; when he was an ensign, it would never have occurred to him to question a request from the ship's Master, even if the task was one primarily for the Sea Mother's eyes.

"For ourselves, there have been no others irretrievably lost except what *The Tidebreaker* has borne," Jasmenal continued. "Our fleet wounded number in the dozens, mostly flash blindness and a few arrow wounds. The Shari on the other hand have lost at least a third of their marine fighting force, with a significant number trapped on vessels no longer battle worthy."

There was no cheer, no celebration of the fact. Only a collective glower, with a wish that these sea fleas just leave, abandon their ambition, making up whatever lie or ruse the Sultan might believe.

"Now I'm sure our captain will tell us when we will send Lieutenant Becan Glethlyn off on her final journey."

Jasmenal's green eyes locked with Rosen's gold, unreadable. To his discomfit every soul in the chamber turned to him, expecting guidance that he was not ready to give. He honestly had given no thought of the practicalities while he wrestled with grief. He'd need to appoint a new first lieutenant as well.

"Thank you, master," Rosen found himself saying. Had she ambushed him publicly to test him? Watch if he cracked? A captain could be removed during war if she, or he, was not up to the task. "We must give Glethlyn's shade a chance to say her goodbyes. Since we are awake, we do not know how long we can linger. But she will know we have no abundance of time to spare. We will give her the night and send her off at dawn as custom."

There was a general murmur of agreement, at both respecting the custom of wake and the urgency of their unfinished duty.

"Until then, return to duty," Rosen said. He was somewhat pleased Jasmenal seemed to check herself, as if she had wanted to add something. Good. She should remember, except in rare circumstances, the ship's master was not the captain.

As the crowd dispersed, many taking more food as they went, Rosen intercepted Jasmenal.

"Captain?" she queried.

"I wanted to thank you, Master, for collating the reports. It would be helpful for me to review them at my leisure."

The pause was less than a breath but Rosen noted it. "Of course, captain," Jasmenal said. "I only thought speed at the time would aid us all." She passed the papers into Rosen's hand. "Only it will aid me in my own duties to have them as a reference."

Rosen didn't hear untruth, or even the shiver of truth bent to her own purposes. This surprised him. Her actions might not have been meant to undermine his authority. "Understandably," he found himself saying. "Ensign Savalis?"

"Ai, Sea Father?"

"When you are finished with your primary tasks, make a copy for our master if you will. Better yet, get one of the purser's clerks to do it."

"Yes, effa," Savalis said, leaving the magi berth with the notes in hand.

There was a cool silence between Rosen and Jasmenal for a couple of heart beats.

"I was only exploiting a chance to do my duty," Jasmenal finally said.

"It was an excellent execution of initiative," Rosen replied.

"I'm glad you think so, captain."

"Still, as tried and weary as we all are, I should have seen this report first. I'm sure it simply slipped your mind. Again well done, Master."

Rosen turned away without waiting for a reply.

He would have left then except for words that seemed to carry:

"Why didn't I catch it?" Glenfar's voice echoed from a bunk where she sat, her sable robes looking more somber than usual. Next to her stood older women of the order, including Ta Taren.

"Stop that," Taren said, not without sympathy. "Do not confuse what you knew then and what you know now. You knew it was danger, and you possibly saved our Sea Father's life. You did not know the type of danger. And even if you had, catching it would not have been wise. It had the force to rip your hand from your arm. Better to shove it aside, if the chance comes again. You cannot return to the past and do anything differently, so you are wasting energy. Think instead of what you will do better. But Sel's bosom, do it without self blame…"

Easier said, Rosen thought. He spent the rest of the day catching up on his logs. Until dawn the chest would be open, then sealed again before the funeral. He let his duties occupy his mind, keeping the grim thoughts at bay. When he retired he hoped tiredness would take him to Glethlyn in dreams. They were not long coming.

Rosen had only dreamed with the dead a couple times in his life; when his mother's mother passed, and when his winter-shepherd Sephus died. They could be startling, a simple dream interrupted by a sudden presence. Many reported that they didn't even realize it was the dead taking leave until they woke. As he fell asleep, no sooner had he woken to dreams than he saw Glethlyn sitting in his chair waiting for him.

"I've seen the rest of the crew," she said. She looked much like in life, still in uniform, but with her hair was free, and her eyes, like all the dead , were black with the hint of starlight sparkling through them from eternity. "I can't tarry, I've yet to visit home. I can hear the singing. So beautiful… One can only resist for so long."

"I'm sorry," Rosen said. Everything he thought of sounded inadequate. His grandmother had lived a full life and her passing was seen as the continuation of the mother's journey. Sephus didn't really understand what was happening. He was just full of joy to no longer feel the arthritis that had afflicted him near the end. His last thought was for Rosen to join him soon. Rosen trusted the joys of the Otherworld would be enough to ease Sephus' disappointment for a couple centuries. But Glethlyn wouldn't have centuries anymore. She was dead before most of her life had been lived.

"Oh, Sea Father, don't pity me," she said standing. "I didn't feel a thing. Though I was quite angry once I understood. I… well, there's no point in going over it. Taran will have to grow without me. I appreciate the affection that drives the desire for revenge. But I see many things clearer from this side. Most of the Shari are slaves to their duty, indentured or driven by the fear of what will happen to them or their families. Some share the deluded Sultan's dreams. Destroy their faith and they will scatter. It was a joy serving with you. Keep it bright, Sea Father. In victory of the Otherside, eh?"

Then Glethlyn vanished and Rosen woke.

Rosen wiped his moist eyes.   He was no longer sleepy and so he rose to write the eulogy.

Chapter 6

Horn and Wake

Pearl swam with urgency. She'd taken a good breath before diving into the deeps, Sharkhook right behind her. She still didn't grasp what was happening; they had been schooling underwater, treading in formation when something had gone wrong with the parley. The only thing she knew for certain was Ta Rau Jethar's horn had dropped into the deeps and needed to be retrieved.

She had sped to the spot the school driver indicated, but saw nothing. Now she was circling slowly down, trying to spy the glint of white horn with hammered gold accents. It wasn't actually a necessity and Pearl took heart that if they had time to retrieve this, their situation could hardly be dire. Then driver sounded to the entire fleet school:

((Dive deep. Strike will burn the water))

Pearl looked back at Sharkhook who sank level to her. ((A Shari ship dares to threaten *The Oaken Blue*)), she sounded.

Pearl would have laughed but needed to conserve her breath. Instead she rolled her eyes, allowing a couple of bubbles to dwerble up. Then she continued her search. Out of the corner of her eyes she saw other divers either skimming the water or, like her, circling around a spot, before abandoning it for another. Above the water currents shifted as the ship's school drivers treading shallowly suddenly dove away from impending danger. Looking down, Pearl didn't see the target, but suddenly her blue green tinted world lit up as a bright flash exploded silently above. In that moment Pearl spied a glimmer of gold, the decorative border of laurel and moonflower worked in metal circling the open end of the horn as it nestled far below in a tangle of seaweed. The next second the light was gone and all was dull again, but Pearl dived unerringly and felt the auroch horn with its cool metal accents in her grasp as she shot up.

Sharkhook sounded to the school the horn had been found as Pearl rose to the surface. The rest of the school was rising now, and, as one, avoided the place strike had flared. The water might still be boiling hot, or a surviving Shari could get lucky. As they rose, Pearl spied figures like themselves

sinking into the water, flouts keeping their hair in a cone on the head out of
the way, if that was needed. They wore scale mail, glimmering gold and
green in the water, and held tridents. As they floated down, controlling their
descent with water essence, they looked much like a soldier on land, frozen
in the middle of a long leap. The glassy sky of the underwater world was
broken by muffling splashes as many humyn fell into the water, some jumping from their burning boats, others already dead. These fell slowly past
into the deep gloom of the sea depths never to be seen again. But the living,
who fought for life, thrashed on the surface, some trying vainly to swim in
their armor, others doing what they could to cast it off before they sank.
Pearl pulled back to tread water from a distance. She could not have explained why: she had felt the minds of Shari slaves in the merchant galleys
beyond and was revolted to the depths of her soul women were kept for such
vile use. But these did not seem like slave masters. The mood of their
minds had no dreams of riches or conquest, just the terror of dying in the
water and the desperation to do whatever necessary to live. Thus it was unfortunate for them a company of marines suddenly swam to intercept them.
Pearl watched in fascination and horror as the humyn were seized, whether
by robe, hauberk or hair, and pulled away from the surface, skewered on tridents, if necessary then pulled down until they were dead from lack of
breath. The water filled with red mist …

((Pearl!)) Sharkhook sounded.

Pearl shook herself, swimming rapidly away from the killing waters, to a
place safe to surface. She erupted between the hulls of *The Oaken Blue* and
The Black Seal, the horn still in hand.

"Well done!" the school leader from *The Oaken Blue* said, a wild looking woman with tattoos of squid tentacles down her arms.

Pearl handed the horn over. "Only doing my duty," she said, then wondered why. She'd never seen herself as particularly "dutiful", certainly not
patriotic. Those she loved, she loved fiercely, but she loved no nation.
What, the Meer, who treated her like a freak for her full figure? Or the Federation who tolerated her mongrelness as useful in service of Tyrum? And
yet this feeling of duty to those she swam with grew, and the reason they
swam together could not be ignored.

Pearl shook herself, black hair spraying droplets. It didn't matter. She could feel camaraderie and connection to other mothers of the fleet without worshiping the Federation and the landed values it endorsed. While they were risking their lives to defend the lifestyle of Ta Mel, she knew demagogues denounced the city of Tyrum and debated the maintenance. Suddenly she felt defensive of her adopted home.

"We're returning!" Sharkhook called before she dived.

Pearl abandoned her thoughts and followed to rejoin their school. Ta Mel was full of "hak". Pearl was her own agent and would be loyal to whom she wanted for as long as they deserved her loyalty. If that was patriotism, she would not debate the label.

* * *

Col sat uneasily next to Freya as she sharpened her black, grimsteel blade for all the good it did. Sparks flew as she drew the stone across the edge, the screech a complaint against its ill and unnecessary use. No metal or stone so far could scratch much less sharpen the blade any further, but Freya found the action soothing and Col was mesmerized as the sparks reflected in the greenish blue sheen of the dark metal, as if looking long and deeply into a mirror of the gods that could show them their fate.

"Would you stop that abominable racket?" Bron growled.

They were waiting on the upper deck, sitting or lying on the floor boards, against a wall Col was certain divided the deck from the heart chamber. Though his active essence was weak, there was a power, like the pressure of a storm against the ear, a shivering of magic in the air reminiscent of static. To either side was open deck space, plenty of room for the volunteers and marines to gather. The marines had gone above to enter the water a while ago. Now there was more room to recline if one desired. This area was to the aft of the ship; ahead were open hatches with a series of stairs leading both up to the tops and down into the lower decks. Around the supports of the companionway stairs, indeed wrapped everywhere practical, was breathing vine, a plant that filtered noxious air. Daylight gave dim illumination from the hatches above, relieving some of the gloom the lanthorns struggled to light. There was constant activity around the hatches down to the main hold, with queries on the state of supplies. A few minutes earlier, a couple healers ran past them to the nearest stair. They returned shortly later with a wounded officer on a stretcher, carrying her quickly to the hospital set up in the crew mess hall.

An explosion was heard, followed by another. Col gathered the solcannons were striking.

Freya stopped whetting her blade. "Sorry, cousin."

Col shook himself. "It's odd," he said. "I thought grimsteel was used in the heart of the ships."

Freya nodded, her long red-gold locks shivering. "Ai. And for the center and edge of Federation swords."

"Then smiths can work it."

"Only in special furnaces, with the strongest sulessence. Even so, the sharpening stones we use are useless for him."

Col rolled his eyes at the gendering of her sword. "Perhaps because it's solid grimsteel, not just dusting, plate or thread?"

"Yes, that's likely. And I've been told by one smith it has qualities of Dwen formed wood."

"How?"

"The hull of this ship, the grains of the outer planks have been condensed, like close grained wood, making it even stronger, whereas what doesn't need it is left for flexibility. The metal in the center is denser than the rest, the edges honed, not by a stone, but every fiber placed there, as if it was grown like wood. And it's one piece."

Col shrugged. "Then it's simple: it was cast somehow."

Freya shook her head. "Cast metal is brittle."

"Cast, then hammered?"

"I think not; there are no signs of smith work as we know it. I suspect he was magi forged and was found in an ancient tomb, perhaps from the time of the feudal lors. After all, it has the ancient sign of the Mother-god, Eurath, on the hilt."

Col glanced again at the cross guard where the simple crossed circle was engraved, or cast, or however made. Whatever its origin there was purpose to the blade.

Then the shouting increased, a change in timbre that meant a new urgency. Col stood with Freya and others, wondering if their time had come. Col's heart hammered. They said the Shari were armored and intended to board. Col felt extremely naked without a helmet or shield. He'd cadged a stiff leather coat riveted with plates of metal at the shoulder and over the breast, but he would need to move fast. Freya wore a little more than he did, a scale mail shirt with a proper gorget and a thick leather girdle belted over her blue and dun striped bracs. Bron, a formidable woman, wore no armor apart from her thick sleeveless leather vest. Both cousins had the front of their hair bound at the top of the head, a common sport fashion among Cambrian tribes. They and the rest seized the grips of their swords, axes, maces or whatever instrument a mother favored as they stood ready to rush above when the crewgirl ran to them, but it was not the action they expected.

"None of that!" she bellowed. "Put those toys down and help draw water from the hold!"

Col didn't know why and none of them asked. Dropping their weapons they rushed to the hatches while above them bright light flashed, followed by distant explosions and women swearing.

"Don't look at it!" Freya said as they worked with two others to pull on a rope raising a platform with two barrels. Col stared straight down, the activity in the dark hold frantic below him as they pulled and pulled. Suddenly there was no weight. Col glanced up; just as he saw the barrel maneuvered to be poured over the deck, brightness like the sun exploded across his vision. Belatedly he closed his eyes, but persistent spots overlayed his vision whether he kept his eyes open or shut. There was another explosion and another one, much louder, that seemed to rock the ship. Somehow he was able to seize the next ropes and pulled with the rest. As long as he didn't need to walk or run he would be fine for the moment.

New fears birthed as Col smelled burning wood. What was happening? Were they dipping into the drinking water to save the ship from fire? Shouts turned into screams; one girl in particular seemed to be wailing longer than the rest. Steam burns, he'd heard, probably from watering the deck. Then the explosions stopped and the shouting was of the normal sort, those in command demanding an account of those below them. The water continued to be drawn but soon the assistance of the volunteers was no longer needed and, after retrieving whatever gear they had dropped, they returned to their place of waiting.

That brief excitement past, they sat disconsolate for a half hour. Then came the news it was over. The Shari had attacked. Many of their ships had been scorched to cinders. Col wondered whether their presence as volunteers was redundant. Surely the cannons could eliminate the enemy much more efficiently than a ragged group of mercenaries.

Then the first shock came: one of the officers was dead. The news shook Col more than he expected. Not so much that she was dead, but that she couldn't be revived. Intuitively Col knew it was the same woman the healers had passed with earlier. It would eventually emerge her wounds were too great for elfyn medicine. What could the Shari have that healers were unable to counter? Perhaps a poison? For differing reasons Dwen and Blue were resistant to poison, especially if plant based, but this was the Gold officer with the kindly laugh. Perhaps she could have fought it if she wasn't aelg. Elfyn were almost immune to poison and many ills that those of humyn ancestry succumbed to. But if she was Sula she would not have been a pilot in the Tyreen navy.

They were dismissed to muster at dawn on the morrow. Col stood feeling lost while the women dispersed. He wished he had something to do. A resentment was brewing, borne of the unexpected tragedy. Even the most mild mannered dreamed of revenge, and anyone daring to look at the less mild, Navi for instance as she came down from the tops, could see eyes that almost glowed with the power of the sun. Col saw Samath and considered joining him to help with the healers, but then watched as Sam embraced Navi. Navi was the one woman Col avoided so it was with relief he saw the divers return.

They ran down the quarterdeck stair and then to the middle deck and would continue until they reached their berth deep in the aft of the hold. Out of them, Pearl exploded, eyes wild, then sighing in relief on seeing Col.

"I heard the ship was attacked!" she said, careless of the water she was dripping.

"Ai, Fish!" one of the volunteers complained, moving away from Pearl's soaked form to protect her weapons. Col joined her and they made their way down to the middle deck and into a small toilet that by luck had hemp towels. Pearl dried the worst of the water.

"I think the commissary has cakes available."

"Sure," Pearl nodded walking out with the towel on her shoulders. "There's no point in getting completely dry until we know we're done for the day. And we might fish later. Are you well?"

"An officer was killed," Col said.

Pearls eyes widened. "How?" she exclaimed. "We have healers and surgeons! Even magi to drag back the dead!"

"Her wounds were too great," Freya said, joining them as they made slow progress to the area with upturned barrels for tables near a kiosk that was being filled with cakes and bread.

Col saw it in Pearl's eyes, not the fear of death, but the fear of not coming back from it.

"What's the point of all that Ta Mel-hak education if it's useless when you need it?"

"Ta mel-hak," a woman echoed in passing. "Very droll."

Col's gut went cold when he saw her black robes and her solstone studded taq. But the magi didn't tarry.

"Perhaps we shouldn't antagonize those who have the power to retrieve souls," he suggested.

"Except apparently they don't!" Pearl glared at the magi's back.

"It won't matter one way or another," Freya put in. "Magi are above petty quarrels with civilians or so I'm told."

Pearl looked like she wanted to argue, but said nothing more. Col had trouble not feeling an almost religious deference to the magi. They were for all practical purposes the druids of the Federation, and druids in Cambria were not to be trifled with, even in *Dún Bhéal*, or Dunvan, the cosmopolitan port city that was most influenced by secular elfyn society. If anything, the magi's self effacing, almost lampoonish antics, made Col more uneasy.

As they came closer to the stove, barrels with bowls and trenchers stood by the queue. Taking one each, Pearl made a face, wrinkling her nose.

"Sausage and bacon again?"

"A hearty and good repast well overdue," Freya said.

Col said nothing, though he agreed. The bags of supplies he and Sam had set aside privately were the only reason he was not utterly miserable with starvation. Whatever was being served he would happily eat, seconds if he had the chance.

While Pearl muttered about landed fair under her breath, he tried to lighten the subject.

"They predicted storm but we've seen aught."

"Careful, love," Pearl said. "Payeen will hear you."

Once they were served thick pea soup and bacon over a round of pan-fried cake, the three of them settled around a barrel table to eat. They were joined by a mix of divers and other crew in a scrum crowding the stairs and commissary.

"No fish?" Sharkhook asked, holding an empty bowl with no enthusiasm.

Freya looked exasperated. "If you want fish, you'll have to catch it yourself."

Sharkhook looked at Pearl. Pearl took a bite of her stew and made another face. "After all that swimming I can't eat this landed pea paste with sausage," she said standing. "Who's game?"

Merock, the driver of the starboard divers, made a fluting sound like a high seal bark ending with a sigh to catch their attention. Eying both Pearl and Sharkhook meaningfully, she said. "Just enough to eat."

Pearl patted Col's shoulder. "I'll be back soon."

Col didn't like her leaving, but if there was a time to fish it was now. The ships were moving back in line and would hold their general position until the morrow.

Pearl paused as she secured her tangles and other diver's gear at her belt, looking over to a male diver who shared their berth. "Perhaps Aeryn could help us. I've heard he swims well."

Then Pearl winked at him, and Col felt hurt. Why was she doing this? Aeryn was quite comely and Col had a pang of jealously. Then he saw the small nod she gave in Sharkhook's direction and Col felt a fool.

Unlike Pearl, Sharkhook took strongly after her Meer heritage. Tall, lean and broad-shouldered, she had no paps whatsoever, her wavy black hair short and untidy, her hands and feet webbed with flukes, a triskelion tattoo on each shoulder. Aeryn, one of only two men among the starboard divers, was built much like Col: about the same height making him taller than the average Meer male, but much shorter than the Meer mother. He had the same blue skin, black hair, and blue eyes as Sharkhook, but Col knew, under his canvas bracs, his nethers were landed, not pouched like many Blue men. Like Pearl, he was shy about his less than perfect Meer form, but Pearl had told Col, in spite of that, Sharkhook had an eye for Aeryn.

Indeed Sharkhook looked nonplussed for a moment as Aeryn joined them. Col wanted to laugh at the absurdity of Pearl midwifing courtship in the midst of a war.

When they left one of the crew muttered, "Sharol might come back with fish, but we'll be lucky to see the other two before dawn."

Col joined in the laughter. It was a simple thing, a joy at something as common as a mother pursuing a man, a touch of normalcy that kept the dread of another battle at bay. This gave a hopeful cast to the other news: clouds rolled over the sky, darkening Sul as She set. But surely they could clear by dawn. Perhaps this was not as great a threat as was foretold. If there was enough to strike with lance and cannon, perhaps the storm would be tardy or miss them altogether.

Their spirits were further cheered when Pearl returned in less than an hour, Sharkhook and Aeryn with her, all bearing the bounty of newly caught fish, in this case three modest sharks. A merry dinner was made for the Blue crew, prepared with no flames. Few ate of this bounty except those who liked fish Meer style. Knives flashed expertly, turning raw fish into delicate strips of pale flesh, drizzled with scented vinegar wine that looked almost appetizing. Col did occasionally eat Meer food, when it was marinated in brine with mustard sauce. But not like this. It was as appetizing as eating raw sliced potatoes. He expected that was how Pearl felt about a meal of boiled peas and sausage.

The wake began in earnest, not a sober thing like in a magi abbey, but loud and alive, well watered with barley-mead and rum. First tales were told of Becan Glethlyn from her youth as a midship to her arrival on *The Tidebreaker* years ago. Apparently once commissioned as a lieutenant copilot, she never served on another ship. Many were the tales of former ensigns and midships she'd teased, but none were told by Ensign Jarroth who was conspicuously absent.

"Glethlyn was like a sister at sea with Jarroth," some soul said. "The spark probably hasn't the heart to wake her."

"She might be to bed early to catch Glethlyn dreaming side," a midship said. Col was surprised it was a boy.

"Ai, girl, ai, might be the case."

"I'm not a girl!"

There were chuckles at this.

"He lays water down like a girl! Take the complement, middie!"

The boy looked both perplexed and pleased with himself while laughter buffeted him.

Flutes and drums started to play. A Gold man in a robe that was smudged from labor made his way to the barrel where Col sat. He had a pewter tankard in each hand; as he arrived, Col recognized Samath.

"There you are, Colm," Sam said. "I got these for myself and Navi, but she's off getting rum."

"*Go raibh maith agat!*" Col said with feeling. "*Tá deoch uaim, ach…*" Col waved at the cluster of women that weren't so much a queue as an impenetrable mob around the barley-mead barrels.

"Something 'good at me'?" Sam said, his pretty face frowning.

"It's 'thank you' in Gael," Pearl put in. "See, I listen!" she added with a smile.

Col said nothing, taking a long drink instead. Pearl's Gael wasn't bad, but his uncle Fenras claimed she had a horrible accent. Samath cadged a stool and sat down with them just as Navi arrived.

Tall, forbidding, with a harsh handsome beauty, Navi looked even more unapproachable than usual. She was mobbed with questions about what had transpired on the tops, the uncontrolled strike that had injured so many. Never one to withhold her judgment, she was now strangely reticent:

"The Shari weapon murdered the lieutenant. Then many Shari died by solcannon strike. I helped make it so."

"That's not how you tell a tale," Sam said.

"I'm not a bard."

"True words," Pearl said.

110

Navi looked down, perhaps thinking of rekindling their hostilities. But she was distracted by a new platter of flayed raw fish, this one marinated in wine and radish sauce. Pearl caught Navi's eye, then smiled in false welcome.

"Would you like some fish?" Pearl asked as if offering a rare treat, knowing Navi was revolted.

Navi didn't take the bait. "As dull as the pea soup with bacon leavings has been, I will somehow manage to restrain myself. Are you finished, Samath?"

Samath sighed. "I was hoping to dance."

Col looked at his friend doubtfully. "This is a tune from the *Sliabh Arda*. There may not be back flips and spinning, but it's its own challenge. Dwen can keep up but I don't know, brother."

"Very well!" Sam said, standing suddenly, putting his tankard down with force. "If it's a challenge, I accept!"

Col chuckled in sympathy. "I learned these dances living in Dunvan. I wouldn't want to steal your queens, brother!"

"Navi," Sam said in a sweet tenor men used to wheedle favors from mothers, sisters and wives, "May I have a loan of a queen?"

Navi sighed. Perhaps thinking it was a cheap price to keep her liaison with Samath, she gave him a queen.

"There," Samath said. "We can make it a bet."

Col shrugged. He was quick on his feet and all the tunes played so far he'd heard before. Feeling he was cheating his friend, he reluctantly put another gold plated coin on the barrel, matching Sam's queens. By chance they both had their heads facing up, portraits of Sunqueens past indifferent to their endeavor. Quicker than Col expected, the first two coins were covered by others. Then Merock was called to manage the stake with Navi.

"*Déithe ár sábháil!*" Col swore. "What have you done?"

"Nothing yet!" Samath said cheerfully as he belted his robes up to his knees and walked to a space on the deck cleared for them. "I'm going to make queens on this voyage, on one road or another!"

Reluctantly Col removed his leather armor and joined Sam, standing a little ways away. He hoped their friendship survived this trial.

"Don't worry, love!" Pearl whispered. "The divers are behind you!"

"So we understand the terms," an Albini woman said. "You dance until one stops, or stumbles or trips. You may call off the contest with all wagers returned."

"I understand," Sam said cheerfully.

"*Tuigim*," Col added.

"Then begin!"

First the drum started, followed by a flute. Col waited for the fiddle and then let his feet fly. It was an old dance, the *sean nós*, as quick and complicated or as simple as the dancer chose. Generally, unlike similar elfyn dances, one kept ones arms at the side, minimizing their movement. Col could tell from the corner of his eye Sam ignored this, using the Dwen form of elbows and hands accenting his movements. But this wasn't a tribal contest in Dunvan. The punters only cared whose feet danced the longest without fail. Sam could ornament his movements all he wanted, they would not care for his artistry, only their queens. Perhaps he would exhaust himself.

Yet even on this deck, with no sunlight to lift his essence, Samath seemed to keep up with Col effortlessly. Col turned in his heel kicks and jigs to face Sam, who grinned at Col's shock. Sam started to add little claps to his performance, matching the claps of the audience. A part of Col wanted to laugh, another part was appalled the desecration of the traditional dance. And a part larger than either, wondered if Col had miscalculated.

Samath, sensitive Gold soul, with no practical essence training, nonetheless had stronger elfyn ancestry than Col. Col worried Sam would dance all night if he had to beat Col.

But that was not how the dance would be decided. In all the enthusiasm of slicing and preparing the shark, a sliver of flesh had fallen unaccounted. Just as Col considered offering a draw, his heel landed on the unseen fish and his foot shot out from under him. With no time to land in any graceful way, the best Col could do was land on his side, catching himself as everyone was taught in the martial form of the Dance.

The music stopped and there was a cheer. Col couldn't believe it. Sam was jumping up and down in excitement, almost squealing, "I won!" Pearl's fallen face was full of sympathy while most of the divers swore. Slowly Col sat up. Sam looked down, almost apologetic, offering his hand. Col sighed at took it, standing up.

"Indeed, you won, brother." Col stood on one foot, turning the other up to scrape the shark meat off. It had its revenge.

"Oh," Sam said, understanding. "Look, we can…"

"No," Col said firmly. "You won. *Maith thú.* Fair play."

They hugged briefly, then Sam was pulled away by Navi, a thin smile on her face.

Col didn't take it personally. It was Pearl Navi was gloating over.

"Let's go count my winnings!" Col heard Sam say as he and Navi left, Navi's arm possessively around Sam's waist.

The divers glowered with disappointment. But when they understood why he had lost, they let the matter fall, for some soul among them had to be at fault. Col himself didn't dispute it because there was a superstition about trying to rob Felkeni, the Goddi of Luck, of his due. The Gael part of him rebuked himself for all but baiting fate. He should have known better. So Col considered the outcome just.

"That was grand!" a crewgirl said. She held a square box that could just about fit a tankard. It was made of wood, its corners reinforced with brass and one side had a brass ring in the center. Col realized it was a hole and the box was an obscura.

"Didn't I warn you about stealing our ghosts?" a fierce Albini woman with thick black hair growled.

"Calm down, highland savage," the crewgirl said casually. Col knew the woman, Bethyn Olden, was the publisher of "Letters of Note", a newsletter for the ship. Olden had tried to recruit Col once she'd learned he was a scholar. But between the constant cleaning he was tasked with and drilling as a volunteer Col had little enough time to spend with Pearl, much less help scribe a pamphlet. As he watched, Olden was slipping a thin sheet of leaden colored metal out of a slot and replacing it with another. "I think I caught the two of you!" she added excitedly.

Col wasn't sure how he felt about that. The Albini woman, Seand inion Morgu, continued to glower at Olden. Her concerns weren't uncommon in Cambria, even in cosmopolitan Dunvan. Col knew it wasn't logical, but there was something eerie about the images captured by the obscura, impressions made on chemical plates, or projected onto special paper to develop in sunlight.   Black and white, the crisp illuminations did give the impression of a ghosts frozen in one moment of life.

"Pity you didn't catch the lieutenant before she passed," Col said. "She wouldn't mind being a ghost on plate or paper now."

"Oh, but I did!" Olden said. "She gathered the middies for a game of rings. I was going to do a plate. But with her gone, I think I should take the plate to the college in Gashora and make paper projections. It might change command's mind."

"How?"

"Command has been most unimpressed with the art," a boy midship piped up. A couple of the middies had gathered to watch the obscura, hoping Olden would capture more images. "They do say, harsh light tells only half the tale."

"And yet magi and scholars have embraced it," Olden said. "I just think the old trolls don't like anything aged less than a millennia."

"I have an obscura," the boy added. "But I wasn't allowed to bring it. Ama said it cost too much to live at the bottom of the sea."

"And right she is," Olden said. "We know what you middies get up to!"

At last, close to midnight, the deck officer commanded them to retire to be fresh on the morrow, the midships chivvied towards their berths by their seniors.

Col followed the divers down to their berth, filled with bunks and awkward hammocks, the three grand portholes still boarded over for the duration of the battle. This time Pearl settled in by Col's side on his lower hammock, though there was barely room to hold them. Nonetheless they dozed off quickly. Col dreamed of vague shadowy ships passing through gray fog, like the ghost ships of the Nords, rumored to take the dead on their way to cold Hel.   Suddenly flames erupted in front of him, and those on the ships had the cast of death, the turban wearing crews emaciated like skeletons, all the more horrific for being still alive. Chains bound them to the decks and their course would not waver. Slowly one of them, dead eyes staring out from under his turban wrapped helmet, looked at Col.   Then there was a flash of light and Col was alone and adrift on the sea, the ruins of a ships floating around him, the dead Shari sailor floating with him, still staring.

Col tried to break away from the baleful gaze, but he seemed to be falling into the grim sailor's orb, like a meteor doomed to fall to Eurath…
Col woke at the sound of an explosion.

Chapter 7

Fire with the Dawn

Rosen woke at the sound of an explosion.

Stumbling out of bed in a fog of forgotten half dreams, he fumbled for his baldric and scabbard before staggering out the door, through the pilot's mess and onto the quarterdeck. In the dim lights of the hanging lamps the deck seethed with women swarming in alarm, eager to get to their posts, the great masts casting shadows over them like trees in a forlorn wood. There was no flame or fire on the Tidebreaker's decks. All was well on the Tide-breaker. For now.

Gripping the hilt of his sword, Rosen scanned the dark murky waters, where the line of Tyreen vessels were almost invisible except for the mast lamps, gently rising up and dipping down with the swells. Dawn was still hours away. Near the center of the line, flames danced on the waters near *The Black Seal*, no, it was closer to *The Oaken Blue*. Rosen murmured, "Too close."

"Indeed, Sea Father," said a woman next to him. Lieutenant Sithinas was, like himself only in her white shirt and slops, the sleeping trousers officers wore to be decent if roused suddenly during the night. She held a telescope as she examined the waters. Rosen slung his baldric over one shoulder before taking the instrument in turn to view himself. The flames danced, rising and falling with the water, like spirits who had made a dark pact with Maer. Was it burning oil? The hull of *The Oaken Blue* appeared undamaged, but the crew took no chances. Water, precious filtered drinking water, was poured down the side as a precaution. At the same time *The Oaken Blue* moved forward, southwards, until her hull was free of floating flames.

"Oil, you think, lieutenant?" Rosen ventured out loud. "Yet it's so strong and persistent."

"My guess, captain, is a type of pitch. It can float and burn."

"Sea Father," Galen said, looming out of the gloom from Rosen's other side. "You are barely dressed."

Rosen looked down. Of course he was without his bicorn and coat, but the shapeless slops covered the essentials. "It's not as if I'm shirtless."

"Thought a mention should be made."

"Thank you for that service, boatswain. Do you have a report that isn't a comment on uniform regulations?"

Galen might have narrowed her eyes in pique, but Rosen was too tired to care. "*The Oaken Blue* seems to be the only target. Divers are investigating."

A whistle sounded from the Admiral, echoing down the line through the fleet. Above a signaler translated, "Brace for aft drive!"

Rosen looked up at the cage; Lieutenant Carvus Sandryn, a Dwen pilot without the usual nut coloring, was in the cage. Her green eyes shimmered as she drove, reaching for one of the cage's twisted wood supports, making Rosen reflectively wince. It was an irrational worry of his that at any moment the wood would twist in her grip. But unlike himself, she was in full uniform and Rosen didn't like the idea of standing in his sleeping clothes for all to see if he didn't have to. So instead of taking the cage he moved to the larboard node, an oval of aqua embedded in the hull at waist level and touched it to assist with the water-essence flowing through the cage and heart to drive the ship. As soon as he touched the blue-green glass, he felt the lap of water against his side, as if he was the ship, along with the beginnings of the counter current of the keel's aura as the pilot on duty prepared to move *The Tidebreaker* aftward, slightly north, to comply with the new order: the entire fleet was to move aft and let *The Oaken Blue* drift ahead. The next moment *The Tidebreaker* began a slow reverse, until they stopped several fathoms back leaving *The Oaken Blue* quite alone.

"I'll take over, Sea Father!" Ensign Jarroth cried, having run up from the companionway in the center of the quarterdeck.

Rosen stepped away, closer to Galen. "What is she thinking?" he muttered.

"Offering herself as a target?" Galen suggested.

"Perhaps." Rosen said nothing more, returning to his cabin and shutting the door firmly behind him. He wanted someone to talk to, to share ideas with, but he couldn't stand to look at Galen, much less talk to her. He knew he was being a child, yet for the moment he couldn't help it. Dropping his baldric on a chair he made for the toilet closet to wash his face. *The Tidebreaker* moved aft again, abrupt, then steady, before stopping. Perhaps Carvus was dressing the line. They would drift in position until new orders came.

Until then many tasks could be done. Rosen had no desire for more sleep. Now properly dressed, he would walk the rounds. Then he would drive *The Tidebreaker* awhile, though in this case "driving" was more a point of keeping her in place. They could not afford to anchor; the need for speedy action could come at any moment. And then, when the light came, the last grim duties would follow.

Dawn came overcast, yet with a narrow window along the horizon for
Sul to shine. It would not be the best light to light the funeral barge, but it
would do. Rosen stood near the cage, having just surrendered it to Lieutenant Remard Haulet yal Rooth, a flukeless Blue pilot with gray Cambrian
eyes. Here he overlooked the quarterdeck as ship's guards helped crew
bring forth the bower from below. The crew gathered much like they had
during the captain's court, standing and sitting everywhere they could, even
on the rigging and spars. Many wore white shawls or stoles, the color of
sending a soul off at dawn. Rosen himself had a length of white linen
draped around his shoulders for this sad duty. Glethlyn's body was
shrouded, a mercy to the eyes. Let them remember her as she'd been:
laughing and merry, not a corpse with a ghastly cavernous wound. Her effects had been packed; they would go to the mother's estate, or, if she had
directed otherwise, to her consort and child. Glethlyn wore the uniform she
had died in. By tradition the clothes worn in death were assumed to be
those best to travel through the Door. That was why heirlooms of great
queens and nobles were considered haunted, though this was rarely sinister.
The most extreme forms were the Soul Swords of the ancient queens, that
carried a portion of their bearer's spirit. Glethlyn's sword wasn't forged by
ancient magi smiths, but it too would be returned to her mother's house; perhaps a part of her laughing soul would live on in it. Rosen knew the shroud
was sealed with a pitch binding, serving doubly as an accelerant once her
bower sat on the water. The funeral bower was a small boat just large
enough for her corpse. Had Glethlyn passed after long years naturally, and
it was her desire to join the sea, it would have been built properly: high
prowed and ornamented, towed out by a barge before being lit. All that
could be spared in the moment was scrap planks woven together with
branches, some with fresh greenery Rosen suspected had been donated by
Ranks Officer Fadwen. The crewgirls steadied the bower near the starboard
wale while ropes were attached to lower Glethlyn at the proper time. Sul's
color changed from red to amber orange, the cloud bank above her neither
growing nor dispersing. Perhaps there would not be rain after all. There
had been no dancing this dawn.

A horn blew, long and deep, and the already subdued crew ceased idle
chatter. They were one now, in battle, in grief, in the great horror that any
one of them could be lost irretrievably. It was a captain's duty to quell the
horror, give it meaning, and feed the thirst for duty always with the promise
of hope. Rosen spoke:

"In remembrance of our good friend, Lieutenant copilot Becan Glethlyn, we thank you for your service and give joy for your journey to the Otherside. May our hopes and prayers go with you to our foreborn and afterborn. As they live beyond the Door, so do we live in Ta Pangeal, what woes may be, we know after is blissful eternity. Let us not be sad for the passing of our brave mother. While we tell of her deeds, she lives with us still, as she tells of our deeds, so we will live ever after. In death, as in life, duty prevails. In Victory or the Otherside. *Sul maj yanin amian.*" [2]

To this last the crew replied as all Tyreen crews replied in the slightly blasphemous apocrypha the Federation Admiralty tolerated:

"*Ar Ta Yifmar maj yanin elama.*"[3]

The proper response was "Praise mother Sul," which some muttered under their breath with little passion. Glethlyn's bower was lowered to the sea, where it would be lit and consumed. Rosen became aware of the silence across the water. Sul had barely traveled ten degrees in her arc under the pall covered sky, casting long shadows of the fleet across the western waters towards home. The gap remained at the horizon, but presently started to blur. Sul's light might not last long.

Rosen's eye drifted to the sea where a couple of divers were towing the bower out to open water behind the Tyreen line. Rosen wanted Glethlyn's remains to stay as far from the battle as possible, at least until they had been consumed. The bower stopped moving, the divers untied the rope to take back. Then they dived, making underwater wake trails as they swam back to *The Tidebreaker*.

"Strikemaster!" Rosen called, to Azar Sernalash, who had moved from her usual position on the forecastle to command the aft crews. "Put our friend to rest."

"Sea Father!" Azar acknowledged. "Crew, strike!"

Both the starboard and larboard turret cannons had been angled at the ready. The next second there was a flash of blinding light. Rosen had lowered his eyes, grateful it would hide the tears that threatened to well. He heard only the steam of the water and his heart skipped, a perverse part of him wanting to give the order to stop before Glethlyn's remains were destroyed, making her passing irrevocable. But of course he did not move. It was just an echo of regret, the last vision of what might have been slipping away forever. Glethlyn had long gone through the Door and was as much at peace as any soul lost in battle could be.

---

2 Sul is our mother.

3 And the Sea is our sister.

Rosen blinked. The bower was consumed with flames. His eyes were drawn to the white hot center of the fire. Almost immediately they cooled to a yellow, as the incendiary sulessence that stuck them faded. The crackling of wood and shroud would soon give way to ash and charred bone. What didn't burn would sink into Maer's depths until the End.

It started then, the Coraco-Aniadan, the hymn of loss and separation sung with a hope to bring a soul home. Rosen never quite understood why it was sung during wakes and pyres. His mother had patiently explained, "Our true home was the Otherside of dreams. By singing we help the soul find their way." Yet magi reported, and many agreed, souls found their way to the Door just fine. His hound certainly did. To this his mother had smiled, saying, "In honesty, we sing such songs to find our own way home from grief."

That made more sense. After all, the dead had passed on, they had heard the singing on the other side of the Door. And perhaps those who sang from beyond the Door did so to remind the living their place was to stay and live. It was known "dread fever", a sickness that drove sufferers prematurely through the Door, could afflict elfyn and elf-born alike. Singing on this side of life helped anchor the living to the world.

Rosen didn't sing. His voice was average to his ear and, living with Korali, he knew the dangers of overestimating one's talents. As was traditional, after the first verse was sung by those with bold voices, then other singers would start mid verse, singing over the first voices from the beginning in a cascading a capella that continued for as many verses as agreed. There were legends of Coraco-Aniadan being sung for a day in the ancient times of the Sunqueens. Even now it wasn't unheard of for an hour to be sung in the passing of heroes and stateswomen or beloved Aeons. And Glethlyn, while she was unlikely to have been an Aeon (few aelg lived past three centuries), was beloved, and so the crew sang longer than the three regulation rounds. Galen's voice, a deep tenor, made him lonely for their friendship. Then he heard the singing echoing across the water and realized the other ships sang with them, faint and distant as if from the magical isles in Cambrian myth. Not one raven croaked nor even sent a crass thought; Glethlyn had more patience with ravens than most. That moved Rosen as much as the chorus that sang around him. It wasn't just *The Tidebreaker's* loss, but all the fleet's loss. Then the tears wanted to come, but he restrained himself. There was no shame; many mothers who had known Glethlyn wept. But he was their captain and they were still at war. Thus his masculine side must be tamed in the service of duty.

A shrill whistle cut through the air and, a fine instrument cleaved by a rusty blade cleaving, the Coraco faltered. Rosen almost welcomed the intrusion, for the tightness in his throat was becoming unbearable. He understood its meaning the second before orders were barked. All singing stopped.

"Look to the dawn, Sea Father!" a Dwen from the tops cried.

It was utter madness. Out of the dawn a fleet of Shari ships sailed, though of course no sails billowed their masts were still resting on crutches. Instead they rowed like the mad, driven by whips or frenzy, at their best speed with a purpose: they aimed for *The Oaken Blue.*

"What in the Deeps do they think they're doing?" Rosen said to no one in particular as officers shouted orders and the crew shed their funeral redes to take battle positions. Rosen roused himself, feeling as if waking from a dream. He was of the living; it was his place to stay and live. He stepped closer to the cage, but didn't relieve Sandryn. Instead he stood by, wanting to see all before making a decision.

"That was actually clever," Glenfar said, the magi virtually appearing at Rosen's elbow.

"Pardon?"

"Sailing with the sun behind them. It would have been devastating with aqua driven ships or against a lesser fleet. As it is, the closer they come the quicker they will find death."

Rosen looked up. Sul had dimmed, the gap at the horizon becoming hazy. "Don't be so certain. Unless you can disperse the clouds."

Glenfar shook her head ruefully. "There are operations to harness and direct the weather. But no elfyn magic since Er can stop the courses of Payeen. You might as well pray to Her."

"If it worked, I'd do it in a moment. What are they doing?"

"If I was to guess, they have ascertained *The Oaken Blue* is our leader. They may think if they can board her, the rest of the fleet will fall."

"And the Admiral has made that easy by drifting forward?"

Glenfar shrugged. "It could be a ruse."

Rosen nodded. "The idea was planted as a trap in dreams. Well, let us hope."

Then a series of whistles sounded from *The Oaken Blue*: the rest of the fleet was to hang back.

"Our suspicions seem to be confirmed," Glenfar said.

"I would feel much better if the clouds cleared," Rosen replied. The gap at the horizon hadn't closed, but Sul was rising above it. Soon it would be overcast for the purposes of the strikers. He became aware of Galen nearby.

"A diver reports a damaged ship sent as a sacrifice was responsible for the explosive fire last night," Galen said. "The water burning might be the first evidence of humyn essence use."

Rosen shook his head. "A trick. If they had essence they would have used it earlier."

Glenfar added, "Investigation of the fire's remains reveal a mix of pitch and naphtha. On a deck it could be devastating. There is pine resin and other materials that make it resist dispersing in water and it cannot be easily quelled."

Rosen, like most of the fleet, had heard the exchange between *The Oaken Blue* and *The Black Seal* on the subject of how the Shari were to be disposed of. He was starting to think the Jackal had been right all along. Their situation must be dire indeed if he and Tresmadore could find agreement while he and Galen remained estranged. Taking a breath Rosen looked at Galen, forcing himself to be both authoritative and congenial, stifling all feelings of pique or misuse.

"Make certain the crew is ready, boatswain."

Galen's eyes flickered in many levels of understanding. They had much to repair in their friendship, but now was not the time to think on it. Galen nodded, and strode off shouting down the hatches.

Lieutenants Sithinas and Sandryn joined them on the stern, looking weary having barely stolen a couple hours of rest the night before. Master Jasmenal took up her place on the larboard stern steps. The ship's guard surrounding the cage hefted their stars. Today might be the day they would use them, but could they burn? The tops and yards were again thick with archers; the strike crew with ready hands on the stone. The essence-powerful Farthal should probably be returned to her post; she might be one of the few souls able to strike on a day like this. But Rosen trusted the strikemaster to make that choice. Most magi clustered ahead on their forecastle gallery, others, like Glenfar, lurking where they might be needed. A couple hovered above highest tops of the ship in the air, robes snapping sharply in the morning breeze. The marines and divers were already in the water. Together they watched as the Shari sped on their misguided course. They would not have long to wait.

* * *

Sea Father Manweth Lanash, driving *The Starshard*, stared at the glowering sky with foreboding as the Shari drove their ships forward in what could only be the most desperate of maneuvers. Surely they knew how fast Tyreen ships could move? Surely they remembered the loss of their many ships laid to waste by the solcannons? What profit did they expect, attacking *The Oaken Blue*, even if by some twist of fate they succeeded in boarding her? Of course it was no small thing for himself that the Shari's target was the same ship his wife's daughter served on. He took comfort Dagmath was a strike captain and not a diver, well out of the Shari's path and in the best position of defense. His faith in Jonsaymanor should suffice; she had a plan, perhaps playing out an ancient duel between leaders to decide the fate of the fleet. However there was not enough faith in the world to mollify a mother, or father, when their child was threatened. Had his sentimentality won over duty, he imagined swearing to Dagmar he would protect their daughter, no matter the cost. Manweth knew the sentiment was a vain one, at odds with his duty, and Dagmar would never demand such a thing from him while he served in the Tyreen navy. But for the first time, though he was a man, he felt the pull of a mother, the compulsion to protect the child of his heart at any cost. Coming on so suddenly it frightened him. Perhaps it was because, before the death of the officer on *The Tidebreaker*, he had not considered any real danger in their venture.

Now Manweth wanted Dagmath far away from the fleet, safely at home like a babe. But she was a woman, not a girl. It was not as if she'd been enslaved to false duty like so many of the Sultan's tools. It was easy for a parent to accept the independence and agency of youth, until dangers became all too real. He rebuked himself for his selfishness; it was disrespectful not only to his daughter's choice, but to himself and Dagmar, who had raised Dagmath to be brave and dutiful, and act boldly as a mother should, that she could teach her own daughters in time. Girls were meant to become women, and the wishing of mothers and consorts never stopped the march of days that would make it so.

Wishing and praying wouldn't stop the clouds either, Manweth thought grimly. He stood on the pilots dais as the clouds thickened, feeling the surge of essence through his feet as he kept *The Starshard* treading in place. The advancing line of Shari ships, a little over three score in all, made respectable time for oar ships, but was a crawling pace for an aqua vessel. This time there was no warning: strike flared from one of the forecastle solcannons on *The Oaken Blue,* and with a crack, the entire bow of one ship went up in flames. Disappointingly, it had not breached the hull at the waterline, nor exploded their store of salts. Manweth worried the pall already reduced the power of the solcannons. The Shari tried to retreat, ships' oars working furiously backwards, fighting their own momentum. Then Manweth was forced to attend to the defense of his own ship.

The Shari line had broken, a large group of vessels targeting *The Oaken Blue*, the rest shifting their angle in an attempt to slide to either side of the other ships bows, hoping to get close enough to board. Archers from the masts above rained arrows down; Manweth saw a black-turbaned captain fall. Dead or not, another humyn took its place screaming orders. A black robed humyn ducked under the bow tent covering the Dragon. Manweth yelled, "Strike starboard!"

Strikemaster Hilla Bratt knew the target priorities: first the Dragon, then the engines, then the hull. The officers were left to snipers. It was as if the sun had emerged from the clouds, so bright was the deck on Manweth's right side for a moment. And while he heard the snapping and cracking of burning wood, it bothered him there had been no explosion. He glanced at the sky, the clouds ever occulting that last of Sul's rays, the scent of rain now filling the air. Then he gasped as if punched in the side.

It had been a rock or some other heavy missile, thrown from a ballista, by chance hitting a place in *The Starshard's* hull that connected to an aqua node. Angry at the pain, Manweth ordered another flare of strike. "Clear them from the hull!" he bellowed.

They had no mercy. One moment white fire lit the air, blinding in intensity. Finally there was an explosion of the timbers cracking in the sudden heat. The light now gone, a blackened hole could be seen through the deck burning into the ship, where flames shot up. The screaming started, as desperate humyn, clothes on fire, leaped into the water. Manweth didn't have time to consider their fate before the next explosion.

This was from deep inside the vessel, blowing it apart, sending bodies and kindling forcefully across the water. Instinct made Manweth duck as a splinters of wood sailed through the air, some lodging in the mizzenmast behind him. Cries around told that not all mothers had been as lucky. Two women limped below decks to where the healers laired in the crew mess.

Manweth shook in a sudden cold sweat, echoes of mortality in the air. The force of the destructive black salts that fed the Dragon was not something he'd experienced so closely. There was a reason firework shops and merchants had strict rules to abide by. Even charcoal warehoused for winter was carefully managed to prevent a disaster of city-wide proportions. There must be barrels of the stuff, so much it had been deliberately made, stored and transported for the sole purpose of conquering Gashora. Every Shari ship could be a lethal bomb. Manweth watched as the clouds thickened.

Perhaps it would be a strange gift from Payeen that sulessence would soon be almost unusable.

But until then they needed to rob the Shari of what salts they could and keep them off the hull. To that end Manweth had the strike-crew light the water around *The Starshard* for as long as they were able.

For he had seen the long ladders lying on the decks of the vessels. After their sulessence was spent, they needed to be prepared for boarding.

* * *

The Tidebreaker was far enough away from the explosion that they were in no danger, but Rosen ducked anyway, feeling foolish as he straightened. A whistle sounded, giving warning about using cannon strike on close Shari ships, reminding the fleet they were full of explosive salts. They should scorch the lot from a distance, then it would be over. Unfortunately the dimming light limited the range and power of the solcannons. They had struck as many of the Shari vessels as possible. *The Tidebreaker*, like many ships, was surrounded again by the white fog steaming off the water. As the enemy vessels made a gambit to engage and surround each ship to board, arrows rained from the tops, clearing decks as turbaned warriors, waiting for a chance to board, fell like puppets with cut strings. Soon the ships were close enough to throw their own volleys of arrows, and though many were shoved aside by magi magic or sunk into the timbers of the ship, some found a mark as a crew was heard to shout or scream in pain. The decks hissed as water was laid down after each strike of the solcannons. While the women had the power, all was done to hit the weak targets of the ships, lancers eliminating as many captains and humyn magi as they could. Then the clouds thickened, the warm light turning subdued gray.

It happened so fast. Rosen felt a chill down his spine. Looking up, he saw no break in the pall, and knew they were at a disadvantage. The time for sweeping cannon action was past. It would be a while before the Shari noticed. From this point forward regulations required cannon strike to be reserved for close defense until the sky cleared. The cannons would each have one charge left, from ambient essence, and then would be unusable. Lancers weren't much better off. The most sulessence virile – those with strong Sula ancestry – could fire a lance in cloud cover, but already the sky was dim. It would be a challenge for all but the magi. Rosen reluctantly had a midship summoned while another volley of arrows from above cut the air.

"Sea Father!" Midship Doren Orenath called from the quarterdeck, saluting smartly up at Rosen. "How can I serve?"

"Retrieve that elf the Marshal sent from the hospital and tell her to report to the strikemaster."

"Ai, captain!"

Perhaps it would make a difference.

"I should ask if my master can spare souls," Glenfar said.

"Yes," Rosen agreed. "Thank you."

Meanwhile the Shari, ignorant of their change of fortune, continued to row defensively until they were out of cannon range. There they drifted to a stop, treading water, waiting for what Rosen could only guess. The truth was, safe though they may be from strike, they were still in the range of Dwen arrows.

The thought of arrows roused Rosen. "Have the archers pause," he said out loud, to Lieutenant Ni-Fionna, the deck officer on duty. "And the snipers to shoot their targets at sight."

Ni-Fionna echoed his order. At the same moment a signal whistle echoed down the line, with the same order in the interests of defense. They were also to advance with speed. The strange scorpion-sterned ships tried to dress their line, perhaps preparing for another attempt to board, but they suddenly had no need to wonder how they would engage the Tyreen. City-ships almost four times the mass accelerated forward at speeds the Shari had never witnessed at sea, and many of their vessels became clustered or swamped. If they had previous damage, repairs fell and the crew was forced to consider braving the waters lest they be pulled under. The remains of one blasted boat drifted on the water, neglected flotsam. If there had been survivors, they were dead now, by water or the marines' hands. At least the Shari were defensive, their gross losses returning them to caution. Ships hardly moving, they fired arrows madly, some finding a target, most falling to the sea. Meanwhile, the Tyreens had a height advantage and used it ruthlessly. Regular archers fired over the ships, and captains, magi and troops were reduced. Only the oardrivers were not deliberately targeted, for the goal was to drive the Shari away. But Rosen worried their bravura would return before they adopted a strategy of retreat. And then, if they did board, if it did come to blows, it would be a far grimmer thing than either side desired.

Rosen gripped the hilt of his sword. He had never used it to kill. He'd fought briefly as an ensign to subdue a privateer, and had used the flat to dissuade a would be thief during leave in Dunvan. Never had he needed to kill. Now he knew, if he fought he must be ready to kill. Dealing death was considered a solemn, grim thing, even a humyn death. The most irreligious butcher prayed to Theedwen, the patron Goddi of Dwenoshire who guarded and shepherded the souls of beasts. When it was time for the harvest kill, they went with prayers through the Door. In myth, that was the first betrayal of the Oneness of Life the hero Jaro learned. Even a daughter of Sul could not evade killing to eat if she wanted to live in the Orb among its mothers. And so, barely a day old yet as fleet as the wind and as strong as a champion, she felled the Great Ram with a thrown stone that she could eat.

Sula were not overly sentimental about eating the flesh of beasts, but neither were they indifferent. It was never forgotten that a death of one had been exchanged for the life of another. This was not to be taken for granted, even with the death of a dumb beast.

How much more grim was it to know they must take the lives of humyn for no reason than their ruler drove them to this situation? If not for the loss of Glethlyn, Rosen would be tempted to reason with the mad beasts to avoid doing something he feared would changed him forever. Once they were in Amer's great bloody hands, the Mother-god of war did not easily release any mother or man.

The pause in action renewed a hope the Shari might flee. Archers on both sides stopped, the Tyreens finding a dearth of clean targets, and the Shari simply couldn't afford to waste arrows. Without the sun's rays, the sea air was cold. Rosen found comfort in his essence connection with the ship. They had glided to a stop and whatever hunger for revenge that burned after Glethlyn's murder, was cooling before the realities of their situation. Perhaps Rosen didn't entirely understand a mother's hunger for vengeance after all.

There was a conceit among society men that by their sex they were somehow immune to the excesses of dark Amer. Korali believed this, explaining it was because they were not ruled by the virile drives of mothers. This was obliviously "hak", as the Shari proved. Unless somehow humyn men were more motherly than elfyn men. The truth was mothers dominated elfyn military history, so of course the majority of heroes and villains would be women. Few men, having to struggle for recognition, would be overcome with the peculiar arrogance that led to excesses of Dark Amer. The absence of opportunity for corruption was not proof of moral virtue.

Nonetheless, Rosen was thankful he was a man, that he had not internalized the motherly entitlement that often went with blood lust. And he rebuked himself for ever dreaming of warlike adventures, as if the fantasies of youth had somehow brought him to this moral crossroads. He would eschew vain fantasies of glory, and denounce blood lust, and yes, he would even kill, but he would take no joy in it. And then he understood the seduction of the mad Mother-god of War. Glethlyn's death had taken them to the brink of blood lust and he had not even noticed. "Death to the Shari". Had he not been thinking in rage, he could never have doomed the entire Shari-tani race for the actions of its enthralled fleet. They were the wrong words at the right time. They had united his ship, but at what cost? Now it felt like he had cursed himself and his crew, tricked into seeking joy in murder by the promise of vengeance. And there was no way to undo it. He could only pray that the wisdom of Sul would shine through the clouds of wrath before they were lost to madness.

It started to rain, light but insistent. Rosen thought to send for his cloak, but it would only hamper fighting. Then the thing that Rosen feared happened: the Shari began to move.

They did not move south to flee back to their reserve line, which hovered now in a foggy haze. Archers filled their stern decks while they maneuvered to rearrange themselves. From the rear a line of about nine ships creeped forward through the haze, through the reserve line, for what purpose Rosen couldn't fathom. They had no archers or deck troops that he could see.

"Sea Father," Glenfar said. "I regret to inform you, they understand we are in some way weakened."

Rosen knew in his bones it was true but resisted it. "How? They have no conception of how essence works."

"No, but they have crude symbolism. To them, we are fire and are strong in the sun. Now it is raining and strike has stopped, they have the idea our fire has been quenched."

"They are more right than they know," Rosen muttered.

"So they see their chance."

The Shari returned to the bold gambit of ships driving forward to surround the Tyreen vessels intending to board. Rosen hoped the Admiral's plan had accounted for the lack of strike cover because *The Oaken Blue* was about to be surrounded. He had no time to worry about the Admiral's ship or any other because three Shari scorpion ships were closing on *The Tide-breaker*.

"Arrows," he said hoarsely as several heavy thumps told him shot from the ballista had struck the hull. Thankfully the rocks had missed the rib-fins.

"Captain?" Sithinas asked beside him.

Panic hunted him. Taking a few shallow breaths, Rosen called, "Ni-Fionna! Tell the masts to fire at will!"

The Shari were closing. One ship was so close it had disappeared out of the cage's line of sight. They had ladders now, not very long Rosen thought at first. Then he remembered they weren't in dry dock. The ladders did not need to be the length from keel to quarterdeck, only from the waterline to quarterdeck. And not even that far; it would be from their deck to the quarterdeck. For that, presuming they could breach the ship's defenders, the ladders had more than adequate reach. Badly shot but still dangerous arrows clattered over the decks here and there. Larboard *The Meer King* twisted out of line, rolling first away on her larboard side, then turning her bows back towards *The Tidebreaker* and rolling starboard at the same time discharging her starboard solcannons all in one volley to effect. The ships crowding her were crippled, one without oars on one side, its tops burning, the other two with small fires on the deck eating through their folded collapsed sail. The strike had even distracted one of the ships circling *The Tidebreaker*, setting their stern deck on fire and causing all their archers to abandon it. Now there were only two ships of immediate concern. Rosen felt he needed to feel the battle and for that he needed to drive.

"Lieutenant copilot," he said to Haulet, "prepare to be joined."

There was no time to change places and it was good to have two pilots if they could work together. "Strikemaster" he called. "How much force do we have?"

Sernalash glanced about. "I'm less one elf! With the magi, we may have one good volley!"

"Save it for the Dragons on the nearest ships!" Rosen ordered. "Strike when you have the shot and spare no cannon!"

"Ai, captain!"

Rosen stepped onto the dais and barely felt the vertigo, his nerves were so high. Then there was a horrible sound of shattering glass, made louder by his connection with the aqua. His arm flared with brief pain. Two rib-fins had been damaged by ballista. He could feel the wake of the ships coming fast, now both out of sight of the top wale. Perhaps they planned to ram? Then it was bright as noon as the starboard solcannons from the forecastle to the stern all discharged at one target, followed by the screams of humyn burning alive.

Larboard was a different tale. The cannons discharged but either were more spent or the strikers less able to compensate for Sul's diminished power, as they did nothing more than flash brightly, dazzling any soul unfortunate to look. Rosen saw two magi rise from the deck to join the one already hovering, the solstone gems on their caps glowing. One of the was Ta Taren. An arrow was suddenly snatched out of the air; others lost speed to fall listlessly. It would be the two adapts to either side protecting the ship's adept as she did an operation: arms out in front, one hand above the other as if they were grasping two oddly placed latches on a door. Then suddenly her arms twisted as if she was turning a great wheel clockwise. There were cries of surprise and a great splash.

"Ha!" Glenfar crowed. "Master threw that Dragon overboard!"

That was something, Rosen thought. The eager volunteers were called up. Officers stood by, veterans resigned to the danger of their positions, confident the healers could bring them back, provided they avoided the deadly Dragon. Others, women barely older than girls, were more aware than ever of their duty to stand and relay orders, even in the line of fire. Swords were unsheathed; axes and maces hefted. The naked terror of the crew, of dying truly and forever, was only matched by their bravery and resolve. While the ship held together they would defend her.

There was a lull while *The Tidebreaker* pitched, dipping slightly to lean starboard. Desperate shouting voices, a cacophony of urgency told Rosen a great bulk of humyn still lived. Out of sight they scrabbled like rats inside a cob wall. Rosen had given over most of the driving to Haulet, reserving himself for steering, or simply feeling the battle through the ship. He wondered why the archers weren't shooting when the air above him sang, arrows and bolts flying, one after the other, and to his satisfaction he heard cries as they hit their targets. Perhaps the crew would be slaughtered and the attempt to board would come to aught.

That was not to be. Rosen felt it through the water, another ship had joined the attack. Arrows leaped into the air, shot high with no intent at accuracy but simply to hamper the Tyreen archers. Cries sounded above as a couple of Shari arrows found a mark, and two Dwen tumbled down out of the masts. One, struck through the leg, landed well enough for it though she shouted in pain. Immediately she was rushed below. The other had simply been grazed in the arm and fallen from surprise. She waved away help, looking around the deck for her fallen bow.

A nearby scream brought Rosen's attention to the node by the larboard stair. Ensign Jarroth gasped and grit her teeth in pain. She'd been hit in the shoulder. It was hard to watch her grimace, tears streaming down her face, white knuckles gripping her sword while she swooned. Rosen looked around for help, but Ni-Fionna was there. Quickly she snapped the arrow shaft to a hands width above the wound, then relieved the girl, shouting for a replacement as Jarroth stumbled down below decks.

The air was thick with dread. Rosen felt a a chill down his neck, like the claws of the demonic Bane trying to drag him into the pit of the Void. He knew he was in danger, elfyn blood sang of speed and grace and the magic of remaking fate by will. At the same time he understood, as he attempted to evade death, he knew he was too slow. Perhaps he would be just injured instead of killed. He spun on the dais in time to see the steel tipped arrow hover towards his face. Then a gold hand plucked it out of the air, tossing it aside.

"Have a care, Sea Father!" Volunteer Hoethnav Roelyn said. She continued in a fluid motion to knock several more arrows aside with the flat of her sword. Even in the dim pall, her sulessence was strong enough that she glowed like a sainted hero.

"Volunteer!" Rosen gasped. "My thanks!"

"All in duty!"

"Wait… Aren't you with the lancers?"

"Little point now! I'll dance to where I'm needed… "

Rosen couldn't argue. Roelyn wasn't the only one. The lancers were scattered around the top wales, using their weapons like pikes. Regular strikers now held whatever weapons they had at hand, though they stayed near the solcannons on the chance Sul might return. Rosen surveyed the ship's guard assigned to stand around the cage, mizzenmast, and skylight. The stars would not be as deadly without the sun. If they were boarded it would be essential to keep the ship running.

More arrows clattered down like deadly rain, or would have if magi were not working to rob them of force. Glenfar had risen in the air to join the effort. It had its own risks; the edges of the flapping folds of Taren's robe had already been pierced by a couple of arrows. The sense of dread grew in Rosen. Suddenly he had an urge to move *The Tidebreaker*'s prow starboard and heave south a fathom, but it would countermand the spirit of the order to stay in line as they advanced.

Rosen would always regret not doing it, the irony being disobeying this order would never have been noted while others would be his bane. At that moment he reasoned if Jarroth could take an arrow, he could keep the ship in its course, whatever his misgivings. Then the time was past and it was too late to do anything but bear what was coming.

A muffled explosion sounded off the larboard.

The Shari arrows stopped.

The Tyreen archers however didn't stop until a missile whistled through the shrouds and rigging, a round shot the same size that had killed Glethlyn. This time no one was caught unawares, evading it effortlessly. It land on the quarterdeck, at the base of the main mast. Except it was no bronze ball, but a clay pot of the same pitch-fire from the night before. It was only luck that when the flames erupted across the deck the strike crew and guards managed to leap clear, midships swinging up into the rigging like Dwen, with little or no damage. The one grim exception was the Dwen who had just retrieved her bow. A hideous scream sounded as Rosen saw the woman below standing with a sheet of liquid fire raking her legs. He was rooted to the spot in horror. A couple brave middies and crew slaked water and sand on the woman but nothing would stop the flames completely. Like the trees she loved, the woman would be consumed.

Then Galen, like a champion laysaid player intercepting a runner, charged across the deck. She caught the woman around the middle, ducking her head to avoid the worst of the fire. Without stopping, she did the only thing that might work and let her momentum take them both over the starboard wale.

Rosen felt faint. Moments later he heard the splash of Galen and the archer hitting the water. Sernalash shouted orders to pour sand on the deck, but the flames were persistent, refusing to be so easily smothered. In desperation more water was thrown down with poor effect; the fire was reduced, but still lived, hot pitch spitting like a nest of mad vipers, a danger to anyone careless enough to step in it.

~Sea Father!~ a soul, probably a magi said. ~It was a ruse! They are trying to board!~

Sure enough grapples sailed over the top wales, first at the starboard quarterdeck, then from Rosen's left, dead larboard.

Instinct made Rosen retake control of *The Tidebreaker*, pushing the copilot's will aside inelegantly. Haulet didn't fight it, redirecting her essence flow to support his actions and whatever the nodes and heart required. Rosen drove the ship sideways, causing it to list abruptly for a moment. Perhaps that would put the Shari off, though it also off footed some of his own crew. It seemed to take forever – one second, two – until finally he felt what he hoped for: the hull of *The Tidebreaker* struck first one, then another Shari vessel. It was impossible to know how they fared, but Rosen hoped *The Tidebreaker*'s sheer mass had caused enough damage, even swamped the smaller vessels as had happened to so many others. Water might not douse the salt powder fire, but it would damage the unused powder.

Great cries and shouts of alarm echoed from the Shari, yet the sound of their attempts to scrabble up the sides of *The Tidebreaker* resumed. For every Shari grapple that hooked, a Tyreen ax was ready to sever the rope. Only when the ladders were finally placed, defended by archers, did the Shari finally find purchase to ascend. Their captain screaming at their back, they were possessed of desperation and battle rage. Lancers speared many but more came. The volunteers finally showed their mettle, fighting the tide, Hoethnav's sword like many flashing almost faster than the eye could follow, cutting down those the lancers missed. The modern Sula war lance was designed to scorch with essence more than stab with force, and so they were not as efficient as they might have been. The crowding at the wale had become untenable. To slaughter the enemy, the Tyreens would need to withdraw enough to let them board, the better to kill the enemy in the open.

As the rain fell, tears from a weeping sky, Rosen drew his sword and prepared to kill.

Chapter 8

Dance or Die

Navi ran with Samath, their spirits high after winning the wager. Samath spun and skipped, then gripped her hand again, pulling her to a stair to the upper deck. Then Navi took the lead, pulling him behind her to their mutual goal: a place they could celebrate together. It made Navi laugh remembering the outraged looks on the diver's faces as the Fish's boy (Codac? Kell?) slipped and fell. Navi would not quickly forgive Pearl for her humiliation floating in the wake of the ship for almost a day.

As for Samath, he was bubbly with delight.

"I'm still quite surprised!" Samath enthused. "Gael and Albani jigs aren't my usual diversion! I prefer Dwen steps and branch jigs."

"You danced well and fine," Navi said as they came to the upper deck.

"You're just saying that because I won and you're richer for it!"

"The one event did birth the other. Both can be celebrated."

They paused at the door of a starboard berth just past the main mast.

"Do you think –?" Samath began, but Navi held a finger up for silence as she opened the door as quietly as possible.

It was dark, the one window a black mirror obscuring the night beyond. To either side of the door stood a rack of three bunks attached to the wall, Dwen formed wood, grown and rooted. Under the lowest cot were cubby holes for belongings; a table stood by the window over a metal locker for letters and effects to be sealed before battle. Hanging over the table was a cheap shuttered lamp, light leaking from the imperfect seams. No other soul was present.

"Where have your sisters gone?" Samath asked.

"They said they were going to raid the Gains table in the deck officer's wardroom." Navi shut the door plunging them into near darkness. She could see well enough with the leaking light, but would have preferred if Lun had been shining. With the rain not even a star could be seen. So she partially unshuttered the lamp, and let the solstone gems light the room with their white glow.

"Oh, yes," Samath said, sitting on a stool by the table as he spilled the coins out of his bag. "I want to count it all!"

"Are you certain that's the best use of our time?" Navi asked as she removed her sword belt and boots.

"You're always so keen," Samath said, with a sly, sultry glance.

Taking the invitation Navi went to him, kissing his neck from behind. "You can count it later," she whispered in his ear.

Thin hands brushed the coins covetously. Then Samath let himself be enthralled and pulled away to one of the lower bunks.

"Isn't yours one of the top ones?" Samath asked as Navi helped him remove his robe.

"Yes. But since they are absent, I see no reason to make trysting more acrobatic than we desire."

Samath was as a man should be: masculine and agreeable, merry in bed, and otherwise out of a mother's way. Barring the awkwardness of his odd friendship with Pearl's boy, his passions always seemed to be in harmony with her own. Samath had no unnatural dreams of fighting like a mother and was pleased to lay back and give himself up. He was the perfect distraction. For Navi had been more shaken by the death of Glethlyn than she let herself admit. True, she leveraged her distant humyn ancestor to claim herself elfborn, granting her the option of citizenship in Tyrum, a city far less demanding than a Sula town or, Sel preserve her, the family estate. But Navi had every intention of living the full length of life a Sula expected to enjoy her liberties. Glethlyn's death was an unwelcome reminder that until the Shari question had been settled, her future was in Felkeni's hands.

So Navi lost herself around Samath, two bright souls linked for a moment. His muted essence didn't put her off and, if she was honest, she was rather fond of him beyond their relationship of convenience. When they finished, they dozed together, sharing a brief dream walking on the sea in sunlight surrounded by fog and mist. It was rather nice to cuddle together, even if the cot was too small. A part of Navi worried she might be too taken with Samath, but there was time enough for that to change. One day he would become demanding and tedious, and she would dread his expectations. Then they would drift apart. It was expected, a part of Navi encouraged it. She'd been close to a man once, and the pain of their final separation was something she intended to forever avoid.

At midnight they were roused by the return of Navi's sisters and an argument ensued as Striker Tellon Braz insisted on her own bunk.

"You can't yield it for one night?" Navi asked drowsily.

"No!" Tellon said. "If you want your boy can join you in your cot!"

Navi sighed and sat up, still naked. "Could you at least step out so he can arrange himself?"

Samath had pulled his robe around his nethers.

There was a collective groan as the women stepped out the door.

"Who would have thought Hoethnav could be so chivalrous…"

"Thank you," Samath murmured. "But I think I should go. Like you say, I'm not much for acrobatics."

Samath dressed, gathered his coins and left with a quick kiss. The women reentered and didn't stop teasing Navi for quite a while.

Navi didn't mind. It was a distraction from the threat of the Door that loomed over them all. And this was a better berth than her first one with smelly Cambari mercenaries always threatening to tattoo her in her sleep. All the women were strikers or lancers, therefore all with strong Sula ancestry. It wasn't that Navi was a chauvinist exactly. She didn't believe Sula were inherently superior to other elfyn tribes. But it was the culture she knew and was the most comfortable with. She hadn't understood that until she moved to Tyrum. Yes, there was less pressure to conform and more liberties to live by private whims, but there was also a diversity that shocked her. Somehow she'd assumed the Blue would always be swimming in the sea, not walking side by side with one on the streets, often smelling of fresh seaweed or worse. And many Cambari and Brownies looked nearly humyn by dress if not for their accented ears and brows. The food was not such a disappointment. Unlike many snobbish Sula, Navi liked sausages. Her own mother was unconventional; perhaps because they lived in a tower crèche and never had a fati, Navi and her siblings were raised on working mother's fare and were no worse for it to her mind.

Still, living in Tyrum had been a cultural shock. Yet, once she'd adapted, Navi found it suited her. At her heart, Hoethnav Roelyn was, to be generous, shiftless. She liked the bright and new, the horizon of possibilities, the ever interesting turns that new knowledge would bring. But Navi couldn't settle to a task, preferring to rush off after the next bright thing and she absolutely loathed the slow pace of study. In fencing, the spark of dancing with the ring of metal on metal invigorated her. And she had a talent with sulessence that led her to study for a while with the indifferent ambition of becoming a magi. The idea was fetching; perhaps one day she could work as a private sorcerer.

But lack of discipline, the fetes, the men, all brought her to the brink of failure in her first year. It was not impossible to salvage her studies, but it would have taken a monumental effort. In distracting herself she discovered her humyn ancestor. And it had been so easy to blame her failures on this individual who had been dead centuries past.

Ama had not been pleased when Navi abandoned her studies. But who was ama to judge her? At least Navi admitted her desire for the easy life of wonder and joy, whereas ama wanted both the liberty of her own ways, forever trying the limits of the law, and still to be seen as a respectable Sula mother. Navi laughed at the thought.

So Navi left her mother's crèche block in Ta Meloshok over twenty years ago and never looked back.

Now she was on a ship in the middle of the sea with all the adventure she ever wanted and more. She had confidence in her ability to fight humyn, no hesitation or scruple against killing them. The arguments about the morality of slaughter were tiresome. They had threatened Gashora and had designs on their mothers. To threaten a mother was to threaten her nation. If the Shari wished not to die, they had only to retreat. They had not. Thus their puny humyn lives were forfeit.

The explosion early in the morning startled her out of sleep so much, she rolled off her bunk and landed on the floor before she was completely conscious. Somehow the women avoided knocking into one an another, perhaps because most of them were regular crew used to working instinctively with each other. Navi grabbed her sword and joined the rest with their sundry weapons before rushing out to learn how dire the situation was.

But it was nothing they could help with. A humyn trick, salts mixed with oil or some such burning on the water to frighten the simpleminded. It was still dark so using the cannons would be out of the question. With no immediate danger, they trudged back to their cabin to dress properly, then ate a small breakfast from stores raided from the galley, before laying down to get some rest before the funeral.

Dawn glowered over them, and the words over Glethlyn's passing worried away at Navi's stubborn optimism. Death dare not touch her, no Amerling would be welcome; she had no intention of passing through the Door before her time. She did not sing, nor did she weep. She had not known Glethlyn, but as an officer she seemed fair minded and not full of her own ego. Navi could not see the irony of this thought at that time. Samath sought her out and she let him cleave to her side, hugging him to her in return. It was a welcoming thing to have a beautiful man by her side at times like these, a reminder after death came the creation of new life. Not that Navi would be birthing anytime soon. She was much too interested in enjoying herself free of obligation from house, or estate. But one day. By then there would be another beautiful man. For now she would enjoy the one present.

However there was no enjoyment after Glethlyn was sent off. The Shari, the damned, cursed Shari, had attacked and Navi was bidden to run to fortify the solcannons.

Stationed on the forecastle, Navi held one side of the cannon holds, another woman on the other side, while a third had her hand at the butt of the cannon, against the cool, honey colored stone. They struck ship after ship, timbers breaking apart blackly, hungry flames consuming the wrecks, and if they were fortunate hitting the bows just so, the reward was a retort of thunder across the water as the front of the ship exploded in a cloud of fire and black smoke. After five strikes, they would change places so that none of their essence was drained by the cannon, all the while enveloped in stream as the midships laid water on the deck. Soon it became an effort, the stone seeming empty of light, the veins no longer hungry for their magic. Navi glanced upward and her worry was confirmed: the sky had betrayed them, thick clouds covering Sul to rob them of force.

Magi were ordered to join them, as well as the mad cavalier Farthal, though she was nowhere to be seen. The magi bought them a few minutes more, but they were dangerous in a different way. Unlike Farthal who became drunk on sulessence, the magi focused all their will to leach every mote of power into the cannon and themselves, including the essence of the strike-crew. Navi knew how to prevent this vampirism, to bend the flow around her aura so she was not drained like a salted fish. But her other strikers didn't have the training and almost fainted.

"Mind your flow!" Navi snarled at the black robed woman as a ray of flaming light pulsed from the cannon to char the deck of a Shari vessel.

"I can strike in this pall or be full of care, but not both!" the magi shouted back.

"Then at least demolish our targets!"

They were all frustrated by the lack of sun. In truth only those strong with sulessence could make any effect now. The Strikemaster herself was forced to lend a hand, until neither she nor the rest of the magi could make the cannons strike more than a blinding dazzle that had no destructive force. So the magi were told to tend the cannons. They had an idea they could increase their charge even in cloud cover. The rest of the strike crew was released to assist the defense of the ship any way they could.

Arrows sang over them as archers showered the nearest Shari ships. Navi drew her sword surveying the best place she was needed while the ragtag mix of volunteer marines were called up, swarming the decks to take their places fore and aft. She would not put herself under the command of either of the volunteer sergeants, the Dwen Brownie Nanyesh Taffelan nor the Prithi mercenary Bronwen mar Cerran. Neither Trees nor barbarians would dictate Navi's course. Navi leapt onto the starboard wale, foot on a ratline while she hung from a shroud, just long enough to see what was coming from below. Shari ships were moving close; Navi jumped down and ducked as arrows were let loose. She spun in place, knocking many out of the air with her blade, surprising even herself. It wasn't all her quickness. The magi hovered above and stood on the ships knees and bollards, either casting the arrows aside, or robbing them of speed. It was an easier operation than many thought. No soul stopped individual arrows, but made a deflective aura around themselves that any free object was flung to the side, in the same manner a small meteor passing Eurath was flung back into the Void. It helped the defenders greatly but could not stop all arrows.

There were cries as some Shari arrows found targets, one a young ensign shot in the shoulder. A couple Dwen tumbled out of masts. The wounded were replaced while they went below to the hospital.

Navi ran, dodging around one of the fallen archers, feeling the flight of arrows almost before they arrived. Danger, her soul said to her, danger to them all because the three arrows she marked were on a dead course for the pilot's cage.

She swung her sword as she ran, leaping first down to the quarterdeck waist, scattering a goodly amount of arrows out of the air. But these were the weak ones, robbed of their power by magi magic. Navi understand she'd had a small Reverie. The deadly ones had not yet come. Knowing where they were to go, she ran to the stern deck, dodging around magi and resting solcannons, taking the stern steps four at a time to be where fate decided she was needed. Everyone seemed so slow: the Brownie copilot who turned the inquire what she was doing on the command deck; the ship's guard hefting their stars; the Cambari volunteers still scattered waiting for action not fathoming in their simple minds it had already arrived. The Sea Father was aware, Navi felt his thoughts, trying to evade possible death that was coming from a steel tipped arrow, knowing he wasn't fast enough. Navi plucked the arrow of of the air, tossing it aside as she knocked others away with her sword.

There were words of thanks, questions about post, but they were not important. Felkeni was again whispering in Navi's ear: she was to keep an eye on the top wales. Of course, the humyn were trying to board. But she must also keep herself away from the main mast. There was danger there. The image of a burning tree filled Navi's mind, overlaying but not obscuring her sight. The part of her soul that understood bellowed at the Dwen woman standing about to climb back to the tops. She'd just found her bow.

A retort echoed, another Dragon striking. A ball sailed through the shrouds but every soul was attuned to the force of its path and leapt aside so it landed on the deck. Except it was not a ball, but a pot of the same fire that had danced on the waves the night before. It slaked the deck like water and the Dwen archer was set aflame. Like many Navi was rooted in horror, at a loss for action. Calling the Cold would not even help for oil and pitch fires needed to be absolutely smothered. The boatswain tackled the Dwen and they both fell overboard.

The crew rushed forward to suppress the fire, but Navi held back. She knew in her bones this was a distraction. Sure enough as the pitch fire was tamed to a spitting smoldering mass the Shari came first with grapples, then ladders. They allowed the first cluster of turbaned warriors to step on deck, pulling back to have more room to maneuver. They came, sun-browned faces with black untidy beards grinning, not in joy, but the maddened aggression that kept fear at bay. Many chanted "Al-ahat!" and other cries, as they stumbled through the gap of the top wale onto the quarterdeck. Their long tan, dun and reddish caftans showed the trials of living at sea and the stench was a miasma to Navi's senses. Some had armor, others only shields slung on their backs. Many had swords, cutlasses, axes and spiked clubs, all held clumsily as they ascended the ladder. If only some magi could push the entire ladder back. Lancers speared the first few humyn and there was a rush by Bron and several Cambari to push the thing off the ship. But it was weighed down with humyn bodies; in this case its rickety construction made it bow inward against the hull, resisting being simply pushed away without falling with it. So Bron ordered her women fall back and let the Shari come to met their death.

As they clambered onto the deck, one turbaned head was struck by the Master's star in one hand, her sword in her other hand slicing across the humyn's belly, his cutlass falling to the deck in the tangle of his own disgorged intestines. The next one came for Navi, lunging with the point of his blade towards her throat. With a flick of her blade she sliced his arm off at the elbow. Before he could even understand he'd been maimed, she reversed her blade across his throat. Blood poured out of his mouth like a fountain, before he collapsed at her feet.

Navi was in her element, dancing, sword spinning, the Shari falling before her as she effortlessly cut through them, feeling the blood of the mother and the passion of war. One Navi cut down by severing his leg at the knee, so he fell screaming like a slaughtered bull. He would die being trampled by his own countrymen who could not afford to stop for aid or mercy, so fierce was their need to take this ship, no sacrifice was too great. The next cut of Navi's sword aimed at a neck on her right, missed its mark, striking off a turbaned helmet while severing an ear. The humyn raised a spiked club. She had plenty of time to swing her blade across her left, making a couple new boarders duck back, cutting through the side of an ax wielding warrior on her right as he fell screaming, then bringing her sword back with force into the side of the now one eared man before his club fell. Except instead of his sides opening to spill with gore, her sword hit a coat of small armored plates. The club fell wide as the man was winded. Navi both felt and heard his ribs break. Gasping he rose, pulling his club back for a strike, only to have a star spike his head from behind. He shivered and jerked under the point that had penetrated his skull, eyes rolling back as bright blood ran in rivulets down his face, to be broken by drops of water.

That's when Navi realized it was raining.

The dead humyn slid to the deck at the feet of the guard who killed him. Navi nodded her thanks, then swung at the next, her sword sliding down the back of a rusted glaive with such force, it struck the hilt, knocking the weapon out of the humyn's hand. The man ducked away, hiding behind the shield he'd unslung. Navi gave him no more regard for the one after was tall and able, in a mail shirt wielding an ax and holding a shield to effect. Aware of the skirmishes to either side of her, Cambari bellowing battle oaths as they waded into the butchery, Navi only had to focus of this one, who paused looking at her uncertainly. His mind leaked so many thoughts: was this a woman or a tall youth? How many had he killed of his fellows to be drenched in blood? And how was he not injured without armor or even a helmet? It should be easy, they looked narrow and fragile. Swing the ax at the head…

Navi dodged to one side, avoiding the ax blow, while rotating her sword in a counterclockwise arc to sever the extended ax hand. It was so quick the humyn had only started to scream when she reversed the blade to sever his head.

And now Navi saw how much blood covered her. Drops splattered her face, the inadvertent taste of tangy salted ichor touching her lips as the head rolled down the stern steps in a series of sickening thuds.

A jab in her left thigh made her jerk back. It was a lucky hit, a warrior lunging after finally fighting his way to the deck, keeping the Cambari horde at bay. Navi's blood was up so high, it wasn't painful, but made her aware she needed to guard her left side as more humyn pressed onto the deck. She grabbed an abandoned ax, swinging it wildly to clear room on her left. The guards using stars kept most of the area around the cage free. Nearby Bronwen's cousin, flaming haired Freya, was dancing with her eerie black blade, working well with the Cambari warrior boy. How his bronze sword lasted this long was a mystery to Navi. No sooner than the thought passed, with the next parry the graceful leaf blade of sword bronze, forged in the Cambrian hills, bent against an iron scimitar.

The mercenary and the boy were nearly surrounded behind the mizzen-mast. They might not be able to hold out if the boy – damn boys who thought they could play at war! – could not guard Freya's back. As odious as Navi considered the entire matter, she would not stand by and let a man be killed.

Navi darted away from the skirmish, leaping on the top wale using a neglected solcannon for a boost. The touch was invigorating, wet with rain, but bright with the memory of the sun. Near the mast shroud a rope hung free from an aborted repair. Navi threw the ax into the center of the ladder where humyn clung to board, pleased it landed in a shoulder, the man falling with a wail to the water. First tugging the rope to be sure it would hold her, Navi grabbed it and leaped off the stern top wale to swing over the deck, sword in hand, landing in front of the boy soldier as a cutlass swung down towards him.

Navi ran the Shari through the chest, no hidden shirt of armor stopping her blade until the hilt hit the sternum. The next second Navi fluorescenced, the excess magic from touching the solcannon discharging to make flames licking the edge of her sword, setting the humyn on fire. The horror of it while he screamed made the other attackers fall back, stumbling to be cut down between pitiless guards and Cambari. Navi kicked the shrieking creature off her blade, snarling to Freya and the boy, "Dance or die!"

Then she was hacking her way back to the larboard wale, a knife cutting her cheek, just missing her left eye. Enraged, she grabbed the offending arm and snapped it at the elbow, the man's scream satisfying as she ran him through, his scream ending in a gasp. She tossing the dying creature aside because two things had manifested: lancers clustering at the wales and a thinning of the clouds overhead. Not enough for cannon strike, but enough that a sulessence powerful individual with a sun lance could light the air for several moments.

Navi trusted the guards, crew and barbarian mercenaries to tend to the remaining beasts behind her. An explosion echoed over the water, but it was distant. She joined the line of women, her cabin mate Tellon Braz happily pressing one of the long solstone glass enameled lengths of metal into her left hand. They aimed together, down at the ladder still thick with human bodies and struck long sustained rays of light that instantly set the ladder aflame. Those at the top rushed to clear it, clinging to the wale as the ladder collapsed, others jumping into the water as the better fate than burning. A voice rose to sing a verse from the Federation anthem with Tyreen errant words. By the end a course of voices had joined, some while still fighting:

Many thought to make us thralled, let me tell a tale:
Of dragon boats from northern lands with sailors tall and pale;
City lights shown like the day as they tried to scale the wall,
With spear and beer in hand we called, "Take care lest you fall!"

Come what may, our ships sail ever on!
To seize the best of rum and men and revel till the dawn!
Come what may, raiding ever on ~
Catch us on the shining seas if you have the speed and brawn!

Many Shari, those who had not fallen back into the sea, lay dead or dying. There were still Shari on the decks, now alarmed they were very much alone. Lancers had destroyed the boarding ladders on the starboard wale was well. A raven was croaking incessantly above. Some grapples remained. Navi saw the tip of a helmet rise into view. By the time she darted over, the warrior saw his mistake and was at a loss. Navi simplified the matter by removing his head. Then she turned to the remaining Shari.

They fought out of desperation until, seeing themselves surrounded and out numbered, they dropped their weapons and fell to their knees, calling out something about "Al-ahat", their god the Ever-sky.

There would be no mercy, Navi thought, finding herself over one vermin, a dull ungrateful humyn ignorant of the sacrifices elfyn mothers made for millennia to keep the Orb safe. Navi grimly pulled her sword back, ready to harvest these sheaves of worthless souls. They had killed Glethlyn, a bright elfborn soul who could not be replaced. In that moment she agreed with the rule loving demagogues infesting the capitol: humyn were a disease that should be eradicated for the peace of all. How dare the humyn filth consider petitioning any god for mercy...

"Volunteer Roelyn!" the strikemaster bellowed. "Stand down! They are surrendering!"

Navi could just do it. What could the Tyreen navy do, float her again? They certainly wouldn't go to the effort of retrieving the animals.

"Roelyn!" Azar Sernalash shouted, almost shrill with rage. "Did you not hear me?"

Navi lowered her blade. She had decided to live in Tyrum and abide by their ways. So she let the woman with the gold eyes and gold bindi shout at her for several minutes, while she stared down at the humyn sullenly. He finally understood he was going to live when his hands were tied and he was led away by the guards, tears of relief streaming down his grimy black-bearded face.

When the shouting was over, Navi walked away. Midships offered water used to slake the decks to wash the worst of the blood away, or as some Cambari decided, to be drenched from head to toe. The battle for the ship was over, though Navi saw the same drama played out on other ships. Not all had been boarded, but enough that Navi sent a silent prayer they would prevail. If help was needed a whistle would sound. For now Navi cleaned her sword and sheathed it until it was needed again.

Chapter 9

Pitch-fire and Steel

The volunteers charged, the rain hitting their faces as they ran up the stairs to the quarterdeck. No wonder the tide had turned against them, Col thought as he fought to both keep up and not lose his footing. Pearl was gone, somewhere in the sea, and Col tried not to think of the danger she might face. For now he had to survive.

They had barely emerged from below decks, seeking the best places among crew and guards when flames erupted nearby around the main mast. The light glimmered off the marines' scale armor as a viscous oily fluid spread to cover the deck, surrounding the main mast with fire, threatening to pour down the stairs below. There was no thought of order and formation as every mother and man dove away from the flames, or leaped into the lower rigging, or, like most of the marines, took the simple expedient of diving overboard. Col slipped and found himself on his side under a solcannon, bright flames near him. Then blows rained on his shoulder as Freya beat out a patch of oil that had slashed on his leather vest.

"*Elam!*" he gasped in thanks, knowing that he'd be bruised in that place.

Before Freya could reply a hideous scream erupted and Col saw a Dwen on fire. She had been standing in the center of the conflagration with nowhere to run. He blinked, numb to any way he could help when a great ox of a woman ran to catch and carry the unfortunate Dwen over the side.

Col stumbled to his feet in horror, watching as the wall of flames licked everything in their path. He and Freya joined women who threw water on the fire; they could not fight if they burned to death first.

"No, you fools!" a crewgirl yelled. "It burns like oil! Use the sand!"

And so they strained their backs throwing buckets of sand across the flames, while above flaming ropes and sail were cut to fall around them. The sand wasn't as effective as with simple oil, but the flames were suppressed, though the fire smoldered, not completely robbed of its force.

"Come on!" Freya urged. They darted and leapt over the bent women and girls up to the stern deck where the rest of the aft volunteers, with Bronwen as their sergeant, scattered amongst the guards and strike crew. Arrows fell dully, robbed of their force by magi, though one pierced the tip of Col's boot cutting his big toe. He gritted his teeth, swearing as he hopped before yanking the arrow out, then rushed to catch up with Freya standing behind the mizzenmast, the skylight oval nearby just as the first turbaned invaders threw grapples over the ship's sides.

Freya shook her head as Col moved forward to help the lancers and others. "We are better out of the way! Be ready when they break through!"

Freya drew her sword and he followed, watching as the lancers skewered Shari as they tried to board, many screaming as they were thrown back to almost certain death. Axes fell on grappling lines, not a few severing hands and fingers without prejudice. Then a ladder was raised and could not be easily thrown back, not even with the mass of women like Bronwen who made the ships' boatswain look to be an average formed mother.

So they fell back to give themselves room to move as the Shari, white teeth flashing in dark faces, advanced over the wales. The fading flames gave them a demonic cast, the tips of helmets touched with blood, cutlasses and scimitars swinging eagerly for a target. None of the first who boarded survived, killed and dismembered so fast many were dead before understanding their doom. Then they pushed through, by twos and threes, cut or wounded but still eager to fight. For a moment Col felt the fear of death, then he stopped thinking as his body reacted to whatever danger came.

"Don't fight the sword, fight the woman," Freya's voice echoed from their training. The humyn that rushed Col raised his curved sword high above to strike down with force. But the humyn was slow, so slow Col wondered if he was in battle trance. It was nothing to slice across the man's front, cutting his robes so they hung in tatters while blood seeped through them. Then, as the sword fell, Col brought his own backwards to cut the throat on the return. He did so well the man's head was half severed as he fell back to the deck, his weapon falling with a dull clatter. It happened so fast, so effortlessly, it might have been a dream. Then another humyn was facing Col, screaming incoherent fury in an alien tongue.

The second was dispatched like the first.

And so was the third and the fourth. Then Col lost count.

There was no way to judge their success. He caught a glimpse of Bron, a Shari leaping upon her. But then Col saw it was not the case: Bron had caught the man with one hand, crushing his neck before lifting him up and tossing him into the sea. Col felt little fear except the worry tiredness might diminish his force. Once he heard Freya gasp; perhaps she'd been cut. But a glance showed she was hale and on her feet so he didn't spare another thought.

Then a new wave of attackers came from the starboard, from a different ship, fresh and full of fury. That was when Col found himself back to back with Freya. They were surrounded and cut off from the guards.

"Dance like one!" she bellowed.

And so they did, back to back, for the moment the need to survive super-seding their duty to repel the Shari or even protect the pilot's cage. Sure and light though their footing was, the rains' relentless drizzle threatened to unfoot them had they not had each others backs for support.

Then it happened, Col's worst fear: his sword parried a Shari blow with a heavy cutlass and it bent.

Col grappled clumsily, the man driving forward with his blade. Col blocked and turned it aside with basic dance moves, cutting his palms. He didn't dare move his back from Freya's as they were still surrounded. Col, still faster than the Shari, was forced to wrestle him. In a couple of moves he'd disarmed his opponent. In another, he broke the arm in a lock and the Shari fell back gasping.

"Why are you dancing with it?" Freya shouted.

"My sword bent!" Col called back, barely ducking a swinging blade.

Freya swore and spun, dancing like a marionette of death, cutting down Col's attackers, while almost impossibly thwarting her own. Her red hair flew and, with the stormy sky behind her, she looked like Moragu, the great Cambrian Goddess of War. She was faster than Col, much faster, and with her grim steel sword that seemed to sail through bodies, she seemed unstop-pable. But without his back guarding her, Freya wouldn't be able to last for-ever. Col cast about desperately for a substitute for his ruined blade, even a Shari cutlass.

Suddenly a light flashed. For a moment Col thought it was a lightning. Then he was looking up at a Sula woman who glowed faintly, as if the de-parted sunlight lingered on her as she swung on a loose rope to land on the deck. The next moment Col recognized it was a blood soaked Navi. Her sword, faster if possible than Freya's, spun and flashed, and with a scream a Shari who was about to cut down Col was impaled through the chest. The next moment Navi's sword erupted in flames, the ambient essence, combined with her battle rage, sparking her sulessence, and the man, still not quite dead, screamed as he fell back, flames enveloping him.

Navi withdrew her blade and raked both Freya and Col with a scathing look.

"Dance or die!" she shouted before leaping to a top wale to confront new invaders.

The Shari around them fell back in horror at the immolation of their comrade. Grateful but shaken, Col had a moment to catch his breath and footing.

"There!" Freya shouted, pointing to a fallen guard who clutched a wound at her side. A crewgirl was taking the brief respite to drag her away below to the healers, a star lying on deck, sword still in hand. "Quickly!" Freya urged.

Col darted forward to intercept the wounded woman before she was taken away.

"Please, emha, my sword is ruined..."

The guard handed it to him.

"Use it well, girl," she slurred before disappearing below.

Col blinked at the absurdity then looked to rejoin Freya. She had moved closer to the dais of the pilot's cage where the Sea Father was kicking a Shari back, before Freya spitted him. On the other side, the lancers with Navi were repelling the larboard invasion with little place to stand. To meet up with Freya Col would have to run around the starboard of the stern deck. It didn't matter how, he had to do it.

He ran, then found his way blocked by fallen bodies, the fighting living and a solcannon. There he took a leaf from Navi's book: grabbing a hanging rope, he leapt onto the starboard wale, and used his momentum to swing to Freya's side only stumbling a little as he landed.

"A fair bit of dancing, friend!" she said. "Shall we trade places? I think I'll be at an advantage there!"

Col shrugged. *"Is cuma liomsa!"*

There was no room to move around each other and so they did a roll
over: in this case Freya bent half over, then Col rolled his back over hers,
thus changing places.

"Much better!" Freya said. "How is the sword?" she added.

"*Togha!*" Col said reflexively.

The truth was he hadn't marked it much, its balance was so good, it felt
as light as air. It was a standard Federation host sword. A keen eye could
see a faint black line, as fine as a hair, on the sharpest edge of the blade.
That was grimsteel, giving them an edge unequaled to even the best forged
steel. The blade wasn't magical in the usual sense. It was no soul sword or
wizard creation. But compared to his ruined bronze blade, it may as well
have been forged by Soltarlu Firewind, the smith of Sul's Court of Heaven.

When the next ragged bunch of Shari came, looking more desperate than
the last, the sword danced with Col's will. These Shari never had a chance.
In moments they were cut down. Col paused, looking at the blood and carnage at his feet and for a moment the grimness of the duty settled on him.
They had lived moments before, humyn not unlike his father's tribe. Now
they were dead. Col's spirit sank and he knew he was in danger, but he
didn't seem able to stop himself.

As if from a great distance, he heard Freya yell, "Look to yourself, Col!"

Slowly, or so it seemed, Col raised his head. A mad Shari charged him,
screaming in rage and fear and fury. In that moment he knew the man was
desperately throwing his life away. Though the hope of victory was long
gone, he could not retreat. While Col's mind seemed to watch from afar, his
body had not forgotten the wisdom of his training. It was like watching
someone else move as Col swung the sword easily across the man's path,
just as an ax was brought down to slice Col's body. Then the man's ax and
hands fell as Col's sword cut off both arms at the elbows.

Suddenly Col was aware of his body and mind again, as screaming filled
his ears, while his front was covered with blood. It was only after Col removed the man's head, releasing him from misery, did he realize it was himself who was still screaming. Col shook but there was no time to think, only
to act. He forced the horror of the bleeding stumps aside and fought, dancing with Freya at his back again. They were like a single force now, the

new sword making Col almost Freya's equal. With the guards, they cleared the Shari away from skylight and mizzen mast.

Then the decks were cleared, light flashing from lances as the clouds nearly parted, enough to give essence powerful women one strike as they sang in triumph. There was an explosion, from where Col didn't know, releasing a flare of blue light. After that the last Shari were repulsed, falling into the sea as ropes were cut and the ladders were burned from beneath them. A few not dead remained, now pleading for mercy. Col saw Navi raise her sword, gold eyes glowing with rage, but the strikemaster rebuked her. Reluctantly Navi lowered her sword. Chivalry and honor would prevail at sea, at least in this moment.

Col lowered his own sword, gasping freely with relief.

"Now you can say you've fought!" Freya said grinning.

Then Col understood. She didn't smile for joy at the dead around them, or the blood slicked deck or the carnage they had delivered. She smiled for the joy that they still lived and Col found himself smiling back. Then they found each other's eyes, his gray and hers gold, and a passion exploded inside him like he'd never felt before. Magnetic and overwhelming, Col felt drawn to Freya, his comrade and battle companion, the woman he had made war with like he made love with Pearl. And when Freya kissed him he wanted in that moment to give himself completely to their passions.

The next moment he pushed Freya away and they stumbled apart.

"Sorry," Freya said. "I was over come – "

"Don't," Col raised his hand. "Don't let's think on it."

Just as sudden the passion fled, though whether it was because the moment had passed or his own guilt, Col didn't know. Like the recent horrors he wouldn't think in it now. Freya seemed to accept this and took the same tack.

"We should help gather the wounded and captured," she said, cleaning off her sword and accepting the water the midships offered to wash her face.

"Yes, of course," Col found himself agreeing, eager to agree to something innocent, as he too cleaned himself the best he could. He looked around him: everywhere there was recent horror in women's eyes, while above ravens croaked, some descending for a quick feast of dead humyn eyes before being waved off by crew. One raven, perhaps piqued at being thwarted, kept croaking, irritated and insistent. The Sea Father, covered with dark splatters of blood, was sheathing his sword and stepping out of the pilot's cage. Navi had returned to her place with the strike crew. But around them, out on the sea, battles still raged. In the gloom of mist and black smoke, half the Shari fleet seemed to be burning.

A whistle went up from the masts, followed by a reply from another ship, Col wasn't sure who. But all regular crew became tense, turning their attention to *The Oaken Blue*. Never had Col expected to see a Tyreen ship in such a state. Black smoke billowed out of a great gapping hole in the front as she listed. A blue glow surrounded her. Beside him a crewgirl muttered, "Sun and Sea, save us! She'll be holding it together with pure essence!"

Before Col could understand the meaning orders, were shouted and all marines present jumped into the sea. For *The Oaken Blue*, the greatest ship on the water and the Admiral's flagship, was being evacuated.

Chapter 10

Wounds

Back in Tyrum, on the white wall that protected the city from raiders and storm, there was a point girls, and some boys, dived off in a dare. The top of the Wall, fifty feet above the sea, was much higher than the freeboard of a city-ship, the distance between the waterline and the quarterdeck. Galen had only dived off the Wall a handful of times. But the experience gave her the confidence to charge with the burning Dwen archer over the side and into the sea.

The first second was the longest: Galen shut her eyes to protect them from both the flames and pitch-fire that had spread to her vest, threatening to burn them together. She held on to the woman, screams ringing in her ear, knowing that with what they'd seen last night, if they both weren't submerged utterly, the fire would consume them.

The next second they hit the water. Instinct made Galen clamp her hand over the woman's mouth as steam hissed in her ears, the deadly mix of resin, naphtha and salts reluctant to cede their alliance with the air. Galen felt pulling and opened her eyes, the water blurry, ready to crush a Shari attacker to death by the sheer force of her grip. But it was just a couple of Blue divers, stripping the Dwen of her garments, correctly seeing they would insist on smoldering and melt to her skin.

Galen was almost out of breath and gratefully yielded the Dwen to one of the divers who sealed her own lips around the woman's, exhaling air into her lungs. Galen decided to surface, gasping for breath.

The roar of the battle assaulted her ears as she tread water. There was another explosion and shouts far away and above. *The Tidebreaker* was drifting, meaning Galen was closer to the stern than she had been. It would be work taking the woman back to the tops, for that was the only way to the hospital now the ports were closed.

A diver surfaced, short black hair shaved at the sides revealing triskelion leaves tattooed on either side of her blue skull, much like Galen's own rams' horns.

"The diver's ladder!" the woman said, and Galen understood. Taking quick strokes she would meet her there and then pull the woman up to the tops.

Galen looked up through the smoke and fog, not fancying the feat one bit. The locked rudder loomed, dividing her way. Above it ascended the galleries, in order from the waterline: the rank's mess, the deck officer's wardroom and the captain's cabin. Above that was the ornately carved and gilded stern deck, sea horses rising on waves between astalyn stars. Two figures were fighting over where Galen floated. Presently one fell over, a humyn without a helmet or indeed one arm. He landed in the water already dead with a slit throat.

There was nothing for it. If the woman didn't get to the hospital she might not live. And if Galen didn't return to the decks, who would keep her foolish childhood friend from over extending himself after Glethlyn's loss? He'd taken his first lieutenant's death personally. Left to his own devices Rosen might try to match the Jackal in his thirst for vengeance. So Galen swam to the diver's ladder and clung to it, praying more bodies would not fall on her before she brought the wounded archer to safety. Shortly, the divers met her, bobbing up, like dolphins hopping.

How they did it Galen wasn't certain. Had she been on dry solid land it would have been easy. Or an unfraught sea with the aid of a rope, boom and tackle. But somehow they did, Galen clinging to the bottom of the ladder, a series of metal holds bolted into the hull. The divers hefted the Dwen woman out of the water to drape on one of Galen's shoulders, steadied by the same arm. Galen would use the other to carefully ascend, jerking to catch each rung like an acrobat. Before she started a cool hand squeezed her ankle; Galen felt a sincere feeling of sisterhood and concern she hadn't expected from a stranger.

"Step with care," the diver said.

Galen glanced down but they had already disappeared below the water.

Arrows hissed above, some clattering on her shoulder. Then like Jaro carrying Myngar's sacred calf, Galen ascended, pulling their weight up with her arm, then taking a step with one foot to launch herself up with a short hop, grabbing the next rung. Thankfully the woman had passed out, making her weight dead. It took Galen a minute to reach the ranks officer's mess.

Unlike the upper galleries, while the windows opened, there was no out-side balcony. Galen gripped the rung she hung on, startled to see faces look-ing at her. The nearest window was flung open and a midship cried out:

"Need a hand, emha boatswain?"

Galen looked up to the long perilous journey above her, and did some quick calculations. She should have thought of it herself! Not only would she be relieved of her burden, but the Dwen would get to the hospital quicker and safer.

"Sparking idea, middie!" Galen said. "Get strong hands and quick!"

The girl darted back in. Soon a collection of senior midships and other crew available came to help, including ship's purser. Emha Jorun Arden-weld was a thin, laconic Gold woman who rarely smiled. She looked much like an officer, except she had black shoes instead of boots and no bicorn.

"A rather ridiculous time for a stroll, boatswain!" Ardenweld said, as they pulled the Dwen woman inside.

Relived of her burden Galen gasped, "Get her to the hospital sprightly! She was burned with pitch fire!"

"We will act with alacrity!" Ardenweld called, then shut the window.

Now able to use both hands, Galen clung to the ladder, catching her breath. Suddenly she felt the wet and cold, chilling her though the breeze was slight. Her burns were also making themselves known – both of her deck shoes were scorched, and pitch-fire had splashed on her calves. It wasn't serious and there would be time enough to visit the hospital later. She scampered up with speed to rejoin the battle. Soon she would be too busy to be bothered by pain and her chilled blood would warm in battle.

* * *

The first wounded stumbled through the open doors of the crew mess, a Dwen archer limping with an arrow in her thigh. The shaft had been snapped off a hands breadth above where it had torn her white sea breeches, now seeping crimson with blood. Eld dashed over to help the woman limp to a bench. Tending this was a simple thing: the flesh was cut and only needed the removal of the arrow for the woman's natural healing to begin. In truth it had already begun, essence rich tissue trying to find a way to seal around the metal intruder or cast it out. But arrows were not slivers and it needed to be pulled out, forcibly if necessary. Fortunately the surgeon was able, opening a case of glass knives to first slice the breech fabric, then feeling the wound to know best where to cut to ease the arrow out.

"Need a draught?" the red hatted surgeon asked.

"Just do it!" the woman bit out.

Without further ceremony, the knife made two quick cuts and the surgeon yanked the arrow out, the Dwen only gasping slightly.

"Wash and seal it, Farthal," the surgeon commanded. To the woman she added. "I want you to sit several minutes under the hand of a healer until bleeding has stopped before you return."

The woman nodded but the surgeon was already examining a midship with an arrow in her arm.

Eld had never worked as a healer properly, yet everywhere she served, it was marked in her record and she found herself dragged back into a temple or field hospital. Her hand hovered over the wound, barely touching, letting her aura seep into the blood, hungry blood that held the motes of air ferried by breath to the lungs. It was the easiest way to fall into a healer's trance. The very fact that blood was exposed betrayed trauma and the need to heal. Eld closed her eyes and slowly her sight was filled with the vision of the small strange world that was the scaffold of life as every scholar knew.

Everything seemed bright red with white stars. In the midst of it all was a canyon size fissure, blinding white where the motes were exposed, air entering without care, always with the risk of bringing invaders to this realm. Already the woman's essence was rallying, a dark crust moving to close, the skin dreaming of knitting in a pattern that echoed its memory of wholeness. That was why this part of healing was so easy: the body wanted to be whole and skin wanted it faster than many parts. Eld just let her essence flow with the woman's, adding speed so the wound would not be open to more injury.

Opening her eyes, Eld felt as if she'd woken from a nap. The nut brown skin was knitted but there was still redness and swelling.

"You know it's not fully healed, right?" she asked the woman. "Wait for the after tending to be done before you return."

The Dwen shrugged, green eyes now free of pain. "I'll be careful, ama," she said sarcastically.

"Get along before I injure you myself." Eld knew it was always the way, on land or at sea, soldier, cavalier or sailor: if the urgency of the hour called, a wound was ignored no matter the healer's advice.

More came, a twisted ankle, easily mended; a broken finger, not so easily, but it was a simple break. Once wrapped in Dwen twisted strips of wood to splint it, the Cambari woman insisted on leaving. A couple of midships with dazzle blindness; they were bidden to drink draughts and sit quietly until their sight returned. Fortunately no injuries like Glethlyn's, no soul was taken early through the Door yet. And then Eld saw Ensign Jarroth helped over to sit heavily in front of the surgeon, her young face twisted in pain. An arrow shaft had hit her in the shoulder. Eld stood to go to her, but was intercepted by a crewgirl, one of the boatswain's mates.

"Farthal? You're to join the strike crew on the forecastle! Smartly!"

"No mind," Prefect Ordryn Mathynwol said as she examined a nasty cut. "We can spare the Pony."

Eld ignored Mathynwol and retrieved her coat, buttoning it as she darted out onto the upper deck. She had planned to just run up the companion stairs, but the activity from the hold relaying supplies looked too dangerous to interrupt. Instead Eld ran the length of the deck to the stair that emerged before the pilot's cage, right on the heels of the volunteer fighters. She had to wait until they dispersed to their diverse stations before she could run up on deck, only to immediately duck as a projectile of some sort sailed over her flouted hair.

There was a crash, followed by flames and a hideous scream. Eld had caught herself on one of the solcannons near the starboard stern steps. The touch, even without sunlight, was calming and invigorating if not for the woman burning alive in front of her. Eld was about to rush, maybe with touch she could call the Cold, the inversion of sulessence that could smother a surface with frost if the air held enough water. But the boatswain was quicker, taking the burning woman overboard into the water. They were in Maer's hands now.

Now Eld's way was barred by a desperate attempt to smother the pitch fire. A motion caught her eye: the window to the clerk's cabin was broken. Was she well? If a pot of pitch-fire had fallen inside…

Eld ran around the stern stair to the main door of the cabin. It was open and that seemed irregular. She rushed in to find Ensign Savalis limping, a smear of blood on the thigh of her white sea breeches as she shuffled papers into a strongbox.

"What in Sul's tresses are you doing?" Eld shouted.

"You sound like our Sea Father," Savalis said. "Bit of wood flew into me. Biggest splinter I've ever had!" she added with a manic grin. "Help me get the papers in the boxes to seal, please!"

Eld had to forsake the words she wanted to say. It was quicker to help and the girl would be willing to abandon the cabin once the task was done. Eld grabbed papers under Savalis' direction, moving like a dervish. The strike crew would have to wait. First she would know Savalis was safely ensconced, at least as safe as could be considering.

After a couple of harried minutes the papers were finally in place. Eld slammed the lid shut and waited for Savalis to retrieve the lock. She had only stepped in front of the broken window when she jerked with a gasp, before sliding to the floor.

"No!" Eld bellowed, catching Savalis' tall, gangly form. Her green eyes were wide, dusky skin yellowed from shock.

"I think I've been hit again," Savalis slurred.

"No, no, no!" Eld repeated like a desperate prayer. A red fletched arrow had sunk into her from behind and into her lower gut. This was a serious wound, one Eld was certainly not able to tend on her own. She let Savalis' body fall against her, then snapped the arrow shaft in half to keep it from catching and making the wound worse. Eld would have to abandon the box, leaving it unlocked, to carry Savalis to the infirmary. A soul was worth more than leaves of paper, no matter how important.

Savalis wasn't completely unconscious. Gripping the younger woman close to her, Eld give her some of her own essence, strengthening both their auras as they limped together. They took the stairs behind the mizzenmast, stumbling down to the upper deck. It ended outside the heart chamber, opposite the door of the deck officer's wardroom. Perhaps Eld should place her there and get help? No, better to make one journey. Who knew what state the healers would be in when they arrived.

WOUNDS

So Eld shuffled down the deck with Savalis, trying to avoid aggravating her injury while at the same time keeping the bleeding inside contained, and the essentials of the nerves and tendons intact so her healing would be quicker. If the arrow had missed her guts, had penetrated nothing but skin and muscle, it would be best. Otherwise the surgeon would have to cut with assistance. Eld worried from the sounds of the fighting and screams of the dying, if there were enough healers for a serious operation. She herself couldn't tell the true state of the wound. She could only give Savalis the grace of her own essence, hoping it would be enough to keep her alive until she could be tended.

* * *

High above in the masts of *The Tidebreaker*, ToKeh perched on the three foot edge fence of netting and woven branches around the highest tops platform while Oleth aimed her bow with precision, waiting for the moment the Shari would be close for the best strike. ToKeh wasn't a fleet raven; he was, for lack of a better word, a volunteer, but one that only heeded Oleth or his own whims. ToKeh had lived in Oleth's house in Tyrum's Tree Quarter for decades, first as a roof squatter, and then as they developed a friendship, as part of the household. Oleth's helper had begged him to go with the fleet and so he did. Though he understood the threat, being a raven, he still couldn't fathom why any thinking beast would come so far to seek such trouble with a greater foe. He'd long since accepted those bound to land did insensible things.

Below the Shari ships drew closer, flimsy boats full of dark faces with succulent eyes. When the living became carrion they would feast, or so the fleet ravens told ToKeh. He was warned one had to be careful to evade the scruple of the land bound to throw carrion to the sea, or worse, burn it.

"Stop thinking on your belly and have care," Oleth chastened, the oak leaves of her yastol low over her head, almost covering it like a helmet.

~fast i can move- faster than walk thyn.~ ToKeh replied, though the sudden shift of the ship made him grip the weavings and rock with his wings half extended for a moment. Every motion of the ship was magnified in the masts.

Oleth laughed. "And you can bob like a chicken!"

ToKeh eyed her beadily. Thyn had humor and thyn ravens, unlike Thyn Elk, did laugh in their way, but ToKeh decided not to encourage Oleth, though he found it funny.

"In seriousness, friend," Oleth continued, "There is a reason the other ravens have taken flight or roosted in shelter. An ill arrow could catch you."

ToKeh scraped his beak on the edge of the basket. ~ what is fast to the land bound is nothing to us.~

"If it was just one, perhaps. But when they come it will be a cloud, and the magi can't deflect them all…"

At that moment an order came to fire at will.

ToKeh hunkered down while Oleth stood, one foot on the edge of the basket, firing arrows as carefully as she could. She was an uncommon Dwen sniper, able to use the unerring arrows that floated on sunlight to find their targets. Their virtue was wasted without the sun but they killed all the same. The air sang a discordant whine of the archers' collective efforts, like a stormy wind forced through the branches of many trees at once, much of the enemy falling to the decks of the strange scorpion ships or overboard into the water. The clouds of green-fletched death should have been the end of the gutlings bobbing in their boats.

However this wasn't a land war. The combination of angles, distance and movement varied the outcomes of normal gambits. Humyn fell, but there were still enough to reckon with when they started shooting back.

ToKeh didn't even think, reacting so fast it was as if he had been transported by magic into the shadow of the weavings. Many archers had to stop shooting, dancing out of the way when they could, others catching arrows in flight. And others let themselves be struck rather than stop shooting; they would keep their post and be tended later provided the wounds were not grievous. Spent arrows fell on ToKeh causing him to cry out like a crow. Belatedly he saw the wisdom of the fleet ravens hovering in the air, above the magi, beyond an arrow's flight.

The arrows finally stopped and ToKeh hopped back onto the rim to look down. His eyes widened as he saw the bronze tube they were calling a Dragon being loaded with its deadly fire.

~the dragon will roar again!~ ToKeh said.

"Not if I can help it," Oleth said grimly, aiming at the humyn loading it.

But then more arrows flew from the Shari vessel, not all robbed of their power. ToKeh swiveled his head, seeing a second boat approaching. His raven sense for speed saw the humyn, then the bow he held, then the arrow as it left the bow, sailing with a doom as certain as a falling egg. And like a falling egg, ToKeh could do nothing to stop it.

~duck, nest lubber!~ he screamed in thought, while trying to knock Oleth back. But all he did was cause her arrow to go awry.

The next second the rude steel tipped arrow buried itself into Oleth's side, the red fletching mocking ToKeh like bristles of dried blood. Oleth sank down on the floor of the tops, her bow dropping from her grip, as she sighed.

ToKeh landed inside with her as the dragon roared again.

~get up! you have to get up! go below! be healed!~ He did not add what he thought to himself, ~not bleed into carrion~.

"Ah," Oleth said, weak from blood loss. The arrow had struck her deep in the side and breathing was a labor, much less moving. "I can't get up."

~sky and scorched feathers, just fall out!~ ToKeh said. ~you'll heal the same!~

Then a dull roar came from below them. ToKeh hopped to look at the flames licking the deck around the very mast they roosted in. A woman started to scream as she was consumed by fire.

ToKeh hopped back. ~up! out!~ he said, pecking Oleth's arm.

She shook her head, her yastol hitting the side of the cage. "I'll be fine..."

But she would not be fine. ToKeh had seen and followed too many shot game in his time to know that Oleth didn't have much time. Her lungs would be full of rich, red fluid and would no longer take air in. The ship shifted and ToKeh twisted to keep his balance. He needed help. At the same time he saw the humyn, the one who shot the arrow and ToKeh imagined what delicious joy it would be if it was carrion.

~I see it,~ ToKeh said. ~I can kill it.~

Suddenly Oleth's hand was around his feet, her grip tightening as death came. "Don't be silly," she said weakly. "You will be shot. I'll get a healer...my shade will serve..."

~let me go!~

"Promise not to seek vengeance. You would be killed before you landed... is something burning?"

ToKeh didn't like to worry Oleth. He saw the fire was being dealt with, the flames were less, the burning woman gone...

~it's nothing. the crew is dealing with it. but the humyn come.~ ToKeh watched helplessly as the humyn boarded, not because they endangered them, but because they would delay getting help.

~let me go! i'll get help!~

But Oleth wasn't thinking clearly. Her eyes had closed, but her grip was still firm. "No tricks, friend. No vengeance. Two of us need not die. All will be fine..." She slumped, eyes closed apparently unconscious, but her grip was still firm.

~dammit can't anyone else hear me?~ ToKeh screamed in thought while croaking as loud as he could. ~can some rotting elfling mother come and help? Oleth's shot!~

~they are firing on the humyn, fledge,~ the rook mother said as she circled far above. ~be patent.~

Then Oleth's hand slacked and ToKeh knew she was dead.

He took to the air, enraged, joining the circle and flying offensively close to the rook mother.

~patience? she's dead!~

~there is plenty of time to retrieve, fledge.~

~how do you know? she's meat, now! and don't call me a fledge!~

~then stop acting like one,~ another raven said as he flew sharply between the mother, making ToKeh check to catch himself.

~rot your feathers!~ he said, before flying back to the decks.

Tokeh hovered around the archers, pestering and pecking those who were not shooting and finally he made himself understood. It was still a while before Oleth's body could be safely lowered because the fire still smoldered, there was no question now of inelegantly dumping her. Only Sula healed well from burning; it was best for any other race to avoid flames in the first place.

So it was a long time before Oleth was found, then lowered from the masts and into the hospital. Then the healers mistook her for unconscious, until ToKeh pecked and croaked. Finally she was attended, but it was too late. He'd smelled it, the rigor growing, the corrupt fluids pooling making her corpse rigid. No elfyn medicine could heal a body past that point, even if the spirit was willing. ToKeh listened to the idiot elfling with the funny green clothed head express her regret and all he thought was how soft and juicy her gold eyes would taste, how quick he could do it. Sky, feathers and shit, she'd even be able to heal, get new eyes, so it wouldn't even be a capital crime. He'd be banished from the Federation lands of course...

But he'd bring shame on Oleth and her household.

ToKeh croaked with the rudest thoughts possible at the blithering elfling, flying in her face so she had to duck as he fled the hall. He'd seen the humyn. The one with the bow that loosed the arrow that made his friend carrion.

ToKeh would have vengeance.

Chapter 11

Stray Rope

Rosen tried to steady himself feeling the flow of the ship's pitch and yaw as she treaded the waves while he and his copilots kept her in place. Grating savage yells from the water below presaged attempts to board *The Tidebreaker*. Rosen wondered if Galen and the scorched Dwen were okay, or if in escaping the burning pitch they had succumbed to another danger. He caught sight of *The Sunchaser,* at the other end of the line, in similar straits as himself, far from her place as she tried to outmaneuver boarding attempts by swimming in circles. Similarly, to starboard, *The Fortunate* pitched visibly as Sea Mother Lenor led a group of scorpion sterned ships in merry circles.

Rosen didn't dare try that gambit. He was only just certain he and his copilots could keep the ship steady, provided the Shari didn't get to the cage and no red fletched arrows hit their target. As the pitch-fire below him was smothered, volunteers covered the decks, dispersing between the guards, crew and magi. Now he felt more secure about their chances. Then, with a great shriek and cry, the first Shari boarded larboard, at both the stern and quarterdeck.

Rosen gripped his sword though no Shari came close yet. They were cut down by mercenaries like Bron, Freya, and Navi, and many of the strike crew who, with no sun, had nothing else to do. At first it was effortless, the dissected bodies falling as blood spilled across the deck, painting even the defenders red. Then with animal savagery the Shari pushed between those being killed, over those dying, before they too were cut down. Still more came. A man screamed as he was almost cut in two by a sword stroke from shoulder to breast bone, fell in front of the cage pillar, gurgling as he died.

Rosen pulled his eyes away, forcing himself to watch the battle to either side of him. The humyn moved frantically, with frenzy; it was hard to know if they fought with skill because most were cut down so quickly. Then several things happened at once:

Behind him the warrior man's blade broke or bent, forcing him to grapple with a Shari. Starboard, a new wave of attackers boarded from a second ship, swarming the marines. In that chaos some of the boarders made their way to the cage, somehow knowing the pilot's dais entwined with blue glass was where the ship's power lay. Stars fell on Shari heads, thwarted from full damage by the turban bound helmets. Still, they staggered with the blows; the cage guards switched to swinging the stars into the enemy's faces with better effect.

"Prepare to yield to the heart!" Rosen yelled to his copilots as they all drew their swords, having anticipated the order. The ship could be driven by the heart chamber alone. They would be limited by the lack of eyes on the sea, their senses restricted to the aura of the ship, but it would have to be enough. Rosen let go of his connection with the ship for at that moment a guard's star had stuck in the ruined face of a corpse and two Shari rushed past her to where Rosen stood.

Sounds faded, the battle around him feeling distant as the warriors charged slowly. Was it because they were humyn? Or had Rosen entered a battle trance? He only knew that, when they came, he could dispatch both.

The first Rosen feinted right, swinging his sword up across the body, slashing deep into the gut. The humyn folded like a puppet with cut strings. Before it fell, Rosen pulled his sword back to slash the throat of the second one. That Shari stumbled back, dropping his sword as he gurgled, then fell over to the deck below.

Suddenly sound rushed back to Rosen's ears. The warrior-boy had managed to find another sword. A bloody melee raged around him, but the cage were no longer threatened. Galen appeared, clothes wet and bedraggled just as another Shari came close. The capstan bar in her hand first knocked his helmet off, then crushed his skull. She bellowed: "Close up guard on the cage!"

Rosen nodded his thanks but was perplexed: the captain of the guard should have given that order. He cast around for sight of Ledranal Mordmhol, a black haired, gray eyed Cambari Gael, but couldn't find her anywhere on the top decks. Meanwhile Galen waded in to take a wounded guard's place, crushing the heads of any Shari that got too close, or else crippling them with blows to the knees and elbows. A strange sound from above made Rosen look up.

There the archers perched, sending volleys of deadly arrows into the decks of Shari vessels. Some of the shrouds and lower rigging were black from being splashed with pitch-fire. Sail had been cut down hurriedly in the rush to stop flames from spreading in the masts. But the tensions weren't even. There was only so much the crew could do while fighting a fire and firing arrows. Rosen never saw the straining rope, but he knew something would snap and could only hope it would not be dire. A suddenly released taut rope could lash a woman like a whip. There was nothing to do but warn the crew and hope:

"Stray rope!" bellowed Rosen as he crouched.

No sooner had he said the words, than the creak turned to a whine, then a screech, followed by a sharp crack. Out of the corner of his eye he saw it whip around, high in the air, over the starboard amidships. Hopefully it would snap in the wind and spend itself. Instead it spun, looping back over the deck. Crew dived out of the way; a humyn was knocked aside, scream-ing as its face was lashed to the bone. Rosen's breath caught as he saw Galen stand up after a swing with her capstan bar only to be in the path of the rope.

She had little time to react. Dropping the bar, she tried jumping out of the way. The rope first slapped her and she was forced to spin to avoid the worst of the blow. Unfortunately that meant diving towards starboard hull while the rope snaked itself around an arm. In her struggle to evade it Galen rolled over the edge and disappeared from sight.

"You have the ship!" Rosen yelled to Haulet. He ran to where Galen had been, still holding his sword. It was absurd she should fall into the sea twice in the same day. The divers could retrieve her, he knew. And Galen was an excellent swimmer for a Gold. But this time a Shari vessel waited. And seeing her fall, images crowded his mind: running with Galen as a boy to the sea shallows to catch crabs; dropping small pots of colored powder on Helanault and her gang from the Wall, running away before being seen; get-ting sick on white brandy in the cellar of The Cup and Pearl before their first fire. Galen would never be his lover, would never wife him, but she was his firm friend and whatever had happened between them on this venture it didn't matter in the moment. She was like another sister and he couldn't imagine his life without her.

Rosen dropped his sword as he reached the edge of the ship, throwing himself over to clasp the rope. Galen hung by a prayer, gripping both the rope and the edge of the hull, the shadowed water dark below her dangling feet, the Shari ship lurking a furlong or so fore of them.

Rosen threw his arm over. "Grab it!"

"Are you mad? I'll drag you down! The Fish can retrieve me! I did it once before –"

"Not with Shari so close! Damn you, grab it!" Rosen shuffled his feet and found what he hoped, a loop of rope tangled with a cannon truck to anchor his foot in. "Go on, you stubborn ox! I'm secured…"

Except he wasn't. No sooner than Galen complied, her strong hand seizing him above the elbow, then he felt himself slide over the edge.

"Damnations, don't let go!" he yelled. If she just climbed up as quick as she could, she could pull him up too. An explosion echoed over the water, so thunderous Rosen almost let go. There was a flash of blueish light. But he didn't have time to worry what it might be; as long as *The Tidebreaker* wasn't in danger. Suddenly two arms seized him from behind and his slide was arrested. This came at a cost; the woman's hands had to reach around his hips to hold on, the front of her pelvis somewhat intrusively pressed against his rear. But as immodest their position was, Rosen was anchored enough that Galen could clamber up, where the three of them collapsed together on the deck. The woman was the missing Captain Mordmhol.

"*Brón orm faoi sin –*" she started.

"No need to apologize!" Rosen replied. Galen gasped for breath; she had a welt across her neck. "Alright?"

A second explosion retorted, making Rosen's ears ring.

"Sul and Maer!" Galen swore. "I'm fine! Provided that Dragon doesn't find us, Sea Father."

"'Sea Father'?" Rosen stooped to retrieve his sword, while Galen reached for her capstan.

"That's your proper title," Galen said stiffly.

"So were being proper now?"

"Would you prefer 'captain'?"

"I'd prefer my friend back."

"She never went anywhere. But she is sorry for demands she had no right to make."

Rosen swallowed. "I know."

"*Cad a dhéanamh sibh?*" Mordmhol demanded, retrieving a star. "*Tá muid ag troideann fós!*"

Rosen and Galen laughed.

"She's right!" Galen said. "We are still fighting!"

Mordmhol returned to the fray, laying about her with her star and sword.

"When all is done I think I will have quite an appetite," Rosen said, looking over the decks. The crew was doing well. The ship would not fall.

"I think you'll find eggs to be unattainable for a while," Galen said.

"The winds of war, my friend, winds of war. Let's finish this."

And so, slowly, like a weaver tending a frayed tapestry, their friendship started to repair. But that it took the threat to Galen's life for Rosen to see what losing her would cost him was troubling. What if Galen hadn't been hit by the rope? Would they continue in their duty, ever drifting further apart? Wasn't it a perverse thing, when the gentle aspects of Solshari and society failed, it took the conflict birthed by Amer to rebond friendship?

Rosen rejoined the cage. The Shari were soon pushed back, the lancers taking advantage of a patch of thinning clouds to strike at the boarding ladders, singing while they burned. Then, at last, it was over. Prisoners were taken and the task of cleaning the deck began. There was much to be done, but he looked forward to having a repast with Galen, a chance to affirm he valued her friendship. Conflict might bring mothers together, but it was better to bond over meat and merriment, not blood. Rosen watched as Navi was rebuked for attempting to kill a surrendered Shari. Yes, there had been enough of the Madness of Ameram for the day.

Rosen saw *The Sunchaser* had shed her attackers. His eyes scanned the sea, noting several other ships who had drifted from the line, some with hulls blackened by pitch-fire or holes made by Dragon shot, all their decks a hive of activity. *The Black Seal* and *The Charred Bronze* in particular were moving towards each other with such speed Rosen worried they would collide. There the water churned and there was a strange openness on the sea. Rosen scanned the water, heart racing. No, it couldn't be, he thought desperately. The open space of churning water was full of divers, beneath them, deep in the water a blue light glowed from below, almost certainly from the fallen heart of a ship.

"No," Rosen whispered. "How could it be?"

His eyes had accounted for all the ships except one. And now it seemed she had been scuttled. What would become of them without her?

Chapter 12

Maer's Watery Embrace

Admiral Jonsaymanor Jansenwol had hoped the first thwarted attack, with its decisive deadly result still smoldering in the waters, would be enough to dispel Shari delusions about their capabilities. When the ships retreated she expected, if not surrender, then a withdrawal. But the Shari somehow guessed, with the pall of cloud and coming rain, the Tyreen fleet was weak. With a grim intelligence, the Shari collected themselves and reformed their lines:

About four-score ships comprised their front line, a score less, the reserve line. Between and center was their flagship, scorched but still sea worthy. Behind these lurked a ragged line of seriously damaged ships that managed to stay afloat. There had been activity in the night, repairs made cannibalizing the worst ships to shore up those that might still serve. Reports told of many barrels being shifted, probably supplies, but barrels of salts that fed the Dragon was heavy on the minds of the Shari captains. When the advancing ships neared the Tyreen line, they broke into groups, their aim to board the towers at sea. A greater group than the rest started to converge on *The Oaken Blue*.

"Tell the strikemaster to strike at will once they are in range," Jonsay said to the deck officer.

"Ai, Sea Mother!"

As the order was echoed, Jonsay cursed the Dragon of Tamask. The good news was, as a weapon of war, it was unreliable, prone to rolling in swells and even exploding if not tended properly. But the suddenness of its damage when it did strike had an unnerving ability to shock and demoralize. While they had sunlight, however weak, Jonsay made it a priority to destroy every Dragon on sight. Care had to be taken because of the salts stored to keep the ships from coming too close. Reluctantly Jonsay came to the conclusion Tamnath had been right all along: had they struck them out of the water on sight the battle would be over, Gashora's safety secured and not a soul lost.

Now they had to strategize with what they knew. The Shari appeared to have learned the limits of the Dragon and were instead taking the idea of their boats being virtual bombs to heart. There was a plan to make one a sacrifice, the intent of scuttling a Tyreen ship. Jonsay had no idea how much powder that would take and had no interest in finding out. It took no imagination to see this new scheme was possible. It had drawbacks: not counting the need to keep reserve ships, there were not enough to scuttle the entire Tyreen fleet if they wanted to save powder for the Dragon's breath. They could not continue their original plan to sack Gashora without absolute victory and that was unlikely. The most the Shari could accomplish was enough damage with the idea of demoralizing the fleet. Perhaps they hoped if they scorched enough ships the Tyreen navy would retreat.

Jonsay had to put her pride aside and consider it. Not a rout, but a retreat north, across the Gashora lane, still guarding it but waiting out the clouds. Jonsay looked up. The pall gathering at dawn was thickening. They would be lucky to get half an hour's worth of strike before the solcannons would be ineffective. If they retreated, the Shari would row after them, in an absurd chase they could not win. But is was better than sailing in circles near ships that were petards on water. The end was certain; it was only a matter of the means.

"Prepare the crew to move aft," Jonsay said grimly. It was not a heroic maneuver, and Jonsay did not like to abandon the forward position she'd put *The Oaken Blue*. She had hoped to keep the eye of the Shari on her, allowing the rest of the fleet to work with less harassment. But this action would minimize risk to lives and their duty would be fulfilled, however inelegantly. "Send to the fleet to prepare to move aft in defensive –"

"Pardon, Sea Mother," Ta Athine interrupted. "Before you send that order, consider the ten ships advancing through their front line."

Jonsay stood near the cage, allowing Captain Otha Jolarund and Lieutenant Tethini Madwol, one of the few male pilots, to drive. Ta Athine had drifted down from the tops where a couple magi still hovered next to the archers. Jonsay didn't need a telescope but she had not noted the subtle movement of these ships. They came from the group of damaged ships and had very little crew. Only the lower oars moved, which made them slower;

they seemed to have only one goal: to float forward. There were no archers, no troops. Even the ballista towers were unfortified.

"How do they know their direction?" Jonsay asked.

"Under the tent is the captain who gives direction. There is also something like a crude raft towed in the wake of these particular vessels."

Jonsay thought for several moments. "They plan to abandon these constructs when they are near enough."

"We think so. And if they linger during the night –"

"Yes," Jonsay said, understanding. They had been lucky. The idea of petards floating in the dark made her shiver. They should be able to retreat out of range. But during the night, without eyes on the sea, anything could happen.

"Sea Mother?" Lieutenant Elush Brawlyn, the deck officer relaying orders, queried.

"Belay that," Jonsay said. There were no good choices, but a messy daylight battle was better than a messy battle at night. "I am joining the cage," Jonsay said, stepping onto the dais with the copilots. She merged her essence with *The Oaken Blue,* her mind expanding with the awareness of the ship, feeling the water lap around her and the wind as if the mast tops were her hair. "We will ease forward. Lieutenant? Strike crews are to deflect attempts at boarding. The Shari scorpions should not touch our hull if we can help it."

"Emha!"

To Ta Athine, Jonsay said, "Inform the strikemaster of those peculiar ten vessels. They are to be destroyed without prejudice if the chance comes."

"Sea Mother," the magi acknowledged, leaving in a swirl of black robes.

The Shari ships separated completely out of line, moving in groups with such speed as they could to their chosen targets. Among the Tyreen vessels singled out were *The Starshard, The Sunchaser, The Sea Bright*, and *The Tidebreaker*. Jonsay smiled at the thought of attempting to board *The Tidebreaker*. Male captains, used to struggling for simple recognition, were particularly fierce when cornered. Less amusing were the cluster of six Shari vessels that bore down on *The Oaken Blue*. By rowing eagerly they came into range quicker. Jonsay felt the almost imperceptible pitch of *The Oaken Blue* under her feet at the same time as all the solcannons facing fore flashed with blinding brightness. The next second brought the crack of ship timbers snapping from the heat. Then came a loud retort and smoke. The Dragon had fired but a splash told the crew it had missed its mark. They struck again, and once more. That unfortunate Shari vessel exploded, a cloud of black smoke rising before *The Oaken Blue* as the crew cheered, the fragments of the ship flying high and floating away as the stern disappeared below the water, the crew floundering without help.

The remaining ships tried to distance themselves from one another, but were too slow. They were at the perfect distance to be picked off. But the next round of strike was little more than a heated flash. The humyn's eyes were dazzled, fabric caught fire, but there was no significant material damage. Above the pall was complete. Sul would no longer be a help from the heavens.

The memory of Jonsay's Reverie returned, the singing behind her, Tergani's voice calling. Whatever path she was on, it must pass near the Door. And she had no knowledge of whether she would live or step through. There were many paths that could lead one to stand before the Door. There was not enough information so there was no point in dwelling on it. The moment would come in its own time. For now, Jonsay felt dread for her crew.

They made preparations to defend against attempts to board. The magi deflected the arrows that came, while *The Oaken Blue*'s archers did their best to clear the decks of the scorpion ships of captains and other leaders, like their false magi. Yet even now, certain the Shari were safe from the deadly light that destroyed many of their ships, the handful surrounding them kept their distance.

Then an explosive retort echoed nearby. Two to three seconds later the hull of *The Oaken Blue* was hit amidships by Dragon shot.

Jonsay felt winded, the veins transferring the force of the hit to her gut. But the impression faded and the damage was negligible.

"That was unpleasant," Jolarund said.

"Indeed. We will endure."

It happened again. And yet again. Jonsay understood. They were trying to breach the hull like a fortification. The trouble was, unlike a trebuchet on land, they could not keep their position steady enough to keep the focus on the exact point. Also, while wood was in many ways inferior to stone for the purposes of forts, it did not shatter, but bent and splintered. Already the ship's woodweaver had sent a team of mates below to watch the damage and repair the wood as they could. It would take a long time to drill through the three foot thick hull and then only if no wood-essence was at hand to reknit the planks.

It started to rain. After almost half an hour the Shari must have come to the same conclusion. They pulled back, but, alas, not to retreat. The arrows had been too effective. To protect those that fed the Dragon they withdrew. Then the Dragons roared again.

Glass shattered and by the time the damage was assessed, more Dragon shot had been fired. This time it was pots of stones aimed at the many berth windows. They did not need to be fired at full force to do damage. Jonsay gave thanks the Shari did not understand the purpose of the aqua folds of glass against the hull, the rib-fins that helped guild the ship, making a rudder superfluous. Some were already chipped and damaged, but they served. Being without windows would be a nuisance, but the woodweaver could cover them with scrap planks.

But they had not reckoned with the enemy's determination. When next the Dragons roared, from three vessels that could still operate their engines, they shot pots of pitch-fire towards any available window. Some landed on the hull, scorching the blue, white and black banding. Others found ingress. The boatswain was fairly screaming for crew to find the fires and smother them with sand, the magi volunteering to call the cold without question.

Through the nodes and veins Jonsay felt the ship shiver as if it was a thinking creature in pain. Two fires were spreading: one in the upper deck, the greater one in the middle deck. The blocked ports were being opened, the wooden door plugs in some cases kicked out to sea. Only three companionways led to the upper decks and the aftmost one was blocked with fire. This was made worse by the center open hatches that acted like a chimney. The gallery windows of the ranks wardroom were shattered to give more options for escape. Jonsay waited as long as she could, praying for the magi below calling the cold so strongly that ice smothered the surfaces of the upper deck amidships and the middle deck ceiling just below the mess where the hospital was arrayed. The wounded were the most vulnerable. But when the fires merged under the heart chamber, Jonsay knew it was only a matter of time. Even if the pumps hadn't been blocked, the pitch-fire was impossible to suppress at its current size.

"Brawlyn, tell the archers to sweep the decks of any Shari ships in range of any living humyn." The order broke Jonsay's heart. She was not a murderer. But if the wounded were to have a chance, they needed to be evacuated without fear of being shot.

The next order was the hardest any Sea Mother would ever give, the one order she avoided at all costs, and the one that could, if things went badly, mean the death of her. But the matter was already dire there was no point in delaying:

"Captain Jolarund, you are to abandon ship. Please, lead our crew to safety. Now."

Jolarund had hesitated. A captain pilot, she'd never had her own ship. She was as loath to forsake their action as Jonsay was. Then her essence was absent, as she stepped off the dais.

"Ai, Sea Mother," she said clearly, saluting then running off as she shouted orders.

The remaining co-pilot took up the driving flow ably, but Lieutenant Madwol looked terrified.

"It will be as well as it can, lieutenant," Jonsay said to him. "There will come a point you must abandon me. When the time arrives, please to not argue."

Madwol swallowed, saying in a shaky voice, "Yes, Sea Mother."

It was understood a Sea Mother was always the last to evacuate a doomed vessel. If every soul could not be taken to safety, she stayed with them till the end. It wasn't always a death sentence; that was why divers were stationed even in the Federation patrol fleet. But the threats of death by arrow or floating pitch-fire made rescue in this theater less certain. Now Jonsay accepted she would come to the Door before Sul had set. She would hear Tergani at least one more time before their journey together in the Orb was finished. Farthal and Gemal, her youngest daughters, wouldn't be asleep for a while. Her eldest Jonan and her son Oni might be awake later than was custom in their tasks volunteering in the city during watchfulness. But her consort Tergani, a powerful wizard in his own right, would feel her passing. She must try to linger as long as possible after her body failed. Try to keep her soul on this side of the Door to say goodbye in dreams. And give Tamnath Tresmadore words to hopefully settle her soul when she took over as admiral.

Around her the deck appeared to be in chaos. In truth it was a quite orderly reversal of their preparations to set forth:

Spars swung as the launches and boats on the skid beams were raised to hover high enough to swing over the water when ready. Healers and magi, with the help of the crew, carried, lifted or floated the wounded into the boats. With them went the midships, though many protested not understanding how dire it was, that no amount of bravery could stop the flames below that creeped around the magical ice that tried to contain it. Once the archers confirmed the death of all the nearby humyn, the divers and regular marines took to the water, jumping off the upper wales without ceremony. Ravens took flight to other ships. Smoke rose from below, driving any soul out of the hold through the hatches that started to warm like a kiln chimney. The woodweaver and her mates threw the last of the wickers, floating rafts of heavy, fused, trimmed branches that many could cling to while they awaited rescue; magi moved to float over them, ready to protect the survivors and assist in their retrieval. The healers climbed into the boats as they were swung out and lowered. Only one boat remained, hovering over the water. This was for the last stragglers like Jonsay's own clerk who had just come to her side.

"Why are you not on that last launch, lieutenant?" Jonsay asked. Flames started to flicker through the hatches of the abandoned quarterdeck.

Lieutenant Amralan said, "There's still room, Admiral."

"What?"

"There's still room in the launch!"

"Is every other soul to safety?"

"Those on the lower deck and orlop have been seen jumping through windows! Any soul left can be retrieved by the divers, surely!"

Jonsay sighed. The fire was weakening the veins, the mix of grimsteel and aqua that transferred essence to drive the ship. A blue glow started to permeate the air and with it Jonsay's senses were expanded to a new sensitivity.

"I feel several souls struggling in the berths. A couple have taken refuge in the baths. Until they are retrieved my place is here. You locked the boxes? Then get on that launch and that's an order! Madwol, you are re-lieved. Go with her!"

Now Jonsay was alone. No more copilots tended the nodes or heart chamber. Suddenly she gasped. It felt like her gut had been punched. Essence flow was erratic, barely controllable. She worried she would faint. There was a real possibility of disincration, an effect of strong essence at the mote level, making part of a substance air or fluid for moments. But those moments would be devastating. Otherwise solid objects would fall apart, food or living stuffs would collapse in gruesome ichor. The essence powerful, whether living souls or objects, resisted disincration by the Prop-erty of Wholeness, as scholars stated it. However, the wild unconstrained forces that were usually used to drive a city-ship could equal that of a pow-erful aging magi. Finally Jonsay understood what had happened: the veins connecting the heart of the ship to the cage had been severed by fire dam-age.

So, clinging to the supports of the cage, Jonsay made herself the ship's heart. She had control again, but didn't know for how long. She felt it now, a prickling along her skin, the timbers of *The Oaken Blue* separating as the aqua glass melted, water-essence sublimating. It wouldn't be long now.

Above the sky seemed to brighten, a cruel jest of fate too late to be of use. Ahead a Shari vessel drifted forward, oars out but not moving. It yawed right, its broadside directly ahead of *The Oaken Blue*. Jonsay could see no soul before it was so close the deck obscured it. A whistle shrieked from a ship bearing on her, *The Leviathan*. There was no one left to rely the code to crew, but Jonsay understood it and was horrified: they had an un-spent cannon and enough light to strike.

As sure as Jonsay knew Sea Mother Solet Tosslon was a quick pilot, she also knew that scorpion ship that nudged the hull under the bows was one of the vessels full of salts. Tosslon wouldn't know the state of *The Oaken Blue*, that nothing could save her, or that there remained souls trapped be-low, including a cat. If there was strike they would all die, the bulk of *The Oaken Blue* crushing them to the bottom of the sea.

Jonsay desperately thought of how she could signal *The Leviathan* to abort strike. The prow of that ship, led by a figurehead the noble whale, gracefully made a final turn towards *The Oaken Blue*.

The solcannon flashed and strike hit the Shari boat surely full of more power than all the fireworks Tyrum used on Recognition Day.

The thunderous explosion hammered into Jonsay's ears. Still gripping the bars of the cage, she fell to her knees while she tried to shake the feeling of being punched in the face. Black smoke billowed up over the prow, obscuring sight as the rain seemed to fall harder. Then, in one horrible lurch, *The Oaken Blue* listed forward as she started taking on water.

Jonsay tried to ignore the pain of the ship she felt as her own. It was taking all of Jonsay's energy and essence to keep *The Oaken Blue*, her sister and joy, together and upright, slowing her sinking for as long as possible. She had no idea if the trapped crew had escaped, no energy to spare to check. As long as the heart of the ship, that magi constructed amalgam of grimsteel, solstone and aqua was intact, she could have bought them more time. Now being the heart, a feat no elf, much less elfborn, was ever expected to do, she would have no energy to tend to her own survival if the divers couldn't save her. As she felt the fires consuming supplies deep in the hold, a peace stole over her. Now death hovered near, there was nothing to fear. It only remained for her to hold the ship together as long as she was able.

When she was gone Tamnath would be capable enough to continue, though Jonsay feared for her soul. Perhaps Tynlar would be the watchful sister, hated at first but eventually thanked for her mentorship. Jonsay desperately hoped she was not the only soul who could restrain the Jackal in the tortured Tamnath. If only Tamnath had confided in her sooner. It was no way for even a warrior mother to live, everyday hungering for the feast of Dark Ameram, every moment a temptation to depravity.

Then, deep in the ship, came a second explosion, almost directly below Jonsay's feet, and she knew her doom had come. The severed heart of the ship had burst apart in the flames, its magic running wildly through everything it could. Loose essence arced like lightning from aqua node to aqua node. Being the heart of the ship would take all of her life force. No one would ever understand how she did it, a feat of magic to rival the greatest magi of the Age of Light. Those magi were Sula born elfyn, with the full birthright of sulessence. Let the demagogues be confounded, Jonsay thought wryly. Her only regret was her death was certain.

Suddenly Jonsay saw her children in the gloom, like ghosts in daylight from a great distance. The girls paused in one of their epic arguments over things the young take so seriously. Then her son, gazing in a mirror uncertain of what he saw on the cusp of manhood, trying to both live up to and apart from his fati. And her eldest, a young woman ready to make her mark, speaking to a group of scouts. She paused, her head turning as if hearing a whisper of a shade. Jonan wasn't without essence talent, but preferred sport…or perhaps thought she was supposed to prefer those things to follow her mother? Oh, child, you must follow your heart, Jonsay thought. But Jonan couldn't hear her.

Yet Tergani could. Jonsay saw a cloud of flame around him. Or perhaps that was his hair in sunlight. Then his deep burning gold eyes looked into hers and she knew without a doubt he both saw and understood.

"My love?" he mouthed silently, eyes widening in horror.

That made Jonsay angry. He was the love of her life and she would never see him again living. They should have had many decades together, perhaps centuries. Whatever conceit Tergani held that he insisted he was aelg, Jonsay knew he would outlive her by centuries. She had been the luckiest woman in the Orb for this noble and humble son of Sul to agreed to be wifed by her. Now there would be no more joy together. In that moment she damned all the Shari to the worst torments of the Bane. They had robbed her of her golden helpmate.

Then the rage was gone; Jonsay had no heart to sustain it. It wouldn't be long now.

The aura of the ship glowed aqua blue as the ship's essence bled out.

Jonsay shivered from rain and shock. Then she was spent, with no more energy to give.

The Oaken Blue broke asunder in an explosion of blue-white light and Sea Mother Jonsaymanor Jansenwol fell into Maer's watery embrace.

* * *

Pearl dived, swimming with an urgency as never before. *The Oaken Blue*'s school herder, Eela shal Looah, had taken charge, sounding insistently that they should spare no speed. The water was unnaturally warm as Pearl swam through the haunting wreckage, seeking bodies of the living. While the ship had broken apart, and the essence discharged had destroyed much of it, there still remained large parts that sank in situ on the soft sea bed, some rolling unhelpfully, making the retrieval of bodies even more difficult. And there would be bodies: some had hit their heads before falling in the water; others were cases of simple drowning. These were the easiest to retrieve, as were many still on the decks. Those further below would have drowned by the time they were found. Still, if they were found quickly, they would return to the living.

The wreckage loomed around Pearl like the broken toys a giant child had flung into the sea, forsaken and unwanted. Many pieces still shimmered with a blue aura where essence bled into the water from melted and exposed aqua. Later would come the great task to retrieve the keel, sunken and buried in muck and slime. The keel and the heart were always retrieved when a ship failed. But in Tyrum's history few varsadmer had been so throughly destroyed.

Pearl spotted a body ahead, a woman trapped under a sundered plank. It was not heavy; Pearl waved a hand over the plank, boosting the power of the turbulence with water-essence to help her heave the plank off before dragging the woman out. It was a crewgirl, dark gold eyes still wide in shock or disbelief. Clutching the back of her vest, Pearl dragged the woman to a group of divers who immediately took her to the surface. Pearl turned back, diving deeper.

Circling more wreckage, she passed two crew women, Cambari, both in woolen bracs, their bound floating hair and whey pale skin seemingly out of place. It wasn't only Blue like Pearl or the diver, who directed the Cambari as they sawed through a section of plank, who could hold their breath ably. There were many such aelg, strong swimmers by the reckoning of the landed, with enough Meer in their blood they could hold their breath for several minutes, but not enough to be divers. They were helpful now: the woman were doughty, among those who turned the capstans to raise anchors. Here their weight was an advantage, allowing them to sink and stand while they worked opening a section of wreckage where bodies were trapped. Bubbles drifted from their mouths as they worked. Suddenly one dropped her end and swam up to surface, the meager amount of air in her lungs spent. The diver took over and the sawing resumed. Pearl swam on.

She came to a section lying on its hull, such that the berths inside opened up to the sea, their floors and ceilings now walls in their disarray. No body remained, but books and bedding scattered across the ocean floor, with the occasional shimmer of a tin cup or goblet that had settled in the weeds. But this was not a salvaging venture. Pearl's only concern was for the living and the dead that hovered on the threshold of the Door. She decided to circle over, taking the length of a sunken lance to scrape around the outer area of this section of wreckage. Mud swirled up like brown fog. Pearl saw a bit of green and white. Grabbing at it she felt the robes of a healer. As she tugged they were still attached to the woman's body. With a great heave Pearl pulled the woman up out of the mud, her golden hair obscuring her face. Pearl grimaced, pulling her head back expecting the worst. There was no point in retrieving a woman with wounds like Glethlyn had suffered. However the woman was whole, apart from being drowned. Her aspect was peaceful in death. Then Pearl heard a voice in her head:

~Swim, you stupid Fish!~

Pearl looked about wildly. The words had not been sounded. Then her ears burn with embarrassment. It was the shade. Oh hak, the woman's shade was nearby.

And clearly offended at the time it was taking for her to return to the living. Stuffing her pride, Pearl grabbed the back of the healer's robes and started swimming to the surface. It was then a school of divers descended on her, swimming madly as if a sea serpent was in pursuit. Pearl sped away, thinking to get out of their path, but it was, Wahoon yal Nomney, the school driver from *The Black Seal*. She glided away from the school to intercept Pearl.

((Sharol Hauktee Yal? Of The Tidebreaker?)) Wahoon sounded.

((Ai. I need to retrieve –))

((Drop her. You can come back for her. You are helping us now!))

Pearl didn't like taking orders the best of times, and certainly wasn't going to be bullied out of the course of her duty.

((I take orders from Merock or Eela. Not any Fish with a loud voice!))

The Wahoon swam close with sudden speed, her eyes piercing and fierce as she grabbed the front of Pearl's net tunic.

((I'm the driver of *The Black Seal* whose captain is now the acting Admiral of the fleet. You'll obey me as you would your own driver or you'll be up for mutiny!))

Pearl thrashed to get away but the woman was at least as strong as she was. Too angry to care about, Pearl sent a sharp stream of water past the Wahoon's ears. It was a trick that worked even with Meer: the water moving at sudden speed was like a shrill whistle. The driver's grip loosed in surprise and Pearl broke away.

((I'll help you after this one is retrieved!))

Wahoon sounded for her school to swim on before bellowing at Pearl, as much as one could "bellow" in sounding:

((We go to retrieve the fallen Admiral, you stupid fishmonger!))

Pearl grabbed the healer's robes and swam up, while sounding, ((A healer is worth more than an admiral.))

Then Pearl swam fast to ensure her escape. She worried Wahoon might tangle her and drag her back. What she sought was a cluster of working divers; there were none near the surface here, but a couple below doing rounds. Pearl sounded loudly, ((Look out above!)) then dropped the healer. As the body sank, a limp doll lost at sea, pale, earnest faces turned up then swam forward to catch her and take her to a boat. Satisfied the healer was tended to, Pearl switched back and dove with speed following the wake of *The Black Seal* school.

Wahoon looked livid, her tangles in hand, the cords waving eagerly like a hungry octopus. Pearl didn't slow for a scolding. Time was truly of the essence. She sped with all of her force, wondering how she'd find the Admiral if *The Black Seal* school hadn't yet. Her breath wasn't fresh anymore. She had perhaps a quarter of an hour before it would be a trial to resist surfacing. One advantage over them was she knew which areas had been searched. Then she remembered an easier way.

The Admiral would have fallen straight down with the heart and keel. Both radiated water-essence. All Pearl had to do was feel where the water was most essence rich, as for retrieving any aqua object, and the Admiral should be nearby. She swam fast, feeling the water as she went, always tacking closer to the strongest source of essence. As expected it brought her through the fields of blasted debris and blackened planks, fallen mast trees and scattered ropes and anchors. Pearl let the feeling draw her to a place a great mass glowed, pulsing gold and blue. It was the size of four barrels, still surrounded by the remains of the black metal bands that had encased the orb of aqua and solstone. This was the heart of *The Oaken Blue*. Pearl paused, hovering around the spot, knowing she was close. Nearby was a section of keel, perhaps three feet wide, still glowing blue with active essence. But it and the heart were fading. Soon only a magi would be able to find them. Then Pearl saw her, on the section of broken keel a couple of mast trees had fallen over, making a kind of bower. There, lying on the bare blue aqua, was the Admiral.

She looked much like many artists imagined the bower of Laifmyr, "He Who Sang by the Sea", the brother of the first Meer Sea Queen, who died in the Cataclysm. The "Lay of the Song of Water" described his tomb hidden in the deep sea, guarded by sea dragons. There were no dragons and it was a poor bower, scattered with mud and debris, but it held the Admiral as she rested, arms flung out, cloths scorched and torn, her body otherwise whole. Pearl's eyes widened with surprise. She rushed forward to waste no time. Both Jonsaymanor's mouth and eyes were closed. It meant, however improbably, she was alive.

Pearl hovered over her, glancing up to see how fast she needed to go. The Admiral had to be moments from drowning. In the dire circumstances of battle, the aqua and her connection to it had extended her breath. Maybe the direct contact with the keel reinforced her unconscious urge to live. In any case, Pearl had a choice: save her now and swim at a disadvantage or keep her breath and trust the healers to retrieve her.

The next second Pearl clasped her lips over Jonsay's mouth and expelled the last of her air into the Admiral's lungs. Then she grabbed the larger woman, thankful for the water's help, and drove them both to the surface as fast as her essence could take them. When there was a choice, preventing death was preferable to retrieval. There was a chance, however slim, the soul would wander and lose their way, or hear the singing beyond the Door and yearn for a bliss and peace rarely found in life. Besides, the water was thick with divers; no one would let her drown.

Yet there was a difference in swimming with one's last air and none at all. Even using only essence, Pearl's head swam and her vision blurred. A lifetime of practice was all that kept her from inhaling water and she knew the moment she lost consciousness she would drown.

Then Sharkhook was there, from where Pearl didn't know. The burden was taken from her and she was pushed up, towards the light, into the cold air, and she breathed deep knowing they would live at least another day.

* * *

Tamnath heard a soul screaming. It was a horrible sound, a woman screaming, nothing motherly, nothing heroic, only loss and bereavement that could never be comforted. *The Oaken Blue* had shattered like a glass bauble before her eyes, taking the woman she saw as both sister and mother away to a watery grave.

Then Tamnath understood it was herself screaming, having abandoned the pilot's cage and nearly thrown herself over the wale, as if she herself could stop Jonsaymanor from falling into the water. Only moments before *The Leviathan* had whistled the Tyreen flagship might be in distress, the Admiral's gambit of using herself as a lure working better than she intended. In a moment Tamnath had herself under control, the horrible sound stopped. She took some comfort that she wasn't alone; her voice may have been lost among so many others who had seen Jonsay disappear into the exploding blue light, mothers of many children and many battles wept openly, all look-ing for some sign, some hope in the churning flotsam that was the ruins of *The Oaken Blue*, that by some grace Jonsaymanor had survived.

From a cavern deep within Tamnath's troubled soul, the Jackal emerged. Tamnath was as far from a literalist as one could be. She never believed in praying to the unseen to do what the living were capable of. And the Jackal was capable of much.

"Get me the diving school herder!" Tamnath roared. A diver appeared at her elbow in seconds. Tamnath looked at the woman with a predatory calculating stare. The thin blue woman was not the one she wanted. "Where's you driver?" Tamnath demanded. Every instinct screamed inside her to act, but she knew what she needed was beyond her talents.

"In the water, emha. Assisting with the rescue –"

"Belay that!"

"Emha?"

"Your first and only task is to retrieve the Admiral!"

"But emha, the Admiral may be dead and others live –"

"Those that live can float and wait. Tell Wahoon the divers are to retrieve the Admiral or not bother returning to *The Black Seal*! Understand?"

The woman backed away, perhaps seeing madness in Tamnath's eyes. "Y-yes, emha."

"Then what are you waiting for? Or do I need to throw you overboard?"

The woman ran aft and seconds later there was a splash.

Tamnath didn't move. She knew her copilots had taken over but didn't care. She stood watching the waves busy with divers evading the wreckage of the Shari boats as they helped crew into launches that had been sent by *The Leviathan*, *The Starshard* and *The Charred Bronze*. Even *The Black Seal* was launching boats. Tamnath didn't care as long as one brought back Jonsaymanor.

The wait seemed eternal. The final acts of the battle continued at either end of the Tyreen line, but no Shari ship came near *The Black Seal*. In Tamnath's mind nothing was as important as this task. No one dared disturb the captain at her vigil. Later she would suffer their pity and whatever else, but at this moment no one dared say a word. For Tamnath had not accepted Jonsaymanor was gone. She was larger than life, she was Tamnath's rock of fortitude, without her Tamnath might have no salvation from the Jackal, that part of her that was a burden and a danger to all that was precious. And so Tamnath waited, and hoped, and prayed even, though her prayers had no form or sense of obsequiousness. Had Maer herself risen from the depths of the oceans to offer assistance, she would have ordered the Mother-god of the Sea as she ordered the Blue diver. Perhaps it was a good thing the Court of Heaven did not literally exist.

Finally there was an eruption of water, most of the divers converging on one of the boats. Ineffable elfyn instinct told Tamnath they had been successful.

"Officer!" she shouted at Lieutenant Nesthet, who acted as deck officer.

"Emha?" Nesthet queried warily. She was shaken by the collapse of the flagship like the rest of them.

"Have the healers ready when the Admiral is aboard! Tell them to inform me of her condition!"

"Emha!"

They would make a room for her, rest her on one of the many tables as they worked, a poor substitute for a temple healing room under an array. Tamnath watched the boat near, Jonsay being held between three divers as a wool blanket was wrapped around her. Ropes and hooks secured the boat by tackle to a yard, hauling it and those with Jonsay, a mix of shivering strike crew, Cambari mercenaries and Dwen. Once over the skid beams, those uninjured within helped to carefully move Jonsay to a waiting stretcher. All this happened within sight of the cage. Tamnath gave the nod to Wahoon, the understanding she and her divers were released to return to the general rescue. Tamnath expelled a breath she hadn't known she was holding and let herself look out at the water around them.

There was a disturbance around *The Starshard*. That ship had advanced towards the sinking place of *The Oaken Blue*, virtually over where she'd fallen. Tamnath couldn't see Captain Lanash on or near the cage. That was odd. Perhaps he'd suffered a hit. Further down the line, *The Tidebreaker* and *The Sunchaser* showed signs of being harried by fire and boarding. Those battles appeared to be abating. Below many souls clung to the wickers floating on the water, waiting to be rescued. The Admiral's barge, full of the wounded and middies, had gone to dock with *The Charred Bronze*. It was no matter to Tamnath. Let the Wolf play nurse to the floundering cubs. Better sport awaited.

In the churn of water around them some humyn thrashed, the dying remnants of the crews that had attacked the flagship. All thoughts of amnesty were forgotten as the water turned red with Shari blood, the marines doing their final duty. For Admiral Jonsaymanor Jansenwol had fallen and her crew wanted revenge. Few knew she was on *The Black Seal*, her life yet to

189

be determined. So Tamnath watched with grim glee, wishing she could join the revel. Instead she became aware of a woman waiting nearby.

Tamnath glanced once to her side, then back to the sea, to the south where the last remnants of the Shari lurked. They would be dealt with in time. The woman wore a white coat, with dark green facings, a green taq on her head.

"Speak," Tamnath said.

"Admiral –"

"Do not call me that!"

"It is true."

"Does she live?"

"Yes, but only just. She is deep in dreams, and we truly cannot know if she will wake. And so *Admiral*," Ship's Prefect Talin Othmar emphasized, "let us not be jealous of our sorrows, nor think they are unique. Of course we will do all we can. But you don't need a healer to tell you command has passed to you. I am merely informing you of Sea Mother Jonsaymanor's state."

Tamnath breathed hard, irrationally angry at losing a pointless argument. "Take me to her."

As Tamnath descended to the upper deck, she felt it was the worst moment of her career. To have authority and rule as a general under a queen was one thing. But to be a queen…to have the entire force and expectation of honor and duty resting solely on one's shoulders … that was never something Tamnath desired. It was too much like motherhood. As much as she loved her daughter, had she been without her mother's house to foster her, it would have been a trial. It was Tamnath's duty to bear the mantel of fleet mother now, to be the one whom everyone looked to for answers, and the one who decided when honor superseded vengeance. The Shari would regret their choice. Still Tamnath would delay any decision until she saw Jonsay with her own eyes.

They passed into the mess hall, walking around the wounded, reminding Tamnath of yet another duty that waited. In the calm between action it was a captain's duty to visit the wounded, to show her respect for the sacrifice her crew made, to never forget every life was precious and none were to be squandered. To Tamnath it was always a burden, more so than others, but now, with her impending ascension to admiral, it was slightly less grim. A woman had lost an eye, but these things were easy to heal, given time. Nothing like the mortal wound that had taken the officer on *The Tide-breaker*. This woman would be given a choice of sailing back Tyrum or staying at the temple in Gashora, to return home later. The rest of the wounded were a mix of those struck with arrows, broken bones and burns. Tamnath took comfort that no soul on board had been lost through the Door, sparing her so far from speaking to the family of the dead.

A sudden coldness took her gut: she was wrong. As admiral she would have to take on that task for the survivors of *The Oaken Blue* should Jonsay not recover. And then Tamnath knew she had sinned against duty, for if there were dead, and they could not be retrieved in time because of her compulsion to find Jonsay, she was as guilty of murder as if she'd killed those women herself. With these thoughts she entered the berth set aside for Jonsaymanor.

"She'll need more tending than the hospital can provide," Othmar explained.

Such a great woman, so virile and strong, she looked small and frail in sleep. Her uniform had been burnt and rent in a great many places, her skin gashed and cut from the explosion and fall into the water. For all that she was whole, except she slept. A male healer was doing his best to dry her hair, a task that would be made easier once the sun returned.

"Sea Mother," he murmured, giving a nod of acknowledgment but not a salute. Healers weren't required to follow naval protocols. Their primary duty was to save and restore the health of the crew.

For reasons that Tamnath would have found hard to explain, while she found most men in mothers' professions a nuisance, male healers never bothered her.

"Can you read any thought?" she asked him.

The man shook his head. "She dreams, but they are so deep and vague, and she does not know herself in them."

The man continued to work, taking bandages and strapping Jonsaymanor's limbs down. It was a common thing for the unconscious wounded on a ship, so that they did not fall out of bed and become injured further.

Tamnath had seen enough. She turned around and made her way back to the upper deck. Seeing a free deck officer she barked at her, "Get Midship Drothmey in my cabin."

For years Tamnath had flouted naval regulations any times it suited her or the circumstances wouldn't earn more than a scold. Rarely would she bind her hair in the naval queue, unless ceremony absolutely required it. She pressed into service a series of midships to help her circumvent the rules; they carried her bicorn when she must wear it briefly, a sop to convention, while the girl in question was rewarded a small gratuity always welcome to the perpetually skint crew. Why was it so important, to have her hair flow wild like the heroes of old? What was this deep part of her soul that refused to be bound? Was it an expression of the prisoner the Jackal made her in her own body and a desire to be free? In any case on this day it must stop. She was the Admiral now and the fleet needed to see her as such.

When Tamnath came to her cabin she left the door open. Soon after Drothmey bounced in, saluting clumsily. She had scraps of linen wrapped around one wrist and the sleeve of that coat was blackened at the end.

"Sea Mother, you sent?"

"Are you wounded?"

"It's nothing, emha. A splash of the pitch fire, but I was able to scrape it off."

Tamnath nodded dubiously, then sat in a chair and gestured for the girl to attend her. "I need a naval braid as fast as you can."

"Oh!" The girl hid her surprise and set to work, though throughout it Tamnath heard her inhaling sharply. The girl was clearly hiding her pain. For all that the naval braid was as good as any. Most unmarried women did their own, but Tamnath knew with so little practice she would have made a hash of it.

When Drothmey was done, Tamnath stood and looked in her glass. Her angular features looked more so, accented brows almost aggressive over eyes that hid a killer. She nodded in approval.

"Well done, midship. Now get yourself to the hospital and do not argue. Bearing pain is a motherly virtue, but only a fool does so without reason."

After the girl left, Tamnath turned back to the mirror. She reached for her neglected bicorn and slowly lowered it on her head. She didn't recognize herself. Was the Jackal still there? Could a simple change of costume outmaneuver her? And did it matter? There was work to be done, Shari to be killed and a fleet to rally. Tamnath Tresmadore would take any help she could muster and may the Mother-gods have mercy on all their souls.

Chapter 13

Tears from the Sky

Raindrops hit Manweth's face as he drove *The Starshard* as near as he could to the place *The Oaken Blue* had vanished, reckless of the stray Shari vessels in his path, some crushed and swamped in his ship's wake. He felt he couldn't breathe at first as he sought his daughter, first on the decks of *The Black Seal*, then in the water around where the flagship had disappeared. Wickers were being thrown down to assist rescue, while divers converged to seek the injured or trapped in the remains of the sunken hulk. The splash of water near the stern told Manweth his remaining divers had joined the effort. Meanwhile skirmishes were being settled on several ships further out.

None of that mattered. How small the world became when a parent sought a child, when their heart hammered to escape their chest in the desperation to know they were safe, that all was well. Then he saw Dagmath floundering in the water. She was an expert swimmer but it appeared she was injured or trapped. Though Manweth was proud of his Prithi ancestry, he was named after the Cambrian God of the Sea for a reason. Without thinking further, he started to unbutton his blue naval jacket while shouting orders to his copilot.

"Lieutenant Selan, with my complements take the cage!"

"Sea Father, are you mad?" Selan protested.

"We're all mad now, lieutenant! We're caught in Amer's embrace, whether we will or no! Let us hope we survive it!"

Once Selan's feet touched the dais, Manweth leapt down, threw his coat aside and dived over the starboard wale.

First Manweth felt the brief joy of flying. Then his arms sluiced through cold water and for a moment he panicked for having not removed his boots. But it didn't matter. As dull as he might be in the sun, his water essence was active enough to drive him without foot flukes, and he could hold his breath longer than most. As the water seeped through his clothes to touch his skin, Manweth didn't feel chilled like most landed, but embraced his senses expanding with the water. He swam to where he had last seen Dagmath.

At any other time, along the white sandy shores near Lethglean, or smaller isles around Been where Tyreens took leisure, it was a simple thing to mark out one's child's essence from others. Mothers were best at this, having the psychic remains of a physical bond, but with practice a man could do well enough. However, the water churning with the desperate and dying, the stink of blood and humyn filth, Manweth despaired for a moment of finding Dagmath. Then he saw her, bobbing in the water. In seconds he could have her in his grasp, though he wondered how to get her back to *The Starshard*. He should grab a wicker, tie her to it and have it hauled up. If he wasn't mistaken her distress was being thrown into the water half concussed.

First Manweth had to reach her. At that moment a hand seized him, strong with desperation, clutching his arm as if life depended on it. A turban bobbed into view and the whites of humyn rolling eyes made Manweth pull back. Manweth had no animosity, no thought of revenge, only of getting to Dagmath. She bobbed once, then sank out of sight. It his own desperation Manweth tried to free himself of the drowning humyn's grip, but he had no leverage. And so he drew a dagger, the service knife all officers carried and he slashed out. He hoped only to wound the man, though he knew in his heart such a wound in unfriendly waters was a death sentence. Then Manweth was free; in moments Dagmath was in his arms.

"What in the thundering abyss and the howling deeps do you think you're doing, Sea Father?" a Blue woman shouted next to him in the water. It could only be Armeel yal Lath, the school herder of his ship. She took it personally if any "landed" took a diver's risks.

"She's my daughter!" Manweth shouted back, treading water more with essence than motion.

"Your duty is in the pilot's cage of *The Starshard*!" Armeel yelled as if he was a green midship.

"Duty be damned!" he found himself snarling back.

"It shall be if we continue like this! Give her to me! I can swim better with a burden. It is unseemly for a captain to flounder in the water like a dead carp!"

Manweth didn't argue further. Dagmath would be in better hands, true. But Armeel didn't understand. When the choice was between duty and a child's life, honor at sea versus the obligations of marriage, there was no choice. The law said only mothers had the possession of their children. Even married consorted men were only given guardianship if there was no estate from the mother's line available. This was so rare in practice men almost never had guardianship, and certainly not without the support of his mother's estate. But the heart did not know the law. To Manweth his wife's daughter Dagmath was as much part of him as if he'd birthed her. And so he had acted as any mother would.

They swam to the aft of *The Starshard*, to the rungs that divers used to climb. Manweth only ascended after Dagmath was raised in a net, gently passed to crew, then to the infirmary. He eschewed assistance, his thoughts unsettled. As usual, Armeel had been right. His place was to stand in the cage and his actions, nobly inspired though they be, had not brought assistance to his daughter any sooner.

A sudden chill hit him, and at the same time he had an urge to glance back. Down below he saw the floating body of a humyn, arms thrown out to either side, as if asking an uncaring god above why he had been brought to this place to die. Blood from a wound across his throat stained his once white garb a ghastly watery pink. Manweth wasn't even sure if it was the same humyn who had grabbed him. If so, what did it matter? His death had been certain, only the reasons changed. Had *The Oaken Blue* not fallen, he would have been doomed by a Dwen arrow or a marine's trident. But the fact was Manweth could have saved him. His daughter's rescue was imminent in the capable diver's fluked hands. Had he not panicked, he would have remembered that and not compounded his error by abandoning his post.

But then it was certain the humyn would have died, for Manweth would not have been in the water at all. Yet the knowledge Manweth could have saved a life weighed on him. Perhaps the humyn wasn't evil; he could be one of the many thralled who had no choice but to do the Sultan's bidding. Now Manweth would never know.

The humyn's face haunted Manweth for a long time after he returned to the pilot's cage.

* * *

And the rain fell as if the heavens themselves mourned at the Admiral's passing below the waves. While some mothers wept silently at their post, Sea Mother Tentynlar Aldwyn had neither the heart nor passion for tears.

The Charred Bronze was one of the great ships, and it took focus and foresight to drive her effectively. Tynlar wasn't for the daring maneuvers the Jackal favored, but in this moment daring and duty merged. It was the hew and cry from *The Black Seal* and *The Leviathan* that aborted Tynlar's initial foray to assist *The Sunchaser* and *The Tidebreaker*. She turned in time to see *The Oaken Blue* break apart and disappear, so the obvious course was to turn her ship in a sharp arc and drive it to assist the rescue. Her divers didn't need orders as they poured overboard to join those already in the water. Orders from the boatswain and deck officers flew back and forth. The women knew their business and Tynlar had nothing to add. It was her belief that a well run crew was managed with few orders. The sea wasn't a nursery and she was no crèche keeper.

That was well for other reasons: Tynlar's throat was so dry with shock it ached. She could not be gone, not Jonsaymanor. She didn't *feel* gone. They would have to wait until dreams to know if she truly had passed …

As the women worked and the injured, dying and drowned were dragged aboard, Tynlar noticed *The Black Seal* floating in place, with little or no activity. "What in the deeps was Tamnath doing?" Tynlar thought, glad to be distracted by her long antipathy. The woman boasted almost constantly about her martial deeds, usually for the venal goal of bedding young men. Now Amer herself clad the sea in her warlike visage, and Tamnath was not to be seen?

Tynlar's Dwen eyes were very good. Tamnath was not in the cage and nowhere on the dais. Perhaps she'd met a grim fate. That we would all be so fortunate, Tynlar thought uncharitably. Commodore Tamnath Tresmadore was like a spawn birthed from Athmod had she trysted with the Bane, relentless and untouchable. Nothing so simple as an errant arrow, or even the Dragon of Tamask, would be Tresmadore's doom. Finally, among the activity on *The Black Seal*, Tynlar spied her, standing at the edge of a top wale, staring into the depths of the sea where the Admiral had disappeared. Her face was full of despair, her unbound black hair flying across her face like lost pieces of her soul.

The sight shocked Tynlar. She'd never been certain of Tamnath's relationship with Jonsay: was it affection or ambition that drew her to the Admiral's circle? It was perfectly possible Tamnath exploited Jonsay and the motherly feelings the Admiral had for those who served under her. Tynlar felt a rare wave of shame that she had misjudged Tamnath's affections. But she also wondered why she was frozen in inaction.

It did happen, even to the most seafaring and battle hardened: a mother froze as if stolen by Reverie and could not respond to the circumstances at hand. However in that case it was the duty of others to replace her until she was herself. That Tamnath still ruled was evident by her crew's deference.

She wasn't trying to save the Admiral, was she?

With that thought Tynlar knew she had guessed correctly. She was both outraged and grateful. Outraged because it was their first duty to save those the Admiral had given her life for, yet grateful because if there was any chance of success, the Jackal would birth it. And so Tynlar turned her mind to the next pressing matter: how to dispose of the remaining Shari, for she was next in command of the fleet.

The Tidebreaker and *The Sunchaser* had repulsed their attackers, both bearing scars from the battle. *The Tidebreaker*'s main mast was scorched, hanging with burnt and blackened ruined sails, the decks still smoldering from the pitch-fire. *The Sunchaser* looked hail enough, though her sides were streaked with blackened ash where pots of pitch-fire had landed, burning with less effect. Sea Mother Maeven Roanteth's broad figure bellowed from the cage, her words indistinct from this distance. But there was something wrong and finally Tynlar saw it: the bowsprit was broken and where once an orb of honey gold solstone rose on a wave of carved, painted wood, there was nothing. A small wound for a ship, to lose its figurehead, but it hurt a captain's pride. Still, there was no urgency. Instead Tynlar looked for the Shari to see what, if any, mischief they were still capable of while there was daylight.

The roving ships filled with salts had all been dispatched, either by strike or in some way scuttled. Sea Mother Lenor, in all of her adventurous and enthusiastic maneuvers – which incidentally contradicted many if not all of the fleet's instructions – had struck many ships while they had the sun, swamped a few more in the rain and captured not one, but two ballista.

They were simple machines, not as big as those used by the ancients, but they meant the strike crew had something effective to do. Unlike the three-foot thick hull of a city-ship that was virtually impenetrable to Dragon shot, the hull of the scorpion ships was comparable to a private yacht. Even with the odd stone the ballista did significant damage when aimed properly, if not to the hull, then to the oars and oarsmen. And that was before the smith was bidden to cast whatever scrap bronze or iron they had into rude balls of shot. Already those crew from Brownie families who had made clocks and contraptions were excited to create this engine. They had all the materials and tools; Lenor boasted they could have two more engines by sunrise. Tynlar was impressed despite her irritation with Lenor's flouting of directives.

But that was all for the morrow. At the moment the reserve line of ships had barely moved. Tynlar wondered if the mathematics of the situation weighed on the Shari admiral. They had come in a flotilla of two hundred vessels to sack Gashora as the first action of the Sultan extending his empire north. The Shari now had less than half that amount of ships intact and at full strength. Damaged vessels were being cannibalized for wood and supplies. The decks of the ships visible were crowded and who knew the numbers of the wounded.

Why the reserve line didn't advance puzzled Tynlar. That was their purpose. The clouds above thinned more and offered a possible explanation. The Shari knew the Tyreen ships were much faster and the solcannons were only weakened by clouds and rain in their primitive understanding. If they engaged now and the clouds cleared, they would be destroyed. So the ships retreated. Most bore the signs of strike damage; many had lost oardivers and were unable to do more than limp back to their lines. Three of the ships involved with the ill fated attempt to capture *The Tidebreaker* and *The Sunchaser* malingered in the water, their crews dead or too few to row. A half hearted volley of arrows flew as marines and crew moved in to capture the boats. Then the Tyreen archers slew any humyn soul remaining still holding a bow. Some fled below into the bowels of their ships. What desperate plan they had could only be imagined. They would not escape.

Satisfied the immediate danger was gone, Tynlar turned her thoughts on how to settle the matter. The warlike part of her, hot with blood and numb with loss, wanted to chase them now, knowing whatever the cost, the fleet could bear it. The sheer mass of the Tyreen vessels could be used to ram the remaining scorpion ships into splinters. But that was needlessly reckless. It would be like a talented yet inexperienced chess player chasing her losing opponent around the board because she had not thought through her strategy.

"Sea Mother, a missive from *The Helix Bow*," a midship said, holding out a folded paper.

Tynlar took it. It was time to put aside grieving and tend to the present. Sea Mother Lusaid Sleath wrote as much, her queries echoing Tynlar's thoughts. Perhaps they would flee. How this matter was to be brought to a decisive end was, of course, up to their new Admiral.

Tynlar felt the water's current through *The Charred Bronze*, bringing the ship in a close arc near *The Black Seal*. Should she send a missive to Tamnath? She was in command of the fleet now. Even if Jonsay survived, she would be no fit state. Tynlar hoped Tamnath didn't resist this duty, or force Tynlar to take decisive command. They had never come to blows, the Wolf and the Jackal, not counting the odd game of laysaid played between ships' crews. They both had an instinct they were deadly to each other and so avoided excessive provocation. But if Tamnath Tresmadore could not fulfill her duty, Tynlar would have no choice but to challenge her.

Tynlar dictated a response to Sleath: they would hold their position, finish the rescue, then prepare to end the Shari when the sun returned.

The message sent, Tynlar felt it was time to expand her sense of readiness. "Midship, fetch my yastol."

Tynlar rarely wore a yastol and found the expectation she should because she was Dwen ridiculous. No Dwen needed a yastol to feel the wind like branches in a tree, or sense the currents and wetness of the air, any more than one walked around with a telescope to accent already acute vision. It was more a cultural matter: Dwen raised in Ta Dwenoshire wore the yastol from their sprite years and so it felt a part of them. Tynlar was raised in Tyrum and its environs. She only wore a yastol infrequently, usually on holidays. Still, there were times she felt the extra passive essence it afforded was an asset, and this was one of them.

The midship returned, holding the crown-like headdress of wood leaves out with one hand. Tynlar took it, giving the girl her bicorn. Tynlar was a traditionalist in some ways; while she was closer related to the Ash Dwen, she had a yastol of oak leaves. She slipped the yastol over her white streaked red hair. The moment it touched her head, Tynlar felt a coolness around her and the air seemed full of life and energy. She breathed deeply as the leaves raised, and the contact expanded her senses, as if she had roots and branches extended to the sky. Now she felt the faint energy of the sun that leaked through the clouds, no matter how gray. It had been a long time since Tynlar was a green pilot who felt simply merging with the ship's heart made her feel like a god. Wearing the yastol, now she wasn't just the ship, but the Mother Tree of Ta Pangeal, as the mystics would say: her sight felt keener, as was her sense of poise and power in the Orb. A tree reached down to anchor itself before reaching up towards the light. She considered the metaphor ...

A cry went up from the waters near *The Black Seal*. Divers surfaced in such number, the water frothed for a moment. A Blue woman with long dark hair gasped as she surfaced with the help of another diver. In their arms was an unconscious woman with a healthy athletic build, her blue officer's coat scorched and torn. It was Jonsaymanor.

With the yastol amplifying the ship's essence, Tynlar was almost moved to weep. She looked to the commodore's ship and was further relieved Tamnath was now roused, no longer in a stupor. They watched as the divers worked with crew to lift Jonsaymanor into a launch. Did she live?

In her heightened state, Tynlar focused her eyes. It wasn't so much the images were clearer as she had a sense of the magic behind them. The limp form of Jonsaymanor was heartrending, but her eyes were closed. That was a good sign. Those who held their breath with reflexive water essence would not be staring glassy eyed. But there was no way to truly know without boarding *The Black Seal,* where the launch was hoisted to the decks.

Tynlar looked again where Tamnath stood but she had moved, striding away with a healer in her wake. They disappeared below. Another good sign? The Admiral was alive or at least retrievable? Surely Tamnath wouldn't bother to go below if only to check a corpse?

Tynlar exhaled. It did no good to wonder when they would know soon enough. Tynlar drove *The Charred Bronze* gently through the water in tandem with *The Leviathan*, both assisting with the rescue. The rain faded to an uncertain light haze and near the horizon, far to the west and home, the clouds thinned. As the hours wore on, the sky took a burnt cast as Sul prepared for her long journey through the Lands of Night.

The rescue was finished, their ships full of survivors and wounded distributed among the fleet. Now came the task of planning the salvage: the keel and heart could not be abandoned, nor the cache boxes. Whether the figurehead would be retrieved, time would tell. They wouldn't try any longer than it took to sort the Shari and make for Gashora.

A red ray of the setting sun shown through the clouds, warming the deck and mast in the light of dusk, as the pall of impending night was about to settle on them. Tynlar wondered idly what the galley might provide. Cold sausage and cheese weren't as much of a trial for her as it was for the Blue crew, but Dwen did not keep high spirits if there were little greens to be had, and Tynlar was no exception. There was still plenty of travel-loaf, a pemmican of dried venison, berries and honeyed nut butter. The Dwen archers were nibbling it constantly. She'd send for some, taking it with a tea tonic; that was the best that could be done until they arrived in Gashora.

The whistle came from *The Black Seal* to dress the line and hold it for the night. Tynlar yielded the cage to her copilots and prepared to take her turn of the wounded. They weren't all her wounded, but it didn't matter. They were on her ship and it was her duty to look after them. But before she'd made her way to the stairs a raven intercepted her.

~auk. i fly from the grim captain.~

Tynlar's though speech was excellent and she knew exactly whom the raven spoke of. She glanced at *The Black Seal* while she took the paper. She did a double take. Tamnath could be seen no where on the decks. It wasn't completely odd; perhaps Tamnath had dictated the missive from the hospital or her cabin. But Tynlar knew Tamnath never retired so soon when her blood was up. Unless it was to slake it with a man. Surely that was furthest from her thoughts at the moment? Tynlar scanned *The Black Seal*'s decks again.

Tynlar inhaled in mild shock. She had found Tamnath, apparently in conversation with the strike crew. Presently she broke away, trotting down the stern steps stairs to the quarter deck. One thing was distinctly different: her hair was bound in a queue and, damn Tynlar's eyes, Tamnath was actually wearing her bicorn. Had Lun himself manifested before her, she would have been no less amazed.

By chance Tamnath glanced over the distance to see Tynlar facing her. She saluted lazily, almost as if they were chums. Tynlar started to worry for Tamnath's health; perhaps she'd been struck by one of the Dragon's shot balls? Tynlar saluted back, then opened the missive:

To the Charred Bronze, with complements, etc.

Jonsaymanor lives.

TT

Tynlar shook with relief. Jonsaymanor lived. Thank Maer and Sul, and The Mother Tree, Jonsay lived. Then Tynlar closed her eyes, until the threat of tears passed. Jonsay lived and all would be well.

But the curse of Amer's blood lust and the Bane's demons of chaos were not yet done with the Tyreen fleet. At that moment another explosion thundered over the water.

Chapter 14

Surrender

Navi carefully stepped around bodies broken or riven into bloody limbs and ichor. She shrewdly looked to where she might be useful with a mind to avoid the gory task of cleaning. Already burly crewgirls swaggered along shouting orders to volunteers and crew alike to pitch in and help, not just with the carnage, but the final suppression of the pitch-fire that stubbornly smoldered.

Navi made for the forecastle, feeling heavy and ungainly as she ran along the edge of the starboard wale, swinging on the edge of the fore mast shrouds before landing between the solstone cannons above the magi gallery. This part of the deck was covered with a revolting mix of blood, cloth, leather and armor, almost as if …

"Well landed, volunteer!" Ta Glenfar said, interrupting Navi's thoughts as the magi floated back down to the deck. Her black vestments were rent with several holes.

"Hak," Navi replied dismissively. "Had the sun been shining, I could walk on Her rays with the lightness of Solshar."

"Hm," Glenfar said, considering. "I didn't take you for a poet. Or to remember that once Solshari was Sul's daughter, not son."

"Bright and Quick were always Daughters of Sul," Navi said. "It was the first Romantics who imagined Bright as a boy. A sop to motherly sentimentality."

Navi helped the strike crew replace lances in their holdings while they conversed, Glenfar perched on the bollards by a cathead.

"So in your philosophy there are no Sons of Sul?" Glenfar asked.

"I'm sure there are plenty, as numerous as Her children are. But I doubt any of them stand with the God Mothers of Heaven."

"What of Myngar's consort, Felkeni?"

"An invention of those who fantasize they can wife fortune."

"Ah, but Ramlachi Eclipse, Amer's consort in war…"

Navi snorted. "A fantasy of athletic masculinism if ever there was. Mark, even Ramlachi gives himself to the only woman who can mind him, the Mother-God of War."

"But what of Theedwen? Meerti?"

Navi shook her head. "Both sons of Mother-gods; their power comes from Eurath and Maer respectively. And Meerti is a myth mask for Laifmyr, "He who sang by the Sea", in all probability a living elfyn man, though the legend of the eternal bower has not been proven outside dreams."

"Then you doubt the Manifestation."

Navi shrugged. "The dragons of the sea and forest predate the Cataclysm and the manifestation of the Thyngalu. Perhaps it is the same for elfyn."

"You are well read on the classics and history, volunteer."

"Thank you, emha."

"Yet my tutors might say strangely lacking in a sense of balance and symmetry. For surely as Mother-Gods rule in a reflection of mortal circum-stance, so too do Goddi reflect the best we imagine in our consorts and sons?"

"I'm no literalist, Ta Glenfar. You are exactly correct: we mothers imag-ine gods in our image and that drives our passions. It is a reflection of our world as we know, not a path in myth and tales we must follow to find meaning. Myth is a mirror of our circumstance."

"How then do you explain Lun, the sole Goddi unmarried, ruling his own domain?"

Navi laughed. "He is what every woman desires at times: all of man that is a beauty and a bane."

"Beware, sister," Glenfar said laughing. "Lun cursed Jaro for less!"

"Rather more, if I recall the tale. Now a less philosophical question, magi: what is that?" Navi pointed to the deck not yet cleaned.

Glenfar looked down with dispassionate white eyes. "The remains of two humyn, courtesy of Ta Hethlion."

"Child, you should have a care speaking a dragon's name lest they hear," a woman said, hovering into view from the bowsprit gallery below to step onto the deck. She was older than the ship's adept Ta Taren. Navi guessed from the force of her aura she might be an Aeon. But then why... "Am I not ship's adept?" Hethlion said, finishing Navi's thought. "The bother, girl. Ambition is for the young and easily bored. Glenfar, you could be of use helping prepare the next Sadol operation."

Glenfar smiled apologetically and hopped down making her way to the forecastle steps leading to the magi berth.

"You had a question?" Hethlion asked. Navi barely glanced down before Hethlion sighed. "Ah. These two unfortunates were brothers. They were abandoned on the streets of Tamask, their Indus mother dying in childbirth, their father refusing to recognize them. Together they survived a cruel unforgiving world, finding employment first as guards, then with posts in the Sultan's armies. They were not the worst souls compared to many in the Sultan's service. Unfortunately, they also attempted to kill a midship and crewboy. They were disincrated."

Navi shook. Disincration was advanced magic of a soul expert with the basic alchemy of life. Certain motes in their essence were so close to air it took only a shiver or twist to change them for moments, removing the solidness that kept a mass or body whole. It was one of the ways an elfyn body could be killed beyond possibility of retrieval.

"Interesting," Navi said, feeling weak.

Hethlion smiled. "Kind of you to lie about it." The magi looked sober. "Their last thoughts were of each other. I must write it down. Your servant."

Hethlion followed Glenfar leaving the deck.

Navi had no intention of lingering near the effects of such deadly magic, nor being pressed to clear the sad gore. So she was pleased when strike captain Lieutenant Olesh Desmet waved her over to the larboard hull at the base of the forecastle steps. With her was Tellon Braz, her annoyance with Navi long past.

"We're looking for bright souls to help clear the captured ships," Desmet said, pointing down at the water. The vessel was a virtual wreck, both side castles burnt and shattered into kindling, though the fore and after decks were reasonably intact. A handful of shields still lined the place where the top oardrivers once sat; broken and burnt oars hung off the vessel's side, but no oarsmen remained. The ship appeared abandoned. It was several fathoms away; one of *The Tidebreaker*'s smaller launches waited below to ferry them. "I know your type," Desmet said shrewdly. "You are not happy unless you are dancing in the sun. Failing the sun, any dance will do. Some

Shari might remain and we should give Sernalash a chance to forget her anger."

Navi glanced at the strikemaster who was not marking them at the moment. "Very well," she said, grabbing a longer length of loose rope from the shrouds. "Last one on the deck is dragon bait!"

The rope wasn't long enough to reach the launch but it didn't need to be. Navi swung in a shallow arc away from the ship's hull, just enough to clear the curve, letting herself slide freely down holding the hemp loosely before letting go, landing in the center of launch in a deep crouch. A second later Tellon landed beside her, a little less solidly because of her deck shoes.

"Not I!" Tellon crowed, waving strands of gold hairs out of her face as she stood, the boat rocking slightly.

"Ai, but she is," Navi pointed up grinning as Desmet's bicorn shook with her head before she started down a rope ladder placed for that purpose.

"It's not as if you were leaving any sooner before I boarded," Desmet's voice carried in pique.

Navi and Tellon exchanged a look. "Dragon bait!" they said together laughing.

"Could you contain your sprites, lieutenant?" the pilot opined. "The Shari have already done their best to kill anyone on board, without the launch being swamped!"

Indeed, the floor and hull was scattered and pierced with red fletched arrows.

"The Shari sent one last volley," a woman explained as Desmet finally joined them.

"We're ready, pilot," the lieutenant said. "Ferry us to our doom."

The launch eased away from *The Tidebreaker*, cutting through flotsam and bodies as it made its way to the vessel. It was so small and barren a soul forgot how much damage they had brought in numbers, decks full of fanatical, murderous warriors. Now there was nothing. It was short, not even half the height of *The Tidebreaker*, barely the size of a Federation patrol ship, though its many oars, even broken and ruined, gave it a business like appearance.

As they drifted towards the Shari vessel, Desmet spoke:

"The survivors have retreated below. Remember you must honor any who wish to surrender." She paused giving a Navi a look. Reluctantly Navi nodded once. "We will round up the survivors before taking stock of the vessel's contents."

Water erupted to either side of the boat as three divers surfaced. One was that damn Fish with the buoys, Pearl. Navi avoided meeting her eye. She hadn't forgotten the humiliation of floating. She'd taken some satisfaction having seen Pearl descend ashen faced from the tops. Sure, Navi felt like a shriveled plum, but Pearl had actually suffered; Meer and Blue generally did not like heights. Navi smirked to herself, but her inner mirth didn't last. There was something about Pearl and her boy (Callas? Cail?) that troubled her. She'd had plenty of men, free rides and harlots, bored helpers and errant sons, but she never defended one like a sister. Well, perhaps a bit; chivalry was always part of the wooing game. But Pearl acted like she'd wifed the boy (Colin?). Navi had never claimed to be "in love". The idea escaped her. Men were unreliable, vain creatures. A mother had to protect herself and be certain any boy knew she wasn't their cache of gold. The closest Navi had been to a man was Lorthai, a harlot in Lethglean. They had several enjoyable months together. Then they fell to rowing: according to Lorthai she took him for grated, wouldn't invite him on hunts, and she expected him to be available when she returned, even knowing the demands of his trade.

The maddening thing was, even as they shouted at each other outside the brothel house (for which Navi would be fined later), even through her anger and frustration (why did men have to be so difficult?), Navi knew Lorthai was *correct* on many points. She *was* acting like a child, expecting him to be her convenience. She hadn't set out to do so, but fell into a habit that felt natural and normal, and therefore didn't seem wrong. And after, he wouldn't see her, refused all calling and correspondence. It baffled her so and she decided to avoid any man who made her feel too welcome in her heart. However good it felt at first, nothing was worth the anguish of the end. That was why, as pleasant as Samath was, she must take care not to lose herself with him.

So she avoided looking at the Fish whose boy, whatever his name was, reminded her of the whole sordid affair. That was the closest Navi had come to being "in love". As Sul willed, she hoped never to fall into that pit of sentimentality again.

They came right up to the hull, near the bows, where a gap before oars made an easy entrance to the deck had it been docked. As it was the deck was ten to twelve feet above them. There was enough pitting and uneven-ness in the hull the crewgirl with them didn't bother with a grapple and rope. She scampered up and took a moment to confirming the immediate sur-roundings were secure. Apparently all was well, because she whistled in the affirmative. A bundle of rope was thrown up, a ladder; she caught it and se-cured it to the deck, then let it fall for officers and crew. All this while Pearl and another diver had pulled themselves onto the launch, while the third stayed in the water. Navi ascended the ladder with the crew and boarded the scorpion ship.

The ship hardly matched that description in its current state. The high hooked stern post had been broken and burnt to the level on the stern deck, much as the fore deck, hardly a forecastle, was bereft of rail or tent, the fallen Dragon just visible at the edge of the deck.

"Be careful," Desmet said. "That could roll off and it's not a feather."

Navi stood a moment near the ship's hull, where a crude anchor was lashed. Looking over the fraught sea, the water seethed with the many mo-tions of the ships, the fleet's activity suppressing the natural waves into moving pockets of washes and swells. There was little wind and the rain had nearly stopped, as the ship rocked under Navi's feet, like a skip used by a Meer scout. It was odd how she felt the mass of this vessel much more than *The Tidebreaker*. Though it was smaller, it felt larger because she could sense the weight as the ship rocked and pitched under her feet.

Navi followed with the rest of the crew, the officers gesturing silently as they searched the vessel. There was blood and bodies of course, scattered arrows from both fleets, red fletched rude steel tips mixed with green fletched Dwen arrows. Navi saw no solstone tipped sniper arrows and that was as it should be; snipers who knew their business found their target. Sniper arrows would sink with the dead to the bottom of the sea to rest for eternity.

The top deck was simple, made more simple by the complete destruction of the castles at the side that had held ballista. One of those broken engines

had fallen on the oar benches. The other was lost altogether, likely overboard. Oar benches ran most of the length of the vessel along either side,
twenty-five in all. Some benches were broken, burnt or covered in blood.
Others still had a sad figure slumped over an oar, one with three arrows in
its back. Desmet drew her sword to poke the creature, making certain it was
dead. This was the first order of business, checking those bodies they saw
were indeed as deceased as they appeared. They had to step carefully because the way was cluttered with bodies, debris, and fallen ladders presumably to the now absent catapult platforms. Down the center, much like *The
Tidebreaker*, there were two hatches, much smaller of course, obscured by
long poles the size of trees sitting on crutches. They were the masts the
Shari removed before battle; in the deck there were round holes of the right
size, with large shims of wood scattered nearby. What a strange design,
Navi thought. At least the masts, stacked and lashed together, blocked any
possibility of attack from the hatches. Once they were certain nothing else
lived on the top deck, attention was turned to the aft and bows of the ship.

Under the stern deck an ornate gilded red and black double door stood
ajar, the dark interior, likely the captain's cabin, seemingly empty. Before
the doors was another hatch with stairs leading below deck. Opposite, in the
shadow of the far bows could be seen stacked barrels, the powdered salts
used to make the dragon breath. One was turned over, black grains finer
than sand covering the wood near more steps leading below.

Navi peered in the dimness under the fore deck. She could smell the still
hot dragon above where, even unseated, it scorched the wood. The fittings
of the ship were brass with ornamented geometrical designs. Navi gripped
her sword as she neared the dim opening with stairs leading below. Nothing
stirred that she could see.

A Blue marine in scaled armor tapped her shoulder, shaking her flouted
head, nodding to the aft of the vessel where Desmet and Tellon prepared to
descend in front of the captain's cabin. Navi nodded and joined her, picking
their way down the length of the ship.

"It's a mystery," the marine said in a breath of a whisper. "We know they
were seen disappearing below."

They joined Desmet and Tellon.

"It's blocked," Desmet said, sneering in distaste. Tellon, though crew, wasn't too eager to leap to the task.

Looking, Navi saw the shadow of a body. It would be graceless here to avoid labor. She stepped down with the marine and they both dragged the humyn body up to the deck. In death all bodies were strangely heavy, as if with the flight of the soul the dross matter weighed more. Worse, the thing stank with sweat and blood and voided fluids. They heaved it to the side, then with a great squelch, the guts slithered out of the man's belly onto Navi's boots.

The marine, curse her to the Deeps, laughed, while Navi, like an offended cat, tried to free herself and clean off the offal.

"Laugh while you may, Fish!" Navi said. "You can take point with the next body."

Then Desmet and Tellon were already descending, Desmet's sword glimmering, Tellon with a capstan bar. Navi and the marine followed until they stood on the lower deck beneath a short ceiling that required them all to crouch.

Behind the stair, aft, were crates and barrels of supplies, mostly undisturbed. The deck opened at both sides, an aisle running down the length where oarsmen would step up to the benches by the hull. It was hard to see how many were left dead because directly ahead of them was a bulkhead and doorway, and steps into a sunken hold. It was dark, the hatches above covered with something solid. Only the filtering of light through the mast holes gave an idea of the size and how many might be within.

They heard a sound, a scrape of metal against wood. All the women stood as still as stalking lions. Beside the aisles outside the hold's inner walls, here would be only one passage through, and presumably a doorway near the hatch at the end, under the bows. They had only to listen to know where the humyn were.

It wasn't just a case of elfborn hearing acuity. They could also control their breath better, even under stress. But there were few sounds to distract a soul. All humyn ships leaked and creaked, so Navi closed her eyes to focus her hearing better.

Then she heard it, not just a breathing but the muffled sounds of a struggle. Navi's eyes flew open as she drew her sword. They stalked forward,

down the steps, into the hold as slowly the outlines of shapes took form.
One humyn, maybe a couple others. Then there was a desperate cry and a
small figure ran forward.

A Shari man ran into the filtered light, little more than a boy, his turban
askew, eyes wide and terrified. Navi raised her sword, but he had no
weapon. He shouted something in his strange tongue. Navi had picked up
a couple of Shari words for trade over the decades, but he wasn't speaking
in a trade bazaar trying to get queens. He shrieked in panic and the only
word she understood was *"Nah!"*

But "no" or "not" what?

He froze a moment seeing the women, muttering a prayer to "Al-ahat".
But whatever he feared from them, he feared more what was in the room
behind him where sharp scrabbling sounds were heard. Raising his hands he
repeated, *"Taslim! Taslim!"*

Desmet seemed to understand. *"Zano bozan!* Kneel!" she ordered, nodding to Tellon to bind him.

If anything this panicked the man more. *"Nah! Nah! Farar kon!"*

"You can run later!" Tellon said impatiently while the marine stepped
forward to help bind him.

"Nah! Farar kon!" the man screamed. Then, between his sweaty fear
and terrified mania, he slipped out of their grasp and ran towards Navi,
screaming, *"Farar kon!"*

Navi was never much for using thought speech. It took more effort than
just saying words. With close friends in youth it was useful for stealth. She
almost required a situation of urgent excitement to understand anything
timely from thought speech. And few humyn were capable of it, though
their thoughts leaked everywhere. But in times of great fear humyn could
project directly into minds. As Navi grabbed the man's wiry underfed arm,
she had a flash of what was in his mind, like magi a had punched her soul:

An aging maned humyn in black robes laired within, barricaded behind
barrels of salts gathered from other ships. A shuttered oil lamp flickered
nearby, and he held a length of cotton rope with salts twined in its strands.
A couple Shari cowered around him; he was clearly a magi of sorts, feared
and respected for his knowledge, utterly devoted to the cause of the Sultan
and the Ever-sky. But Ali, the man Navi held, did not want to die. He

would take his chances with the dread she-devils of the sea. With them he'd have a chance. Here he was doomed ...

Navi let the man go as she bellowed like a Sea Mother: "The room is full of salts and a mad humyn is going to strike them! Flee!"

She lunged to grab the marine, pulling her backwards and throwing her towards the stairs after the fleeing humyn who was already out of sight. Tellon looked at Navi in alarm, blood smeared blond hair glimmering just as a flame flared. Desmet had just stepped forward, finding her way blocked by the barrels clustered in a barricade in the center of the hold. She stepped back, understanding the truth of their situation. Navi had to trust they could flee on their own time as she dashed to the upper deck.

Leaping through the hatch, she was appalled to already be on the heels of the marine. Damn Fish! They never ran well. Navi grabbed the woman's shoulder as she ran, hoping to throw her forward and overboard. But she never got the chance.

The entire ship exploded beneath them. Navi felt a sudden great pain on her right side. Then she was flying, alight with fire like a phoenix before falling into the cold and dark. She knew nothing for a long while.

Chapter 15

Knaves at Sea

Col felt he was run off his feet helping the crew with the cleanup after the battle. He'd retrieved his poor bent sword, its beautiful leaf blade lines forever marred by a deep crease. He had straightened it the best he could, but such damage never truly healed without a forge. When he had time, he'd ask the smith if it could be reforged on ship. Until then he worked, collecting the burnt and broken debris, scattered weapons and effects from both sides. The Shari's possessions would be confiscated, and, especially the arms and armor, studied by military scholars when they reached the mainland.

As the day grew late and the sky darkened, Col joined the women washing and sanding the deck to clean out the blood, but they would not let him help collect and dispose of the gory remains of bodies. "It's mother's work, butcher's work and not a thing any man should be forced to do," one crewgirl said.

Col didn't argue like the ravens trying to barter and bargain over humyn eyes and entrails. The truth was, now the heat of battle was abating, his stomach wanted to rebel, but there was nothing in it. Still he maneuvered himself close to the top wale in case he lost mastery of his body. That's where he found the officer huddled underneath a stern stair, clutching a leather case of letters to her chest.

She had to be one of the refugees from *The Oaken Blue* distributed for berthing among the fleet. Her blond hair was in disarray, her bicorn lost, and, while Col wasn't conversant with insignia, the helix twining a star on her coat's shoulders meant she was at least an ensign. Something about her suggested her duties were not mean. She appeared to be trying to stay out of the way but at the same time seemed insensible to her own muttering.

"Emha?" Col inquired.

"The boxes are locked. I'm sure of it. I have to tell the divers to find it!" she finished. Then she looked up at him, startled at his presence. "Do you think the Sea Father is available now?"

"I don't know." Col looked around uncertainly. "You can talk to the boatswain, I think. She's the meaty one with tattoos ..."

"Was on the *The Oaken Blue*," the Gold woman explained. "She wouldn't come. I left her there…" The woman's eyes trailed out over the water. "I left her…"

Col understood. "You were following orders. There's no shame in that."

"Yes, orders…. I sealed the cache, but it was too heavy to take. No room. This," here she gestured to the mass of papers in her hands, "Is all I could seize. So much could be lost…"

"I'm sorry. Perhaps you should wait near the captain's cabin?" he suggested. "I think it's through there, behind the wheel."

"Yes, yes that would be sensible. I was the Admiral's secretary you know." She paused to rearrange her papers before standing. "I apologize, effa. I seem to have lost my hat. Very careless of me."

"It's no matter," Col said at a loss. She obviously thought he was someone else.

"What's going on here?" a Blue officer queried to Col's gratitude.

The Gold woman snapped to attention, saluting. "Ensign Amralan, emha! Reporting from *The Oaken Blue*!"

"Lieutenant Ni-Fionna," the Blue officer replied. "You may be at ease and free of duty until the healers say otherwise."

Amralan relaxed slightly. "Very generous of you, emha! As I was saying I lost my hat. Regulations state an officer must be properly attired at all times …" She trailed off, looking confused.

"Volunteer, please escort the ensign to the hospital," Ni-Fionna said.

Col relieved to be ordered clearly. It wasn't just being faced with Amralan's pain and loss, but the feeling of helplessness in the face of such anguish.

They were at the mess doors when she stopped.

"Do you think the Sea Father will have extra paper? I should be writing this all down. I can remember it perfectly, but it needs to be written down. It's my duty, you see. I was the Admiral's secretary…"

Col didn't like to think of himself as a shirker, but he decided there was little honor lost in helping her.

"I have paper, but it's in my quarters. I'll get it but you need to go inside so the healers can tend you."

"Thank you, effa! Thank you very much!"

Col wanted to wait for her to walk through the door before dashing down. Then he remembered business he had with one of the infirm. As quick as he could Col found the guard who lent him her sword. She appeared to be asleep on a table.

"Are you wounded?" a healer asked sharply.

"No," Col said, somewhat taken aback.

"Then begone until this mess is sorted!"

"I wanted to return her sword."

"Then leave it. She must sleep now. You can express your gratitude later."

Col left the sword by the cot. "Thank you, emha," he whispered, hoping her soul could hear.

"Knave!" another healer barked. Col spun around, alarmed and offended, but the healer was yelling at another man. "Where are the fresh mosses?"

"I think someone is bringing them…"

"Well find out!"

Col made a careful retreat. Cultural chivalry aside, some women were driven to bullying when conditions excused them. He was sure the healer was a perfect gentlewoman in times of peace, at least he hoped so.

Now Col ran to a companion stair. He didn't spare time informing anyone. If he was quick he would return soon enough. Of course the berth was empty, all the divers being on duty. He wondered when he'd see Pearl next. He retrieved his satchel with his papers and neglected book. There hadn't had nearly enough time for all the writing he'd planned. Even his portrait of Pearl wasn't finished. He left his bent sword on his hammock and rushed back to the hospital on the upper deck.

Amralan had wandered back outside the mess, looking forlorn but no longer muttering. Col decided it wouldn't hurt to take a moment to run up the steps to the quarterdeck to look over the wale. He was rewarded with the sight of Pearl standing on a barge near one of the captured Shari vessels. He waved, but she didn't see him. No matter. They'd see each other soon enough. He trotted back down to the mess hall. Amralan still lingered.

"Ai, emha," Col said, announcing himself. Then from the forecastle above someone called, "Col! What are you doing down there?"

It was Freya. Her sword was sheathed, her hands covered with blood and bile. He could almost smell the general stink of death, and not the romanticized taint of blood some hunters took joy in, but true offal, waste and bloody manure. His nose had become dense to it among the reek. Col dreaded rejoining the work crew. It was then a male voice behind him said, "Volunteer, I believe you're wanted above."

Col spun around, annoyed and ready to retort. There were few men on the ship who had authority he was compelled to obey. So it was with shock he found himself face to face with the Sea Father.

Col aborted a retort and forced his face into a semblance of humble obedience. Captain Gathelyn was taller than him by almost a head, with a mix of both motherly and manly traits Col found disconcerting. Perhaps it was because the men he knew who were motherly were Cambrian humyn cousins. It was not possible with maned faces to see anything but a man, even if he was hunting and fighting. And Captain Gathelyn, while nowhere near as brawny as his first mate, was able to hold his own against a mother. His height and broad shoulders gave the expectation of seeing a woman.

In spite of his surprise, Col had a better instinct for politics than Pearl and no urge to tempt fate.

"Pardon, Sea Father," Col said. "I was lending the Admiral's clerk my papers."

Col was satisfied to see the captain mark the information, interest flickering in his eyes. "Then do so and return to duty."

"Right." Col took the satchel off his shoulder, and opened it to extract his book.

Then an explosion echoed over the water causing all the ravens to take flight. Col let himself be dragged to deck by the captain while flaming splinters of wood fell on them, but they were shielded from the worst by the quarterdeck. Amralan fell with others to the deck. For several fearful seconds they waited, but no arrows flew, no further explosions sounded, no screams of the wounded were heard. Shakily Col got to his feet with the captain, the Sea Father with hand on sword as he ran up to the quarterdeck. Col followed him.

The crew was stamping out any flaming debris as the boatswain shouted to the captain:

"Ship's fine! The same can't be said of the recovery crew!"

"The recovery crew?" Col echoed. Then he understood.

Throwing his satchel down to the upper deck, Col ran down to the larboard wale, leaning over as far as he could, desperate for the sight of Pearl. She'd been standing on the launch by the Shari vessel. Now there was no vessel, only burnt and smoking remnants that sank as he watched, though a burning shell remained white hot, almost too bright to look at. Around it the water burned, leaking pitch-fire from the stores of the destroyed ship. While he heard the captain shout orders behind him, he searched the remains, the barge, anything that might be Pearl.

Then he saw her bobbing in the water. Was she swimming? Floundering? It was hard to tell in the haze of black and white smoke. It wasn't clear anyone had seen her, or if any of the divers dared to go near the fire on the water. Damn cowardly Fish, Col swore to himself, imagining they'd abandoned her. Then she disappeared from his sight.

He couldn't bear it anymore. Screams surrounded him as he unlaced and discarded his boots. He had no illusions about his swimming skills and without essence, footwear was a hindrance. Then he jumped off the ship into the water.

The guilt of his stolen battle kiss drove Col on, as of he'd jinxed his fate by letting it happen. If he lost Pearl … he couldn't think on it. Col hit the water, the force of it cold and sudden, making him want to gasp, knowing he couldn't yet. With great effort he pulled himself up to the surface. He was certain he'd seen a diver's form. Not a body, just her form. He thrashed in the water, trying to avoid flaming debris, or worse, the floating flames from the pitch. He was forced to dive again before he had fully caught his breath. It was there in the cold water, he realized exactly how exhausted he was from the battle and how not being in his element, he risked pushing himself past endurance. Soon it was all he could do to keep moving, to keep afloat. With sudden clarity he understood he could die. And if he was having trouble finding Pearl, what were the chances he'd be found and revived in time? But it didn't matter. He'd save her or it would be the last thing he ventured.

Then Col saw Pearl, clear as day, her wild black tresses around a face drawn with worry. Behind her it was bright, but he was cold. Then Col felt tendrils binding him. Perhaps it was a dream. Perhaps he was dying already and a kelpie was dragging him to the deeps. Then he knew no more.

* * *

From the time Samath was separated from Navi when the Shari attacked he was kept quite busy. He reported to the hospital, where a couple of girls with serious dazzle blindness were being treated, while supplies were checked and organized. There was a concern the draughts would run out so they were counted again. And then he set to work with a couple of Dwen men from the woodweaver's mates who made long strips of thin wood that Samath sorted by length. These would be used for splints to stabilize broken bones. They shared their travel loaf with him; the strange mix of dried meat with nuts and berries was tasty and filling. But he missed bread and looked forward to retrieving his cached food from his berth later. Then the prefect made a business of reordering the tables, to the surgeon's irritation. It was a matter of who was to be immediately tended and who must wait. Samath understood the idea but was ignorant of the details of temple protocol.

So he set to cleaning with the men until another task was foisted on them: they were to cut up blankets and soak them in a barrel of water to be prepared for drawing heat from burns. Healers could also call the cold, but in a very small way, making coolness around a wound that needed it. It seemed prudent after the pitch-fire attack on the deck and the horrible scream of the wounded archer. For a long time they didn't know her fate until she was brought in, heroically rescued after falling overboard. She was laid on a wet blanket that was then chilled, while her limbs were wrapped to draw the heat from them. The worst was her feet and legs where she had stood. But every part of her had some wound from burning, face and shoulders much less, though most of her hair was gone.

A healer opened her mouth and poured a draught down her throat, with a touch of essence making her body swallow. There were many draughts: some for pain, some for sleep. Many sped healing and this seemed to be wisest. The faster she could be made whole, the more space to tend another.

"The trouble is burns heal best with an array," a male healer said.

"Well, we don't have one!" the prefect snapped. "Get two more anchors!"

An anchor was a healer who assisted by offering her, or his, essence. Samath wondered if there were enough souls in the makeshift temple. There might be a score? Perhaps a little more? But not all of them were adepts. Many, perhaps half, were novices. Maybe the magi would help if it came to it. Samath hadn't any doubts about their preparation until the officer died.

The sadness clung to him as he returned to work with the Dwen. It wasn't right for a soul to leave the Orb so soon. Still he couldn't hate the Shari for it. It would be as senseless as hating a wolf that had eaten a stray sheep. That was it's nature. The nature of humyn was to lash out without wisdom, led meekly by the boldest and loudest of their tribe. One might as well hate a fire-panicked herd for trampling crops. That was why Samath's grandama said management was so important. Humyn could have wisdom, but needed to be free of both want and sloth. Either allowed the venal among them to thrive. And grandama knew: it was doing charity works in Cambria that she'd trysted with an elfborn Dwen druid. She was surprised as any of the household it led to the birth of Samath's mother. Working with the wood calmed him, though his wood-essence was as passive as all the rest: just enough to feel, never enough to make magic.

They stopped making strips as the first wounded were brought in: burns, more arrow wounds, some struck by flying splinters of wood, broken bones and cuts from sword and axes. It seemed most of these were Cambari boldly engaging with minimal efforts at defense. What would Col say? Samath had never taken an interest in his Cambrian ancestry, in fact he didn't know for certain which tribe or nation his grandsire had come from. The Albini? The Picti? His family had strong Gold ancestry so it was nothing more than a curiosity one discussed at a fete. But from living in Tyreen he understood the general warrior culture that in past times was happy enough to die gloriously in battle as to win. The modern Cambrian claimed not to be as reckless; the evidence spoke against this.

The elf was there for a while, then she was called away. For some reason the prefect didn't like the cavalier. That was odd because Samath had thought Prefect Mathynwol was a bit excessive in her Sula pride. Maybe it was because the elf had sole Sula ancestry. This could be hard to reconcile for an aelg bigot: for if being Gold put Mathynwol above other elfborn backgrounds, surely she should subordinate herself to a shining Sula. But of course the bigot's entire concern was to dominate all others in her sphere and be subordinate to no one. That Lancer Farthal was not much impressed with Mathynwol's authority didn't ease relations.

So later, when the Farthal returned with a seriously injured young officer and Mathynwol unwisely sniped about the "pony" returning, Samath was eager to escape the cavalier's rage. In a stroke of luck he was sent away with a healing novice to prepare designated berths for serious cases.

Leaving the mess the sound of battle was deafening, yells and screams mixed with the constant clang of metal on metal, be it sword, shield, ax, mace, star, or lance. Now and then, near and far was an explosive retort of the Dragon and a fog of smoke and black powder hovered everywhere, not thick enough to obscure vision, but heavy enough to feel averse to breathing. Samath ran after the young woman to where the berths ended near the companion stair at the center of the quarterdeck. The berths were to be both opened and made ready for wounded who needed greater tending. The door to the starboard berth stood ajar as expected, its bunks and bedding waiting for the occupant's return.

"What will we do about the effects?" Samath asked.

"Never mind that!" the novice said. "They can be retrieved later. Go the larboard berth and see that it's ready for use!"

Samath first looked around, but there seemed to be no activity in the dimness. He ran across the deck, around the stairs to the berth, a spent arrow rattling down the steps as he passed. Reaching the door he grabbed the latch and pulled it open.

For a second Samath didn't understand why a Dwen woman in a long rough linen robe was sitting on the end of a cot while another tried to stop the bleeding from a deep scalp wound. Or why one's sword was curved, or the smell of musk that overwhelmed him.

The next second Samath knew he should slam the door shut and scream for help. But he wasn't quick enough. So the humyn, who had somehow found shelter to hide here, spied him and the one standing lunged.

Samath was quick but had no training. A strong meaty hand grabbed his arm but he twisted free, only to fall inside the room. By this time the wounded one had stood, a crude mace in its hand. Then they pulled away, Samath still huddled by the door that was slightly ajar.

Their thoughts bled and even without thought speech he understood they saw him as a prize. He lept to his feet, first startling them. Then they re-laxed and grinned. They could wait until the ship was taken. Then emerge with this concubine. Had they not fought enough?

Samath shivered with revulsion and tried to move to the door. Then the one who grabbed him rushed forward, using the weight of his body in the closed space to both slam the door shut and pin Samath to it. The maned mouth exhaled foul air and hands groped Samath. He swung to slap the creature like he wound any forward woman, but it had withdrawn suddenly, looking at the place Samath's robe covered his nethers with confusion.

The men started arguing in Shari, a language Samath had no knowledge of at all. He tried to think what Col would do. Suddenly he seized the latch, but now both humyn grabbed him, pulling him back insistently, throwing him over a bunk and to his utter mortification pulling his robe up to expose himself.

There was laughter and more arguing as Samath twisted away infuriated. "Don't touch me you filthy unwashed beast!" he yelled.

They laughed, without understanding, only taking joy he was discom-fited. Then the one with the weeping wound made a motion to loosen a trouser-like garment under its robes. The other humyn looked dubious. Was the thing going to urinate on him, Samath wondered in horror?

Samath tried to get to his feet, but the first humyn grabbed him, and tried to push him down on the lower bunk, tried to pull up his robe again. In the struggle contact with his flesh and essence made Samath understand in a way no magi training was needed:

They were shocked he was a man. He was so beautiful. What a waste, they should just kill him before he gave them away. But no, the other one said. They could use boys like this and some will pay. He would show how. Not as good as a woman, but when women are few …

Samath screamed long and sustained. It wasn't so much fear as outrage at the thought they would dare to force themselves on him. So piercing was the sound the humyn let go, the other trying to cover its ears, all thoughts of lust gone. Samath had no skill with a sword and besides it still hung in a sheath at its belt. But the mace had been dropped on the other lower bunk and any mace was basically a club. Samath snatched it up and started swinging wildly.

The human who had held him ducked the first blow, it landing into one of the bunk supports. But the second blow broke its hand, and then its arm. Then Samath swung around, leading with the mace, to hit the face of the humyn who would have violated him. He rained the mace down on its head again and again, careless of the blood splattering his robe, only knowing he would be safe when it did not move.

When it was over Samath stood shaking. A scream behind him made him spin towards the door in time to see the other humyn fall from a capstan bar crushing it's skull. He held the mace, forgotten, in a nerveless grip, breathing hard.

"Tresses!" the crewgirl swore. "Are ye alright, effa?"

Samath nodded while more women converged.

"How did they get down here?"

"Sweep the deck for more swine!"

"What happened?"

"Was almost killed by two humyn."

Samath didn't correct them as the mace was gently taken away and he was led back to the mess hall. The novice was upset the other berth would need cleaning now, but was otherwise kind.

"You need a tonic," she said leading him to a bench.

Voices argued around him. Irritation at sensitive Luns. Samath didn't care. He sat with a tonic shivering for a long time, not marking the activity around him.

Samath had never been raped, much less by a man. The idea of being violated by a man was alien and revolting. Not that rape wasn't revolting in itself. But there was something particularly vile about a man turning on another man, as if taking on a corrupted mother's role, he could advance himself at the expense of another of his sex. But he had once been at a Garden of Lun with too much drink. It was in Lethglean and well managed, so he was spotted and culled from the masked crowd before any soul could take advantage of him. Yet he remembered one woman's eyes behind a fox mask, hungry and waiting. He had been trying to walk away from her when he stumbled and sat hard on a bench. Too young and proud to ask for help, he watched as she made her way to him, hunting, stalking, waiting until she was sure before the final pounce.

And then the men of the temple who hosted the garden surrounded him, helping him stand, guiding him out of the grounds, into the temple proper, to ask him where he lived and the name of his estate. The fox woman had faded so fast he though nothing about it until the next morning when he was rested. Then he understood what had almost happened and shook the same way he shook now.

His mind compelled him to remember the men, their smell, how they assaulted him and finally the blood and the mace.

The shaking stopped. Samath finally understood. It was the lingering terror of not knowing he could defeat such a foe. Looking down at his hands he felt a growing pride. With it came a knowledge he didn't need to depend on a woman to protect him. Perhaps he would ask Col to teach him more. Or Navi. The idea amused him and he smiled.

"You seem recovered," a healer said.

Samath started. "Yes, yes I'm better."

"Then I must ask you to yield the bench for others."

"Oh! Of course!" Samath said leaping up.

Signal whistles sang. Samath didn't quite know what that meant, but most thought it signaled the battle was over. He was stiff and wondered how Col fared. With that thought, when put back to work to help organize and inventory, he maneuvered himself so that he could walk through the infirmary. Risking rebuke, he malingered as much as he could, taking his time walking through the wounded, all the while scanning faces until he was sure he hadn't seen Col. That was a relief. He was also pleased he hadn't seen Navi, but he had no doubt Navi could dance on pitch-fire if she wanted to.

"Put those here!" a crewboy barked, pointing to where the linens Sam held should go. "What are you doing weaving around like a drunk on Recognition Day?"

"I, um, was looking for…"

"Sul save us, your lover? She's alive or dead, and if dead she won't be for long. So focus on your duty, volunteer. You can be a love sick boy when we reach Gashora."

"Yes, effa," Samath said reflexively, feeling embarrassed.

"We need flasks from below. Ask the purser where to find them."

"Yes, effa."

"And I suppose when that is finished you can have leave to wash that robe. You've had a shock, but you handled yourself ably so you've no reason to malinger.

Samath understood but the rebuke still rankled. Whatever adventure he'd been hoping for, he'd be happy when he returned to land, away from the fleet's rules and discipline. Perhaps it would be different if they sailed for pleasure. Oh, it didn't matter. He looked forward to Navi's return. What tales they would have! And then it hit him: he was hungry! His figure be damned, he would gather a hearty repast, as soon as the galley had food available.

Samath sighed as he trotted through the ship fetching this or that, idly wondering how long he walked in one day doing his duties. Finally the solstone lamps were opened and he knew evening was coming. He was retrieving more towels when he saw the red warmth of the sun streaming through the open door of an upper deck berth. He went inside not intending to tarry too long. The room was one with a window on the larboard side he was sure (he still confused larboard and starboard now and then). It was a small room, but it had a large window and the light peeking through the clouds was the last before the sun disappeared. Sam put the towels down and opened the window, feeling the cool air. He hadn't been on the top deck since the morning. It was nice to see Sul even if the view was shared with battle scarred ships and floating wreckage. Then the sun disappeared and he smiled, thinking of dreams and the coming night.

Well, Samath at least hoped his coming night would be filled with more than dreams. Though where he and Navi could retire was uncertain. They would find someplace. He reached for the window to pull it shut. Then he heard an explosion so loud it seemed to knock him off his feet. There was a whistling sound and then he fell.

Or it felt like Samath fell. He was still standing, feeling shocked in his soul. Looking out the window he saw the black clouds of the smoldering wreckage of a ship. A Shari ship. He didn't understand. Suddenly everything seemed to be in a fog. The solcannons couldn't have struck it. There wasn't enough sunlight. It was time he got back to his rounds anyway. He reached out to shut the window, but it passed through his finger tips.

With dread Samath looked down to see himself lying on the floor, a splinter of wood having sliced his throat. His blood spread around his head like a halo; when the healers got to him, he'd be weak. It could take a long time to build blood if no one could share. Oh, he didn't want to share blood! It was a ghastly thought, the ghost of another's blood in one's veins, but it was better than death.

Death. So this was death. Samath looked around, the fog making sense now. It was spirit fog, thoughts unformed or in transition. He knew he should go to someone, but no one would be sleeping and it was very hard for even a strong spirit to alert the living if they were awake. Samath was only a mediocre dreamer. Perhaps he could go to the magi. Someone said they always had a dreamer on duty.

But then maybe he wouldn't be found in time and he would have wasted it when he should be visiting his mother or his sister in Dwenoshire. Except he didn't know where she lived. Could he just wish himself to her? Was that how it worked?

Samath sat down on the narrow cot like bed, slightly surprised he could do so. He supposed it was a dream bed. Or perhaps it was dead too... He should try to get the attention of a healer. Then he heard it: the sound of singing.

It was as if the best voices of all the choirs that had ever lived had joined with an orchestra of master musicians playing harps and flutes to make a sound that went through the soul, singing of loss, longing and joy all at once. Legends said any who set eyes on Laifmyr asleep in his bower would forever hear the singing of his soul. This was exactly what Samath always thought it should sound like; so many playhouses getting it wrong, only harping on the loss and longing, but forgetting the joy, the pure bliss of a burden left far behind and the anticipation of a world of wholeness where none truly died.

Samath tried to sigh, but he had no need to breathe now. He decided he would sit and wait in the company of voices from beyond the Door.

Then the Door opened in the air near him and he was bathed in a blinding light, the singing was stronger than ever. Samath knew he shouldn't step towards it, but the voices soothed every hurt and worry. It was like a symphony of cool water on an over hot day and he couldn't get enough of it. And so he walked to the Door …

Chapter 16

Shepherding Ghosts

Rosen couldn't stop the silly boy from diving into the water. He was too far away, and who would expect a landed Cambari to dive recklessly into water with flaming pitch-fire? A crewgirl near the wale looked at him askance and in horror, as if she might be blamed.

"The divers will find him!" Rosen called out with an assurance he didn't feel. "Go where you're needed!"

"Ai, captain!"

Rosen looking into the water below, the darkening shadows scattered with floating flames and wreckage. Even the launch was gone. Had it been a mistake to investigate the ship? Whistles sounded from the mast tops, a signal to the rest of the fleet to beware while he felt *The Tidebreaker* move away, to avoid the fire touching or, worse, adhering to the hull. The survivors of *The Oaken Blue* repeated the tale it was pitch-fire within that had led to that worthy's destruction. So Rosen was one less a boat; he dearly hoped those that had been on or near the Shari vessel would be retrieved alive.

It was out of Rosen's hands for the time being. He noted the Admiral's clerk Amralan was on her knees gathering her papers, the boy's satchel on the floor nearby.

"I have to mark it all down," he heard her mutter. "I was the Admiral's secratary you know."

Rosen trotted down the steps from the waist to just outside the mess cum hospital.

"Yes," Rosen said, hoping he sounded soothing. "Let me get you an escort to take you to my cabin. Perhaps you can help my clerk. Then you can take all the time you need."

A midship was collared for the task and Rosen watched them retreat aft, feeling forlorn. Ensign Amralan was in shock, clinging to her duty like a wicker to keep her sanity afloat, and the keen knife of grief at bay. Eventually she'd need a healer. Later he'd find her a berth, but for now he surrendered his refuge.

Yet what refuge remained? The Admiral, though not dead, was so far in sleep no one knew what would become of her body or soul. Rosen walked to the stern deck and watched the last of red Sul disappear below the horizon, the end of another day, the start of another night journey. Did Jonsay-manor walk with Sul? Perhaps visiting her family in Tyrum by dreams? At least all of their loved ones were safe, at least they had that comfort.

A racket drew Rosen's attention to a group of Dwen harassed by a raven. He looked up where the ship's ravens had resumed roosting in the tall masts. There was an aura of disapproval from them. He never quite understood how they managed themselves. Naval custom left them to it; the ways of Thyn were not the ways of elfyn. Rosen also knew there were a handful of "volunteer" ravens in the fleet, friends of crew who joined for curiosity or companionship. The only orders they followed were their heart. If Rosen could guess, this raven was upset its "elfling" was injured. He was glad when it calmed itself; Thyn could be banished from the fleet. There were laws that could banish Thyn from the Federation, but they were more a thing for the books than a practicality. It was nigh impossible to banish individual Thyn from civilization, much less a Thyn-raven. A flock mother would have to police the skies and Thyn never understood the need for organized lawful-ness. Thyn "law" consisted of harrying, the organized harassment and driving off of an unwanted individual. The policing of unwanted Thyn in the Federation defaulted to something similar: no effort or expense was made to track down individuals. But if they were caught, they were driven out of the area. Exceptions were made for Thyn who had turned murderous. They were treated no more harshly than murderous elfyn, except with less of a drive to capture them for trial.

Rosen watched as the raven was taken below with a body the Dwen car-ried. A series of croaks followed by flapping of wings told Rosen many ravens had taken flight, some wheeled around towards the water, eager for the free grisly meals that awaited. It would be dark soon. The whistle sounded for the dusk watch and Rosen bestirred himself. He had no time to brood. As well as checking the watch list, he had a task he'd put off: the ap-pointment of a new first lieutenant. While the decks were being cleaned with salt, sand and water, Rosen called a meeting of all the copilots in the pi-lot's mess.

Solstone lamps glimmered dully in the subdued mess, the light fading from the skylight above. It, along with the lamp gems, had received much less sun than usual. Lanthorns would have to be lit sooner, perhaps before midnight. The pilots were in the seats they usually took at meals. Rosen stood at the head of the table. Usually, as now, there was no chair, allowing one to address the table with ease. Three Gold women sat on along the starboard edge of the table, leaving the empty seat near the table's head empty. That had been Glethlyn's, though formally it was where the First Lieutenant sat. Lieutenant Tracan Bawn Ní Ban had a Gael grandmother of Blue ancestry who lived in Dunvan. She was Gold in every way except her eyes, a stormy silver gray that matched her temperament. The youngest of the pilots and only out of the Academy the last year, she was impetuous. Rosen's preference was that she be either in the Heart Chamber or drive during calm weather. The woman next to her, Lieutenant Loran Galyn, could have been Glethlyn's sister, except she was quiet and studious, though known to be an excellent card player. Lieutenant Borthyn Eladwol was the last of the former quartet, who sat holding her bicorn on the table. It had vines wrapped around the crown, an ornamentation not strictly within regulations. As a soul with not only Dwen ancestry but active wood-essence, she was allowed to wear a yastol instead of the bicorn. Instead she made a project of attempting to do both. The woodyvines shifted and curled under Eladwol's disconcerting yellow green eyes, the tendrils like a cat trying to find the most comfortable spot on a bed. Her right eyebrow was ornamented with a spiraling Tenes tattoo.

At the end of the table, back to the doors and opposite Rosen, sat Lieutenant Hocta Mert , a unique Dwen Brownie because in fact she had no Shari ancestry. Though Mert retained a thick Dwen accent, the humyn in her family's past were from Azhinazu. The Azhins were said to descend from the refugees of the Tahmery, when the culture fell millennia ago to wars between the Fars and Indus. Now the Azhins, a mahogany skinned clannish humyn, lived a simple life in the jungle or along the coast, trading freely with local Dwen, both communities working together to avoid the slave trading merchants from Sharitan. Mert didn't wear a yastol, and her hue was so dark it almost blended with her jet black hair. But her green eyes were striking, almost glowing with a blue shimmer. She preferred to work in the heart chamber; she claimed to often feel nauseous piloting from the cage. On the larboard side of the table, next to Mert, were Lieutenants Sithinas and Haulet. Sandryn was taking the first watch in the cage while a couple older ensigns tended the Heart Chamber. Sitting a space away from Haulet was Jarroth, looking forlorn. As a training pilot she was often invited as a courtesy. She stared at the seat Glethlyn would have taken, lost in her thoughts. She seemed even smaller without her usual spirits.

"Ensign, you're not required to be present," Rosen said.

"I'm not allowed, Sea Father?"

Rosen sighed. "As I said, you're not required. This is a pilot and command matter. But you can linger if you like."

"Thank you, captain," Jarroth murmured.

"Strike that!" Bawn said. "Doubt any of us will be here long. Here, lets get you some cheer."

Jarroth's cup was filled with lime grog, which Rosen hoped had less rum than this mess usually made off with.

"I'll try to keep this brief, as I hear dinner will be served within the hour."

"Another desperate attempt by the galley at chill fire cookery?" Eladwol ventured. A chill fire was charcoal burning in a hearth, usually in the morning, but sometimes in the eve, to drive damp out of a house.

"First the Dragon of Tamask and pitch-fire, now tureens of bland pea soup and stale bacon," Galyn added. "Not sure which of the three is deadlier."

"Are we certain they are not being Shari spies?" Mert asked. "Here to destroy morale?"

"Yes, your complaints about the galley fare has been noted," Rosen said testily. "I'll treat you all to a grand meal at The Sun Tree when we return to Tyrum. Assuming all you fine mothers don't die of starvation."

There was laughter; even Jarroth cracking a small smile. Before more witticisms were made, Rosen pressed on.

"With the passing of Glethlyn the post of first lieutenant has been vacant. It should not remain so any longer, so we may ..." Rosen trailed off as the door opened and Master Jasmenal entered the mess with Prefect Mathynwol.

"What is it?" Rosen asked, imagining either a navigation crisis or another death, possibly both.

"We became aware of the discussion over who is to be appointed first lieutenant," Jasmenal said. "And thought it prudent to be present." She didn't take a chair, instead perching on the corner of the table nearest Mert.

Rosen was annoyed. "I could see why you might think some metaphorical navigation was in order. But I don't think any soul present needs a healer."

"But, Sea Father, remember the food!" Bawn said.

Both Jasmenal and Mathynwol seemed impervious to the spirit of the lieutenants' laughter. Jasmenal's face remained calm, calculating with coldness, while Mathynwol stood arms crossed, slightly behind where Mert sat, like a mother returned from a long day to find her household in foolish disarray.

"We are just here to observe, captain," Jasmenal said smoothly, with politician's ease. But her eyes were those of a hunter.

"Suit yourselves," Rosen said.

"And besides, the Pony and our surgeon seem to be allied against my instruction," Mathynwol added.

It took Rosen a moment to think of whom the prefect could mean. "Lancer Farthal? What's she done now?" Rosen was starting to regret hosting the Marshal's agent.

"She came in with your secretary, shot through the back."

"What?" Rosen's heart raced, crowding out clear thought.

"Don't trouble yourself, Sea Father. It's a simple matter of keeping her asleep until she's tended. She's not dead."

"Then what was their concern?" Rosen demanded.

Mathynwol shrugged. "Bleeding within. But it's easily stopped, drained. And we've plenty of blood to share if it comes to that. The arrow can be cut out later."

"But they disagree," Rosen ventured.

"Surgeons always think they know best."

"I'm inclined to think they know best about surgery," Rosen said with reluctant diplomacy. "Please keep me informed. Now to the matter for which we are gathered. As you know a first lieutenant must be serving honorably, be respected by the crew, and have the skill and temperament to work with the crew master in managing the ship. She must also have the experience to be prepared to step in as acting captain if, fate forbid, I am incapacitated. Sithinas, Sandryn and Haulet are all capable on the first counts. However Sithinas is the most senior."

Jasmenal made the smallest sigh. For some reason it irritated Rosen.

"Pardon, Master Navigator, is there an objection?" Rosen demanded. "I was under the impression you'd forsaken your pilot's duties."

Jasmenal blinked slowly, her face emotionless. "If that is your will, captain, then it will be so."

"How supportive of you."

"Should she not be read?" Mathynwol asked.

Rosen was baffled. "Why?"

"Reading for truth is procedure for Admiralty advancement," Jasmenal said. "It's no different from the readings we have by lot every quarter of the year."

"Yes, Master, truth reading to manage duty in the hosts is something Admiralty or Command does in confirming a promotion. It is not necessary in an active theater at sea or in the field."

"Why not just speak plainly of your true concerns, prefect?" Sithinas said, green eyes glowering.

"Oh here we are again," Mert said, her tone that of one bedeviled by tediousness. "This Gold idea that the Forest is always after revenge, and too every Brownie harbors a love for the abandoned desert lands of her foremothers."

"It's not unreasonable to confirm those with Shari ancestry have no loyalty to the Sultan," Mathynwol said defensively.

"It is when that soul was birthed and bred in Tyrum!" Galyn said.

"See, you must do what I do," Mert said to Sithinas. "Tell the tale of your household to remind Golds, whose memories are not as long as trees. My grandama came –"

"– From a distant land of savannas, fleeing a forced marriage on a Meer maleen," Eladwol said.

234

"– To settle with her Meer consort near Azhinazu, where one of her daughters wed a Dwen," Galyn continued.

"And that daughter in turn birthed a girl who learned she had pilot talent –" Haulet added.

"I don't need a ridiculous Brownie ballad!" Mathynwol snapped.

"Ah, but you forget: I am not 'Brownie'. Our household is Azhin, Yorub and Meer," Mert said. "And we are being no more Shari spies than Sithinas." To Sithinas Mert added, "This is how you must speak to Golds with bad memories."

"Pity we never get to hear the whole tale," Bawn added.

Rosen said nothing for a moment, hoping the silence would speak for the moment. Mathynwol's face was ugly with dislike but she said nothing more. Mert leaned back in her seat with a thin smile, reveling quietly in the prefect's discomfiture.

"As instructive as that stratagem is, lieutenant," Rosen began, "no officer or crew is obligated to recite a litany of their ancestry for the idle interest of any asker, and certainly not a soul they do not answer to. As for truth reading, the minds of mothers and men are their own unless they are called to account for some offense. I have no reason to believe any of my officers have sympathies with the enemy that would conflict with their duty. And since you, prefect, know even less about the souls who serve in the cage, neither do you. That is the end of the matter.

"Lieutenant Copilot Dwool Sithinas is now *The Tidebreaker's* new first lieutenant. Glethlyn's cabin is yours if you will –"

"With respect, Sea Father, while I am grateful, I will stay as I'm berthed for now."

Rosen nodded. "As you wish. Any further questions?"

The pilots all chorused a subdued, "No, Sea Father". Mathynwol said nothing, glaring at no one in particular a moment before stalking out. She might have slammed the door behind her except at that moment a tureen and several platters were being carried to the table by several midships. Jasmenal slipped out without a word. It was the most subtle insolence; what had they both come for except to induce discord?

"Sea Father, will you take your meal here or in your cabin?" Midship Orenath was asking. She held a rather large covered tray.

"In my cabin, midship," Rosen said. "I'll eat it later. Congratulations, Sithinas. I regret this honor was more fraught than it needed to be. I'll leave you all to your dinner," he added, excusing himself.

Back on the quarterdeck, in the chill of coming night Rosen looked with trepidation towards the darkening shadows around *The Black Seal*, lanterns twinkling like fallen stars dancing around her decks. For better or worse, they were in the hands of the Jackal now. Tales of dark Athmod sprung unbidden to Rosen's mind, a particularly grim collection of myths. Athmod was the Mother-god of strategy and mischief, a trickster and shape shifter. Birthed from the ill considered trysting of Amer and Lun, while she was a great asset to her mother in the war, Athmod was ultimately only loyal to her base ambitions and desire to rule the Orb as a tyrant. She was decapitated by Jaro of the Dawn. Unlike Jaro, Sul's daughter sent to live a hero's life in the Orb before returning to her heavenly home, Athmod was a true immortal and could never die. Her living head was flung into the deeps of the Void where it lives still, screaming forever while her mind whispers the joys of malice to those foolish enough to listen.

This was all part of the myth, "The Rape of the House of Lun", where, after Athmod had her way with the princes of Lun, she birthed an army of new Bane demons that threatened the civilized world. The tale was considered tawdry by the most ardent defenders of the classics. Yet it best described the feeling of foreboding haunting Rosen now that Sea Mother Tamnath Tresmadore was at the helm of the fleet. Admiral Jonsaymanor Jansenwol was the fleet's mother and hero, both a comfort and an inspiration. Tresmadore, in contrast, was both warrior and bane. She would hunt for victory, but at what cost? Rosen was thankful the worst of it seemed over. Surely there would be little time for the Jackal to feast. Soon it would end and they would be in Gashora where the Admiralty would leash the Jackal.

A flapping made Rosen aware of an arriving raven. It dropped the folded missive in his hands and didn't wait for a reply. It needed no reward, there was plenty of carrion in the sea.

The missive was from *The Black Seal*: every captain was to get their affairs in order so that by dawn they'd be ready for the final action.

Rosen pocketed the missive and ascended the stairs to the stern deck. On his way to the cage he made a point to touch all the nodes. The veins were fine, as was the heart. A sharp sadness smote him as he thought of *The Oaken Blue's* heart lying in the deeps. It would be retrieved in time. For now his duty was to care for *The Tidebreaker's* heart, and it shined strong and true. He relieved Sandryn and stepped into the cage.

Merging his essence with the ship was more comforting than Rosen expected. He worried all the tiny hurts would overwhelm him, but though they could be felt, especially the fire damage to the mainmast, on the whole the ship had weathered the battle well. A little scraped, slightly concussed, but nothing a healing draught and some rest couldn't cure. He smiled to himself, imagining the ship as a wounded sailor, doughty of course, like Galen but more beautiful. Of course Galen didn't have anyone to blame but herself if she was going to shave her head and cover herself with barbaric tattoos...

"Can I interest you in a drink, Sea Father?"

Rosen opened his eyes to see Glenfar. "Sorry, magi, not in the cage."

"A pity," Glenfar said, breaking a bottle seal. "It's a gift of mead and I cannot promise any will be left when I'm done."

"You deserve it no doubt. Helping shepherd ghosts?"

"Not as many as we feared." Glenfar looked troubled. "For some it was harder that usual, herding them back. The death and despair and desperation. There's a couple of Cambari on *The Helix Bow* who could have been retrieved, but their spirits fled into the joys beyond the Door. That time wasted we lost others who were ready to return..." She raised the bottle. "Not all. This was a gift from one who snapped her neck as she fell into the water. It was an easy retrieval after hanging her. You should see the shock of the novice healers who've never seen the hanging."

Glenfar laughed as mothers did when tragedy and absurdity met. "Hanging" was a necessary precursor to revive the drowned. "No point in dragging a soul back if it can't breathe," Rosen had overheard a healer expound once. It was simple: the body was hung from the mast or rafters, or held upside down while their mouths were stretched open and lungs palpitated by essence or force until water washed out. It was an inelegant affair; after the body was laid out, followed by revival.

"What's it like, bringing back the dead?" Rosen asked. He'd always been curious but had never been friendly enough with a magi or healer to ask.

Glenfar considered. "It used to be a bit frightening. The singing from beyond the Door. If you've seen a loved one off, you know. It draws you the first time. We are warned, of course. Foolish girls think they can walk through the Door and come back. It seems so possible. But once your mind has crossed the threshold, the body dies. We lost a student when I was in school. She was driven to find her grand dame. Some questions of unfinished family business. Well, she has her answers, for all the good it's done anyone breathing ...

"In training we were never allowed to help Threshold Work if we were sad or grieving, or even ill. The Door doesn't open unless the soul is separated from the body, but once it is, it can take any soul that chooses to walk through it. And if a soul is stubborn... Oh we've had those. Usually children who don't understand they won't be able to return. But sometimes it's silly boys who think they're doomed to die of unrequited love. Then the door becomes a spirit gale and it takes the force of a magi adept to resist its pull. A strong wizard can force it shut, but I know I can't. I just pray when I'm helping retrieve them they want to come. Generally we hold onto them until their body is breathing again. Talking helps. Ask them about something they yearn for. Make a dream image. Anything to distract them from that singing. The experience has ruined all theatrical works on the subjects for me. No mortal musician can imitate the haunting beauty and terror of the music beyond the Door."

Rosen thought about how his winter-shepherd had run through the door. True, the singing was beautiful, but Rosen felt no compulsion to follow. "You said they are fleeing through to the Otherside?"

"They don't truly wish to die. But many of the crew have never seen real combat, where they knew they would have to kill. The unknown shock of the Dragon and the pitch-fire ... the constant fear of not knowing what danger will come next ... this wasn't an ordinary action. This was actual battle. The healers are calling it soul shock. It weakened the soul's anchors. The need for solace and the dread of returning to battle, makes the pull of the

Door stronger. This can be worse for those with strong essence. At least no Cambari on this ship were lost irretrievably."

"Except for those couple on *The Helix Bow*."

Glenfar shrugged. "They were confused more than in despair. Whatever we may say of our humyn granddams, they were anchored strongly to the Orb by a love of life."

Rosen smiled at the irony. It was the humyn part of elfborn that kept them tied to life. "So any new intelligence?"

Glenfar's brow furrowed. "There is a thing, but I may not speak of it until more is known. I can share that a Shari vessel has fled both the battle and their own fleet."

Rosen was surprised. "Truly?"

Glenfar nodded. "We're watching them, dreamers investigate to see if it's part of a greater strategy. Yet so far all evidence is the captain of that sole vessel has decided to flee, with a hope he and his crew will be assumed dead when the Sultan hears of the fleet's destruction."

"What is their bearing?"

"South, and a degree west."

"That's an ill course. If they pass Sea Home and seek mischief, the Meer will not be kind."

Glenfar shrugged. "They'll have plenty of time to correct for more hospitable lands. I suspect they're simply avoiding the Sharitan coast."

"Yes," Rosen mused. "That would make sense. There are many lanes they could take, through the Shoals, south of Azhinazu. They would do well to find a refuge past Nomclar and destroy their ship." Rosen felt a strange kinship for the fleeing Shari and a deep hope they would escape. Surely Tresmadore would agree they posed no threat. And if they succeeded, perhaps more Shari would flee the Sultan. The idea of the Sultan's subjects and slaves fleeing gave Rosen a pleasure he could indulge without shame. He knew it was a fantasy, but the thought gave him hope.

They fell silent, and Rosen embraced the simple joy of piloting. They were not moving so much as coasting in formation on the prevailing current, not keeping an exact position, but close enough to reengage the remains of the Shari when dawn came. And when dawn came it would be grim, the balance of the Shari's ledgers would be paid and there would be no escape.

News came of the crew sent to investigate the Shari ship. One humyn survivor was interrogated by Sithinas, a scrawny man who seemed to be grateful for simply being alive. His name was Ali and he was very keen that they know he tried to warn the crew. It had been a trap, a desperate gambit by those who believed the she-devils of the sea would eat their souls and it was better to die "as men", whatever that meant. Rosen assumed the meaning was close to "as a mother", but the concept sounded strange. Mothers had a native ambition and drive deriving from the need to provide and protect their children, not to mention the passion to make them in the first place. This was the basis of civilization. A man's native drive could best be described as finding the right mother to protect and provide for him, not that this undermined individual ambition. Rosen was aware he was not considered a normal boy, but that was separate from his deep passions. Even he felt the urge to find a woman to shelter him, if only for a night.

The Shari was placed with the other prisoners in a storage room, a handful of survivors from the battle. What would become of them had yet to be decided. They had surrendered, and so were entitled to the privileges of prisoners: simple healing and food. But Rosen wondered if the honor of the fleet would be tested soon. If too many had been lost irretrievably, there was little chance of forgiveness.

"I must retire," Glenfar said. "On the morrow," she added, walking away with a yawn.

"On the morrow," Rosen murmured.

He would sleep soon too, though where he wasn't certain. Perhaps the gallery bench of his cabin, depending on where the clerk had settled. The next couple of hours passed calmly, though not quietly. Work was still being done, ropes repaired, planks shored, and there was an attempt between the woodweaver Fadwen and the scribe Bethyn Olden to construct a ballista under the guidance of a magi. If they finished before dawn that would be its own accomplishment. Rosen imagined this was the calmness of a mother watching children at quiet play, their activity reassuring her of their health, their strength. Rosen know his crew's spirit, whatever had happened, was stronger than ever.

When the whistle for the watch ended and Rosen stepped off the dais, he felt a gust of wind, a determined breeze, that blew the remnants of smoke and haze around him. Above low ragged clouds were suddenly rent, revealing the bright stars. A collective sigh rose in the masts from the Dwen on watch and some mother started singing a sad ballad, a lament of the loss of the Mother Tree:

Roots still tell
of a time when we stood
drinking deep from the well
in the grove dreaming far
as the reach of the stars

Quiet the grove
all the children are gone
the last mother asleep
past the Door in the deep
beyond all the Orb's dreams

Songs we had
of a joy for the life
in the shelter we found
under leaves of the wood
while snow covered the ground

The dragon called
all the last of the clan
to gather their treasures
for the journey ahead
to homes dreamed yet unfound...

This part of the ballad was called "The Journey" and had over a hundred verses in Dwenifee; the entire lament, perhaps a thousand. In the Sula version usually only the first few score were sung. If Rosen stayed to listen, he'd still be standing at dawn. He owed it to himself and his crew to be fresh for duty on the morrow. He yearned for his cabin, even if he was forced to sleep on the deck. But the last grim duty of the day awaited, and it did no good to put it off: he must review the wounded.

The mess was full of healers at work, some at gruesome tasks like the re-pairing of bone. A Gold woman lay on a table in a deep sleep, while her nearly severed upper arm was only attached by a tendon and some flesh. Without a healer she would have lost it, for a limb had the same limits of death as the body. But she was lucky to have healers nearby and the wound was clean. A short small bar of grim steel was inserted into the marrow of the upper bone, while the rest of her arm was manipulated by two healers, so that the lower bone was joined over the rest of the grim steel bar. Then Talyn Alharn, a surgeon in a red taq, did the fine flaying of flesh around the wound with glass knives so that they could mark how well the tendons joined as the healers used essence to reknit the connections, the flesh grow-ing like Dwen manipulated plants or branches. Only when the gross mus-cles were attached to Alharn's satisfaction, was the skin closed up. Dwen assistants wrapped splints of wood scrap around legs and arms, ankles and elbows, even necks, to immobilize those who had such extreme surgery. These served better than the frames used in Ta Mel hospitals as they fitted the patient perfectly.

Those who lived were in good spirits, even the blind, knowing their con-dition was temporary. Rosen said little as he walked through the ward, though many women murmured their appreciation; there were no seriously wounded men.

Suddenly a raven called sharply, between a squawk and a croak, and something more painful. It was only by ducking Rosen escaped being scraped by the great black bird as it flew recklessly out of the hall.

"I apologize, Sea Father," a healer said. "It is not a fleet raven and he was distraught. She came too late." The healer gazed at the first of the irre-trievable Rosen laid sight on, a Dwen archer naked from the waist. An ar-row had pierced her side. She looked peaceful in death. "Her body was de-layed, trapped in the tops..."

Rosen nodded soundlessly. Ultimately it didn't matter why. She was dead, as dead as a humyn, but she shouldn't have died, not this young. He looked at the rest, a couple Gold lancers he would learn had fallen into the water after being wounded, also delaying their retrieval, and one Blue.

With Glethlyn that would be five total, five mothers he'd have to account for when they returned.

That made him remember Ensign Savalis.

"She's fine," Mathynwol said in bad humor. She'd reluctantly led Rosen to the table where Savalis rested, still asleep. Next to her sat the cavalier, looking drawn as she watched the ensign's face for signs of awareness. Rosen felt Lancer Farthal would rest easier once Savalis woke. It was a sentiment he was completely in sympathy with. "With our Pony at the vigil, I'm sure your clerk's soul knows how to stay on this side of the door."

"Kindly remember Farthal is the Marshal's agent," Rosen said. "Her title is 'lancer', not 'pony'."

"The point is your secretary will be fine. Excuse me while I tend to others, Sea Father."

Rosen sighed.

"Thank you," Farthal said. "But in truth I care not what an arrogant bigot says."

"That may be, but I do care what the Marshal's agent might report."

"Sadly, our worthy Tantilaan would be indifferent. I feel I could sleep if she would just open her eyes a moment."

"She wasn't treated by our prefect?" Rosen asked.

"No, she needed a surgeon. Quicker than your prefect wanted. It …" Farthal's voice cracked. "It wasn't a simple wound. There was a lot of cutting to free the arrow. More to heal the damage within." Farthal stared at her hands. Rosen saw they were covered with drying blood. "And she will need more blood. But that can wait until she wakes."

Farthal fell back into her silent vigil. Rosen rested one hand on the elf's shoulder in solidarity. If any bright soul could call Savalis home, Farthal could do it.

The surgeon, healer Alharn, was beckoning him. Rosen remembered the explosion, and realized there should be more wounded.

"Those that boarded the Shari ship…"

"Before it went up like a firework show on Samhain in Dunvan?"

"Yes."

"Not all are accounted for. Of those that are, we have a marine with a scorched back. You should let her sleep; the nature of her wounds means she must rest on her fronts. There is one more, but it is grim."

"Oh?" Rosen looked over the ward.

"We've put her in a cabin alone. It seemed prudent. She might drift if we don't keep an eye on her. Her wound is challenging. She will have to find a way to live, because we can do nothing more."

Rosen followed Alharn out of the mess with trepidation as they walked the length of the upper deck to a cabin at the end of a line of berths near the place the volunteers had waited for battle. What wound could be so tragic? Even horrific burns healed in time. Only the complete removal and destruction of a limb …

Then Rosen knew someone had been maimed in the explosion.

Rosen gazed on the woman sleeping peacefully on a cot, the lamp hanging from the ceiling giving her face a soft, gentle cast. In this light it took him a moment to recognize her as the brave but arrogant Hoethnav, the same volunteer that had snatched an arrow out of the air meant for him. For a moment he forgot her treatment of men and felt a kinship and sorrow, that, had she been awake she would not appreciate. Her long gold hair was in disarray, much of it singed, classical elfyn features almost a death mask if not for the rise and fall of her breath. A light blanket covered her and Rosen couldn't tell what she was missing. Both legs were clearly present.

"How is she wounded?" he asked.

Alharn pointed to Hoethnav's right side. There, almost hidden in shadow, Rosen could see the cover was flatter than it should be, going up all the way to just below her shoulder. He forced his mouth shut so he did not gasp at the horror of it.

"There was nothing we could do," Alharn said in a quiet voice. "A diver retrieved her lower arm, but it was scorched black. Completely cooked, as was the stump."

The endless horror of living maimed made Rosen ill. He could understand the desire of some shades to avoid returning to waking life. A wound like this could only be a cage of pain and doom, more so to a mother like Navi whose ego was invested in her physical virility.

"Does she know?" he asked.

"She has yet to wake, Sea Father. And when she does… Well, her su-lessence is strong. I'm inclined to keep the room shaded for sunlight until we know she's not a danger to the ship."

Rosen looked at Alharn. "She's not a magi. That I know of."

"Nonetheless, her rage may be an inferno. Remember the effect of the lancer's grief? Honestly, I'll be surprised if the bedding survives. The best we can do is have water nearby."

"Have a watch," Rosen said.

"We've made arrangements, Sea Father."

Rosen nodded, then retreated. His duty done he walked to his cabin. He was pleased Amralan had eschewed his bed, taking her sleep on the galley bench.

Rosen's table had been taken over by her books, ledgers and journals and open ink bottles, all crowding around his still-covered dinner, now cold. Rosen capped the bottles, stacked the papers, then set to eating dinner, an-other adventure of pea soup and sausage, the pan fried cake on the side. While he ate, he wondered how he would finish his own logs. He'd have to take them to the mess table without. There was a subtle rap on his door.

"Enter."

The door opened. It was Galen.

"Sea Father, we've a cabin for the clerk."

Rosen nodded wearily. "Let her be until the morrow," he said gesturing to where she snored quietly.

"Very well," Galen said. "We've another loss."

Rosen looked up. "How?"

"They carried up the body of a Gold boy. He was already stiff. It seems he was by a window when the ship exploded. A shard of wood sliced his throat and he was lying there, unmarked for a while."

Rosen sighed. Another soul gone, another life to account for.

"Galen?"

"Sea Father?"

"Would you stop that?"

"Just trying to keep an even keel, effa."

"It's not the ship commons. Formality is not necessary."

"Yes, Sea Fath –" Galen mouth twitched, suppressing a smirk. "Yes, effa."

"I suppose. Now tell me, how many were lost on the ship?"

"We're not sure," Galen replied. "We can't find a diver. Hoethnav… you've seen her?"

"Yes."

"Well, she was lucky. The Blue marine that was with her, her back was burned to the bone. They're not sure if she'll survive. The others, Striker Tellon Braz and strike captain Olesh Desmet…"

"Yes?" Rosen said, looking up sharply. Braz and Desmet had often made merry with Glethlyn and her quartet.

"Sorry. They didn't get above the scorpion ship's deck fast enough. There was nothing left of them. A magi has been called to contain one enraged shade. I don't know which of the two. It is the greatest irony, though bodiless, are having no trouble resisting the pull of the Door."

It was a nightmare from myth, shades that refused to be banished from the world because of a great wrong. What could healers or magi do? Force them through the door? It seemed too cruel.

It was too much. No wonder Glenfar was exhausted.

"Wake me before dawn," Rosen said. "And, Galen?"

"Yes, effa?"

"We have much to discuss. When duty allows."

Galen nodded solemnly, saying nothing more as she closed the door behind her.

Rosen forced himself to finish his logs. Then, removing only his boots and jacket, he lay down, suddenly more weary than he ever remembered. The day's events took their final account of his strength and found him wanting. He fell into the dreamless sleep of the exhausted.

Chapter 17

Adrift

Col dreamed walking on the ocean floor, through a forest of wavy blades of iris shaped leaves, greenish blue and well over thirty feet tall. Every step into soft sand puffed into cloudy dust and the light was filtered like dappled shade. It was cool, his soul was calm, and he hardly noticed he had no trouble breathing under water.

That was how Col knew it was a dream, for no elfyn could breathe water like a fish. He looked around; these water dreams usually included Pearl, whether because his feelings for her tacked his dreaming in tandem with hers or she, pursuing him, drew himself into her own dreams. He peered up at the light that must be the sun, an indistinct brightness flickering through the water surface. Then he heard Pearl's voice from a distance, "Get up!"

Col swam towards the light. He didn't so much swim as leap up with the intention of rising, continuing to drift upwards, through the leaves, until the water was thin and clear. But he couldn't rise further. The sun seemed just out of his grasp, the mirrored underside of the surface taunting him and suddenly he couldn't breathe anymore …

"Get up!" Pearl yelled, dragging Col over the lump of wood by the shoulders of his armored vest. Reflexively Col tried to grasp something, anything, and found a couple of breaks in the planks, though he feared he'd just given himself splinters.

Now Col took stock of where he was and it was grim. They clung to a chunk of hull, long and uneven with an odd, almost squared corner rising up at the edge. It was just large enough for them to hang on to. Pearl kneeled on the top, where she had more leverage. Now awake he scrambled up, dripping water and chilled. To his chagrin, the entire plank sank slightly.

"Maybe I should hang off again?" Col suggested as he shivered.

"No, you don't!" Pearl said sharply. She never spoke to him like that. He looked at her, wet hair tangled on her head, one side of her face smudged, perhaps with a small burn. Her blue eyes were wide and alert as she scanned the water. "I had you strapped by my tangles, but they broke. And of course the fin arrived at the same time."

Col felt a chill that had nothing to do with being soaked straight through with water. The weight of the metal plates didn't help matters. But perhaps it was fortunate if Pearl's suspected danger. He looked around. Though the sun did indeed shine, low, and presumably in the east, they were surrounded by thick mist so that nothing distinct was seen. If she was correct...

"Perhaps it was a dolphin," he offered.

"I sounded in their speech. It did not answer. And they rarely travel alone, dolphins."

Col nodded, trying to feel braver than he felt. He was a good swimmer close to shore. But out in the open sea he was just a liability. "Maybe you should just kill it."

"I will. If I have to. But it's large, love. As long as the barge I was with."

Col's feelings sank. Most sharks were small things. It was only out in the sea, over the deeps, that the great mothers dwelt.

Finally Pearl creeped forward on her knees, ready to reenter the water. Her belt was free of tangles; she only had hooks and a knife. Then Col noticed the other side of her face was scraped and raw.

"Your face!"

"It caught the explosion, a burning plank. I was dizzy a moment, but I didn't need rescuing, especially from a flukeless landed boy!" She shook her head in exasperation.

Col hugged his knees together. "This is my fault."

Suddenly Pearl kissed his cheek. She smiled. "I'm not mad at you, love, but for you. It was sweet you tried to rescue me. But all you've done is put us both in need of rescue. I had to swim with you a long way to avoid the pitch-fire. By then we were too far to be found by divers and it was night. I didn't dare leave you in stupor, even lashed with the tangles." Pearl looked around at the eerie wasteland of fog. "I suppose we drifted. Really, you should have known the divers could retrieve me even if I'd been concussed."

Col's mind filled with dark reproach. Because he did know, and yet at the time ... "I was certain you were lost to me."

"Not so certain or your wouldn't try to rescue me."

"Oh don't be so damned literal for once!"

Col blinked. Pearl was looking at him, slightly shocked. "Sorry. I, I felt I was going to lose you and then I'd never be able to... Damn everything!"

At times like this he'd excuse himself for a walk, or stride a short ways to vent energy before returning to converse calmly. But neither of them dared to move on the ruin of planks barely large enough to hold them. "Pearl, when the ship exploded, I felt you would be lost to me forever and that was my punishment for ... for letting Freya kiss me in the heat of battle."

Immediately Col felt both relief and despair. He had confessed, but they were going to die. He didn't look at Pearl, at his sea goddess that he had betrayed in a moment of weakness.

"She kissed you? Or did you kiss her?" Pearl asked.

"She kissed me, but I ... I was inflamed by it. Nothing else happened, there was no time for anything else to happen ..."

Gently Pearl placed an arm around him and pulled his head on her shoulder.

"Don't be a guilt-ridden fool. I know you love me. I think of other men. In dreams or waking. But I chose you." Pearl kissed the top of Col's head. "Let us make a pact: should either of our passions fade, we will break with the other honestly. Never to dwell on it until it turns to poison and hate."

"Yes, that seems fair and wise. You're not angry?"

Pearl let him go and shrugged. "I'm glad you told me. I'll watch Freya more closely because I am a woman. But no, I'm not angry. I must in fact have the very best taste in men; every mother wants mine!"

"Does that include the Remora?"

Pearl arched a brow. "Perhaps effa would like a swim."

Col laughed, then stopped suddenly, pointing to a spot twenty feet away. The fin reappeared now, turning suddenly to swim around them. A swell rocked their improvised raft. Pearl now had a knife in her hand, moving to a crouch on her feet scanning the water. Col drew a dagger but didn't dare shift from where he was for fear of capsizing.

"The matter of our wooing in life seems to be at an end," Col said watching the water. He'd seen the shadow of the beast. It wasn't a behemoth, but it was only himself and Pearl. "At least we have the sturdy benefit of a Dwen hull for our funeral bier. No one to light it, of course..."

"What did you say?" Pearl asked sharply.

"Well, we're all alone, so there's no one to put us properly to rest…"

"No, silly, the hull. You say it's Dwen shaped?"

"Well, yes, see how the fine fibers are interwoven? A Shari hull is just planking hammered together."

"All landed contraptions look the same," Pearl muttered, now feeling the hull for something. "I thought this was a piece of the Shari ship…"

Suddenly she slipped headfirst into the water.

"Pearl!"

It was useless. Now Col dared to move to his hands and knees, wondering what possessed her. The fin made a pass again, corralling them like wet sheep, then, to Col's dread, it made right for them.

The gray skinned beast, a simple shark grown large by hunger and time, raised herself out of the water, mouth open, hundreds of teeth forever growing around a deep, dark maw. Col didn't think, rolling to the side, then to his feet, making the entire plank tip. He instinctively shifted his balance, to his own horror leaping towards the beast. And then his body's experience and the need to meet the danger took over. Perhaps too, his desire redeem himself in the eyes of the woman he loved drove him to act swiftly, driving his dagger into one of the beast's eyes.

Col was no fool. He knew he could not wrestle the beast and to try would be his death. Instead he dived into the water, holding fast to his dagger for he might still need it. But the water turned red and the beast, surprised it could be stung so, swam away, its whipping tail cutting the back of Col's leg.

His sight underwater was not good, but nonetheless he saw Pearl floating in front of him, holding the hull, sounding something. It was a haunting sound that reminded him of Cambrian tales of the Selkies. He smiled and shook his head.

Pearl grasped his front and forced them both to surface. "What are you doing?"

"I stabbed it's eye!"

Pearl let him go. "Well done, my war-king. Now clamber up on top before it returns. I found a node of aqua. I think I can drive the water to propel us!"

"But where?" Col asked. "We can't see anything in this mist!"

"It's burning off," Pearl said. "Your eyes above water are better. Stand and see if you can find the fleet."

It was a good thing Pearl was in the water, Col thought. He also gave thanks to his foremothers for his natural grace. In moments he pulled himself out of the sea and stood on the planks, the water sloshing over his feet. Pearl was right, the mist was dispersing, ragged tatters drifting on the ocean breeze. Finally he saw the fleet, east and south of them, dark spots above the horizon, the occasional sunlance flashing.

"There," he said, before gingerly lowering himself. Something in the corner of his eye made him do a double take. It was his turn to shout:

"The shark returns!"

"Don't move!" Pearl ordered as she spun around in the water, then dived.

And this time, no matter how painful it was to wait, he obeyed. First there was nothing. Then the water swelled as the beast thrashed around in circles close to the surface. Col hung to edge of the planks with one hand hoping it wouldn't get bit off. Then the surface of the water erupted in sharp narrow streams, as if an invisible sword's edge was slicing up through the waves. Col was sure Pearl was using the slicing streams, water-essence like a cutting tool. The fin surfaced again and Col gripped his dagger, but the shark had had enough. The ocean was wide and there was plenty to eat that did not cut with metal barbs and water magic.

Pearl surfaced, throwing her hair back with a gasp. "Now, if nothing else wants to eat us, I think we can rejoin the fleet!" Pearl sank to her neck, feeling under the broken hull. "This was a piece of the launch. There's one small node of aqua…Ahhh!" she cried out.

Col said nothing. He knew touching the aqua brought on visions of the Cataclysm to those sensitive with water: the fire, pain and death of a world, that they nonetheless had to adapt to live in. He knew the stories, all the tales. Anyone who pretended to scholarship could discuss the Cataclysm, the defining event in elfyn culture and history, in detail. He was not sure he'd want to experience a vision of it.

"How any soul can pilot for hours, I'll never know!" Pearl said, looking grim. Slowly Col felt the hull moving. It was not as smooth as a boat, or even a curach. It bobbed quite a bit on the waves, but he could see they would make better time than if they tried to swim. Or rather if he tried to swim.

"Pearl," Col said. "Why not just swim back and get a barge for me? The fog has cleared, though I think I see flashes from the solcannons…"

"It's the battle again. I'm not leaving you," she said tersely.

"But isn't it tiring? I heard them explain how the heart and keel are connected. The aqua veins are made to help essence leverage."

"Are you going to bore me with mechanics while I'm saving our lives?"

"My life. I was stupid enough to jump in the water."

"I brought you," Pearl said, full of self reproach. "The diver's berth is underwater. It's only luck that Shari Dragon contraption didn't strike when we were sleeping."

"I begged to come, remember?"

Pearl didn't answer.

Slowly the small dark shapes resolved into the familiar forms of ships. Col heard a croak and from high above. A raven wheeled over them.

~troubled?~ it asked.

Col refrained from his first sarcastic response. Yes, he thought, hoping his poor thought speech was enough. Please send a barge.

~will fly,~ the raven replied and made its way back to the fleet.

It took over an hour for a launch to retrieved them.

"Come aboard, my fine sea rats!" the gold driver said, while a crewgirl helped Col step off the wreckage. Pearl had already pulled herself up and into the boat. "Mind, we'll have to stay clear while the good mothers of the fleet clean up these miscreants! Drifted far did you?"

Pearl nodded, uncharacteristically reserved.

"It wasn't bad," Col said, happy to sit down on the planks, a wool blanket wrapped around him. "Apart from the shark."

"Now that's a tale you'll be telling me in payment."

"It's a short tale."

"It's a short trip. Aren't you Cambari all poets? Even the men? Out with it lad, a lay of the Sea Rats and the Shark."

Pearl, recovering her spirits, laughed while Col told their tale, the ships looming ever closer. What would Samath say? For himself, Col was certain he'd had enough adventure for a decade.

Chapter 18

The Dragon's Final Breath

The dawn sun rose over a misty sea of thick fog, but all that mattered was the sun did shine and there was no cloud in sight. No time was spared: each captain rallied her ship, the crews able and active. Decks were stoned clean of remaining blood, archers returned to their tops and perches, and the marines and volunteers, after tending to the wholeness of weapon and body, stood at the ready, though it was not expected the volunteer fighters would see action this day. For every strike crew was in high spirits, gleeful at the return to life of their companion creatures, the solcannons. There was much blank strike and discharge for both practice and joy until they were told to save it for the battle. Lancer Farthal had even returned to serve amoung. Rosen wondered for a moment where volunteer Hoethnav was before re-membering she was in no state to fight.

There were also the ballista built during the night on a handful of ships, more or less ready to be tested.

On *The Tidebreaker*, the woodweaver Fadwen worked with Olden to ma-neuver the contraption on the far aft of the stern deck, between the turrets. It might not be the optimal placement for the oversized, torision crossbow, but it was the only place for it. If it was needed it would be the ship that must move to clear a target. Barrel bands had been reforged into the bow, scrap wood twisted and formed to make the stock and moving parts. There was even shot for it: random stones from the hold, usually dedicated to ballast, and Dwen crafted bolts of hardened wood.

Rosen had been assured by both Ardenweld and Jasmenal the materials used were scraps and hadn't compromised the ship. He remained dubious. Were they really carrying almost a barrel's worth of unneeded loose rock? In any case, a couple hours after dawn every crew member was ready to fin-ish the war neither the Tyreens nor the Federation had sought nor wanted, but were now responsible for ending.

At the third hour after dawn the Tyreen line floated at the ready, specks of the Shari fleet just visible on the horizon. The drums beat to quarters throughout the fleet, their minds and purposes as one. On the top decks, when all crew stood by their stations, the drums stopped, and the ship's adept, Ta Taren, stood on the forecastle facing the pilot's cage, as if addressing the captain and crew. Taren would be relaying the prelude all orders from their new Admiral Tresmadore on *The Black Seal,* as well as strategy agreed on from her council. Instead of conference with their new admiral by planks or ferry, the news had been communicated by sadol operation the night before, then written down on a leaf of paper that Taren read from, her voice amplified to be heard by all on the top decks:

"Missive relayed from The Fleet Admiral, Captain Tamnath Tresmadore, with complements, etc.

Firstly, our new Admiral expresses her commendation of the execution of your duties so far and her confidence you will continue to do so until our task is done.

Secondly, she gives word of Sea Mother Jonsaymanor's health. She lives but is lost in dreams. So regard her in your prayers until she returns to us.

Thirdly, today our final task begins. The Shari, displaying tardy wisdom, plan to rout. However, their actions have come at a dear cost, and their ships must be prevented from causing more mischief. Therefore we will engage the Shari one last time. Their ships are to be destroyed or crippled. Those who survive will be given the choice of surrender or annihilation.

Await *The Black Seal's* signal to engage. That is the end of our Admiral's missive.

In addition, our order must impart some grim news: we have discovered a small fleet heading to Tyrum."

Taren paused, waiting for the expected murmur of alarm to subside.

"This may not be as dire as it sounds. There can be no more than a handful of vessels. Their feeble cartography has given them the idea Tyrum is a tiny island, distant from the mainland. It is is possible they will be unable to find Tyrum. However, the Admiralty and patrol fleet have been warned. Tyrum should not be caught unawares. We are assured the ships guarding the harbor are more than equal to the task of defense.

Lastly, as some have heard, a Shari vessel has deserted. Even now it has sailed south out of sight, last seen with sails full, going as fast as the winds and currents can take it. Since they have abandoned their aggression, it has been decided to let them escape. We pray this gives pause when the next fool in Tamask thinks to wage war on the Federation. That is all."

A whistle rose from *The Tidebreaker*, joining other ships at about the same time: *The Black Seal* was being informed the missive had been announced. There was a pause, then *The Black Seal* whistled directives: advance on the tenth. Strike on your own time once in range. Do not let your vessel be surrounded. We stop only for signs of surrender or until all of the enemy have been destroyed.

As the last notes faded, the drums began. Rosen stepped in the cage, merging with *The Tidebreaker's* heart. Lieutenants Mert and Bawn stood nearby, ready to co-pilot.

Galen was leaning against the rail forward of the cage, by one of the deck solcannons; she had just finished her rounds checking crew readiness.

"Have we ensconced the Admiral's clerk in her new quarters?" Rosen asked.

"She's berthed and bottled with the Marshal's agent."

"Is that wise? That was Glethlyn's cabin."

"Better than taking a cabin for one of the seriously wounded. I've one of *The Oaken Blue's* woodweaver's mates berthing in my cabin. We'll all be like jarred onions before it's done."

"Fine," Rosen said, imagining what Farthal might write about the accommodations.

"A healer convinced Amralan a restful potion would do her good," Galen continued. "We're still missing two crew, Sharol and the Cambari boy."

"Col," Rosen said.

"Yes, probably."

Rosen frowned. "I thought he at least would be retrieved by a diver."

Galen shrugged. "He hasn't been found."

"Send a raven out."

"Yes, captain."

"So, is it true what is being said of Tresmadore?" Rosen asked.

"That her wanton locks are now in a naval braid?" Galen replied. "And she, now our most noble Admiral, wears her bicorn like a proper officer?"

Rosen glanced at Galen. "Well?"

"Ah, Sea Father, why would she not?" Galen said deadpan. "She who is our Admiral and must set an example."

Rosen shook his head. It must be true. The woman known as the Jackal must have done much soul searching to put aside her childish habits. Perhaps they would make it out of these trials without further scathing.

The drums had stopped and the Tyreen line was moving fast enough that froth churned at the ship's bows. As the minutes passed the scorpion ships grew larger. They were no longer in line, clustered together, perhaps from salvage and repair work. The most notable thing was many had reset their masts, though they had not rigged sail. Rosen knew they were sighted when the ships separated, rowing into a jagged line, many ships floating freely, apparently abandoned.

"Strike crew is to clear floating ships as a priority," Rosen called to the deck officer. He looked over the sea, as she relayed to order to the Strikemaster. He would not let *The Tidebreaker* risk the same fate as *The Oaken Blue*. He wouldn't even risk crew. They had decided captured ships were to be examined by magi before boarding.

One magi approached the cage. It was Glenfar, looking tired, pale eyes weary, her robes ripped and rumpled.

"Are you certain you should be about?" Rosen asked.

"I have no desire to sleep with strike discharge above me. I don't think anyone can rest until its finished."

Rosen, wondering about the news, asked, "Did you speak with the sadol in Tyrum?"

"No, but I was one of the circle. It sounds worrying, but put it out of your mind. The harbor fleet..."

"Yes, the harbor fleet will scorch them out of the water before they set foot on the shore. Sorry, that is not reassuring, whether from you or Taren. We were caught by rain clouds. Tyrum, much like coastal Cambria, has fickle weather. If they're surprised..."

"It's not as if they can win, Sea Father!"

"No, but they can cause as much damage as they have with the fleet. The dragons did not tell of this."

"Perhaps the flotilla hadn't separated yet."

Rosen sighed. "Yes, that must be it."

"Or the Thyngalu are in conspiracy with the Shari."

"Sul save us from clever magi! I should throw you overboard."

"Let me remind effa, magi do not answer to command, but serve the nation in an advisory capacity under the charter of the Sunqueens …"

"Then I'd advise your magi-majesty to keep her feeble jests to herself."

Glenfar took a broad step to the side. "Men in command have such a fragile temperaments," she murmured, eyes glittering with mischief.

"Careful, stargazer," Bawn put in. "Our Sea father can lash you to the bone with his tongue."

"Yet I am compelled to keep my dignity and not respond," Rosen said archly, like a laird of the queen's court. "And shouldn't you be hovering?"

Glenfar looked up to where half the magi were floating around the ship's tops, just above the archers.

"We're dividing our essence," she explained. "Any arrow or shot will be swept around the hull's aura. But some of us need to stay on the deck to anchor the operation."

"I see," Rosen said, not really understanding how it worked. As long as the magi did, he was satisfied.

Several more moments passed as the Tyreen line neared the Shari vessels, now rowing forward. They were still a threatening number, a couple to three score not counting the drifting ships. But the Tyreens would not underestimate the danger again. Sun glimmered on the swells between them, reflecting a promise of the heavenly ordained judgment at hand. There was a flash starboard, followed by a loud crack, a retort of timbers split. The next second a thunderous clap as a cloud of black smoke billowed between *The Fortunate*'s masts. Sea Mother Lenor had destroyed a ship trying to creep around the line.

A couple seconds later, they were only several furlongs away, the scorpion ship oars working in tandem driving the Shari closer to death, as if offering themselves as sacrifices.

Azar Sernalash called out: "Sea Father, we are within range!"

"Strike at will!" Rosen called out.

The bows lit up like noon. There was no need for Rosen to think of any clever strategy. They had the sun. With mother Sul victory was only a matter of cannon work. They aimed for the center of the enemy's bows, re-warded with several explosive retorts down the line. Scorpion ships that were not shattered apart sank suddenly, either bows first or to hover at the deck line, oardrivers on the lower deck drowning if they could not escape. There was no stop to allow the enemy mercy. While the line continued clearing the enemy with the fore solcannons, many ships used their aft and turret cannons to finish off survivors in the water behind them. *The Black Seal* and *The Exalted Unicorn* in particular were ruthless about leaving the sea bereft of life in their wake. Screams and cries of the injured and dying drifted across the water. After several more moments, with more strike, the water ahead was again covered with clouds of black smoke and steam. More importantly, the sea worthy scorpion ships had been reduced by half.

And the Tyreen fleet continued to advance. Maybe the Shari didn't know how many ships they'd lost in less than a quarter hour. In the next five min-utes they lost seven more. The Shari were not yet without teeth. Sharp re-torts of the Dragon being fired echoed, most shot falling into the water. Then there were sounds of shattering or crunching glass, the rib-fins of ships struck by Dragon shot or stones launched by ballista. The bows lit up again as the solcannons struck, steam rising from the decks as water was laid down.

Then it happened, an actual clever tactic: a Dragon roared just after the last strike. The ship was ahead, a puff of dark smoke ejected as a ball sailed directly at *The Tidebreaker*. Every soul in its path ducked or dodged, except for the magi who increased the essence of their operation to slow and deflect missiles. Rosen felt it as a force against his ears, pressure in the air shifting as the powers of the Orb were redirected with elfyn purpose. The bronze ball, a sister of the one that had killed Glethlyn, visibly slowed, dipping in the air as it sailed half spent over the observation walk, then to the forecas-tle. Ta Taren reached out to catch it, but this was a mistake. She bellowed in pain as in the next second her wrist snapped and she collapsed to the fore-castle deck.

Glenfar fled the stern deck, running between the strike crews to join the magi helping the ship's adept. Even half spent the shot from the Dragon was dangerous. Rosen remembered Taren warning Glenfar against doing such a thing. She must have thought the operation had made the shot tame enough.

Taren went below to the hospital, and was replaced by another magi. Glenfar returned, white eyes blazing, taking the stairs to the stern deck three at a time. The ship rocked under him as Rosen was about to ask how Taren was, but Glenfar had her own agenda. She seized the small deck solcannon and attempted to yank it free.

"That is being screwed tightly to the rail," Mert warned her. "And is heavier than it is looking…"

This only slowed Glenfar down a few moments. She looked at where the solcannon was attached. The next second metal clasps and screws flew apart with a clatter, allowing her to pull the small solcannon free.

"Mert is correct," Rosen said, not wanting to have the fifty plus pound weapon fall on a midship below. "They are heavy…"

"Not with Eurath to help carry it!" Glenfar said as she floated up through the masts to the amazement of the archers.

"What are you doing?" the magi replacing Taren yelled.

"The order was to strike at will!" Glenfar called in reply.

Rosen was glad it was out of his hands. What could he do?   He kept the ship steady as he watched Glenfar fly out over the nearest Shari vessels. He worried she would be hit by strike, or just as badly, make the crews hesitate. But they worked in tandem: the crews struck and if any survived she struck down at them. This seemed to go well enough until she was hovering too close to a ship as it was struck by a solcannon from *The Meer King*. Glenfar was thrown, but didn't fall, floating on the air until she could control herself again. But she lost hold of the solcannon and it fell into the sea.

A magi emerged from the decks below. Ta Taren had returned, her right hand and arm swathed in a splint of wood vinings, looking as if she was slowly turning into a tree.   In short order she bellowed so that all could hear:

"Ta Glenfar! Return to the ship instantly!"

Meanwhile the Shari had no more than thirty warships left.   Out powered and out maneuvered they pulled back to cluster together, making a rosette of ships facing out, surrounding their battered flag ship. This did not count the damaged ships that drifted, nor the three merchants floating less than a quarter of a mile away. New orders whistled: *The Meer King*, *The Fortunate* and *The Leviathan* were to clean up stray vessels and wrecks. There would be no petards left for the unwary. As those vessels broke out of line to seek out their new prey, *The Black Seal* ordered the rest of the fleet to cease strike and form a half ring around the remains of the Shari Fleet. They were to remain out of arrow range and wait for more orders. A retort echoed across the water as one of the ships being cleared exploded.

The Shari ships were overflowing with rescued crew, the vessels riding low in the water, with no hope of outrunning the Tyreen fleet, even if Payeen herself blew into their sails and the way was clear. Then the order came for the fleet to turn clockwise and show their broadsides to the enemy.

A city-ship, when driving forward, had two to four solcannons available to strike the enemy ahead. Tactics often used the first strike to clear the way, and the solcannons amidships to pick off stragglers. But with a stationary target, it was much more deadly to use broadside targeting, where seven to ten solcannons were available for a single volley of strike. And given the Shari propensity to move forward in attempts to board, this meant they were in a trap with the only escape back south. Rosen wondered why Tresmadore kept the south open, then remembered ringing an enemy with strike increased the chances of striking ones own forces.

The Black Seal edged forward. A whistle rang out: strike once on command.

What was Tresmadore planning? From the vantage of facing inside the arc, Rosen saw an officer take a step up to the forecastle of *The Black Seal* to stand among the magi. Ta Rau Jethar had returned. A black robed woman helped the officer hold a speaking horn and Shari words echoed out, being translated by ship's crew as before:

"Greetings again, Sea Host of Sharitan, brought here unwisely by the Sultan Darav Ormaz Damaski, pretending to authority as Shah of Tamask, Khan of the Indus and Suzerain of Azhinazu and the Cathanites, and styling himself as Sheikh of the faithful of Al-ahat. These are the foolish claims of a greedy, delusional ruler. As Ambassador of the Tyreen Navy, we warned of your aggressive course and gave you the chance to abjure it. You have faced the full wrath our host and know victory is impossible. By your actions you have doomed your ships to destruction. They are now ours to dispose of. Show wisdom and surrender now and we will spare your lives. Show more resistance and you will burn to death."

The last words faded. What would the Shari do? Rosen wondered. True they had lost most of their fleet. But still they faced ten ships less than their own. If their reason for not fleeing before was overwhelming numbers, that reason wasn't made much better when numerically they still out numbered the Tyreens. Rosen was certain the Sultan had never set eyes on a varsadmer and thus would not be impressed with excuses.

That could have been in the Shari admiral's mind. Or the captains of these ships decided for their own reasons. Whatever it was, three ships moved forward, not to maneuver to escape, but straight out of the ring, rowing fast. This time Rosen saw one of them, missing the fore tent, loading a Dragon.

The whistled order "strike" echoed.

The next second Rosen covered his eyes as the sun seemed fall among them in a blinding glare.

Moments after everyone ducked as at least twenty Shari vessels erupted in clouds of black smoke, the sound as deafening as a thunderstorm. Splinters of flaming wood rained down for several moments. Other ships sank in the water, scuttled by strike, and still others began to burn, as pitch-fire leaked around the water. The flames leaped higher, burning bright with smoky blackness, newly wounded screaming, dying and drowning as they waited.

The Black Seal whistled to hold their strike.

What was Tresmadore playing at, Rosen thought with feeling? He would rather kill them outright that watch them burn to death. Even yearning for vengeance, for Glethlyn's death to have meaning, he didn't have the heart to burn this many of the thinking and living alive. But he knew the Jackal did.

He suspected the only reason she didn't proceed was in honor to Jonsaymanor. The wailing slowly abated as the wounded died, the living desperately seeking refuge on any vessel not in flames.

"Perhaps you did not understand," a new deeper voice said in Shari.

Rosen was mildly surprised to see Tresmadore holding the horn. Rumor was true; she wore her bicorn and her dark hair no longer flowed free.

"You came to attack our nation without provocation," Tresmadore continued. "It is only because of Federation naval codes of chivalry that you are still alive. I will happily and with great joy annihilate every single Shari if your surrender is not immediate."

By grim luck the admiral of their flagship, the same soul who had mocked them, still lived. The flagship was as overcrowded as the rest. Its oars suddenly dropped limp in the water. Some thing shinny was being passed forward to the fore of the vessel. At the same time oars were dropped by all remaining ships afloat. At last the admiral, now scorched and grimy with soot, stepped forward with the horn. His voice echoed feebly across the water but was understood:

"There is nothing else to say. You see we are at your mercy. We surrender. Dispose of us as you will. Only I ask, for the sake of my men, that if you have merciful souls, do not think returning us to failure and shame is a mercy. Take us as prisoners or kill us outright. That is all."

The fleet did not relax yet. The Shari were allowed to rescue and put out their fires, but they were watched carefully. Rosen wondered if they figured they might escape while in captivity, or even have an opportunity to overpower their captors. If so Tresmadore was not taking chances.

The crew on the Shari warships, of which now only five remained whole, were first ordered to dispose of their arms and armor, to be thrown into the sea. Because of the custom of wearing cloth over mail, this required the entire remaining Shari survivors to almost strip naked. Helmets and shields were removed, but not required to be disposed of. Bows were to be unstrung and broken. After, they were allowed to dress again before the next labor: the pouring barrels of salts into the sea. It must have hurt any who had taken such pride in the Dragon, especially the false magi, now sitting as useless as any other aging humyn without rank. The Dragons themselves were also thrown into the water, save a couple to be returned to *The Black Seal* for examination. They waited over an hour while the Shari were defanged, ready to respond to any mischief. The magi were sent to hover over the decks, scanning minds for hidden suicidal stratagems, the idea being they would be able to escape relatively unscathed. The Shari seemed to huddle together before these black robed visages that glowed with visible gold auras. What dread magic had their admiral doomed them to? But there were no thoughts of sabotage, for the magi reported the enemy was completely subdued.

Only then did the Tyreen fleet breathe a collective sigh of relief. It was over. The Shari were defeated and Gashora was safe. All that remained was to dispose of the prisoners.

BOOK IV

Chapter 19

Dreams and Draughts

Navi stood near a blazing inferno. Where it was, whether on land or sea, she didn't know. She held up one hand, shading herself from the brilliant light, yet there was no heat. She thought nothing of this for a long while, and this was odd. With that awareness she woke to herself and she wondered where exactly she was.

There was mist everywhere, or perhaps it was fog. It was hard to tell if she walked by a shore, or waded in a shallow pool, or, improbably, walked on the wide blue-green sward of sea waves. If she could see that at least she'd know for certain she was dreaming. Shadows moved through the mist; women shouted, screamed, raged, then ran away. Every so often a haunting melody of horns and pipes drifted on the air, both enticing and repelling her, the hairs of her neck standing on end. Suddenly the inferno abated, flames flickering down, then swirling into a hole of blackness before disappearing. It wasn't exactly dark, but with the inferno gone everything seemed dim and lifeless. Then the mist parted and Navi saw a healer sitting on a stone bench nearby.

"Hello, Hoethnav Roelyn," the woman said. "I am Talyn Alharn, a surgeon on *The Tidebreaker*." She wore white robes, but they weren't accented in the usual green, but red with a red taq. Her aura was Sula strong or possibly a Gold with a more powerful aura than most. They appeared to be in a temple garden. That's when Navi knew she was indeed dreaming.

"Am I dying and you're trying to draw me back?" Navi asked, looking around for the Door.

"No, volunteer, you are alive. But you are wounded grievously. I thought it wise to discuss your condition before you wake."

Navi looked down at herself. She wore a short tunic of the kind she liked when taking exercise or holiday relaxation. It was sleeveless and she wore nothing else; even her feet were bare. Very carefully she sat down at the far end of the bench. The illusion of chill stone was quite realistic.

"So…what? Am I burned so horrifically no man will look at me? Surely the temple in Ta Mel can set me right, though it take years to do so."

"They would indeed, if that were the case, volunteer. However I regret to say your wound is unrecoverable."

Navi stared at the healer. Her face was a study of professional sympathy, carefully free of pity. "Why am I not awake for this discussion?" Navi demanded.

"Two reasons: the first is you are under a draught for your own rest. The second, when you comprehend your fate, the rage may be uncontrollable. You remember the incident with the grieving cavalier. I am hoping to mitigate a disaster."

"I see. You don't want me to burn the ship up."

"That is the idea."

Navi looked around. The mist was slowly clearing. It looked like they were sitting on the edge of a great fen. "Then tell me and be done with it."

The healer needlessly took a deep breath: "You have lost your sword arm. It was severed by the force of the exploding ship. Though we retrieved your hand and lower limb, it was burned to the point no living flesh remained to connect it. I am sorry."

Navi shivered, feeling the truth in the healer's words. It was said lying in dreams was impossible, but Navi suspected most people didn't attempt it because dreams were such malleable things. She looked down at her right arm, as whole as she remembered it. It felt strong, healthy and hale.

"How much do I have left?"

"Your shoulder and a few inches."

Navi shivered. "Thank you … for trying to save it."

She walked into the mist, eager to get away from the healer, from anyone. She tried not to think of what no arm meant for life. It didn't seem real. She was whole here. Music rose on the wind. She looked about, like a hound scenting the air. The Door. Why not? Perhaps it would open for her. She ran towards the sound, not knowing what she would do if she found it. She saw a light , as if streaming through a tunnel. But when she neared, it shut and the singing stopped.

Maybe she had to wake and feel the full horror of it for her soul to flee. But she dreaded waking. If she could avoid it wouldn't that be better? And then, what if this was all a bizarre dream?

At the thought the fen faded and she felt as if she was being dragged back through a long tunnel. Soon it was dark and she couldn't move. She was lying down, light covers over her, or most of her. There were no covers over her right arm.

Navi's eyes flew open. It was the light before dawn and she lay on a cot in a small room. One wall had the usual three bunks. There was the sharp smell of lant and vinegar. Someone was moving around in the gloom; Navi saw the outline of a woman. She felt like the same soul she'd met dreaming. The round cap on her head certainly looked red even in the dark blue watery gloom.

"Both awake now, for better or worse," Alharn said. "We'll be shadowed by the line and that's something. But I think it's wise to keep the window covered. You must excuse the berth. A couple of Shari managed to find their way to lair here. Their removal was quite messy."

Alharn looked down at Navi, her professional sympathy still in evidence. "Do you remember our conversation in dreaming?"

Navi looked up at the ceiling, fearful and trapped. She could still feel it, her arm. She flexed it. It was fine. And then she understood why the covers didn't touch it. Because it wasn't truly there. And the moment she dared to look would make the loss real. And then the rage would begin.

Navi closed her eyes, then opened them looking down her right side, though she didn't move her head.

As expected the light blanket fell across her but dipped at her side with no arm to fill it out. The shock made her want to scream. Had she not been told already, she knew she would have. What was the point in stoic bravery if one has already lost? There was no reward for grimly accepting a maimed life.

She closed her eyes again and tried to stop her suddenly fast breathing. She hadn't noticed she was hyperventilating. Alharn leaned towards her, trying to give her a draught. Navi shook her head, pulling away, easing her eyes open. "I want to know why I still feel it! I can move it, flex my hand... Why?"

Alharn shrugged. "It is a thing of the mind. It imagines you should have an arm and still believes that you do. Do you feel pain?"

"No." Navi flexed her arm again, raised it above her head and marveled that she saw nothing, because there was nothing to see.

"That is something, at least," Alharn was saying. "Sometimes the pain lingers. I know it's not much comfort, but your dream arm is as real as dreams. With training some can use it waking, in sensitive essence work."

"Feeling auras and glamors?" Navi barked. "I can be a cheap fortune teller, laying hands over a growing belly to tell if she'll birth a girl or boy…"

"It can be much more than that, but I'll let a magi explain if you're interested."

Navi sneered but said nothing. Having magi training, she knew the surgeon was right. It was in fact the part of the soul that dreamed that gave a wizard the leverage to do magic. But Navi wasn't interested in being sold a concern in a half life. Looking around, she asked, "Where am I?"

"In a berth prepared for the seriously injured."

"How thoughtful. I thank you though in honesty I feel no thanks and will happily return to my berth…"

Navi tried to rise and was overcome with dizziness. To her chagrin she groaned with a bone deep pain.

"That is ambitious of you, but you'll be berthing here for a couple days at least. You have been bruised virtually all over your body. And unless you had a bottom bunk, you will find it difficult to return to your berth. Your effects will be brought to here. There is no argument, though it might be good to try to walk around this eve, just to loosen your joints."

Navi nodded, feeling suddenly sleepy. And then the entire battle rushed back into her mind.

Still drowsy she asked, "Where is the Fish?"

"Who?"

"The marine I was dragging out when the ship…"

"Ah. She's been seriously burned. If she keeps away from the Door she may survive."

"Whole?"

"Yes. In time. She must be sent to a Temple."

"Damned Fish," Navi said nodding absently. "And the rest?"

"One diver is missing. The others with you on the boat... There is nothing left of them."

Navi froze in horror. Tellon Braz, Olesh Desmet, it didn't seem possible they were so utterly gone. Damn everything to the deeps, they were good women. With no body left, did their shades linger? Legends told of vengeful spirits when the body was not shriven properly. In Sula society the meeting before the Door was expected. Would they be able to do it? Or would they go through the Door leaving their households bereft?

It was too much. Sleep was pulling at Navi again. She tried to ask another question, but her mind had drifted. Then she was running across the fen while the fog rolled in.

Navi was fast and strong; even the muddy ground barely hindered her, though she felt the extra effort. She welcomed it, had always welcomed the test of physical prowess, whether against an opponent, herself, or simply the elements. Then the fog parted and the sun shone, and it was like flying; she felt she could run like the wind without rest, forever.

A figure appeared by the shore, rapidly coming into focus, a man standing with his back to her. He had gold hair, and of course she knew him. Though Navi wouldn't claim she wooed him, she did desire him, she did enjoy his company and the thought of losing his company made her anxious. Samath stood like marble, wearing a sleeveless long tunic with fine trim, something simple, expensive and elegant. Such a thing was common for a boy to covet from the merchants of Ta Meloshok, and therefore in dreams they would indulge themselves. He even had ribbons hanging off the shoulders. Navi slowed as she neared him, her bare feet light as she stopped in the wet sand. Samath had no foot prints to mark the direction of his arrival, and still he was strangely motionless. Navi had to circle to face him.

Navi was alarmed. "Samath?" she inquired, but he said nothing. His face was like a marble statue, more perfect and beautiful than in waking, and his eyes, like tawny-eyed stones, were blank, looking back at a shore far out of sight. Navi reached for him. At her touch, he crumbled into mist and drifted away.

Navi cursed. The boy chose an odd time to be coy. Navi had to resign herself to facing him first in waking, to him seeing her maimed. To him never wanting her touch again. She looked up into the bright sky over the endless beach and bellowed with rage.

Navi woke.

The light in the dim room was brighter and Navi was alone. She thought she heard flutes and drumming; did they Dance again? But no, it was another action, maybe another battle, this time without her. However Navi had an opportunity, though how long depended on the Shari. She wore nothing under the blanket, but saw her clothes and some effects on the bottom bunk across the cabin. Carefully she sat up, feeling unbalanced. Yet she was able to dress herself. Bracs were just a matter of balance; the shirt was the worst. She would forgo her tunic vest. Dressing wasn't so difficult, but moving reminded her of her living horror. She considered her boots, and decided to not bother with the buckles and laces. They wouldn't be needed and in fact Navi wouldn't need anything more if she was successful with her plan. The only thing that bothered her was walking around and being seen with a stump that was the remains of her arm. She still avoided looking at the wound. Stripping the blanket off her cot, she draped it over her shoulders like a mantel and set out for the hospital in the mess hall.

There was a moment of disorientation when Navi stepped out of the cabin door. Shouts and bright flashes from above told her the battle continued. She felt the ship pitch and list, not greatly, but enough to know the pilots weren't driving for the comfort of the crew. Between the brightness of the open hatches and the orders shouted from the cage, Navi figured she was on the upper deck and very close to her destination. At least all she needed to do was walk down the length of the deck, close to the cabin doors in case debris was blown or fell in. She made it to the hospital unscathed.

Now Navi's native conniving took over. An infirmary was a mobile temple with the blessing and bane of temple rules. Everyone had a task all managed by a prefect, a woman to be avoided. Healers were generally wiser than magi; both could read minds and truth, but a healer had an instinct for the gray areas that weren't deliberate lies so much as self-deception. In short, a healer might be able to guess a soul's full intentions before they themselves knew. Navi intended to avoid any keen mind by blending with what they expected to see.

The far recesses of the hall, where food was served in normal times, had returned to some semblance of their former arrangement, bare tables waiting to hold platters heavy with food come next meal. But the nearer part of the hall was still lined with benches on one side. On the tables in use for surgery, a couple of patients lay, thankfully deep in the dreamless sleep of a draught. The rest of the tables were lined against the far wall, covered with long cloths, so that even the heads of the figures were hidden. Navi shivered. There were not many, but she knew they were the dead, lost beyond the Door. Anyone who could be retrieved would appear to be sleeping.

Suddenly a woman cried out, sitting up on one table. Her wide-eyed stare was made all the more alarming by her visage, a matted tangle of blood-soaked red hair with Cambrian tattoos across her face. Two healers and a magi tended her; the healers gently pushed her back, while she murmured, "*Bhí mé san Oileáin, Oileáin na Availin! Tá siad ann in fhírinne! Canann siad …*"

"Yes, they are real and they do sing," a healer said, "But you will live a while yet in the world …"

Resentment filled Navi. The woman was whole so of course she should live. Navi faintly heard the healers confer among themselves:

"That is the last to retrieve."

"Well, then I will take my leave," the magi said.

"Thank you …"

Navi pulled the coverlet around her, feeling ill at ease. The ghost arm felt so real. Now that she had no passage or stairs to navigate, she expected to be steadier. Instead she felt unbalanced, stumbling when her feet should be firm. She stopped to feel her bearings. Then she understood. While she may feel her arm, because of its absence her balance was off.

Navi took a deep breath. It wouldn't do to rage and give herself away. Instead, under the guise of pouring water from a pitcher she eyed the place where healers stored the draughts, a chest on a table at the edge of the hall. It was unguarded. And why should it be? The draughts for sleep were not a thing for recreation, not like brandy or the herb of hunger and bliss. Mothers knew enough could kill a soul. At least that's what Navi understood. It would be a simple and elegant way to go through the Door. Taken before sleep, she'd be irretrievable by dawn. But there were too many healers working about at the moment. Navi's eye was drawn to the tables where a woman lay unconscious, while two healers attended, while a red-hatted surgeon was operating on the lower right arm. It was Alharn.

The limb was grotesquely open, pulled almost in two like a broken wooden doll. The meat glistening red was kept clean and living by the touch of the two healers, while Alharn inserted a small bar of black metal into the marrow of one side of the larger bone. The smaller bone was whole, perhaps cracked, but not cut in half. Navi noted the raggedness of the flesh under the arm and realized it had been almost completely severed except for the smaller bone. The skin on the back of her neck crawled. This is what they would have done with her, had enough of her arm survived to be reattached. She had heard of the operation: a small bar of grimsteel was set into the marrow, made in such a way its harsh essence kept the healed limb from withering, giving it a chance to become whole and strong again. But some were forever haunted by dark dreams, either of the Cataclysm or deep haunting fears of the soul. In rare cases, they became such a torment, the woman chose to have the limb severed forever. Navi watched as the bone was set, both halves joined by the bar of grimsteel, the line in the bone fading to almost nothing as the healers drove essence through the woman's body to knit the bone just enough to stay in place. Sudden forced healing was a shock. Only the minimum was done, then nature was given the rest of the task. But as they manipulated the flesh and muscle, cajoling it back into its proper place, Navi couldn't help thinking the healers would be doing the dragon's share of the task. The important thing was they were distracted. Slowly, Navi walked over to the table with the chest, neither looking right nor left, her senses keeping her alert. Still, she wasn't at her best. Tiredness filled her bones and her other senses were far less keen. She had just put her left hand into the chest, fingering three vials to retrieve, when a man's thin but strong hand landed firmly on hers.

"Those are to be distributed as needed," the man said. Navi was slightly surprised he wore the green robes of a healer.

"I, um, was looking for a draught," Navi said.

The man arched one brow dubiously as he eased the bottles out of her hand. Like most men working as mothers, he didn't smile. "And you needed three?"

Navi looked down at him blankly. She wasn't used to explaining herself to men. "I'm not a healer."

"No, you're not." The man closed the chest with a firm snap. "Your actions have the air of mischief. I know our surgeon herself is attending you. If you need a draught ask healer Alharn."

Navi glared at him. Did male healers get wooed much, she wondered. Were they as prim and unattainable as the Solshari of the poets? This one had a lean drawn look. But sometimes that was a hidden cache of passion. The berths of healers could be dens of debauchery for all she knew.

There was a horrible scream from above them, sounding quite close. It made Navi shiver. She knew someone had been seriously wounded. Part of her was grateful for the distraction; her actions would be less marked. But then the ship's adept staggered in, holding her right hand to her chest, reluctantly supported others of the Order.

Navi had a conflicted relationship with the Order. The fact was she could return anytime she wanted. They were not an exclusive society, using a bad study history as reason to bar future schooling. But a soul would be queried to see if they had matured in their commitment. It was only pride and temperament that kept Navi away. In addition to avoiding the shame of failure, Navi hadn't been ready to devote her time to the still meditations required to attune to the forces of the Orb. At the moment the more immediate concern was her schemes being exposed by a master adept.

But the ship's adept was quite distracted by her broken wrist. She refused a draught for pain.

"I've dampened it enough myself!" Ta Taren snapped. "Just set and wrap the thing!"

The ship's prefect was not known for her easy manner, but she and Ta Taren had a friendly acquaintance.

"Magi make the worst patients," Mathynwol said calmly as she held the wizard's wrist.

"And the Temple is full of condescending tits!"

"The words of a woman with her pain well in check. Wrap it tight," Mathynwol added to a Dwen crew. "Our wizard is certain to battle dragons next."

No sooner was the arm made rigid in a swath of wood tendrils than Ta Taren left.

The distraction gone, the male healer looked over to Navi, perhaps wondering why she lingered. Navi turned away. What did it matter? She would not be pitied by a man, and definitely not by a man whose profession was to pass out sympathy. Navi stumbled, aborting a curse. She noticed it was quiet. She thought she heard the sound of a speaking horn in the distance. Were they actually speaking with the savages again? One might as well reason with a brick. There was nothing for it now. She would save the draughts she begged for and that might be enough. About to leave, she noticed a low cot out of the way with a figure with flouted black hair lying face down.

Navi instinctively knew it was the marine she'd tried to save. Her torso was bare, the blue skin on her back covered with deep cuts and burns, looking raw even though the surface of the flesh had been healed. A faint sheen of ointment covered the massive wound; her head was turned aside on a small pillow. She seemed to be asleep, but stirred as Navi approached.

"You look like a flogged slave," Navi said.

The woman grunted then fished a handled mirror from underneath her cot so she could look at Navi with ease. Navi's reflection hovered greatly foreshortened under the woman's shoulder, their faces apparently side by side. Except for a sheen of sweat, the woman looked well enough.

"Oh you," she said. Her expression was hard to read, as was not uncommon for Blue or Meer.

"Is that an ancient Meer expression of gratitude?" Navi asked.

"Yes, I am forever in your debt and you can also marry my son, as soon as I birth one." She grinned, sharp teeth shining bright white in the shadow. In a serious tone she added, "I am grateful. I hear the rest were lost."

"Yes." Navi still found it hard to reconcile. "The diver with the buoys may return. She's too fast for the Keeper of the Door."

"You still haven't forgiven her for making a fool of you."

Navi grunted. "I floated, but she was masted and the worse for it. On that count, I'm more than even. Is it painful?"

"It's dull. That's what the draught does, make it dull and everything else dull as well. I feel wrapped in a thin shroud of glass and the light pains my eyes. But all that is preferable to feeling the full pain of the wound. And you? They said you were wounded badly."

Navi pulled up a stool and sat, keeping the blanket wrapped tight. "I'm well enough. My body feels like every inch was beaten. The blast I expect. I'm better now."

The woman nodded. "I felt that too. It was more painful at first than my burnt dorsal. They say because so much flesh is gone, there is less to feel. I heard the shrill boy rebuking someone; was that you?"

"Perhaps."

The marine smiled. "There are places to buy draughts in Gashora that will not question why."

Navi furrowed her brow. "But healers shops will ask and read ..."

"There are other shops, wandering merchants trading in many goods. Anything for a price. There is supposed to be a blessed abundance of them in the Shari quarter, but Sul knows how much is quackery. Better are the foreign merchants, Dwen if you can get them." Here her voice lowered so Navi had to lean in: "They often avoid scrutiny by omission for they aren't citizens of the Federation, are they?"

Navi made a noise. "You'd think bureaucrats would consider that gambit."

"Its not worth the trouble if the shop sells sundries and only has a small percentage of apothecary stock. As I understand it."

"I thank you. That will be helpful. Mind yourself, fati returns to scold us..."

"Excuse me, emha," the man said, glowering down at them. "I am pleased corporal Madrash Imer Yal has society. However it should be limited for she needs rest."

"And new draught?" Madrash said hopefully.

"It is time," the man confirmed. He unstoppered a bottle and put a reed straw in it so Madrash could drink as she lay.

"Then I bid you farewell, Hoethnav. Forgive my indisposition and go with my gratitude."

These were formal sentiments and Navi felt awkward she couldn't return them as gracefully. "You are welcome to my service."

Navi stood abruptly, brushing by the boy healer. Explaining her discomfort would have been difficult.

Partly she was embarrassed by Madrash's gratitude. Mostly she was resentful. Had Navi not grabbed the marine she might still have her arm. Why did she lie about the seriousness of her wounds? She wanted no pity. None at all. Every girl played and dreamed at being a hero. No child played at being maimed for life.

Navi looked at the woman whose arm had been reattached. She slept while a Dwen crewboy under a healer's direction used wood-essence to twist strips of lathing around the limb, like had been done with the magi. In that moment Navi felt a kinship to this woman, as if it was her arm that had been saved after all. By living whole, a part of Navi would live on with the woman, when Navi was gone. There was no question of her leaving, only of the time and method. Navi made her way back to the cabin.

Navi would visit her mother before she passed through the Door. That much she should do whatever words had passed between them in life. Wastrel came to mind, as did Navi's own rejoinder of hypocrite. She smiled. It didn't matter now. The path of all life led to the Door.

Near the cabin Navi passed an open door and glimpsed the sun shining over the sea. Her face relaxed, softening a moment, the light a balm on her scorched soul. Sul knew what was beyond the Door. Not even the Magi had ever made the journey back from true death. But they did know ancestors sang at the threshold. Navi had heard them. She dearly hoped that wasn't all they did in the Otherside, or she might be in for quite a tedious eternity.

Chapter 20

A Sacrifice for Victory

The top decks were the first to cheer, joined by a raucous chorus from the decks below as the word spread: the battle was over and they had won. Women hugged each other, and they were soon invaded by the volunteer mercenaries who rushed up to see for themselves.

Rosen gave the order to the deck officer to officially announce the ship could be at ease. Strikemaster Sernalash was already instructing the strikers to clean and tidy their stations: the stone was to be polished clear, water and sand for slaking refiled along with myriad tiny things that contributed to readiness. The archers climbed down and the mast crew removed additional perches and supports placed for the snipers. Fadwen and Olesh were quite disappointed their ballista wasn't needed, but the Cambari took an interest, suggesting a demonstration or wager. What wouldn't Cambari wager on?

The magi descended back to the ship, many clustering around Ta Taren who was in the foulest of moods. While many younger adepts marveled at her wood-woven splint, an older woman was heard clearly saying, "That was a very foolish thing to do, Ship's Adept."

"Yes! I am well aware!" Taren snapped, clearly enraged with herself for her painful miscalculation.

Ta Glenfar added, "I was told trying to catch a shot was unwise and something about how it could rip one's hand off."

"Yes!" Taren said, her voice resonant with a dangerous agreement. "You are quite correct, young adept. And do you know what else is unwise? Fluttering about like a sprite from a child's tale where even a blind archer could pick you off!"

"Oh, but you see, master, I was coordinating with our archers by thought —"

"I meant the Shari archers, you delirious, fey sparkwit!"

Many crew had edged away from the magi with a mixture of alarm and amusement. The older magi, Ta Hethlion, was calming the Ship's Adept. Rosen was relieved soon after that august body of wizards retreated to their berth. The only thing worse than one essence-enraged cavalier would be a group of essence-enraged magi.

In wondering where the cavalier might be, Rosen set eyes on her walking towards him. They exchanged a look; very slightly she nodded her head towards the pilot's mess then disappeared from sight below the deck. She looked haunted and spent. He turned the cage over to Lieutenant Bawn and made his way after her.

Rosen paused on the quarterdeck, noting the door of the secretary's cabin was ajar. Inside glass covered the cot, floor and desk, the metal strong box full of papers but unlocked, the lid having fallen back on the deck, some leaves sliding free. The clerk's log book was still open, a blot on the end of the last hurried lines, the pen placed in its holder. Savalis was nowhere to be seen. Rosen gathered the stray papers and, finding the lock, looped it through just to keep the box secure. He felt unsettled. Her presence was always in this room, so much so the cabin was permeated with a constant feeling of urgency, lest the clerk miss any activity on the ship that should be recorded. Now it felt empty.

"Pardon, Sea Father," a young voice said. "Savalis not returned yet?"

It was midship Roni Alhern, one of the few boys serving in the fleet. He was a Gold boy, barely past adolescence and he looked indistinguishable from his fellows, except perhaps being narrower overall. In his hands were a couple of short leaves, the missives of the ship's activities jotted on scrap paper to be recorded.

"No, midship." Rosen replied. "She has not returned yet. Leave them as you would."

The boy dropped the leaves into a basket for that purpose.

"Oh, and midship?"

"Yes, Sea Father?"

"You did well to think of drawing more water from the sea to slake the decks."

"Thank you, Sea Father! But twas only doing my duty!"

These modest words were belied by the glow around the boy's face, pleased as he should be his actions were noted.

"As you were," Rosen said. The midship saluted and disappeared.

Stepping out of the secretary's cabin, Rosen shut the door behind him, looking briefly across at the master's cabin. She'd just exited and walked to speak with the deck officer. The words were indistinct, but affable, the two women laughing as they parted, speaking easily as if raised as sisters. It was an awkward, unfriendly truce he shared with Jasmenal. His mind still lingered over her presence during the appointment of Sithinas as first lieutenant. As far as he knew, unlike the prefect, Jasmenal had no quarrel with Sithinas nor a hidden bigotry against the copilot's distant Shari ancestors. So what had been her goal? She'd defended the cage with the guards ruthlessly; for that Rosen was grateful. Then he was certain it wasn't him she defended, but the ship. Jasmenal would save the ship because she saw herself as its captain one day.

Rosen strode to the mess doors. It was a waste to linger on thoughts of Jasmenal plotting mutiny. She would do as she would, and he would meet it if it happened. Young voices echoed from within; when he opened the door he saw the cavalier surrounded by midships, Ensign Jarroth nearby, her right arm in a sling. The sun shined down from the skylight as if they were standing in a high mountain meadow.

"I like melon best!" one girl piped.

"Orange!" another countered.

"Apple!" added a third.

"They don't make ices in apple, sparkwit!"

"Do! I've had them in Dunvan!"

"Let's not all become sparkwits by calling each other sparkwit," Farthal said. She still smiled, but her voice had lowered slightly, a mother giving gentle correction. "Else there may be no ices for anyone."

"And that would be a true tragedy, so it would," Jarroth added, herself taking on a commanding tone, though she wasn't old enough to lower her voice effectively.

"Sea Father!" a midship cried on sighting Rosen. They all jumped like wet oats in a hot skillet, saluting smartly, Jarroth using her left hand.

Rosen saluted back. They seemed well enough though they looked ragged: deck shoes were scorched, jackets torn and frayed, a couple of girls without jackets all together. Two had bandages over one eye, along with the usual assortment of cuts, bruises and scrapes during an action. Many faces were still smudged with dirt and char.

"Ensign," Rosen said to Jarroth, "Please take these fine midships to be cleaned and dressed before returning them to duty."

"Ai, Sea Father!" Jarroth said, full body at attention. "Midships, with me!"

They ran out so full of enthusiasm, the door was left ajar. With a sigh, Rosen shut it.

"Thank you, lancer, for indulging our middies," Rosen said. "I'm only glad, among all the losses, it was not one of the girls."

Farthal's face was blank, her friendliness evaporating with the midships' exit. "There is a boy among the midships."

"He is, as the Gaels say, grand. Already back to ferrying clerk's missives."

"That is well."

Farthal fell silent and despite the bright interior of the mess, Rosen felt a chill.

"So, lancer, though we have won, there is much to do," Rosen continued. "If you could state your business with me?"

Farthal closed her eyes, an elfyn effigy standing in the sun, bright and beautiful as only the Shining Ones could be. She shook a moment, then her gold eyes opened, staring into Rosen's as if willing him to know, to save her from speaking the words. He knew before she spoke, a shiver that shook his entire body with dread: "Ensign Moradrin Savalis has passed beyond the Door."

Rosen didn't move. He could hear distant whistles, commands, women shouting. A laugh. Someone above on the stern deck explaining the workings of the ballista to any who would listen. Then it seemed the voices were just noise, audio illusions from a mind broken from being too long at sea.

"But the surgeon removed the arrow," Rosen said, his voice thin and pleading.

"She bled too much within," Farthal said. "It weakened her and her spirit was confused, refusing to anchor because she mistakenly thought she had logs to finish. A magi was called to assist but it was too late…"

"No," Rosen said. He yanked the door of his cabin open, the wide expanse of the sea facing him, expecting to see Savalis perched on the long bench below the gallery's windows. She would need to eat something. She never ate enough. Of course she wasn't there.

Rosen cast about, seeking his clerk in every corner. This had to be a cruel jest. Did Savalis not think he'd discipline her with watches because she was the ship's clerk? But no, he was wrong to be angry with Savalis. She was too dutiful for such a prank. Jasmenal put her up to it. Few ensigns felt secure enough to deny the requests from a master navigator. Masters could be disciplined, he could court martial her and have her replaced, though it was up to the Admiralty to uphold his ruling. That would teach Jasmenal to plot to remove him from command.

"Captain?" Farthal queried from the doorway. The elf sounded concerned.

Something inside Rosen collapsed. He looked back, surrounded by the trappings of his command, worth less than sea spray compared to the loss of a soul. His eyes prickled with waiting tears, his voice a bereft thing he didn't recognize as his own.

"But we won," he pleaded.

"This is why elfyn do not war with each other," Farthal said. "Victory always has a sacrifice, Amer will always take her due in blood. And every soul lost weakens our collective duty to the Orb. But this is no comfort. Savalis is gone with Glethlyn and many others. The only way is forward and in remembrance. I tried to give your clerk my own essence to help her live. I'm sorry it was not enough. I will leave you."

The elf was gone, though for how long Rosen didn't know. He stood by his desk, near the place Savalis herself often hovered, snacking on whatever was offered, always in good spirits, good company though restless to return to her duties lest some important action of the ship fail to be marked down. He felt numb. Then, in another bid at hope the idea came: he should visit the hospital. Perhaps Farthal was mistaken. Or Savalis had been found after all. They could all laugh about this dreadful mistake. Another mark against the Marshal's agent and her perpetual interference.

It was no use. Rosen didn't move because he knew this was not a trick, or jape, or prank, from the Marshal's agent or the master, however covetous she might be of his post. Savalis was dead, passed beyond the Door, and no soul who passed that way ever returned to life.

First the tears fell, then Rosen sobbed, weeping without restraint sitting on the gallery bench Savalis had used only a couple days before. Why it rent his soul more deeply than Glethlyn he didn't know. Perhaps it was his efforts to keep her from danger, if only through the sharing of victuals. Or that he knew she'd gone so suddenly she was unable to say her goodbyes even in dreams. Her household would not know she was gone until they arrived at Gashora and the list of those who passed was officially given to Command. He sobbed harder, knowing they would hear of the victory and think Savalis still alive to return for days after. They wouldn't even suspect her absence in dreams because Savalis barely gave herself time to sleep, much less travel in dreams. It was a cruel thing, all the crueler because they had won.

"Sea Father?" a voice said.

Rosen's head snapped up. It was an ensign, Sorani Aldweth, one of the few male officers serving on *The Tidebreaker*. He was Gold, not a pilot, serving well enough under the orlop deck officer. Unfortunately for Ensign Aldweth, he'd caught Rosen vulnerable in a way he never let a woman see on duty. His pride offended, his grief invaded, Rosen shouted, "Get out!"

Aldweth vanished and Rosen slammed the door shut. It hurt, a physical pain deep inside his gut, as if he was a mother who had miscarried, a piece of her heart ripped from her with the body of the stillborn babe. Like death before a soul's time, miscarriage was a rare thing. Both were mourned more than the stupid gross humyn who murdered Glethlyn and Savalis could understand. Gone. She was gone, and no amount of tears would bring her back.

Rosen had stopped weeping when someone knocked at the door. He said nothing, hoping they would go away. Perhaps Jasmenal would call for his removal from duty. The idea was madly amusing. Perhaps he should let her. The door opened. Only one soul dared to enter without the captain's reply.

He looked up at Galen, concern in her face. She slipped in and shut the door softly behind her. She offered a folded missive of the kind delivered by raven.

"Ensign Aldweth was to deliver this," she said.

Rosen took it but didn't open it immediately. Galen waited. He knew she was giving him time to compose himself.

"Shall I share news of how the fleet is disposing of the Shari?"

"Yes," Rosen whispered hoarsely. Anything to not have to speak.

"After disarming them, the ships were boarded and inspected for lingering salts or other mischief. A guard has been placed on four surviving warships, the Shari bound and are being counted. The rest of the ships have been destroyed."

Galen sat next to him, leaning her capstan bar against the bench.

"The logistics of carrying prisoners hasn't been planned for," she continued. "We'd generally assumed the Shari would flee. Many mothers think they should all be thrown to the sharks and rays, for haven't they done enough? Why should they benefit from our chivalry?"

"Naval code," Rosen said shakily.

"Ai. It's not for their benefit, but for our honor. The Admiral, that is Admiral Jansenwol, would want it this way."

"Ai."

"So we've a problem of how to house the sea fleas and sand druids. They're packed like jarred pickles on the scorpion ships, and won't survive like that til Gashora. There's a clever idea to house the prisoners in the merchants. See the irony? The plunderers become plunder."

Rosen nodded but didn't laugh.

"And you'll not be surprised the ravens are happy enough. Carrion aplenty floating on the sea. Sea Father?" Galen paused until Rosen looked at her. "You need to open that. It's from *The Black Seal*."

Nerveless fingers unfolded the paper.

> With complements, etc.
>
> Expect your person on the B.Seal within the hour as witness to questioning.
>
> Prepare crew to assist salvage. Other duties to be detailed.
>
> TT; A

Rosen was on his feet. "When was this delivered?" he asked hoarsely.

"When you terrorized an ensign, about a half hour ago?"

"I need a launch prepared," Rosen said, replacing his bicorn.

"It's waiting."

He looked down at Galen, her brow furrowed with concern.

"Do you want me to come?" she asked.

Rosen shook his head. "Prepare the crew to help with salvage. Tresmadore alludes to something else. I have to go."

"A moment." Galen went to his private toilet and retrieved a towel damp with water. "Your face," she said, handing it to him.

Rosen didn't argue, having no idea what how he appeared. He wiped it once, the coolness reminding him he was alive. "Elam," he said, then left for the launch.

The sun was still bright, though the air smelled of salt and sulfur. Rosen strode quickly across the quarterdeck, ignoring eyes or glances, imagining the conversation hushed as he passed. He was feeling the beginnings of shame in how he treated the ensign, another man with the same challenges as himself. They would both have to bear it; surely his brother in trials knew by now there was no time at sea to sit in solar rooms tittering apologies over flower infusions and teacakes. The launch was already hoisted and hovering over the larboard waist.

"Want to hop in before we lower it, Sea Father?" a crewgirl asked.

Rosen shook his head. "Thank you, I'll descend by ladder."

"Ai, captain!"

It was always better if there was time to maneuver a ship by the yards carrying as little as possible. As the long boat descended to the water, Rosen walked to where two crewgirls were looping and hooking a rope ladder. A couple moments latter the launch pilot called out she was ready and Rosen descended.

They first cleared the front of the Tyreen line before turning sharply to speed across the bows of many ships to *The Black Seal*. South of the line the four remaining scorpion ships rested, surrounded by boats and launches, their decks thick with prisoners. Beyond, the three merchant ships seemed closer, two Tyreen vessels near them, perhaps towing them. Another smaller ship, barely more than a large boat, had drifted far to the north, threatening to go behind the Tyreen line. It had to be the mysterious aqua yacht; one of the city-ships turned in pursuit.

"Aye, captain," the pilot said, "That'll be *The Fortunate* chasing the miscreant. Sea fleas will be lucky not to be struck out of the water."

"No," Rosen said under his breath. "We need that vessel. It's aqua driven. The magi will want to know how."

"Ah so, Sea Father? Then I'm hoping that fact has been shared with our worthy Sea Mother Lenor. Else they'll be naught left but a sea pyre!"

Rosen hoped that as well. Then they were pulling near *The Black Seal*, other launches lingering. Of course Rosen wasn't the only one summoned. A ladder was already hanging. In seconds Rosen climbed to the deck.

The Black Seal was a larger ship, and yet seemed smaller with the crowded top decks. Where the crew wasn't working on the decks, the shrouds, or the solcannons, souls clustered, many wrapped with blankets, both Albini tartans and the dull Tyreen blue service wool. These must be the refugees from *The Oaken Blue*. Grateful but bereft, they held tin cups of rum or tea and nibbled on whatever snacks were available.

"Sea Father Rosen," a green eyed Gold woman said in greeting. It took a moment for Rosen to recognize Lieutenant Braille Aledan, a deck officer. He remembered she was close to Tresmadore. "You are expected."

Rosen was sure what she meant was, "You're late." But Aledan didn't seem to be snipping, briskly motioning for him to follow. The ladder had been placed so he climbed to the fore of the waists amidships of the quarter-deck; it was close to the skid beams where one of *The Black Seal*'s launches still rested, the others presumably in use. They walked the length of the starboard waist, to just past the main mast, the place a captain held court to discipline crew. Instead of standing above, at the rail before the pilot's cage, Tresmadore sat on a chair just before the cage pillar. She held her sword in one hand, idly tapping it on the deck before her for emphasis and intimida-tion. Three Shari kneeled before her, hands bound at their backs, wearing little more than linen trousers and kaftan style shirts, all stained with dirt and blood. Their heads were bare, black untidy hair thick with sweat and grime. Around them was a loose assortment of crew and staff, including captains from *The Helix Bow* and *The Sunchaser*. Sleath and Roanteth nodded in greeting. Rosen forced himself to jerk his head in response. Two magi lurked behind Tresmadore's shoulders.

"Sea Father," Tresmadore said, looking up, tapping her sword, making the captives wince. "You're late. What kept you?"

Tresmadore was almost unrecognizable. Her hair had been tamed and with her bicorn she was the image of the perfect officer. The triskelion on her shoulder insignia had been replaced with the Tyreen sea queen. She did not look pleased, her gold eyes glimmering with a blue sheen, stormy water over the sun. Somewhere the Jackal still lurked, biding its time.

"Apologies, comm – Admiral," Rosen said. "I was delayed."

"Then you should have had time to bring your clerk." Indeed the other captains had an ensign or at least a midship with them.

"Again, apologies," Rosen said. "My clerk – " His voice caught. He'd be damned if he wept in front of Tresmadore.

But Tresmadore sat back, face suddenly blank. "No matter!" she said. "The notes shall be passed anon. We are almost finished. Be sure to have one appointed as soon as duty permits."

"Yes, Admiral," Rosen said.

"Now, where were we?" Tresmadore said rhetorically, swinging her sword up to rest on her shoulder. "For those of you not fluent in Shari, this," she pointed her sword at the middle of the three humyn, "is Komar Zan, the admiral of the Sultan's flag ship. He's had a shift in mood since he tried to kill Ta Rau Jethar a couple days back. These other two are the surviving captains of their ill thought out mission. They've confirmed there is a flotilla seeking Tyrum. If they're lucky, they'll be burnt out of the harbor like the rest of these sea fleas. They've been remarkably truthful. *The Fortunate* is about to collar the aqua yacht. Komar Zan claims the man driving that vessel had a vision of victory over the She Devils of the sea. Yes, that's what we're supposed to be. Even you, Captain Gathelyn. Clearly humyn Reverie is hardly reliable."

"Bear in mind, Sea Mother, this might not have been a true Reverie," one of the magi said. "He believed this Hadi had a vision, but as we know, the Sultan's so called magi are often court frauds."

"And if Hadi can Reverie, that means he is not humyn," the other magi put in.

Tresmadore frowned. "Elfborn?" she asked.

"He would have to be."

"But didn't you tell our Admiral he wasn't?" Tresmadore looked at one of the magi.

"I said he had not the knowledge. But it could have appeared so because he does not think of himself so."

Tresmadore barked several words of Shari at Komar Zan. They spoke for a short while.

"It says Hadi is the son of a respected Sheik, his mother the daughter of a prosperous farmer given as a concubine. This Hadi has an odd skin hue, dark and dusky with a strange blue hue. Ta Wolast?"

The magi behind Tresmadore's right looked intently. Komar Zan looked around in alarm, as if hearing something strange. His mind was being read; Zan would hear the other mind as noise like a breeze or the buzzing of insects. He started to pray, bowing and looking to the sky.

"Now he wishes the Ever Sky to deliver him from this terrible fate." Tresmadore sighed with boredom. "So?"

"His image of Hadi is very probably an aelg soul. His brows are sharply accented and the humyn Zan feels a soul force he cannot explain."

"Very curious, don't you agree, Sea Father?"

Rosen wondered why he was being singled out. "I'm sure we all have an interest, Admiral."

"But I'm putting you in charge of interrogating this Hadi, as soon as *The Fortunate* stops chasing him around the water."

"Me?" Rosen said slightly shocked.

Tresmadore stood and sheathed her sword.

"The fleet will be busy with salvage for as long as it takes. I'd rather not spare any more than one ship to the task of organizing and managing the prisoners. And the captain with those responsibilities might as well interrogate this Hadi. It will save time. The three merchants will have to be investigated and cleared as well – "

"With all due respect, admiral," Rosen said daring to break in, braving Tresmadore's quelling glare. "I'm not certain I'm suited. I don't even speak Shari well – "

"That will do, captain!" Tresmadore said. "I've made my decision. You've plenty of opportunity to show your initiative and you've plenty of crew who do speak this sand druid cant fluently. And take these three with you when you return to *The Tidebreaker*. I want the stink off my ship before supper. More orders will follow anon."

Rosen stood frozen, outrage almost getting the better of him. Tresmadore, not having heard his acknowledgement, started to turn her head, the Jackal searching for prey. He forced himself to say, "Ai, captain!"

Not "admiral", not "Sea Mother", but simply "captain", mimicking the same snub Jasmenal gave him daily. But Tresmadore smiled thinly, darkly amused, eyes glittering maliciously the sun.

"Pardon!" Rosen amended immediately. "Ai, Admiral!"

"Winds away, Sea Father! Winds away!" Tresmadore said with a laugh. "Just get this rubbish off my quarterdeck!"

Rosen was at a loss at how he was going to manage the three bound humyn. The ship's guards prodded them to follow, the other magi, Ta Athine of *The Oaken Blue*, explaining where they were going. After that they went willingly.

"They will not give you trouble, Sea Father," Athine said as the crowd dispersed. "The admiral, Komar Zan, in particular feels a care and responsibility for the welfare of his men. The other two will be compliant as long as they are not given a reason to think they can escape."

Rosen nodded and followed the guards herding the prisoners. They were being unbound to descend to the launch.

"I'd watch them, Sea Father," one woman said. "The magi knows best of course, but they are also angry and resentful. They might bolt in madness."

"I understand." Rosen followed them down into the boat.

The men sat in the stern uncertainly, eyeing him. Rosen gripped his sword, a reminder of his authority. The move was marked. A launch wasn't the best place to fight and he didn't feel comfortable sitting with them.

"I'll stand for the journey," he told the pilot.

"Ai, captain," she replied.

The water was choppy and Rosen had to concentrate to keep his balance. The prisoner's eyes never left him and he understood the guard's concern. Sure, under threat they were tame. But a part of them was always seeking an opening, ready to charge like a bull. Only when they had pulled alongside *The Tidebreaker* did he relax.

Rosen didn't ascend first. "Get the guard!" he called up. "We have prisoners! They are to be bound instantly when they step on deck!"

Hand still on his sword, he jerked his head to the rope ladder. Understanding, they climbed and were secured in custody without incident. Only then did Rosen ascend.

"*Cad a tarlú?*" Mordmhol demanded, looking at the new arrivals with disgust.

The lesser captains shrank away from her, wide-eyed and fearful; the admiral less so, but still wary. Komar Zan may have never seen such a large, strong woman, but he himself was not a small man.

"Put them with the rest, guard captain," Rosen said. "I'll explain later."

Rosen walked to the aft of the stern deck, wanting to clear his head. The wind was getting brisk as the day wore on. Galen joined him and he explained what Tresmadore tasked him with, laughing joylessly.

"Why us?"

"Come, my friend," Galen said, resigned. "It has to be someone. Maybe Tresmadore thinks a man would be a better keeper."

"Doubtless that's exactly what she's thinking. And she'll still have the use of our best divers for the salvage."

"Ah, it's not as if you'll be nursing them yourself."

"Won't I?"

"I don't think she's doing this to slight you," Galen added.

"Please convince me of this."

"She's just choosing larger ships for the salvage. They have larger holds."

"*The Fortunate* is the same rate as *The Tidebreaker*, and the overgrown sprite that drives her gets to chase down the mysterious aqua yacht."

"I see you will not be convinced."

"No, boatswain, not today."

"Then leave it to me," Galen said. "Organizing prisoners isn't different from organizing crew. We have regulations to guide us."

"Do we have food as well?"

"Supplies were retrieved before some ships were scuttled. The merchants should have more. I should get to work. We won't be able to move bodies before the morrow, but we should have a count and a plan. Oh, and I took the liberty of putting Amralan into the secretary's cabin. I'm sorry if it's a shock, but the purser's clerks aren't as experienced and it keeps her busy."

"Yes, of course," Rosen said.

"Look!" Galen pointed to a boat approaching from the north and west. "I think our lost volunteers have been found...

Rosen nodded then strode to his cabin and slammed the door. Thankfully it was empty; the clerk with her papers was gone. He was behind on his logs but it was the books of regulations that he was seeking.

Prisoners. He'd never had more than a couple, villains detained until transportation for trial. Now and then crew who found themselves brigged for one reason or another. This was different. Prisoners of war and the rules of honor were to be applied scrupulously. For a second Rosen wished the Shari had resisted to the end and had been annihilated, sparing him the inconvenience. He had no time to bemoan his fate as he needed to review codes he hadn't read since his naval exams. At least he had Galen, that was a blessing. Galen would organize the mess so it would be manageable. The matter of food troubled him. It would do no good for morale to win the battle and then have to explain to the crew they were on starvation rations for the cause of chivalry. It would be enough to make a mother mutiny.

That sobered him. In spite of his grief, in spite of his offense at being designated to the masculine task of fleet's keeper, he needed to avoid even jesting about mutiny. Morale was high, they had won, they had done their duty. Any trial now should be presented as a minor inconvenience until they reached Gashora. The women should dream of honors, fat purses, and eager men, not the ignoble task of shepherding the very humyn who killed their fellow mothers.

Rosen read intently, understanding the war wouldn't be over until they reached Gashora's harbor.

Chapter 21

The Thralled

Galen left the stern deck at a slower pace, trotting down the stair to the skid beams. The crew was about to raise the launch.

"Castan!" Galen shouted at a thin, tattooed crewgirl, one with obvious Cambrian ancestry and equally obvious webbed hands. "Leave it in the drink!"

"Emha?" Castan queried.

"It's a long tale," Galen said. "We're going to make a crèche for our Shari guests. I think we've enough time before sunset to investigate the merchants. Give a better idea of how to sort the lot tomorrow. How long do you think it'll take to collar some volunteers?"

"Could be quarter of an hour. Half might be best. Better, to be sure."

"An hour then. Will return anon."

Galen swung her arms in rapid wheels, ending in a stretch, feeling her breast bone crack. She was among the larger women in the fleet, those who wielded capstans like boy's batons. She hadn't set out at the beginning of her sea faring career to be the image of a mother sailor, but now she embraced the life. Yet there was something missing, a part of her that wanted the society of the family house, for was not that the basis of motherly civilization? Her estrangement from her own mother had driven her into a neurosis this need could be met by birthing a child. And that had nearly destroyed the friendship she held the most dear.

She took her time walking to the mess hall. In a strange way she had the Shari to thank for the precarious salvation of her friendship. Had she not nearly fallen … Well, there was time enough to think on it later. Rosen would be worrying about his dereliction of duty if he but missed a comma in the naval code. Galen had no such worry. The only reason her mother permitted her to play at sea in her youth was her studiousness; she was as knowledgeable about Federation legal code as she was about knots. This studiousness transferred easily to the academy, and though she had no talent or interest in piloting, she was aptly qualified to manage crew. If Rosen wasn't so stubborn, she'd happily quote him the exact parts of the code as they related to prisoners. She respected her friend's solicitousness, his desire to be treated as a mother's equal, his refusal to be pandered to, but she knew Rosen would give the management of prisoners over to her in the end. Thus her impatience for him to come to what was a foregone conclusion in her mind. No, the prisoners would be no problem. What troubled her was within.

Galen entered the hall, full of wounded, healers and volunteers. As the only light came through the open galley doors, lanthorns hung in abundance. Tables covered with the shrouded dead drew her eye. But they were numb to her, their passing not yet real, especially Savalis. She understood why Rosen felt that loss was a personal fault. His clerk had been young and keen, a bright soul who was gone. Galen would mourn her like the rest later. Now she felt the fear of the living, the fear she had succeeded in her ill-thought-out venture.

"Boatswain?" Prefect Mathynwol queried. She was washing her hands in a basin. "Hope you're not planning to foist that Pony on me again."

Mathynwol was a trying woman, tedious in her status consciousness. Galen knew, while they were both Gold, Galen's tattoos earned her the low class of a Cambrian savage in Mathynwol's books. Fortunately, a crew master equaled a ship's prefect, and so Galen could regard Mathynwol's opinion with contempt at no risk to Galen's own station.

"I'm here to speak with the surgeon," Galen said.

Mathynwol grunted, then called out, "Alharn? If you're finished stitching up reckless Cambari? Our boatswain needs tending."

The hint of a sneer flickered over Mathynwol's face before she moved to tend another midship. How did she know?

"Emha Sellisyn," the surgeon Alharn said as she walked over to Galen. "How may we serve you, Boatswain?"

"I need to speak about…"

Galen broke off. Her eyes, always quick to catch mischief, saw a tall figure exit, a woman wearing a blanket like a mantel. She followed the figure's path backwards to a table where a woman lay, her arm newly splinted with Dwen bound wood. "Was that volunteer Hoethnav?"

"Yes," a man's voice confirmed. A male healer had joined them. "I think she was trying to liberate an extra draught or two."

"Hmm," Galen said frowning. Theft was a serious issue. Though allowances were made for the wounded, women like Navi took allowances as rights.

"Boatswain?" Alharn said. The woman wore a red taq, and, like many of her profession, red accented robes "that hid the letting of blood".

"I need a word privately, surgeon," Galen finally said.

Alharn nodded, the man returning to his duties as they moved away from the benches of waiting wounded, and the tables bearing the dead. They were in the fore part of the mess, where food was served. A door beyond led to the beakhead deck and the compost canisters under the magi gallery. The lanthorn light was weakest here; soon they would be replaced with proper solstone lamps for the night.

"Take a stool," Alharn said, grabbing one for herself. Soon they sat facing each other. "Give me your right hand."

Galen blinked but did as she was told.

"Breath evenly, boatswain. Relax and be still."

"I haven't even asked you what I need."

"Oh come now. You think healers are cloistered from gossip? I'm only surprised you haven't sought us out earlier. Do you fear or anticipate it?" This last she said as she placed her right palm low on Galen's hard muscled stomach.

"I ...I don't know. It would be best it wasn't, but if it was?"

"It would be awkward, yes. You could be rid of it. No draught necessary this early. I could do it now. You wouldn't even notice. Though you would shed in the next month."

"Yet as awkward as it would be, I'd want it."

"I see," Alharn said. "Well, if that were the case, I'd suggest a long journey after our return to Tyrum to inject some, shall we say, doubt into the source of the begetting?" Suddenly Alharn pulled back her hand, releasing Galen. "But that will not be necessary. You are empty."

Galen sighed in relief. As much as she wanted a child, it would have been a further strain her friendship. Now they could move past it. Perhaps she would humble herself and take his suggestion of hiring a companion.

"Thank you."

"None needed. I am happy for you that this melodrama is at an end. Oh, no one judges you, not truly. I have unwisely had my way with our brother healer there." Alharn eyed the man. "Discreetly of course. Then my berth is unlikely to be invaded by middies with urgent messages. I will have to explain myself when we return."

Galen had sympathy for the surgeon. "Will you? Isn't this just the passions of war?"

"Yes," Alharn said. "But the passions of marriage do not survive dishonesty. Perhaps my consort will be forgiving. However history has shown he will retire to his mother's house for a year. That's about as long as he can stand to be in the same house as his fati."

"Surely a hero of war will be granted some leniency."

"We'll see. In any case, your worries are at an end."

Galen left the hospital feeling surprisingly light hearted, so much so she felt guilty. Mothers had died, others were maimed or lost, but she was elated she wasn't growing with a child begat by her best friend, a child that would have doomed them, or rather him, to the eternal wagging of tongues. With that done, Galen could organize the prisoners with a clear head.

She smiled to herself as the launch ferried her with the women Castan picked to the first of the merchant ships, happy to lose herself in this task, though Rosen worried it demeaned him and his crew. At least it would be easy; few times were citizens or subjects of the Federation permitted to lord themselves over humyn, exploiting their awe and fear of elfborn. Now that might be the most efficient path to management as long as all other matters of honor were upheld: humane feeding and berthing, free of exploitation or cruelty. They should be kept busy. Tasks like cleaning, cooking and managing their own toilet would keep them from mischief. As they said: working hands made a thoughtful mind.

As they neared one merchant ship, the high painted prows in red, black and gold speaking of dreams of elegance, the barge eased into its shadow. A grotesque beast, with a gilded gargoyle like face, served as a figurehead. It was strangely silent, oars slack, absent the industry of sailors giving the ship an empty, haunted aspect. The merchant galleys were much like the scorpion warships with respect to beam and freeboard. They were almost twice as long, with only one top row of oars, and two stout fixed masts shored up and bound at their base with smaller poles. The sails were slack, as if the action of raising had been interrupted. A more primitive people, say from the island tribes in the south sea lanes, or Azhins from the deep forests of Azhinazu, would be filled with awe at seeing these vessels. However Galen's eye could see the rudely joined planks, the flaking sun-scorched paint and the many small things that said, though this was a great effort of engineering for humyn, it was a mocking imitation of their betters. These vessels were also older than the scorpion warships, weary planks bearing scars of barnacle infestations at the waterline.

The worst was the smell. It took no imagination to fathom the source: a mix of ripe, unwashed bodies and crude ship hygiene. As the pilot maneuvered the launch close to the hull, the water next to them erupted as a diver surfaced.

"Al met and welcome!" the woman said, bobbing briefly before hopping out of the water to grab the sides of the boat, making it wobble slightly.

"Ai, you!" the pilot objected. "We didn't survive the Shari to be knocked in the drink!"

"Sorry!" the woman said. She still held onto the side, but let most of her weight fall into the water. "Just wanted to update our boatswain on what to expect."

"You're with *The Tidebreaker*?" Galen asked. The woman did look familiar. For a Blue she had Sula proportions, shoulders broad but not as meaty as a Meer, her muscles ropey, sharp and lean. Though her bosom was virtually absent, like Sharol she wore a hemp net tunic with knee length laced canvas trousers. Her flukes were modest, her hands having less webbing than Castan. Most notable was her skin, a compelling Blue with Meer shading that made it darken near the joints. She had extraordinary green eyes, the blue sheen merging completely with a Sula gold beneath. But what marked her in Galen's memory was the triskelion leaf tattoos on the sides of her partly shaved head.

"Alsauk Yal Horah at your service," she said with a smile. "But everyone calls me 'Frye'. I'm with the larboard divers. Last we met you were a might preoccupied."

"Ai, I was," Galen said. The sun seemed suddenly warmer, though it was late in the afternoon. "Well, you'd better tell us what you know."

"Observe yonder," Frye waved a couple furlongs away where two other merchants floated at odd angles. "They've all been checked by magi. No minds lingering over hidden salts on the lot. Those surrendered sprightly in *The Fortunate*'s wake, the captain and small guard throwing their weapons into the sea as ordered. *The Fortunate* has gone on after other prey. It was *The Meer King* who secured the other two merchants."

"And this one?" Galen asked.

"The tale is when ordered to surrender, the captain and his fellows defied our worthy Sea Mother Sharethan, waving his sword dramatically it's said. So he was struck dead by a lance. This caused the humyn on deck to panic and flee below. It's any soul's guess what the state is."

"Thank you, Alsauk."

"Frye," the diver corrected. Her eyes glimmered with mischief but no malice.

Sul help her, Galen thought. Did Sharol have a sister?

"Thank you, Frye," Galen said, lowering her voice to discourage unwarranted familiarity.

"You and the sea are welcome!" Frye said, smiling brazenly before releasing the boat and rolling gracefully backwards into the water.

Galen didn't know why she stared after Frye's wake, but something in her soul stirred.

"Boatswain?" the pilot queried.

"Right!" Galen said, shaking herself. "Get us as close as you can."

In short order a couple of crewgirls, with a combination of skill, agility and the forceful application of hooks and picks, scaled the hull to the deck where they were thrown up a folded rope ladder.

"Why didn't we bring any Dwen?" one opined.

"*Na bí buartha!*" the other said. "The splinters are probably free of cobra venom!"

"Hurry up!" Galen bellowed. "Sul won't tarry for us!"

A couple moments later the ladder snaked down, the wooden slats clattering against the hull, then hung swaying over them.

"Sorry, boatswain," one of the crewgirls called. "The hull bows out much like our own!"

Galen grunted. She thought little of the climb, spending much of her time being half suspended in some way or another over a deck, making her comfortable with the flexibility of laddered ropes. No, she was more concerned for the anchoring, that the vessel wasn't rotten in a way that the entire thing would give way. Luckily the wood was sound enough. She pulled herself up, followed by the rest of the boat crew.

In addition to the two crew girls there were four ship's guards. Galen decided after the losses on the sabotaged Shari ship, to only risk proper crew and those contracted with the navy formally. The guards all had Cambrian ancestry to some degree. The guards attracted such women, gallowglasses for the Federation who yearned for adventure, but had no interest in the hand-to-mouth mercenary life.

There was a strange cooing noise as they explored the deck. The dark worn wood was not much wider than the scorpion warship. There were no side castles, but both stern and bows were built in a way to suggest cabins and berthing. Like the warships, oar benches lined the sides of the hull, their space and proportions suggesting more than one man at an oar. No bodies lingered, and while the smell was not pleasing, there was no scent of death. Only when she climbed up a stair to the top of the fore platform did Galen see the body, the captain lying flat on his back, sword still in hand, empty eyes staring at the sky. Half his face was burnt to ash, a charred hole through his neck and upper lung, the precise targeting of a sunlance at close range.

Galen looked down at the rest of the group. A guard was looking into something like a small tent that sat aft on the starboard, towards the middle line of the ship just clear of the oar benches. Galen felt anxious. The Dragon of Tamask had lurked under shelters at the bows of the warships and now every shelter seemed suspect. The guard pulled her head back. "Looks like a primitive galley!" she called.

"That explains these chickens!" another said.

Sure enough, next to the galley was a pen of sorts. Clearly there had been other animals but all that was left were two birds. Galen made a note to return them to *The Tidebreaker*. Down the center were hatches and the expected stairs to the below decks.

"Should we go below?" one guard asked.

Galen shook her head. "I want to know why the doors are closed fore and aft. You two," here she selected two guards. "Stand outside that aft door and watch the hatches. The rest, with me."

Galen had her capstan bar in hand. The guards drew their swords, the two crewgirls hefted maces, diamond-headed exotic rods scavenged from the battle. Sul shone redly, her rays bent to blood by the smoke and late hour as they approached the door of the bow chamber, ornamented with snakes and peacocks. Galen lightly tapped the door. There was no reply, but their keen ears heard the intake of breath, fearful thoughts hovering in a haze just beyond. Galen nodded once, then kicked the door in.

It flew apart in splinters, the panels hitting a couple of the human huddling within. They cried out but not for Ala-hat as expected. Many looked Shari, but their clothes marked them as Cathans or closely affiliated with that seafaring culture. The Cathan trouser was of a different cut, less flowing, closer to the Federation sea breeches, and they preferred a variety of felted and cloth hats to turbans. One man stumbled forward blinking, hands open in surrender.

"No burn!" he said in broken Hiltekash.

"Do you speak Shari?" Galen asked in the Fars dialect.

The humyn spat. "Yes, we speak the cursed tongue of the tyrant!"

"Why are you here if you think the Sultan a tyrant?" Galen asked. She had a notion but wanted to feel the truth of his words.

The humyn laughed without mirth. "My brother, you have fought and defeated the Sultan's creatures and you need to ask this? Those who refuse will be thralled like the wretches below. Better to serve as his sailors freely and have some compensation. But I say to you, my brother, vow to treat us honorably and we surrender into your hands. Only do not send us back to Tamask. We want no more of the Sultan's war with the Vardashi and yearn only for our home and our wives."

Galen was pleased to feel no false words. Regulation required a complete interrogation by a magi, but for now she felt they could be trusted to manage themselves.

"Tell me of the wretches below."

"Well, my brother, the Sultan following the wisdom of the arts of war, fills his warships with brave warriors at the oar. But for his vessels of trade, he is stingy, preferring those he does not need to pay with pension or honors, better yet those indentured or enslaved. The men below are such. Beware! With them are the captain's men who may be a trouble to you."

"And why have they left you alone?" Galen asked.

The humyn grinned. "Without us to sail the ship, they are going nowhere. We shut them out." He glanced ruefully at the broken door. "They had some idea to outrun your fleet. But we have eyes, my brother, and knew this was not possible."

One of the guards laughed. "My Shari isn't good, but is he calling you brother?"

Galen waved at her. "Trust me, leaving humyn to their assumptions will make this easier." In Shari she asked, "Is the captain's cabin occupied?"

"Not by the captain!" The humyn laughed collectively at this. "If any are within, perhaps one of the women."

"Women?" Galen queried, keeping her temper in check. She had no illusions about the status of Shari mothers. Though this humyn was an ally against the Sultan, it did not preclude him having Shari attitudes. Often the oppressor infected their victims with their moral poison.

"Yes, brother, some captains drag their whores to sea with them, thinking this is a pleasure scow. They say some are thralled or captured or concubines. I do not know. Sometimes they are shared, but our captain was jealous and kept them for himself and his lieutenants."

"Very well, thank you –"

"I am Hanno," the humyn said. He grabbed the shoulder of a younger humyn, one of whom had been hit by the door. One eye was red and soon to be black. "This is my younger brother, Himli." Himli smiled weakly. "Remember that we help. We want no war with Vardashi."

"That's good," Galen said. "I am Galen, the crew master of *The Tidebreaker*. That is a ship. Stay here under guard while we investigate below."

The guards, who had been standing outside the captain's cabin, chanced the door. They shook their heads.

"Nothing and no one!" one called.

"Come up here and watch our friends," Galen said. "They're just sailors and don't want trouble. So far I believe them but regulations require a watch before they're interrogated. The rest of you, let's go below."

301

There were two hatches with stairs. After conferring with Hanno about the layout below, Galen chose the foremost one, thinking it less likely she or the other women would get trapped without an easy retreat. The stairs were barely more than crude ladders, leading into a hold filled with provisions, mostly barrels of drinking water. The light was dim and shallow breathing echoed in the stuffy air, the scent of unwashed humyn almost overwhelming. They had all descended when a voice shouted, "*Qif!*"

It meant "halt" in one of the Shari dialects. Galen's eyes, sensitive to light as any Gold, saw the outlines of a figure, probably armored, with a turban-wrapped helmet, light glimmering along a slightly curved saber. She hefted her capstan bar, less elegant than a sword but more than equal in weight.

"Your admiral Komar Zan has surrendered!" Galen called out in Shari. "Drop the sword if you want to live!"

The humyn laughed. "I will not surrender to demons of the sea! What of you, are you not men?" he addressed the wary figures in the gloomy hold. "Fight and I will make you free men!"

"Maybe you shouldn't have thralled them to start," Galen growled. She could feel it. The humyn would charge soon. "Try not to kill any forced to fight," she added in Hiltekash. Then with a roar of "Al-ahat!" it lunged, sword swinging.

It was a tight space, so Galen kept the bar close to her, swinging with a snap of a wrist down to break the humyn's femur. He fell screaming, his sword clattering to the deck. The guards wadded in behind her but it was unnecessary. There was a scuffle as men swarmed the only other two armored humyn, disarming and subduing them.

"Here! Take them!" one of the humyn said. "They work for the Sultan! We do not! Take them!"

It was easier than Galen had a right to expect but she was glad. Those thralled to oar were much leaner than most of the Shari fighting force, fed just enough to work. They had many tales: some were Bedu, from the same Oasis Flats that produced the prophet who founded the cult of the Eversky. Others were slaves captured from the Indus mountains, the Scorpion Hills or the shores of Azhinazu; or debt slaves from Tamask to Cathan. Like the sailors they had one passion: to see their homes again. Galen didn't even know if that was possible. For now the aggressive humyn were stripped of armor and arms and restrained, with the exception of the one with a broken leg. The pain of his wound would keep him docile.

"It'll need a healer," a crewgirl said.

"Ai," Galen said. "More than it deserves. Move them into the captain's cabin so they're kept from the rest. Then take stock of their supplies." She switched to Shari. "Jaffa?" she asked the humyn who had led the others in subduing their old masters. "You know Hanno?"

"Yes, my friend! The sailors are good men we have no quarrel with. Only the Sultan's creatures."

"I'm going to task you to work with the sailors to keep the peace tonight. Guards will stand at the captain's cabin. I know you have just grievances. But we cannot let you molest or abuse them."

"We have food and water and our freedom," Jaffa said. "We are blessed by the true Al-ahat, the abundance of the sky that is never ending. That is enough."

"We're staying the night?" one of the guards said.

"Can't be helped," Galen replied. "Divide yourself into watches. I'll have food ferried over. I still have to inspect the women."

It took a while to understand that the berth for the women was not just under the captain's cabin, but the entrance to it was through a hatch in that same room. The injured humyn glared at Galen as she passed him to a narrow stair at the back, just wide enough for a woman to walk down. Here as in the captain's cabin, every non functional surface was inlaid with ivory and rare dark woods, bordered with intricate carvings of beasts and merriment, all gilded. The roof was much the same, beams accented with retching demonic faces. What made it obscene to Galen's eyes was not the wasted opulence, but the carelessness: soot marred the paneling, stains soiled the furnishings, and burns and wax covered most surfaces. It spoke of riches quickly gained and indifferently valued, that as transitory as all wealth was, more was to be had and thus care was neglected of what was possessed. There were few things considered to be sins in the modern elfyn mind, but waste was one of them.

At the bottom of the stair was a small passage, just large enough for a door. Hanging above was an oil lamp. The door had a simple latch. Galen put her hand on it, then paused.

It was not the wisest idea to enter without company. But no mind beyond hinted of aggression or malice. There was an anxious wondering of their fate and that was to be expected. Above Galen heard the guards speaking in Hiltekash with someone, directing them down below. Then they returned to chatting in Gael, one saying sharply:

"Na bígí dána, amadáin móra!"

Galen hoped the prisoners didn't try the Cambari too much before she returned. She hammered hard on the door. "Hello?" she said in Shari. "You are safe now! You are all guests of the Tyreen Fleet! I'm entering now!"

Galen pushed the door in and had a glimpse of a room much like the cabin above, with cots and cushions littering the floor. There were several humyn women, with varying shades of skin, from a Sula gold to the deepest Dwen nut brown. They huddled together wrapped in thin blankets over light silks and printed cottons that had lost their luster from their time at sea, looking nothing so much as grubby colorful rags. Many had cheap brass jewelry, bangles and bells. A couple wore the bindi, the decorative forehead dot that marked them as members of the Indus tribes. Others had the curled fringe Asherite women wore, though now their hair was lank and frazzled. They all had the drawn wary look of hunted prey; few were taller than Galen's shoulder. At the sight of Galen they huddled closer together. One woman stood apart from the rest, in a far corner. She wore a green sari and veil, her dark scented hair pulled back and carefully bound in coils. She notably had more flesh than her sisters, not because she was fat, but because they were far too thin. It marked her as someone of privilege. Galen immediately knew it was prudent to question her, but the chance never came.

From Galen's left, partially concealed by the door, a figure flew at her, frenzied, and desperate, something metallic in its hand. It moved fast, reckless for its own safety, or perhaps hoping even in failure to find death. But as fast as it was, it was still humyn. Elfborn reflexes told her in a fraction of a moment where her attacker was, that her attacker was female and that she wielded a sharpened metal tool of some kind. Galen turned with speed, her mind marking the woman's rage and hate, her hands deftly grabbing the wrist with the weapon, then spinning her whole torso to slam the woman up against the other side of the door.

"Hak and damnation to the deeps with Shari rats!" Galen bellowed, still holding the woman pinned high on the wall. It had all taken less than a second. The women scattered away, against the far wall, crying out in alarm. Above feet thundered down. In seconds deck officer Lieutenant Rondaleth rushed in, sword in hand.

"Boatswain! Isn't that one of the thralled?" Rondaleth lowered her sword, looking perplexed.

"A sand flea assassin!" Galen snarled. "She jumped me as I entered!"

"Oh, I see!"

Galen squeezed the woman's wrist until the metal, a twisted handle from a spoon, fell with a clatter. In the corner of her eye Galen saw the green saried woman back away, eyes darting. Only then did she let her attacker go, dropping her like a worthless doll.

Galen breathed hard while Rondaleth shouted at them in Shari more fluent than her own. The woman who had attacked her huddled against the wall near her feet, holding her wrist, but her dark eyes were full of defiance. Her long black tresses were uncovered and unbound, and she wore the loose linen pantaloons so many boys were fond of for beach walking. Her face was marked with scars from burns or lashings, but her white teeth bared up at Galen, surprisingly whole. Galen waited until Rondaleth was finished with her harangue before starting her own.

"I don't know the reason for that foolishness," Galen started in Shari, "But if you'd all prefer to stay slaves we'll happily leave you on a boat to drift back to the Sultan!"

"That's not true, boatswain," Rondaleth said in Hiltekash.

"They don't know that!" Galen growled, pleased to see the women shrink back. Except for the one with dark deadly eyes. She just stared like an insolent cat.

Rondaleth sighed. "There's a misunderstanding."

"Enlighten me."

"They think you are a man."

"The other prisoners are embracing me as their 'brother' and didn't want to fight, but this half starved chit thought she'd retake the ship by herself?"

"No, boatswain, I think she assumed you were here to use them."

"What?"

"Or take them upstairs to be used. That seems to be how they tell the tale…"

Galen looked down at the woman, barely the size of a healthy adolescent girl. She understood but her blood was still too high to feel sympathy. It didn't help at this point the woman-girl spat on her feet.

Galen smiled, more of a grimace, reminding herself of the codes of war. "If you can kindly rectify their misapprehensions with your infinitely better Shari…"

Rondaleth uttered a stream of rapid words, pointing emphatically at Galen's bosom a couple of times. Galen sighed. What was there to do? The Shari woman-girl looked up suspiciously, following Rondaleth's gestures, then slowly stood. Galen took a step back. Maybe that would convince the creature she meant no harm. Suddenly the woman spoke.

"These are man's arms!" she said grabbing Galen's biceps.

"First she wants to kill me as a seducer, now she's fondling my arms," Galen opined.

"No one said Shari were rational," Rondaleth said. "They don't seem to believe you have any bosom."

"I'm not going to drop my breeches to prove my womanhood! They'll have to take it on faith!" In Shari she added, "We wish you no harm. But any more obstructive actions and you will be treated like prisoners and put to hard labor!"

The women said nothing, giving her sly looks. They still didn't believe she was female. It wasn't that Rondaleth or the guards above for that matter, didn't have their fair share of muscle. They certainly could toss about any one of these under-fed women like rag dolls. Galen supposed it was her almost utter lack of bosom that women of her development had. Rondaleth still an expected female form, a narrowing of the waist these women were familiar with, the only great difference being Rondaleth had a mother's shoulders. The attacker moved away to stand against the wall, though not close to the woman in green.

"Now that's settled," Galen said, "you will have a chance to wash on the morrow. And there should be food soon."

Suddenly the attacker blurted something rapidly, pointing to the woman in green. But the key words were unfamiliar to Galen.

"She says that woman will collaborate with the Shari admiral," Rondaleth said. "Apparently they are lovers."

Galen turned in time to see the green garbed woman rush at her accuser and spit at her. Like a cat, the wild girl leaped with sharp, uneven nails, clawing for the eyes. In a moment Galen was between them, pushing them violently apart making them fall. "*Qif!*" she bellowed in Shari.

The women looked up, resentful, but crawled away from each other.

Galen continued in Hiltekash, letting Rondaleth translate:

"While you are under our charge you will abide by Federation Naval code, which has punishments for fighting and disrupting duties. You will be taken care of, fed and watered like guests, but you will also be expected to do simple, honorable labor to offset hardship to our fleet. When we reach Gashora you will be released into the care of the city authorities where you will be free to chose your destiny. Until then you will abide by our laws or face discipline."

Galen deliberately left the nature of discipline unstated. They would never be flogged, nor even floated, but the worry of what might be would prevent trouble making. She looked at her attacker and the admiral's lover, until they lowered their eyes, submitting to her authority. "Do I need to have you bound?" she asked in Shari.

They both murmured in the negative, "*Nah*", standing to take diametrically opposite places in the room.

Galen picked up the metal handle, then motioned to Rondaleth they were leaving.

Once the door was shut Galen asked: "What are you doing here?"

"The Sea Father was anxious how you were getting on. And an officer should be in command of a captured vessel."

"That's true." They made their way up the stairs. "Tomorrow I want a magi to read them all, especially Komar Zan's lover. If she's a saboteur, keep it quiet so we can watch her. I'll introduce you to the sailors and freed men. They should be cooking later. Make sure the prisoners and women eat, but keep the women separate for now."

They exited from the captain's cabin until they were standing on the deck and the eve was upon them, Sul turning red as she neared the western horizon. The fleet's ships were finishing the salvage for the day, drifting between each other like swans gliding on a lake. The merchant ship felt lively now, smoke rising from the modest galley as the humyn cooked and chattered and laughed. It was like a holiday. Alas, Galen had been too slow, for the poultry had been slaughtered. A simple but hearty meal of flat bread, olives, pickled fish and stewed chicken with red and yellow spices was shared by the humyn. Galen was surprised it smelled more appetizing than the pea soup and bacon the Tyreen fleet's cooks seemed determined to punish them with.

Then Galen remembered the guards needed their food organized, but that had been done; Rondaleth had brought supplies of cold meat, bread and cheese for the night, and also a Gold crewgirl who cheerfully explained she'd be grilling food on the deck for their crew. Galen left in dubious humor: while she was glad the vittles had been sorted, she was resentful that she'd been robbed of exotic fair and a good grill, which was both her specialty and something her palate yearned for. When they sailed on patrols or ferried goods there was always time for a good grill in the sun.

Galen sighed. She'd done all she could for the day. When she returned to *The Tidebreaker*, after checking the ship's affairs were in order, she'd draw up a plan of management for the prisoners. That should keep Rosen from brooding too much on the task foisted on them by their new Admiral.

Chapter 22

Uisce Beatha

"...Mar sin buaileadh é,
isteach na doimhneacht,
shlíoc sé leis."

Col finished his composition, pleased he was inspired under such conditions. The launch brought them to just below the diver's ladder and they were about to bid their rescuer farewell. The pilot frowned, as if considering how to pick her words.

"I suppose it will do. One does what one can with a battle on. Can you catch the rungs?"

"Ai," Col said, unwrapping the blanket he'd been given. He was cold but no longer chilled. Even the pain from his cut leg had faded.

"Up you go then."

Pearl waited with a strange expression, somewhere between amusement and disbelief. She nodded for him to go ahead, perhaps worried if she wasn't behind him he might fall. Sighing, Col stepped on the rungs and started climbing. Halfway up his curiosity got the better of him.

"Very well," Col said. "What was wrong with it?"

"I didn't say anything was wrong with your poetry, love," Pearl said, but she muffled a snort.

"Yes?" Col said in pique. "Don't choose this time in our adventure to refrain from airing your opinion."

Pearl snickered, then cleared her throat. "Maybe it's more elegant in Gael," she ventured.

"But?"

"If I understand, and we both know I'm by no means a druid or magi on the subject ..."

"*Lean leat ...*"

"The last lines are: 'and thus defeated, into the deeps, away it slunk'."
Then Pearl, unable to restrain herself, hooted with derision.

Col wondered how she could laugh like a mad *bean sí* and still keep her hold on the diver's ladder. But she had rescued him, so forgiveness for mocking his poetry would come in time. They climbed onto the stern deck with Pearl still laughing.

"You try composing a ballad in a short time after almost becoming a shark's lunch!" Col said crossly.

"Oh ho!" Pearl continued, as they climbed onto the deck. "Beware the craft of the Cambrian Poet, for, like their drink, one is as likely to cough it up as imbibe! 'Away it slunk!'"

"May our merriment never end," Col said. "As much as I love being the source of mirth, I'm after retrieving of my satchel from the Admiral's clerk."

Or that had been Col's intention. This part of the stern deck, usually open between the two turrets and their solcannons, now had a contraption in the middle, just before the oval skylight rising from the deck. The wood-weaver Fadwen and Emha Olden were explaining the function to excited midships and other idle crew.

"It's a pity it was never used," one girl said.

"*Is trua sin*," added a guard.

"Not such a pity Sul's return meant it wasn't needed," Olden said. "But yes, a disappointment our nightly labors were unnecessary. We may do a demonstration for amusement this eve."

"It's a catapult!" Col blurted. "I've only seen them in books."

"I thought it was a large crossbow," Pearl said. "Don't catapults lug rocks with slings?"

"There are many kinds," Fadwen said. "The twisted rope distinguishes it from a bow…"

"*Brón orm!*" Pearl interrupted with a smile. "*Caithfidh muid amach!*" With that she pulled Col away to the stern steps.

"Ai! That was interesting!"

"To a landed barnacle maybe."

"I can't help notice your use of Gael is to either charm my relations or avoid trouble."

"But don't you need to retrieve your papers?" Pearl said innocently.

After querying several crew, they were directed to the secretary's cabin. It made sense; perhaps Amralan was working with *The Tidebreaker's* secretary. But at the door Col found Amralan puttering around the cabin, arranging papers. A cot was at the side, under a window in the starboard hull. The other window, looking down the deck to the bows, was broken, shards of glass scattered across the floor. There was a desk and a high scholar's stool, baskets to organize missives and the usual assortment of pens, ink bottles and other tools a scribe needed. A heavy iron box was sitting on the floor just before the cot, one of the lockboxes documents were sealed into in the event the ship was lost.

"Sorry, effa," Amralan said. "The box wasn't locked. Careless. All could have been lost. Like with the Admiral…"

Col exchanged a look with Pearl. Neither of them knew what to do.

"Are you sure you should be here?" Col said, wondering if the healers had tended Amralan.

"Yes, middie, don't you see the work to be done?" Amralan was opening a large ledger, placing it on the angled desk. "Messages are piling up and the mess will have to wait."

Col didn't know the details of a ship's secretary's duties, but he had gotten quite good at cleaning. With all the loose glass, he worried Amralan would cut herself in her state. "Then how about I sweep up the glass?"

"Sparking idea, young effa," Amralan said absently as she made some quick strokes of a pen in the ledger. Col knew enough that she would be marking the change in time and scribes. Pearl helped by picking up the larger shards while he searched for a small broom. Suddenly Amralan said, "Oh no!"

She was looking right at Col as if seeing him for the first time.

"What?"

"Go to the infirmary instantly, young effa!" Amralan said. "You're covered with cuts and bruises and not fit until a healer says otherwise."

"I feel fine!" Col objected. "I've only a couple of splinters…"

"Come along," Pearl said, pulling him away. "You do look a bit of a mess. Perhaps you can raise the spirits of the wounded with your poetry!"

"*Fág é!*"

"Go on!" Amralan said. "Don't argue or you'll face discipline, midship. Return if the healers release you."

They made their way to the mess, pausing near a rubbish barrel so Pearl could throw away the broken glass. Contrasting to the activity above, the hospital had a dim restful feel, lanthorns giving everything a warm fireside glow. There was no moaning as was the case after a Cambrian battle; though mostly a sport among the athletic and keen, it still had its share of injuries. Whatever romance Col felt for his father's people, it was born best in a world with elfyn medicine. Those with simple wounds sat on benches out of the way. A couple tables were red, the ghastly remains of surgeries, and some women had haunted eyes, as if they had walked the low roads and returned, barely believing they still lived. They were the retrieved, now to be known as twice born. Col shivered. Then he remembered he'd last seen Samath helping the healers.

Col looked around for Samath, eager to tell him of his adventures. He would be jealous. Or perhaps not; Samath seemed happy with his expected role as a man. Still, he would be entertained and Col was keen to speak with a soul who was not sniggering at his prose. But Col didn't see him. Vaguely aware Pearl was trying to engage a healer to examine him, Col wandered through the mess hall, expecting at any moment to see Samath in his smudged robe, his cry of welcome, perhaps a rebuke for him being distracted. There were Dwen men helping the healers and a row of tables in the back with figures under white cloth …

No, Col thought to himself. He shivered violently looking into the dimness beyond. Those tables held those lost beyond the Door. He would not walk forward, he would not learn something that he could not unknow, Samath would call out to him any moment… Then he saw the fold of a linen robe at the edge of the white shroud and ran forward with a cry.

Women did not wear any kind of robes on the ship while at duty and all of the men Col had seen, crew and volunteers, wore bracs or sea breeches. The companions wore robes, but they would not be near the battle, would they? At the table, Col stripped off the white cloth. And there lay Samath; his eyes had been closed and he had a horrible wound at the side of his neck.

"What happened?" Col tried to shout, but he sounded faint and hoarse. "How? He was safe here …"

A healer was by his side, a man. He firmly took the shroud from Col's hands and replaced it.

"My regrets volunteer. It was an uncommon accident. When the ship exploded, a shard of wood struck your friend through an open window."

"But it's nothing!" Col yelled. "A simple cut any novice could close!"

"Yes, but he was not found until his blood had drained and his spirit fled." The healer, though petite and thin, was surprisingly strong for his size. He firmly pulled Col back. "Please do not disturb them. They will be shriven at the right time."

Col yanked his arm out of the man's grip. He burned with rage, now without words. Poor Samath, he thought. Now hidden under the shroud, Col had a strange worry he'd have trouble breathing. "It's not fair," Col croaked. He scented Pearl before she put her arms around him, all mirth forgotten. He clung back, wanting to keen. He'd never understood it before, the keening of the Meer. But even with a quarter of Meer ancestry, he wanted to keen. Samath had been a good companion and now he was dead.

Col let Pearl cradle him, his grief stuck in his throat. Then he pulled away.

"What do you mean, they will be shriven at the right time?" he called after the healer.

"At dawn is expected."

"*Seafóid,*" Col said.

"Pardon?" the healer said.

"*Déanfaimid anois.*"

"*Cad a dhéanamh muid?*"

The captain of the guard had entered. She was a formidable woman, perhaps hearing raised voices she thought she should intervene. Col saw many eyes taking an interest and decided speaking in Hiltekash was best.

"The healer says the dead will be shriven at sunrise. But then they should be waked now! Not all of us have the benefit of dream visits nor knew of their deeds. They shouldn't be burned unknown like waste ..."

"Oh, for the sake of Sul!" the prefect said. "Mordmhol, get this hysterical savage out of my infirmary!"

The guard looked between them, then scanned the hall. "See, my fine prefect, it's not your infirmary. It is the Tyreen fleet's, who is beholden to the Admiralty. Your authority diminishes as the infirm are healed. And in diminishing, those parts not in use become free. *Mar shampla, thall ansin.*"

313

She pointed to the large recess where food was usually served. Col knew it was used for examinations if privacy was needed, but as Mordmhol pointed out, this was less frequent.

"That needs to be available for extra wounded!" Mathynwol objected.

"There be no more wounded for the day, *maith an bhean*," Mordmhol said.

"Don't 'good woman' me! How would you know?"

"The day grows old and all have been rescued and accounted for. Even if there be need, you've enough space as you are. And the boy is right, the dead should be waked properly." Mordmhol called behind her to another guard, "*A Mhaeve! Tabhair an t-uisce beatha!*"

"I will not have whiskey in my hospital!" Mathynwhol shouted.

"But it won't be in your hospital," Mordmhol said. "It will be in the bows next to your hospital."

"Alharn!" Mathynwol called to a surgeon. "Is this acceptable with you?"

"As long as they stay out of the way, I see no harm," Alharn said. "Do keep your traffic to one side of the hall as you come and go."

"*Ar ndóigh*," agreed Mordmhol.

And so it was done. Cambari of all tribes had gathered in agreement, and even those who did not claim those green hills as ancestral lands stood in support. For this time it wasn't just a Gold officer, however well liked, but souls the crew had known. They gathered near the dead, much like in the commissary, around barrels for tables, sitting on benches and stools available. Food was brought up, bread with sausage and pickles. Many made traveler sandwiches, washed down with whiskey, or barley-mead for those who did not find *uisce beatha* to their liking. The Sea Father would say words on the morrow, thanking the dead for their service, wishing them well on their passing. But this eve they celebrated their passing comrades life, their hopes, their dreams, their deeds before their end. That was how Col learned of the attempted rape of Samath by two stray humyn and his bold actions that killed one before he was rescued. Then Col found himself weeping quietly with overwhelming sadness. He'd never be able to tell Sam how proud he was. Pearl sat near, herself solemn when a diver called Frye related the loss of a marine, killed by the same explosion that led to their misadventure. Several souls from the strike crew, including the gold eyed

Brownie strikemaster came to lay two shrouds down for the two women lost so completely there was nothing left to bury. They were joined by Mistalryn the bard, and what Col was sure was one of the working male companions, the only men besides Sam to wear robes. He still looked glamorous, but in a weary way; he was propping up a limping woman dressed a bit too dashing to take seriously if it wasn't for the very real leg wound and a hand wrapped with bandages. They were pitch-fire burns. After an hour the whiskey and tales had dulled the hurt. He yearned for sleep. Then a thought came to him.

"Does Navi know?" he wondered out loud.

Pearl shrugged. "Where is she anyway?"

"Volunteer Hoethnav?" a healer nearby asked.

"Yes."

"She is berthed privately because of her wounds. I'll get Alharn."

Soon the surgeon wearing red was approaching them. "Are you friends of Navi?"

"Not exactly," Pearl muttered.

"We know her," Col said.

"Then perhaps you can return this to her." Alharn held out a sword in a still damp sheath, pieces of the charred, ruined baldric still attached. "The divers retrieved it. It may give her solace. I warn you she is maimed and will not welcome your company."

"Maimed?" Pearl asked. "How?"

"Her arm was destroyed. There was nothing we could do."

"Oh."

"I suggest you make your visit brief."

While the surgeon gave Pearl directions, Col drew Navi's sword, feeling it rebuked him by just holding it. It was an elegant thing, more so than Freya's grimsteel, though not balanced as perfectly as the guard's sword he had borrowed. An old fashioned enameled grip ended in the head of a python, with an orb of solstone in its mouth. Like many Sula weapons, the flat was enameled with solglass. It was an old weapon, perhaps several hundred years, but still good, only now showing wear along the blade.

Abruptly Col sheathed the sword, following Pearl. This would be the most discomfiting moment of their adventure. He disliked Navi intensely, but this, the loss of an arm, he'd never wish on an enemy. She was arrogant and proud, but she had also fought bravely and Col, as Cambari, respected that alone. And she had saved him. The old rules of honor haunted them all. Like it or not they were linked to her. There were more obligations to war than flowery brave words and dying nobly. The bravest had to live in the aftermath.

Col swallowed as they came to the door of the cabin. Pearl eyed him solemnly. He nodded. She knocked.

"When do healers bother to knock?" Navi called in annoyance. "Enter or begone."

Col shivered, his neck hairs raising. He would rather face a wounded dragon in its forest den than a vulnerable Navi.

Slowly Pearl opened the door. It was a typical crew cabin, three bunks against one wall. The bunks had been removed from the other wall, re-placed by a cot. Navi stood with her back to them, looking out the window, a blanket wrapped around her. This cabin was in the ship's late afternoon shadow, so it was dim. It was not obvious which arm was missing.

"Sorry," Col said, "We're not your healer."

Navi's head snapped around. Col was astounded how her face could pass through so many expressions in a matter of moments: surprise, anger, suspi-cion, contempt, then finally, curiosity. Col might assume it was an elfyn thing, but Pearl was never so mercurial. Navi's eyes had fallen on her sword.

Col stepped into the room and quickly set the sheathed sword on the cot as if it was a snake that might bite him. "The divers retrieved this."

Navi's eyes flickered up to meet his. Her words were flat and cold. "My thanks." Then she returned to look out the window. "You have done your duty. You can go now."

"There's one more thing." The words caught in Col's throat. His hesita-tion made Navi turn her head back, now impatient.

"What is it?"

Col mastered himself. "Samath. He's irretrievably dead."

Navi's eyes widened in shock. "What?"

"He was injured in the explosion. Something flew and cut his throat. They didn't find him until it was too late. I ... We thought you'd want to know."

Navi's face was a mask of marble, the mask mothers made when they pretended not to care. Abruptly she turned her back to them. "He should never have been here," she murmured to herself. "Silly boy."

Col didn't know what more to say. "Thank you for saving me. Earlier, in the battle."

"Leave!"

As Pearl pulled Col away, he felt the danger if, by some ill wind of fate, they witnessed Navi weeping. Was it possible? Did anyone live to tell that tale? He let Pearl lead him away, he didn't care where. Soon they were in the diver's berth, empty because of the salvage that still continued.

Col sank to the floor thinking of the hole in his life, of Samath, cheerful and happy, with nary a care, confident in the strength of mothers to protect him. Samath who saw adventure as a series of romances, war just the backdrop in his personal tale of finding women to woo him. Samath, with his wiles, who had cajoled Navi into rendering a grudging apology. Samath who had simple tastes and a good heart. Perhaps Navi was right, it had been silly of him to volunteer, but he had, and that was worth something, wasn't it? His death was as simple as his life, and suddenly Col realized he knew almost nothing about Samath, where he was birthed, where he lived. He was just a boy who hopped on a ship looking for adventure. His death was unheroic, meaningless, and for all that the more true. There was no heroism in death. No one was actually spared by the dying of a mother or man; it was the action of protecting, not the death itself that had meaning.

And Col felt rage too, for though only a part of him was elfyn, it was enough for him to resent the early leaving of any soul that should have lived for at least a couple of centuries. What was said to mark elfyn from humyn, evidence to the contrary be damned, was that elfyn did not die, but lived eternal. It was worse for Col, because through Cambrian tales, romances of elfyn glorified by the simple, he had internalized the belief that elf magic could fix everything. Now the magic had failed and no amount of raging would change that.

Overwhelmed with grief, Col found himself sobbing in Pearl's arms. She sung a lay he could not understand for it was in the Meer dialect and he had never learned to speak it. But the tones were soothing, and spoke of the great peace of the wide ocean that embraced Eurath. Col didn't know how long they sat there, but at last he felt too empty of tears to weep.

At some point he slept, waking to find the berth full before climbing into his hammock properly. When the call to rise came, he didn't move. He wasn't crew, what could they do to him?

"They gather above to burn the dead," Merock said. "Any soul who wishes to assist, report to the boatswain mate."

The divers filed out but Col didn't move.

"Come, love," Pearl was saying, gently shaking the netting. "We have to say good bye. You'll regret it if you don't."

"Since when do you care for the customs of the landed?"

"We all say good bye to those who have passed through the Door. Come along. Remember we live and you're not alone."

Col nodded dumbly, easing out of the hammock, letting himself be led. In a moment of absurdity he remembered the clerk still had his papers somewhere. He decided they were safe enough where they were for the moment.

Chapter 23

The Rites of Passage

It was just past dawn as the fleet prepared to send the dead off in a custom as old as the seafaring cultures of the western island nations. Even the Nords of the far north sent their dead to the Otherworld on burning pyres, on land or by sea, depending on local custom. It was possible the humyn adopted this custom from Sula. Rosen wasn't certain. He did know the current custom dated from the times of the Sunqueens, even before Selastimor the Great took it on herself to be immolated as she lived that she may make the journey that no magi had yet achieved: walking through the Door with a living mind and returning to tell the tale.

Of course Sunqueen Selastimor was never heard from in waking or dreams. Now it was known once one passed the Door, there was no return. Yet fire was still seen as the path to Sul's palace in heaven, at one time reserved for queens and heroes of the nation. There was a point in history the pyre was so regulated, it was considered prideful to volunteer one's mother to be burned in death without an agreement by lot. Gradually only those disgraced were refused the pyre. Many Sula were quite superstitious in believing they would not pass over completely if their flesh was not reduced to ash. Old stories of wandering ghosts on the high plains did nothing to dispel these fears.

There would be no such fears on the sea. Here the dead were always burned, excepting in extraordinary circumstances where burning was not possible. They would follow Glethlyn on their bowers, consumed by flames while the fleet observed the rights of passage.

Many women welcomed these times as a way to grieve without diminishing their pride. That thought brought the beginnings of grief, the knowledge, for all of being elfborn, they were mortal, and that the righteousness in duty did not make one immune to the dangers of extinction.

Rosen watched Galen move, directing crew, organizing the bowers, chivying the divers, always with Meer expectations of time, reminding them of the schedule. The deck had been stoned and the crew assembled in the brisk cold of the dawn breeze, all wearing their least soiled and shabby clothes. That was the signal for the ritual to begin.

The naval ritual of the rites of passing were so well known Rosen hardly needed to think on it, especially after Glethlyn. The words he spoke to the crew from the stern deck now seemed empty and hollow, as if he was a Brownie automaton made for the amusement of children. However he'd arranged for the Aeon magi, Ta Hethlion, to lead the main dedication. The magi had been the high priests of the old realm. Many still felt the order was better suited to preside over these rituals. Rosen also felt the women needed a mother's voice and with the loss of Ensign Moradrin Savalis he had no heart for the task. He watched Savalis' bower in particular being prepared, then lowered as Hethlion intoned:

"The soul birthed in the Orb must one day pass through the Door.
Be it after an Aeon or too suddenly soon
know we will meet again after the End..."

A Cambari poet, one of the volunteer fighters, stood nearby, face covered with dark blue paint, hands open as if to catch blessings from the sky as she echoed Hethlion's words in Gael:

"*Caithfidh an t-anam a bheirtear isteach sa domhan lá amháin dul tríd an Doras...*"

Some aelg, who had lived with humyn, claimed the rote of ritual was comforting. Others did not fathom this. Humyn did not understand the truth of the soul's passage through the Door; how could they be comforted by what they did not know? Rosen knew both his and Galen's mother, both strong Sula households, would never accept any death before two centuries.

Hethlion's voice, steady and solemn, finished the dedication:

"...Until that time distant and unknown,
We bid you this life farewell,
Giving thanks in your passing for your friendship,
Loyalty, bravery, and society that without,
Though in sorrow we are bereft,
We shall remember in our hearts always and forever."

In the same moment the Cambari finished, ending her prayers in the fashion of the monastery coda:

"In ainm an Mháthair,
agus le Sula Bríd,
agus ár spiorad le cheile…"

Most of the crew chanted: "Always and forever", while those following the Cambari echoed her last word: *"Áiméan."*

The souls had already passed, of course, those who had time, already spoken to loved ones and made their wishes known. These rituals were for the living, not the dead, and the sun shining above through indifferent light clouds cared neither one way or the other.

The ships were motionless; the fleet was arrayed in a loose line facing west, the direction of hope, longing and loss, for though Sul rose with promise in the east, She disappeared each night west and a tiny part of every mother wondered what would happen were She not to return.

They were to strike as one. Already, as Rosen stood with Galen beside him, the bowers of the shrouded dead were steadied by divers, before pushing the craft out into the range of fire. Minutes passed in silence. The drums began, strong firm blows on cowhide. Along the Tyreen line they drummed as they put their dead out. Some ships had none. *The Black Seal* had more than its share from *The Oaken Blue*.

And then they were all floating away together, ready to drift into eternity. A whistle sounded and the drums stopped. The divers had withdrawn.

Another whistle rang out, this one from *The Black Seal*. At the sound, Strikemaster Sernalash called:

"Crew! Hands ready… Strike!"

The lancers, including the Marshal's agent, aimed and the sad flotilla flared brightly, the bowers engulfed in fire. As the flames leaped higher, a fiery line across the western path of the sea, the Blue started to keen.

It was a rending haunting sound, piercing to landed ears. Meer did not weep, and many of the Blue shared this trait. Thus when overcome with emotion, keening was their only release. Rosen resisted for as long as he

321

could before turning his head aside to diminish some of the tones. The Cambari had no such reservations. They bowed their heads respectfully, but with hands firmly over their ears. All the landed were grateful when most of them dived into the water, leaving only two behind: a male with eyes swimming in tears, and that talented but troublesome diver, Pearl Sharol.

"How is that for amusement, lover?" she said, to her boy. "I look too humyn for maleen society, but I cannot weep."

Pearl walked to the edge of the larboard waist amidships. The keening continued underwater, the haunting sound rising through the timbers of *The Tidebreaker*, echoing in the sea and in their souls, just outside of their understanding. Rosen felt that if he listened long enough he could make out words his soul had forgotten from a lost dream. Then Pearl sang part of the Keen Song and no translation was needed:

> *"He's gone to the Sea*
> *and taken my heart*
> *doomed to this life*
> *while forever we part~*
>
> *down falls the rain*
> *on a world that is gone*
> *weeps now the sky*
> *now the burning is done~*
>
> *I watched as he fell*
> *his soul spent and gone*
> *away though the door*
> *without worry or wrong ..."*

The song was attributed to the first Sea Queen mourning her brother, Laifmyr, after the Cataclysm. Pearl had a shallow voice, with only one tone; Rosen suspected it sounded best underwater. It was a long song, in a plain droning chant that, sounding underwater, would carry for miles. There was much more, but suddenly Pearl stopped and dived over the wale after the others.

Rosen was relieved Col didn't follow her. They barely survived the consequences his last foolish romantic gesture. Now there was a painfully trite ditty to memorialize the event spreading through the ship, getting more ribald as it passed from soul to soul. Maybe it was a good thing that the crew could find humor, however crude.

As the Coraco began, they sang and Rosen let himself become lost in the shared grief around him. Their voices echoed over the waters as the dead burned. Galen's tenor was strong, as was the bard's highly trained dual range. Few casual singers bothered to learn the discipline of "singing in two voices". Some elfborn couldn't do it at all. Many sang low or high, with an overtone. Many more preferred to speak in one voice and sing in another. It was said the Federation Marshal rarely sang because, though her voice was like a dragon, her song would be envied by Solshari himself, and that worthy did not consider that a compliment.

As the fleet sang, the flames fell, becoming paler as the sun rose in her traces. Soon all that was left was the smoldering husks of the bowers. At a sign, in a flash these were obliterated with one strike of a cannon, the remains now part of the wind, sun and sea. The last notes of the Coraco ended.

Rosen called for the crew to be dismissed, an order Galen echoed. The crew returned to their many tasks, the work of the salvage driving discipline to return after the chaos of battle. Meanwhile Rosen felt he knew just enough about prisoner management by naval codes that his instinct to turn it over the Galen had been more correct than he'd imagined. She remained oddly cheerful at the news they would remain the Shari's nanny until Gashora.

"You're not troubled?" Rosen asked.

"Nay, Sea Father, not at all," Galen said. "They'll be as placid as lambs before all is done."

"Tresmadore wants me to interrogate the yacht pilot. His name is Hadi."

Galen grunted, frowning. "Well, if he's a prisoner, we should know about it soon enough. If you have no need, I should see how our guests have got on during the night."

"As you were."

The stern deck felt crowded. It didn't help matters the ballista still laired on the deck. It had been pulled against the aft of the stern hull, thick lengths of wood looped around one foot and its bow to secure it. Similarly the strike crew was securing the solcannons and their trucks with chains, so their lengths hugged the hull. If needed, they could take some salvage. Already two crew girls with some Cambari volunteers were lugging tarps up to the deck. Mert was piloting, an easy task alternating between treading and gliding closer to the working divers. There was only one launch now; Rosen watched as a handful of healers piled in it with Galen, presumably to examine the prisoners. He might be able to beg a loan from a larger ship, say *The Starshard* or *The Charred Bronze*. The women bearing the tarp neared and he moved to let them pass.

Why was he lingering, Rosen thought to himself? They were gone. Savalis was gone. There was no time to sit with one's grief at sea. The ship always needed tending, always something beckoned. He saw the elf Farthal standing out of the way in the starboard turret, her flouted hair buffeted by the wind. She leaned on a solcannon, looking north. He knew she hungered for land as much as he hungered for peace of mind. They would neither be satisfied until the fleet reached Gashora.

Rosen left the stern deck. He would need to wait for Galen's report and the launch's return before he could do anything directly with the prisoners. Until then his logs needed tending.

Chapter 24

Bedeviled in Bonds

Galen sat with the relief guards in the bows of the launch near the pilot. Aftward sat the healers with their bags of draughts and other tools. She was pleased to have been kept appraised of the prisoner transfers by raven. Ships were to all be sending what healers could be spared, as well as supplies. Crewgirls would follow to work out the most efficient way to tow the lot. They could be lashed or wood bound together. However it was to be done, it would be a slow and awkward business sailing with the prizes to Gashora.

Reaching the cluster of captured ships near the merchant galleys, Galen set to investigate the vessels individually. She'd sent Lieutenant Rondaleth a missive and was pleased to see her waiting on one of the fire scorched decks. A lean Dwen with Sula eyes, Rondaleth didn't wear a yastol, though her reddish brown hair was pulled back as if she might. The freshly brushed deep blue naval coat had one black scorch mark marring a sleeve. No prisoner could be seen. On the stern and bow platforms stood naval guards, spares recruited from other ships.

"Ai, and how do the leaves fall?" Rondaleth called out as Galen climbed a rope ladder to the deck.

"There are no falling leaves on the ocean, Wildling miscreant!" Galen called back. Though unnecessary, she was grateful for Rondaleth's hand to pull her up the last step. "Unless it be on a hearty breakfast. And then I would say they fall with welcome."

"Perhaps after we review the sea rats," Rondaleth said. "There's supposed to be an abundance of vittles waiting in the galley. What's your pleasure?"

Galen smirked mirthlessly. "A full purse, a full flagon and a full bed."

"What every mother in the Orb wants, ai? Sadly you must settle with the last of my golden mead."

"That will do, when we come to it."

While the guards climbed aboard, Galen and Rondaleth walked the length of the scorched and broken deck to the captain's cabin. The doors were ajar, within the floor was covered with sea soiled bedding and filth. A darkening red patch might have been where a body had fallen. Above and around the ceiling and walls were covered in gilded ornamentation, craft work celebrating the ambitions of the Sultan's creatures.

"There's nothing like the squalor of decadence," Rondaleth said. "It's said those with sudden luck after a life of lack are wont to offend fashion by gilding their food, but this ..." She gestured around her. "This is an affront to aesthetics."

"The rulers of Sharitan are jackals," Galen said. "They steal from others then wish to profit by taking credit. But to my mind the art is no worse than an embellished romantic painting."

"I'm a stoic, I suppose," Rondaleth said. They both looked down the stairs of the open hatch forward of the captain's cabin. "Let us meet our guests."

The stairs were narrower than Galen was used to, but some helpful soul had hung a couple of lanthorns. Shari were partial to oil, however it was decided they should not handle any incendiaries if it could be helped. They were in a type of antechamber used for storage. To either side, along the hull, ran an aisle next to oars and benches. This could not be seen at a glance because most of the hold was taken up with a room that ran down the length of the ship. Its entrance was an open doorway before them, wide, sturdy steps leading down. Light leaked from hatches above, dimly illuminating a huddled mass of humyn. Galen knew from intelligence there would be a doorway exactly like this at the other end. She took one of the lanthorns down and carefully stepped down into the hold.

The Shari sat packed like rats, a row on each side, with just enough room to lay down, as some had done. These came to alertness when Galen entered, sitting wide eyed, whites glowing in the gloom. Their hands had been bound in front. Galen watched, felt the mood, eyed each soul as well as she could. She was sure a couple had loosed their bonds but had the wit to be subtle. Where would they go? Did they consider revolt? They had the mass to take over this ship if somehow the guard was caught unawares, but that was all. Galen looked at them more closely, while they stared back mutely.

They were all men and were wretched. Turbans of all colors were covered with grime, tunics torn, bloodied and foul. Many did not have shoes, but unlike Blue suffered for this, some missing toes, or nails ingrown and festering. Others had simple wounds bound in foul cloths, not serious now, but that could change. It was hard to read their dark eyes: did they welcome the Tyreens as saviors, freeing them from the Sultan's wars? Or were they resentful in their defeat, believing their just cause thwarted by demons? Whichever it was, they marked Galen and her every move. Using her crew voice, she bellowed in Shari, "Stand!"

They stood, responding with a respectable degree of discipline considering they were hobbled by bonds and wounds. To Rondaleth Galen said, "Stay alert while I walk down the room once."

It was a risk Galen knew she could take. She wouldn't let many others do this. They had no weapons and being bound would not be able to fight. But even if one of the two who had loosed themselves – and Galen marked them – attacked her, their death would be a useful lesson. For though Galen was committed to discharge her duty to the prisoners lawfully, a part of her wanted the visceral vengeance of killing, the feeling of the life of an enemy fading in her hands. Were she to be so provoked, that killing would be both satisfying and lawful.

But no man was so bold. Some shivered, others breathed prayers under their breath. They all stank of sweat and urine. She finished her walk and, seeing nothing she didn't expect, returned.

"Are the prisoners in the other ships the same?"

"As I understand."

Galen sighed. "We're going to have to review them all for certainty. Warn the guards, a couple …"

A voice interrupted as they withdrew, rapid and contemptuous, but the Shari words were clear: "*Shaitan.*" Devil. "He" was a devil.

Galen understood. She was physically formidable, but she often forgot the aggressive tattooed horns over her ears had a demonic effect. Amusing still was the persistent assumption with the humyn she was male. However it made them docile. More swiftly than one might expect for a woman of her size, Galen spun on one foot and lunged into the room at the source of remark, ironically one of the two men who had loosed their bonds.

"It is so!" Galen growled in Shari, seizing the humyn's tunic so he couldn't escape. "I am your Devil. Do not forget!"

To the man's horror, she wrenched the rope looped loosely around his wrists and retied it, so tight a knife would be needed to release him. Horror struck, he stumbled away. The other prisoners shrunk from her. Satisfied, Galen left.

"Boatswain," Rondaleth ventured as she followed. "That binding…"

Galen cut her off. "He won't be tied for long. The first thing to organize after we tour the other ships is bathing. Do it in groups of twenty at a time. We'll need more guards. And barrels for water. And lant."

"You think there's enough?" Rondaleth said wrinkling her nose.

"Salt as well," Galen added. "After their bodies and clothes are washed, the healers can inspect them. We don't need disease to spread. Those too wounded to work should be berthed separately. The rest? You'll like this. The rest will clean this hulk out from top to bottom. By this eve I want this ship berth to smell like roses."

"That's ambitious!"

"Oh, before they work we'll feed them. Tonight they'll be too exhausted for mischief."

Rondaleth took out a signal whistle and started sending for what they needed from ships nearby while Galen was ferried in the launch to the other three captured vessels. They were much the same, one more demanding of food and water, another in the midst of staging a rebellion. Those wanting refreshment were reassured they would be watered after bathing. Their spirits raised in thanks made Galen unprepared for the attempt to over power her and the ensign on duty on the next boat. One Shari died from a snapped neck, the other, run through with a sword. It wasn't dead, but wouldn't live long. Galen left it up to the healers on whether to heal or retrieve it.

That done, she told the driver to take her to the merchant galley to meet Rondaleth for a late breakfast.

When she arrived the healers were tending the freed men, freshly washed and agreeable, waiting on the oar benches in turn. There was a surgeon and the ship's prefect from *The Charred Bronze,* ten healers in all. Every so often a humyn leaving would exclaim their thanks to *Al-ahat,* or one of the many other humyn gods, before bowing deeply to the healer who waved them briskly on. That would be simple healing, pain vanishing from bruises and strains, or perhaps an old wound being corrected, the ache now forever gone. The same drama played out on the other two merchant galleys, in one case a soul was moved to sing.

"Well, they're cheerful at least," Rondaleth said as they ate just outside the door of the captain's cabin. They made a meal of cold ham, cheese, sausage and pickle on fresh flat bread, a gift from the sailors of a paste of mashed chickpeas.

"And they cook reasonably well," Galen said, devouring her food without prejudice, washing it down with mead. "I was expecting some sort of curry."

"We think of curry as Shari or Brownie food, but curry spice originally came from the Indus tribes. There's a real issue of the food and water supplies, boatswain. Whatever our Sea Father and Admiral are thinking, it's not sustainable. The galleys, except for one, were fortunate to have little damage."

"Which one was damaged?" Galen interrupted.

"See that one? With the peacock figurehead? A plank was ripped out. No one knows when, but it was flooding on the morning of the first engagement. They lost a couple of souls, I think. But it was caught before the ship was lost. It's still sitting low. Should I call for crew with a proper pump?"

Galen shook her head. "Need to finish with the prisoners first."

Another couple of launches came with supplies to clean, and water was drawn up into great tubs on the decks of the warships with buckets of bath salts and weak lye powder. While Galen would have taken satisfaction in forcibly hosing down the prisoners, they were for the most part left to their own devices. Each group was wary, some thinking the tubs were to drown them or some other torture. They were guarded while their bonds were cut, then told to wash. They only hesitated for modesty, though it was mostly male crew that had been sent for this reason. The shouting guards were women, not that most of the humyn could see the difference. The guards became so irritated, the Shari decided it was safest to strip off their clothes and surrender their bodies to the brushes and rags left for them. Once started they forgot their shyness, the relief to being clean overcoming inhibitions. If it was any comfort, Galen would have told them their nakedness was not attractive to any of the elfborn crew. Most of the men came from a breed that was quite hirsute, more so than Cambrians, or maybe it was that dark hair that made it seem more abundant. That, and their manes, made them revolting to most women in the fleet. Only a few, men just past adolescence, or by chance of fate, were hairless enough to be considered objects of prurient interest.

Of course, to Galen, all men were unattractive. They struck her less as potential partners and more like clumsy animals. She never thought herself bigoted but the lack of dignity given by clothing, in her post funerary mood, invited uncharitable thoughts.

The clothes too were to be washed, something many Shari objected to. Galen caught some words, though whether serious or made out of nerves it was hard to tell:

"You are to take care of us. You feed us, wash our clothes. It will be like home."

The comment elicited laughter from his fellows until the guard he was addressing grabbed the tunic and threw it overboard to flutter briefly before falling into the water.

"Nothing to wear, so nothing to wash. Just like home," she said.

Thereafter no Shari objected to washing.

Galen wondered if she should rebuke her, then shrugged. She would have done the same thing.

It took the better part of an hour for the washing. Once finished, the Shari wore little more than loincloth wrappings around their privates, some simply wearing their trousers wet. Their other garments hung over benches and wales to dry. The day was now cloudless and would have been hot except for the strong breeze. The first healers arrived, finished with the galley humyn and now ready for the challenge of the prisoners.

In the ancient Tahmery, and among the Indus for that matter, women as scholars and healers were not unknown. However in modern Sharitan those were old customs of a dead, decadent culture. It was learned men who were respected, rightly or no, for having physician skill. The Cathans had no such prejudice against women of learning, often having whole families of practicing healers. There was even a rumor the rich and powerful of Tamask preferred Cathan healers for their person, while publicly praising the Ever Sky and the court magi. All this explained why the Shari rankled at being examined, guards wrestling some to sit, forcing them to be still, even though a healer's initial examination was little more than laying of hands and examining the courses of the mind. Galen had to help some of the more reluctant patients becalm themselves. She was called *"shaitan"* more than once. Only after enough of the Shari hadn't died of fright or been transformed into toads did the panic over the examinations cease. Finally Galen could relax and just observe. That was when a healer approached her.

"Al met," the woman said. *"The Tidebreaker*, correct?"

"Ai, Boatswain Galen Sellisyn."

"Healer Marleth Morn, *The Helix Bow*."

"So how are the patients?"

"Once they understood they feel better after, they are compliant. Though some will mutter charms to ward off our demonic magic."

Galen snorted. "That's expected."

"What are we to do with chronic aliments, emha?"

"Hunger and exhaustion? Tell us which and we'll remove them from labor."

"I was thinking of tooth disease and cataract," Morn said. "It's not many, but it's easy to fix. They are our charges. On the other hand if there's no urgency, it can be left to the Temple in Gashora."

"If the pain or blindness prevents them from labor, treat it."

"There are a couple that can't be treated," Morn said. "Teeth are rotted to the nubs. But lesions can be filled and kept from spreading."

"Do it. They should be grateful, but I expect they will resent this as all things."

"I think they resent most women examining them 'like animals', I believe was one thought. Do you know a great many of them lack foreskins?"

"It's a conceit of desert cultures and fanatic stoicism," Galen said. "I used to bother our captain about this as children. It was...well, he was being a brat and so was I."

"Sea Father Rosen?"

"Carry on," Galen said.

It was an old battle between Galen and Rosen, one of the few that had got out of hand. He'd discovered her aversion to the birth chamber, born of her discomfort with the fact, if she ever wanted a child, she'd need to coit a man. Rosen needled Galen with birthing accounts, his excuse being, as a girl, surely she shouldn't be bothered about the details if she was to be a mother. This fastidiousness was long since gone, the gore of blood and birth lost in the reality of blood throughout the life of any woman of action. Galen laughed at her past self. She had her petty revenge, retaliating by expounding on the grotesque customs of circumcision, an invention of desert humyn tribes concerned with the lack of hygiene, yet not wise enough to move themselves to a land with more water. It was an extreme solution, grotesque enough for males, but utterly barbaric when applied to females. But Galen had swallowed her aversion for the joy of finding something Rosen visibly recoiled from, which was hard to do. He had been a tough boy, knowing to share in girl's activities he couldn't afford to look weak.

Even now that was what drove Rosen, the fear he would look weak. A wave of regret washed over Galen for their indiscretion. Thankfully it was fading in the past and that was a blessing. She would do this task well for him. Tresmadore would be pleased and then perhaps they could rest a little.

After a quick breakfast of oatmeal provided by reluctant cooks from several ships, those prisoners fit to work were chivvied to the task, first clearing out the holds, bringing barrels, crates and bags up to the deck to be sorted by crew, a necessity to know what was needed to feed them. Water, when it was good was left as it was, in clay amphora near the oar benches or the barrels in the hold. It would keep the ship stable. In fact care had to be taken in balancing movement on the relatively shallow draughted vessels.

Once all supplies were brought from below, the men were set to work cleaning the hold. Filth was thrown into the sea, the planks below salted and scrubbed. Some chuntered and moaned but neither Galen or the women watching them cared, provided the work continued. A couple times work slowed and Galen was forced to use the starter, the end of a length of rope, as thick as a walking stick, that in times before Recognition was used to beat lazy crew. The sharp crack of the hemp hitting the deck next to where an insolent individual stared up defiantly at Galen was enough for the humyn to redirect his course to industry. The Admiralty forbade the flogging of prisoners but not the threat of the same. It was not a pleasant task, driving these beasts to work, but it had to be done.

After came the upper deck. The supplies had been stacked to the side, secured by ropes and tarps. Broken wood, benches, fallen arrows, and the last of the bodies had already been cleared. The deck was now to be stoned and sanded, something that Galen herself needed to demonstrate. She had not realized Shari ships were not stoned, but it made sense. The vessels were not so large and there wasn't an imperative that the surface be as smooth as possible to move solcannons quickly. Nonetheless, they would stone, and those that could not stone, scrubbed with sand, as well as clearing the captain's cabin out. Only the tops where the guards watched were spared. By late afternoon the prisoners were exhausted. They were fed again, more oatmeal, a grain many were unfamiliar with. Yet they didn't complain; unseasoned and bland, it was something, though some muttered about "slave food". After eating they were allowed to dress, some rewrapping turbans around their hair. Then they were returned to the hold and bound again. After the attempted revolt, no chances were taken. Spare blankets had been brought, many older and thin. This was a sop to morale, the crew and volunteers being offered new blankets if they donated their old ones to the prisoners' keep. One might say bedding wasn't essential; the sheer amount of bodies in the hold produced enough heat to keep them from chill. But it would becalm them.

Near sunset Galen stepped back onto the galley where Rondaleth was stationed.

"They're calling the ship *Ta Azaduta*," Rondaleth said, as she dipped scrap bread crusts into a bowl of mashed chickpeas mixed with lime and salt.

"*'Azaduta'?*" Galen queried. "Freedom is '*azadi*' in Shari."

"Ah, but not among the Cathans, who share a dialect similar to the Asherites, both of which claim some relation to either Fars or Bedu. Though the differences be small, beware of mistaking them lest an offended Cathan correct you with a tongue sharper than the bite of an asp. You may inquire how I came by this knowledge."

Galen laughed looking to the bows, where Hanno waved at her.

"My brother!" he called. "You come, you eat!"

The Cathan sailors and free Shari all looked much better. Smiling made their rough maned faces less savage looking. The galley had also been cleaned, though not to such a degree. They were not prisoners and the top deck had not suffered damage during the battles. They were motivated by concern for their own comfort in the coming night.

"I cannot!" Galen called back. "I must return!" She gestured in general to the Tyreen ships nearby.

Hanno laughed, calling, "You work harder than a slave, my brother!"

"Still hasn't figured out you're a mother?" Rondaleth asked bemused.

"It keeps them cheerful. How do the women fair?"

"They bathed and seemed affable, but the wild one has a complaint. She has insisted on speaking with our captain."

"Has she now," Galen said. She admired the spirit of a Shari woman who somehow had not been broken. But Galen hadn't forgotten the attack. "Did the healers examine them?"

"Ai. They are all bound for the temple in Gashora. Not just because of the use they endured. Their minds…well, they say they might be a danger to themselves if they didn't have adjustments.

This was probably true. Adjustments of mind were administered for shocks and frights, especially with small children and animals who did not have the understanding to calm themselves. This would be much more serious. There was a rumor in the aftermath of the Battle of Gate Step there was the most adjustments given to mature souls at a time. Galen wondered how many of the crew might benefit. Perhaps they should all be examined.

"I haven't seen any star gazers," Galen said.

"Oh ai, they've been too busy with sadol operations. Should be a couple coming on the morrow."

"Well, I see my launch coming," Galen said. "The captain should be inspecting tomorrow. Are you settled well enough?"

"Ai, we have a good watch, fine vittles and plenty of mead and black rum. It's like having my own command."

"Just don't lose the run of your ambitions, lieutenant."

"Never fear, boatswain, never fear. Good eve."

As she drifted away in the evening gloom, Galen imagined the clustered scorpion warships lurking near the merchant galleys as shadowy hulks, vessels of dreams and damnations none of them could yet escape. Looking on them she felt foreboding. If in the night the warships were all swallowed by one of the great sea dragons, a Thynamar, it would be no loss in Galen's mind.

Chapter 25

Shackled

For a moment Hadi thought they would win. Seeing the great Vardashi flag-ship fall apart with blue fire had excited him. His prophecy was becoming true! The Sultan would have his victory and Hadi would have his revenge! Now all was lost; Hadi watched as Komar Zan submitted to the She Devils of the sea.

Where had they strayed? True, they had been surprised by the bright weapon that smote their ships with the rays of the sun. Komar Zan had been angry, even clumsy messages by flags somehow conveying his rage at being caught by surprise with this fire magic. But rain quelled it. That should have been their hour of victory as many of the Vardashi ships were swarmed with hardened warriors. Yet the Queens of the Sea were adept even without their magic; they had their own men to repel the Sultan's troops, pale warriors like those from the northern lands of gloom, and other bright warriors like the guard who challenged Hadi in the Port of Djinn years ago: tall, gold haired with an aura of a sainted prophet. Over the years Hadi had managed to convince himself that warrior had been a man, other-wise he would have to admit the Sultan's fleet had been defeated by Var-dashi women. And not with tricks or seduction, but by some raw force that defied everything the clerics of Al-ahat said was truth. He knew many cler-ics and magi of the Sultan's court were delusional fanatics or crafty mounte-banks. Still, much of their wisdom was based on the folk culture that had prevailed in Sharitan for centuries. That wisdom said woman did not defeat man except by sly trickery worthy only of cowards.

Whatever they were, the Vardashi were not cowards. And with the return of the sun they took their vengeance, destroying ship after beautiful ship, crafted with hard won knowledge, turned into so much kindling. Hadi knew it was over when Komar Zan made a defensive circle. Perhaps he prayed one of the fireships would do more damage, take another Vardashi vessel to its grave. But they understood the danger and eliminated them all from a safe distance.

Hadi had been creeping his own boat by water magic away from the bat-tle and north since the failed attempt to storm the ships. There was a flotilla still free, perhaps he could meet with them. At least he'd be in the direction he was sure would take him to his father's lands. Through the water glass, Hadi felt the waves undulating, bearing his small ship up and down. It was indescribably pleasant, this feeling of being one with the water. If only he could enjoy it. Instead he must somehow make an escape. Many were the tales of the Sea Queens who killed brigands and pirates without mercy. Hadi didn't expect to be spared, and in fact was surprised the rest of the fleet hadn't been put to the fire magic.

"What are you doing?" one of the crew demanded.

Hadi stood on a platform at the bows of the ship, a sort of sunken gallery, the bottom of which was threaded and infused with the water magic glass. For this venture he wore a helmet under his turban, a light mail shirt beneath his robes, at his belt a jewel handled sword the Sultan himself had presented. The man was one of his guard, known to the palace through his father, also a respected sheik.

"Calm yourself," Hadi said, with a confidence he did not feel. "We will find the flotilla and return to help."

"Bah!" the man said, sneering. "You are a coward! You have the magic of Al-ahat! His vision has brought us this far. Did you not call the rain before? Do it again and save the fleet!"

It was true Hadi had allowed, even encouraged, the idea that he commanded water magic for Al-ahat. This simple creature would not believe he had no power no matter what he said but he preferred not to fight it.

"Al-ahat's ways are inscrutable to all but Himself," Hadi said. "We will return in the night and rescue the captain – "

The guard spit at Hadi's face, making him dodge to avoid it. "Snake words! They speak of you, conniving and clever as a Vardashi. The Goat-eared Djinn."

Hadi's ears burned, his face prickling with old shame.

"Perhaps the Sultan will see the truth, that you've been a spy for the Vardashi all along – "

In a flash Hadi drew the light sword and sliced the blade across the guard's throat. So fast he was, the man couldn't even scream, clutching his neck, red rivers of his life leaking through his fingers. Wide eyed with impending death, the man sank to his knees.

That would not do. Hadi couldn't have him interfering with the fragile water glass beneath his feet. With his other hand Hadi yanked the creature up by the front of his mailed shirt and hefted him over the edge of the pilot platform. The guard rolled over clumsily, falling into the water with a splash. Thus the suspicions about Hadi's motives would drown with the man.

Above Hadi, on the main deck, was a cry of alarm. There were two other guards, as well as a couple of sailors of no consequence. Hadi cursed and stepped up to the deck to meet the guard. His mind was full of rage and confusion; the dead guard had been his friend.

"What have you done?" the man shouted, drawing his sword, a curved thing better suited for cavalry.

"He was a traitor," Hadi said. He didn't expect to be believed but said it to buy time.

"Liar!" the guard cried, swinging his blade.

Hadi stepped aside, adroitly avoiding it. He was the first to admit he had no great skill in fencing. But he did have Vardashi speed. Quick as an asp he stabbed his opponent in the neck. The man fell gurgling to the deck. Hadi turned away and was hit in the face with a fist, knocking him to the deck to fall awkwardly on the second guard's body.

The fist was actually holding a sword and had missed cutting Hadi's neck by pure chance. Hadi rolled, evading a swipe at his head, then neck. Then he ducked to pick up the sword he dropped. On rising he jumped out of the way of another slash before cutting up and severing the last guard's head.

Blood spilled across the deck, but this was no matter. It did not interfere with the water magic. Meanwhile the Cathan sailors huddled in terror. He could almost feel their thoughts: perhaps they should jump into the sea and take their chances with the Sea Queens?

"I will not stop you if you wish to flee! But stay understanding you serve me, not the Sultan!"

They nodded uncertainly. This was not a surprise. Hadi knew most Cathans hated the Sultan. "Then clean this up! We sail north – "

"Look!" one of the sailors cried.

Hadi's piloting had been interrupted and in that time someone from the Vardashi fleet had taken an interest. One of the great ships was turning towards the merchant galleys, bearing down on all of them. Hadi jumped down the steps on to the platform in the bows, feet, aura and essence instantly in contact with the water magic. He turned the yacht north with one goal: to flee. Maybe it wasn't him the ship was after. Surely the merchant galleys would be a better prize. Who knows what riches their captains had brought with them. And there were women...

Hadi cursed his foolishness. Of course they wouldn't be interested in the women. But perhaps tending to them would slow them down. If Hadi could drive the yacht far enough, long enough, maybe they would give up. It was only a tiny boat compared to the leviathan Vardashi vessels. He prayed they thought him as unimportant as a sand beetle in a bazaar.

It was not to be. For a good half hour Hadi drove the yacht through choppy waves, the sea more vigorous than the coastal routes usually taken. And though he'd put much distance between the yacht and the Vardashi vessel, there was now no doubt it followed him. There was some business with the merchant galleys. But another vessel was tending them now, the first ship again in pursuit, a relentless hungry wolf at sea, determined to feast its fill.

"Pray to your gods!" Hadi said to the sailors. "We may not be long for life!"

For Hadi expected to be burnt asunder by the fire magic for his refusal to surrender. Not that he had explicitly been given the chance. However it was expected. It was the way with the Sultan's forces against cities that resisted. The first armies, driven by the twin ambitions of Al-ahat and dreams of empire, razed resisters. By the time the Sultan rose to power they had become merciful out of practicality. The conquerers, a mix of ambitious clans from the fertile basin and pastoral tribes hungry for gold, often lacked the skills to exploit the economies of their new territories. Slaughtering people to seize land one could not use was a waste, as well as a weakness. If the land was not firmly occupied, it could be taken back. Thus the practice shifted to simply slaughtering all the armed defenders.

Hadi had no illusions of his use to Vardashi. If anything he expected to be punished for daring to use their magic against them. How did they execute traitors? he wondered. Why had he not sought this knowledge? He did not even have poison to save himself from the certain torture that was coming. He could dive into the sea. But if they wanted him, he knew they had better swimmers by far than himself. He did have a knife. Was he brave enough to use it on himself, to cut his own throat as quickly as he'd cut the guards? He did not want to die. All of his dreams were failing, all of his ambitions come to nothing. At least he would be with his mother again in the paradise the Vardashi called "beyond the Door". Or was even that way shut to him for what he'd done, for making war on their nation?

A horn sounded, long and deep, the kind calling the high steppe tribes to war. Then a voice speaking in Shari bellowed like thunder from the sky: "Flee no longer and surrender!"

Hadi looked over his shoulder and quailed. The prow of the great ship loomed over him, waves of water flowing in swells away from the massive hull, almost directly above him the largest anchor he'd ever seen, lashed to the ship. If it were to drop, he and the entire yacht would be destroyed. At the head of the bows, rising like cresting a wave, was the figurehead of a dancing or flying man, holding a gilded wheel over his head. This was the closest Hadi had been to the great ships, like forces of nature parting the waves, larger even than whales. How had they ever imagined victory would be theirs? Great curved blades of blue water glass sat in the hull along the water line. Hadi instinctively understood they gave the ship's water magic more leverage and maneuverability, in addition to the driving keel. His boat would be swamped by the force of the vessel, even drawn under by its passing. The sailors screamed for him to stop, but he drove the yacht on. Better to die in the water than burn by fire.

"There's no escape, you ridiculous sand druid!" the thunderous voice echoed over him.

Hadi was made bold by desperation, given hope by his keen feeling with the water. The swells that threatened to swamp his boat he made his allies, riding through them like an expert fisherman navigating stormy waters. The wave, the swell, the flow, even the force of the Vardashi vessel all spoke the wordless language of water, the birthright his hated father had gifted him. He felt the way by droplets, his boat could safely strike past, learning to push the water to his advantage as he'd never thought to do before, minimizing counter waves that hindered his passing. It was exhilarating, perhaps he

341

would escape after all. He laughed. Vardashi water magic was his to command!

Unfortunately Hadi had much to learn. While he was quite talented, his experience was negligible compared to a Tyreen pilot. Being so close to the ship put the yacht into *The Fortunate*'s aura. Both being aqua vessels, their water essence started to interact in ways Hadi could not have predicted. The usual course was the lesser vessel's pilot, on feeling the closeness, worked to evade the larger vessel, using its wake swells to help keep distance. But the reverse was possible: the greater ship, with greater essence leverage could push a smaller boat away – or draw it closer. To Hadi's horror he felt his boat slow to match the ship's speed and then virtually stop. Ropes were thrown down, landing heavily on the deck, followed by figures in white trousers and blue vests, sliding down like expert mountaineers. Some had strange bars of metal, the same weight as a small sword but blunt and heavy. Others had whip like ropes. Hadi stood facing up from the pilot's platform, sword out, daring any to come forward.

The voice bellowed out in the Vardashi tongue, "Remember, my fine sea fleas, we want him alive."

Hadi could feel the Vardashi around him thought little of this. Their unfriendliness was palpable. A couple glared with strange green eyes, wearing crowns of leaves on their heads; the others were similar to the golden Vardashi of the Port of Djinn, perhaps not quite as graceful or tall, but still with a magical force to their auras. Like Hadi, all their brows and ears were accented to some degree. In that instant he saw his tragedy: it was not the recognition of his sire he wanted so much as a place he could belong, a place he was no longer alone.

A splash behind him made him spin around. He had a second to note a woman with black hair bound on the top of her head, blue skin like the sky, wearing a shimmering shirt of scale mail, before the trident in her hands caught and wrenched his sword from him, throwing it in the sea. Before he could cry out the others set upon him and soon his hands were bound with a magical vine that wrapped itself around his wrists like a living thing. He was defeated; there was nothing else to do.

The women called up their success, his sailors surrendering, also bound, but perhaps not as firmly. They were hauled onto the greater ship by ropes like sacks of flour, deposited on the wide deck in front of a tall whip thin figure with gold hair and eyes, and the energy of one forever young. She grinned, a young woman, pleased to have her prize. A horn was in her hand; it was her voice amplified like thunder that hounded him. Her garb was stranger yet: an indigo blue coat cut close to the body, with a skirt in the back like a swallow's tail; fitted white trousers and knee high black boots; a black hat with gold trimmings on the front and sides that seemed to match the gold on the shoulders of the jacket, a star and a sea horse, perhaps insignia of rank. She wore a sword and her eyes blazed with excitement as Hadi was brought before her, seized as soon as he stepped on the deck between two burly savage looking women who he understood to be guards. The captain spoke while a Vardashi in black robes translated.

"The captain says, 'you sure did give a chase and that's the truth!' You are welcomed aboard *The Fortunate* and your vessel shall not be abandoned."

It was true. As they spoke his yacht was being lifted by ropes and yards out of the sea to hand lashed at the side of the ship. The sheer ability of another ship to do such a thing had Hadi in awe.

"And myself?" Hadi asked.

"You and your companions will be taken for questioning. I suggest you are truthful. I feel you understand lying would be futile."

Hadi said nothing. They were shoved down a stair wrapped with a strange plant to a lower deck. It was so big a small village could gather in the space. Before Hadi could wonder more at it, they were put into a room with a guard, forced to sit down on the bottom part of a tower of cots. They were given water, and escorted to a toilet area once. It was all strange. It took Hadi the longest time to figure out the strangest thing: the ship did not stink. There was the smell of burnt salts of course, sulfur and charcoal. But it did not stink of sweat or grime, and the clever toilets did not even require the changing of buckets. One was only bidden to throw water down them.

"What will they do with us?" one of the sailors asked.

Hadi tensed, expecting a rebuke, but the guard said nothing. They were only shouted at if they tried to stand. "I know not," Hadi said. "But you should know what the one said is true: lying is futile. You are Cathan sailors. While you bent your backs to the service of his Eminence, your lack of love may save you."

Hadi didn't know why he was reassuring the men. He felt some guilt for terrorizing them earlier. In honesty he felt guilt for killing the guards. Now he understood, their intentions to report his actions to the Sultan were in vain. He should have laughed at it. Years of terror of losing his station could not be undone in a moment; he only knew nothing could keep him from his personal quest to find his father.

In the evening one of the women in blue came with a magi. For a wild moment Hadi thought one of the hated wise men had joined with the Vardashi. But no, the gold eyed woman's robes were of a different cut, silver tracings glimmering in the fabric, her round, flat-topped hat studded with four golden diamonds that seemed to glow. One could feel her soul force. Hadi resisted praying to Al-ahat, cogent that such a thing would not help his case. The sailors had no such reservations, muttering to their pagan gods for deliverance. Hadi heard the sound of scraping across slate in his mind, then wasps. The magi looked between them with terrible eyes, eyes that saw into the soul, then asked the sailors in Shari, "How did you serve the Sultan?"

Of course they betrayed the Sultan, their service, their very presence at sea. They would not have come to war against the Vardashi. Cathans knew this was foolishness, but they had no choice. This last was only partly true. The sailors had been chosen from the best who worked in the shipyards of Tal-al-Amlot, offered a portion of profit after the sack of Gazhor. However it was true their service to the Sultan would be compelled one way or another. The magi listened without interruption and told the guard in their tongue to remove the sailors from the cabin. Then Hadi was searched by another guard, bidden to remove his turban, robes, armor, even his shoes, until he wore nothing but his linen pants. The guard roughly patted him, seeking hidden instruments or weapons. But even his eating knife had been taken from him during capture. He shivered slightly wondering if now the torture would begin.

"Do you harbor any idea of escape or sabotage?" the magi asked suddenly, her voice seeming to ring through his head though she had not raised it.

"I...I will not if I am treated honorably," Hadi managed to say. "For asking a prisoner to not wish for escape is like asking a bird to forsake the sky."

The woman in the blue coat laughed. *"Nach bhfuil sé dána?"*

Hadi did not know this tongue. He'd been careful to not reveal he knew some of the Vardashi language though was never as fluent as his mother. It was a language they used between them in his father's house. But this was strange, like nothing he'd ever heard.

"You are to understand, provided you have no designs on escape or mischief, you will not be bound. Do you agree without reservation?"

"Yes," Hadi said. He felt a pressure against his head, the magi sorcerer seeking his mind to confirm his compliance. Then the pressure was gone and the magi turned to the other woman, telling her he would be docile and should be washed and fed before being delivered to the sea king.

Hadi hid his surprise. "Sea king"? Had he heard correctly? Or was it "sea father"? It would be strange after all these adventures to learn the Vardashi She Devils were after all ruled by a man. He was taken away to a room with both toilets and washing basins.

Now free to observe his surroundings Hadi gave himself to wonder. Wood seemed to grow in decorative joins as it met both the ceiling and the floor. Warm lanterns hung, light flickering behind spiraling filigree, while the harsher bluish light of the sky filtered down through massive hatches along the centerline of the ship. There was more than enough room to walk without bending his back, many of the Vardashi being taller than himself. Paint was sparse; a dark blue with orange trimmings covered the walls to either side with doors. But most of the wood was uncolored, though it shone with rubbing and oil treatment. Like the Sultan's fleet, many fittings were copper or bronze, all shining brightly with disciplined care. The crew was a separate wonder.

For the first time Hadi saw what he was sure were the Hybernat barbarians from the northern lands of gloom. He had read about the woven hatchwork patterns of many colors, wool trousers with bold stripes, the heavy rings of twisted metal around their necks, not something their slaves wore, but reserved for the honored. Their skin was not as whey pale as Hadi expected. Perhaps it was sunburn from their voyage. But they indeed had many tattoos though Hadi did not expect them to have the same ears and brows he shared with the crew. Were all the Hybernat Vardashi as well? Many of these warriors bound their hair on the tops of their head with brass rings or thongs. They stared at him with unfriendly gray eyes, smooth faces reminding Hadi of the femaleness that belied many of their muscular limbs.

After washing Hadi was returned to the room and allowed to dress. Not unexpectedly his armor and helmet was gone. Food was brought to him, a wooden bowl with a pea soup mixed with a sausage like meat, along with water in a tin cup. He ate and drank, grateful of this care. One of the lanterns was hanging, burning low as the light outside the window faded. He was left without a guard now and so went to look.

It would have been a magnificent view, like in a tower floating over the water, except the hulk of another ship loomed near, blocking his sight. Still it was interesting, the hull rising from copper plating at the water line, up a body of white painted planks to alternating bands of blue and black, what looked like two towers flanking the tops of the aft stern. The setting sun glowed gold and red through many engines on the upper deck that housed long bars of honey colored glass. This must be the engine of fire that had destroyed the Sultan's dreams. Masts rose like the tallest trees, Vardashi among them like sailors everywhere. Now Hadi saw they did have sails, but were tightly furled, used only infrequently. He wished he could see the setting sun, see the sky unhindered one last time. For whatever the Vardashi sorcerer had said, he was certain when the morrow came his life would be over. He had never forgotten the burnt, twisted figure outside the walls of the Port of Djinn. Whatever offense that wretched soul had caused the Vardashi, surely Hadi had exceeded his crime.

The cot was more comfortable than Hadi expected, the blanket warm though it was thin. So he slept and dreamed of times past, and of memories his mother imparted through her dreams:

> When his mother Lamia carried Hadi, she began to dream as a Vardashi, and a true vision showed her the path of her fate before it came. She saw herself coming before Sheikh Parviz Chabahar abu Ameleth and his court, saw herself waiting, head veiled and bowed, the perfect humble and modest woman. The man, who she only knew by name and title, was not hideous, but he had the hard eyes

of one with little pity to spare in his dance with ambition. He set down a letter, a letter from her father that offered his daughter as concubine in exchange for favors in both trade and court.

Lamia understood this vision was her salvation. She had thought of fleeing, of even throwing herself into the sea. Briefly she thought of returning to the Port of Djinn. But she would not be pitied. She also did not trust the Vardashi, even her friend Telshorn, would understand the plight of a woman in the Sultan's realm. They would expect her to act like a man, demand her rights of motherhood! No woman in Sharitan had rights by being a mother except by the whim of a man. And no man would write the letter she had seen, not even her father. He cherished her in his way, but her duty as a daughter was to be his chattel. Father had his own ideas on who would be a best match. Her panic grew when she knew without a doubt she was pregnant and no marriage would be arranged in time to save her honor. So it was with a mix of sadness and joy that she saw her father die in a fit, a pleurisy of the heart not uncommon to the aging prosperous man, his indulgent life choking his heart.

Lamia worked fast to write the letter her vision foretold, sending it with a messenger, waiting anxiously for weeks. Meanwhile she retrieved the cache she had saved for herself, now hidden in her jewelry box, enough funds to flee to the Port of Djinn if all was lost. Then her prayers were answered: she was summoned to the Sheik's house, escorted by her brothers, the letter read and all came to pass as she had seen.

Finding her pleasing, Parviz Chabahar accepted her, and soon bedded her. It was a thing painful and unpleasant, nothing like her Vardashi lover Linastola. But to Parviz his cynical soul had finally found love. Some Vardashi magic in her aura moved him to obsession. In the days following he decided to marry Lamia. No concubine she, but his true love gifted by Al-ahat! Lamia was now a wife, much to the displeasure of Parviz's former favorite, Shadra.

Even before Hadi's birth his life was at risk. One night Shadra attacked Lamia with a knife in an attempt to blind and disfigure her. Now visibly pregnant, Lamia had the senses of a Vardashi. With a strength Lamia never knew before, she overpowered Shadra. Lamia had no animosity for the other woman. She was fighting for her own survival in the cruel world men had trapped them both in. Lamia pleaded with Shadra to stop, that they did not have to be enemies. But Shadra would not stop and tried to stab Lamia's belly. Catching the knife, Lamia turned it, still in Shadra's hand, sinking it into her stomach. Shadra died gasping, Lamia looking down sadly, understanding how woman must fight woman under men to secure the safety of herself and her children.

Lamia ran, screaming for help, that Shadra threatened to kill herself in despair at being abandoned. So that was the tale accepted when the woman's body was found. Lamia became head wife, befriending all, though friends of Sharda remained wary. Hadi was born much later than Lamia expected, a blessing to her tale. The child a boy, was healthy but strange. Lamia made a show of praying to Al-ahat to grace her boy with a cure for his odd coloring and Djinn features. Lamia made Hadi wear the turban at a young age. Then Lamia had a vision of Hadi as man, but with no beard. He wore the robes of the magi and stood at the hand of the Sultan explaining some device of war.

Lamia had been relieved. They would be safe. Hadi would be safe and honored, even being begat from Vardashi which no one must ever know. And this was life for both Hadi and his mother. Status gained with Vardashi magic, lost to a small degree with his grotesque birth, retained in fragility by Parviz's lingering affection.

Hadi woke in the dark, the lantern burnt out, alone with his thoughts. He was glad to have not dreamed further, of his mother's final days, of her pining for Linastola who had long forgotten her. In spite of his precarious promises to abjure thoughts of escape, the rage against his father returned.

With the light of dawn he was taken to relieve himself and given more food, this time a pan fried cake to be washed down with water. Then he was forced to wait again as the morning light grew. The ships outside moved like swans in the Sultan's gardens, engaging in various tasks, boats being raised and lowered. A loud knock sounded and Hadi turned to the door. It opened and a guard stood with the same woman in the blue coat. Neither seemed to speak either Fars or Bedu, but the guard forced shackles over Hadi's wrists then pulled him out of the room. Once he followed her direction she let him walk on his own. They were going back to the deck above, under the sky.

The black robed sorcerer was waiting.

"I apologize for your shackles," she said. "It is the regulation of the Federation navy when handling belligerent prisoners of a certain class. "Do you still agree to abide by the terms we discussed before?"

Hadi hesitated. "I have no plans to escape. Where would I go? But if I see a chance to follow my course I will take it. I served the Sultan true, but now I serve my own ambition."

"And that is?"

"To find my father and bring him to account!"

"Interesting. Well, down you go. The chains should give you enough play to navigate the ladder."

Hadi looked below. He could barely see the boat because of the curve of the ship. It seemed much farther down than he remembered.

"Don't look," the magi said. "It will be easier on your mind."

"*Déan deifir!*" an impatient guard said when Hadi hesitated. Slowly he made his way down, fearful of falling and not being free to swim properly. Once in the boat, they made a choppy journey past ships obviously engaged in salvage. He watched while a great object just out of sight in the water was wrapped with ropes and towed to a nearby ship. Then it was pulled up by the yards, a beautiful length of blue-green glass over three feet thick and as long as one of the boats. It spilled water like a cascade as it was carefully raised to the deck. Hadi realized the Vardashi might be working a while if their goal was to recover the entire wreck of the fallen vessel. Soon they were under the figurehead of a golden dolphin and Hadi was climbing aboard a new ship, the ship of the sea king, he assumed.

It was much the same as the other, important persons – officers? – in blue jackets and black hats striding to and fro between crew that wore wore anything from the blue vest and white leggings to the savage garments of the rude Hybernat. A guard as meaty as the rest seized him on his arrival, all but dragging him, not below decks, but into the shadows under the stern. Instead of a door to the captain's cabin as expected, they passed by a small cabin, its door open, where a scribe worked furiously cribbing notes she was given by youths who ran to and fro. Nearby was a wheel, for what purpose Hadi did not know, behind it a narrow stair below. But that was not their path. A door was ahead and once opened they stepped into a room filled with sunlight.

It was as if Hadi was back at the traveler's inn in the Port of Djinn. This room was made for dining, a large table taking up its center, surrounded with the throne like seats the Vardashi preferred. A couple women in blue coats sat at a meal with bread and some sort of meat. On entering they stood, hands clutching their swords, gold eyes glaring at him with reproach. The guard leading Hadi hammered hard on the door at the end of the room.

"A chaptaen! Tá an cime anseo!" the woman shouted.

There was a pause before a voice called out, "Enter!" in Vardashi.

Hadi was led into a wondrous chamber with windows spread out before him so the sight of the sea was unhindered. The room was as well made as any he'd seen, with every comfort: a large bed to one side, partly hidden by a curtain, desks with papers and quills, more chairs and cabinets and even a chessboard, though no pieces were in sight. A sumptuous bench padded with red velvet ran beneath the windows, and short steps led to a gallery should the captain wish to take air or craved privacy. To the far side of this chamber the walls curved out, inset with more windows. These were the towers he had seen from outside. A presence made Hadi shiver and then he laid eyes on two magi like sorcerers, lingering next to an important looking desk, the chair empty. One, with pale almost white eyes, Hadi felt was young, her power strong but wild. The other did not look exactly old; she looked ageless, perhaps there was the beginning of creasing around her eyes. But those eyes were more terrible yet, gilded glimmers of the sun's wisdom fallen to the earth to burn the unworthy and wanting with stark truth.

Hadi shivered, swallowing, his throat suddenly dry. He'd finally spied the captain, or who he assumed was the captain. A figure had stood so still in the gallery, back to them, Hadi's eyes had slid over it. Now it turned, with the strange gilded black hat, stepping up from the gallery to come to the table. If this was a man, he was one of the most beautiful men Hadi had ever seen. His eyes were first gold, then blue. No, it was a blue sheen –

Hadi couldn't tell. His long black hair was braided like all the officers' in a kind of pony tail. This man moved with a fit grace, without the bulk of the guard whose hand still grasped him, but dangerous. He took his throne behind the desk.

"Tell him to sit," the man said. Even his voice had a different quality to Hadi's ear: lower than a woman, but higher than a man.

Hadi began to sit on the stool placed before him by the guard then cursed himself. The motion was marked by the sorcerers.

"I do believe he understands us," the older one said.

"Does he," the captain said. "Then maybe we can finish quicker than we thought."

"I confess to lack fluency," Hadi said, keeping to Shari. As he expected his mind was surrounded by noise, his truth and thoughts being examined. "My mother, she understood your speech much better. I can read some, but have little practice speaking to Vardashi."

"He has a student's understanding," one sorcerer said. "It might be best to use Shari for clarity."

"Fine," the captain said. "Tell him who I am and why he's here, Ta Hethlion."

"You are in the presence of Captain Gathelyn of *The Tidebreaker*. You are to answer questions about your involvement with the Sultan's aggressive actions. Will you speak willingly and truthfully?"

"Yes," Hadi said. What loss was there now? Even if the flotilla made it to the isle of Sea Queens it was doubtful they would survive, much less rescue him.

"Well, that makes things much easier, don't you think, Sea Father?"

The other sorcerer was setting up a table for writing.

"Ready, Ta Glenfar?" The captain said.

"Ai, Sea Father."

"Then let's begin."

"First, what is your name?" Hethlion asked.

Hadi told them everything: his mother's story, how he came to be, his rise in the Sultan's court, the making of steel, his reconstruction of the water magic ship. At the end the captain stared at him, eyes darkened more by their blue sheen, the gold absent. Finally he spoke very simply and carefully in Fars, apparently wanting Hadi to understand him:

"Do we understand that you lied about your vision of victory all so you could settle a score with your sire?"

Something about how the captain asked this made Hadi quail. The man, so beautiful but yet a man, was angry. He stood and so did Hadi backing away, limited in his retreat by the bulk of the guard who had brought him in.

The captain started shouting, passionate words of grief and outrage, so fast Hadi could not catch all of them. He gestured at the bench under the windows, someone dear had sat there and was gone. Hadi tried to cling to his own rage, at his father's abandonment, his justification for everything he'd done, for everything his mother had done, to find the destiny he'd been robbed of. But the captain was too angry to care. And why should he? He only knew Hadi was an enemy who caused the deaths of those close to him.

The sorcerer said soothing words and the captain stopped raging. Instead he stared at Hadi, hatred in his eyes, as if he could set him aflame like their fire contraptions. Finally he asked, "Does Komar Zan know of your deception?"

Hadi shook his head violently. "Do not tell him!" Hadi, his eldritch Vardashi-born strength aside, was sure Zan would kill him.

"Why not?" The captain was yelling again. "I should have you shackled side by side so you could both discuss your many errors at length! But you are lucky to be a privileged belligerent. You will not be culled or tortured or despoiled because Command wants you brought to Ta Mel alive. You might even have your wish if they can find your sire, if only to understand how a wretch would think waging war was a reasonable solution to petty familial drama! Get this child out of my sight!"

And so Hadi was dragged away from the captain's wrath and put in another cell, but this one had no window. The lamp hung beyond his reach and shackles remained. Otherwise it was much like the room in the other ship. He felt he would have a long time to reflect before he finally reached Vardashi lands. For the first time since he committed to this venture he was not so certain he wanted to find his sire, this Linastola. He was now a man without a country or clan, and no leverage to make demands.

Yet Hadi was alive in spite of all, even if at the whim of the Vardashi. How it would end he didn't know. It had been all of his making, exploiting the Sultan's desires of conquest for his own ends. Had he failed because this was based on a lie, an immoral beginning for a just goal? What had Telshorn said? That his quest was in vain? Perhaps Hadi had been mistaken after all.

Hadi sat in thought a long time, considering his past and future to come.

Chapter 26

Salvage and Supplies

Rosen's day began long before dawn, taking the last watch of the night. The sun was barely above the water, just starting to warm the air, when he and Galen stepped into the launch with Ensign Sorani Aldweth, the male officer Rosen had raged at in his grief. He needed a clerk by his side, the purser could not spare her own, and Amralan was best where she was. Working as ship's secretary calmed her soul and kept her mind from the mistaken conceit she was to blame for abandoning Admiral Jansenwol. Aldweth was qualified and his deck officer, Lieutenant Loran Glendwol, said he could be spared. It would be an awkward journey, made more awkward in that their destination was *The Black Seal*. They climbed aboard while Galen continued in the launch to check the prisoners soon to be inspected by magi.

Admiral Tresmadore had sent for all the captains to meet on the new flagship to breakfast together. It was understood to be a working meal, for there was much to do before continuing to Gashora. The issue of supplies had become urgent: almost six hundred prisoners would not feed themselves. Ideally the supplies on the warships should suffice, but much was damaged or spoiled. The Tyreens themselves had little more than enough provisions to reach Gashora. Then there were the freed women and men on the galleys, who, being fed only enough to work, had even less to spare. Water was their bane for they had no seadrinkers or even stills. Every ship was filling barrels from the sea, filtering the water as fast as they could, drink vines being grafted and grown by those with the wood essence and skill. But filtering still took time, at least a day per barrel. Ideally this would be done as they sailed.

That was not yet possible because salvage was not finished. Most of the keel had been retrieved and many of the rib fins. There were still strong boxes unaccounted for. They sat around the pilot's mess table, Tresmadore sitting at the head, extra chairs and stools crowded around as they snacked from platers with cut fruit cakes, breads and cheeses, slices of sausage and ham, and one platter dedicated to raw fish. The sunlight filtering though the ample skylight was cheerfully bright, in contrast to their sober discussion.

"As you know," Tresmadore was saying, "Every ship's clerk carries a waxed leaf of paper inside her coat with a list of the ship's lockboxes. Do we have that list with us, Captain Gathelyn?"

Rosen was caught off guard. His mind was still on the prisoner report that Aldweth held. "No, Admiral," he replied. "It must still be in Amralan's possession. She's serving as my ship's clerk."

"We need that to know the exact number left and where to search for those still missing. Send a copy as soon as you're able."

"Yes, Admiral."

"Now is a good time as any to submit your requests."

This had been whistled the eve before: captains were to bring details of both their abundance and deficits and redistribute supplies accordingly. Aldweth stood to drop the leaf of paper with the rest, awkwardly reaching to avoid jostling Rosen. They had not made a peace and Rosen didn't know how to without pandering to Aldweth's sex. How often had he himself been yelled at as an ensign for no reason with never a hint of apology? It disconcerted him that he did not know how to resolve this. But more than that he realized Aldweth had barely eaten because of it.

Once Aldweth returned to his stool Rosen said brusquely, "You won't be any use to me starved, ensign. Here, take my plate and use it."

"Yes, Sea Father. Thank you, Sea Father."

Aldweth snatched a portion of ham, cake and cheese just as the flurry of submissions ceased.

"Now we estimate – ," Tresmadore paused to look at notes her own clerk passed her, " – to have another four or five days of salvage. How are we supplied for the fleet?"

This was directed to a burly woman in a kilt, bronze eyed, with hash and dot tattoos on her cheeks. Her red hair was coiled in braids on the top of her head and she wore a leather apron over her blue sea vest. She stood arms akimbo, as if impatient at the intrusion in her day.

"How many ways do I have to sing the ballad?" the woman growled with nothing of the deference expected for a captain, much less an admiral. "We do be skint, and I'll guess the tale is the same all on your ships. Maybe iffin you be getting stargazers to work the lances and coal, they can manifest more vittles. But I doubt Sel herself could work enough magic to feed our lot."

"For those of you not acquainted, this is our ship's cook, Emha Carredeth Banat. She was a chef in a Dunvan bistro for decades and is reputed to be a culinary genius."

"*Is ealaíontóir mé!*" Banat said proudly.

"Yes, you are an artist," Tresmadore allowed. "Your freedom with a publican's son was less appreciated. In any case, artistry and brilliance will not keep you from starving with the rest of us. So what do you suggest we do?"

It was hard to tell if the cook was thinking or seething. "It's obvious, isn't it?" Banat finally said. "Fish."

"Fish doesn't keep without salt," Captain Roanteth said.

"And we may need to send the divers far if the water hasn't cleared," Sleath put in. The mix of blood, sulfur and salts had polluted the immediate area.

"Oh, what can we do?" Banat said sarcastically. "If only we were able to move our presence on the sea from one place to another! And salt! It's not as if we're not surrounded with it! *Amadáin!*"

"That will do," Tresmadore said, but she smiled with amusement. "For those of us not so brilliant, how can we fish and store it quickly?"

"Pickled garum," Banat said, somewhat mollified by the pandering to her expertise. "Still won't keep like proper salting, but should get us to Gashora. And we'll need even the drunken supplies from *The Oaken Blue*. They'll be barrels of water, cheeses the fish haven't eaten and even the oats and wheat. Bread and flour will be done for of course, but the rest shouldn't be left."

Tresmadore sighed mightily. Rosen understood. He too wanted to get to Gashora and be done with the adventure. But it was senseless to forage harder when there was food to be retrieved.

"And Admiral?" This was from Manweth who had stood.

"Yes, Captain Lanash?"

"The weather seems to be amiable, but the currents less so. We may take longer that expected even if we were to leave for Gashora today."

"That will be impossible if we're to tow those Shari scows!" Lenor said.

Tresmadore was quiet while the captains murmured in general agreement. Finally she laid predator's eyes on Rosen. "Now is a good time to review the report on the prisoners and our special guest."

Rosen nodded to Aldweth who stood and quickly walked to pass the papers in question to Tresmadore.

"Thank you, ensign. We seem to be blessed with the presence of fine men today." She flipped through the leaves, distributing some to aides as she spoke. "Tell us about the prisoners, Captain Gathelyn."

Rosen summarized the report, detailing their berthing. "They are compliant and rendered harmless, Admiral," he finished. "As we speak magi are sorting them by character."

"Maybe the number can be culled," suggested the Blue-skinned Welansha of *The Dragon*. "That will save some supplies."

"Alas, that is beyond our scope," Tynlar said. "Once they are prisoners, our duty is transport and delivery. If any are doomed for death, their executions will be done by the Admiralty or Command."

"Too true, commodore," Tresmadore said.

It took Rosen a moment to comprehend. Of course, now Captain Tentynlar Aldwyn of *The Charred Bronze* was the fleet commodore.

"The cull is to be left to Federation authority," Tresmadore continued. "But what of the merchant galleys?"

"Yes, Admiral?" Rosen was uncertain what she was asking.

"Your crew master reports the humyn able, having no loyalty to the Sultan, and, most importantly, with ships virtually intact. 'They only desire to see their homes again' it says."

"Yes," Rosen affirmed.

"How many of these souls are there?"

"Just over two-hundred?" Rosen said.

"Two-hundred less mouths to feed. When the magi are finished with the prisoners, have the merchant crews examined. They cannot be freed without every soul passing an order of clearing. Once they have we can release them."

There was a general sound of agreement.

"However, that does not solve all our problems. We have four captured vessels in various states of damage. One will be towed or lashed to be taken

358

for further study. The rest scuttled. Because we cannot make speed while dragging primitive war ships. So I must ask a sacrifice from every ship here: find a place for, what is it?"

"Twenty-nine," her clerk replied.

"Make secure berthing for two score and ten prisoners. We share the load, we sail faster. Now tell us of this Hadi who has been the cause of so much mischief. He's aelg, correct?"

"Yes," Rosen said. "His mother was the daughter of a Shari farmer. She met a man from Meridian by the name of Linastola in a place called the 'Port of Djinn'."

A look crossed Tresmadore's face which then became blank and stony. "I know the place," she said softy, as if for a moment forgetting she was in a pilot's mess crowded with watching captains. "I know the place," she repeated more firmly. "We call it 'Jaret Harbor', named after the nearby township, though they have no true harbor apart from subsistence fishing south of the coast."

"Wasn't that where you worked on a merchant skip all those years ago?" Belshorn of *The Exalted Unicorn* said. "She somehow got lost in the desert for days – "

"Yes, it's a thrilling tale," Tresmadore cut in. "But we don't have time. Tell us more, Gathelyn."

Rosen related the substance of his interrogation the day before.

"Are we to understand the motive for causing so much chaos is a boy angry with his fati?" Jendalis of *The Sea Mare* demanded.

"He feels aggrieved," Rosen affirmed. "His mother had few choices as a woman in Sharitan growing without marriage to a man."

"Then his anger should be with the men who rule Sharitan!" Manweth said. "Not with a country that has never caused it hurt." Manweth sounded harsher than Rosen had ever heard him.

"I'm not for flogging," Roanteth said. "But some souls could benefit."

"There's one thing I was told by Ta Hethlion, after the interrogation," Rosen said. "Hadi looks like an adult man. His intelligence is as mature as any student starting studies, but he has the wisdom of a youth. Hethlion says it is partly from being shunned for his aelg features. Even so, he is no more mature than an older youth. If he was humyn, he would be fifteen to seventeen at most."

"I feel so much more at ease knowing a virtual child was the cause of all this destruction," Sleath said with a sarcastic sneer.

"Indeed," Tresmadore said. "However he is a privileged belligerent and it is for Command to decide his fate. As is their so called admiral, Komar Zan. You've done well so far. Organize the distribution of the prisoners, Gathelyn. As for the rest of you, it seems we'll be in these waters longer than expected, maybe a week before we can sail. So get your divers to work before we starve. To duty."

"To duty," the room echoed and they stood making preparations to leave. "Rosen?"

It was Tynlar. "Al met," he said. "Congratulations on commodore."

"It's not as if there was an allotment or vote. We're leaving aft fleet commander unfilled until we reach Gashora. I just wanted to say I'll be sending you a spare launch."

"Elam," Rosen said with feeling.

"To duty." Tynlar nodded to the ensign politely then left.

"Have you eaten enough?" Rosen asked Aldweth. He hesitated. "Grab what you want and be quick."

"Yes, Sea Father."

The launch brought Rosen close to a merchant, *Ta Azaduta* painted in white near the bow where a grotesque gargoyle figurehead leered. A rope ladder of a sturdier sort, one with slats, had been attached. Rosen smelled the scent of frying fish.

"Al met Sea Father!" a guard called down. "There's plenty if you're hungry!"

"We ate, thank you!" Rosen replied. "Tell Rondaleth I'm here!"

He climbed to the deck, the launch withdrawing with the ensign back to *The Tidebreaker*.

"Captain!" Rondaleth said, striding out of the aft cabin sucking on an olive. She had no hat.

"Where is your bicorn, lieutenant?" Rosen asked.

"Ah that. A tragic tale. I set it down within and I don't know where it's got to!"

Rosen looked at her dubiously.

"It's true, Sea Father. Dratted Shari I expect."

"The Shari stole your bicorn."

"Or the Cathan sailors. They're a merry bunch."

"Aye, the Cathans are a great bunch of lads," a guard put in, a twinkle in her eye.

Rosen sighed. With the passing of the battle, pranks would return. "I expect it will manifest," Rosen said, eying the Gael guard pointedly.

"Aye, it's likely," the woman said shamelessly. *"Na bígí buartha."*

Rosen looked around the upper decks. Humyn sat on oar benches chatting while doing tasks like mending. Nearby was a sort of open grill galley. This was where the fish was being cooked. At the far end a cluster of humyn intermingled with some divers from the fleet as they held more fish up, freshly caught.

"Look like sharks," Rondaleth put in.

"I'm surprised there aren't more," Rosen said. Most sharks were small, but they needed to be wary of a larger mother. There had been enough blood in the water to draw them for days. "Where's Galen?"

"Below, being given a tour by one of the Cathans."

"Well, let's join her."

The ship was old, well made for what it was, but quite primitive in ways. The stairs were little more than ladders, narrow and built with the expectation of being regularly replaced. Below the hold was dark, light leaking through the edges of the hatches. A couple small lamps burned near men too injured to work above. They smiled and nodded at him, white teeth flashing in the dimness. On either side of the hold thin blankets lay or were rolled, with sandals or shoes nearby and other meager personal effects.

"Captain!" Galen said. "I was just about to go above. All seems well enough."

"Ai," Rosen echoed uncertainly. "It seems sparse."

"This is what they're used to," Galen said. "They could do with more clothing. And a top off of their water."

"They'll need more than that," Rosen said. "We need to prepare them to voyage on their own."

"What?"

As they returned to the tops Rosen explained the low supplies and how they were to allow the free Shari cleared by magi to go their way.

"Well, they'll be happy," Galen said. "All they want – "

A hideous shrieking sound echoed from the bows. There was a struggle, a cry, and Rosen could just see a humyn figure being lifted over the hull by the ropey arms of a whip-thin diver. She wasn't as tall as most, but that didn't matter. Essence dense muscle made her as strong as a leopard. Her black hair was shaved on each side revealing triskelion and leaf tattoos.

"*NEE MISE DO HALEEN!*"

It was Gael sounded above water to scream in the open air, hurting landed ears.

The humyn shrank back, unsure of what to do while the one the diver held flailed, kicking his legs, trying to gasp for air.

"Diver!" Galen bellowed. "Release him!"

An inarticulate screech echoed out of the diver's mouth, sharp canines and incisors bared, then she tossed the man to the deck where he gasped.

"I do not understand, my brother!" he said to Galen in Shari.

Galen made a motion for silence, glaring at the diver. "What happened?" she demanded.

"Oh, is he your pet?" the diver demanded. "Then you should leash him! We bring them fish and our thanks is he thinks I want gold for my time?"

"He was trying to pay you for the fish?" Galen asked. "I still don't see –"

"No, not for the fish! He thinks we – or at least I – am a jockey of some kind.! That was fairly amusing until he refused the truth of his wrongness and thought to seize me for his own! I don't know why it was me he felt so amorous for, but I think the slow-witted creature understands now!"

Rosen didn't know what to think. Most of the divers were hearty women. Looking at them he thought he understood. This diver was a little shorter and thinner than the rest, much closer to what humyn expected a woman to be. Thank Sul Sharol hadn't been present. She'd have taken the humyn over to a watery grave.

"Galen? Explain their mistake and that none of our crew works as companions. This should not happen again and any humyn acting in this way will be put with the prisoners."

Galen spoke firmly in Shari, accented by Rondaleth, who was more adept with the subtleties of the language. The humyn had come shakily to his feet, grinning nervously, apologetic though still not really cognizant of what he'd done wrong. Rosen caught some of his words:

"My brother, I apologize for offending. The woman, she brings fish and smiles. I think we feel the same, but she is your woman?"

Galen closed her eyes, praying for patience. "No, Hanno, she is her own woman. She feels nothing and wants nothing from you."

Hanno bowed deeply, "I apologize my brother."

"And I am not your or anyone else's brother!" Galen barked.

Hanno's maned face looked hurt and confused. "I – I do not understand."

The diver threw up her hands. "Come on sisters!" she called from near the ship's edge. "We came to deliver fish, and we've done so. I came looking for a good woman. But there there seems to be a lack of real mothers present."

This was said looking straight at Galen, who seemed to have forgotten Hanno.

"Wait!" Galen said, but the divers jumped into the water and disappeared. "Frye," she added. "I didn't realize…"

"What?" Rosen asked.

"Frye is…like me."

"You swim well, but I imagine Frye is much better."

"No, you idi – " Galen broke off in respect of Rondaleth's presence.

"Oh." Rosen understood. "Well it's not like you're the only sister in the fleet…"

Galen glowered at him. Of course she knew that. Sel preserve him! He was slow. Frye had come looking not just for any woman, but Galen. He had no idea what the shape of this melodrama might be. And he planned to keep himself from being entangled the best he could.

"Well, I'm sure there will be chances to amend misunderstanding," Rosen said. "Is there anything else I should see before we tour the prisoners?"

"Yes," Galen growled. "The women. The former slaves."

"The ones who thought you were a man?"

"Yes."

Rosen shrugged. "In a place where men are built like mothers it makes a sort of sense. 'My brother'."

Galen turned on him, looking fierce. "Any more japes, 'Sea Father'?"

"You don't need me," Rondaleth muttered, withdrawing. "I'll just sort out the rest of lunch…"

"Sorry," Rosen said quietly.

Galen turned away, stomping in her deck shoes into the cabin and down a narrow stair. They came to a door. Voices could be heard, but they quieted. Someone made a shushing sound. Galen hit the door once.

"Our captain is here to meet you!" There was no objection so she opened the door.

Rosen's first impression was of a bizarre theater troupe of costumed dancers, their multicolored clothes having seen better days. There was a hint of rose and jasmine in the air. The women froze, suddenly silent, look-ing at him with wide, dark eyes. As he and Galen entered they withdrew, huddling together near a large platter that held the remains of bread, mashed chickpeas and fish. They seemed clean enough; most had head veils, which they pulled tight around them as they looked at Rosen. Soon many relaxed, losing their guarded way, except for one, a wiry girl with a scarred face who stared at him suspiciously. She was also wearing a bicorn.

Quicker than Rosen liked, she rushed up to him, coming barely up to his shoulder. Galen barked for the girl to stop. She withdrew slightly, then hit him on the chest with the flat of her hand. In a second Rosen seized her wrist as she was about to repeat the blow.

"Perhaps you can explain who I am?" Rosen said through gritted teeth. The girl tried to yank her arm back, but Rosen wouldn't let her yet. Though he knew her mind was coming from a place of disadvantage, a lifetime of fighting women to prove himself wasn't easily forgotten.

Galen barked in Shari again, gesturing to his uniform and sword. Rosen caught the word for captain. An aloof woman in green silks appraised him as if he was someone of note, while the others exchanged looks and rear-ranged their veils, some bowing and smiling. The savage girl stopped strug-gling. Only then did Rosen let her wrist go.

But she said something in rapid Shari, her eyes running over Rosen's front in a way that made him uncomfortable. Some of the other women smiled.

"Boatswain?" Rosen said in a tone that she knew meant he was expecting an explanation.

"The rabid child said 'this one is a man'."

"I see. And the others?"

"Find you attractive, I think."

Rosen groaned inside. "If I ever wanted to be ravished by humyn women I suppose this is my chance."

Galen shrugged. "You'll find they would expect you to take a more, um, motherly role."

"So I'm in a room full of Hallaults. Thank you, no. Has the admiral's lover made mischief?"

"She hasn't had a chance. Remember, Komar Zan is on the ship."

Rosen nodded. "Tell them... they will have a choice soon. To continue on with us to Gashora or return with the Cathans."

"I don't think that's wise," Galen said.

"It's what Tresmadore is offering. We don't have enough supplies to feed ourselves, them and the prisoners."

Galen said a couple of words in Shari, and withdrew, shutting the door. They hadn't seemed so wretched, Rosen thought. But something urgent was on Galen's mind.

"I put Hanno in charge of the free humyn," Galen said. "I thought they were safe with him and the sailors. Now I don't know. Frye could snap his neck, or jump into the sea. But these – " she gestured behind her, " – these women would be at the mercy of even their fellow wretches if he truly thinks any woman who smiles is seeking to tryst with him."

Rosen thought a moment. "But don't you think they should have the choice?"

"They do not know what they are choosing! They would be exchanging one trap for another."

"One could make the argument we are trapping them as well."

"At least our snares will not involve pressure to tryst whether they will or no."

"Very well," Rosen agreed, yielding to Galen's understanding. "For now. When the magi come…"

"Ai," Galen rumbled. "We'll know the truth of all their souls, including the vain creature in green."

Soon they stood back in the stern cabin. Rondaleth's voice could be heard from above; she was standing with a guard chatting about the weather.

"Look," Rosen said. "It wasn't your fault, this humyn."

"Yes, Hanno, 'my brother'."

"It isn't as if you read Hanno or knew his mind. And it could have been a misunderstanding…"

"Come, friend, we've all been humiliated in failed wooing. Being rejected is not shameful. But refusing the truth of rejection is a peculiar arrogance."

"Yes, you're right. I just don't understand it."

"Nor I. But we don't need to to denounce it."

"Hail and well met!" Rondaleth called as if she was addressing the Orb. "Mind that first step! It's quite high!"

They walked out on deck to see four black-robed figures float up from a couple of launches, to step gracefully on deck.

"Sea Father," one woman said to Rosen in greeting. "Ta Athine late of *The Oaken Blue* in service. With me are Ta Wolast, Ta Ronel and your own Ta Hethlion."

"Taren is still sulking over her arm, Sea Father," Hethlion said. "Try not to hold a grudge."

"I have every faith the magi are the most adept to manage magi business," Rosen said.

"What I want to know," another woman's voice said, "Is what smells so good?"

Rosen was surprised an officer was climbing the ladder.

"These humyn don't cook badly. Maybe we should put them to work in our galleys!"

A shiver went down Rosen's spine. First they saw her hat, then the shoulders of her blue jacket, shoulder boards once decorated with a triskelion and crown, recently replaced with the sea queen of an admiral. He knew before before she stepped on the deck who it was. It filled him with dread, but he couldn't have explained why to any living soul.

Ta Hethlion added, "Oh, and for some reason our new Admiral, Sea Mother Tamnath Tresmadore, decided to join us on our way over."

Chapter 27

Reviewing Scruple

Tamnath resisted the urge to wince as Lieutenant Aledan played a flute. They lounged on the stern deck in the starboard turret after the captains had returned to their ships, all of them having some time to spare in their duties. It wasn't that Aledan couldn't play; she was an adequate flautist, technically sound, though not inspired. No, it was the notes sounding in the air that disturbed Tamnath's thoughts. Tamnath wasn't even clear on her thoughts, a barely conscious roiling mass that wanted to be left to their seething quiet. And with each note Aledan disrupted them, silt disturbed in eddies of troubled water. Tamnath tried to distract herself, stood to look out at the fleet's industry in the wake of their victory. Among the working vessels floated the charred remains of the scorpion ships, worthless flotsam left to the whims of Maer.

The salvage continued apace. Much of the larger pieces of aqua from *The Oaken Blue* had been recovered, as well as the acorn figurehead. The keel pieces would be laid out along the unused decks of the larger ships; the broken heart had been hoisted by *The Charred Bronze*. Because of their need, a stream of supplies was also drawn up, much surprisingly intact from the ship's collapse: barrels of salted pork and sausage, sacks of potatoes and roots. They expected to find some rounds of cheese saved from the scorching heat, though this would not hearten the fleet. Already women grumbled they were fasting on cheese and ham. They would welcome the coming supplement of fish.

The divers would be enriched in this venture. For even as they did their fleet duties, they were solicited to retrieve personal belongings, a priority low on the navy's agenda. The practice was discouraged as it led to predation; it was a short step for the mercenary diver to return belongings for a reward to collecting them in sundry to be sold as dear as she could get away with. Tamnath knew before they set sail again there would be claims on sold and found goods by their rightful, or alleged rightful, owners. Traditionally what was not claimed, the captains received a cut of. Thus objections from the command staff were often minimal.

Yet even if *The Black Seal*'s divers found the Great Pearl of Waelune, without the Admiral, their true admiral, to Tamnath it would be a worthless prize. Soon she should be reviewing the prisoners, a task she thought tedious. She'd wait until the final report after the magi had examined them. At last Aledan was finished and Tamnath released the breath she hadn't known she was holding.

"Well and goodly played!" Lieutenant Nesthet said. "'Dancing Jenny' was a favorite of mine as a girl."

Tamnath turned away from the fleet and sauntered back to the table to pour herself a cup of lime grog.

"I know you have Cambrian sentiments," Tamnath said. "But a ditty about a crippled humyn traveling to Ta Mel for healing is trite work at best."

"You object to the concept?"

Tamnath winced. "It's so sweet it makes my teeth ache. In life humyn are all ungrateful swine. I'll have the pleasure of meeting them soon."

Aledan laughed and leaned towards Nesthet as if in confidence, "Our Sea Mother prefers something grim and shrill, like "The Call of The Dark Druid."

"Your Sea Mother prefers civilized music," Tamnath corrected.

"Ah," Aledan said. "The March of Amer it is."

Tamnath laughed suddenly, snorting a bit of her grog, then took some cut cheese. "Not on that reed, and certainly not by yourself. 'The March of Amer' cannot be done justice outside an arena or theater."

"On that we agree." Aledan set her flute down and also took a portion cheese and olives from the plate. "So what are we about today? Apart from expecting an abundance of fish?"

"Ai, my friend. Make space on the forecastle for some 'artistic' culinary work ahead. We need the stern clear for divers and amidships for gross salvage. Nesthet, check how the commissary is able to assist. With all the lance and lens cooking, they may need to keep the coal fire going."

"If I never eat pea soup again – "

"You might starve, my friend!" Aledan finished. "We can't afford to be choosy!"

Tamnath laughed. "It shouldn't come to that. Oh, and prisoner accommodation needs to be made. We don't want them too deep, nor too close to the top decks. Nor in the way. Maybe the lower deck? I'll be inspecting the prisoners at some point."

"You didn't tell Gathelyn," Nesthet said.

"Oh, our dear Sea Father expects I'd be along sometime. Perhaps not so soon. It will be interesting to see how he gets on."

"Interesting in that you find his dislike of your person amusing?" Aledan ventured.

"You don't approve."

"I don't understand. If he's an over bold man out of his depth, let him succeed or fail as fate decrees."

"But Felkeni might be partisan, being a man himself…"

"Sea Mother," a gravelly woman's voice interrupted. The speaker was a tall and thin Dwen, wiry and dark. Her yastol was a strange thing, the leaves not the more common oak, ash or maple, but hawthorn, complete with thorns rising from the base. Aggressive red glass beads were woven through with wire; actual berries wouldn't survive long. In any case no one could mistake Boatswain Elashayd for a man, though once as a prank crew had placed hawthorn flowers in her yastol. She was both Brownie and Dwen. Usually Tamnath wasn't fond of Brownies and their current belligerence with the Shari didn't mollify her opinion. Still she respected Elash: the crewmaster knew every plank and knot of *The Black Seal* and never a mast had cracked while she served.

"Yes, Elash?" Tamnath murmured.

"Now we are becalmed, the Tree Head of the mast crew wishes a moment of your time."

Tamnath's roiling thoughts threatened to boil over. Men, troublesome men. If the twig of a boy hadn't wanted to be taken by a mother, he shouldn't have lingered in her cabin …

Tamnath inhaled and mastered herself. "It will have to be this eve," she replied, her voice even and light. Confidence was what the crew needed to see. There was abundant gossip over the men she took to bed. But which one and how was a matter of discretion. By attempting to use force with Rhondalyn she'd broken discretion. The honor of the Forest must be appeased, the boy as well, and probably the Tree Head's purse, Tamnath thought sourly. She should have just paid the boy for his service and have been done with it. "I need a launch within the hour."

"Sea Mother," Elash acknowledged, then withdrew. Tamnath caught Nesthet looking at her. The lieutenant looked away quickly but she was still smirking.

"Yes, lieutenant?" Tamnath asked. "Share with us your amusement."

"I only thought that when the navy hires companion men for a venture, they shouldn't be wasted."

Aledan snorted. They both knew Tamnath avoided prostitutes.

"And have you exercised this philosophy?" Tamnath asked.

Nesthet laughed. "In the first two days, of course. Where else can you have a harlot for free?"

Aledan looked scandalized. "But surely you left a gratuity?"

"Why? He's being paid plenty by the Admiralty. And all the green girls are afraid to use him for fear he'll laugh at their clumsiness. So he's getting a pleasant time by hardly working at all!"

Tamnath smiled, amused, but she said, "Remember, as officers have an example to set. A couple of queens may lighten your purse, but it will raise the esteem of the navy in his eyes. We don't want the harlots to mutter that we're a fleet of skin flints, do we?"

Nesthet leaned back and snorted, now in bad humor. "I am skint."

"You wouldn't be if you didn't keep losing at Gains," Aledan said.

"And any mother that bad shouldn't be playing at all," Tamnath put in.

"You know, perhaps we should have left you stranded on Oracle Isle," Nesthet shot back. "How is your Meer lover anyway?"

The lieutenants took turns mocking Tamnath lightly. She let them while her thoughts turned dark. Aslynari, the beauty of the sea, the source of peace and dreams she'd not known since a child. But she had not dreamed about him for days and she felt abandoned by his absence. Before the battle she had burned and slaked herself with the Dwen. With the battle done, the burning would return. For her own reasons, Tamnath didn't want to use the hired companions. And she didn't dare risk another liaison with crew or a volunteer. It made her angry. The world was full of men but she was not al-lowed to touch what was within reach.

Or was she?

A thought came, some would say grotesque, but it was not against naval or Federation law. Given the mind of the humyn, they might enjoy it. Shari men, even their aelg descendants, the Brownies, were known to be harlots. But were there any suitable?

Tamnath's tastes leaned solidly on the elfyn side. Once Aledan had commented that Manweth's mane looked "striking". But to herself humyn males looked best when they had passed boyhood by a handful of years, but no more. Only a few had an elfyn form and lack of mane further into adulthood.

"So what's trysting with Meer like anyway?" Nesthet was saying. "Obviously they don't all drown their lovers."

Tamnath smirked and stood. "If you're ever privileged to woo one, you'll find out."

"Are they like Blue men? They look odd, like girls with over long clefts. But they say when they open up, they look normal, right?"

"I'll let you wonder while you tend to your deck," Tamnath said. "If you're very well behaved mates, you both might get a surprise."

"And months before Hal Suldan," Aledan put in. She also stood. "We are so privileged to serve on *The Black Seal*."

"You know it and well," Tamnath said as Elash approached.

"Your launch is ready," Elash said.

"Thank you, boatswain," Tamnath said. "I will see you worthies anon."

Tamnath descended to the launch. As she pulled away from *The Black Seal*, Tamnath looked across the water. To the west of the ship, the divers worked with crew and volunteers, boats ringed around the area. They were still bringing up aqua, but one vessel was collecting a goodly amount of barrels. Several ships treaded water in the south. The open sea was hardly ideal. Tamnath had hoped to be done by the eve, the next at the most. But with the prisoners, the free humyn and their dwindling food reserves, that was not going to happen. She was impatient to sail directly to Gashora.

Since that could not be, Tamnath considered the prison ships. She wanted the Sea Father out of the way. The sooner he finished with his task and the prisoners were allotted among the fleet, the better. His mere presence was an irritation, a demand on Tamnath's senses. She would keep it brief, ensuring both of them could remain dignified.

The barge sailed past *The Tidebreaker*, and Tamnath waved a lazy salute at the calls of "Tresmadore" from the crew. No doubt they loved their Sea

Father, but she was a celebrity in her own right. Long before she enrolled in the academy they were telling tales of her merchant days in the wilds of the South seas. As a Tyreen officer, the tales only grew. One benefit of her early adventures was her fluency in Shari, though she was more adept at some dialects than others. It would be handy when questioning the captives.

As they neared the merchant galley, close to another launch full of magi, Tamnath wrinkled her nose. She scented the common caustics and lye washes used for cleaning, with a lingering musk of humyn sweat. And strangely a waft of rose attar. She could only imagine what it has been like before. Now there was a stronger scent, that of cooked fish. If she hadn't eaten already, it would be welcome. The black robed figures stood and floated to the deck, their launch withdrawing. One was speaking as Tamnath climbed the ladder, scampering up like a Dwen to stand on the uneven deck while a magi she didn't know announced her arrival.

Tamnath made a couple quips about the fish, while the boy captain stared at her as if she was a boarding pirate. Near him was his bison of a boatswain, who had a reputation for cultivating a productive crew. Part of Tamnath was put out Rosen gave himself up for this child hungry girl-lover while rejecting herself so prissily on Oracle Island. But she cared not; she was here for other prey.

"Admiral on deck!" a lieutenant cried from the top of a stern platform where she stood with a guard. She saluted, which Tamnath returned.

"Where is your hat, lieutenant?" Tamnath inquired casually.

"Alas, stolen, Admiral!" the lieutenant called back. "Some villain among us, I expect!"

Tamnath looked at Sea Father Rosen.

"It's likely a prank, Admiral" he said. "I've been assured it will 'manifest' in time. We didn't anticipate your arrival so soon."

"No," Tamnath said with deliberate obscurity. She could not care less about uniform regulations. But the exchanges told her the mood: his officers and guards were bored, the boy himself was uncertain and anxious, and the magi, well, were magi. They walked among the humyn, apparently in friendliness. A couple descended below deck. "So, captain, everything in order?"

"Yes, Admiral." Perhaps Tamnath imagined it, a hesitation to call her "admiral", an echo of his earlier corrected snub. The beast inside her stirred. "Should I show you around?" the boy captain asked.

Tamnath looked at Sea Father Rosen, then past him. He stood in the doorway of what would be the Shari captain's cabin. She'd take him there and it would happen quickly: once the door was shut, she'd put a dagger to his throat, force him remove his baldric then bind his hands with the belt at the post of a bed. He would not shout out for shame; he would know all his efforts to make his way in a mother's world were for naught. Buttons would fly under her knife before she tore his sea breeches down, and she would take her time settling over him. It would be a ravishing he would never forget...

The sun was suddenly bright, making Tamnath blink. Blood pounded in her ears. She was still standing on the deck with the Sea Father facing her. But his reserved expression of dislike was now colored with puzzlement, his demonic boatswain sliding her eyes to the side, about to say something.

"Yes!" Tamnath said forcefully, trying to remember the last thing before the dark reverie.

Rosen's face returned to its reserved tenseness. "Very well. They're below decks – "

"No," Tamnath said, trying to make it sound like a decision instead of a sudden thought. "I misspoke. Bring them here, in rows. I want to see them in the sun," she added by way of explanation.

"Admiral," the Sea Father acknowledged. Then he said words to his boatswain to organize and bring up the humyn. The lieutenant trotted down from the stern platform to stand nearby. No one engaged her, Gathelyn didn't introduce her. They shared their own private moment of awkwardness while the lieutenant attempted conversation: "Nice feathered sky, ai?"

No one answered her. Part of the reason Tamnath didn't want to go down into the hold with the Sea Father was an irrational fear that being in close proximity she'd lose control. It felt worse than ever now the battle was over, the hunger, the burning. If she only could have a swim; that might take the edge off.

The humyn came, many and varied, sailors mixed with Shari oarsman and servants. Tamnath recognized the sailors as Cathans; they would have been pressed into service in some manner. The Shari tale was simpler; unlike oar rowers for the warships, merchant galleys used, a mix of slaves, the indentured and criminal. That was part of why, even though they were not enemies of the Federation, the magi needed to sort them. It would be irresponsible to return them to their humyn herds if they were counter-social in anyway. The boatswain chivvied the humyn in two rough lines. Tamnath heard a magi explaining in soothing tones their admiral desired to meet them. And so the large and untidy beasts gathered before her, smiling eagerly, the most unlikely of souls to grant her celebrity. There was some attempt to enforce a disciplined silence, but they were too excited. Bright eyes, with gapping teeth, exchanged muttered whispers: is this one a woman? they wondered. Surely with hard lion's eyes a man? A youth yet unbearded, who rose by boldness and bravery above others? No, Vardashi do not have beards, one corrected another …

Tamnath walked forward slowly, aware the Sea Father was following her. It didn't matter and might even be useful. As she expected most were hirsute creatures. They seemed either lean and starved, or round with a central fattiness that could be the stress of want or the excess of the idle. Humyn, moving no essence and using less energy, found it easier to store fat than any elfborn. It was nearly impossible for elfyn to hold extra fat; their essence needs simply burned the excess. One could say humyn were like the lesser celestial partner of a planetary orb, a passive, reflective companion drawn irresistibly into an elfyn orbit. Yet even in the case where elfyn were drawn to them there was an element of mutuality to the attraction. It was rare for humyn to let themselves be taken by a powerful elfyn mother. Such encounters could be overwhelmingly terrifying. By the same token few mothers would seek out a hairy sloth of a male. Most trysting was not done between heroic mothers and humyn peasants, but, say, a traveling tinker and a sailor, the more humble of each race. For this reason demagogues often denounced such pairings as diluting the purity of elfyn blood. As Tamnath had no intention of marrying or birthing from this lot, such thoughts didn't bother her.

But other thoughts did. Though unpracticed in thought speech, the humyn minds were so permeable, so open, Tamnath could not ignore their collective mood: they were grateful, they were glad. Yes, they saw she had the face of an angel and that confirmed in their minds she was sent as their salvation.

In Shari one of the oarsmen cried out, "Praise our salvation! Praise Al-ahat for sending the Vardashi *almilland* to deliver us!"

Tamnath blinked as if waking from a dream. Her dark compulsions were forgotten in that moment as she felt strangely moved. It wasn't the words – words were cheap and false. It was the feeling. They truly did want nothing more than their freedom, to return home where ever that might be. She could almost feel the jackal within whining with disappointment. Still, Tamnath was used to wrangling celebrity.

"You honor me!" she found herself saying. "And we honor you! You have been brave and have endured many trials under the Sultan." Many spit at this, cursing their former master. "So let it be known, as soon as you can be fully supplied, you shall be released to return home as you will!"

Tamnath might as well have announced a wedding between the two most popular clans in their communities. Any pretense at ordered discipline vanished and the humyn started to shout and dance for joy, adding more praise to herself, Al-ahat, and other pantheons : Lakshmi, Danu and Baal. They pressed bowls of food into the hands of the magi, who of course never refused food.

"They've been washed well, Sea Father." Tamnath finally said.

"Yes, Admiral. They've also been tended by healers. Those supplies – "

"Will come soon enough, Sea Father. I will to speak with the magi. Then we should tour the prison ships."

"Ai, Admiral."

A change had come over Tamnath. It wasn't softness exactly. But no matter the hungers she bore, she would not exploit these simple creatures. Perhaps it was her racial chauvinism: by acknowledging her as their salvation, she felt the obligation between them more keenly. In any case, the hunger would wait for a more apt target. One of *The Black Seal*'s magi was present, Ta Wolast. Tamnath went to her.

"Have you tasted this ?" Wolast said holding a flat bread wrap. "It's not as rich as their usual fair of yogurt mint sauce and the garbanzos are missing lemon. The fish is an excellent addition however."

"Perhaps we should let them cook for us," Tamnath said. "How do you report their state?"

"As expected. Relieved to be out of the Sultan's clutches. Overjoyed to be leaving for home."

"All of them? No culls?"

Wolast signed. "Alas, there are a handful. They should be transferred quietly."

"Obviously."

"Oh, I think you will find it will not be well received, Admiral. The humyn who leads the sailors, Hanno, is one of them."

Tamnath frowned. "They can surely sail without him."

"But will they? And it appears he's something of Boatswain Galen's pet."

That was awkward. Tamnath didn't want any more trouble than necessary and *The Tidebreaker* was hosting the Marshal's agent. "How bad is it?"

"Why is he to be culled? Hanno is an agreeable charming individual and an expert sailor. But he is twisted. Though married he has harbored an obsessive fascination with his sister's daughter since she was a girl. He imagines they are lovers since she was a child and acted out this abomination in every way. His sister does nothing because he is a respected sailor and provides for their family. The child bears it."

Tamnath's fine feelings for the humyn's gratitude vanished. She shook with suppressed rage, feeling dirty for having let herself feel sympathy.

"Yes, Sea Mother, it is a revolting offense to the soul. But more importantly, were we to release him – "

"The poison would spread," Tamnath finished. "More young mothers would be disenfranchised, boys under his influence corrupted."

"Yes, you grasp it. The Cathans were not always thus. But the pressure of the Sultan's empire twists the shape of their culture, crippling their sense of wholeness. They cannot escape the economies of slavery while under the Sultan's rule. Once it's accepted that souls can be chattel, any relationship may be corrupted by exploitation. Hanno is just one of many, but he must be culled. The Orb will be better for it and the Cathan herd will breathe easier."

"What of the prisoners?"

"They should be finished. Would you like us to accompany you?"

"No," Tamnath said. "The Sea Father and his staff should be sufficient."

"Very well."

It took almost another half hour to organize the review of the prisoners. The Sea Father of course wanted his crew and staff present, and Tamnath herself needed, if not a clerk, than an aide willing to serve. Finally Ta Ronel of *The Oaken Blue* volunteered. Not an ideal choice for Tamnath; she would have to speak carefully around the magi boy. But he would serve for the moment. When they boarded the first ship, the prisoners had already been taken back below, while magi conferred with the Sea Father. They stood aside to wait for their own launch.

"Ten more to be culled," Gathelyn said to his boatswain.

"Bring them," Tamnath said out loud.

"Pardon, Admiral?" the Sea Father asked.

"Those to be culled. I want to see them."

Tamnath waited while guards retrieved them. It would be a perfect solution, using the culled. They weren't long for the Orb in any case. She sat on an oar bench while she waited, the scent of ammonia sharp.

"It's quite clean," Tamnath remarked.

"Working hands make for less mischief," Ta Ronel said, while withdrawing a leaf of paper and a charcoal pencil. "What in particular do you want scribed?"

"Names. I will tell you which ones. There will be conditions and they must agree truthfully."

"I see."

A line of figures emerged from one of the stairs, roughly led by two guards. The precaution of binding their hands in front had been taken. Once they were above and shoved into a row facing aft, below the fore platform, Tamnath stood to examine them.

They were clean, but ungroomed. Uncertain dark eyes furtively glanced at her, perhaps wary of being put under a spell, with one exception. Thinner than the rest, he glared sullenly, then his lips twisted in a smirk, as if harboring a secret he dared her to seek out. For a second his eyes roved over her, as if trying to spy the woman in this bold manly creature. Tamnath could almost feel its thoughts: if only he could test himself against the creature, he would know. Even a bold woman fell before the vigor of man…

"Why is this one to be culled?" Tamnath asked.

A waiting magi stepped forward, considering the humyn. "Ah, this soul is a shifter. You know the kind…"

"Scroungers that make queens turning their barracks into a marketplace, yes. The navy discourages them, and only partly as a courtesy to the purser."

"Well, in this one's case he shifted the usual things: food, wine, – coffee is popular – , and other sundries soldiers need. But his biggest profit was selling captured women and children to be … used."

Tamnath's skin crawled, her aversion reflexive. Harloting was mostly a male concern in mother cultures, the odd jockey not withstanding. The men were never beholden or sold like chattel. It was not just an offense against the man's household, but his mother's estate could sue a badly run house into penury. The idea of children sold for such a purpose was, if possible, worse than the violation of mothers. Tamnath's hands were hot, the sun dancing on her skin, and she yearned to draw her sword.

But a sly inner voice bid her to welcome this gift. The creature was not as hairy as most, and, once groomed, would be acceptable. Tamnath let herself match the humyn's leer, and felt pleased when its own faltered.

"Ta Ronel, mark its name down," Tamnath said.

The rest were not worth her consideration, being too unattractive no matter how they were groomed. As they were returned below Tamnath called a guard over and instructed her to bring up any others of a similar aspect. The Sea Father's face was full of confusion. It didn't matter, as long as he and his crew obeyed. The ones brought forward were younger or looked so, thin and lean. The tallest ones she'd reject; a couple had straggly pathetic manes that could be shaved off. One Tamnath could almost use as he was. She waved the two tallest to be returned then told Ronel to take down the remaining ones names. While the magi cribbed, Gathelyn appeared in the corner of Tamnath's eye. He looked suspicious and scared. As if he was trying to screw up his courage. Tamnath could always sense fear.

"Yes, Sea Father?" she said nonchalantly.

"With respect, Admiral, what are your intentions with these men?"

Tamnath smiled at the turn of phrase. "Well, I assure you I have no intention of wooing them. They will have a chance to labor as men often do."

"Doing what?"

"What a harlot does, if you insist on bluntness."

Then a thing happened that surprised even Tamnath. Gathelyn stepped to place himself to block her way.

"What are you doing, Sea Father?" Tamnath asked in a lazy drawl.

"You have given me the charge of these prisoners, Admiral. It is my duty to ensure they are treated according to the rules of war and honor. Not taken away to be ravished in private."

Tamnath let the corner of her mouth curl in a sneer. "My, what a lurid mind you have, Sea Father. The niceties will be observed. That is why we are taking names. They will not, ahem, 'serve', unless they choose to."

"And how can they?" Gathelyn demanded. "Admiral?" Tamnath smirked at the tardiness of boy captain's honorific. "They are our prisoners. They would do anything to ease their lot. That is not a choice but coercion."

Suddenly Tamnath was enraged, but she kept her voice icy and cold. The magi Ronel had returned and was listening. "Why do you care for the honor of Shari culls?"

"These are not culls – "

"How many are your dead?" Tamnath interrupted. "You do not know the Shari mind. This is a thing all men in Sharitan claim to yearn for! Or so they boast and their prophets promise them unlimited lovers in paradise. They themselves see their chastity as a small thing. So if they choose to harlot in their brief lives, I will not be troubled by it."

Still the Sea Father didn't move. Tamnath had to give that he was a brave.

"And would this be a choice you found fair?" he asked. " If you were a captive? Would you accept a woman offering to trade your dignity for comfort?"

"But I am a woman," Tamnath replied. "So the question is ridiculous. It is not my fault the true fate of men is to feed a mother. Now stand aside."

Gathelyn shook his head. "I can't. Duty compels me to stand. I will not allow these men to be used in contradiction to chivalry."

Tamnath glared at the silly man. Ronel, now finished, stood uncertainly by. Tamnath let herself think. The boy truly wasn't going to stand down. And she knew, as she'd read the codes herself, he was within his rights to have concerns. He perceived his charges wouldn't be safe and it was his call. And, damn her, she'd given him that authority.

Still, a mother always found a way. Ta Ronel, being a magi, ventured diplomatically:

"Sea Father, while it is irregular, it is not necessarily exploitive. I'm sure our Admiral has every intention of only recruiting those read as willing... "

"Exactly!" Tamnath said. "Thank you, Ta Ronel, I will take that with me. Our Sea Father has done a great service by reminding us all protocols should be observed. Carry on!"

Tamnath smartly turned away and headed to the ladder, brushing past the boatswain. It was best she get to the launch while her temper was even. As the launch returned her to *The Black Seal*, rocking on choppy waves, she cursed Sea Father Rosen. The boy had made his point, but she would have the men. Now it was a contest that she had to win. She would wait a few hours before visiting the other prisoner ships. A simple review with a clerk and her own crew. She couldn't wait long; they were due to be divided up between the ships. In this way she would make certain The Black Seal's portion would be suitable for service.

Of course they would be read for compliance. They whole matter was unlikely to be brought to fruition before the salvage was finished. But before they sailed to Gashora, Tamnath would have a man in her bed for every night of their journey. Her passions would be slaked, and the Sea Father's prudish scruples wouldn't stop her.

Chapter 28

Baiting a Jackal

Rosen shook as he watched Tresmadore navigate the ladder down to the barge. Sul dimmed a moment, a wisp of cloud crossing Her face. At his side Galen inhaled to speak but he spoke first.

"Get them below."

"Very good."

And still he shook as clumsy humyn feet shuffled back into the hold. What was he going to do? Showing down Tresmadore wasn't a victory but an invitation to her vengeance. And why in Sul's name had she gotten the conceit of taking humyn to her bed? Her ship had a companion, probably two. As he understood it, men willingly fell into the Jackal's bed. Failing that they were a week from Gashora, a fortnight at most if the salvage dragged. Sel's bosom, could she truly not wait? There had to be something darker behind it, a need for conquest. Amer shadowed the Jackal and never more so than now.

It was almost time for luncheon and so they left the warship cum prison scow, not for *The Tidebreaker*, but for the merchant galley christened *Ta Azaduta*. Rosen wasn't yet ready to return to his ship with Tresmadore weighing on his mind.

Once in the captain's old quarters, they ate ham, cheese, and olives from the guards' rations.

"I see your bicorn has returned."

"That savage one was given it by a guard," Rondaleth said. "Took a lot of convincing that she couldn't keep it. Oh, the fish should be cooked soon," Rondaleth said. "We need to gift the humyn charcoal and teach them how to cook with it, if we are to release them.

Rosen nodded. "It would also be good for them to get fresh air and exercise."

Galen grunted. "Once their labors are done. It's important they know discipline and what is expected of them. Yes, even the mothers. Perhaps especially the mothers."

Rosen smiled slightly, remembering Galen's first report. "Still miffed you were nearly assassinated as a seducer?"

At that moment several Shari approached the door and bowed holding flat bread laden with garbanzos and fish.

"That one is Aqila or Aqi," Rondaleth said as she slathered white sauce over her portion of fish. "She's from the Bedu tribes in the desert hills. I think she was captured young and never truly tamed. She has repeatedly complained to one of the guards that Indri will not do her share of the work. That's the one in the green veils, the admiral's lover. If you want a lesson for discipline, you might start there."

Galen's reply was masked by her sudden interest in her plate. As usual Rosen marveled at how much she could eat while he took the same portions Rondaleth did. "Mind, the women will be transferred ere long," Rosen said.

"They're not being released?" Rondaleth asked.

"The healers insist they are first bound for the temple. After that, they may go where they will."

"But surely it would be quicker to simply sail with their countrymen. Even if not to Sharitan, it will be a closer journey to Cathan or Nomclar."

Rosen looked at Galen. She lowered her eyes, focusing on eating to delay her own coming confrontation with matters of honor. "It's come to my attention the freed women may not be as safe with their freed countrymen."

"Oh. Should I keep the humyn below when the women come up for air?"

"Just keep the guards close," Rosen said. "There is another matter."

Rosen shut the door and briefly explained what had transpired with Tresmadore. When Rondaleth spoke, she kept her voice soft in case the guards might hear.

"Sea Father if I may venture…You are not close to Tresmadore."

"Much like the sky is not close to the sea."

They were all silent a couple moments before Rondaleth asked, "Do you think duty is threatened? I despise saying the words. Tresmadore has been a worthy mother for all I've known her. But her actions have the cast of obsession."

These were Rosen's exact thoughts. And yet, being Rondaleth's superior, he felt duty bound to reassure her, tempted into comforting lies. But who would they comfort? Her mind or his ego? He took a middle way and cleaved to the truth:

"Our Admiral's words were unnerving, true. I hope they're an expression of the burden of duty and nothing darker. We should not gossip but look to protocol as our guide." Rosen took a sip of the mead Rondaleth had provided. "What do you think she is doing?" he asked Galen.

"At a guess? She's looking for explicit permission. I suspect she'll come back using magi to prove their minds are their own."

"Well, that would be fair, surely?" Rondaleth said. "Then we'd know the men weren't coerced and could decide."

"Perhaps," Rosen murmured. "We'll see."

Even the prospect of a magi reading didn't put Rosen at ease. They would have to be separated from Tresmadore, made to feel safe. Blast it, a room would have to be set aside and he'd have to insist Tresmadore not speak with them until those who agreed were ready to go. Rosen didn't relish facing off with her again. And leaving the prison ships felt like abandoning the battle field. Tresmadore said she'd be back. But when?

Galen stood. "I need to settle a matter with the sailors. Do we have an idea when they will be released?"

"Once they're supplied I suppose," Rosen replied. "Could you call a raven? We need other matters clarified."

"Like when the Admiral is returning?"

"Ai."

Soon a raven fluttered down and Rosen was able to scribble a passable missive on a scrap paper leaf. Waiting made Rosen feel vulnerable and exposed. Then he berated himself for cowardice and decided to take his mind off these concerns by letting Rondaleth explain the management of the ship. They had guards of course, but the humyn seemed to be managing fine left to themselves. They explored the supplies in the hold. There was twice baked bread with most of their nutrition burnt out of them; dried fish and cured meat, and sacks of dark powder that Rosen thought for one alarming moment was the salts that fed the Dragon. The earthy smell gave him a hint.

"Coffee?" he asked Rondaleth.

"Yes," she replied. "Upper class Shari seem to breath it for sustenance. They give their dregs to the servants or slaves."

"I had some once as a boy visiting a Brownie house. It was very bitter. I didn't like it."

"It's brewed differently in Gashora. With cardamom or orange flower. Sometimes fermented with rum or brandy."

"What a waste of good brandy."

They returned up top in time to see the women let loose, two guards nearby as ordered. They looked cautiously to either side, shrinking a little as the men, spying them, called out boisterously. Rosen didn't get all the words but there were expressions of welcome and something about sisters. They didn't wave, instead pulling veils closer around them. Spying the officers they seemed to relax a bit, sitting on the oar benches while men rushed towards them with food. This the guards intercepted.

"The guards will serve them," Rondaleth said. "At least while the three culled remain on board."

"Yes," Rosen said, feeling sad. He looked for Galen and saw her speaking with the sailors seriously.

Meanwhile the women were losing their shyness, high spirited with nerves and eying Rosen almost flirtatiously. They giggled softly as they ate, with two exceptions. Indri, still in green veils, walked with a mincing prim tread to sit apart from the women, like a princar on a throne. She appraised Rosen coolly with kohled eyes and inclined her head, but did not smile. Neither did Aqi , who stood tense, looking around as if to confirm there was no enemy in sight, arms down but at ready, walking like a gladiator expecting a fight. She had lingered so that Indri could go past, before choosing a bench farthest from her. Rosen, not wanting to put her ill at ease, or Sul help them, give her a reason to think she was in danger, stepped further away from the women.

In the sunlight, the humyn males ate while they chattered in their many tongues. Rondaleth was explaining what Rosen already knew from geography: the Sharitan empire encroached on many humyn lands and territories. Wars over influence, resources and vying creeds had festered in the Fertile Basin for centuries. Now it had spread to the South Straits, Nomclar, Cathan and beyond. They weren't even the wars of the ignorant over want. Those among the settled Fars, Bedu and Indus knew the arts of irrigation, the rotation of fields, the basics of tending animal waste to enrich fertility.

There was no famine and no need, only the greed of rulers arrogating enti-tlement to comfort, riches, and slaves. Most of the humyn were caught in this storm that did not spare the peoples from the farms and cities or even those, like Aqi, from pastoral tribes in the arid hills, trying to live their own ways before the Sultan conquered them.

Rosen watched them carefully, settling on an oar bench amidships. Un-der the watchful eye of the guards and crew the women and men slowly started to mingle. It might raise morale if they had a bit of society. Those who stayed with the fleet, whether by choice or fate, would almost certainly settle in the Shari ghettos of Gashora. The more determined might try to re-turn to their homelands by road but it was not advised. If captured by the Sultan's troops they would likely die horribly, after being tortured for infor-mation. They weren't to be told, not yet, that if the Federation did not think them trustworthy, they would not be allowed to leave. In that instance, if they escaped and were caught, they risked being killed without ceremony. Humyn did not have elfyn rights under Federation law. While there were specifics uniquely applied to humyn, generally they were treated like all Thyn, or thinking-beasts: they were not to be harried, harassed or killed without cause. But neither was there a need for a trial if one was killed in an act of mischief. It was sufficient for the slayer to be read as being within her rights.

While return was ill advised, Rosen knew the draw of humyn to their place of birth was powerful. He felt sad watching the women shake out their veils, the men slashing water liberally on their faces, some unwinding and rewinding turbans. Though now they smiled in the sun surrounded by a sparking sea, free for the moment from bad dreams and future cares, many were doomed to return and die.

Or simply die. Galen walked to where Rosen sat, sitting on the next oar bench, looking subdued while a humyn started to play a flute.

"Where did they get the instruments?" Rosen wondered.

"It's how they keep count and pace oaring. There's been concern on the galleys about the flutes and water. We're really releasing them?"

"You heard our Admiral. How are your associates?"

Galen's jaw twitched. "I told Hanno he and others had been chosen in ex-change for freedom of the rest. They were surprisingly credulous. Apparently paying tribute with slaves or captives in exchange to avoid being despoiled is a common enough thing. I may have implied one day he might be allowed to return. It's not a complete lie; perhaps he's one of the humyn who can dream before going through the Door."

They fell silent listening as between the flutes and improvised percussive instruments, accented by singing and clapping, a traditional dance ensued. Unlike Cambrian dancing to reels or Dwen jigs, either solitary dancers or paired groups, the Shari seemed to favor dancing in lines or circles together, often sinking low on one leg, then the other with a practiced athleticism. Soon the women were laughing, and with some encouragement they also danced, but not with the men, only with each other. They spun with their veils circling each other a while, then returned to their benches, laughing shyly together.

Except for Aqi. She did not dance. Rosen saw her walk to some men and say something strident and loud. An older male came forward. The others fell back while Aqi exchanged words with him. Whatever matter it was, her face was stoic and unfeeling. Rosen heard the words for thanks or gratitude. Then Aqi pulled away from the men. Perhaps she and the man were of the same tribe.

It was odd to Rosen that Aqi was the only female humyn to do this. The other women looked warily at the men, coy in a way Rosen imagined alien to women. The men, on the other hand, were growing more boisterous, like youths trying to impress an object of desire. The song became more energetic, the dancing more daring. Rosen almost laughed; they were preening.

A movement made Rosen start. Aqi had leaped up to perch next to him, standing right near the hull.

"Be careful," Rosen cautioned, then felt foolish. She didn't understand Hiltekash.

Aqi looked at him, then sat down, hugging one knee. She pointed at him: "Captain," she said flatly.

"Yes," Rosen replied.

"Yes," Aqi echoed, nodding her head. Dark eyes bored into his. Then she looked at Galen and pointed. "Woman."

"Sel preserve us," Galen muttered.

"Yes," Rosen confirmed wearily.

Aqi laughed. "No woman like man in Sharitan."

"No, I expect not," Rosen agreed.

"You've have a new friend," Galen said.

"We've agreed you're a woman."

"Grasped that, has she?"

Aqi stood up, making Rosen nervous. It was a long fall and though she'd probably live, the divers would be cross if they had to rescue her.

Aqi jumped off the bench as graceful as a cat and said, "Taevol, captain," before walking back to the singing men.

"Who's teaching her Hiltekash?" Galen asked.

Rosen shrugged. "Humyn aren't stupid. I expect she is listening and learning."

Now a clattering rang out from the humyn group. A couple of women were dancing in a circle, with tiny cymbals on their fingers, the men clapping loudly. It was strange but energetic. A couple of the crew and guards who had come to watch started clapping as well.

"Perhaps we could get them some proper instruments and have them perform for the crew?" Galen shouted. They had to raise their voices a bit to be heard.

"Perhaps," Rosen said. "But I doubt they'll be here long!"

"Do we know if the Admiral is returning?"

"I haven't – "

A scream went up from the women. They ducked and ran into the captain's cabin as black shapes descended on them, the sole exception being Aqi who found a rope to wave overhead, warding off the attack. The men followed her example, shouting at the dark birds that swooped over them. The ravens had been drawn in part by the shiny cymbals and costume jewelry of the women. Rondaleth was calling for calm while one bird circled to land on the wale near Rosen. It dropped a missive on the oar bench and eyed him expectantly.

~from seal and black,~ it thought, hopping once. ~return words?~

"A moment," Rosen said, snapping the missive open. "And if you could avoid scaring the humyn like the pests you are, it would be appreciated."

~it was funni.~ The raven croaked unapologetically.

The missive was more personal than most:

With complements, etc.

Your diligence is noted. The matter in question will not be resolved until salvage is finished.

Regrets for the lack of clarity. Await my next anon.

TT; A

"She's not returning today," Rosen said out loud. "Away with you!" he added to the raven. "There should still be plenty in the sea."

"So what do we do?" Galen asked, while the ravens landed on the edges of the hull staring at the humyn who seemed barely convinced they were not devils.

"She says to wait for her next. We finish the salvage first."

"At least her priorities are sound."

Rosen grunted. "I expect her priorities are that of a politician. Whatever happens, we need to supply the galleys and organize the prisoners for transfer."

"What's happening to the ships?"

"I think they'll be scuttled. Except for one. I'll probably be forced to tow it," Rosen added sourly.

"Imagine how this will keep the Marshal's agent busy."

Rosen froze. The Marshal's agent. If anyone could reign in Tresmadore's buccaneer approach to naval codes, it would be the Federation Marshal's agent. "Yes, my friend. I think we can make an asset of the Marshal's agent for once. We're done here for the day."

In the next couple of days the merchant galleys were supplied and sent off, the red-topped sails of *Ta Azaduta* leading the three ships south at dawn one morning. The brothers Hanno and Himli had an emotional parting, Hanno having written letters for their families with a promise he would return, the gods willing. They would never see each other again in life.

The women kept on the merchant galleys were transferred to makeshift rooms on *The Tidebreaker* partitioned with scrap and salvaged wood on the lower deck, near a toilet and washing area. This did not suit one of the hired companions being somewhat close to his berth, which was already a dubious arrangement, farthest aft on the deck and within the arc of the tiller. For the sake of his sanity Rosen was thankful the rib fins had been spared and the tiller remained locked. If any man of trade was Rosen's polar opposite it was one who sold his company in bed. Speaking with him was much like weathering one of Korali's tirades as the companion opined the proximity of the unfortunates diminished the atmosphere of romance. There was much sighing and expressions of regret that Rosen could agree with in a strict sense. In contrast the humyn women seemed happy enough, especially once they discovered they could walk where they willed.

The humyn men were another matter. Hanno and the couple of humyn from the galley destined for culling were given the courtesy of a cabin, for Hanno had labored honestly and helped keep the peace on the galley. Unlike the women they did not have free reign, but were brought up daily for fresh air and some exercise. The prisoners would be even more restricted. They were also to be kept on the lower deck, but in a brig built of iron mixed with Dwen twisted wood. There were to be two jails, one against each hull, narrow and long, with room to house up to a score of prisoners each, sitting or lying side by side. No locks were available so a door of iron bars would be twisted shut with wood-essence using long branch lengths. And there would be guards day and night.

Meanwhile salvage continued. The majority of aqua from *The Oaken Blue* had been retrieved, as well as the solcannons. The anchors were left as well as the chain rode that would be unneeded and add extra weight. Some effort was made to fish for rope. Rosen didn't fathom it; hemp grew so abundantly there was never a lack. But Fadwen explained there was always a need of fibers for repairs. The barrels of supplies were allotted like the rest, more to those who needed them. It wasn't until the very end of the week the last lockbox was retrieved. Only then did operations shift to prepare to sail again.

During this time divers and others adept at fishing were kept busy adding to the fleet's larders. First it was sharks of all sizes, the carrion in the water acting as the perfect bait. When they had diminished, it was sprats and whiteing. Volunteers recently battle proven found themselves put to work gutting and deboning. But many came from coastal fishing communities and thought nothing of it. Once deboned and filleted, the fish were laid in a sun plate to gently roast in the sun. The sun plate, a long platter shaped grill, fitted with mirrored angled sides, was a ubiquitous tool every house helper had on a roof kitchen. It was possible to roast fowl with a sun plate, but that needed a spit. These had been cobbled together on the top decks, for both the abundance of sunlight and the sheer amount of fish that needed to be tended. For this purpose there was only a grate; all the fish were thrown on to grill.

Strike crew did the actual roasting, the natural effect of the sun's rays concentrated by mirrors enhanced with essence. Fish could be cooked in minutes, but full cooking was not wanted. After salting and searing, mead or barley-mead must was thrown over the lot, hissing while honey scented steam wafted over the decks. Then the fish was thrown into barrels, topped with vinegar and wine, and sent to the galley for storage. Unlike true garum, these would not keep long, but it should be enough to get them to Gashora. It wasn't exactly an unpleasant process, but after a couple days the scent of fish and vinegar permeated the ship. Once the barrels filled the balance of meat needed, the fleet was ready to leave.

Now the prisoners would be divided and the spare Shari vessels destroyed. Ensign Amralan worked with Ensign Aldweth dividing the prisoners from a list. Rosen didn't inform them of Tresmadore's intentions, hoping in the ensuing time, the Jackal's keenness had waned. She wanted the prisoners sorted and that's what he'd done. He had also requested the presence of the Marshal's agent as an observer, even to his own ear sounding painfully casual about the matter. He was certain Farthal was not fooled. When the time came to join them in the launch, the cavalier was kitted out as if meeting a skirmish, complete with sword and lance. She was only missing her horse. Rondaleth was also with them because of her fluency in Shari.

The weather was fitful on the day they met Tresmadore on one of the prison ships, uncertain if it wanted to rain, blow, shine or do all at once. With Tresmadore was an aide and the magi Ta Wolast.

Rosen felt like a midship again, about to be inspected. Galen must have shared this mood as they both snapped to attention with far more ceremony than was warranted. Farthal stood a step behind them, neither respectful nor insolent with their Admiral, threading a fine needle between duty and dislike. Then Rosen stepped forward to met Tresmadore.

Tresmadore's face was unreadable, her eyes burning darkly. A ray of sun eased from the fitful sky to cross her face, and still she seemed to be in shadow, her troubled soul a dense cloud in the brightest light. She stared back at Rosen with naked antipathy and something like smugness. Behind her the clerk took a leaf of paper from a folder and stepped forward with the Admiral.

"Sea Father," Tresmadore said.

"Admiral."

Then Tresmadore spoke quickly and crisply, making it almost impossible to interrupt:

"My clerk has the list of prisoners to be transferred to *The Black Seal*. Have a guard retrieve the prisoners and bring them here where they will be read to confirm their willingness to take on lesser duties."

Rosen said nothing. He felt himself shaking again and feared his courage would fail him. Tresmadore's false cheer turned to impatience.

"Did you not understand, captain?" she asked.

"With respect, Admiral, I think it wise I am present when they are retrieved."

Tresmadore sneered. "As you will."

Rosen strode forward, bringing a guard with him. He also called for Rondaleth to join him. She fairly leaped to his side, the tension in the air a palpable thing. They quickly descended into the dark cramped hold before Tresmadore could think of a reason to object. From the constant cleaning it smelled of vinegar and lant.

"If I may ask Sea Father…?" Rondaleth ventured.

Rosen waved her quiet, nodding in the direction of the clerk. She was a prim Gold woman, the kind more at ease in a library than in a battle, but Rosen guessed she was loyal to the Jackal.

Rosen said casually, "You're fluent in Shari. It will be helpful."

He cursed himself for not thinking to bring one of his own magi. At the steps into the hold, the guard shouted for the prisoners to stand.

"This is the list?" Rosen asked the clerk, eying the leaf of paper in her hand. He would have to be as quick as a raven.

"Yes, Sea Father – "

Rosen yanked it out of her surprised grip and gave it to Rondaleth. "Have the prisoners step forward when their names are called."

The clerk glared at him, no doubt thinking uncharitable thoughts about bold men. Rosen didn't care. With no magi of his own, he saw one chance to do his duty honorably without further incurring the Jackal's ire. As long as he didn't disobey her orders, he was safe in his command.

The men came forward and stood in a row, all clearly the youngest or fairest of their kind. Yes, the Jackal's intentions were clear. Rosen stepped forward into the dim light of a fading lanthorn. "Lieutenant, please translate."

"They're supposed to go topside now!" the clerk objected.

"They will, lieutenant. In just a moment. This won't take long." To the humyn Rosen said:

"Men of Sharitan, you were my prisoners and I had a responsibility for you, which is now coming to an end. We are about to sail home, forsaking your vessels. So you will be divided between our own vessels. My Admiral, who waits for you above, has an offer of service on her ship, of a way to lessen your labor. But you may find this work undignified. If this is so, you do not have to accept it. Then you will be alloted to other ships where you will work hard, but be treated fairly. The Admiral's offer is your choice. If your refuse there will be no punishment. When you go above, you will be questioned by a magi to determine if you both understand and your will is truly your own. Be clear and honest. Those who find the Admiral's offer desirable will be transferred to her ship and I will have no power over your fate."

Rosen stopped. He hadn't prepared to speak and was unsure if he'd forgotten anything. And he worried if he spoke on it would only make them more anxious. Rondaleth's translation wound down. When she was done, he asked, "Do they have questions?"

He waited while Rondaleth spoke in Shari. He knew he was close to insubordination, but felt this couldn't be rushed. The men looked at each other. One said something, looking from Rondaleth and Rosen.

"He says he'd prefer to stay so sees no point in going up."

Rosen felt like he was about to step off a cliff. "Very well. He may step out."

As the man scurried to crouch in the darkness with the rest of the prisoners, the clerk broke in, "Sea Father! I must protest! They were to be taken up – "

"And waste our Admiral's time? Any more?"

Under his gaze, a couple more left the line, after first bowing apologetically. One said something rapidly.

Rondaleth translated: "It is a fool who takes a free gift from an enemy."

Rosen's heart pounded as he waited a second more. But the rest stayed. Rosen was relieved in a way. Had he returned with no men, he could only imagine Tresmadore's wrath.

"Very well," Rosen said. "Clerk, first strike the names of those staying from the list. Then you may lead these up top."

The clerk sullenly obeyed. She'd be within her rights to complain about his actions, but the worst he'd get under naval law would be a rebuke. Rosen walked ahead of them, eager to be out of the dimness. His first sight, as expected, was an irritated Tresmadore.

"Apologies, Admiral, for keeping you waiting," Rosen said quickly. "They are coming."

Tresmadore wasn't fooled. She knew he'd done something and would want to know what. Well she'd have something to discuss with her clerk on their journey back to *The Black Seal*.

The humyn emerged, some wary, others apparently pleased to be in the open air. The clerk was soon herding them into a line, her voice strident in the way of a callow mother with little authority. Here she might well be a god to these wretches. After days of cleaning and stoning the ship, they no longer laughed at the authority of a mother.

Rosen stepped to speak with Farthal while Ta Wolast was called to examine the humyn, her black robes billowing as she passed them. Visibly the men shivered, feeling her power.

"What did the Marshal say?" Rosen asked.

Farthal's gold eyes glowered. "She found it – Pardon, I should not repeat that. She is concerned only that they agree free of coercion. I am not to interfere unless that condition is violated."

Questions were asked and the task put to them clearly. None objected; there was even one who grinned. This did not completely surprise Rosen.

Had he been a more suspicious soul, he might suspect the magi of being so loyal to Tresmadore, she bent the truth. Her actions said otherwise. Wolast pointed to one man and said, unequivocally, "He speaks against his will."

Rosen nodded to a guard to return the humyn below.

"See, Sea Father?" Tresmadore said, as if reading his thought, "It wasn't a sham. You didn't need to drag the Marshal's agent here. I took the further step of instructing the magi show to them exactly what is being asked of them. So, scruple, honor, and duty have all been served, have they not?"

"Scruple perhaps," Farthal said. "Honor and duty are in doubt."

Tresmadore and Farthal locked eyes. "What says the Federation Marshal, lancer?"

Farthal paused, then said, "The Marshal demands they are free of coercion."

"And that condition has been fulfilled. Hasn't it, Sea Father?"

"So it appears, Admiral," Rosen said stiffly.

"So it appears?" Tresmadore mocked. "First you object like a prude uncle invited to a garden, then you scurry behind your superior's back to complain to the Marshal over a simple matter of prisoner management. Now you refuse to admit your concerns were unwarranted?"

"With respect, Admiral, I believe – "

"Ta Wolast!" Tresmadore interrupted. "Please confirm to our delicate Sea Father the humyn have agreed to harlot themselves of their own free will."

Wolast sighed. "It is true. A couple are even eager. Though they may not completely understand they will not be dominating any mother."

"They'll understand soon enough!" Tresmadore laughed. "I'm glad we've finally come to an agreement, Sea Father. Sul grows old today and there are thee more ships to retrieve willing prizes from. Now you know scruple will be observed, your presence will not be needed. Organize the launches to distribute the prisoners. That will be all."

Tresmadore didn't wait for Rosen's salute. The men, looking slightly bewildered, were guided to the ladder to one of the boats waiting below. Tresmadore had brought her own launches to retrieve, as she said, her "prizes". Rosen felt sick. It was their choice, but it wasn't honorable to his mind. If Dwen had captured Sula men and offered they harlot themselves for kinder treatment, Federation mothers would be in arms, calling for the Forest to be burned down. It wouldn't matter how willing the men were; the very idea of asking the men to harlot with no remuneration in a time of war was offensive.

Rosen had done what he could. Until they reached Gashora, the Jackal would rule the fleet as she willed.

"Sea Father," Rondaleth was saying. "Are we finished?"

Rosen shook his head. "With our Admiral's pantomime, yes. Whistle for the launches and tell the ships to expect their new guests soon."

"Ai."

Rosen hadn't quite moved yet, staring at the boats taking Tresmadore and the men with her to the next prison ships, until she toured them all and returned to *The Black Seal*. Would she use them all? Or would she share her "bounty"? The idea twisted his stomach.

"It was done as fairly as it could be," Galen offered.

"It shouldn't have been done at all," Rosen said. "With any luck, she'll get scabies."

Galen guffawed mirthlessly. Rosen wished he was the type of man to tell Galen to spread that as a rumor. The Jackal deserved it.

But if a bold man was considered a nuisance, a gossip was unforgivable, never mind young officers excelled at the craft, putting the common consort to shame. The launches came and groups of prisoners were barged to each ship in turn. It took most of the afternoon. At last Rosen returned to *The Tidebreaker* to watch the prisoners being secured. They seemed cheerful, partly because, once in the new brigs, they were unbound. But mostly they acted like tourists, marveling at the make and crafting of the ship. Rosen returned to hover near the pilot's cage, while Galen made certain all was ready to be underway. The salvage was finished, the top decks cleaned of fish and stoned for good measure. Whistles sang out; *The Leviathan* and *The Charred Bronze* eased forward towards the three Shari vessels huddled together. Several flashes of light flared from their solcannons, followed by thunderous cracks as the timbers of the ships split and went up in flames. A faint cheer echoed over the water, giving the last vestiges of Shari ambition a viking funeral.

The one ship spared to be examined by scholars was already linked with a tow line to *The Tidebreaker*. Rosen was still uncertain how it would fare. New whistles sang out and the ships pirouetted and maneuvered into their line positions, facing north. They could not set off with the joy of surging through the waves, yet still, Rosen relieved Bawn so he could pilot. It wasn't his watch, but he needed the distraction of duty, the feeling of moving the magic of the ship, his ship, the only place in the fleet he could control. Rosen tried to let go of his grim thoughts about the Jackal, giving himself to the joy of piloting. The sun was falling west when the fleet was in position. Another series of whistles sounded and they were underway, north and east, Gashora bound.

Chapter 29

Trading on Dignity

The catch of harlots was so large that Tamnath put aside her anger with Rosen. Lieutenant Selis Torin ní Fia, the ship's secretary, seemed more upset with the war king than she was. Perhaps Tamnath would let her have one of the men. There certainly were plenty. As for Rosen Gathelyn … Well, being bold may be how Cambrians let their men behave, but if the Sea Father kept being a nuisance, he'd find himself with something less pleasant than minding prisoners.

As soon as the humyn were aboard *The Black Seal*, there was the matter of grooming. They were docile enough, though gaping in wonder at the vessel and the technical craft they'd never seen in their lives. The crew also paused to gawk, something Tamnath put an end to with Elash's help.

"What are you all staring at?" Elash bellowed, the thorns on her yastol bristling. "This isn't a tour barge! Return to duty!"

However only crew needed to obey. Officers like Aledan and Nesthet didn't help by staring.

"I'm afraid to ask," Nesthet said.

"Consider them as diamonds uncut," Tresmadore said. To Elash she added, "Have the guards put these in the new brig for now. Then send for the companion. I want them washed up in an hour."

"I have to admit, they don't smell as bad as I expected," Nesthet said.

"That's because these are the most masculine ones." Tamnath watched them disappear below decks, still gawking at the ship. "By the time they're finished, they should be worthy to serve in a House of Lun."

Aledan's face went grim. Before she could speak, Tamnath said, "Don't look that way. They've been read as being willing, in exchange for no labor. And this way Nesthet's empty purse will have no further demands on it."

Aledan looked after the men. "They know you want them to harlot?"

"Explicitly. I should thank our prim Sea Father for leaving no doubt in their minds what's expected."

"And we pay them nothing?"

"Did you not hear the ballad of Nesthet's empty purse? Of course not. They are laboring as prisoners. It's simply a different type of labor."

"I'm not sure companioning is covered by regulations," Aledan said.

"It's honorable labor," Nesthet put in. "Isn't that what men always say? But I'm not sure. I'll wait until they're cleaned up."

"Ungrateful little troll," Tamnath said. She wasn't offended. They always bantered like this, their affection channeled through jibes.

"Please, Sea Mother, not the plank!"

"That depends on your management." But before Tamnath could follow up with more queries, a man was approaching.

He looked annoyed, as too many pampered men did. A blue mantle, trimmed in gold, covered a long tunic of gold brocade on white linen. His hair was tri-plaited and he had a circlet on his head, a romantic accoutrement of an ancient prince. If he hadn't been on board, there was nothing to suggest he was a harlot, except perhaps an abundance of flashy pendants and rings.

With grace and practiced style, he inclined his head in an aborted bow: "You called for me Sea Mother?" His soft voice was completely at odds with the furrow of annoyance on his brow.

Whether that was because Tamnath never used him, or Nesthet's failure to leave gratuity, Tamnath didn't know or care.

"Yes, thank you for coming, Effa. Elash will show you where the prisoners have been taken. I'd like you to direct some of the crewboys in making them presentable."

"By which you mean?"

"Maneless and elfyn."

"Oh. I'm not sure I'm an expert in humyn toilet – "

"You're a man, aren't you? Make them look civilized."

He – Tamnath couldn't remember his name – didn't look happy. But he said, "Very well, captain."

"Thank you."

After he left, Tamnath said, "Now let's leave this place of misery and sail to Gashora."

It took several hours before they were ready to sail. The salvage had to be secured and it took an inordinate amount of time to collect the divers who, between retrieving valuables and fishing, were in a frenzy of profiteering. However they'd use their gains, Tamnath didn't know. Divers appeared to live hand to mouth, in primitive dwellings, considering the sea their true home. Even the Meer maleen cities, as they were called, were little more than a group of huts floating on the water. If Meer and Blue didn't have to breathe air, Tamnath suspected many would never leave the water.

That brought her thoughts to Aslynari, cool yet fiery, and how she felt alone without him.

Was their tryst just a whim? Was that why she no longer dreamed of him? Or had he been forbidden from traveling to her? The emptiness gave an edge to her overdue passions. With perhaps more aggression than was needed she chivvied the crew, made Elash drive harder so they could be sailing before the sun set. As the whistles sounded, Tamnath estimated they'd make good time, well into the night. Elash informed her the humyn were ready and indicated she would act as escort. Nesthet had gone to some business on the middle deck, so Tamnath collared Aledan to accompany her to the lower deck.

"Very well," Aledan said. "Just to see them."

"You might like what you see."

"I might," Aledan said, sounding reluctant.

They made their way down to a room near the tiller where some of the humyn had been taken, while the rest waited in the brig. Entering, even Tamnath was shocked at the success.

They looked wary and shaken, perhaps because they had been shaved and their hair washed out, some of them still damp. Or it could be because the three crewboys who had assisted the companion were all carrying a rope starter. Tamnath was certain she saw welts on one humyn's leg.

"Effa," she addressed the companion, "I hope you have not been beating the prisoners contrary to regulations."

"No more than they earned!" the companion shot back, eyes flashing. "That one groped and molested me!"

"Did he?" Tamnath eyed the man. He looked familiar apart from the growing bruise on his chin. Tamnath stepped forward and he shrunk away slightly, uncertain. Grabbing a shoulder, she spun him around, and pulled his hair off the nape of his neck. There the skin was faded, the pigment removed in a pattern of the letter "T" for "*tenaiya*", the word for "kill" or "cull". More gently Tamnath turned the humyn back to face her. He was delightfully almost unrecognizable. Except for the glower of his dark resentful eyes. Yes, this was the same one. "Is it true you attacked my ship's companion?" she asked lightly in Shari.

The humyn sullenly glared at the elfborn man. "That is not a woman!"

Tamnath laughed loudly to the irritation of both men. "My apologies effa! There seems to be a misunderstanding. I think they were hoping you were a woman."

The companion did not find this at all amusing. Tamnath noted the sleeves of his robes were tied above the elbows for labor, and his trilock plaited hair more frazzled than he usually permitted. He looked more like a glamorous scullery knave than a courtesan. Amber eyes narrowed as he said, "That is utterly ridiculous!"

"Obviously, I agree. You go to such lengths in your profession to project enticing masculinity. These, however, are used to a cruder expression of their sex. I expect this is the most groomed they've ever been in their lives."

None wore what they'd come in, instead being covered with plain undyed shifts of muslin or hemp. Their feet were bare and... Tamnath paused, once more looking over the humbled one for the cull. Now stripped of body hair, his face was elfyn enough, his body narrow and lean. He was only slightly taller than her shoulder. There was another, almost as good, but his features were sharp and reminded her a bit too much of the boy captain. That might be a pleasant game, to take a harlot, pretending he was the Sea Father. But she didn't want that just yet. Now she wanted a simple escape. And this one had soft lips. She could imagine herself –

But Tamnath had no need to imagine. "This one," she said to a crewboy. "Put it in my cabin and feed it a plate of something. Olives and cheese. It'll get more later."

"Admiral."

"After it eats, tie it to stay out of mischief. What about you?" Tamnath said to Aledan. "Are they good enough?" Tamnath caught Aledan looking at the one she rejected. "I see." Tamnath grinned. "Put that one in Aledan's quarters. Oh, stop acting like a stoic." Tamnath slapped Aledan on the shoulder like a mother driving a daughter in sport. "A mother at war has needs and grim are the tales of those who ignore them."

To Elash, she said, "Return these to the jail and feed them something light. Get the rest cleaned and prepared. They may be 'laboring' later. And don't worry, effa," she added to the companion. "Your extra labors will be compensated."

That task finished Tamnath withdrew, Aledan quietly in her shadow. Now, as Sea Mother and Admiral, Tamnath had to display discipline. Oh, did she want to take the man now. But the crew must see she wasn't a slave to this want. First she met the tree head of the mast crew about the matter of the Dwen boy. She said the usual things that adhered close enough to truth to work: she regretted her forceful encounter (true), was sorry the man was offended (true), and reassured the driver it would not be an issue again (all true). Tamnath felt she was buying time with her soul; if she paid the tithe of humility, she could reap the rewards of passion. Yet when she was done, the rage returned, the anger at being thwarted, though the incident with Rhondalyn happened almost three weeks past. For the first eve since *The Oaken Blue* fell she didn't visit the Admiral, instead returning to her cabin. The man sat on a stool, hands bound, a crewboy standing nearby.

"You can go," Tamnath said, dismissing the crewboy. Once he was gone she locked the door and removed her baldric and coat. The humyn stared at her, uncertain and suspicious.

"Do you speak Hiltekash by any chance?"

He stared at her blankly.

Tamnath sighed. She would have continue in Shari. Pulling the thong holding her queue free, she unbraided and shook out her thick dark hair while she spoke. "I don't like this language."

The man's eyes hardened, his mind harboring strong opinions. "You speak the tongue well enough."

"With great reluctance. Your country is a place of misery, torture, and filth. But you, well, you cleaned up well enough."

The man didn't know what to do. But he looked at his bonds. "You will keep me tied?"

Tamnath considered it. It was a fulsome activity, playing with bonds. "Perhaps another time."

She strode over and pulled out her service knife. The humyn eyed it worriedly. "First tell me why our magi say you are a criminal and degenerate."

"What?"

"You were judged, remember? Sometimes the unwitting don't notice. You may recall remembering the acts."

"I remember no crimes," he said defensively. "I thought of our prizes and trade. So much good for the plunder and women and their spawn."

"Girls and boys," Tresmadore offered. "Children."

The man shrugged. "If their gods could not protect them, that is not our fault. By victory we know Al-ahat gives us the right to spoils and slaves. They are at the mercy of the faithful and owe the victors submission and loyalty."

Tamnath was revolted, but the Jackal within smiled. "What an interesting philosophy. How does this syllogism work when you lose?"

The humyn looked up with contempt and hate. And, strangely, the firmness of his member was visible under the cloth of the robe. Tamnath could feel it, a rebellion to defend the truth of his misguided creed. She cut the rope. The next second the humyn lunged, grabbing one breast and trying to seize her around the waist. She backhanded him with her left hand so forcefully he flew to land crosswise on the bed. Dark eyes widened in shock and terror.

Tamnath knew his kind. The humyn was not frightened by any physical hurt, only that his world that said woman was a slave of man had been shattered. This time it wasn't the Tyreen ships, or elf magic, or guards or even the magi sorcerers. All that could be borne in his mind if he clung to the belief that, without these supports, he as a man could defeat Tamnath as a women with brute force. Without that axiom his sense of purpose crumbled and with it any remaining resistance.

"What do I do?" he asked, avoiding her eyes.

"You? You do nothing." Tamnath removed her sea breeches but left her shirt on. The man looked shocked, looking at her then away. "Don't tell me you're a virgin."

"I... I have only had women in bondage."

"Ah yes, the women and children you sold."

"Just women. No young ones."

"Truly, you are one with great scruples."

"You beat me then you mock me?"

"Don't cry me a ballad. Your pathetic attempt to overpower me is a violation of the agreement you entered. Perhaps I should send you to another ship, with instructions to have you laboring on the deck stoning every waking moment."

Stoning was work for meaty, vigorous souls. The humyn was already shaking its head. "I am sorry! I do not know what came over me."

"Not to worry. Just remember: by victory we have the right to spoils, and you are at our mercy and owe us submission. Is that not how the tale goes?" A light faded in his eyes, the last embers of rebellion dying. "Now lie back."

Tentatively he did, on a bed likely softer than he had surely known. Tamnath stood over him and finally threw her shirt off. The humyn's eyes were wide, from shock or arousal she couldn't tell. His shoulder length black curly hair splayed around his head like a dark halo, his skin almost elfyn smooth. The hemp shift was rumpled just above his knees, trapped by his weight on the bed. Tamnath yanked it up.

She'd never trysted with a humyn. For a moment she recoiled. His member looked twisted and strange at the end; he was missing his foreskin. But Tamnath had known of this custom and it didn't interfere with anything important. What mattered was he was half full. This was another reason to take the younger prisoners; passion was never far from the surface. Grabbing him, she squeezed him gently. She was an experienced seducer and he responded.

The man gasped and Tamnath's nethers ached to be fed. When he was firm enough, she held his wrists down and slipped herself over him. He gasped again, eyes wide as if looking at a terror beyond her shoulder. And then she forgot about him, the only thing that mattered was possessing him and feeding herself in the act of devouring. And as Amer took Lun on the shattered plains after the defeat of the Bane, so Tamnath took this man, until there was nothing left in either of them.

405

* * *

In the eve Braille usually looked forward to retiring. She'd pipe a bit before sleep, write in her journal about the journey, always with a thought to amuse family. Being officer of the upper deck she would usually have a dedicated assistant, but the battle and losses had spread them thin. Now Tresmadore's scamp braided her in the morning for a gratuity. One of her best deck officers was still in the infirmary from pitch fire burns. Preparing to go underway without her at hand been a challenge. But they had managed and Braille looked forward to enjoying a bit of brandy with acorn milk. Though it was far from obvious, Lieutenant Braille Aledan was Dwen.

Her blond hair certainly didn't advertise it, nor the warm hue of her skin. It was in her green eyes, though they had a hint of gold, warm flecks in pale emerald. Braille was always called Gold by those who didn't know her because Sula culture had declared that best though her sulessence was feeble. But she could also move wood and that was enough to be accepted as Dwen. Though Braille lacked the pilot talent and so never would captain a Tyreen ship, she did take joy in placing her hands against the hull of her cabin, feeling the ship in a way even Tamnath would find alien.

But Braille would have to forgo these pleasures because Tamnath had foisted one of the Shari concubines on her, and woe to the women who hesitated to boldly tryst with an available man in Tamnath's presence, lest she be jibed as a sister lover or worse.

Braille liked Tamnath, was even fond of her, but they had drifted apart. What had drawn her to the celebrity captain had worn thin over the last decade, a tune repeating the same notes into banality. Maybe this was the same with all celebrities; the closer one was to the fire, the more one felt roasted. It wasn't just Tamnath's unending but predictable activities of wooing, merriment and sport. Braille was older than her captain, now Admiral, and at nearing half a century started to consider the future. She'd like to manage an estate household, with or without a helper, and she'd welcome children. But she had been hesitant to let any grow. Her thoughts in focus, Braille saw she had held an anxiety of being mocked for pursuing a respectable mother's life. Never mind Tamnath had a daughter of her own living with Tamnath mother's sister. Braille's resentment deepened at the hypocrisy of it all. This last stunt, foisting a Shari harlot into her bed, put her at the limit.

When Braille had the lower deck, she had returned briefly to the quarter-deck to review the final tally of the salvage. Standing by the great fragments of the recovered keel from *The Oaken Blue* was almost a spiritual experience. It was beautiful in the last rays of the setting sun, great hunks of greenish blue glass, like solidified sea water glimmering with fiery highlights. Braille was glad she had no Meer ancestry to see visions of the aqua's origins. The living tales of the Cataclysm were sufficient. These pieces would be transported back to Tyrum, either to be used for a new ship or broken up further to repair old ships.

Braille finished her count, marking pieces to be moved to the upper deck, then gave the report to the ship's secretary. She considered visiting mess hall and those she knew in the infirmary. Instead she walked to the room that had turned into a shrine. A healer was sitting very still by the side of the cot. Braille wondered if she might be trying to reach Jonsaymanor in dreams.

Indeed their Admiral and mother of the fleet had the cast of simple sleep. A waxiness to her complexion gave away that something was not well, her breath shallow, and her robust frame seemed to have shrunk. Jonsaymanor's essence was burning to keep her alive. How long it could go before she was spent, Braille didn't know. She wasn't as close to Jonsaymanor as Tamnath. But still she felt the loss. Braille's throat tightened with emotion. The healer became aware of her and spoke while still keeping her vigil:

"There is no change."

"Can you see her?" Braille asked.

"From a distance, as if in a fog. But anytime we try to get close she drifts farther."

"You haven't heard the Door?"

"No. That is a good sign. It shows she has no desire to leave. But if she doesn't return in a month, her body will be spent. Sometimes there is a light. We think another dreamer is trying to reach her. We will take all the aid offered."

Braille nodded. "How can she live? I thought without draught the life of a woman is limited by a fortnight."

"True. We have been trickling." The healer elaborated at Braille's puzzled expression. "It involves a tube or a reed placed in the upturned mouth. A healer encourages the body to swallow. By this method Admiral Jansenwhol 'drinks' thrice a day. We are considering adding tonic, but it is risky. Her wounds are not common and there is little to guide us in treatment."

"We trust you will do you best. That is all duty can demand."

"Pray to Sul it is enough."

Braille left the room. Suddenly she felt quite hungry. She had no desire to eat in the wardroom so she collared a midship to send a platter to her cabin. Only when the girl was out of sight, did Braille remember why she was hesitant to return to her berth. Now there was nothing for it. If she didn't return the Shari boy would assume the largess was part of his payment and Braille wouldn't have supper.

And so Braille returned, thankfully passing neither Corma or Tamnath. She nodded to the couple of officers eating in the wardroom before striding to the door of her cabin larboard, the larger of the turret rooms. She tried not to think how her cabin was directly under the captain's bed, thankful for the sturdiness of the ship's beams; their thickness prevented sound from carrying much. The Eldest of the Orb knew when Tamnath would take her man and what that would entail.

Braille paused with a hand on the latch. Well, if she didn't feel in the mood, she could always return him. It wasn't as if he would tell. But if asked he would tell, since Tamnath was fluent in Shari whereas Braille's Shari was simply serviceable. She sighed and opened the door.

The cabin was spacious for a ship, but nothing like the captain's. Braille was glad she hadn't been forced to share. She did have a quarter arc of the turret windows, complete with a curved bench below, but there was little to view now it was eve, a hanging lamp with fresh solstone gems making the glass black mirrors. Reflected was her writing desk and chair, a small cabinet and somewhat larger chest, a small table and a bed slightly larger than a cot against the longest wall. Nearby clothes hung on hooks. The humyn huddled on the floor at the end of the bed, crouching over an empty plate with crumbs and the scent of olives.

He was striking and surprisingly elf-like. Of course, that was why he was chosen. He looked up surprised. Braille saw he held one of her tin cups with a white liquid. He had just put it to his lips.

Braille shifted her eyes to the cabinet where her drinks were kept. It was closed, but he had to have been at it for the crew would have given him nothing but water. In that same moment she moved, faster than the humyn could follow, snatching the cup out of his hand.

"Stupid, greedy savage!" she exclaimed, holding the cup and breathing hard. "You could have killed yourself!"

He shrank away, stared at her blankly, while she kicked the door shut with a boot.

"This," Braille said emphatically, "Is acorn milk! Only those of Dwen ancestry can drink it without being poisoned. Even I have to not overindulge."

He continued to look at her blankly, relaxing a bit now he didn't think he was going to be struck.

"You don't understand one note of what I've said, do you?" Braille tried parsing the words in Shari. "This drink. Poison to you, to humyn. Not to me." Here she swallowed it, the sweet bitter milky liquid soothing on her throat. She added, "To make it safe acorns would have to be leeched of their flavor first."

At the sound of his language, the humyn's eyes lit up. "You speak the language of the Blessed Lands!"

"Cursed, don't you mean?" Braille said. She put the cup down and opened her cabinet to retrieve a bottle of sweet wine.

"Perhaps," the humyn replied. "I would not have chosen this journey."

"So why did you come?" Braille asked while filling her cup

"We go where the Sultan commands."

"You could not say no?"

He laughed. "Yes, if I wished to die with pain."

"Couldn't you escape?" Braille was curious what drove the average Shari sailor.

"Escape where? The Sultan rules all of the lands of Lin and Alon. His reach has subdued the Indus and the Cathans. Those he desires in the mountains and wastes his troops find. Even the Bedu can't evade him forever.

Those in the cities are slaves to the gifts of his industry. I weave and spin. Where am I going to flee to in the badlands? What use would I be to myself or those that herd for generations?"

"You weave? How does a weaver end up on a warship?"

He shrugged his shoulders. "I find myself in prison. I am given a choice. Sail for riches or slave in the mines. Only a fool choses the mines."

Braille was intrigued. Before she could ask another question there was a knock. She let the midship enter to put her supper on the table: sun pickled fish, vinegar spiced wheat, with boiled potatoes and bread. The girl glanced at the humyn but said nothing.

"Emha."

"Thank you," Braille said.

After the middie left, Braille locked the door. She looked down where the humyn still huddled in a half crouch. He had lowered his eyes and gone silent. Braille stooped, took the empty plate from the floor and brought it to the table.

"Are you still hungry?" she asked.

He looked up, eyes wary, and nodded. His eyes were odd, flat, without the depth of those who moved essence. Yet they seemed to reflect Braille's magic back at her, moving her in a way she couldn't describe. She felt calm inside, as if her soul had let out a long sigh and could finally rest.

Braille blinked. The shift was distracting, a rude thing meant to cover the wounded when their own clothes were soiled. While Braille separated a portion of her meal onto the other plate, keeping more of the fish for herself, she asked the humyn, "What is your name?"

"Firas," he said. "Firas son of Gabi."

"Well met, Firas son of Gabi. I am Lieutenant Braille Aledan. By naval custom you will hear most call me by my estate name Aledan. But within this room you may call me 'Braille'."

"Brahhil."

"Close enough. Now let's get you something less appalling to wear."

Braille scanned her hooks looking for one of the robes, a rustic green light wool, with gold embroidery. It was well worn but it would do.

"Here," she said, holding the robe out. "And stop huddling on the floor."

Firas stood up and took the garment hesitantly, opening it first. "You are tall," he said.

"Not as some. Go on."

She expected him to shed the muslin. Instead he put the robe over it, making an odd yet stylish effect. It wasn't too dissimilar from something a Tyreen Dwen might wear at home. While Firas said nothing his posture indicated he was more comfortable. His wavy black hair had been sheared evenly just below the shoulders, now laying against the robe collar, touching it hesitantly. His face had been shaved, his dusky skin reddened, but he couldn't have had much before because there were few mane producing pores on his chin or cheeks. Firas' face was almost classical, only his nose was a bit larger by proportion than an elfyn or aelg. Other than that ...

"Sea Queen," Firas said, "Is it permitted I may eat now?"

Braille started out of her musings as she retrieved the stool from her desk for Firas, herself taking the chair. "Sit," she instructed. "And you don't have to call me 'Sea Queen'."

Firas looked at the stool as if it was a strange beast. The chivalrous mother in Braille almost came around to help him, but she stopped herself. That was ridiculous. She wasn't wooing him. So she sat and tucked in. Firas finally sat down.

"We do not have chairs," he said. "Except in noble houses. And magi who think if they sit like Vardashi they will see Vardashi wisdom."

"Obviously that was a failure," Braille said.

"Or perhaps the failure was of our Sultan, may he have mercy on us, ears who are deaf to wisdom."

"Something we can agree on. You were saying you were in prison. Why?"

Firas picked at his food with his hands. Braille felt it would be unwise to give him a knife, but she retrieved a two pronged fork.

"Thank you, Sea Queen." This time Braille didn't correct him. "This is like tabbouleh," he said of the vinegar spiced wheat.

"It was waterlogged and salvaged from the wreck. Supposedly our master cook on *The Black Seal* is a 'genius'. It was considered more efficient than trying to dry and mill it. You were saying?"

411

"I was caught in a house of pleasure. No, it is not what you think. I was not there to find love. I was seeking my sister."

Braille heard his voice shift, like one navigating a great pain. She waited for him to continue:

"We were very close when we were young. She…was taken by bad men against her will. I was too young to protect her. Our father, he is a hard working man but strict. He cast her out. I cannot forgive him."

Braille wasn't sure she understood but asked, "Why did he cast her out?"

"She had brought dishonor. It is the men who have no honor but women pay."

"Where did she go?"

"Where all women with her fate go, to the streets, from man to man. I saw her now and then, gave her bread if I could. Once father caught me. He was angry. I …" Firas ate some more. "He was always angry. We work hard but have very little. He says 'we do not waste bread on whores'."

It was a word Braille always had trouble interpreting. The idea of female companions wasn't alien. They did exist, "jockeys", romantic figures pandering to the ideal of how a man wanted to be wooed. Sometimes they were hired by women to keep consorts entertained while they traveled. Braille was sure there was one on *The Tidebreaker*. Occasionally male crew would opine *The Black Seal* should get one and Braille could see their logic. But they were a small group and Tamnath ignored them, finding it amusing: "If they want to be taken, their are plenty of crewgirls willing to have them and not at the expense of *The Black Seal*'s purse."

But "whoring" as Braille understood it was, in Sharitan, only a thing women did and was seen as disgraceful. And yet it was in such demand it upturned Braille's understanding of economics.

Taking herself out of her thoughts, she asked, "So you saw your sister now and then…"

"And then she was gone. I did not see her for months. After the rains I know something is wrong. She would not leave the city without telling me."

Braille nodded for him to go on.

"So I ask around. And find her last friend is serving in this house, but the men will not let me speak with her. So I sneak in at night and was caught." He sighed. "I was doomed from the start. She is gone. I don't know where."

"And they imprisoned you? What for?"

"Theft."

"Did you explain?"

"They did not believe me. They think I am stealing favors not money. The house is owned by a rich sheik close to the Sultan's court. So I am told to slave in the mines or fight at sea. They also threatened to take my manhood. But I think that was just a cruel joke to frighten me."

They had finished the food. Braille got another tin cup and poured some more wine, giving it to Firas. He took it in both hands. When he tasted it his eyes widened. "What wine is this?"

"They make it in Meridian, a province near the heart of the Federation, a great island in the Ath river before it becomes the Hethlyn flowing to Gashora."

Firas looked confused.

Braille waved a hand. "That is where they brew spirited brandy. It's more wine than brandy, but the brandy keeps it sweet."

"It is like a drink of gods. Or devils."

"Too much will do things to your head." Braille appraised Firas before her next question. She wasn't a notary but had a sense for the truth. "Why did you agree to our Admiral's offer to companion for her crew?"

"Is that what you call it? I am a companion?"

"It is more polite than harlot. Or as you say 'whore'."

Firas thought for a long time. "I admit the idea is strange. Rich women of great nobles have lovers. They give them trinkets. But never does a woman pay for a man like that. The one who groomed us, he is a 'harlot'?"

Braille smiled. "A companion, yes. It's not such a disgrace in the Federation."

"No, his finery is fit for a prince. He is paid well I see. There are sometimes – I do not like to say it, but nobles will keep boys for a similar purpose. But they are wretched."

Braille took a moment to absorb what she'd heard and tried to keep her rage in check. It was a grotesque distant outrage and there was nothing to be done about it in the moment.

"Do you think yourself wretched now?"

Firas looked her in the eye for the first time. "No. I feel ashamed. I know what purpose I was brought for. I agreed less for comfort that was offered and more because I did not like the company of those men. I could do nothing about their sins, but I could escape them, so I did."

"You are ashamed of abandoning them?"

"No, Sea Queen. I am ashamed because, though your admiral has made it clear we are to be like whores, I find myself moved by your presence. This should disgust me or terrify me, but it does not and I do not know why. But I know there are worse things than being the plaything of a Sea Queen."

Braille's feelings of calmness, excitement and comfort returned. Firas was drawn to her essence as all humyn were. The power was said to be overwhelming. For herself, Braille couldn't fully explain, but there was one way to get to the root of the matter.

"You call me 'Vardashi', your word for 'elfyn'. But most of us in the fleet are not. We are aelg or elfborn, our foremothers having married and trysted with humyn. To you there may be little difference; elfyn and aelg both use magic humyn cannot. But elfborn are less powerful. What we are feeling between us, for I feel it too, is what our first foremothers felt. It doesn't have to be shameful." Braille stood and came to Firas, leaning over him slightly. "But I am about to retire and there is only one bed."

Then she kissed him and found no resistance.

Firas let her shed the robe, and though he hesitated at first, he pulled the shift over his head. Even his body had been stripped of hair. It must have been a humiliating process and Braille doubted the companion enjoyed it either. Then Firas lay back while Braille undressed and unbound her naval braid. When she returned to the bed, Firas reach out to touch her hair.

"It is like sunlight spun into silk," he said. "And has fire in the light."

The lamp certainly drew out the hidden reds in her gold hair, the forest meeting the sun, as if the last rays of dusk had filtered into the room before Sul dipped into the sea. Braille could imagine their bodies touched for a moment by the red light, her pale gold skin over his dusky darkness. But Sul was gone, having left them to their privacy.

Braille kissed Firas again and the calmness filled her. He was uncertain, but shy men were not beyond her experience. And once she was around

414

him, they knew the rhythm of lovers since time began. She felt in joining that their fates were joined. It was a romantic conceit of course, she was simply past due for a release, Tamnath for once being correct. Yet it felt like something more, the beginning of a journey Braille didn't know the end of and this excited her. There was too much certainty in her life and not enough living for the moment. And so she gave herself to the joy of it. When they finally fell to sleep there was no doubt Firas had also found it pleasant.

* * *

Firas had never known such a feeling. Being taken by the Sea Queen was like being ravished by a Djinn, her power was overwhelming, her very touch enflaming his spirit. He was at once both drunk on and terrified with the pleasure he felt. And then she was done.

He didn't mind she hadn't continued until he spent himself. Part of him was worried he would die if the pleasure had been any greater. And there was always a price for gifts that seemed godlike. He was simply glad for a moment of joy, with a goddess of the sea and away from the foul and rude men he was forced to serve with. And so he let himself fall into sleep, the goddess settling at his side.

Firas fell into dreams, dark and murky, his soul sinking down to a place where demons dwelt. But they were not demons, they were men, they were his crew and he was back among them, as they sailed to meet the Vardashi. It happened one night, the captain was in good humor and had decided each of them was to have a woman to share. The one given them wore a blue veil and had dark kohled eyes, and while she did not struggle, neither did she smile. Firas knew the fate of such women, their stories like his sister, taken young against their will and forced by a man to whore for bread, or else driven by calamity into poverty. Firas lusted of course, every man did, but he had no interest in partaking of fruit that was stolen, not given freely, or at least paid for honestly. He knew some women were thralls and to be thralled to whoredom was abhorrent, no matter the decrees attributed to the prophets of Al-ahat claiming those captive to the faithful could not be raped.

But the men Firas served with did not care what he thought. He cleaned their weapons, polished blades and mended "like a woman" and though he had been given a knife and mace to use, when he wasn't rowing on the lower deck – hard back-breaking work – he was assumed to be of little use. Once the battle began the magi who tended the Dragon employed him to measure the powdered salts because he had a meticulous eye. However, all these tasks, while needed, had little value to the ordinary men who dreamed of plunder and concubines. Now they had the use of a woman and didn't understand why Firas would not.

They jibed him and the threat was clear: he would use her or they, when they needed a woman, might use him. Whether it was a real threat Firas would never know. For his own reasons he was too frightened to find out. And so he put himself inside her, thrusting while she looked blankly over him like she did with all of men who used her. After they cheered at "making him a man", he let himself fall out and wither. They were all wretched but it could be worse.

Then the dream took him to the depths of Hell, to the slums of Tamask were he lived in the shadow of buildings of great wealth he'd never set foot in. Like noble veiled ladies, they marked not the fortunes of those who lived on alms, prayers and the whims of fate. Or the wretched who preyed upon those even more wretched.

Firas had been just thirteen summers, his voice was between a man's and a boy. He was running for his life. He had some idea what the older hooligans sought, while they shouted after him, speculating his sister had been a whore. They were bored and full of blood with low morals. The feeble earnings they made serving the wealthy were enough to assert themselves over others. Those who did not submit to their arrogance they punished.

And so Firas ran but he was blindsided and caught. And, though he fought wildly, he was hit until the pain made him limp with weakness. Then they took him like a woman. The pain was horrific, worse than any of the beatings from his father. Firas screamed but no one came. And, as Al-ahat willed, he survived, but his father must never know for Firas knew his father would kill him. Being passed from attacker to attacker, he'd forgotten the pain, how long it went on...

Suddenly a bright light surrounded him and the attackers were gone. The glow diminished and he saw his Sea Queen. She grabbed his hand and pulled him up.

"You've been drawn into the wake of my dreaming, but you cannot control it. It can take you to bliss, or to the worst places you've ever been if you do not know how to walk in Dreams. Hold on, don't let go."

And slowly Firas rose, light as air, and the dank foulness of memory left him. He was saved. Looking at his Sea Queen's determined countenance, gold glowing tresses floating around her, how could he have thought the Vardashi demons? They were holy and she had saved him from Hell and that was all that mattered.

Finally they stood on solid ground, but still Firas knew he was dreaming. The Sea Queen wore something strange, loose leggings like those in the north and an open vest. Perhaps this was what she wore on land. Firas himself was wearing the dun tunic of his youth, though now he had a man's body.

"We are on the level," she said. "The place where dreamers start their journey."

Around Firas he saw the deck of the ship, but just beyond, where the sea should be, was a wide plain of grass as if the ship sailed on land. "The appearance of traveling dreams depends on the mind of the dreamer and the collective minds of those powerful nearby," his Sea Queen continued. "I think the fleet yearns for land."

Firas laughed, finding it all strange. "It is like being in a different land," he said. "The light is different though and I feel I could fly."

"Some do. But dawn is coming and I will be called to rise soon."

She pointed east where the sky was the pale dusky blue of predawn, but wondrously, the light of the sun shone up at them from below the horizon, filtered by the sea water. Then Firas let himself be pulled by his Sea Mother's grip, the scene fading to darkness.

Slowly Firas becoming aware of his own body, still lying on a bed. He opened his eyes and it was dim, the lantern above fading. He felt wondrously refreshed.

A moment later his Sea Queen rose and somehow moved over him, extracting herself gracefully from the cramped bed. After first splashing her face with water from a basin, she dressed with alacrity in all the strangeness of Vardashi garments of war.

"Firas?" she said.

"Yes, Sea Queen?"

"Stop calling me that! Braille or even emha."

"Yes, Brahil Emha."

Braille laughed. "Very well. Do you wish to return to your other friends waiting to serve?"

"Where would I go?" Firas asked.

"You can stay here. You might be rousted by a crewboy come to clean. You should take the chance to use the wardroom toilet. But if you go back, expect to be passed around. That is what you agreed to."

"To be used by other Sea Queens."

Braille sighed as she donned the long blue coat. "Yes."

"I like it here."

"Then that's settled."

There was a knock. Braille unlocked and opened the door. A girl entered, a young woman, looking much the same age of Firas' sister when she was cast out. The girl was also dressed like a sea queen, though she wore shoes instead of boots.

"Come in, middie," Braille said. She sat on the throne-like chair while the girl acted like her groom, first combing Braille's long, gold hair, then deftly weaving it in a thick, short braid that was bound at the neck to let the rest of the hair fall freely. Then Braille stood and let the girl brush first her uniform, then her strange narrow hat. Finally the girl left, perhaps to groom other sea queens.

Braille buckled her baldric and sword, not quite looking at Firas when she spoke:

"Were those your memories or fears?" she asked.

Firas would not have answered any other woman. But Braille had rescued him from the nightmares. "As I said before, there are worse things than being a plaything of a Sea Queen."

Braille looked up, her expression unreadable. "The part with the Shari crew...you despise their company."

"Yes. They will be cruel to those that are not strong enough to fight them."

"As cruel as those those men long ago?"

Firas could not speak. Speaking would make it so and he had tried to forget for so long he almost had.

But his lack of words told his Sea Queen all she needed to know, for Vardashi were wise in the ways of minds. A whistle sounded.

Braille looked directly at Firas. "I will send food. If anyone asks for you, tell them emha has said she is not finished with you."

"Yes, Sea Qu – "

"Ai!" Braille interrupted, waving a warning finger.

Firas smiled. "Brahil Emha. Yes, Brahil Emha."

"And that is as good as we'll get for now," Braille said. She donned her hat and left, closing the door firmly behind her.

Firas fell back on the bed. Never in his life could he remember lounging to rise at his leisure, and certainly not in a bed so well made. He worried at first of falling back into dreams. But hadn't Brahil said he was drawn into dreaming by her mind? He should be safe. Besides he wasn't sleepy. Instead he rested feeling the luxury of it, as the light brightened, indirectly lighting the quarters, until through the curved windows, past the shadow of the ship, he saw the light of dawn reflecting off the windows of the ship beside them, to the west. The room would be in shadow until late afternoon. His curiosity was piqued about the other ships.

Walking naked to the windows, Firas stared out. He couldn't see them all from this vantage, but he saw enough, the proud sapphire prows cutting through sea foam, driving a path with their magic reckless of where the sea flowed or the wind blew. Falling back one vessel towed the surviving warship, pulled along by great cables such that, like a tired nag, it seemed to struggle through the water to keep up. Was it the ship Firas had served on? But it didn't matter. All the prisoners were either wretched like himself or rogues, bullies with supple spines for those above and cruel blows for those below.

Firas was in no doubt he had been among the wretched. But he had escaped and had no intention of ever returning. He raised his hand to make a very rude gesture to his former captain and all who were loyal to him. He smiled, such a thing would get him whipped in Tamask. Then his eye caught something below the window.

There was a cushioned bench where one could sit. On it lay a flute. Firas had played the flute as a child, had been reckoned as very good, but his father had not liked it. Any time away from weaving was time wasted. Firas learned never to bring reeds back from the river. But this flute was not a reed. It was a finely made thing of wood, but Firas could not fathom how. There was no mark of tools on it, no scoring of the lathe, no chip marks of a whittler's knife. It was as if it had been made so, as if fruit of a strange plant. Hesitant of its magic, Firas picked it up.

The flute seemed to hum on its own, channeling the air through it as if it breathed. Nothing happened to him, though Firas didn't know what he feared. To be struck by lightning? Turned to salt? Gingerly Firas set it against his lips and blew.

The note was purer than any he had made before.

Firas sat down on the seat to better handle the instrument. He did the scales, trying to hear how the flute sang, and every note was sweet. If he had this flute he was certain he could have played at the Sultan's court and left weaving behind forever.

So Firas played like he'd never played before, the music a pure joy to make, unwitting that keen elfborn ears wondered at the source.

Chapter 30

Wings of Vengeance

Rakki was grateful to scour the great pot and do the many the lesser tasks the galley crew put to them. Demeaning tasks, slave's or worse, women's work. For he felt, by falling out of the line of "special" volunteers, he'd barely escaped with his soul. From a boy he had been told of the she-demons that would rob a man of his vigor, and weren't they now enslaved by the Sea Queens, defenseless and at their mercy? Yet, like women always did, they tempted men into their beds. But Rakki was no fool; while he yearned for comfort, he had no intention of making it easy for the Sea Queens to work their dark magic on him. For why else would a woman demand a man to her bed? Women did not feel the pleasure of the loins like a man did. A woman only sought such a thing for a man's purse, or, if she be a virtuous woman, for marriage. If anyone asked him, Rakki was certain they would never again see the fools who were taken away.

Rakki would have much preferred to remain at home in Tamask, where he served in the guard of a Sultan's retainer's house. But when the Sultan demanded his service – for Rakki had once been a sea man and was expert with a bow – no one denied what the Sultan demanded. And, were he honest, he admitted the treasure they were promised from sacking Gazhor made him dream of riches and freedom. Perhaps a farmstead where he would have a wife and children. And slaves to fan him like a noble, and horses and asses. And he would have grapes and make wine, for while he worshiped Al-ahat, the old god of rain and plenty raised to a new glory, he was not of the stoic cult that eschewed liquor and many pleasant foods. For years it was feared the Sultan would take the prophet's dietary scruples up and then men like Rakki would never be able to eat pork again.

Instead his Eminence had taken up the whim of war and expansion. Darav Ormaz abu Damaski saw himself diminished compared to his ancestors, and with his advisors, had concocted a plan to raid the Vardashi and steal riches from Gazhor. It was known that the plan at first had lukewarm reception at court. But in the outer lands, the deserts and high mountain, tribesmen openly laughed, though rarely within earshot of the Sultan's troops. They had not forgotten the stories of the Vardashi and how they called fire down on King Maccadan in ancient times, after the great loss of the one and only attempt to invade Vardashi lands under the general Kurus the Magnificent, who was himself captured.

In fact many of the nomads in the mountains, and south near the Azhins, were rumored to trade with Vardashi, strange women and sometimes men from the eastern forests who wore crowns of leaves, and others said to come from the sky. But Rakki thought that as silly, an exaggerated legend of a djinn. There was even a time he doubted all the tales of the Vardashi, children's tales, parables of the mighty and greedy fallen from grace.

Rakki doubted them no more. Now he found them inadequate to describe the reality. There were so many tribes of Vardashi here, and only some fit the description of tall gold haired goddesses of fire with burning eyes. Some swam and looked fish-like, others swung between masts like monkeys. Still others were covered with tattooing and strange tartan fabrics known to be worn by barbarian tribes of the cold lands, far north and west. Perhaps some were, and the tales of bearded men in dragon boats were wrong. Many things were exaggerated by travelers. The Vardashi were all strange, but the presence of particular ones made the hairs on Rakki's neck raise. Like the dark-robed magi who looked so similar to the magi of Sharitan and caused wonder in many of his fellow prisoners. The learned said Sharitan owed much of their knowledge to past generations who made friendship with the Vardashi. Perhaps that was how the magi started, a pale imitation of these Vardashi sorcerers. Shari pride objected to the idea, but Rakki couldn't help wonder. If so, the Vardashi magi were orders of power beyond anything Rakki had seen in the Sultan's court. They knew minds and walked in dreams. He much preferred the Sea Queen's crew that didn't use magic so obviously.

For instance the captain who had charge of them. He was a man, though he barely looked it, his features, like all Vardashi, were pointed and feminine, belying their lethal grace. Not that Rakki himself was great barrel of a man. He had always been thin. But he worked and was strong and let his inadequate beard grow as much as it could so as not to draw the attention of perverts who could not get women. But there were women who liked fey boyish features in their men. Rakki was certain this male captain was popular with them. Perhaps he was the admiral's lover and that's why he was trusted with the prisoners. In any case, he was a man and that made Rakki feel safer surrounded by what he saw as vengeful demon women. Perhaps this Captain Rozin had his own magic and that was why he was treated with favor.

Rakki finished the kettle and was told to take it out to dry. There were doors that opened onto a small deck at the front of the great ship. To either side were round "houses", a place for the composting of waste. In the center, through the small deck, the bowsprit, as thick as a tree, rose at an angle, as if pointing the vessel forward. He'd tripped against it once. Rakki would have liked help; it was quite heavy and the wind was strong and chill, but he learned early on to never show weakness and would only ask of those he trusted. Alas they were dead, or maybe on one of the other ships. He would not know until they got to Gazhor. As he turned to reenter, his thoughts flew back to the battle:

Their spirits had been high with blood and fear. There was barely enough room for him to pull his bow and no point in aiming for anything in particular. They used mass tactics, shooting in waves hoping to overwhelm the enemy as best they could. They had been told to aim in the masts, for that was where the deadliest Vardashi arrows came. Though they too used mass tactics, the Vardashi had archers who could kill a flea from several furlongs away. Rakki had seen their captain fall with these arrows and so felt he was doing his duty by shooting as fast as he could. He saw his arrow fly and, improbably, remembered its flight into a nest where it struck a Vardashi archer.

Rakki shook his head. Was he dreaming? He'd never known where his arrows landed. It was impossible. Then a voice in his head cried:

~you~

He turned and found himself beset by one of the great black ravens that roosted in the Vardashi masts. It was as large as an eagle, and he barely saw it before pain erupted in the left side of his face. He knew he'd been blinded and tried to protect his remaining eye. But in doing so he exposed his throat which the raven tore at with its feet beak. Rakki barely sounded a strangled yelp when he felt his throat torn open, again and again, as if the bird knew ripping open his jugular would be his death. And all the while he saw the scene of where his arrow landed, in the side of a woman who was this bird's companion and a red rage filled him. It was the raven's rage. Then Rakki understood. Like a loyal dog, the raven avenged its master. If he wasn't dying himself he would have felt pity for it.

Losing blood fast and unable to speak, Rakki fell to the deck. His last thoughts were of the sky and flying free. This must be what it was like to be a bird...

Then Rakki died.

* * *

ToKeh flew past the guard and magi who ran to investigate the commotion. He ignored their demands to return. He knew he had to fly fast, before the fleet ravens had been alerted. ToKeh was a good flyer, but he didn't fancy evading an entire flock trying to take him down for the reward of a few morsels of meat. The mangy crows could all rot. He had taken vengeance and it felt good. He only regretted abandoning the eyes.

ToKeh flew adroitly between the masts and rigging, making it harder for a pursuer on wing. But no one followed him, though many minds watched him. Then he heard the fleet mother's mind:

~they demand you turn back.~

~they let her die! they can rot and so can you!~

~you can't fly to tyrum. it is too far. you will die.~

~as will the foolish one who follows me~

ToKeh knew the fleet mother wheeled high above him, but she made no move to intercept him.

~if this is the fate you choose, may the wind lift your wings and never fail you~

And that was all. ToKeh was free, for all that mattered.

So ToKeh flew on, west and north, into the sun of a dying day, for as long as he had strength.

Chapter 31

Walking the Wale

The next day the sun shined brightly, the wind blowing fast but steady. Had they still been sail driven it would have been considered auspicious. As it was, Rosen felt everything had settled into an equilibrium, though the sight of the scorpion warship being towed out the aft window of his cabin felt ominous. Being by far the smaller ship, most souls wouldn't be able to see the whole of it from the top decks of *The Tidebreaker*. But here, especially in the predawn, it seemed to bear down on Rosen, a vengeful ghost of thwarted Shari ambition.

Rosen put it out of his mind and joined the Dance for the first time since the battle. In his spot high on the stern, he had an even better view of the galleon, being forced through the waves by the towline, like a shark caught by an over ambitious fisher. He rebuked himself for the distraction, focusing on the slow turns and sudden blows, but he was spent in mind and body. The crew participating were fewer than usual. At the end, when they were all done, he noticed a small dark skinny figure among the crew milling to seek the baths or the mess. It was Aqi, in crew breeches and vest, her faded Shari rags gone. She was speaking with a flouted marine and a Gold captain of the strike crew, Lieutenant Tamithryn. Rosen smiled. Dancing was good for the soul, even if there were feats beyond the ability of humyn. Perhaps now she was forcing them to teach her more Hiltekash.

As Rosen trotted down the stern steps he called out to Galen chivying crew below: "Boatswain!"

She looked up.

"Have breakfast set up in one of the turret decks! It'll be a fine day!"

"Ai!"

Soon Rosen changed into his uniform and was sitting under the open sky at a table with Galen, the marine captain, Arlesh yal Ahlool, Strikemaster Sernalash, Woodweaver Fadwen and Ta Taren, her arm still wrapped with wood strips. They were serving themselves as the captain of the guard, Mordmhol and Master Jasmenal stepped in to join them. Soon their plates were heavy with fish, a cracked wheat salad, potatoes and bread. Taren struggled a little at first, but they helped her fill her plate. After that she just used essence to shift food if she needed to, eating with a fork in her left hand.

"Wasn't the Admiral's clerk Amralan invited?" Rosen asked, spearing some of the fish.

Galen swallowed. "She's poring over the salvaged notes. Wants them organized and annotated. I think it's an obsession."

"It's all of the Admiral she has," Rosen said sadly. The times he'd talked Amralan she never met his eyes, feverishly working with little sleep.

"Our prefect should have someone engage her," Taren said. "She is grieving and while this method is not lethal, if she doesn't eat or sleep it can lead to mania."

"Yes," Rosen murmured. "And where is our prefect?"

"Overseeing the reordering of the mess, I believe," Jasmenal said. "Soon the crew will again be able to eat in the luxury they were once accustomed."

They laughed. Then Fadwen, Ahlool and Sernalash gave brief reports of their domains while the food disappeared. In addition to the savory main meal, there were blanched shrimps and a salad of sea greens with thin sliced onions and olives.

"Our cook is getting creative," Rosen commented.

"*Is fearr liom cais agus liamhás, in fhírinne,*" Mordmhol said, fingering samples from a platter of sliced cold meat, cheese and sausage.

"You'll be the only one enjoying that repast on our return voyage," Rosen said.

"We'll restock in Gashora, surely," Galen said.

"That depends what the purser rules." Ardenweld had sent her regrets, feeling too busy with accounts to come above to breakfast with them. Rosen would need to look at her books before allowing luxuries. He dearly missed eggs, but they needed oats and other supplies that had become dear. He reached for his cup of honey mead when a sound made him stand and look around. Something caught the corner of his eye. Rosen leaped up in alarm.

On the edge of the captured ship being towed a figure hung off by her hands, making her way with care perilously over the sea. Admittedly the fall into water wasn't far on the smaller ship, maybe twenty feet. Looking down Rosen saw two divers treading water. He didn't know what made him angrier: that it was happening in full view of the fleet, as they sailed at cruising speed, or by having divers below was proof of premeditation. And they always fell. Even the best of them couldn't navigate the bowsprit, though since the Shari vessel lacked one, perhaps it could be done. This was a common prank reserved for new crew members, usually egged on in a dare for some coin. Such things had been strictly forbidden in the lead up to the battle. The defeat of the Shari made many women lax.

"Boatswain!" he bellowed.

Galen was at his side in a second. "Ah. Yes. Who is that?"

"I don't care who it is!" Rosen was feeling apoplectic. He almost called for a telescope to spy the figure closer better. Then he recognized her and was, if possible, more livid. "It's that mad Shari girl!"

"Ai," Galen said with maddening calmness. "Aqi."

"I know her name! I want to know why she's walking the wale!"

"I'll send a raven. I see an officer standing on the stern."

Galen was right. That soul was about to regret the watches she'd be standing.

"No," Rosen said tersely, gritting his teeth. "Lower a launch."

"Ai, Sea Father."

At that moment there was a splash. Aqi cried out, sputtering as the divers converged on her.

"She didn't do too badly," Ahlool said. "For a humyn."

Rosen fumed. "Announce my coming!"

Galen collared one of the Dwen crew, explaining the situation, while Rosen stalked to the diver's ladder. While he was halfway down to the water, he saw the Dwen run on the towline, agile as a squirrel, then leap on the ship's deck. Rosen had to hang on a rung for a couple minutes for the launch to meet him. In an emergency, he might have done the feat the Dwen just had, but he thought his rebuke would be dampened, quite literally, if he fell into the sea.

Galen went with him. No sooner was he on the deck of the warship, was the officer, strike captain Lieutenant Tamithryn, greeting them apologetically.

427

"A free humyn was walking the wale!" she exclaimed. "Can you imagine?"

Rosen said nothing at first. He tried to push aside his fear of what Tresmadore would say, the snide sneer that would creep into her voice though otherwise she would be civil. And the naval code! Sul and Maer help him, deliberately endangering a prisoner! Then he remembered Aqi was free and his blood calmed a bit.

"Who's responsible, lieutenant?" he asked with deadly calm, suspecting the answer.

"Well, Sea Father, no soul is ever forced to walk the wale. It's a challenge given and accepted."

"Lieutenant, I just abandoned breaking fast with my command crew because of this foolishness. Don't waste the Tyreen navy's time. Who gave the challenge that was accepted?"

"I think a challenge was understood by the humyn in question during a discussion with Corporal Eshela and, um, myself."

Rosen stared at Tamithryn. He didn't trust himself to say anything yet. This was the time Galen would usually start bellowing. But Tamithryn was an officer and outside the crew master's discipline.

High spirited voices and laughter indicated the divers were fishing Aqi out of the water. The first was the marine Eshela, grinning as she pulled herself onto the deck. She leaped to attention on seeing Rosen.

"She was game, Sea Father," Eshela started.

"Was she?" Rosen interrupted acerbically, finally finding his voice. "And how exactly did she agree to this?"

Eshela was Blue, much like Pearl, and looked mostly humyn, but with little bosom. "We were talking about naval customs. She wants to join. We said it's complicated, humyn don't usually join... and then she was walking the wale."

"Just like that?" Rosen felt something was missing from the story as he looked between the strike captain and the marine. "You were having this conversation on an abandoned warship? How did she know about the wale?"

Tamithryn blinked her gold eyes nervously. "Well, we told her only brave, strong women could join. That there were tests. And then..."

"And then you described walking the wale as one of these tests," Rosen finished with gritted teeth.

"We thought she'd be frightened off, Sea Father!"

"When has mother's pride ever been frightened off with a dare?"

Tamithryn shrugged helplessly. "Shari mothers are different! They've been taught to be passive like boys …"

Rosen ignored the casual sexism, saying, "Yet somehow this lesson didn't take with Aqi."

At that moment Aqi arrived, climbing onto the deck dripping wet like a half drowned cat. Yet she was grinning and, though she shivered, she swaggered across the deck to stand by her "mates" Tamithryn and Eshela. Aqi looked at Rosen, then imitated the attention posture of the other two. It was absurd. She was almost a head shorter than all of them, had more the body of a youth than a woman, but it couldn't be said she didn't have spirit.

Rosen exhaled and said, "So explain how Aqi got onto the wale."

Corporal Eshela blurted, "We didn't want her to try on *The Tidebreaker*, for obvious reasons – "

"Yes," Rosen said.

"So we came here, thinking once she understood… Anyway, she just leaped up. We didn't have time to stop her –"

"You brought her here. And she's humyn," Rosen said, now looking at Aqi. Her muscles were wiry ropes and she had little fat, for a humyn perhaps too little. "No humyn can move as fast as elfyn, few as fast as aelg. Thus you were inattentive."

"She has a will," Eshela blurted. "For instance she insisted on dancing…"

"Dancing is not walking the wale and risking death!" Rosen stood over Aqi, who stood even more rigid. Part of him wanted to laugh. He hoped his Shari would be sufficient. "So you want to join the crew?"

"Yes, oh captain!" she said loudly. Everyone present on the deck had gone quiet. As maddening as it was, keeping occupied was good for morale, as much for the prisoners, or the former prisoners, as for crew. "Why do you want to join my crew, Aqi?"

"They are women, but they are strong! I want to be strong!"

The answer moved Rosen. No matter how much the Shari had tried to beat the mother out of Aqi, she was indomitable. But he couldn't let sentiment rule. There were practical concerns about ability and loyalty.

"But we killed many of your race," Rosen said. "Do you not fear us?"

"I was stolen from my people by the Sultan's men and saw my father murdered before my eyes. I take joy in the death of the crew that slaved me and I fear nothing, oh captain!"

Now the silence had no hint of restrained merriment.

"Boatswain?"

"Yes, Sea Father?" Galen said. Her tone was that of an ancient retainer, eager to correct a fault of honor for her princar.

"In older times girls journeyed on ships, before they were proper crew. Assign such tasks to this one and put her on the watch roster. She will serve as a ship's helper until we get to Gashora."

"Yes, Sea Father."

"Crew Aqi!" Rosen said sharply in Shari.

"Yes, oh captain!"

"You will serve until we reach Gashora."

"Yes, oh captain! Thank you, captain!"

Now that was settled, there was the matter of discipline. "Let the new recruit observe her first floating."

Eshela and Tamithryn looked aghast, both about to object, but thought better of it.

"Yes, the battle is over, crew!" Rosen said, letting his voice carry to the tops of *The Tidebreaker* that was now clustered with gawkers. "Discipline is no longer suspended. And you will be disciplined for unnecessarily putting the life of a humyn in danger. Corporal Eshela, you are in the boatswain's care. Lieutenant, you're with me."

"How long, you think, Sea Father?" Galen asked.

Rosen knew Eshela would be masted like Sharol. "Until this eve."

After they returned to *The Tidebreaker* Rosen reviewed his logs and was reminded of another possible matter of discipline. Once Eshela was ensconced in the tops and Tamithryn was given a rotation of duties by the strikemaster, Rosen waylaid Galen.

"What is it now?" she said. She wasn't angry but was clearly quite busy.

"The diver Alsauk Yal Horah of the larboard divers."

"You're supposed to call her Frye," Galen said with a sigh. "Everyone does."

"That glum?"

Galen shook her head. "I think she was trying to– It doesn't matter. What about her?"

"I need to question her. She attacked a free humyn."

Galen stopped abruptly and faced Rosen. He was a bit taken aback.

"Only after it groped her!"

"Very well, but they were still in our charge and the matter must be documented properly."

"Is this you? Or a worry Tresmadore might manifest any minute to interrogate you?"

"A bit of both. Look, I know it's awkward for you. The rabid pet and the would be lover – "

"Frye is not my lover!" Galen said a bit louder than was necessary. A couple of crewgirls averted their eyes and hustled on their way.

"Congratulations my friend," Rosen said. "As if there isn't enough gossip."

"What do you want me to do?" Galen demanded.

"Send Frye to my cabin, with an available magi to read. You may as well ask for Glenfar. Taren will probably be grateful."

"Ai, captain!" Galen said and stomped away.

Things had been so easy battling the Shari. The peace had its own dangers. Rosen knew Galen wasn't actually angry with him. But the knowledge that Hanno would be culled had hit her hard, further complicated by meeting Frye. Rosen frowned in thought, walking to his cabin. It wasn't fair. Galen deserved to have a romance free of complications. Had Hanno not been twisted, his evenings would be spent reassuring her, yes, she was a woman any sister lover would desire; of course she should ask Frye to share a meal, there was no profit without a venture. But now his actions might kill whatever spark still lived.

And so Rosen sat at the table waiting while Glenfar hovered behind his left shoulder again, acting as a legal notary to read truth. Galen was present as well, sitting on a stool.

"When do you think she'll arrive?" Rosen said. "I'd like to take the cage within the hour."

"Well, she's a diver and she's Blue," Galen ventured. "I did tell her as soon as she was done sorting netting. But you know divers."

"Not personally."

"They have a flexible understanding of time."

Rosen sighed.

"The Meer do have a clock," Glenfar said. "It's tidal and rather large. The Conclave use them in their great maleen cities to time fishing patrols. Of course nothing that could be used to mark precise minutes."

"Thank you, Glenfar, for that wisdom," Rosen said.

"Someone's coming," Galen said.

They heard the heavy footsteps of one who did not walk gracefully on land. The next second there was a pounding knock.

"Enter!" Rosen called.

The latch turned and the door was shoved open to bang against the wall.

"Sorry," Frye said. She looked at the door as if it was at fault as she stepped in. She was barefoot and dressed in the netting and canvas most divers wore. She had a crest of short black hair, the sides of her head shaved to reveal a pair of triskelion leaf tattoos on her blue skin.

"Close the door, please," Rosen said. Unsurprisingly the door was shut with a heavy thud. "You're not under discipline, however there are questions about your action on the *Ta Azaduta* before it left."

"Yes, Sea Father?" Frye said, glaring at Galen briefly.

"You attacked a free humyn. I need to know why."

"I didn't attack any soul," Frye said. "I was defending myself from an attack and that is a very different thing. The clever magi should know."

"She's right," Glenfar said. "They are very different – "

"Glenfar!" Rosen interrupted. "Just tell us what happened, Volunteer Alsauk."

"Fine. We were bringing fish to share. At first the humyn was thankful. Then he invited me to stay with him. I thought at first it was primitive hospitality. But his thoughts bled. He already imagined I was looking at him with desire. And when I tried to disabuse him of this, my own fellows telling him I'm a sister, he was so certain in his delusion, first he offers gold for my time like a jockey. Then imagines I am being coy so he grabs my waist. Then I grab him and he misunderstands no longer. Clear enough?"

Frye was openly belligerent. Divers had a unique relationship with the Tyreen navy. Some were crew, but most were like Yino or vagrant workers, signed up for a journey. Volunteer divers had the option of being released in the next Federation port; they could return but only if there weren't marks against them. Frye had been so offended she apparently did not care.

Rosen turned his head to Glenfar.

"Magi?" he asked.

"Oh, she's being completely truthful."

Rosen had to ask the question. "Did you feel the humyn threatened your dignity as a mother?"

"Yes!" Frye hissed.

"Did you feel the authorities present acted with alacrity?"

"No, I did not feel it so." Frye glared. "I felt the boatswain was more concerned for her humyn pet."

"I see," Rosen said. He felt deeply uncomfortable. The dignity of the mother was sacrosanct. But he also didn't believe Galen would lose the focus of her duty for so little a thing. "What satisfaction do you want?"

"From whom? The humyn?"

"The humyn is already under censure and confined."

"Confined?" Frye said. "Didn't they all sail off to magically lands in the south?"

"Not Hanno," Galen interjected. "He is destined for judgment in Gashora for other reasons. He is to be culled."

Frye's face changed, her fierce demeanor vanishing in wonder.

"And the question of satisfaction was from my command crew, not the humyn," Rosen said.

Frye stood tall and a little cocky. "Fine, yes. I do want something. I want your boatswain to tell us true she was not defending it."

Rosen wanted to close his eyes.

"I was not defending the humyn, Volunteer Alsauk Yal Horah," Galen said. "I was shocked and did not know what had transpired. The Sea Father was given charge of the prisoners and free humyn, and I was concerned you might kill him. I see your actions were well within your rights. I only wish you had lingered for me to explain."

They waited a moment, Galen and Frye in a tableau, coming to a détente of souls. Rosen could almost feel the tension bleed out of the room. He had his answers and he suspected so did Galen.

"That's all completely truthful as well," Glenfar put in.

"Thank you, Glenfar," Rosen said. "I suspect that will be all, unless Volunteer Alsauk has anything else to add?"

"Yes," she said, giving Galen a slight smirk. "Call me Frye or don't call at all!"

Frye swaggered out without waiting to be dismissed, the door banging against the wall.

"Boatswain," Rosen said patiently.

"Yes?" Galen looked stunned but pleased.

"I don't want to hinder any liaison. But kindly find a way to speak to Frye about protocol. And also how to open and shut doors."

"Why not mast her?" Galen asked.

"Oh no, my friend," Rosen said standing. "This is your task and yours alone."

They went their separate ways for the day, and Rosen had a pleasant watch driving *The Tidebreaker*. In the afternoon he caught up on his logs. As evening came he was walking with Rondaleth on waists to the forecastle when a raven soared with speed from the bows, flying overhead, and away from the fleet. A whistle went up and all the ravens took flight, circling high above the ship's masts. Something disturbed them. A guard came running, her face white.

"Sea Father!" she gasped, gesturing towards the bows. "A prisoner – he's dead."

Rosen let Rondaleth investigate, instead watching the raven fly like an arrow through the masts of the fleet, as if worried it was being pursued. It continued beyond, tacking a course directly to Tyrum, though it would be its doom. Ravens did not usually kill alone. But Rosen knew this one had. He waited until a couple of magi brought the body forth, a grisly thing missing one eye, it's jugular savagely ripped open. It was carefully laid down as

healers rushed forward to see what could be done. Rosen's spirits sank as
Rondaleth spoke:

"No one knows why, but the raven attacked him while he was laboring."

"Can he be retrieved?"

"Too early to tell. The healers can mend the body..."

"But the soul may not return."

The thought was wearing. Of course a magi or healer would have to
trance and then herd the humyn soul like an errant sheep. They were easily
lost in the dream world. Rosen dreaded writing in his logs that eve. He also
had a vague anxiety that he should notify the Admiral of his irregular volunteer. He decided to say nothing unless he was asked. It wasn't as if he was
pressing Aqi into service.

Looking up, a raven seemed to drift his way. Rosen realized it wasn't a
trick of his mind, but the black bird was diving for him.

Rosen agilely stepped aside, impatient with raven acrobatics, at the same
time deftly taking the folded paper out of its beak.

~well dodged, elfling~ the raven said, as it flew off.

"I yearn to impress," Rosen muttered. He opened the paper, a brown
scrap from a leaf book used for notes. It read:

Black Seal, with complements, etc.

Sea Father Rosen, concerning Prisoners.

Have Magi review minds.

Some cruel – few will speak.

May duty prevail, etc

B. Aledan; L. Up. Deck

Rosen frowned. It took him a moment to recall Lieutenant Aledan. She
was one of the Jackal's cronies; she'd met him on *The Black Seal*. Rosen's
spirits sank. Was it a trick? A ruse? Another, heavens help them, prank?
Rosen didn't trust any mother who served under Tresmadore. He shook his
head, trying to think clearly. It would be a blot against duty to send a captain on an empty quest, but it would be a small blot. Surely they weren't
that bored at sea yet. He needed a magi. But it could wait until after the re-

trieval of the humyn soul. They could investigate what the cryptic message claimed.

The next day Rosen was lunching with Rondaleth in his cabin when Glenfar informed them the humyn was lost.

"Truth be told, the ways of humyn souls aren't entirely known to us," Glenfar said as she sat down and helped herself to some of the olives and cheese. "I've retrieved shocked birds and a Thyn wolf, but death had been very recent, in a manner of minutes, and they had not gone far."

"Mind your portions," Rondaleth said. "The boatswain will join us soon and she has a healthy appetite."

Glenfar waved her hand. "There's more in the sea and that garum fish will last some time. What of the other task, Sea Father?"

Rosen frowned. "I've been told there is trouble among the prisoners."

"By whom?"

"That's not for me to say at the moment. But Galen will be bringing the Shari captain here... Ah, I think they have arrived."

There was scuffling at the door. This betrayed the humyn's presence because Galen, for all her size, was as light on her feet as a Dwen sprite. The door opened, Galen entering first, followed by Komar Zan, hands bound and flanked by two guards. He was no longer wearing a turban; it had been decided that the extra lengths of cloth were a risk in prisoner hands. Still his dark hair was tied back with a scrap of rag, his mane, wanting care, was growing in wild and unkempt. Still his tunic and leggings were clean. The prisoners continued to be kept busy. Rosen swallowed and set his fork down, wiping his hands and mouth with a napkin before speaking.

Without taking his eyes off the humyn, he said to Glenfar, "I need you to read his thoughts."

Glenfar set down her cup. "What am I seeking?"

"Evasion, if what I've been told is correct." Rosen said to Komar in Shari, "Thank you for joining us, 'admiral'."

Komar Zan bowed low. "Oh captain, I am blessed by your attention."

Rosen stifled a sarcastic reply. Besides, his Shari wasn't subtle enough for jibes. "Tell me how it is around your fellow prisoners."

The Komar looked confused.

"Are they at ease? In good spirits? Do they fight? Do they want for anything?"

Here Komar's eyes fell on the table, still abundant with sun baked fish, olives, and cheese. "You eat well, oh captain. As you should. It would be a kindness if we, unworthy as we are, could have some better meat."

Rosen turned to Rondaleth and asked in Shari, a signal she should answer in the same, "What are they fed?"

"They are given a bowl of porridge for breakfast. Bread and salted fish for dinner. And water of course."

"We hear the others on the galleys were allowed fresh bread and fish," Komar interjected. "As much as they wanted."

Rosen paused before answering. "You mean those you kept as slaves and thralled?"

Komar bowed his head, but Rosen was unsure of its meaning. Was he admitting fault? Bowing to Rosen's authority? The mix of self effacement and entitlement was hard to parse.

"This thing you say, is true, oh captain. Our ways are different. We have persons who have offended the law and displeased our Sultan, and they find themselves bound to service."

Rosen frowned. "This is not the tale the mothers tell."

The captain looked confused a moment, then smiled. "Ah. The women. But a woman's tongue is often wayward."

"Is it?" From the corner of Rosen's eye Rondaleth and Glenfar looked dubious, as if Komar was unbalanced. Rosen didn't feel so merry.

"How are the mothers who were slaved to you wayward?" he asked.

"Ah, you misunderstand, oh captain. They are not owned by us, but are the thralls of the Sultan to serve his troops as he pleases."

"Oh, so not personal slaves, but they are slaves. And presumably have offended the law or the Sultan to deserve this."

Komar shrugged. "Perhaps. I do not know how they have come to this fate. Al-ahat gives the victor dominion over the vanquished. It is their fate and I am powerless before Al-ahat to alter it."

"But you are not powerless over how you treat them," Rosen said. He was impatient with Shari literalism. "What did you feed the slaves and thralls?"

Komar's confident demeanor faltered. "Is this a court? Am I being judged?"

"Answer the question!" Galen bellowed.

Komar glared at her resentfully, the living proof mothers were not fated for slavery. "We gave them porridge."

"How much?" Rosen demanded.

Komar sighed. "A bowl a day for the women."

"An entire bowl," Rosen said, his anger stirring. "Imagine, they were literally awash in luxury."

"The men at oars were given more!" Komar said defensively.

"Two bowls?" Rondaleth asked.

"The warriors would eat the best," Galen put in.

"We are stronger!" Komar exclaimed. "We had the power of life and death. And to those beholden to such power, they should be humble and not make demands! And those who judge us as gods, as the prophets say, they will be judged themselves – "

"We are not gods," Rosen said, cutting over him. "But we are a greater power." Keeping his eyes on Komar, in Hiltekash he said to Glenfar, "Can you make a glamor or vision?"

"Pardon?"

"I want him to see the Cataclysm. Now. Anything to scare this arrogant wretch."

Glenfar didn't answer and Rosen took that to mean she had it in hand.

"We also have the power of life and death," Rosen continued in Shari. "The truth is you are only able to stand here making excuses because we have rules of war and are bound to them by chivalry. By your own philosophy, you should not have offended us."

Slowly the quality of light was changing in the cabin. In the filtered rays of sunlight, a form coalesced, at first a small ball of light no larger than a fist. It was high above the table and it took a moment for the Komar to notice it. He blinked, wondering where the light came from, then looked in astonishment and fear. Then the light expanded and became a window into the past that dominated the room. In it vast tracts of lands could be seen, forests, mountains and oceans. Rosen continued talking, keeping his gaze on Komar who's eyes widened as the Dying Star fell and set the sky on fire:

"We are elfborn. Our foremothers moved the powers of the Orb as our nations do to this day. You cannot fathom the many times during the course of history your race has been saved from annihilation by ours. Yet your Sultan, the foolish man no older than a boy in our reckoning, sought a war with us without provocation. Worse, he was arrogant enough to believe he could make our cities slaves to his empire. You should not have offended us. Tell me again what you said about humility?"

At this point in the vision the Thyngalu, the great dragons of the air, had manifested. An individual was larger than any of the city-ships, their wingspan easily as long as the line of the fleet. Komar cried out as one seemed to fly at him, jaws open, large enough to swallow a village. Out of its maw lightning flashed, striking the meteor that fell to Eurath. There were many more flashes of lightning, much of the Dying Star destroyed, but of course not all, for its final fall into the sea was what birthed aqua. Glenfar's vision was adequate, not as solid and real as in a carnival or theater, but enough that when a dragon apparently flew out of the scene, diving suddenly to swoop directly at Komar, the humyn fell prostrate covering his head with his hands. The vision faded.

"You have complained about food, 'admiral'," Rosen said, his voice hard and demanding. "But you've said nothing about your fellows' good spirits."

Slowly Komar raised his head. "A trick of the light," he muttered. "Vardashi magic."

"Your fellows," Rosen insisted. "How are they in spirit?"

"As well as they might be being Vardashi prisoners and at the mercy of fate."

"There are not those who make mischief for their fellow?"

Komar stood tall again. "I still command, though my fiefdom be small. My men act as men, not beasts."

Rosen didn't know what else to ask. He didn't like Komar, though he wasn't as insufferable as Hadi. But Rosen believed he really cared for his crew.

"Guards, return him to the brig."

Once they were gone, Rosen asked Glenfar, "Well? What did you discover?"

"Besides my food you've helped yourself to," Galen said. She sat down and started to eat.

"He is annoyed about the food, that's one truth," Glenfar said. "No, it's important, Sea Father, because it give me a counter measure of his other thoughts and responses. He doesn't understand why you are so offended about the slaves. That's another truth. He in turn is truly offended at the suggestion he didn't have the loyalty of his men. Can I ask now why you interrogated him?"

Rosen shook his head. "I was told, I don't know, it was implied they might be torturing each other?"

"If they are, it's very subtle," Galen said. "They looked fine on the surface."

"Perhaps they're needling each other over their tattered garb," Rondaleth suggested. "Boys can be cruel."

The women laughed.

"Yes, of course," Rosen said acerbically. "How cruel I am not to allow them baubles and cosmetics."

This produced more laughter, and talk fell to other matters of the fleet. Rosen let the issue fade and cursed Tresmadore for setting her lackey up at his expense.

Nonetheless, he and Galen decided to tour the lower deck. Two Shari men labored at stoning, Aqi standing over them, a starter rope in her hand. In sea breeches and vest, she could pass for regular crew at a distance. A couple guards stood nearby.

"Is it wise to give that particular humyn anything resembling a weapon?" Rosen asked.

At that moment one of the men paused and muttered something. Aqi sliced the air with the starter, smacking the deck with a loud crack, making the man jump.

"You work!" Aqi barked in Shari. "Or I hit!"

Reluctantly the man resumed stoning.

"I doubt she'll be using it on us," Galen said continued casually. "She seems quite keen on discipline."

440

"Yes. Possibly murderous. Make sure she's watched carefully. She might be too enthusiastic about disciplining her former masters."

Galen laughed. "Yes, captain. But you have to see the humor."

Later Rosen found himself stuck in his cabin facing a blank log page and his own discomfited thoughts. What was he to write about the day? Should he mention the missive from Aledan? He suddenly decided he would. His interrogation of Komar might be questioned, especially on the point of using a vision to frighten him. Well, he wouldn't have thought to question Komar if it wasn't for Tresmadore playing games. The death of the other humyn was clearly out of his hands. How was he or anyone to know a raven would take revenge? He couldn't remember it ever happening before. Had the raven been that close to one of the dead? It was definitely revenge, for the bird had left all the meat, even the eyes.

Then there was the matter of Aqi. Rosen sighed, letting the tension ebb away. In comparison, the matter of Aqi seemed small and amusing. He couldn't remember exactly why he'd been so angry about it. Still, floating, rather masting, was the right thing to do. They needed to return to fleet discipline.

When he was done, he had a drink and took a walk up to the forecastle, standing on the observation platform over the bowsprit. In times past when ships were smaller and at the mercy of the wind, the spray from the sea blew over the crew. It sounded very romantic in poems, but must have been quite chill. The wind was strong enough as it was and Rosen was grateful for his wool coat. Lagging behind the fleet felt strange, looking at all the aft blue keels, as if they were fleeing him. A figure waved off the stern of a ship to Rosen's far left, northwest of their course. He peered at the bronze ship plate, so far away he was glad for the setting sun's light: it was *The Starshard*. Rosen smiled, waving back, then Manweth disappeared, probably for supper. He missed Manweth. It would be good to get to Gashora if only for the society of other captains.

Rosen didn't have a night watch so after supper, he eschewed Galen's attempts to bait him into playing Gains. Instead he took to bed early. It was time he should try to make the dream journey to visit his household. If he could confirm they were safe, it might shake the feeling that they had not yet escaped all danger.

441

Chapter 32

Burning Souls

Rosen woke in the place dreamers often started their journey, a place that looked much like where one slept. But the farther one traveled from it, the more it changed form according to the mood and power of the dreamer. He was wearing sea breeches, but instead of his coat was a loose, sleeveless tunic with a cord belt, and his hair hung loose, the top locks bound by a thong. He felt free and the dream air seemed fresh as he walked along the deck and then down to a place on the water where seven magi stood in a circle, the waves lapping around their feet. Rosen found he himself could walk on the water, though he was cautious. It was not unknown for a dreamer, remembering some anxiety, to wake in panic.

"Are you wanderer or crew?" the nearest magi asked. Her black robes billowed around her and her eyes glowed golden. Nothing of her features were clear, the light around her bent and blinding though their was no single source to explain it. Rosen assumed it was the essence she used that caused this effect.

"I'm crew," Rosen said. "But I have no need of the Sadol. I will find my own way."

The magi turned from him and the entire circle seemed to waver out of focus, as if it had fallen below a shallow lake. As Rosen thought it, a lake appeared by him, with a grassy path leading to a distant hazy plain. Rosen thought of his family: his mother, Therald, and his sister, Trezmen, amd, almost reluctantly, Korali. It was the right choice. Strong emotion connected dreamers over great distances and Korali's well intentioned meddling produced the strongest emotions. Slowly the haze resolved itself into the three black peaks of bare rock that overlooked Tyrum. Rosen thought he could see the faces of the white Wall. Only then did he truly feel how much he missed home. But before anything else appeared a figure ran towards him. To his relief it wasn't Korali.

"Al met, brother!" Trezmen said, throwing her arms around him. He returned her embrace, and the place where their hearts met glowed with warmth. Then she pulled away and exclaimed, "What took you so long? Ama was worried and Korali... well, was being Korali."

"Did he sing about it?"

Trezmen laughed. "He's too busy. We all are! The Shari you were too lazy to finish off are coming and we're organizing! Even Korali has joined a men and boys work group. And just hours after loudly proclaiming at dinner the men who left to serve the fleet were 'frivolous boys seeking romance and adventure'."

Rosen started to laugh then stopped at the implications of what Trezmen was saying. "So they haven't arrived yet?"

"Well, they are humyn. They're probably still paddling around the isles near Lethglean. I don't see why Federation Patrols haven't scorched them out of the water."

"Hopefully they will." Rosen felt the beginnings of panic, but he had to remember there was nothing he could do. They had to trust the ships in the bay to defend Tyrum. "You know about the Dragon of Tamask, right?"

"Yes," Trezmen said wearily. "We've been transcribing notes as fast as the fleet magi send them. This is the first night that sleep is my own. It's a deadly beast and has killed many as I understand."

"Try not to let them use it," Rosen said. "It's fed by saltpeter powder; water will destroy that. Or better, strike a boat and the salts will consume them."

"Yes, that's been discussed, I think."

Rosen felt a little relieved. "Good."

"So what are you wearing now?"

"What's comfortable to my mind. Much like yourself." She wore her typical calligraphic pajamas, her hair bound on her head to keep it out of her face while she read.

"Well, are you going to show me around your skip?"

"My *ship* is but a pale dream," Rosen said. "We could go to my cabin. What's ama doing for the defense?'

Before Trezmen could reply, a pall descended over them. Rosen looked up at what looked to be black clouds. Instead it was billowing smoke from a great fire, flames just barely seen through the haze. Rosen's skin crawled. His sister spoke first.

"You should see to that," she said.

"Why? It's just a nightmare."

"It feels like a burning soul," she insisted. "Not just a dreamer."

Rosen wished Glenfar was here and was put out the thought of her didn't make her appear. But someone else did.

"She's right," the tall blond woman said. Like Rosen she wore casual land clothing. He didn't recognize her at first. By her side was a dark-skinned humyn male who looked alarmed, a tourist in a strange land. The woman's gold hued aura shined strongly. A bright aura in dreams was a sign of excitement or passion. It took Rosen a moment to understand the man with her was Shari. More puzzling, he too had an aura. Or perhaps he shared hers? Did humyn have auras?

"Are you listening?" the woman barked.

"Lieutenant Aledan," Rosen said, finally recognizing her.

"Didn't you get my missive?"

Rosen was uncertain what to say. "You mean your jest?"

Aledan's eyes flared. "That isn't a jest!" she said pointing at the fire. "It's a soul burning on your ship!"

Rosen looked with horror and suddenly metal bars wrapped with Dwen-twisted wood snapped into focus, darks shadows looming behind them.

"Brother," Trezmen said. "You need to wake up."

Rosen sat up in bed like a marionette jerked by the strings of its master. His heart pounded as he stumbled out in his slops, grabbing his coat and baldric. He was halfway down to the middle deck, when he realized he'd forgotten his hat. It was quiet and nothing of the dark deck dotted with swaying lamps suggested that a tragedy might be in progress. Lieutenant Rondaleth met him near the stair by the jeer capstan.

"Sea Father! Why the urgency?"

Rondaleth was fully dressed, on a late night duty. For a moment, she was backlit by a lantern, giving her a demonic cast.

"Have you heard any disruption? From the prisoners below?"

"No. The Cambari had a late night *céilí* near the commissary. The guards came up to stop a brewing fight. I think they're still there."

"What?" Rosen looked down the length of the deck to the darkened stove at the fore. There were two figures sitting at a table. Something clattered, possibly dice. He was livid. "Come with me!"

The ship's guards didn't notice their approach as they chatted in Gael.

"*Ha! Is cailliúnaí thú! Arís!*"

"*Tá tú ag séitéireacht,*" the other grumbled. "*Le draíocht, is dóigh.*"

"The only magic that should be happening is watchfulness!" Rosen barked coming into the light.

The guards leaped to their feet. "*Athair na Mara!*" they chorused.

"Why are you not below watching the prisoners?"

"*Bhuel, níl siad ag imeacht,*" one began.

"Of course they're not going anywhere!" Rosen said. "But they still need guards nearby to watch them!"

"*Ach, ní bagairt iad leis an gcriú –* "

"But they are a threat to each other! Come on!"

Rosen ran down the companion stair to the lower deck, the guards and Rondaleth at his heels.

This area, once used for drilling and other tasks in preparation for the battle, was always dark at night, just a couple lanterns hung to walk through with ease. Now the dark was full of breathing, fast and slow, now intakes in surprise at their arrival. Like strange thickets of wood and iron, the two jails lined the hull at either side, fifteen or so humyn in each. Eyes glimmered, lowering as some who had been standing crouched. As his eyes adjusted, Rosen saw them better.

"You," he pointed to one of the guards. "Get a magi. Ask for Ta Glenfar." The woman left. "You're Dwen right?" he asked Rondaleth. "In spite of those gold eyes?"

"I can move wood, captain. But I can't form much."

"I don't need a sculpture. Just to open the door."

"Ai, enough for that."

"Good." In Shari Rosen shouted, "Komar Zan! Step forward!"

There was a rustling in the brig along the hull starboard. Komar did as he was asked, gripping the wood boles that acted as bars. "Yes, oh captain? How might I serve? Alas forgive us our poor hospitality."

A couple humyn chuckled at this.

446

They fell silent under Rosen's glare. As his eyes swept the chamber, figures shrank away from him, like the leaves of poisonous plants withering with blight. Rosen made his face stony, raking the men's faces, wary, sweaty, their eyes bright. Several pulled thin robes around them, perhaps to protect them from his elfyn magic. Now Rosen felt it, the last thread of unwoven fate presaged by Reverie, the final dread after which, he hoped, his soul could feel at peace again. He heard quick steps behind him, one heavy, the other, the light foot of one used to walking on air. He felt Glenfar's aura before she spoke.

"Not there," she said. "In the other cage I think is what you seek."

Rosen turned away from Komar Zan, and crossed the deck to the larboard side. The humyn shrunk away shivering. Nearby a whimpering could be heard. "Open the door," he said to Rondaleth.

She sprang forward, perhaps troubled by his grim face. His left hand clenched on the hilt of his sword. Once the wood locking vines were unwound the door swung open easily. Rosen stepped inside.

It was dim, with only light from the deck lamps, and while long enough to fit the humyn, it was barely six feet wide, enough to lie side by side with some space. Most had been sitting cross legged. But figures at the end huddled in crouches, looking wary. One sitting nearby one was grinning. When he saw Rosen's eyes on him, his smile vanished.

On the other side of the deck, one of Komar's companions called, "Who knew Vardashi entertainments were so thin the King of the She-devils would seek us out – "

"There, Sea Father!" Glenfar said loudly, striding into the room. They shrunk further away from Rosen, and actively scrambled out of Glenfar's path, clinging against the hull. They saw a magi of great power. Rosen followed to the very end where Glenfar was pointing near the grinning man who had stood. He was somewhat fat, which was a feat given the work and sparse rations. Rosen looked at him closer. His leggings seemed to be disheveled, as if he'd returned from relieving himself.

"No, not that one," Glenfar said impatiently. She was now next to Rosen. "There."

She pointed down to a thin man huddling next to the bars woven into the hull, pulling away from Rosen and Glenfar. Fear in his eyes, his back was to the hull as he hugged his knees. That's when Rosen saw his trousers were also in disarray.

Rosen blinked, his mind frozen a moment as it revolted against the knowledge. His jaw clenched as he tried to speak.

"What has happened, magi?" he asked, already knowing the answer, but like a child looking for comfort, he asked anyway, hoping to be told things were not so.

"He has been outraged." Glenfar crouched down and forced the man to look at her, holding his chin. "Who did this to you?" she asked in Shari.

He pulled back and spat at her feet.

"No matter, I will find out."

"There is no mystery," Rosen said with disgust. "The smiling jester betrays her guilt. Or in this case, 'his'." Rosen stared at the man again, who now grinned in that maddening way all youths did when caught at something and weren't sure if they would be punished or praised. Except the humyn was no youth, his face covered with a ragged black wiry mane. His breeches still drooped making it look obscene. Rosen wanted to be sick. He turned from the humyn and shouted at Komar in Shari, loud enough to rouse the deck: "Did you know this thing happened?"

"What has happened? You lock me in a wooden cage, how am I to know what is in the other cage?"

Rosen grabbed the no longer grinning humyn and dragged it out to stand near the companion steps, within Komar's sight.

"Ah, I see. Men have needs. Some more than most. If some yield to them like women ..." he shrugged.

"'Yield'?" Rosen growled. The center of his body was on fire, except for his belly which felt like ice. "Magi! Did this man wish to 'yield' willingly in anyway?"

Glenfar stood in the door of the larboard brig, her young face like wax. "No."

"Do not tell me lies, 'oh' captain," Rosen roared. "No soul wishes to 'yield' to another like this."

Komar's eyes hardened, as if addressing a prince being told a hard truth. "True men do not let themselves yield," he said.

A sneer worthy of the jackal possessed Rosen's face. He looked at the man, barely more than a boy, fit but thin, having want of food for who knew how long. Then at the jester he still held, whose smile had faded, its dull humyn instinct informing him he was in danger. Fat-covered muscle made him useful, at the oars, if he wasn't a warrior. In a contest of strength the boy never had a chance.

"And this is what you call keeping the peace?" Rosen demanded. "Letting your men abuse each other? You spineless coward."

Those words hit home. "How am I to blame for what happens in that cage when I am imprisoned in the other?" Komar objected in a rage.

"And you!" Rosen said, pushing the fat humyn from him to stand on the deck. Rosen heard the sound of steel withdrawn from a sheath. The humyn backed away, no hint of smile now, his eyes strangely staring at Rosen's waist. "Why did you need to rape? Are so possessed you can't touch yourself? What is it with followers of the Ever Sky, your 'Al-ahat', that you claim men are superior in all things but you abuse your fellow man – "

The humyn was stuttering. "These are not men," he laughed nervously. "They are soft like women –"

The rage consumed Rosen. He was only slightly surprised to find his sword was drawn, in his hand. Much like the battle, things seemed slow. The abomination grinned obscenely at him, hoping for quarter, for some sympathy, perhaps in a deep belief that, though Rosen was Vardashi, as a man, like all men, they shared a sacred bond.

If so, the humyn was quite mistaken as well as delusional: this bond had not helped the ravished boy, who was some mother's child. And the idea that men were united in some horrific mad war against their own mothers was a perversity. It offended Rosen like an open leprous sore, a disease that needed to be eradicated like the demonic Bane from myth. Rage took Rosen. While the doomed humyn stood, Rosen ran him through so deeply the hilt of his sword hit the creature's sternum. Dimly he heard men scream and yell, huddling even further into the hull, as if it could swallow them.

But there would be no escape. Looking into the humyn's eyes, Rosen watched it die, feeling a dark satisfaction he'd never known even during the battle. "Begone foul thing," he said, as if exorcising its soul from the world. "Begone and rot in the void with Athmod!"

Blood welled up between its lips, dripping down over its chest, onto Rosen's hands, its revolting warmth like acid touching his skin. The humyn said nothing and soon the dull light in it's eyes faded, and the weight of its body pulled down on Rosen's arm.

From the corner of his eye Rosen saw Glenfar looking aghast. There was also a growing murmur telling him those berthed on the deck had left their cabins to investigate the commotion. Slowly the rage ebbed. He tried to pull his sword free but it was stuck. Rosen made a growl, a brutal animal noise, he wasn't aware he was capable of. He had to grab the hilt with both hands and both pull and kick the body off, sharply breaking its ribs so the chest cavity lost its grip. His white sleeping slops were stained crimson but there was nothing for it. He turned to face the horrified Shari and spoke:

"In our land death is the punishment for forcible seduction! It matters not if the attacker is a woman or a man, though it is usually a woman. Nonetheless it is a rare crime because we are a civilized people!"

Part of Rosen was aware his words were somewhat undercut by the growing pool of blood at his feet, and the wet droplets that had splattered his face. "You felt ill used before? Overworked and mistreated? Tresses, you have no idea how fine you've had it! But instead of showing grace and gratitude you act like diseased beasts. Thus you will be treated like beasts!"

"Except for these who I will take from the room," Glenfar murmured. Her look was hard; she would challenge him but she didn't want the fight and hoped he didn't either.

Rosen nodded stiffly, pausing to let Glenfar collar the victim and a couple others she'd identified as past victims. In the face of Rosen's rage they were compliant.

With Glenfar gone Rosen appraised the prisoners. They were rightfully fearful. But it wasn't enough. They'd been fearful before, but that didn't change old foul habits.

"Lieutenant?"

"Yes, Sea Father?" Rondaleth said, looking at the dead humyn.

"I want to know where the lower deck officer is," Rosen said.

"Here, Sea Father," Lieutenant Colma Selimor Uí Rosa said, approaching also wearing sleeping slops. Her gold hair was loose but she did wear her coat.

"I'll save the question of why your deck wasn't more attentive for later, lieutenant," Rosen said. "Right now organize crew to dispose of this. Rondaleth, get crew with wood-essence and the lathing like they used in the infirmary. These cannot abide civilly, so they will be bound."

"Yes, Sea Father," Rondaleth acknowledged.

Within the hour all the prisoners sat with hands tightly bound to the wood bars of the jails, legs and knees thrust through the gaps by necessity.

"There!" Rosen said when the crew was finished. "We can finally sleep in comfort there will be no mischief for the rest of the night or any other night under my command!"

"But we can't lie down!" Komar objected. "This is cruel!"

"Is it?" Rosen said, striding over to glare down at the humyn, knowing he was utterly humiliated. "As cruel as when one of your men have a way with your mothers?"

Komar blinked resentfully, sneering as if to speak but said nothing.

"No, of course not," Rosen said. "Just be grateful I don't toss your filthy hides overboard. Now there will be silence, utter silence for the rest of the night. If anyone is heard, the guards will gag you."

Rosen strode out, the guards leaping out of his way, Rondaleth at his heels.

"If they soil themselves – "

"They can clean in up in the morn," Rosen said coldly.

"Sea Father, you know they cannot sleep that way. They will suffer."

"Good."

The rage started to ebb. By the time Rosen was back on the quarterdeck he felt empty. Looking up the night sky was clear, struck with bright stars. The Dwen would be in high spirits at the sight. Above he heard the strains of a night lay, one of the long hymns Dwen sang in the high trees during holidays, especially at the winter solstice on the night of Hal Suldan, or Yafelram Astersh, the Long Night of the Stars.

Rosen looked up and spied the Great Bear and her cub whose tail ended in the Guiding Star. Nearby Selis, the greatest wizard of elfyn legend, sat on her throne and watched the winding path of the dragon swimming in the stars between the Bear and her cub. As a small boy Rosen always wondered if that annoyed the Great Bear and if she wished Sel would do something to mind her dragon. There were no known Thyn bears, but perhaps in the heavens it was different. And then a bright flash crossed the sky, a shooting star, and the Dwen cried out as if a firework had exploded.

But to Rosen it felt like a comet of ill omen, a sign of his personal cataclysm. For he had violated his oath, and the enormity of his sin only began to settle on his soul. He had been honor bound to protect the prisoner's life. As for the humyn's crime, that was for a naval tribunal to determine. Surely it would have been marked for the cull? In his rage he hadn't checked. In any event, Rosen was not empowered to mete out capital justice to Federation prisoners. It was bad enough one had died by the hand, or rather, beak, of a grief-mad raven. To slay one in cold blood …

However Rosen's blood had not been cold. It had raged white hot with a mother's outrage. Now he shivered, the possessing anger spent, and he wondered at his mind. Had he gone mad? And what would the dawn bring? He would have to tell Tresmadore. He expected no mercy. At any other time he would have dreaded the humiliation of submitting to the Jackal, but now he was too spent to care. There was no comfort, not in his mind, nor his ship, nor even the heavens. No star could guide him on the path across the raging sea of his life that lay ahead.

Returning to sleep Rosen dreamed he was walking in a fog on the sea as if it was land. The fog was thick, having a life of its own, and clung to Rosen as he made a slow way through it, for his feet were heavy, as if he wore boots of lead. Suddenly a figure rose up looming over him, a great fat humyn with hunger in his eyes, a burning desire to possess Rosen for his own pleasure, to force itself obscenely inside him. At the revolting thought, Rosen ran him through with his sword. The humyn laughed and to Rosen's horror seemed unaware it was dying, it's fat, sweaty hands still reaching for him. Only when Rosen twisted the sword the caricature of a person collapsed, sinking to its knees and dragging Rosen down with it. Desperately Rosen tried to pull out his sword, but it was stuck. As he struggled, he heard his sister's voice from far away:

"I saw him, yes, but it was fraught."

Rosen looked up. He could see them, his household sitting for dinner. He knew it was dinner because there was no sunlight, only the house lamps and street lights shining. Ama sat as she always did at the head of the table, but crowding her plate were papers and books, neatly arranged to not disturb the repast. His sister too had what seemed her entire studies arrayed around her, a bit less neatly and she was strangely dressed, in that she was dressed at all. Gone were her student lounging pajamas. She looked somewhat like a clerk with outdoor wear: boots and a short cape as well as a leather belt crossing her front. Was that a baldric? But most astounding was Korali, who wore loose bracs with a belted tunic as he served. A long knife hung from his belt. Equally astonishing was Korali allowing the women to clutter the table while he served.

"Perhaps you should try visiting," he said to Ama. "An older soul might be able to travel far."

"I'm not that old."

"You know my meaning. You'll be less distracted by fancies –"

"I don't have fancies –" Trezmen interrupted.

"You should tell that to the boy clerk who follows you about."

"He's my scribe!" Trezmen said. "He's supposed to follow me about! That's what the council assigned him to do."

"I think he's got a rather soft duty," Korali said, finally sitting down. "I'll be drilling in the forum with the regular men." Korali shifted uncomfortably in his seat. "Oh, I don't know about being so constricted in these bracs! How does Rosen manage it?"

Rosen had assumed it was simple dream, but this sounded too present. Tyrum was preparing for attack. He tried to walk towards them, but he could barely move, his entire body now as heavy as his feet. And still he couldn't pull his sword from the body. A cold hand grabbed his. With alarm he saw it was the corpse seizing him.

Rosen let his sword go but it was no use. The corpse's hand gripped him hard, its flesh burning him like acid. In no other way did the corpse express life; it neither groaned nor stared like in a ghastly tale. It just held Rosen in a deadwoman's grip, and, inexorably, it started to drag him down, the voices fading until everything was dark, gloomy silence. Rosen tried to scream but no sound came from his mouth. In desperation he imagined his cabin, the crystal decanter on the table, the aft windows, the hanging lamps, the node of aqua near his bed. Slowly, with great effort, he rose out of the miasma and woke.

Rosen opened his eyes and gasped with relief. Sitting up, he was surprised not to be in a sweat. His pulse raced. He didn't know the time, but, with no desire to sleep again, he rose and freshened up. He spent the morning poring over his notes, correcting his log, but the last half of the page for the previous day remained blank. He knew what he had to do but was uncertain of how to do it. There was a knock.

"Yes?"

"Sea Father?"

It was Galen's voice. He unlatched the door and sat back down.

"You didn't dance," Galen said, sounding concerned.

"No." Rosen had written about the Shari killed by the raven. Blast the bird or praise it, he didn't know which.

"Should I send for breakfast?"

"I –" Rosen wasn't hungry but it was good for ship's society: breaking fast was the time a captain took to discuss matters with her senior staff. Then he thought, damn society. "Have the table placed in the turret deck like the other day," Rosen said. "But I doubt I'll have time."

"A fleet sails on its gut, Sea Father."

"Thank you for that aphorism, boatswain. If you must know–"

Rosen was interrupted by a single sharp knock. Before he could answer the door opened and Ta Taren stepped in, her face as grim as an executioner. Her arm was finally free of the wood splinting. Taren looked solemnly at Rosen, neither angry or fearful.

"Duty compels me to seek you out, Sea Father," Taren said formally.

Rosen nodded waiting.

"Glenfar has informed me of what transpired during the night."

Galen looked at him sharply but Rosen just nodded. "Go on."

"The body cannot be disposed of recklessly. It would call into question the duty of the blameless under your command."

"Body!" Galen exclaimed. "What body? What in the screaming Void is going on?"

Rosen held up a hand for her to be quiet. "Glenfar did her duty."

"And I must do mine, Sea Father. I must inform the Admiral, if you do not."

In a way it was a relief. Rosen no longer had to wonder how he would do it, for the time to do it was now.

"That will not be necessary. I will go to *The Black Seal* today. I am only setting my affairs to rest. Thank you for your solicitousness, ship's adept."

"Our duty is service to the Orb," Taren said solemnly and left.

Galen was bewildered. "What did you mean, "you're setting your affairs to rest" ? You sound like an Aeon ready to walk through the Door."

"Galen, friend, I killed a prisoner," Rosen said. She was speechless. "I murdered a humyn under my protection. I – there was a reason, but it wasn't my choice to make. I need to go to *The Black Seal* when I'm done here. When I return, I may no longer be captain. I expect that will make Jasmenal jolly at last. Please do me one last service."

"Yes?"

"Send a raven to *The Black Seal* telling the Admiral I must speak with her. Then have the launch lowered. I will leave my recommendations for acting captain on the table. Damn it to the deeps, who am I jibing? It will be the Master. Jasmenal will have *The Tidebreaker* at last. I may as well put her name down. Go on, there will be plenty of time later to speak. I have to finish these before I go."

Galen nodded, looking sad and bewildered, but she obeyed.

Rosen's mind wandered back to Tyrum, to the vision or dream of his household, It gave him comfort they were, at least for now, safe. Then he chided himself for being indulgent and set pen to leaf, eager to get what might be the last acts of his command finished. It was then it hit him: if he lost his commission the sadness it would bring to his mother and her house. That thought brought him close to tears. He no longer cared what the Jackal would do to him. The idea of his mother's disappointment was unbearable.

Yet he would have to bear it and bear it alone.

Chapter 33

The Blind Night of Ambition

It wasn't exactly dull to Tamnath, taking these men: they were willing if grudging, or perhaps just shy from the fear of it. They were not used to coupling with powerful women, never mind the added ever present terror of magic, the essence they could never understand. For Tamnath, she felt an echo of normalcy waking next to a male body. There the similarities ended. One or two of these had some enthusiasm once they felt pleasure. But most were simply compliant, pleased perhaps that, at the end of it, they had not been transformed into some wretched creature.

Tamnath sat up, looking at the still sleeping dark form next to her in the early dawn. He likely only slept because of exhaustion in trying not to sleep earlier. There remained a superstition about Vardashi sucking the souls out of men while they slept. Utterly ridiculous, Tamnath thought. If this was a thing she could do, she'd do it while he was awake to savor the terror. For isn't that why demons did such things? But the greater question was why, demon, aelg or elfyn, she'd have any need for a humyn soul.

Now a man's body, that was a good motherly need. She had in this way indulged herself, done things many brothels demanded a steep sum for. Not because such things were necessarily hurtful, but they were seen as less dignified or degrading, and no man defended his honor louder than a harlot who felt misused. But these men, true to their arrangement, made no objection, whatever the act. It had a satisfaction of its own, the echo of a long ago hunger for vengeance feeling slightly sated. The first, the arrogant trafficker for the cull, had been the best. She might recall him when her need for variety was sated. Meanwhile she'd enjoy the regular release, a simple pleasure she'd earned after the duties of the day were done. The first few had taken the edge off. Now she was almost bored. She felt she was missing something but she didn't know what. Or rather she avoided thinking on it, lest she expose herself.

Still, they smelled strange, these Shari. Though the harlot had cleaned them well, their humyn musk lingered. Tamnath was glad they'd been shaved; aelg with hair instead of down tended to have more scent. Whether this was desired or not depended on individual mothers. Tamnath preferred her men to smell male, that is, hardly at all. If she needed to scent sweat she'd go to a laysaid match.

Tamnath rose and dressed for the Dance. It was good to be seen and not just to prove these minor indulgences weren't interfering with duty. It raised fleet morale. And it distracted her troubled mind. She'd send a crewboy to make sure it was out of her bed by the time she returned to dress for duty.

The air was crisp and fresh, with a light breeze from the fleet's passing. By the time Sul burned through the pink clouds of the dawn's haze, the Dance was finally finished and Tresmadore had retreated to her cabin. Relieved it was empty, she dressed leisurely. That was when she heard it again, the strain of a flute below her. Aledan rarely played at this time and so it made her wonder. When the Midship Drothmey entered to braid her hair, for a moment she could hear the tune louder before the door shut.

"What is that, middie?" Tamnath asked.

"Flute, Admiral," Drothmey said as she deftly divided Tamnath's long dark hair into three tresses.

"Sul, preserve us. Yes, I know it's a flute, but who can be playing it in Aledan's cabin?"

"Oh, probably be the boy she's taken to."

"What?" Tamnath was tempted to turn around. "She's wooing one of the crew?"

"No, emha, he's one of the Shari you brought back."

Tamnath had trouble thinking of what to say. "She's wooing a Shari?"

"Well, I don't know about that, emha, but she's very taken with him. He's not to leave."

"Isn't he?" Tamnath was torn between bewilderment, disgust and curiosity. Once the middie was finished she stood. "I think it's time I meet this boy. If he's that good, he should be in my bed, not my lieutenant's."

"Yes, emha," Drothmey said automatically.

Stepping out of her cabin Tamnath walked through the pilot's mess, nodding her acknowledgement to the morning greetings from her pilots, and out on the quarterdeck. She stood a moment watching her crew. They worked steadily, with good cheer, neither hurried nor lazy. With Elash driving them, they'd never be idle. Tamnath couldn't recall seeing Elash ever being still now she thought on it. Slipping between the wheel and mizzenmast, she turned to trot down the stairs that would end in a passage between the deck officer's wardroom and the heart chamber. As the senior upper deck officer, Aledan's cabin was the largest on this deck and its entrance was through the wardroom. Thankfully it was already empty.

Tamnath felt a thrill of excitement as she walked to the door of Aledan's cabin and grabbed the latch. It would be amusing to catch them together. Tamnath had never been one to ride men with her fellows present, but long ago Aledan had been, before she started to become a bore. Tresmadore squeezed the latch and pushed the door, but it was locked.

The fluting stopped. Tamnath let her hand fall, now even more intrigued. At first there was nothing: they were listening. Then boots approached. Tamnath leaned back, trying to look nonchalant as the door opened. The aggressive suspicion on Aledan's face made Tamnath want to laugh.

"Admiral!" Aledan amended, aborting what ever sharp words she'd prepared, perhaps assuming it was a prank.

"Are you going to huddle in your quarters all day? We're to breakfast on the decks."

"I'm hardly tardy," Aledan said, then seemed to understand she was being baited. "I'll join you anon."

"Yes, but perhaps you could explain who exactly is fluting so early in the morning?"

Tamnath pushed past Aledan to see the Shari boy, the one she passed over, backing away to the turret windows. He no longer wore the rough shifts they'd been given, but a long pale cream tunic, that was well made but had seen better days. His hands were lowered; in them he held Aledan's flute.

"I will be there momentarily," Aledan said, with an edge to her voice.

"I'm certain you will. I was just curious. It was this humyn playing? Not yourself?"

"Yes." Aledan looked neither at the boy nor Tamnath. She seemed tense. "He plays well. It amuses me."

"Oh!" Tamnath said. "It amuses you. But we have a bard who's far better than a clumsy humyn. However, if he's so good, he should play as we breakfast."

459

Aledan said nothing, her eyes still glaring. Tamnath could feel Aledan's hope she would leave. Yet she didn't say so fearing a hunt would start.

"Then perhaps later I could sample what you've been enjoying," Tamnath added.

Aledan's eyes snapped up, flashing, and Tresmadore saw it: the deadly mother, the dragon, the wolf, the great bear who would kill to protect her brood. And Tamnath laughed out loud.

"It's true!" she barked. "You're taken with it! Tresses! Sul preserve us! Get on the stern deck, lieutenant! I don't care about your Shari lover. But I do want my officers in attendance in a quint! And don't forget our morning entertainment!"

Tresmadore stepped lightly out the door of the wardroom, nearly flying up to the stern deck in good spirits. It was absurd and she would have much amusement at Aledan's expense. The extremes of such levity she restrained in the presence of the guards, magi and other command staff. "Yes," she said graciously, "Amazing how it can play, isn't it? Then I understand monkeys can be trained to do similar tricks, so perhaps it's not as fantastic as it seems..."

Tamnath watched Aledan's eyes, seething at the insinuation her lover was little more than a beast. But the truth was he was a beast. Tamnath knew the mirth she mined was unworthy, but she also believed she was doing Aledan a favor, however brutal her methods. It was a fancy, a chimera, a fantasy of Aledan's delayed passions. She couldn't possibly harbor a desire to woo the wretched creature. But the things she said were in Hiltekash and the beast had no idea how she spoke of it. So when the rest of the staff left and it was just Nesthet, Aledan and herself, Tamnath could speak clearer.

"It really is amazing," Nesthet said as she sliced an apple. "You'd think he had an elfyn soul, the way he plays."

"It's a pity he can't play anything besides Shari doggerel," Tamnath said. "Perhaps the bard should give him lessons."

"Perhaps," Aledan said noncommittally.

"Boy," Tamnath said in Shari. It faltered and stopped playing, looking at her warily with nearly intelligent eyes. "Do you enjoy being used?"

His eyes flickered between Aledan and Tamnath. "I agreed to serve."

Tamnath nodded. "That's correct. But do you enjoy it?"

"Making sport with a humyn is unworthy," Aledan said in a low voice.

"How chivalrous," Tamnath switched back to Shari. "She's being chivalrous you know. Doesn't think I should ask you questions about serving. Perhaps you'd like to return to your crew."

The human's eyes widened, as if in panic. Tamnath hadn't expected that. Did he truly prefer it here than with his own people? "So answer me if you don't want to be returned: do you enjoy being used?"

"I am pleased, yes, to be of service," the humyn muttered.

"He doesn't sound pleased," Tamnath smirked. "Perhaps he's bored. Nesthet, you want to taste him?"

"I'm not finished with him," Aledan said loudly. "Is there anything more to my duties today, Admiral?"

"I covered the basics with the rest."

"Good," Aledan said, standing. "Firas!" she barked at the humyn, like a raw recruit. He stood quickly from where he sat, instinct warning him to stay close to the woman who kept him. "Follow!" Aledan ordered in Shari.

"Taevol!" Tamnath said mockingly, snickering as they left.

"He doesn't look too bad for a humyn," Nesthet added.

"Pity she won't share," Tamnath said, feeling a sense of mischief. "How many have you had?"

"A couple. Didn't have time for more with the watches…"

"Well, if you fancy him, remember he did agree to service any woman who wanted him."

Nesthet looked nervously after Aledan. "Are you trying to enrage Braille for your amusement?"

"Sister, what do you think Braille is doing?"

"I don't like to say, but she seems besotted."

"And do you think that's a healthy thing considering the object of these affections?"

"Honestly? It's not where my passions lay. But if our foremothers never had such urges, we wouldn't have been birthed, would we?"

Tamnath shook her head and rolled her eyes. "You hope to be her first witness at the wedding?"

"Sel's bosom, it won't come to that, surely!" Nesthet exclaimed.

Tamnath wondered. Looking up, she saw a raven make its way around the masts and then dive for her. She knew the japes of these birds. Holding one hand up, palm facing outward, she let a burst of light fluorescence from her aura, causing the raven to veer in alarm.

~a low trick~ it thought petulantly as it landed in the middle of the table, knocking over Aledan's empty goblet.

"Your race isn't the only one to pull feeble jests," Tamnath said, taking the missive from its beak. Opening the paper she saw writing she rarely had reason to read, the hand of Captain Gathelyn. The lines were steady, quickly written, and the message enigmatic:

With complements from *The Tidebreaker*, etc.

Regret intruding.
Duty compels this captain to surrender command.
will be there within hour with full report.

RG; SF

Tamnath waved the bird away. Nesthet stared with naked curiosity. "Who is it?"

"The boy captain," Tamnath said, but didn't elaborate. As Admiral she was much more careful of what she shared. Until she knew more it was prudent to keep it to herself. "Perhaps at last he's prepared to be taken like a man," she quipped.

Nesthet laughed as expected; many were the jests they had in the past at Gathelyn's expense. Whatever drove the strange man had to be serious indeed for him to offer his resignation before they had even reached Gashora.

It would have to wait of course. Tamnath walked by Aledan as she conferred with Elash on some point about the inventory of the aqua. Aledan pretended to be unaware of her, but Tamnath knew better. They'd never been this much at odds. Part of Tamnath was troubled. Another part of her wanted to go to Aledan's quarters and ravish the Shari boy. What could her lieutenant do?

Yet a strange wariness crept on Tamnath. She'd seen the murderous eyes of a mother in her friend's face. Only a fool challenged a mother and truly, there was no reason to. Still part of her was distracted by it; it rankled that she felt restricted, hemmed in, as if Aledan dared to encroach on territory rightfully hers.

But the boy wasn't rightfully hers. It was these thoughts that made Tamnath concerned for her mental balance. Surely as healthy as it was for a mother to rule her domain, there had to be a limit to that domain? The idea no such limit existed invited a mad hunger that would consume all, friend and foe. And still a part of Tamnath's mind saw limits as a subjugation, a weakness, a challenge to be defeated. What in the screaming Void was wrong with her?

These uneasy thoughts were kept at bay by driving *The Black Seal*. Gathelyn would arrive soon enough. Until then Tamnath would lose her mind in the piloting of one of the fleet's greater vessels. Driving the great varsadmer, a city-ship, was said to be the closest to feeling like a god. Some reported the feeling of an Eirok flyer to be more so, but since Tamnath had no talent with wind-essence, she'd never know. She moved like one merged with the most powerful craft made by elfyn skill, her life force literally carrying the lives of the crew to Gashora. Tamnath had heard many times her talent was extraordinary: she felt the water and more. With the rib fins to leverage her essence, she could push water around her like the best Blue divers, effectively driving the ship faster if needed. And while she couldn't literally feel the deeps, the coolness of the water was communicated through the veins, thus in a way she found a kind of peace. Like a leviathan, she drove forward, standing on the dais in the pilot's cage alone. Most copilots felt uneasy sharing the cage with her and with the battle behind them it wasn't necessary. She'd almost forgotten the conflicts of the morning when she sensed Elash approaching her.

"Sea Mother!" the boatswain called. "Sea Father Rosen has arrived!"

Tamnath turned the cage over to Lieutenant Braun and leaped down. "What is his mood?" she asked.

"I cannot fathom," Elash replied. "He looks drawn and weary."

Tamnath made a noncommittal noise, adding, "Direct him to my cabin."

"Admiral."

Inside her cabin Tamnath waited. It was a serious issue for the boy captain to abase himself. And while she didn't feel a need to impress him, she did feel such niceties as offering drink should be observed. Bitter rum was traditional for solemn occasions, but possibly presumptuous until she knew more. She took out a bottle of white brandy, a misnomer as it was distilled from cider, not grape wine. It was harsh, at least as it was made in Cambria. One of the few things Cambrians did well, particularly after they acquired better stills with the help of elfyn engineering. White brandy had no business being a light sweet helpers' drink and this was mothers' business.

There was one knock and Elash opened the door, letting Gathelyn enter before closing it again. Tamnath hadn't sat. She wanted to appraise the Sea Father on her feet. He did look drawn; perhaps he hadn't slept much. He snapped to attention briefly and saluted. Tamnath lazily returned it.

"At ease, Sea Father," Tamnath said as she poured two goblets. His eyes spied them, perhaps musing on the meaning of the choice, but Gathelyn said nothing yet. "Sit, if you wish."

The Sea Father shook his head. "I think I would like it to be done," he said.

There was a thinness to his voice that matched the wan cast of his face. He was already unbuckling his baldric, removing his sword, the ancient symbol of authority an officer carried, for as far back as the days of the Sun-queens. A Federation officer only surrendered it if they had debased their duty in some way. Gathelyn carefully set the sheathed sword on Tamnath's desk. He looked oddly bare without the baldric. If he left the cabin thusly, by the end of the day the entire fleet would know they had one less Sea Father.

"That's a dramatic gesture, captain," Tamnath said. "Tell me why you think you must surrender your command."

And he told her. Tamnath turned away to look through the aft galley windows to listen clearer, that his male form wasn't a distraction. It worked better than she expected. In truth his voice was middling and never had that pleading edge men often did. If she put aside their long animosity, she heard anguish that was no different from any mother in similar straits.

It was a foul tale and Tamnath felt the truth of every word. She could almost see it, catching the Shari beast after outraging its own, Gathelyn's rage and confusion, for Tamnath would wager he'd never faced such perversity, the soul rot of those who would embrace rapine. For a long moment Tamnath felt frozen, as if in that instance she had seen her soul reflected back at her, clear for the first time at how much carrying her burden for so long had almost cost her.

Still listening she reeled inside. She could not judge these beasts without judging herself. She claimed to have never surrendered to the urge, but by how fine a thread? She'd have raped Rhondalyn in dreams had he not been so adept at waking. The compulsive visions of rapine had become more and more frequent, to the point she'd been possessed by one in the presence of Jonsay's magi trained consort, a man few women could match in mind craft. Tamnath wasn't a fool; she knew Tergani kept her at arms reach from his wife's brood because of the shadow over her soul. Tamnath never blamed him for it. It was a truce of sorts – they kept their distance and maintained a peace.

Except there was no peace for Tamnath, nor for the boy captain, Rosen. Now he knew what perverse and twisted Bane still roamed the Orb in the souls of the damned. He was no longer innocent, he could no longer think all evil was caused by lack and desperation, but must live knowing there were those who desired evil for the joy of it. Rosen had finished his tale and stood silent and still, awaiting her judgment.

Tamnath turned to face him. "Why did you join the academy? Did you always want to be an officer in the Tyreen navy?"

Rosen looked off footed, not expecting the question. "I never thought of it like that, Admiral. I discovered I could pilot. That is my joy, piloting. And it seemed sensible the best place to learn to master that was the navy."

For a moment Tamnath sensed they were siblings, sharing that one joy of piloting. Yet it didn't explain everything. "You could have stayed a co-pilot. Many women do. The balance of joy but without the responsibility for an entire ship."

Rosen shrugged. "It seemed logical…"

Tamnath sighed. "You aren't aware you crave ambition."

"I don't crave ambition –"

"Horse tits. No one takes the exams to captain a varsadmer without ambition. Certainly not a man. It's a trial of its own, ambition. Which is more dangerous: the mother aware of her craving who lets it drive her out of control, or the mother who claims none while it drives her just as hard? Either of them are uncentered, vulnerable to a sudden unexpected gale." Tamnath shook her head. "I'm hak at reflection. But I do know if you ignore your deepest drives they will drive you. Then if you are not careful, you will break on rocky shoals in the blind night. Think on it."

Rosen nodded uncertainly.

"In the meantime," Tamnath continued, her voice hardening, "Get your damn sword off my desk. I don't need boys littering my furnishings with their baubles. Besides, if you leave like that, the fleet will set to gossiping and I want fleet morale eagle high. Not to mention the hassle of appointing your replacement. So secure yourself."

This was understood to tend to one's uniform as Gathelyn did immediately, fumbling a bit in surprise he wasn't being removed from command. When he was finished, Tamnath offered him the other goblet.

"Go on, don't be such a stoic. Any mother would have been offended as you were. Many have done what you did for far less cause and kept their command. In truth you will probably be court-martialed when we return to Tyrum. But I will leave your judgment to the Admiralty and Command."

Rosen took the goblet then drank the lot in one gulp. Tamnath smiled wryly. It was really regretful. Rosen indeed appeared to have the soul of a mother in a man's body and it must be a hard fate. Tamnath resolved to not to add to his hardship.

"Is there anything else, captain?"

"No, Admiral."

"Then, I'll request one thing of you to secure both our duties: send me a complete report of the event and aftermath."

Rosen started, remembering something. "The body. How should we dispose of it?"

"Strike it. And feel no regret. Return to duty, captain."

"Yes, Admiral."

After Rosen left, the day felt strange to Tamnath. They made good time, the blue keels sluicing through Maer's waves. The divers, always dancing with fate, wanted to fish, but now they were forbidden. At these speeds, even the fastest divers would be left behind and Tamnath didn't want to slow for anything. It was even a challenge driving a launch, for it had to jump with a heady speed or else be piloted by essence strong women who could link the smaller boat with the ship's aura. A compromise was made, the launch towed in *The Black Seal*'s wake, the divers agreeing to be anchored with ropes. It was awkward but Tamnath understood even the garum packed fish was too cooked for a Meer palate.

Late in the day a raven came with a small scroll case from *The Tide-breaker*. Tamnath took the rolled leaves out. She was feeling a strange peace she couldn't explain. Perhaps she was growing into her duties. Nesthet entered to query about dinner, informing Tamnath the mess hall was being prepared, an infirmary no longer needed. That was good for morale; the crew should eat as one, with bards and merriment. Nesthet asked about Rosen, but Tamnath waved her away. She'd discuss it later. Nesthet, realizing Tamnath was in the mind of her duties, left after passing a missive from the lower decks. Tamnath nodded absently as she scanned the leaves of paper Rosen sent. When she finished she opened the missive and went cold.

There had been another death, a prisoner who was found hung. The name looked familiar. Tamnath jumped up and lunged for her other papers, notes and other documentation, but there was only one page she needed, the charcoal list of prisoners who volunteered. And there he was, marked for the cull, the first she had taken.

Tamnath's gut was full of ice as she read the rest of the report. The humyn had begged to bathe repeatedly and the guards thought nothing of it. They let him thinking it harmless, but this time there was no crewboy to watch. No one could have predicted what happened next. The prisoner did not come out and the door had to be forced. He had hung himself, smuggling a turban cloth made into a noose. The magi were still investigating. The soul refused to return, feeling it had been debased and fouled, and could only find honor in death. Then, seeing the humyn was marked for the cull, they let the soul pass through the Door.

Debased? Befouled? Damn the thing, Tamnath had only used it like any man who wanted to be used. And it killed itself? Why? It wasn't like it had been forcibly ravished. And certainly had a better fate that the unfortunates it had slaved as harlots for profit. But Rosen had been right, back on the ship, when she'd been driven to possess the men: their agreement was compelled by their circumstance. Had they not been prisoners, the one who chose suicide would not have agreed at all. Their choice was an illusion to scruple. The humyn had seen that truth and couldn't live with it.

Tamnath shook as she stood. She had driven that humyn to suicide as surely as Rosen had run through the ravisher with a sword. She knew it wouldn't fall as hard, the means wasn't as stark. It had been a slaver and was marked for death. But, as it wasn't Rosen's place to act as executioner, it wasn't her place to drive it to that end. Her soul would feel the burden and there was little to lighten it.

Little, but there was one thing. She left her cabin and made her way to the brigs on the lower deck where the humyn were kept. A Gold crewboy stood by, speaking with the guards. His eyes widened in fear on seeing Tamnath.

"Sea Mother! We had no idea – "

"Calm yourself, crew. The matter is ended and there will be no discipline. Are they all present?"

"Yes, Sea Mother! Except for one…" The man pulled out a folded leaf from his vest and looked it over."

"Firas," Tamnath said, surprised she remembered his name.

"Yes," the crewboy said after a second.

"He is well where he was," Tamnath said looking over the humyn.

Three others she had used avoided her eyes. Was it truly that awful? She had lost count of how many men over the years who spoke of harloting as a great party where being paid was just a happy chance. Of course these men had never harloted professionally. Real harlots, "companions" as was the polite phrase, had a more mercenary outlook. They did what they did to make queens. If that meant kissing women in their privates, so be it. If it meant making merry with a lonely Aeon whether she took them or not, that also was agreeable. Harlots knew their business, but they rarely had cheerful souls. Tamnath usually eschewed them for that reason. Then why did she take these, who had no cheer whatsoever?

The startling answer was because she could. The Jackal was hungry and she fed it, and for a while she had relief. But no joy. And she had driven one further into misery, even if by one metric of justice his misery was deserved. Tamnath was no less responsible for the wellbeing of these prisoners than Sea Father Rosen. The crewboy waited, perhaps wondering who the Admiral desired next.

"Listen carefully, crew: these are released from service. They will stay here for now, but are not to go with any more women.

The crewboy looked surprised, but said, "Yes, Admiral."

It was a small thing. Too small to assuage the tide of regret that threatened to breach the inner dam of Tamnath's soul. But it had to start somehow. She had to escape the Jackal. And she had to do it without Jonsay, because Jonsay was lost and might never return.

Then Tamnath felt despair and did the thing she'd avoided for days: she went to Jonsaymanor's side. The healers left them alone and Tamnath was glad. She couldn't weep though she wanted to. Though whether it was because she felt damned or because Jonsay looked so fragile, she didn't know.

"What will I do?" she whispered, knowing no response was forth coming. "I'm lost inside and I don't know what to do, mother."

And still Tamnath couldn't weep. Instead she sat there long into the evening. Nesthet sought her out, said the hall demanded her presence to preside over dinner. Tamnath told Nesthet to do it if she wanted. She felt her command was a sham. Not only was she further from peace than ever, but unworthy to command the fleet. But unlike Rosen, there was no one above her to surrender to. She would have to bear her feelings of unworthiness, at least until they reached Gashora.

Chapter 34

Flintsun

After the dead were sent off the volunteers were allowed much of the day at ease, the only true tasks being the repair of arms, gear or clothes. Col retrieved his papers at last after making himself useful to Amralan as she took on the duties of ship's secretary. But soon she was officially assigned a male officer to assist her and Col was without employment.

Col knew idleness would only bring on brooding so he sought out Bethyn Olden. Not only was he put to work scribing copies, but he helped write several columns for *Letters of Note*, enjoying in particular the description of the building and operation of the ballista. He also made notes to be paired with Olden's obscura images once paper projections were made in Gashora. Midship Roni Alhern often helped, being keen as he had been forbidden from taking his own obscura on the voyage. Col noted Olden understood the ghost catching contraption well enough she might be able to build one, but Alhern had a talent for catching images at the perfect time.

But these were tasks best for the evening, when the sun was gone and other labors had ceased. And soon there was no lack of labor, for Pearl and the rest of the divers were fishing as much as they did during the harvest seasons in the fall.

"Tangles aren't enough now the sharks are gone," Pearl said one day. "Now we have to use nets and herd them with water essence."

Col was watching as a net was hauled to the waists amidships, heavy with whiting. Most of the fish had already been killed through water essence by the divers, but a few still flopped. As they were spilled into a great bin, these were fished out and clubbed by crew before being shoved on a plank of wood before him. He had a muslin apron like many of those at this task, and his knife. Most of the Cambari volunteers were part of the flaying. This wasn't a fine skill to serve raw fish in the Meer fashion. Their task was to behead, gut and cut, whereon the fish halves would be passed to those expert at making fillets, many Blue or from the galley crew.

"Well, it's in your hands now!" Pearl said, pecking Col on the cheek before running aft to join the divers leaping back into the sea.

"It's not work we've not done before," Freya said cheerfully beside him. "In Besh anyone can make quite a few queens working the late harvests!"

"Ai," said Col. "In Dunvan as well. Though it's for silver *trice*." He fished out an inch wide silver coin with a triskele of the Cambrian Island Alliance on one side and a harp on the other. There were other coins used in Cambria with rings, crowns, fish and stags, but the *trice* was the main currency in Dunvan.

"We save our silver for home," Freya said as they worked. "It's limited in Besh to buying cargo directly from quay mongers. Queens are limited in a different way at home."

"Ai," Col agreed. "Some merchants still won't take 'fairy gold'. '*Is fearr airgead trom na ór éadrom*'." *

Freya laughed, the aphorism being well known even to those without Gael. The modern queen was a fiat coin, gold plated bronze, the value representing solstone, the actual basis of the Federation monetary system. But the concept of currency by representation was still held in suspicion by most Cambrians.

Col tried to keep the conversation light. His guilt over their kiss had abated but an anxiety lingered Freya might still pursue the issue. For her part, she did nothing untoward and Col hoped that would be the end of the matter. It saddened him a bit because he liked Freya. But clearly they could not be just mates, friends without passion; there was too much chemistry between them looking for a way to manifest.

Once enough fillets had been made, they were thrown on a grill where the strike crew seared them with an abundance of mead and vinegar. Then the lot was packed into barrels and the entire process continued. Col understood they were literally laboring for their sustenance. The crew spoke openly of concerns that food could become scarce. If waste had been watched before, now it was relentless; even the leavings of sauces at meals could earn a lax crew or volunteer a verbal lashing.

It wasn't just fish they worked to preserve for the trip to Gashora. Grains, oats, wheat and barley, had been salvaged from *The Oaken Blue* and divided among ships by need. *The Tidebreaker's* potatoes were diminishing fast and so they received some of the largesse. It was a dubious gift. The grain being so water logged, the only thing for it was to break it – Dwen did

472

this with a type of long flat wooden wand they dragged through the wet grains, at the touch of which they broke apart – cook it, strain it and mix it with spices, crushed garlic and vinegar or wine. The more cosmopolitan crew said it was much like the dish tabbouleh from the Fertile Basin. Whether the prisoners would agree, Col didn't know, but it was pleasant enough. Personally he was much more pleased that barrels of potatoes had also been salvaged, their time in the salt water giving them a unique but not unpleasant brine taste. One day the Cambari volunteers, greatly supported by the guards, convinced the strike crew to roast potato wedges on the grills. They were some of the best chips Col had ever had.

And finally the salvage and food preparations were over. They sent off the free Shari in style, cheering the *Ta Azaduta* as she led the merchant galleys south, with the hope the ships bore their new masters to a new and better life. Then the fleet turned to sail to Gashora, pausing only to strike the Shari warships into ash.

That evening was the first the mess hall was returned completely to its purpose. Col took up sundry cooking and cleaning duties, but without Samath there was little feeling of adventure or joy. Now he was paired with a Dwen man from the mast crew who had strained his leg and was forbidden to work in the tops until it was fully healed. He was introduced as Ardhen and had the opinion that should be enough.

"Colm mac Fionnbarra ó Síoran?" Ardhen echoed as they polished a table in the wardroom.

"Just 'Col'. And actually, I used 'Ní Síoran' when I came aboard," Col clarified. "It's more Sula."

"Yes," Ardhen said, his elm leaved yastol bobbing as he nodded. "A mother root name sounds more respectable, even in the Forest. But there is none that are needing to know my root name, so 'Ardhen' must do."

"Yes, I suppose." Col said, watching as Ardhen stopped to touch the wall. Above, part of the wood that had cracked grew back together.

"So, tell me how are the trees being where your fati lives in Cambria?" Ardhen asked.

"The trees?" Col echoed. "I'm not sure what you mean."

"The forests, are they thick? Is it full of life? Or do humyn be cutting and burning without care when they could practice the coppicing of tame trees?"

"My father's tribe are merchants mostly, so I don't really know."

"Hmm, living on grassland cleared in the past, I am thinking."

"Probably."

Col learned to steer conversation away from farming, hunting or anything that might include a forest, past or present. He was tempted to ask for a different cleaning companion until one day Ardhen said without prompting:

"I was working with your friend Samath in the infirmary. He was being a bright soul. I am sad for you he is gone."

Col didn't know what to say, but was touched. Dwen were odd to Col, distant but direct; defensive of plants and trees, but careless of comfort with the elements. Once during a light squall of rain, Ardhen ran up to the tops to stand in it, smiling with other Dwen as water ran down their faces, those with yastol, leaves held high, some with their mouths open to the sky. Col watched from the shelter of the stern; some of the other crew laughed but the Dwen did not care. Col could swear when Ardhen returned his green eyes were brighter. In any case, they had both known Samath so Col accepted Ardhen's society, as strange and awkward as it was at times.

One benefit to having a Dwen mate was Col being one of the first "unrooted" to have the newly sprouted greens. With the battle over, the side boards returned, long shallow planters placed in the sun, sometimes attached to the hull. There was no soil of course, but the Dwen made a filler of bast threads, wood shavings and seaweed, that was sufficient for the sproutings of lettuce, purslane, kales and cresses, with particular success with garlands of watercress. Even with forced sprouting by wood essence, there was no time for roots or fruit. Still, adding just a dash of vinegar and salt, the greens brought normalcy to meals.

In his free time Col spent sunny days on the upper decks, out of the way, feeling the wind blow through his hair, enjoying the illusion of freedom. They sailed in earnest for Gashora now, not even slowing their pace for divers to fish, though some managed. When the air was dry he'd finish his notes of the journey, descriptions of crew and other items of interest. But he had yet to write of the battle.

Col knew he should write while the memories were fresh. It was an important part of history and, as a scholar, a duty he should embrace. But when he tried to describe the events, the horror and loss, the images overwhelmed him. Instead he started to draw a face. Hours later that he recognized it as Samath. Then for a while he could not draw again, instead taking joy in exercise by drilling with the other volunteers for sport. They were still technically serving, but with no battle in the offing, no one was fussed about what they did. However space was limited now the lower decks housed prisoners in the makeshift brig.

Sometimes, when Pearl was away, it was lonely but Col didn't mind. Calm was needed to return them to their own minds. Many took the time to dream, visiting relatives in Tyrum or elsewhere. Col had tried, but whenever he'd found himself walking the halls of his house, all was silent and dark, and neither his aunt nor uncle could be found.

So Col traveled further, to the lands of his father, but, while he saw him, it was in the distance, a field surrounded by mist, and so much of his effort went to trying to catch his attention, when finally his father marked him, the surprise woke him, for he vanished at that point. Col himself woke disappointed, swaying in his hammock in the dark divers' berth. Then he spent hours watching and drawing the fish that swam past the window, the wood planks to protect it during the battle long since removed. He wanted to paint them someday; the image was magical and arresting, and few not Meer or Blue had been treated to such a scene.

In the days after work with the fish was finished, Col avoided Freya out of respect for Pearl, except when drilling or surrounded by volunteers. He didn't see much of Pearl except at night and she spoke little of dreaming. But Col suspected she too was visiting family and clan. During the day Pearl and Sharkhook spent most of their time scheming to fish within regulations while the ship still sailed. Other ships towed launches for divers. They decided to troll with tangles attached to nets. The results weren't consistent.

"Writing another lay?" Pearl asked approaching Col where he sat. She was dripping wet.

"Stay away from my leaves!" Col said, recoiling automatically.

Pearl laughed and leaped up to perch next to him, but not so close she'd drip on his book. "We caught a few mackerel," she said. "We'll have to eat it fast."

"It wouldn't last long anyway," Col said, detailing Samath's nose. Samath had a far more elegant nose than Col's. "Vinegar grains and garum fish for breakfast, lunch and dinner, with cold meat and cheese. And whatever stew the cook will invent. Any fresh food is welcome."

"Perhaps an orange?" Freya said, appearing at Col's side. Without thinking he took one of the proffered fruit.

"A fruit of the sun! Thank you!" Col said. Then he saw Pearl smile tightly at Freya and added, "Perhaps you can spare some for the divers?" he added.

"Verily," Freya said, fishing a couple more out of the sack in her hand. "I didn't know divers ate much fruit."

"Sometimes we like a change," Pearl said, still watching Freya, her face neutral.

"Well, there's plenty and if they're not taken they'll go off. We found them lost behind barrels of arrows. I'll see you at drill!" Freya added to Col. She walked on, offering the largesse to more crew.

"Sorry," Col muttered, returning to drawing.

"Winds away, love! This feeling is my burden." Pearl peered at his work. "That's interesting. Is it a real face or imagined?"

"It's Samath."

"Oh." She watched him work. "I don't understand drawn figures well. I'm sure its very good."

Col smiled. "High praise from a blind Meer."

Pearl inhaled for a retort or perhaps a tease, but at that moment every raven launched into the sky with a deafening croak and flew in one black mass north, slowly disappearing.

Pearl jumped down from the wale, looking alarmed. Col closed his book and put it in its satchel. The Dwen were climbing the masts. "What is it?" Col shouted at a nearby crewgirl. "Why did they leave?"

The woman waved him silent, naked excitement on her face as she watched a Dwen scamper up the mainmast. A small telescope was thrown to her, and she caught the spinning instrument while standing on a spar high above the deck. But she didn't put it to her eye yet.

Suddenly the Dwen put a hand out to her left, tying to block the glaring sun. Then she brought the telescope up. A moment later Col heard her voice cry "Call it!"

Before another sound was made, whistles sounded from the ships slightly ahead and were taken up aft. The Dwen cried, "Land fore!"

Col joined the rest of the crew on deck who clustered on the forecastle and behind the bowsprit, some women climbing as high as they could on anything available. But Col could see nothing.

"Damn Trees are pranking us," one woman growled.

"No, I see something!" another said. "Sul's glow flashing above the sea!"

"That will be Felkeni's torch aloft over the harbor!" Freya said. "We'll revel tonight, eh?"

"Yes, we will," Pearl added, appearing at Col's side.

Thank the Gods their journey was almost over. Freya seemed unfazed, inviting Pearl and Col to the planned *céilí* of singing, drink and tales near the commissary. A proper revel, not the stuffy bard entertainment expected in the hall.

Col maneuvered himself away, beckoning Pearl.

"We don't have to go."

"Of course we'll go! Cambrian hospitality is legendary. And serving Meer fish will be easier there."

"Provided scraps aren't dropped to trip dancers!"

Pearl laughed. "We did apologize! And we were punished enough losing the wager I think."

Col sighed, looking back to where it was claimed land had appeared. Then a gasp went up, a young officer, barely an older than a girl, pointed high in the sky. Sul hovered a little after the mid point of the day.

"The flintsun!" the girl cried, and after a moment the crew echoed it. The clouds that hovered around Sul's rays had a misty quality, thin enough that Her brightness was hardly diminished, but with just enough that at four points, almost exactly to the compass directions, blazes of light reflected off the clouds. A glowing ring connected them, much like happened to the moon, except rings around Lun were of dubious portent. However the flintsun was a sign of the blessings from Sul's court in heaven. It was said a flintsun shined on the coronation of Sunqueen Selastimor the Great, her deeds seen as proof of her hallowed soul. Thus the flintsun was the national flag of the Federation. If only there was a rainbow too, the sign of peace marking the end of the ancient war between Sul, Maer, and Eurath, then Col would know all the gods smiled on them, not just the matron of the Federation.

Still, it was a good omen. Something inside Col relaxed. They had survived. Now he was eager for land under his feet, to see the wonders he'd read about, like the great statues of Myngar and Felkeni who stood in the harbor to greet visitors to the city. He'd seen paintings of course. Did they really tower over ships in the harbor, like gods stepping among them? But it would be a while before he saw them. As he secured his satchel, Pearl took his hand and squeezed it, looking intently into his eyes. He felt warm. Yes, there was time to find some privacy. They made their way to the stair leading below decks.

Then they were thrown off their feet as the entire ship lurched as if in the throes of a great quake.

Chapter 35

Sadol Rite

After the dead had been sent off, consigned to both flames and water, Eld retreated to the starboard turret, leaning against the chained solcannon, the touch of its essence-hungry stone cool now it was at rest. It was a windy day, her flouted hair flying about her head aimlessly. She wanted no company, no thoughts. The sadness from the grief and loss around her settled in her soul, so much so thinking on her own loss was nearly overwhelming. Looking north, over the white-flecked waves that diminished to the horizon, Eld thought of the Battle of Gate Step, so far away but only a little more than a month ago. It was too much madness in so short a time, with so little reprieve. Poor Moradrin. She had been confused into passing through the Door, thoughts of her duty always driving her, even in dreams. Had they understood the danger…

It was pointless flogging oneself with recrimination. Ensign Moradrin Savalis had been in a healing sleep like anyone after the surgeon's knife. Ideally, when her body was weakened near death from the bleeding within, her soul would have sought out a magi or healer. Instead she sought out the ship's ledgers, always needing tending. That task was now given to the ship's secretary from *The Oaken Blue*, a male ensign assisting her. Eld had no heart for the work for it reminded her of how she had failed Moradrin.

So she stood apart from the crew in the turret on the stern deck, the sorrow filling her soul. They had been so lucky in Falls Gate. Not a soul lost on either side. Not even some that might deserve it, Eld mused, remembering the three Eurthani soldiers that had tried to rape Seth. A part of her she wasn't proud of whispered, at least they were aelg. But that wasn't true. She had heard of magi and healers lost, and most of the magi appeared to be as Sula as herself, only the creed of the order making them appear separate from Sula society. And did it matter what essence force a lost soul had? They were lost years before they should have gone through the Door, and their lives could no longer enrich the Orb, nor aid in their duty to protect it. It was a loss, not a sacrifice, for a sacrifice implied an exchange. The exchange of a life, even to protect life, diminished them all. And thus war was to be avoided and those who conspired to wage it censured as harshly as possible.

Already she guessed in Parliament the Voice was being called on for retribution against Sharitan and the culling of the humyn nation. It was grim
business, a cull; it had been proposed before, but with the loss of souls it
was inevitable to happen in some form. Even some of the prisoners present
had been alloted for the cull. Eld knew from her healer's training they
would be brought to the Temple, separated and put at ease. Then they'd be
given a drink with a quick acting poison, usually a hemlock. Once dead,
the remains were burned. The same was done for rabid Thyn who resisted a
cure. Humyn were usually culled when it was confirmed they were dangers
to mothers and children. But if the Federation approved a cull in Sharitan, it
would be broader, including any humyn who harbored plans to war. It
would be an ugly thing apologists of the Burning would flock to. Eld
wanted nothing to do with such a thing. But as a cavalier of the Federation
Host she would have little choice if she was sent.

At least it would be on land, she thought. She was so tired of the sea. In
a garrison, on a day free of duty, one could ride far out of sight, forsaking
any unwanted company until one was due to report again. But on a ship,
even the wonderfully spacious *varsadmer*, there was nowhere to escape. So
even free moments never felt truly free. Eld hated it and couldn't wait to return to land.

Yet even those on land were fraught. The worst was the Marshal. Before
the battle Eld had reported in dreams almost every night to the detriment of
her sleep. She continued to dutifully jot down notes about the ships activities, but she had no intention of meeting Tantilaan in dreams that eve. She
would sleep and if she dreamed, it would be of her war sisters, or hopefully,
Seth.

Thinking on Seth moved her. Eld wanted to hold Seth so badly, and
frankly do more than just hold him. When she stirred it was late afternoon.
She stood just as a Gold officer entered the turret deck.

"Sernalash has me checking on you," Lieutenant Mellasan Tamithryn
said. She was one of the strike captains.

"I'm leaving," Eld replied. "I've brooded enough."

"I'm trying to avoid it," Tamithryn said. "It's too horrible."

"Yes."

"You know there was nothing left of Olesh Desmet. Or Tellon Braz."

"They were on the ship that took Hoethnav's arm," Eld said.

"Ai!" Tamithryn shivered.

"That is more troubling to my mind," Eld confessed. "If we pass, we need no body. But if we stay, we need all of it."

"Truly said, but feelings don't always match truth."

"Also truly said. I'll remove myself. Anon."

Eld decided to find a healer to see if she could be useful. It might also give her perspective to see those who still suffered. The infirmary was greatly reduced, the mess hall being prepared to return to serving meals. Eld heard crew grumble, some needed to move in with others as their cabins were consolidated to make space for the worst of the wounded. But there were still a couple tables and a space to treat small things. When she arrived a midship was being treated for a sprained wrist.

"Must you wrap it with wood?" the girl asked. "It feels fine now."

"Until you swing on ropes or do more handsprings, young emha!" It was a male healer who Eld marked before as capable, competent and intolerant of foolishness.

"I can't do handsprings with this woven around my wrist!" the midship objected.

"And that is the point! Return in a couple of days and if you haven't been reckless we may remove it. Go on!"

The midship glared at the man, but said nothing, running out to return to duty or play.

The healer marked Eld's presence. "I usually have patience with children."

"But they're not children anymore," Eld said. "Adolescence is a fraught time."

"Indeed. Mathynwol isn't here."

"At last Felkeni smiles on me."

The man laughed. "She really doesn't favor you."

"Was she savaged by a horse in her youth?"

"Oh no, cousin. It's nothing to do with that. You're what she imagines herself to be."

"Sula," Eld said shaking her head.

"Pure Sula," the healer corrected.

"That is a tenuous argument," Eld said. "Elfyn are only one race, divided into tribes after the Cataclysm. Our differing talents are a reflection of our differing duties. And duties can't be pure. They are something done, not mulled over to feed ego."

"Oh, has our Pony returned to share some of her wisdom?"

Mathynwol stood over the healer as he busied himself with ordering draughts and bandages, not meeting her eye. Eld faced Mathynwol, trying to hide her dislike.

"No, I came to wonder if I could be of use."

"As a barbarian recently reminded me, the hall is diminishing in its capacity as a hospital. So, um, well perhaps you can be of use. That copilot has been trying to bother me for an hour."

Eld looked over at the woman who entered. She was Brownie or Dwen, one of the darkest hues, skin almost matching her dark hair; her green eyes had a blue sheen. But it was her mind Eld felt: wary, angry, vengeful. Not the sort that led to murder, but the kind where a soul would wait for an enemy's humiliation and then take joy in it. Otherwise she had no malice, and certainly none directed at Eld.

"You're a pilot?" Eld asked. Mathynwol seemed to have vanished.

"Yes, I am being a pilot. Hocta Mert, being in your service."

Mert's Dwen accent was heavier than most aelg. The last Dwen Eld knew with a thick accent was Talfi, the owner of the public house The Rowan Oak back in Falls Gate Keep.

"It appears the prefect has vanished," Eld said.

"It is being like magic," Mert said flatly.

"Ai," Eld said. "You seem well enough. What do you need?"

"My arm. I am thinking it was being hurt hitting a helmet. I am told it is nothing but to wait and all will heal. But it is sore still. I am not wanting the hammer."

"No," Eld said seriously. "Any healer avoids that. Take your coat off."

They sat together on a bench while Eld held Mert's left lower arm. It did seem whole to the eye, but at a touch Eld knew something was amiss. The two long bones that twisted in a half helix with each other sat properly in their places, but the smaller bone was riven with a crack. And it was not simple, but on a diagonal that, with any strong force, would shatter in a spiral. Fluid gathered already, swelling to protect it. Eld had been worried the bone had broken subtly and was healing off course. This was both better and worse: better that more damage had not transpired, yet worse because it could have been fixed properly when Mert was first treated.

Eld took her hands away and called for the male healer. "This arm has a shadow break."

The healer looked astonished. "But Mathynwol examined it yesterday."

"Not very well," Eld said glowering. No animal would have been left like this.

"Is there something you want to share, Pony?"

Mathynwol had returned, apparently not having gone far to start with.

Eld stood, bringing herself to her full height, allowing her anger to brighten her aura.

"You are a healer," Eld said with a carrying voice. "Not any healer, but a prefect of this ship's temple. How could you have missed this arm's shadow break if you examined it properly?"

The prefect's face turned ugly. "I don't have to answer to the Marshal's creature in my infirmary! Were you treating the wounded as they poured in? Missing a shadow break among all the burns and deaths is not unknown, Pony! Which you would know if your business wasn't prancing on horses and sucking at the Marshal's – "

"My name is Elderyn Farthal, lancer of 125th Cavalry Host and I serve the Marshal under protest!" Eld roared. "The rest of your words are a stitch of lies and half truths to hide bigotry that has undermined your duty!"

"How dare you!" Mathynwol protested. "I'll report – "

"Please do, emha prefect!" Eld shouted. "And be certain it is read for truth!"

"What in the heavens is happening here?" The surgeon Alharn had entered.

"Healing," Mert said flatly. "It is being said there is pain before wholeness."

The male healer covered his face in his hands to keep himself from bursting into laughter.

Mathynwol breathed like a dragon, her gold eyes glaring hatred at Mert and Eld together. She did not advance, though Eld felt a part of her wanted to attack the upstarts in her realm. Yet neither did she retreat. Alharn carefully stepped between the prefect and Eld.

"Allow me to treat our copilot," Alharn said. "There is little to do for the rest of the day. If you wanted to retire, I would happily – "

Mathynwol turned away, striding out without another word.

"What is the hurt?" Alharn asked.

"A shadow break," Eld said forcing her voice to be calm.

Alharn beckoned Mert to feel the arm. She frowned. "Soreni, get the wood and someone to bend them."

The male healer left.

"You should have come immediately on feeling soreness, lieutenant," Alharn said.

"I did," Mert said pointedly. "She is saying it is nothing then avoiding me."

Alharn seemed to collapse in on herself. "I am sorry. Sealing the bone should be easy. I want it wrapped because you've used it more than you should. Farthal, please act as my anchor."

"Certainly."

The bone properly sealed, the marrow forced back to its proper course, a Dwen assistant wrapped the arm under Eld's guidance.

"Why didn't you press the matter?" Eld asked.

Mert smiled joylessly. "I try to avoid Golds with excess Sula pride. She is having much. You, almost none. Why?"

"I'm not certain I have an answer," Eld said. "False pride is a contradiction at odds with duty. There is no one of us whose talents rise greater than our collective duty to the Orb."

Mert nodded. "A good answer. Now look, I am growing into a tree. My thanks." She smiled at her wood bound arm before leaving.

"Look, Farthal," Alharn said, drawing Eld aside after Mert left. "Your help was appreciated. But this event has force me to consider an uncomfortable action."

"You must go to the captain to report dereliction," Eld guessed.

"It would not be my place to share such a thing with you," Alharn said. "I thank you, but for now, I need you to leave the infirmary."

Eld nodded. It didn't matter to her. Any task was much the same while she was stuck on the boat. She walked up to the quarter deck, then the fore-castle. At least she'd take a look at the sky while it was still light. Crew smiled at her, the Dwen in particular, one woman in a yastol laughing on sight then offering a bite of travel loaf.

Eld took it with thanks, not realizing how hungry she was.

"Good?" a Dwen ranks officer in an oak leaf yastol asked.

"One wouldn't think dried fruit, walnuts and elk meat would be tasty to-gether," Eld said. "But Dwen know best."

"Yes, we do! Woodweaver Aflelett Fadwen," the woman introduced her-self. They clasped hands like war sisters. "I know who you are. The hum-bling of that woman was a long time coming. You've made many from the Forest cheerful. Ai, Frye, what brings you up from the deeps?"

"Bold women who sing the truth!" a Blue diver said. She was very humynish, shorter than many Blue, her black hair was shaved on both sides of her head revealing leaf tattoos. "Even if you are the Marshal's spy!"

Frye offered her hand and Eld took it. Very slightly Frye's smile faltered. Fadwen laughed.

"Fine!" Frye said. "You were right!"

Eld looked between them mystified.

"She was hoping you were a sister," Fadwen added with a chuckle.

"Well, no one's seen her even talking with the companions," Frye said defensively.

It was Eld's turn to laugh. "The Marshal has kept me so busy, between her tasks and the battle, what soul has time? And were I to have a romantic turn, I would look cheap as I'm skint. I was not allowed to bring any coin."

"There," Fadwen said. "You are not the only soul to suffer disappoint-ment."

"Speak not on disappointment!" Frye said glowering over her shoulder.

Eld followed her eye to where the boatswain Galen was working with crew around an anchor. Frye stared longer than was warranted. Eld could feel her willing Galen to look up. And when she did Frye snapped her head back, adding in a loud voice, "The sea is abundant with fish!"

Eld understood but kept herself from laughing with Fadwen. "Let me tell you friend, acting like a Lun is not the best way to impress a sister! Women like us are too few to play games."

"Except games with humyn pets, rabid though they be. I care not! There's fishing to be done. Alas we have nothing between us," Frye added to Eld. "You have a man, don't you?"

Eld smiled. "Yes."

"It's so disappointing. Taevol!" Frye strode to the stern deck where some divers were gathering.

Only then did Eld see Galen glaring in their direction. "You're a sister as well?" Eld asked.

"Oh yes," Fadwen said.

"You don't happen to fancy Frye?"

"Hah! We had a brief liaison. But she has no roots. We are better as mates."

"You might consider informing your boatswain of that in a subtle way. She surely isn't glaring with envy at me."

"Oh, was she?" Fadwen looked but the boatswain had turned away. "You've no idea of the drama that births on a ship, Farthal."

They parted as the evening watch rang. Eld made her way to the pilot's mess, now truly hungry.

That night she tried to find Seth in dreams but he wasn't in any of their common meeting places: the glade they trysted in at Falls Gate, his rooms in the commander's house, or any of the dream roads they had taken. Finally she saw a man, bright and elegant in plain white robes, running towards her. But it wasn't Seth. It was Silalin, the head keeper of children in her family estate.

"Emha Farthal!" Sil exclaimed. "You haven't visited often enough!"

"It's not for lack of want," Eld said. "The Marshal – "

" – Has compelled you with sorcery to join the fleet lest your honors be withdrawn," Sil said, clearly with disapproval.

"It was an Eirok wing and the threat was only implied the once, but yes."

"The Estate received a letter from your commander, Major Selind Alhern. It reads quite apologetic. I think she's equally annoyed and would really like her best cavalier to return."

Eld laughed. "I appreciate your partisanship, but I'm not that unique."

"You were offered a commission for your leadership during the Battle of Gate Step. That sounds quite notable to my ear. Your mother won't stop regaling any soul who will listen. And our dame, well she has plans when you return." Dame was the title of the elected head of a family estate. Eld's grandama was the current dame. "So when do you return?" Sil asked.

"I know naught for now. I'll be pleased to just step on land."

At that thought another white figure seemed to approach them on the white road. Seth at last?

"We heard news of the fleet's victory today," Sil said.

"What of Tyrum?"

"They are still in watchfulness."

"There's a flotilla of the same miscreants on their way. If they don't get swallowed by a kraken."

"How many?"

"A handful I think. Nothing the Tyreens can't manage. How are Traith and Shedann?"

"Your birthed are as well as ever. Though quite put out at not seeing their ama. Children don't understand marshals and duties and all that."

"I know. Herd them to me tomorrow night. I will put aside all unless Athmod herself returns to make war."

"I'll keep you to that. Isn't this Fiorseth?"

The white figure wasn't Sethshorn, but Eld's service horse Fiorseth. Like Sil, she glowed with an aura of a real dreamer. Fiorseth had no bridle or saddle, as bare as she'd been foaled. The mare reared, then her hooves landed in front of Eld and she began to aggressively nuzzle her.

"I think you're about to go on a journey!" Sil said. He smiled, pulling away and fading.

Fiorseth made a deafening whinny. Animals that were not Thyn did not have speech even in true dreams. But their desires were felt and obvious and Fiorseth's desire was for Eld to mount and gallop without restraint. No sooner was Eld on her back than the mare's hooves flew, carrying them down the road faster than a diving hawk.

It was the best for both of them: Fiorseth was without any binding harness, and Eld had no concerns about their course. Mist, mountains, desert or
marsh, it was all deamscape. The worst that could happen would be passing
fallow darkness or deeps, places where dreamers were dragged down by fear
or despair. But Eld could keep them both from such pitfalls by her essence
alone. So they galloped and Eld finally felt free of the confines of the sea.

They left the road far behind, flying over a grassy plain. Ahead a wood
appeared, growing as they neared, the sky suddenly darkening. Eld worried
a moment it was a dark fallow, but their spirits were too high, Fiorseth was
full of excitement and joy. Eld saw they were joined by other horses, a great
herd of horses also with auras. They were dreaming together, some horses
determined and clever as Thyn.

~the elfling is funny~

It wasn't a thought exactly. Speaking in dreams was all thought. But
Thyn minds had a different feel. Eld was astonished by two mares who
passed them, one blond, one black, clearly looking at Eld who was the
source of their mirth.

~an elfling rides free~

~but does it dare enter~

Only then did Eld wonder what was in the wood, a new anxiety. But it
was too late. They were already among the trees.

They were old trees of an ancient orchard all horses dreamed of. Heavy
apples hung in their path. Fiorseth leaped, snatching a golden fruit off a tree
without breaking stride. They flushed out shadows. For a moment Eld
thought they were rats. Soon she saw them clearly: a wolf, wild hounds,
several lions, even elfyn. All these were small, no larger than a large cat and
they ran before the thundering herd, screaming, howling or roaring in terror.
And Eld understood: these were the fears of horses and they were chasing
them down, running them off. She understood what the mares meant, for
had she mistreated a horse, she might be among those terrified by the vengeful herd. And then Eld saw Roel, the arrogant officer she'd defeated in a
duel at Falls Gate Keep. Fiorseth didn't like Roel; Roel was dismissive and
harsh with horses. And so Eld joined Fiorseth's joy at running down the elf.
The only regret was it most certainly wasn't the real Roel. None of those
driven by the herd had the aura of a living dreamer.

Still it was cathartic. They ran their prey over rocky plains, up mountains to the very tops of the snowy peaks high in the night sky, until all the enemies of horsekind were driven off a cliff, screaming and calling as they fell for eternity. But the herd didn't stop, continuing on over the peaks, leaping into the stars to then thunder over plains of dark stormy clouds like the herds of Payeen. The clouds parted at the horizon and the rising sun blinded Eld. She felt herself fall, no longer on Fiorseth. Then she was on her cot and she slowly woke.

The dream was refreshing and Eld felt ready to meet the day with optimism. Salvage continued an activity Eld would be no help with. By noon there was a great industry of fishing afoot and Eld found herself with the strike crew preparing to grill fish en masse on the upper decks.

"You grill?" Galen asked.

"Not as much as I like," Eld confessed. She'd shed her coat, rolled up her sleeves and wore a leather apron like Galen and the ship's head cook, a Gold woman, Salyndwen Mearat, called 'Sel' informally. There was a competitiveness in the air Eld hadn't expected. Galen apparently grilled all her food when not at sea and Sel considered herself an expert and seemed to think her honor as a cook was being challenged by both Eld and Galen.

"Just remember, sparklings," Sel said, "this isn't fancy grilling. We're trying to feed a fleet not impress the visiting governor's consort."

Sel was eying the bottle of mead Eld had requested.

"Food can be tasty and filling," Eld said noncommittally. "I would have preferred must, but there was none."

"Ha! Must! Mead! Vinegar is good enough for them!"

"I like to think that we're keeping the peace," Galen said. "Because if I have to eat one more bowl of pea-stew with salted pork, I'll lead a mutiny myself!" Galen had a bottle of rum and honey on hand.

There was laughter and then the fish arrived. While they bantered, the crew was cutting and cleaning the fish, large sharks that the blood in the water had drawn to them. When the filleted flesh was ready it was thrown on the grills in layers. Helpers sprinkled salt over them. Then the women drew the sun down in their own ways:

Galen used her firelance, a brass wand tipped with solstone, to direct the reflective light in waves over the fish, searing them so they slowly cooked from the outside. Sel made a flaming barrier around the fish, passing her firelance to char them in waves. Eld simply drew the heat underneath until the fish sizzled, then waved the firelance over them, forcing the heat below to return to scar the surface. How it was done was a matter of preference. The important thing was the fish were to be cooked, but not too cooked. Once hot, they splashed their marinade of choice. The grills hissed and clouds of scented steam wafted over the decks. Once most of the liquid was had burned off, the fish were piled into barrels and the process repeated.

They were at it for days, eventually joined by more women with the su-lessence to grill. Eld noted however that those piling the fish in barrels cleverly made sure there was a mix of fish from the tasty grills – hers and Galen's – and those considered amateur or simply dull. It took a week to be finished with both the salvage and the fish. By then the novelty had been lost and Eld was glad they were done.

On one night Eld made good on her attempt to reach her children. She waited on the white road under a misty sun. She felt Traith and Shedann before she saw them, but with them was not Sil but an imposing essence-powerful woman in black robes and wild silver hair.

"Elderyn!" she called, holding a hand of each child. They tried to run forward but she kept a firm grip.

"If I let them go who knows where we'll be." the woman added. The robes were magi robes, but she wore no hat.

"Grandam!" This was Orith Farthal, the oldest mother of the estate just shy of a decade before ascending to Aeon. She had been dame for almost a century before retiring to leave the running of the estate to her daughter, Reythyn, who was Eld's grandama. Orith was a wizard. Though she never finished magi schooling properly, she'd worked as a sorcerer, among many other things. No one liked to shine a light on it, but Orith was something of a rogue. Eld thought she'd have been perfectly happy among the Tyreens. And children adored her.

"It's ama! It's ama!" Eld's children chorused. Traith was just leaving her sprite years around fifty; she liked to dress like a "grown up". Shedann was a little younger and saw no rush to act mature. He was happy to continue wearing loose child tunics. In his hand was his tree doll, Vineflower.

Eld rushed to meet them and they jumped into her arms with ease.

490

"Where were you?" Traith demanded.

"We've been waiting forever and ever and ever!" Shedann added.

"Sil said you had duties!"

"I hate duties! So does Vineflower."

"I must agree, some duties are worthy of dislike," Eld said. "Regretfully, that is what makes them duties."

"It is good to see you," Orith said. She looked as she did in waking, her four centuries hardly showing except to make her hair bright silver white. "Mind, the estate expected to see you in waking. Certainly you are overdue for leave."

Eld sighed. "It's a long complicated tale and we don't have time. So, meteesh, have you heard that ama flew like a bird to join the fleet?"

"Truly?" Traith said, enthralled with the idea. "How?"

"Did your arms get tired?" Shedann asked.

"No silly!" Traith said. "Ama's too strong to get tired."

"Everyone gets tired."

"Verily, my advocates!" Eld interrupted. "If you want to, you will soon know for yourselves." To Orith she added, "I need your help."

"Yes, you do." But Orith wasn't looking at Eld. Following her eye they could see what seemed to be a dark misty cloud descending.

"Lancer Farthal?" a thin voice called.

"You know this soul?" Orith asked.

Eld shook her head, not trusting her voice.

"Well, that won't do."

Eld jumped back clutching the children as a sheet of flame as high as a mountain leapt up between Eld and the cloud. Then it vanished and the cloud was gone.

"If I had real breath, I would be struggling to catch it!" Eld exclaimed.

The children giggled. "Do it again, Ta Ori!" Traith said.

"You didn't want interruptions did you?" Orith asked innocently. "Now what do you need help with?"

Eld described the Eirok wing, the woven white bones, some gifted by dragons, all a rough shape of a bird. Eirok flew it by driving wind essence through the spaces, making it rise to fly as high and far as the magical power of the flyer. The children watched in fascination as Orith manifested the form of a wing by will.

"I have actually seen one you know," Orith said. "But your memories make the construct more solid. There, I think we're done."

"You want to fly?" Eld asked.

"Yes!" the children chorused.

"How do we get in?"

It was unclear to an outside eye. There was a place in the top to settle into the center. Eld placed the children in, with herself behind. She had no wind-essence, but Orith had made the construct responsive to her mind. In dreams she had only to grab the struts like the flyer Lekatol and the construct would obey her will.

"Ready?"

"Yes!"

"Wait, I want to make sure Vineflower can see!" The rope ends of the tree doll curled to attach to a strut, the black eyes of the doll looking out as if it was alive. "Okay!" Shedann said.

"I'll keep duty at bay!" Orith called.

"Elam, Ta Ori!" Eld said with a grin. Traith secure in her lap, Shedann in front of Traith, Eld grabbed the struts and they launched into the dream sky.

The children cried with delight as they skimmed clouds. A tree rose ahead, large as a mountain, and they had a thrilling time sailing between its many branches. Then they skimmed mountain peaks and plains and finally over a vast ocean coming to an island that might even be Oracle Isle. The entire journey was much more pleasant than it had been for Eld in waking. There was wind, but no biting cold, ice or rime. And even the wind wasn't as powerful as in a real wing, where it was almost impossible for anyone not Eirok to look out during flight. They flew and laughed and eventually the night ended. The children refused to leave and so they flew together until wakefulness forced them from the dream.

When Eld rose, happier than she'd been in a while, her mood was elevated for a couple of days. Then the Sea Father confided in her a concern about the prisoners: the new Admiral, a brave but troubled soul, had a plan to offer choice men to harlot themselves in exchange for comfort.

Eld wasn't so much offended as confused. Surely *The Black Seal* had a ship's companion? Why would an elfborn mother lust after such creatures? It was obscene, even if Tresmadore was choosing the most masculine by an elfyn standard. Reluctantly, Eld decided to meet the Marshal in dreams. It would not be until after the salvage that Tresmadore would collect her harvest.

Their usual meeting place was the sadol in Tyrum, that appeared like a lantern lit stone chamber, with an arched roof. Around them were eleven menhirs, the magical force of the chamber so powerful it would look exactly in dreams as it did in waking. Thus the stones shimmered, the ground beneath covered with many shifting symbols as they danced. Sadol work was called the Fold or Folding, from whence the greatest wizard who ever lived was known as Selis of the Fold.

Eld stood in the center of the circle. Soon Tantilaan appeared. This time she was still dressed for duty, standing in a black coat, with gold accents. Field Marshal Egalsh Tantilaan had served as a cavalier so she also wore a flout. Though they appeared to be alone, the glow around each stone was the aura of a waking soul working the sadol.

"The errant cavalier returns!" Tantilaan said.

"Emha!" Eld acknowledged.

"'Emha'!" the Marshal echoed. "I've an interesting tale. Would you care to hear it?"

"Yes, emha."

"I sent a magi to collar you because you've been tardy. And what did she report? Someone close to your dream person banished her. What can you tell me of that, Farthal?"

Whatever Eld said, it must be the truth, for lies were almost impossible to pass in dreams.

"That might be my grandam," Eld said.

"Might?"

"You say this person banished a magi. I don't know of a banishment."

"Fine, Farthal, what do you know?"

"My grandam was with me while visiting my children. She might have perceived an attempted intrusion. The children had not seen me for a couple of weeks and she was not pleased."

Tantilaan looked at Eld, staring steadily, considering. "And your tardiness?"

This Eld had prepared for. She went into detail about the salvage, and supplies, the challenges in the infirmary and organizing prisoners.

"…And so we've been quite busy preparing to leave for Gashora."

"You're reporting they didn't bring enough food?"

"There was a delay leading up to the battle. Contrary currents if you recall. In the rush to set forth, I'm sure arrows and such were considered more important."

"Aelg incompetence," Tantilaan snorted. "This will be investigated thoroughly, I assure you."

"Yes, Marshal."

"Well, I think that is all."

"Emha! Excuse me emha. There is another matter."

"Yes?"

"The prisoners."

"Should be lucky we deign to let them live. What about them?"

"Tresmadore is offering to allow some choice individuals to … work as harlots in exchange for comfort."

First Eld was pleased Tantilaan looked shocked. Then the Marshal burst out in laughter. "Well, it's not much of a surprise! Aelg will tryst with anything. That is why they're the mongrels they are."

Eld was stunned. She was sure Tantilaan wouldn't have spoken so in public. She always knew the Marshal was a bigot, but the coarseness shocked her.

"Come, Farthal, I know you're a sensitive poet and a chivalrous soul. But these humyn aren't real men. They're barely more than animals. If a Tyreen captain wants to do what her foremothers did, it's hardly a matter to object to. Else we'd not have aelg in the first place."

"But, emha, being prisoners it is not dignified labor."

"As long as they are not compelled or coerced, I care not Farthal. If that is all we should meet again soon when– "

494

Eld used every part of her dream skill to sever the connection, waking instantly in the dark. She marveled she could dislike the Marshal more than ever. She was ashamed when she had to inform the Sea Father Tantilaan did not care. All Eld could do was watch as an observer, ensure the particulars of regulations were obeyed, that the humyn did indeed go willingly to harlot.

It took Eld several days to get over her disgust. And then she decided, if she couldn't find Seth, she would visit one of the companions after all.

The cabin on the lower deck was aft and larger than most, though its exact form was hidden by hanging silks and tapestries to lend an air of mystery. There was a custom of making a mark on a slate outside the door. When the man was ready he would open the door and ask the next woman to enter. Professional prostitutes and courtesans almost always had training to read truth, so names weren't needed, only the confirmation one had made a mark. The earliest one could mark the slate for the eve was after the Dance. Eld skipped the dance to be first, annoying a couple of deck officers.

"When she's done with him, they'll only be kisses for the rest of us," Lieutenant Glendwol of the orlop deck opined when Eld entered.

"Welcome, cousin," the man said. "I am Castelyn."

Castelyn had the cultivated deliberate glamor of an entertainer. He was dark Gold, perhaps with Dwen ancestry, a hue more bronze than gold. A narrow face was framed by bright locks tied with gold ribbons, the rest of his hair hanging free. His eyes were lined with kohl, something boys did to be daring, but adult Sula men rarely indulged, and his lips were gilded with glimmer paint. Eld had forgotten how strange it was most men on the ship, being crew, did not bother with glimmer. Castelyn wore a white loose Tyreen tunic, cut wide to flair from the chest, sleeves fuller than the kirtle-shirt worn by most Sula men. Over the tunic was a robe of silvery blue silk, with diamond patterns in gold. Castelyn sat on a chair by a table, the table next to a low, wide bed, surely the working desk of harlots. Lamps hung from the ceiling but they were fitted with amber or red glass so the room always hinted of the setting sun.

"Sit," Castelyn said, directing Eld to a chair on the other side of the table. "Would you like a drink?"

"I can drink anytime," Eld said, but she sat down for politeness.

"In a hurry?"

"Not that much." It had been a while since she'd visited a harlot, but remembered her manners.

"So what does the hero of the Battle of Gate Step desire?"

Eld thought. She wanted Seth. The surest way to put off a companion was pining over another man. "The bed."

"I see. It's early in the eve. But you are the Marshal's agent. I'm sure it will be agreeable."

Eld had remembered the stake Glethlyn had loaned her. It was more than enough to leave a gratuity, but she automatically added more coins than she might have. It was the game soldiers played with harlots. One paid until the man could pretend no payment had passed. And woe be to the soldier, sailor or cavalier who was discovered to be cheap. Harlots' gossip was deadlier than a parliamentary scandal.

As soon as Eld dropped the coins on the table, Castelyn stood, letting his robe fall off him. "The bed" was understood to mean trysting. After the robe fell, Castelyn sat down and removed the tunic. He wore nothing underneath and was already prepared to conduct business. Eld surprised herself at how quickly she disrobed, for the moment firmly putting Seth out of her mind. He was far away, apparently avoiding her, and they would come to an accord in the future. Now she wanted release and Castelyn was available and accommodating. He laid back, welcoming Eld to embrace him.

Leaving the companion's cabin, Eld felt more relaxed than she'd been in a while. Part of her regretted not waiting longer for Seth. But her mind found it easier to do her banal duty, marking the operation of the ship in the hated journal the Marshal desired. She chose to avoid dreaming that night. If she couldn't meet Seth, she had no time for the Marshal. She could wait until the next night. On waking Jarroth hammered on her door to deliver a missive.

"It came by our sadol," Jarroth said. "Who is it?"

"The Marshal, of course," Eld growled. "She wants me to report through the ship's sadol at noon.

"That's sparking!" Jarroth said. "I've never had missives from the sadol. They're only used for duty."

Eld sighed. "I wish I had your enthusiasm."

The day dragged with dread. The woman was in her dreams. She only now thought the ship's sadol would be good enough?

An older magi, Ta Hethlion, escorted Eld to the magi berth when the time came. Already the five circles on the larger circle were occupied by magi. Instead of stones, the sadol was carved into the wood of the deck and filled with grimsteel and possibly aqua. The room was dark, the two windows covered, and solstone lanterns hung to highlight the center of the circle.

"Wait until the air bends," Hethlion said.

Eld had many questions but decided to watch. The five magi who stood around the circle had closed their eyes. At first Eld just heard them breathing. Then it sounded like more than breathing, like a wind in her mind, much like when thoughts were being read or sifted for truth. This was the collective mind of the circle. Now the magi were breathing as one, their thoughts harmonizing together. A collective operation of minds could do much more than one mind alone.

Eld glanced down. She though she saw a ripple near the floor. But it was just the air bending, like a wave of heat over the grimsteel scoring. And then Eld felt the air fold.

A soundless humming could be felt off the participants, their auras almost crackling. The center of the circle seemed to shift and that's when the ghosts of symbols past and present appeared on the floor, all the scripts known to the learned, some lost, some yet to come.

"Step in the center," Hethlion said.

Eld swallowed and did as she was bade.

For a second frisson ran over her skin, as if lightning had passed through her. Then it was gone and she stood at the center, the Marshal before her as if they were present in the same room.

"I'm surprised that worked," Tantilaan said. "These ship sadols really do have capability!"

"Emha, I'm told they are not as stable however," Eld said. "So we should be quick."

"Right you are, Farthal. This has been a productive venture."

"Yes, emha," Eld said as tonelessly as possible.

"Now it's time for you to return."

Eld didn't understand. "I expected to be returning with the fleet after Gashora."

"No, Farthal. I have no intention waiting that long, not with the rumored Shari flotilla possibly en route. No, you will be returning."

"How?" Eld asked. "Emha?" she added.

"I'm considering it. I just want you prepared."

Eld was tired. Even the prospect of a commission didn't feel worth pandering to the Federation Marshal. "With respect, emha, I will not step in a wing again. No, not even for a commission. I could have died in the cold air. Or by some accident of weather. I will not risk robbing my children of their mother needlessly."

Tantilaan stared at Eld, clearly not pleased. But something gave. Perhaps it was because she herself had children. "No need to get tetchy, Farthal. I wasn't thinking of a wing. Besides the wind fairies seem to be scared at the moment. Something about a prophecy with a bear and Ameram. They've all fled to the mountains. There is another way. I'll message you anon once the details are sorted."

Eld left wondering what madness was to come. The missive came in the morning: when Eld came to Gashora she was to immediately go to Lomastal or Howl's Peak, wherever that was. A courier would wait for three dawns at the mother stones. If she missed them, she was to use the Gashora sadol speak again with the Marshal. The last thing Eld ever wanted to do was speak with the Marshal again.

It was with a mix of relief and anxiety she watched the ravens leave the ship. Land fore was called. It would be over soon. She could just see the shore, her Sula eyes better than most while the sun shined. It wasn't actually Gashora, but a crop of land before the bay. Still their journey was near the end.

Near but not over. Eld had been helping the strike crew clean the solcannons when the ship lurched. Chaos and panic threatened to take over. Something was in the water, something that terrified the prisoners. A Sea Djinn. It was ridiculous. There were no such thing as sea spirits and Djinn were an entirely different sort of legend. Only when Eld laid her eyes on it, a saucer of glittering black with a domed crystal window, did she change her opinion. If anything, none of these elfborn knew they should be more afraid, not that it would do them any good. What they needed was the entire fleet to turn around to face the thing. Then they might have a chance.

For Eld had seen the motto of the quartered circle on the side of the craft, the sign of Eurath used by the Imperial Legions of Eurthantal she had battled in Falls Gate. Why the Eurthani were here, she didn't know. But she knew they were hostile. There was no time to tell the captain or anyone the whole tale. Only to warn the danger was real and to help loose the solcannons. They did not have solcannons in the field at Falls Gate. Maybe it would make a difference. The Eurthans, damn the Eurthans! They would always come, their dreams of empire never sated, until such a time they were humbled. Let this be the moment, Eld thought as they prepared the solcannons to strike.

Chapter 36

Sea Tank

Deep in the waters off the continental shelf, exploring a bay slightly north of the Gulf of Sharitan, the sea tank hovered, like a great dome of crystal and metal, or perhaps a bell, as they were nicknamed by their crews. But such a bell would be the size of a sea stack shore rock, equivalent in volume to a Tyreen ship. The mass of such tanks, with their smooth glittering grimsteel skins, topped with a clear crystal dome, another crystal serving as the bottom, was far, far greater. Add to that the legs curled under the circular rim, like a malformed crab, one was left with the impression of a saucer-like vehicle, both sinister and elegant.

The women who fortified the tank shared this eldritch tone with their vessel. Their eyes, whether blue, green, red or gold, glowed with a light from within. Most had dark-hued skin, their hair tended to be lighter. At a casual glance some might have been taken for Shari. But their accented ears and brows betrayed them as elfyn. They, of course, were the norm in their country, the deep and distant Eurthantal. The quartered circle, the sign of Eurath, was everywhere: the buttons of their uniforms, the simple signs and directions above doors, on the hilts of their weapons, especially the service sword the captain wore, like all officers in Her Imperial Legion. It was even on the outer hull, next to the bell's identification and motto. Stories of Our Avatar's Holy Empire of Eurthantal had spread far, though few understood their skills and resources, or the banal nature of society and politics that made them agents of expansion. Like women in service to any state, these women had a sworn duty to perform and they did it with a mix of extreme piety, causal patriotism, modest enthusiasm and occasional boredom.

"Nothing is there," the captain said, leaning over the shoulder of a sergeant. Both their uniforms were dark blue, but the officer's was accented in gold, while the sergeant's was trimmed in dark yellow. Sea Tank crews were the only women in the Imperial Legion who wore uniforms deviating from Garrison Red or Field Grey. It was notable the Eurthantian Empire had no concept of a "navy". Firstly, the majority of Imperial infrastructure was subterranean, thus while there were underground seas, there were no vast oceans with shorelines to inspire the concept of a water based military power. Secondly, water was simply another type of mineral or "earth" to navigate. The tank crew had many essence tools to do this, all based on their affinity for using minerals to extend their senses. The captain watched a section of a table extending from the hull like an angled desk, where the sergeant was trying to give form to what she had sensed. The black glassy surface should hold an impression in lines of glowing light, indicating form, direction and depth. But all that could be seen in the glass was wavy chevron lines, fading as they watched.

"They were there!" the sergeant insisted, her eyes glowing brighter with agitation. She sat back hard, pulling her fingers through close cropped, white hair. The captain stood up straight, her own hair tightly wound at the top of her head in a bun, echoing her restrained, thin lipped expression. She had no time for fancies.

"I know we're overdue for leave, but a dream of salvage prize is no substitute for the rewards of honest pious duty."

"How much would it be worth anyway?" a corporal asked as she monitored their depth with a periscope like instrument. "We're speaking of a primitive humyn vessel made of slivers."

"Planks," corrected another woman. "They use planks of wood."

"'Ris, are you possessed?" the corporal said, disbelieving. "Wood? No one would make a boat out of wood. Aluminum is less expensive. Even pure astrella is less expensive."

"Not to lithogs. They have to dig up metal with primitive tools and have no masons. Tree cover the Athlantal abundantly."

The corporal paused, her mind processing the ramifications while the captain spoke.

"It's unicorn dung in any case, if the vessels aren't there. There's no minds or essence so there is nothing." She sighed, herself somewhat disappointed.

"That is not true, captain," a woman said. "There are minds. But they are not to the south-southeast. They are north-northeast and the essence is strong."

The new speaker who had entered the piloting circle was dressed entirely in black, with knee high boots, as if she was about to go riding. This was her uniform when on duty, and she was always on duty for such was the fate of a slave of God. Very slightly tension in the crew rose, older women forc-

ing themselves to not look, younger ones, unable to resist the thrill of glancing once at her, their eyes irresistibly draw to the red mark on her jacket, a
heraldic triple flame in the center of her chest. Then they looked away, acting as if they had not glanced, hearts racing, anxious if they had been regular in their prayers. This woman and others like her were feared throughout
the Empire as Our Avatar's eyes and ears, their task being to hunt out and
eliminate heresy and any threats to Our Avatar's realm. No mind, except the
most powerful of wizards, was safe from them. In the absence of a priest,
they were to be obeyed like God Herself.

The captain did not like this new woman in her vessel. It distracted the
crew, and herself, for that matter. But she accepted it was her duty to accommodate the Torch. In addition to protecting the Empire against God's
enemies, these slaves gathered intelligence that helped expand the influence
and prosperity of the Empire and Her subjects.

"You can sense them, Watch Officer?" the captain asked.

"Yes," the woman said, uncharacteristically looking up. In public at
least, Watch Officers gave the impression they had no need to look where
they were going using a combination of feeling minds and enhanced essence
training specific to their duties. But here, in the deep waters, her senses
were blunted and so she looked up through the clear crystal ceiling, trying to
reconcile what she was feeling with a target. "Raise the Bell, captain."

The order was blunt and the captain felt new tension in her crew. Their
fear and piety made them want to obey the dread woman instantly, but discipline told them they needed to be commanded properly. Only were their
mission to somehow become a defense of Our Avatar's awe would the
Watch Officer be permitted to directly order crew.

"Pilot," the captain said, clearly but without haste, "Raise the Bell."

The room was little more than a circular mezzanine around the pilot's
well, sinking ten or so feet down to where a woman sat holding great handles rising out of another smooth desk-like surface extending from the wall.
She had two assistants in the small room; below them the floor, a circle fifteen or so feet across, was clear quartz. The sea bed, though only a hundred
feet or so away, was hard to discern. Slowly the sea bed became even more
obscure until it vanished altogether as they rose.

The captain walked to where the Watch Officer stood and joined her in gazing up through the round window. They had been floating casually up until an hour ago, when the sergeant claimed to sense the wake ripples of a vessel. But the Watch Officer also sensed something. Perhaps there was a prize to be made from this journey after all. Otherwise they were overdue to return to port and the captain's consort was always annoyed when she was tardy. His mood was mollified if it resulted in a profit.

And so the women observed together as the water around them slowly lightened from the variegated dark blue-green to a much lighter aqua. This was only because the greater skylight, called "sun" by lithogs, was ascendant. Otherwise the water would be as black as any deep. It was for this reason the pilot relied on the feel of the water and depths sensed through the skin of the Bell and not on sight. Slowly they discerned the shadows, then the undersides, of floating lithog vessels. But they were like nothing the captain had seen before.

One was typical, smooth planking with a basic keel of savage design, its hull free of barnacles. It must be newly built. The amazing thing was these were built not by wild fay, but humyn. The captain wondered how they did it. Perhaps they had elfyn masters. But the other hulls, while dim in shadow, shimmered metallic as the Bell skin, except copper not astrella black. More fantastic, their keels were bright blue, as if made of sapphire. And if the captain read their wake lines…

"Sergeant!" she shouted. "Mark those vessels!"

"Marked!"

"Speed?"

"Almost thirty rings!"

"Astonishing," the Watch Officer said. "They use essence and are driven by minds."

"Elfyn?"

"Strange ones, but yes. We need to study them. Capture one."

The captain wasn't sure why she wanted to object. She also thought the prize would be rich; any vessel with a smooth wooden hull would be priceless for the materials alone. But she did want credit for the prize. Had the Torch not been there, she would have said the same.

"No need to feel threatened, captain," the Watch Officer murmured. "I'm not interested in glory, only information."

The captain ignored her annoyance at her thoughts being read and strode back to the sergeant's station to monitor with the crew.

"So we're going for a prize, mam?" the corporal asked. "Only they're very large, the blue keeled ones."

"Prepare the claws," the captain ordered.

"Ai!" the mechanic replied, touching a panel. The Bell vibrated slightly as the claws folded around the top window raised slightly, prepared to extend to grab whatever was desired. Unlike the under claws used to walk the vessel crablike onto a dock for repairs, the top claws were designed to give way under stress. The greatest danger of a sea tank was being breached and decompressing in the depths. While it was true all pious crew members were entitled to be revived by God in the event of death, the fact remained tardy retrieval would mean permanent death. For this reason sea tanks were often called coffins and their crews water ghosts.

The captain didn't feel she was putting the crew into mortal danger. They'd be near the surface and they vastly out powered whatever these vessels were. Even though the ships also used magic, the Bell was powered by earth essence, and the captain, through both experience and cultural chauvinism, took her vessel's superiority for granted. Still, there were precautions to take.

"Prepare to harden the water," she ordered. "Pilot, slow to hover."

"Slowing to hover," the woman's voice echoed from the well.

"What about the crew?" the mechanic called. Like all of her kind, she had a niggle to inject into her fellow's grand schemes.

The captain glanced at the Watch Officer. Being not a cruel woman, the captain would be happy if the savages fled, leaving their bounty behind. But the Torch probably had other ideas.

"It is custom even for savage captains to remain for as long as they can on their vessel," the Watch Officer said. "That woman will be the most valuable to extract for intelligence. The rest can be euthanized."

The captain nodded curtly in acknowledgment. Privately she hoped the lithogs fled. The wanton killing of animals was generally despised as a waste of God's creations. She never quite understood why wild elfyn and humyn were not accorded the same sympathy.

But now was not the time to indulge in private scruple. She had a crew to drive. They were good woman and deserved the prize that would be divided according to merit and rank. Even with the Torch looming over them, their spirits raised in anticipation of profit. She glanced up one more time, scanning the strange blue-keeled vessels. Not all were the same length. Spying a smaller vessel near the rear of their wake she selected one.

"That one," the captain said to the sergeant, indicating the wake pattern that matched what she saw above.

"Drag or snatch?" the sergeant asked.

"Drag," the captain said.

"Won't they follow?" the corporal asked.

"We'll be too fast," the captain said. Then she added, "And besides, our Watch Officer needs at least one of them alive."

God's slave didn't contradict her; the captain took that as a good sign. "Ready, claws."

"Ready!"

"Mark our ascent. Pilot, raise the Bell at capture speed. For God and Avatar."

"For God and Avatar!" the crew echoed, cheering more from the anticipation of profit than fervent piety.

Not that it mattered. Their spirits were high and their victory secure. After this venture the captain looked forward to a long leave. Perhaps with the prize money, she'd take her consort to the Holy City, Halgon. They hadn't visited in a long time and they could stay with his dynasty on the way. She got on well with her mother-in-law as they both shared a passion for tunnel hunting. It would be a good trip.

With these thoughts the captain smiled as the sea tank rose through the ethereal blue water to their prize.

Chapter 37

The Sea Djinn

Rosen stood on the stern deck, taking a moment from the duties of the day to reflect how far they'd come. The weather was brisk, the wind lively, and had he needed sail, they might have done almost as well as driving by aqua. But he was glad for the aqua keel and rib fins, without which towing of the warship would have been more fraught. As it was *The Tidebreaker* only lagged a little behind the fleet. Though the waves were choppy, the ship was steady and even. Not so much could be said about his career.

Rosen still marveled at Tresmadore's treatment of him, the closest she'd ever come to speaking to him as an equal. Part of him wondered at her state of mind. But he had to accept, for whatever reason, her duties as Admiral had sobered her, revealing a side he never guessed existed. It didn't change his fate, it only delayed it, but it did allow him to save face and enter Gashora a hero. Vindictive admirals did not extend such courtesy. Captains who had done worse had been brigged and shackled, but most were simply removed from command and suffered in ignominy until they returned home to be court martialed.

The word weighed heavy on Rosen. It didn't mean one automatically lost their command, but Rosen knew he was guilty. His only hope was that the Admiralty or Command took pity on him and declared his mind afflicted by war. He despised the thought, but he despised more the idea he'd be shamed in his mother's eyes.

That brought Rosen's thoughts back to dreams. Like many crew he attempted to travel home and was met with empty houses and absent halls. There was a fire burning in the harbor. Perhaps battle raged there. Or their minds were distracted in preparations. And so he was left wandering his ship instead, avoiding private rooms, but he walked to the lower decks and was pleased the souls of the prisoners looked at him darkly with resentment.

"You," Komar Zan had said to him. Rosen was surprised the humyn was aware, but it was not unheard of. "You come to gloat."

"If you want to call it that, yes."

The coldness in Rosen's heart was satisfied, but it was a grim place. He had left, walking back up through the dream ship, climbing the masts to look at the stars. Great dreamers could leap into them and travel the paths. This was how the magi of old learned that the world was an orb and the fast stars, and Sul and Lun, were sister orbs all dancing in the Void by their paths of attraction. And what of the slow stars, Rosen had wondered? Once it was thought there were other, more distant sister orbs. But the truth was in their light. Like Sul, they shined out of their own being and so each one was a sun. The unknown question was how many had orbs dancing around them, and of those orbs, how many lived with a robust source? For it was known the orbs of Amer and Payeen were bare, though there was dream life and it was said to be strange. But the orb of Myngar, the greatest of the sister orbs, had lesser orbs of her own, worlds of water, ice, and fog.

"Your thoughts, Sea Father?" a woman asked.

Rosen started out of musing on his dreams to see Glenfar standing near.

"My thoughts are in the heavens, where I feel I'd prefer to travel if I had the skill."

"It's dangerous work," Glenfar said. "Few modern magi take the risk, the old texts being so thorough."

"What is the danger?" Rosen asked.

"The distance and anchoring. Expending essence can exhaust one. That's why healers have anchors, who keep operators connected to the waking world when retrieving souls. In the Void it is easy to lose one's direction if one loses focus. Usually a magi will simply rebound back and wake with a start. But occasionally a soul wanders too far. This is why, during tests, Lun, Sul and the lesser orbs of Payeen and Solshar are the only ones traveled to."

"Not Amer?"

"Amer is fraught for many reasons. Only strong magi attempt it. It's said long ago there were anchors made of etheric metal, that allowed magi to traverse the very stars like stairs set into a mountain side. Well, perhaps not exactly like that, but you understand. But the secret of etheric metal has been lost. Assuming it ever existed."

"You don't think it did?"

Glenfar shrugged. "Many are the myths of Er the Great. Yet ruins have never been found, in waking or dreams. Visions, yes, very vivid and consistent. But such things can be made by many minds wishing strongly for it to be so. Personally I believe the old magi before the Cataclysm were women of uncommon mettle and nerve who were simply not afraid of dying in pursuit of knowledge."

"Whatever else, that was probably true."

"So you have forgiven me?"

Rosen looked at Glenfar. She had no anxiety or concern, her only offer being friendship to accept or reject. "There is nothing to forgive." Rosen looked away, at the waves, then the waists where some of the Shari had been brought up to stone parts of the deck in the sun. Crew, including the irrepressible Aqi, chivying them. "It was your duty to report my…excess. A captain is not a god."

They were silent a few moments.

"What will happen?" Glenfar asked.

"The Admiral has been gracious to leave my doom to be decided on our return to Tyrum."

"That is gracious. And not congruent with what I've been told of Sea Mother Tamnath's temperament."

"The Jackal, yes," Rosen said wryly. "I think commanding has changed something inside her. But I don't know her, so I could not say what."

Suddenly the ravens croaked and took flight as one, almost due north. Rosen's heart leaped; the birds would only have flown off so suddenly if they spied land. The crew was ecstatic. Rosen saw Ensign Jarroth speak excitedly with Sharol and her warrior poet.

Glenfar smiled at him. "It is true, Sea Father. Our ravens have seen land!"

"Is it Gashora?"

"We're close. Near the garrison at the horn."

Above, "Land fore!" was shouted and whistles from other ships confirmed it.

"Ah look," Glenfar added, looking skyward. "A flintsun. Sul blesses us."

Hardly had Rosen glanced at the phenomenon, than a cry came from one of the Shari prisoners. Then all the prisoners were screaming and running in panic. One had just been restrained from diving into the water by a crew and guard. As he watched Aqi ran to an officer and was yelling and gesturing, as panicked as her countrymen.

"Glenfar?" Rosen said, hoping the magi could understand their minds.

"The Shari, they fear Sea Djinn, a spirit in a bottle roving the waves that steals souls."

"Is there anything they don't fear stealing their souls?" Rosen muttered.

He strode aft looking over the stern down into the water around the scorpion ship. Rosen's skin crawled. Something moved in the water with great speed. It was round and at least as wide as *The Tidebreaker*, with an eerie glow in the center. It passed the Shari vessel on starboard, then came abreast *The Tidebreaker*, perhaps a couple of ells under, water swelling in its wake. Then it sank out of sight.

"Get Galen!" Rosen shouted as he raced down the stern steps and ran along the starboard waist, trying to spy the vessel. "Sound the alarm!" he shouted at Ni Fionna as he darted by. Then the entire ship lurched as if Maer herself had shook it and he was almost thrown into the sea.

The bells were clanging; distress whistles screamed as Rosen fell tumbling to clutch at a shroud to avoid going overboard. Around him Dwen and other crew fell, yet somehow landed on their feet. The ship shivered again and women shouted in alarm. The prisoners fled below decks. The loudest shouts were from the bow where crew clustered with magi, Ta Taren at the fore, looking down in horror. Rosen shoved them out of the way, climbing on to the bowsprit observation platform for a better view. What he saw made him grip the ropes for dear life.

The Vessel, whatever it was, had risen out of the water, a great saucer-shaped crablike thing of dark glittering metal, except the center that glowed with a bluish white light. Rosen saw it was a window, which meant they were not spirits or djinn, but a craft driven by women. On its side was the sign of Eurath, the quartered circle, and strange lettering, confirming this was no spirit apparition, but an artifact of mothers, driven by mortal intelligence. Around the window, folded against the hull, massive arms with claws at their ends. Four of these rose and sought to grasp *The Tidebreaker*'s hull, irrespective of the rib fins.

Rosen screamed, "Strike crew muster! Strike at will!"

Women ran to unchain the solcannons, but the magi were faster. Chains were ripped out of their wooden loops, and two solcannons were dragged as close to the hull as possible, aiming down at the contraption in the water

510

nearly kissing the ship's bows. The glare of sunstrike made blinding reflections off the black metal and the water hissed as hot steam rose to envelope them. But it was no use. They may as well have been children aiming mirrored sunlight at a stone wall. With a horrible shudder the claws of the vessel sank into the hull, shattering some of the aqua rib fins.

"Be wary!" a voice called out with authority. It was Farthal running to the forecastle taking the steps three at a time, her flouted hair streaming behind her. "It's an Eurthani contraption! It might use blue strike!"

"What's blue-strike?" Rosen shouted.

As if to answer his question a peal of thunder exploded around them as if they were sailing in the midst of a thunder cloud. At the same time a blue-white bolt of lightning arced from below, presumably from the vessel, and struck the top of the foremast. There was a horrific crack of wood as the mast snapped just above the tops platform, the mast crew leaping away for their lives. Rosen looked up from where he stood just below, still on the observation platform. He knew he should run but for a moment was overwhelmed. The broken part of the mast fell, timber tangled with ropes and furled sail, and if he didn't move he'd be crushed.

"Sea Father!" someone screamed. Rosen's body obeyed where his mind had become sluggish. He leapt back to the top of the forecastle, falling on the deck just as the mass crashed down, breaking through the observation walk to crash onto the beakhead. Women shouted "Stray rope!" as rigging gave way and ropes snapped, and crew ducked out of the way.

"Really, Sea Father!" a voice said from a looming black robed figure standing over him. "Had we not slowed its passage, you'd be in the infirmary!"

"My thanks, Ta Taren," Rosen said getting shakily to his feet. He looked over the ruin of the foremast and what remained. It was repairable, assuming they were given time.

"Be ready to aim sunstrike at it!" Farthal was still shouting orders to magi and strike crew, sounding more like an officer than Rosen felt at the moment. "Get Dwen to activate wood essence in the hull! Together they will bleed it of power! You want to see it turn green!"

More forks of lightning discharged. One struck near an aqua node; the glass shattered with a flash of blue light. Farthal and a magi struck with solcannon, a low sustained broad beam of light. It would have little force, but force wasn't their intent. They swept it over the path of blue strike, drawing it, for while it acted like lightning it was some sort of essence. Others seized lances to help those with the solcannons until the blue strike, falling in on itself, changed color, becoming a pale emerald green, before dispersing into a glowing ball that fell down towards the water.

Rosen was heartened that the line of the fleet had slowed, *The Black Seal* turning in her traces to face him while *The Meer King* and *The Fortunate* bore on his position to render aid. He ran larboard to look down at the progress of the vessel. That's when he felt *The Tidebreaker* move. Its claws were deep and it was pulling aft; it was trying to capture his ship!

Never had Rosen felt so personally assaulted while in command, nearly powerless to defend himself.

"Every pilot available to the cage or nodes!" he yelled. "You!" he shouted at a Dwen. "Release the tow line!"

If this eldritch horror managed to fish tail *The Tidebreaker* around, it might sink the ship the Admiralty was so keen for.

Galen appeared at his side as he looked down at the progress.

"Divers are inspecting it!" she shouted over the chaos of a near panicked crew. "Should I send the marines?"

"I don't know." Rosen shook his head but he had no thoughts. What could a group of armored women with tridents do? "First let's see what the divers fathom – "

A scream from the water told Rosen something had gone horribly wrong. They watched as the water around the vessel turned strangely white, surrounding one diver while the others either sank or swam away as fast as they could. In horror he realized it was ice. He didn't know how, or why, but the water was freezing. Just then, two figures pushed passed him, the reckless diver Pearl and her boy, Col.

"They need help!" Pearl said.

"I'll hold a rope," Col added.

Rosen grabbed them both by the backs of their clothes, hoping Pearl's netted tunic wouldn't rip again.

"The divers are trapped and you will be of no use!" Rosen shouted, pulling them back.

"Throw down the ropes to the water!" Galen bellowed. "I want crew and volunteers with axes! Sprightly!"

Meanwhile the ice spread, trapping a couple more divers. The rest had disappeared below. Rosen leaped out of the way as women rushed to the sides of the ship with axes. Led by Galen, a mix of souls in tartan kilts, striped bracs and white sea breeches slithered down ropes and ladders to rescue the divers, a rare event. *The Meer King* and *The Fortunate* were close, their solcannons facing *The Tidebreaker*. It was a dire thing to be rescued at the face of a solcannon.

"Use all your force to resist the pull!" Rosen yelled at the pilots. "Ensign!" he called to Jarroth, who was looking askance at the shattered node. "Never mind that! The signalers need to tell the ships to aim at the vessel, not the water! Our divers are still trapped by essence rime!"

Jarroth nodded, running adroitly between the crew to the main mast, calling up his orders. With relief Rosen heard the notes sounding over the water.

The Tidebreaker pitched, rocking slightly as the tow line was released. Now it seemed the ship was being pulled even faster starboard, east and south, with an apparent desire to drag it away from the fleet. Rosen lunged to a node, joining the effort and for a moment felt more powerful than ever, he and his pilots driving *The Tidebreaker* like never before. For a moment he thought it was working. He considered they should change tactics and pull the ship away. But between the claws, feeling as if they were in his own skin, and the cold ice – so cold it threatened to take their collective breath away – the vessel was annealed to them like a great malignant barnacle. For maybe a moment they arrested their movement. Then a burst of force yanked the ship around, the pilots of the grim vessel deciding they needed more essence and had plenty to spare. They all fell to their knees, and half of the women stayed there, still pouring their life force into resisting the pull. He heard the shouts and screams of the women working, the divers in agony. The strike crew stopped attacking the vessel, instead carefully striking the ice to free the divers. Meanwhile the air flashed with strike as solcannons from *The Fortunate* discharged. Rosen could feel the strike scorch the hull, heating the water in *The Tidebreaker*'s aura, but if it had an effect on the vessel, it did not slow it from dragging the ship around. Now the bowsprit faced due east, perpendicular to their course, slowly turning the ship south. Rosen knew in that moment what Admiral Jonsaymanor Jansenwol felt before *The Oaken Blue* collapsed: the horror, the despair, the knowledge of what she was duty bound to do: Rosen needed to give the order to abandon ship.

He wanted to weep. The feeling was no less as the crew swarmed up from the water, carrying injured divers, one half frozen to death, others shivering with chill. One swore at her rescuer, a blond Cambari woman.

"You clumsy ox!" a Blue woman screamed.

"I said I'm sorry!"

"You're sorry! I won't be able to swim for weeks! Look at it!"

She held the grisly half of her severed finger that still had a bit of fluke attached to it.

"They can attach it," the Cambari said sheepishly. "It's not forever."

The worst though was a Cambari rescuer who was waving off help from her fellows. She stumbled and fell and with a gory crack, half severed her foot. It was frozen solid and she had to be restrained and carried because she could not feel the pain.

Rosen felt he was about to fall into Reverie, a welcome escape from what he had to do. The ultimate shame of a captain. And they had been so close, so close to Gashora, to a safe harbor …

Galen was shouting, Rosen couldn't tell what, but she and several crew started swarming to the fore of the forecastle, then onto the cathead an anchor hung from. An ax fell down again and again with much swearing. There was a scrape and snap of chain. Rosen felt the anchor's full weight jerk on the cathead as the rope securing it was severed. Now it swung first fore, then aft, a deadly one ton pendulum. Rosen saw Galen's intent as she perched on the timberheads with a large mallet in hand: she'd release the cathead and the anchor would fall on the fell vessel.

Rosen held his breath. The mallet fell, and the anchor, the weight of a small pied-dolphin, fell on the swing aftward. Sadly it missed hitting the vessel from above, swinging just over the crystal dome to land with a deafening clamor on the saucer's end, a demonic hammer hitting a gong. Galen fell back to the deck, her hands over her ears as were Rosen's and many of the crew. *The Meer King* had come level with *The Fortunate* when he was able to look over the side to see what Galen's actions had wrought.

It was hopeless. Though the anchor had dented the black metal and broken much of the ice, the eldritch contraption was still attached. *The Tidebreaker* was still being pulled away from the fleet. Like the water around the grim vessel, Rosen froze.

Suddenly a Gold face with insistent blue-green eyes was close to his, her presence demanding, her voice commanding him to meet the moment:

"Sea Father!" Master Jasmenal shouted. "You must make a choice!"

Rosen felt he was dreaming, and not just because Jasmenal had called him 'sea father' instead of captain. "We can't fight," he said. "We must assume the vessel is hostile and the crew must be saved." Rosen's eyes swam with tears. "Give the order to abandon ship."

Jasmenal nodded once then disappeared. Galen was standing there solemnly. Then she was in motion, anticipating the crew's need, giving orders herself. The side-bridge planks were freed and the more steady *Meer King* eased closer trying to match *The Tidebreaker*'s speed to link their decks. This would be for the quick and able, like the midships that had been called up and assembled. The healers were clustered near a launch being raised by a yardarm, the magi ready to help them levitate the seriously wounded. But before more could be done, whistles sounded insistent, with ear piercing urgency. The side-bridge was dropped, falling into the water and *The Meer King* pulled away rapidly. But why?

In a mix of alarm and wonder, Rosen watched as one of the larger ships drove in a wide circle, larboard and west, then turned with a speed east so sharply it listed in the water. The rest of the fleet kept their distance. Rosen ran to the pilot's cage, sensing what was about to happen, feeling he needed to be connected to his vessel to react effectively. He and his copilots still tried to resist the vessel, but it only slowed their turn to the south. Somehow Rosen knew once they faced south, it would be over. He gasped in anticipation, the ship almost upon them, finally seeing the figurehead of a rampant sealion.

What in all of Athmod's screaming madness was Tresmadore doing? *The Black Seal* came closer, starboard hull facing *The Tidebreaker*'s bows, the path of her arc dangerously close to snapping their bowsprits like two mounted champions tangled in a joust. Then Rosen understood.

The ram was archaic and obsolete. Some Shari and Cathan ships still had rams, as did elfyn river and coastal ships in feudal times. Tyreen ships didn't ram, but the larger vessels had protrusions fore of the keel, a breaker, to aid in shepherding water currents that assisted speed and to prevent a ship's keel from striking rock. Made of solid bronze, though blunt, they did protrude enough to spare a hull. And the breaker was at a perfect depth to strike a half submersed vessel. With *The Black Seal*'s head of speed, and weight of the vessel, it might be a match for the contraption.

Foam rolled off *The Black Seal*'s bow as Tresmadore drove her ship with speed in a way that a city-ship was never meant to be maneuvered. A horn sounded from the decks, a warning of imminent collision. Rosen had a moment for a wordless prayer, wondering at Tresmadore's madness. He saw her, improbably standing alone in the pilot's cage, holding the frame with both hands, her hat lost in the wind of her passing. Rosen finally found his voice:

"Brace for impact!"

The horn blew again, like a beast calling to its mate.

"Pilots, disengage!" Rosen ordered.

Rosen worried they could all suffer shock if they were connected to the aqua when they collided. If this worked, it was possible *The Tidebreaker* wouldn't survive. City-ships hadn't been built to battle each other. As far as Rosen knew nothing like this had been done in the history of the Tyreen navy.

The Black Seal bore down. They were a furlong away, the hull a blur as they closed. Rosen felt like someone was swinging an ax at a crab that had attached itself to his nose. Then *The Black Seal* collided with the thing that had seized *The Tidebreaker*.

The sound was deafening, more thunderous than the anchor falling on the vessel. Then a horrible screech followed of metal and splintering of wood. *The Tidebreaker* shivered violently and any soul standing was thrown off their feet. For good measure solcannons discharged at close quarters, blinding many. Rosen closed his eyes as the air heated; Tresmadore seemed determined to melt the black metal hull if possible. In counter point was the sound of shattering glass, followed by the hissing of shards hitting the water. Then *The Tidebreaker* stopped shivering and rocked in a shallow pitch, finally free.

Rosen stumbled out of the cage and ran to look over the wreckage of the bowsprit. He stared down just as the round vessel, now ripped from *The Tidebreaker*'s hull, drifted away then suddenly sank out of sight. The light from the top dimmed, and finally disappeared.

With it went many shards of aqua. *The Black Seal* also rocked as it drifted passed, its momentum carrying it on, but the rib fins along most of its starboard had been shattered leaving wood and pins. Even some of the copper sheathing had been lost. Tresmadore stepped from the cage, yielding it to a copilot. Looking back, she saluted Rosen. Belatedly he returned it . Never had he been more grateful for the Jackal and her reckless bravery. He stepped away from the bowsprit and looked at the magi around him. Many were helping the crew put things to order after the aborted evacuation.

"I need a magi, if any soul has a moment," he said.

In moments Glenfar stood by his side.

"Yes, Sea Father?" she inquired.

"Tell me if they are gone. The vessel."

"If they're elfyn – "

"They're elfyn!" Rosen said with feeling. "They used essence to make the water freeze. Sea water does not freeze easily! And the Marshal's agent seemed to know them. Are they gone or no?"

Glenfar closed her eyes, concentrating. "They are elfyn," she said. "Strange. They are angry. Confused. Disappointed. They'd expected a prize? But their vessel is damaged so they are – "

Glenfar broke off and yelled, hands gripping her head so fast she knocked her taq off. "I need an anchor!" she yelled. "A wizard is hunting my mind…"

Rosen caught Glenfar's arm as she sank to her knees. Ta Hethlion and another magi rushed to her. Glenfar gasped with relief.

"What happened?" Hethlion asked.

"There is a mind," Glenfar said, her face shining with sweat. "She is powerful. But now far enough away to lose her hold. I've never felt anything like it. She was trying to learn everything she could about us in that brief time, like reading a book as fast as the wind, and burning every page once she was done..."

Glenfar looked horrified.

"Get her a draught," Hethlion ordered.

"What's she done now?" Ta Taren asked, returning from some task.

"Thank you, Glenfar," Rosen said. He withdrew to let the magi manage their own.

"So they're gone!" Galen said appearing at his side.

"Yes!" Rosen smiled. "They're gone! What's our status!"

"Well, you can see the wreck on the beakhead. The rib fins have been damaged, but they still can guide us into the bay. The keel sustained no damage. And we need to weigh the anchor..."

Rosen strode to a node while she spoke and felt the truth of her words. The heart was sound, the keel was whole and while there were missing or broken aqua ribs, they had plenty to get them to Gashora. "We need to attach the tow line to the warship again – " Rosen started to say.

"Sea Father!" a woman interrupted. It was the Woodweaver Fadwen and her eyes were full of panic.

"What in Sul's flaming tresses is it now?" Rosen said.

"Hull breach! Larboard side! The hold!"

Rosen looked at Fadwen aghast. Then he ran for the nearest companion stair. Galen bellowed at him to stop, but he would have none of it. Within less than the space of an hour he had thought he must abandon ship. *The Tidebreaker*, the sister of his heart, was not going to sink from beneath him if Rosen could prevent it.

Chapter 38

Damned to the Deeps

Rosen ran down the steps from the forecastle to the quarterdeck, then down the closest steps under the skid beams where the launches rested. From there he took the upper deck center companion stair in line with the main hatches to the middle deck, feet flying, hands tearing leaves of breathing vine in his passage. At his heels were Fadwen with a couple of Dwen crew, presumably able and skilled with wood-essence. The bells clanged again, with the same urgency as the attack from the strange vessel: crew was to gather essentials and prepare to abandon ship. In this Rosen and those with him were a hindrance, running in the direction opposite from the masses. He did his best to slide by women as they ascended, while he may very well be leading the woodweaver and her mates to their doom. At the lower deck Lieutenant Colma Selimor met them, questions on her lips, but he spoke first:

"Prepare to evacuate! Get crew and livestock above decks! Only take essentials!"

"Effa!" Selimor acknowledged. "What about the prisoners, effa?"

Rosen hadn't paused, already halfway down the next stair. "Get them up top with the rest!"

In honesty Rosen hoped all could be avoided if they acted fast enough. On the orlop deck, the proper stair ended. It was smaller narrower steps that led into the hold. But the deck was already awash with a thin sheet of water from a puncture higher in the hull. They stood at the intersection of several cabins and store rooms at the fore: Galen's cabin was near the hull larboard; Fadwen's, almost a mirror starboard. Taking much of the center of the deck amidships was the sail room, a wide space to dry and repair rope. Aft of that would be the cockpit and pump room, more stores and cabins, including the purser's. That worthy appeared, a Gold woman, Jorun Ardenweld.

"Hurry!" she called behind her. "You are going retrograde, Sea Father," she added to Rosen. "Should I ask why?"

"No time!"

Rosen heard water pouring. Their final steps took them into the belly of the ship stacked with barrels of water and crates of other supplies, the scent of the recently stored garum fish heavy in the air. The cavernous hold was felt more than seen; only a few lanthorns hung to give enough light to know the way. Doorless rooms, shelves and partitions cast shadow, so one felt as if caught in a maze. During loading, solstone lanterns were brought down to work and organize. Rosen stepped onto the deck with a splash, the water already a foot deep. Had they been in the middle of a great voyage he would have despaired for the food and other necessities the water threated to ruin. But Gashora was within sight, and, provided they survived, this damage would be reimbursed. He followed the sound of pouring water knowing this was the path to the breach, hoping it could be stopped. The hull was so thick, surely the hole at least would remain stable. But the strange vessel's claws were strong and until he saw the damage, he had no idea what repairs would be required. They sloshed through the rising water, mildly surprised it wasn't worse. Finally they came to the break in the hull and saw why.

It wasn't as bad as Rosen expected. Water poured out in a quick moving brook where the deck ended. The hull bowed out in a convex wall marking the lines of the ship, oak planks, joined and woven together. Six puncture holes in a circle nine feet wide had bored into the three foot hull and crushed or scraped out a jagged crescent shaped hole in the wood. They looked at the place water poured through, spraying like a small cataract. If not for the ice still clinging to the hull, filling the claw punctures like frozen grout, the hold would be half flooded.

Still the ice was melting. Sounds behind him told him more women were coming. Fadwen and the Dwen crew were clinging to wood supports and partitions, not for support as he thought, but to feel the damage through the ship.

"Get wood!" Fadwen shouted to her mates. "Any wood! Scavenge if you have too! It won't hold for long," she added to Rosen. "One can feel the ice loosening – "

Suddenly they were bathed in the white light of a solstone lantern. Rosen saw the wound clearly, above their heads, like a great creature had bitten into the hull. Ice, white in the light, black rime in shadow, melted, rivulets of water joining the largest gap where a small waterfall from the sea poured in.

"Sea Father?" one of the new women asked. They were burly Cambari. "The boatswain says we're to drag you out if necessary!"

"Oh, does she?" Rosen replied, both touched and annoyed. "Well, she's not captain! Help the Dwen gather wood! It needs to be sealed while we still can! Then the pumps can work– "

Spray hit them all when the weakened hull broke open, the water pouring in doubling in volume. They were all soaked by the burst. Now the hold flooded in earnest and Rosen knew if they didn't stop it the water would be up to their necks in minutes.

The prospect of giving the order to abandon ship rose again. Rosen wanted to scream. He'd be damned to the deeps if he forsook his ship now. He looked around, thoughts racing desperately. The Dwen were sloshing their way back with wood after dismantling a couple of walls. His eyes fell on a table. He seized it or tried to. Had he been as meaty as the Cambari he could have done it; his arms were long enough. The women saw his efforts and came to help, half carrying, half dragging the table to the hole, holding it up and throwing their weight on it, desperate to make a seal. Rosen found himself side by side with a dark haired Cambrian woman who looked vaguely familiar. They tried to hold the table steady to seal the hole, but it was too low.

"Set it down!" Fadwen called. The Cambari slammed the table on its legs as close to the gap as possible, helped by the water crashing on it, soon to be hindered when the water rose high enough the table would float. Before that happened the Dwen swarmed on it, standing together to try to seal the hole while water crashed over them. Rosen assisted the Cambari in keeping the table down, their backs against it with all their weight, wet to the skin while the flood rose above their knees.

Rosen bellowed, "Will some damned Tree weave this hole shut?"

He couldn't have done it without the women. It took four stout bodies not counting himself to keep the table in place. And still the Dwen had trouble, the force of the sea making it hard to seal the wood. They finally dropped the planks to touch the hull directly, extending fibers to close the gap, while the sea pushed through insistently. The water was at Rosen's thighs and he wondered if he would drown. Perhaps he'd wake on *The Black Seal*, his crew rescued by the Jackal.

"Oh, for the love of Sul!" an irritated voice echoed. The light brightened above them, centered on the ruined wood where water still poured in. Suddenly the air became quite cold. "Pull your hands away from the hull until I tell you elsewise!" the woman ordered.

It become so cold Rosen worried they would freeze. He looked up at the jagged hole to see thick ice form at the edges, creeping inward, the cataract reduced to a trickle until it stopped. The hole was now filled with solid ice. Ta Taren hovered on the water nearby where she had called the cold.

"Don't look so astonished, Sea Father. Once your boatswain explained the situation, the solution was obvious. No! Don't step down!" Taren added to the Dwen. "It's not truly sealed!"

The wood planks they'd struggled with flew up from where they were floating as Taren pressed them over the ice.

"Go on, seal it! Then we can all get out of here!"

Rosen and the Cambari held the table steady while the Dwen worked. Under their hands, the wood bent and molded, interweaving with the hull, covering the gaps and sealing the edges. The Dwen women jumped down with a splash, Fadwen last.

"It's done, Sea Father," she said. "But such a seal is weak on the inside. As soon as we can, a patch should be applied outside."

Rosen nodded, weak with relief. "Well done, woodweaver. And my thanks to you, Ta Taren and the rest."

But the magi had already left. Rosen would have sunk down to rest on the floor if the water wasn't so deep. "Carry on," he said, hoarsely. He turned to thank the Cambari, a mix of crew and volunteers. It was then he recognized the woman who had stood next to him. It was the black haired Albini miscreant Rosen had disciplined for her androphobic disrespect before the battle.

"Volunteer Seand inion Morgu!" Rosen exclaimed.

"Aye, Sea Father!" she said, grinning. Her bizarre black pigtails now drooped and her kilt was as waterlogged as his own clothes.

"You never finished floating."

"And 'tis not a wise hunter who reminds a rankled boar of her presence."

Rosen sighed. "I assume that aphorism sounds more elegant in native Albini."

"That it does. Can you manage?"

The water was nearly waist deep and very chilled.

"Thank you, volunteer, yes. Go help with the pumps."

"Aye, captain!"

Rosen waded to the ladder stair, aware that the strange Cambari who once mocked his command was at his elbow, ready to catch him if he slipped. Seand's sincerity was affecting. He reached the stair without incident and Seand strode off to join the loud voices of crew gathering near the well under the pump at the base where the main mast met the keel. The pump would be checked for faults before the women took turns at the handles in earnest on the lower deck. Climbing up to the orlop deck Rosen felt the weight of water in his wool coat, his boots squelching with an unseemly noise. His white sea breeches were no longer so, all the stray dust and grim, barely seen by the eye, released by the water to wash them in a dye of pale gray muck. With horror he remembered these were his last sea breeches: one pair, battle worn, was still in need of mending; the other blood soaked, stained accidentally from changing out of the slops after killing the Shari. Those had yet to be laundered. Rosen needed a new pair of breeches.

"Sea Father!" Emha Arthenweld exclaimed as if he'd been retrieved from death. "Are we to assume this means we do not have to pack our trunks and abscond?"

"You assume correctly, emha," Rosen said. "But as you see I have another need."

"Yes," Arthenweld said, appraising Rosen's clothes. "Luckily the supply cupboards sit aft and away from the hull."

Arthenweld beckoned Rosen to follow her to the supply rooms while she shouted at her clerks and helpers. "Cease your labors at egress! It seems the ship is not doomed to the deeps. Return everything as it was…again. Really, Sea Father, regardless of the many tasks waiting me when we dock, when we get to Gashora I'll be stepping on the quay just to confirm we've actually arrived."

They walked around the sail room, following the starboard hull, coming to the space of the cockpit, clustered with crew at tasks. It was a short walk beyond where more cabins and store rooms were arranged in a horseshoe. In the middle was a companion stair, both to the hold and the lower deck above. They came to one of the rooms with an iron reinforced door. Arthenweld opened the lock with her purser's keys and took a lanthorn as they stepped inside.

"Good of you to get here early, Sea Father. After the battle there was a mob. Many types of garments aren't available. Everyone wanted a scarf. They're gone. Let's see what remains."

Many of the high shelves in the narrow room were bare .

"Ah, here we are." Arthenweld glanced at Rosen's breeches. "Those are women's breeches."

"Yes."

The pile of new, crisply folded white breeches sat on a shelf indicating they were for men. Next to them, in the place above the label for women, there was nothing. "Sorry, Sea Father, the women really have had a time of it."

Rosen's jaw clenched. There were many reasons he eschewed men's breeches, not the least being how the closure accented access to his privates for all to see. The buttons that ran up both sides of regular breeches, were instead clustered in a rectangle at the front. The advantages for male crew were obvious, but it also the implied they were ready for sexual use.

There was nothing for it. What Rosen was wearing was filthy and he was duty bound as a captain to be as presentable as possible at all times.

"Have them sent up to my cabin," Rosen said with a sigh. "I need to inspect the ship."

"Very good, Sea Father."

Rosen started the long climb to the upper deck, his water soaked coat dragging on him as he went. On the lower deck was shouting and chaos. It was somewhat expected as the news they weren't going to sink caught the crew at odds. There too were the women working the pumps, water drawn from the flooded hold to pour over to the scuppers, draining out of the ship. But something about the tone further to the bows made him pause before continuing to the middle deck. There were blows and cries, the sound of a melee... Was there a fight?

"Sea Father!" Lieutenant Selimor called, rushing to him. "The prisoners tried to break free! Not to worry! The guards have it in hand – "

"*Bígí stadán!*" a guard roared. There was a whistle like the sound of a whip, followed by a cry.

" – With the help of volunteers."

Rosen moved so he could see something of the mess. Among those subduing the Shari was the slight form of Aqi, wielding a starter rope as ably as any pirate captain of the past.

"I'll leave you to it, then!" Rosen said. "I expect a report once calm has returned."

"Yes, Sea Father!"

Taking a companion stair to the middle deck, it was much the same, minus fighting prisoners. Finally Rosen emerged on the upper deck, near the heart chamber.

He stepped away from the stair so as not to impede crew rushing down to assist with the pumps. He could see the doors to the mess hall had been thrown open, figures in white and green telling him it was once again an infirmary. He ran to the mess, needing to know how the crew had fared.

It was almost as bright as outside, every lamp available open wide hanging from any place possible. Women moaned and screamed in pain, the surgeon as busy as during the days of battle. Rosen spied the diver whose finger had been chopped off in her hasty rescue. She sat on a bench, drowsy, her repaired hand bound in wood strips to immobilize it, her body swaddled in a thick wool blanket. The Cambari woman who rescued her sat by her side so she didn't fall, while drinking from a tin cup and speaking with another crew member.

Rosen slowed as he heard hideous moaning from a table where the woman with the ruined foot lay. It was ghastly, the broken frozen flesh thawing, the bones from where the toes attached to the ankle sticking out like a badly cut fish fillet. The surgeon Alharn stood near, attended by three healers, but she had a look much like Rosen's when he had spied the eldritch vessel: shock, bewilderment and knowing he was at the frontier of his experience. The moaning ceased. One of the healers said,

"She's asleep."

This acted like a tonic and Alharn came alive. "It's only frostbite," she said, talking herself out of shock. "Only more severe than we usually see." She wiped her brow, then yanked off her red taq, tossing it impatiently away, as if it hindered her thoughts and essence.

"Keep the flesh from separating completely!" Alharn ordered. "We'll first attach then renew the flesh in stages. Someone get a Dwen! The wood splints must be woven as we work!"

Rosen moved on, passing divers still shivering in thick blankets, fighting the deep cold that could rob a body of all heat. Others had frozen or partly frozen limbs resting in cool water, slowly being warmed to see what damage had taken. Rosen read somewhere that to heal these required many treatments. If the flesh had died, it was less repairing it as regenerating and replacing it so enough lived to thwart gangrene. The work continued until the limb was whole enough that blood could flow and breathe through it properly.

Then there were the women blinded by the close range strike. Simple flash burns would be healed in a couple days. Those whose corneas had been scorched would be moved to the Gashoreen temple. At this pace, there were as many casualties from this alien attack as in the battle. A sudden thought made Rosen stop a healer, a petite young man.

"Have we lost any through the Door?" Rosen asked.

The man glanced at a couple of tables with unconscious women. The Lancer Farthal stood next to a healer and a magi conferring together.

"Not yet," he replied. "But they are in a dire state. Both frozen and deep cold. We need to get them to a proper temple with an array as soon as possible."

He rushed away to assist other healers. Rosen resumed his trek to the quarterdeck with a heavy heart.

On emerging, the clement sea air felt cold, and sent a bone deep chill through Rosen. He faced the wall of a vessel's hull looming over him. Before he could identify the ship, an enraged Galen confronted him.

"Blazing Plains above!" she shouted. "What in the Deeps do you think you were doing?"

"Thank you, boatswain, for your concern," Rosen replied lightly. "Is that *The Black Seal* alongside us?"

Rosen hadn't stopped moving because he didn't want to feel colder than he did. This forced Galen to follow, swallowing whatever scoldings she had as crew was within earshot.

"Yes!" Galen said, putting all her frustrations into the force of enunciation. "I was going to send for you!"

"No need now."

Rosen climbed up the larboard steps of the forecastle, and stood to face the wall of *The Black Seal*'s hull rising at least ten feet higher than *The Tidebreaker*. Tresmadore stood at the edge of her vessel on the starboard waist amidships, agile as ever. There was only a couple of furlongs between their ships. Tresmadore looked quite windswept. While her hair was still in a naval braid, she had lost her hat.

"At last, Sea Father!" she called, sounding impatient. "A damn funny time to go for a swim!"

Rosen felt defensive for a moment. Then he realized she was bantering. The Jackal was bantering with him. These were strange days.

"My apologies, Admiral," Rosen called up. "Had some bother with an eldritch sea sprite! Very careless of me!"

"That it was! Also you've lost your corn!"

Reflexively Rosen raised his hand. He couldn't remember when he last felt his bicorn on his head.

He shrugged. "I am but following the example of my esteemed Admiral!"

To his surprise Tresmadore imitated him, her hand reaching for a hat that was absent, her eyes shocked to find it gone. They said nothing a moment, then laughed as one.

"Never liked the damn things anyway!" Tresmadore said. Her tone changed, ready to discuss business. "I'm broken, Sea Father! Starboard rib fins shattered! And I've cracked the aqua on the keel! We sail at the mercy of Payeen! But you and the rest of the fleet need to get to Gashora instantly! The mischief we saw could be part of something greater!"

Rosen looked north at the rest of the fleet, their line significantly distant, with the exception of *The Meer King* and *The Fortunate,* who had lingered to render aid. But they too were turning north to rejoin the line.

"And because our black feathered friends have abandoned us," Tresmadore was saying. "I need you to deliver this to *The Charred Bronze!* Sea Mother Tentynlar Aldwyn will be acting Fleet Admiral until I rejoin the fleet! Elash?" Tresmadore spoke to a woman just out of sight, but Rosen saw the top of a yastol.

Suddenly a tall, thin Dwen woman stepped forward. Elash was the Jackal's boatswain of many years. She whistled in three perfect notes to "catch", not at Rosen, but at Galen. Galen nimbly stepped forward, snatching the scroll case out of the air, nodding at her counterpart. Elash stepped back out of sight.

"Those are my orders!" Tresmadore added. "Rejoin the line immediately and deliver them Aldwyn!"

Rosen paused in thought. "What if I towed you?"

Tresmadore's eye brows raised in amusement.

"It's not far and it would be faster!" Rosen added.

Tresmadore laughed, but she wasn't mocking him. "And I would be towing the Shari ship, all of us in a ludicrous sea train!" She shook her head. "No! More of these dangers could lurk! Better only one ship is lost than two! I will pray to Payeen, trust my wits, and follow with unfurled sails! But thank you, Sea Father. We will see you anon! Fanswar!"

With that Tresmadore saluted and withdrew from sight. *The Black Seal* slowly eased away. Only after she'd disappeared did Rosen realize he'd forgotten to thank her for rescuing him.

Before they could sail again, the tow line to their Shari prize had to be rejoined. The small ship lingered in the water askew where it had been completely spun about by the whirlpool of *The Black Seal*'s passage. Rosen would learn later that the Shari vessel being cut free had inspired the aborted prisoner revolt. A complete account of damage and repairs was already being compiled, Amralan and Aldweth scribing down dozens of notes within the hour. And the pumps needed time to work. He didn't want to sail until most of the water had been ejected. Meanwhile the tangle of broken mast top, ropes and sail was being separated and removed from the beakhead. The crew would have much to keep them busy in Gashora.

Rosen walked to the stern deck, looked over the aft end of the ship, and watched a while divers and Dwen reattached the towline. Nervously he scanned the water, his eyes imagining every shadow another eldritch sea horror come to do battle. But there was nothing except the green water reflecting a blue sky. He turned away and returned to his cabin.

Stripping his jacket off felt like a relief. Not only had the blue wool become heavy, but, in half drying, it threatened to shrink and felt to his form. His boots were full of water; this he poured into the basin. Then Rosen could peel off his shirt and breeches to dry himself. He looked like a mad druid in his mirror, his naval braid so disheveled it threatened to unravel. Rosen yanked at the tail, the thong long gone and only kept in place by matted tangles. After a couple painful pulls it came loose and he felt relief as his hair hung free. He understood a bit why the Jackal had let her hair fly wild for years. Then he lay down, thinking to rest a moment.

Suddenly he heard a knock and leaped up, alarmed he'd fallen asleep. The door opened and he searched vainly with his hands for his sword, but it was only Galen. She spied him, raised her eyebrows, then shut the door firmly behind her. Rosen fell back on his bed. They'd lost any shyness over nakedness long ago.

"You scared me out of my wits!" Rosen said. "Yet I give thanks because I seem to have fallen asleep."

"I thought I should check on you," Galen said, making free with his liquor store, pouring herself some barley-mead. "Repairs have been made, the tow chain is reattached, the anchor sitting where it should and we're ready to sail. There is some urgency with a handful of wounded, so I thought you'd want to be away instantly."

"Yes," Rosen said. "You're right of course."

Rosen rose and dressed in the new breeches that had been left on a chair. He forgot they were men's until he had them around his waist, where they felt snugger than normal; he missed the hip room women's breeches gave him. There was one consolation: his privates, for perhaps the first time since his commission, felt comfortably free. He turned to Galen, pulling on a shirt, and asked the question that haunted him: "Tell me honestly: how much do I show?"

Galen glanced very briefly, whether in respect of modesty or her usual utter disinterest in male anatomy. "I've told you before, I can't see a difference. The only reason they seem accented more is the buttons are on the front. Once you've tucked your shirt and donned the coat, you're obscured."

"Only from the rear."

Galen's mention of a coat brought Rosen to the next dilemma: the coat he wore wasn't yet dry. The other, worn in battle, had not been returned from laundering. Which left only one to wear.

"Scare up the crew laundering at your first free moment," Rosen said. "Before I'm forced to go naked."

"That would boost morale," Galen ventured. "You're wearing the dress coat?"

Rosen had donned a coat with gold trim on its sleeves, collar and tail.

"No choice. Can you do me a service and braid me?"

Galen smiled wryly and stood, indicating Rosen should sit. He usually did his own hair and it felt strange, her briskly brushing it. The last he remembered someone brushing his locks was Korali before taking him out on his first Moon-meet. Galen had a much firmer hand. Rosen almost regretted asking. He felt every strand of his hair pulled from his face so firmly he wondered if he'd be able to smile or blink again. The braid was wound with a new thong. He supposed he should be lucky he wasn't serving in Admiral Katlyn Moru's fleet, where, in time of war, so committed to discipline in dress, she forced her officers to seal their braids with tar.

"Done," Galen said. "You're ready for your gala."

"Very well," Rosen said, with a laugh. "Let's fanswar."

It was the best of all fortune Rosen looked both fresh and smart, his clean uniform giving him a comfort and confidence that seemed infectious. Women smiled and laughed as they worked, their voices lively and hearty. Galen parted from him, while he trotted up the stairs to the pilot's cage. Far to their larboard and west, *The Black Seal* had pulled away to maneuver and make her own repairs. The sun was falling behind the still bare top masts, where figures dancing among them worked feverishly. The great rudder had been unlocked. He knew the great wheel below the sterndeck would also be unlocked, women like Galen put to work turning it by direction and compass on command. Tresmadore stood in the pilot's cage; even though she could not drive her ship without inducing exhaustion, her pilot's senses were still superior. Suddenly white sails unfurled, blossoming over the masts like billowing silken flowers, their edges golden where the sun's rays touched them. Tresmadore would drive the best she could with the keel, assisted by the wind. The most taxing would be steering by rudder, but Rosen had seen

Tresmadore sail before. He had no doubt she'd come to harbor quick enough, provided the "sea djinn" did not harry them again.

Rosen stepped up to the pilots' cage, about to relieve Lieutenant Sandryn. But Master Sonan Jasmenal had just stepped up the larboard step for some business. Their eyes met and he hesitated.

Jasmenal looked as harried as he had before his nap. A master – much like the purser – wore an officer's coat blank of shoulder insignia. Instead there was a gold anchor and compass on her lapels. She chose to wear boots, but many master navigators wore shoes; neither she nor the purser wore a bicorn. But Jasmenal kept the naval braid from her time as a lieutenant copilot. Her expression was unreadable. She nodded up at Sandryn.

"I think our Sea Father is ready to fanswar," Jasmenal said.

Sandryn snapped her head around. "Captain! We wondered where you were!"

Rosen walked to the cage as Sandryn stepped out. "Gossiping about your betters is an offense against duty," he said lightly.

"Ai, surely Sea Father," Jasmenal said. "They were just concerned you had drowned."

"But not you, master?"

Jasmenal gave a small smile. "Of course not. I know you're far too stubborn to drown." Her smile faded and she added in a quieter voice, "You saved her."

"I wouldn't presume to take that much credit," Rosen replied. "It was Fadwen and her mates, and of course Ta Taren. I only – "

"I know what you did," she interrupted. "I was told. Thank you."

Jasmenal turned away, stepping down before he could reply. It was probably best as he had no idea what he could say. Their long rivalry appeared to be at an end and that was surely a good thing.

There would be plenty to do once they came to Gashora. For now Rosen wanted to enjoy what was left of the journey. Stepping onto the dais he felt the ship like a living thing, and, like many crew and himself, bruised and tired, but still filled with spirit. Looking forward, beyond the bowsprit, the rest of the fleet was far in the distance. Rosen smiled. It would be a bit like a race.

A whistle sounded above. The crew was ready.

Rosen called out "Fanswar!" and drove *The Tidebreaker* forward to Gashora caressed by the warm light of the setting sun.

Chapter 39

The Smiling Sun at Midnight

When *The Tidebreaker* rejoined the fleet it was night and it seemed they had
sailed to the shores of a land with blinding lights hovering over them, obscuring the stars and making the shadows strange. The fleet was waiting
just outside the bay, before the feet of Myngar and her consort, Felkeni, tall
dark effigies that would dwarf many buildings, their details lost in shadow.
But the lights they held aloft were as bright as the Sea Queen's orb above
the Wall in Tyrum. Such light was a blessing making the work easier. Without the ravens, ships whistled queries and requests with simple orders. The
seriously wounded were to be ferried to the city instantly. *The Charred
Bronze* received Tresmadore's precise instructions from *The Tidebreaker*:
she would join them anon; until then they would wait in the harbor so they
could enter the city as one.

Rosen hadn't expected they would be working in the dark, but Felkeni
made it easy, his towering form holding a solstone torch high above the water. The rest of the colossal statue's details were lost in the strange light and
extremely foreshortened figure. Felkeni's torch had been helpful to sailors
for centuries, and the bases of both Felkeni and Myngar, artificial islands
where they stood, were still used as ferry stations. In times past, ships
moored waiting for dawn before pulling into the harbor.

But these days it was impossible to miss their destination, the multitude
of illuminated towers sparkling like a cache of jewels in the water's reflection. The docks fairly glowed, street lights making them brighter than even
those in Tyrum. They ran to curve around the bay in the far east, and then
too in the opposite direction north-west. Following the shore the lights
turned west, broken in places where lesser rivers from the great delta at the
end of the Hethlyn poured into the sea. From that direction were the lit
arches of many bridges, lending the entire city an air of a glittering chimera
out of a dream. Many Cambari spoke of this view as being the true source
of tales of the Shining Ones, but it was probable all Sula cities contributed to
those Cambrian myths. In the morning they would dock along the nearly
straight length of the quay, in the middle where the streets lead into the heart
of the city.

As soon as they made contact with the fleet, Rosen turned the cage over to Lieutenant Bawn. The launch to ferry him to *The Charred Bronze* was lowered, the other being prepared on the skid beams, the priority being the worst of the wounded. Galen shouted out orders and Arthenweld made a rare appearance above deck to organize requests for supplies they needed from other ships. It was a cold night and Rosen had sent Ensign Jarroth on a quest to seek out his lost hat. Lancer Elderyn Farthal stood with him above the ladder to the launch.

"Thank you for your service," Rosen said. "The middies will be sad to see you go."

"What!" Jarroth had returned holding a bicorn. "But you promised to take us for ices, lancer!"

Farthal laughed. "I would gladly stay to obey such an order, my fine ensign! Alas, the Marshal has demanded I take a different path. I will not be rejoining the fleet."

"But you promised!" Jarroth said, hugging the bicorn fiercely. "You promised Glethlyn's ghost."

Farthal looked askance at Rosen.

"You did promise," he said.

Farthal sighed. "I will arrange for someone to do the task."

"It won't be the same," Jarroth said. Her eyes were both sad and resentful.

Farthal gathered the girl in a hug, so easy and gentle, yet not diminishing her station. Jarroth hugged the elf back. Then Farthal firmly pushed her away. "That is the nature of duty," she said. "In duty we abide and shall not be parted. In Victory or the Otherside."

Jarroth nodded, her face determined, without tears. "In Victory or the Otherside." She turned to Rosen. "Your bicorn, Sea Father."

"Sul and Maer bless you," Rosen said.

"Yes, Sea Father," Jarroth snapped to attention and saluted them both. Then she left to assist the deck officer.

"You really can't stay?" Rosen asked.

"I was of the impression the crew would be happy to see my wake," Farthal said.

"They'll be happy to lose the Marshal's agent. But many will miss the elf."

They climbed down to the launch, and it pulled away to give the boat lowering with the wounded clearance.

As they drifted between ships under the glittering lights, Rosen had not realized how forlorn he felt when *The Tidebreaker* was separated and attacked. It was comforting to see the gilt names lit on the aft of the vessels. He even felt a burst of goodwill towards those captains he was unfriendly with – *The Lunat, The Exalted Unicorn* – just for being present, for confirming he was not alone. The others in the launch, a mix of clerks and crew destined for other ships for sundry reasons, marveled openly at the Rulers, as statues of Myngar and Felkeni were known to Gashoreens.

"I wonder how they were built?" a midship said.

"Think it's ash-lime, like the towers, surely?" another soul answered.

"The scaffolding would have to be a forest, ai?" another said, jostling Rosen's arm for agreement.

"Ai," he said, not wanting to give himself away by elaborating. In the dim light his identity and presence had been forgotten. Rosen smiled to himself as the boat carried them, gently rocking on the calm water. He felt like the new midship he'd been years ago when everything was fresh and exciting.

The launch pulled alongside *The Charred Bronze*. Rosen and Farthal disembarked, the vessel drifting on. They climb up the diver's ladder which seemed longer not just because the ship was taller than *The Tidebreaker*, but in the night, with the dazzling lights from the shore, Rosen felt disembodied, like a spirit of a constellation walking among the heavens. Then he stepped through the gap in the aft of the stern deck and into the light of a lantern. A chorus of "Sea Mother" echoed around him. He wasn't even annoyed at being mis-gendered. In fact it made him more comfortable about his new breeches; apparently Galen had been correct. Farthal stepped off the ladder behind him. Rosen noticed a smaller ship sitting close to the larboard bows. Before he could investigate a familiar voice jibed:

"What in Maer's deeps has washed over my deck?" Blinking in the light Tynlar snapped into focus, the white streaks in her red hair glimmering in the light. "And why have you brought the Marshal's agent?"

"We'll just have to mind our secrets," Rosen said.

"Indeed."

A moment later Tynlar embraced him. He returned it, surprised at his hunger for the camaraderie. Then he remembered his errand and pulled apart.

"This is for you," Rosen said, offering Tynlar the scroll case. "You are to act as Admiral until Tresmadore catches up."

Tynlar frowned, "Catches up? What? Is she caught by that thing haunting the waves?"

"She was damaged saving me. Saving my ship."

Tynlar looked at Rosen with sympathy.

Rosen shook his head. "I'm grateful. There was nothing we could do, they were too powerful."

"The so called 'sea djinn'?" Tynlar added dubiously.

"That's what the Shari call them."

"They are Eurthani," Farthal put in. "The same belligerents we fought in the Battle of Gate Step."

Tynlar looked between them, her expression even more doubtful. "Eurthani are a myth told to frighten farm lot children into not straying."

"I'm not going to argue with you, Captain Aldwyn," Farthal said. "I've met them, fought with them, and even made peace with one. The vessel had the sign of Eurath on the hull, made of the same black metal they use for all their arms and armor. This should be in reports from Command. They are elfyn and we were lucky to escape."

"And one of their minds, a wizard I think, attacked a magi." Rosen added.

Tynlar's face was drawn in thought as she motioned them to follow her. She led them to her cabin, Farthal shutting the door behind them. But they were not alone.

The Charred Bronze, being a larger ship, had a much larger captain's cabin. Tynlar's aft galley had a padded window bench so wide it could be used like a cot by at least a couple of souls. Her bed, hidden by a drape, sat in the entire space under the larboard turret, the other turret filled in the same way with a table for dining. This wasn't just for comforts, but allowed more space for society and conferences on the larger vessel. At the table sat a woman, by her uniform an officer in the Federation Patrol Fleet.

Like Farthal, she was Sula. Neither Sula had a halo or visible aura at the moment. It could be the night, or perhaps they weren't as essence strong as the Exiles, known to be talented even among their tribe. But the officer's gold eyes reflected the light with a quality that seemed to radiate more than they received. Her skin was a pale warm gold, impervious to tanning and her hair, white blond, was worn in the same naval braid as Rosen's except with guardlocks on either side of her face bound with gold helix clips. The cut of her uniform was similar in style to the Tyreen navy, certainly the navy breeches and boots were of identical make. But the coat was white linen, trimmed in black and gold; the sword hanging from her baldric was the same as any officer in the Federation host, the pommel solstone instead of aqua. On her head was a sea circlet, a type of seer's helm. In the early days of the magi, many wore circlets and helms with solstone mounted in such a way a queen or magi could elegantly exploit the power of the sun, culminating in the great helms of the Sunqueens. The most basic of these, the seer's circlet, was a polished cabochon of solstone mounted in a gold or brass circlet, such that the stone sat over the center of the forehead, with no backing so it touched the skin. In ancient times, such mountings were often between the half spread wings of a dragon or eagle. Here it appeared to be waves, as if the stone was Sul setting in a watery trough. The woman had been drinking from a goblet, but when they entered she stood smoothly with a grace Rosen found unearthly.

"Don't worship her," Tynlar said. "She's a mother like the rest of us, and no more holy than Farthal."

"But she's a Helix," Farthal said. "That makes her nobility in the Federation Host."

"Indeed?" Tynlar sat and gestured for Rosen and Farthal to join them. "This is Captain Anglyn Sevitah, but they call her 'First and Seventh'. Sevitah, this is Sea Father Rosen Gathelyn of *The Tidebreaker*. And the Marshal's agent, Lancer Elderyn Farthal, who I must add is much more presentable than when she joined the fleet on Oracle Isle."

Sevitah nodded at Rosen, but snapped her head in Farthal's direction.

"Are you the same lancer who fought in the Battle of Gate Step?"

"Yes," Farthal said, sounding weary of her celebrity.

"Well done!" Sevitah said. "We'll need more souls like yourself if these Eurthan ants come back for more mischief!"

"They already have," Farthal said. "By sea."

"Wait!" Tynlar interrupted, addressing Sevitah. "You're saying Command has confirmed the existence of the Eurthani?"

"It's in the reports – " Sevitah cut herself off. "I expect they haven't been shared with the Tyreen navy yet. But yes, the Eurthans are not a myth. I've had to admit 'Emha Damar' isn't a fraud after all."

Rosen looked at the other women, but they were as unknowing as himself. "Who is Emha Damar?" he asked.

"A local celebrity," Sevitah said. "She regales her admirers with her adventures and exploits, and men– Well, men do what they do with charismatic women of that sort, no offense, Sea Father. She makes flints sparkle plenty, and the stories are true, if broadly told. But I had assumed her exotic visage was glamor and cosmetics. Her eyes positively glow like a demon's."

"Damar is Eurthani?" Farthal demanded.

"She's always claimed to be," Sevitah said. "Oh, she's not a villain, I assure you. That matter was put to rest when the um, unhappy, mothers and wives of her lovers, tried to sue for seduction. The men are mad about her and need no coercion to fall into her bed!"

"She has the Touch?" Farthal queried.

"Possibly? Do Eurthani have the Touch of Lun? They certainly wouldn't call it that."

Farthal did not look mollified but said no more on the subject.

Sevitah poured Rosen a goblet. "I had not known there was a Sea Father in this fleet."

"There are two," Rosen said. "Sea Father Manweth captains *The Starshard*."

Sevitah nodded. "There are some men in our navy. Not many, but some. How are the leaves, wolf friend?"

"I'm acting Admiral," Tynlar said. She was reading the scroll. "We'll be floating in the bay until *The Black Seal* joins us. Tresmadore wants us to sail in as one at dawn. The wounded have been sent ahead."

"Well, that's what we've been waiting for," Sevitah said. She drained her goblet and stood. "This will give the council time to prepare your welcoming and get the wounded to the temple without obstructions. I'll return to *The Crane*."

"Pardon, emha," Farthal said, also standing. "I need to go ashore and make my way to the mother stones at Lomastal."

"Howl's Peak?" Sevitah considered. "I can't take you there, but you can get a coach on the quay."

"As long as I'm there by dawn."

"Then the Marshal's agent is welcome on *The Crane*. Thank you for your hospitality, Wolf. And of course for your service to our city. Expect that to be repeated in the coming days until your ears tire of it. Cherish the moments while they last. They will sustain you in the times your duty feels unappreciated."

"Cheerful as always," Tynlar said dryly. "We will meet at the fete?"

"As Sul wills. It was a pleasure to meet you Sea Father. Tae."

Once Sevitah and Farthal left, Rosen asked, "First and Seventh?"

"A tired jest for those who can speak Sulanilish but have no respect for the language."

Rosen thought of the name, then understood. The first syllables of her birth and root names sounded like "one" and "seven" respectively. He assumed the circumstance of acquiring this nickname was more interesting than the feebleness of the quip.

Rosen took a sip of his goblet. It was golden brandywine. "A bit strong," he said.

"She's Sula. Anything less and she'd mock me for serving water."

"What a model relationship of respect and trust."

"It was fraught one time. Remember the tale of the patrol officer who tried to cite me for dumping?"

"Because a green crew accidentally tipped a couple of barrels into the harbor?"

"Yes. That was Sevitah. It had to go before a tribunal because neither of us could be read properly for our rage-filled thoughts. Afterwards? Well, what can you do except pour it into the sea. We took a libation of friendship and have been like sisters since. Quarreling sisters occasionally…"

Rosen nodded. The libation. He and Galen should do that. They could put it all behind them…

"Your thoughts seem heavy," Tynlar said. "Do you wish to unburden them?"

Rosen looked up from his wine. They were friends but he was uncertain what to share.

"Or perhaps we should retire," Tynlar offered. "The wine is strong and dawn comes soon."

"Yes it does." Suddenly Rosen knew what he wished to speak about. "I think I will be removed from command when we return to Tyrum."

Tynlar looked shocked. "Don't be ridiculous. Make no mistake it was ill considered and I do wish you had locked your cabin before letting Galen… well, as you say. But if every captain was removed from command for ill considered trysting, there would be no fleet!"

"No, not that," Rosen said. "It's much more serious."

And he told her what happened with the Shari prisoner.

Rosen felt Tynlar's mood; she was sympathetic of course, but was a committed disciplinarian. He couldn't expect her to offer empty comforting words. The best to expect was, seeing he'd taken responsibility, she wouldn't need to drive it home further. Tynlar knew there was no need to salt the wound.

When he finished, Tynlar asked, "What has Tresmadore said?"

"She's allowing me to stay in command until we return."

Tynlar nodded. "You know, she hates the Shari."

"I think most of the fleet does now."

"No, she's hated them for years. I don't know entirely why, but when she served on a merchant vessel in her youth, it's said she saw things. I suspect that is where her sympathy comes from. But expect none from the Admiralty. Honestly, some mothers look for reasons to remove men from command. And you have given them more than Manweth has."

Rosen's head snapped up. "Manweth? Whatever did Manweth do?" In Rosen's mind it was impossible for Manweth to shirk his duty.

Tynlar smiled wryly. "Like a mother, he abandoned his post to save his wife's daughter."

"What?"

"It was after *The Oaken Blue* fell. He dove into the water. It wasn't necessary, the divers were already there. His feelings overrode his duty. Any mother might have been tempted. But in my experience, the judges in the Admiralty are less impressed by a mother's urges in a man. I am not judging you or Manweth, just being honest about what you should expect."

Though it smote him, Rosen was grateful. This was why he spoke with Tynlar: she would tell him the truth of any situation. Now he knew and could prepare. He would serve as best he could until they returned, and then he must expect to be dismissed. Perhaps he would have the sympathy of the court. He hoped for that at least, not so much for himself as his household.

"I'm sorry, friend," Tynlar said.

Rosen shook his head. "No. War has harmed many more worse than me. However justified I felt, I brought this on myself. I have no regret it is dead, only that I did it contrary to my duty."

"It would have been for the cull in any case. For that I'm annoyed with you for not thinking clearly. Such are the passions of Amer and why war is to be avoided. Will you return to *The Tidebreaker*? You may stay, my cabin is large enough."

Rosen realized how tired he truly was. "My crew should be signaled," he said yawning. "Yes, I'll accept your hospitality. But I should leave before dawn."

They talked a little while longer of nothing in particular before Rosen, after removing his boots and coat, took a blanket and settled down to sleep on the seat below the gallery windows. Tynlar shuttered the lamp. The last thing Rosen saw before dreams were the warm glittering lights of the city-ships swaying in the harbor, rising to merge seamlessly with the stars in the night sky.

After an indeterminate while, Rosen woke in dreaming and found himself standing in a great hall through which a white queen's road ran. Improbably, the hall was filled with a forest of trees, and at the zenith of the domed ceiling was a round window of solstone, like many palaces and ancient buildings that still stood in Ta Meloshok. Rosen had never visited the capitol city, but he knew from books and paintings what the palace looked like. As he wandered down the road he became aware he wasn't alone.

Tynlar walked by his side as did her friend the pony sized Thyn wolf, GaTHu.

"Is this the ancient palace?" Rosen asked. Both he and Tynlar wore casual civilian garb of bracs and tunics.

"It is a palace," Tynlar said. "A memory shared in the dream of many minds of what they imagine the palace looks like."

"But surprisingly accurate," Glenfar put in. She looked exactly as she did in waking but did not wear the hat or veil, her white blond hair flowing freely. "Apart from the trees. Like in simple dreams, it feels like the palace because it's meant to be. And it seems most of the fleet is present."

Rosen looked around and this seemed to be true. The walls of the palace faded in and out, sometimes becoming mist over an ocean, then bleeding back into stone. Above, the roof had the same property, parts of it fading so that stars shone through. Through the round window a red star shined brighter than most, but did not twinkle. A ghost of a blood stained woman in ancient armor hovered near the star. She reached out with a gauntleted hand to a shaggy beast, also walking the celestial ways. It snarled as she tried to grasp its tail, a great bear who stood on her hind legs and roared under the guiding star of the north. It was a vision, but Rosen didn't understand it's meaning. Amer and constellation of the Bear Mother were rarely close in the sky. The vision faded and the roof of the palace hall was filled with hovering forms wrapped in tendrils of light, at first too bright to look at. They resolved themselves into elfyn in misty robes shining with starlight, their fantastic headdresses twined out of pure light.

"I've met them before!" Rosen exclaimed. "They told me they are elfyn but I wondered if it was just a simple dream!"

"They are the Twilight," Farthal said. Rosen almost didn't recognize her without her cavalier garb. She was on a dappled white and gray horse. Rosen wanted to know more but Galen appeared.

"I was having a pleasant dream," she growled. "Then I woke up to into this magi inspired fete."

"Don't blame us!" Glenfar said. "Some source of essence is folding the dreamtime."

"Yes," Ta Athine said, the ship's adept of the late *The Oaken Blue.* "Sel, the matron of our order, is not called Selis of the Fold for naught. A singular soul wielding a powerful source of essence is bending our minds to it, drawing sleeping minds…down to Eurthantal?"

This last ended as a question. As soon as Athine said it two things happened:

First a great light appeared below Rosen's feet, below everyone's feet, the ground they stood on in dreams turning as transparent as water. This light came from the earth, like the sun shining out of the Source that fed all life that birthed from Eurath. At the same time, above them, where Sul would shine over the solstone window at high noon, the light from the Source was reflected a thousand times. Then the light changed shape, taking the form of the symbol of Eurath, a flaming quartered circle, brighter than a flintsun. A feeling of openness and connection swept over them all, something Rosen had only known briefly at times in his life: when his hound passed through the Door; on the best days of piloting in the brightest sun; the first time he'd been taken by a woman. And yet the feeling was more than all of these together, a pure spiritual bliss. A new vision appeared, replacing the sign of Eurath, a messenger of Sul from legend, as they were depicted in art during the Age of Light, a flaming being with two pairs of wings, sent from Sul's fiery country plains to speak directly to their souls.

But the words were obscure, coming from a great distance. Still they touched their hearts and they understood: they all, mothers and men, were sisters and brothers under the rule of Sul, birthed by Eurath, nurtured by Maer. As children of the Mother Gods they had this in common with all life in Ta Pangeal. And it seemed that, with this message of fraternity and hope, there was also a rebuke for falling to the temptations of war. Finally they heard some of the spirit words, so powerful they made a soul quake:

– FOR WE ARE THE ANGEL CORATTA AND THIS IS OUR REVELA-TION TO THE EARTH: WE ARE ALL AVATAR'S OF HER SOURCE AND THE TIME THAT THOU SHOULDST DEPEND ON OUR BODY FOR WISDOM IS COMING TO A CLOSE IN THE EONS TO COME. IT WILL TAKE EACH OF US AS AN AVATAR OF HER GRACE TO BIRTH A BET-TER WORLD. IT WILL TAKE EACH OF OUR SOUL'S WISDOM TO MAKE A BETTER WAY. KNOW IN ALL YOUR WORKS AND SPORT, IN ALL YOUR SORROWS AND JOYS, THAT YOU WERE BIRTHED OF GOD

THE MOTHER AND SHE IS THE SOURCE OF ALL WISDOM AND HOPE WHATEVER THE EVENTS OR TIMES –

As they felt the Door open, a singing echoed so sharp and true they would dream about it at times throughout their lives. And the name they heard that echoed through them would be remembered for eons, though they knew not yet who it was: Coratta.

Then the Door closed and the light faded. The multitude drifted away, falling back into sleep, or waking slowly, savoring the feeling of the divine, some souls weeping as they felt joy unknown since childhood. Long would people speak of this night, even those in the Orb who had been awake felt moved. Many would forever envy those who had seen the messenger with their dreaming eyes. Before Rosen woke he saw Her Humble Majesty as he had never seen her in life, clad in shimmering scale armor, the dragon helm on her brow. She stood under where the messenger appeared, her aura so strong she herself glowed like a small star. Waves of sadness touched Rosen amidst the wonder as a hand reached up to where the Door had been.

"Farewell friend," he heard the queen say. "We will not forget."

Magi and scholars would walk in dreams trying to divine the path of the messenger and from whence she came with conflicting results. Some thought she was an Aeon who had passed over, but no Aeon was recorded in the Federation to have died exactly on that night. Others said it was a magi swept away while traveling the stars. But again, the order knew of no soul missing. Others, the Literalists, who were few in modern society, took what they saw as proof that the Mother Gods did exist and renewed their search for more evidence in the texts of ancient poets. Eventually the truth would be found, but would only be shared with the wisest for it put many in the Orb at risk. For now it was enough to accept they had been blessed to share a great vision reaffirming their collective duty to the Orb. When Rosen woke, he felt as if he had been reborn and he could look at the world with fresh eyes. Even knowing his fate, his heart was lighter, and he believed he could bear anything knowing that he did not bear it alone.

And so in the early hours, bidding a drowsy Tynlar farewell, Rosen returned to *The Tidebreaker* just as the rosy light of dawn touched the horizon. It would be a grand day. The dream had brought hope and fellowship into their souls, confirming the faith Gashora had put in the Tyreens. The city was saved, the enemy defeated, and for better or ill, all would come to account, under an honest sun.

Continued in

Sulamar
Part 3

Glossary

Military Ranks

Tyreen Navy	Federation Host	Cavalry Host
	FM-Field Marshal	
Adm-Admiral	Gen-General	
Com-Commodore	Maj-Major	
FCom-Fleet Commander		
Capt-Captain (pilot)	Capt-Captain	Capt-Captain
CaptS-Captain (standing)		
LtP-Lieutenant copilot		
Lt-Lieutenant	Lt-Lieutenant	Lt-Lieutenant
En-Ensign	En-Ensign	Ct-Cornet
Mid-Midship		
RO-Ranks Officer	Msgt-Master Sergeant	
	Sgt-Sergeant	Sgt-Sergeant
AC-Able Crew	Cpl-Corporal	L-Lancer
S-Sea Crew	Ft-Footer	

List of Characters, Places & Terms

A'Yinomehey: The Bereft of the Forest. See: Yino.

Ach-lune: Meer escort, leader of the Shoal Guard

Achalep - Olympic styles games, once every 20 years

Aefan, Niamh Ni: (capt) Sea Mother [The Quicken]

Aelg: elfborn. Anyone with both elfyn and humyn ancestry.

Aelgyn: category in scholarship describing hominid races with vocal language in the Orb: Elfyn, Humyn, Orukyn. Aelg are sometimes included, but are more accurately a cultural group.

Aeon: an old, essence powerful elfyn individual, usually 500 years or older.

Aeryn: Blue diver [Tidebreaker]

Aftcastle: raised deck at the aft, stern deck

Age of Light, AL: reckoning from the first Sunqueen to the abdication of HSM Daris.

Agha: Shari address of respect.

Ahlool: marine captain, Arlesh yal Ahlool [Tidebreaker]

Ai: common expression of acknowledgment and agreement. Used informally for "yes".

Aiyn: formal, ritual or legal form of affirmation.

Akren, Aleth: the elected Mayor of Tyrum, or Amynvar

Akren, Gayinsi: consort to Aleth Akren

Al-ahat: the ancient god of rains and plenty worshiped by humyn of the Fertile Basin for centuries. Recently in Sharitan, elevated as the sole deity in the monotheistic patriarchal cult of the Ever Sky.

Al-Swenthia: highland pastoral steppes of the Mother Continent

Alansatal: the south east province of the Sulani Federation.

Albini: humyn in Cambrian highlands. Culture is much like Scots

Aldweth, Sorani: (En) clerk [Tidebreaker]

Aldwyn, Tentynlar "Tynlar":captain and Sea mother [Charred Bronze]

Aledan, Braille: (Lt) Gold; Deck officer [Black Seal]

Alharn, Talyn: healer, surgeon [Tidebreaker]

Alhern, Selind: (Maj)Commander of Falls Gate Keep

Alhern, Sethshorn "Seth": lover of Elderyn Farthal.

Allia: large ornamental flower in the onion family

Altans: mountain range in the center of the Mother Continent.

Ama: Informal word for mother. Used like "mum" or "mom".

Amador: loan horse of Elderyn Farthal

Amenrah: name of the alphabet in Sulanilish and Hiltekash. Taken from the first letters.

Amenram: var. Amenrah

Amer: planetary Orb of Mars.

Ameram: also, Amer, Mother-God of War in elfyn mythology.

Amerlings: "Reapers of Souls", legendary figures who stand at the threshold of the Door after death to divide the worthy souls from the unworthy.

Amethia: sub arctic land north of Cambria

Amiantal, Ta: (The Mother Land): name of the Mother Continent.

Amloth: descendants of ammonites, cuttlefish with giant spiral shells.

Amphermones: elfyn pheromones that advertise sex and sexual compatibility. Could explain why there is negligible sexual dimorphism, at least with the terrestrial tribes.

Amralan: (En) ship's secretary [Oaken Blue]

Amynvar: a mayor, usually head of a city or town council.

An: elfyn word for "one".

Aqi (Aqila): Bedu slave girl.

Aqua: sea glass formed on the ocean bed from the Dying Star's impact. Imbued with water-essence.

Ardenweld, Jorun: purser [Tidebreaker]

Ardenweld, Teled: consort of Jorun Ardenweld

Ardhen: Dwen, mast crew [Tidebreaker]

Arlesh yal Ahlool: marine captain, [Tidebreaker]

Armeel yal Lath: diving school herder [Starshard]

Ash-lime: cement

Aslynari yal Mathrisash: son of the Meer Emissary

Aspect: ritual makeup used by the ancient monarchy to show their mood to the public. Retained in theater and domestic service.

Astalyn: Helix Star. Ancient symbol of the Er and regarded as the symbol of the collective Elfyn tribes.

Ath: (snake) one of the two major rivers in the Sulani Federation.

Atham, Athum: the planetary Orb, Uranus. Named after Athmod.

Athine, Ta: magi, Ship's Adept [Oaken Blue],

Athlantal: The lands on the surface of the Orb.

Athmod: Disgraced Mother-God of shape-shifting and chaos. In early myths she is a trickster deity, Athmod the Dancer. Only later does she becomes venal and malicious. Beheaded by Jaro for her crimes. Athmod's head was then cast into the Void.

Auroch: Cambrian cattle

Avatar, Our Holy: ruler of the Eurthantian Empire.

Avigon(Afeegon): Mythical city in the center of Eurath.

Azhin: resident, usually humyn, of Azhinazu. Humyn Azhins are related to Waudans. Ancient Azhins of the Pharon culture were the first rulers of Tamask.

Azhinazu: land in the south of the Mother Continent, covered with jungle.

Banat, Carredeth: Ship's cook [Black Seal]

Bane: myth: demonic host threating the Orb in the early Days of Life. Metaphors for Evil. Also, a slur against Eurthani invaders.

Barada: River in Sharitan.

Barkcloth: a Dwen fabric.

Barley-mead: the most popular beverage in the Sula Federation, barley-mead dates from the first settlements on the Bright Plains. It is brewed like mead, from a 50/50 mix of honey and barley malt sugar. Ale-mead is a cheap substitute of ale mixed with mead; it is illegal to sell ale-mead as barley-mead.

Bawn (Ní Ban), Tracan: (LtC) copilot [Tidebreaker]

Bazhar, Honn: (Capt) Sea Mother of the The Pied Gryphon,

Bazhel: butler serving the admiral's household. Cousin of admiral

Beakhead: fore of a ship including the bowsprit and figurehead.

Bedu: indigenous tribes living in the deserts and wilds of Sharitan. Often exploited by the Sultan. Similar to Bedouin.

Been, Isle of: island just east of Tyrum dedicated to shipbuilding. Sounds like "bean".

Belshorn, Honerat: (Capt) Sea Mother, buddy of Tamnath. [Exalted Unicorn],

Bereft, The: one of many names for the Yino or Wildlings, descendants of those displaced from their ancestral forest lands after the God Storm of 999 YL.

Besh: coastal city in the Ethynsul

Bicorn: cockled naval hat worn by officers.

Bindi: decorative dot worn in the center of the forehead by Indus tribes.

Black Ramothyn, The: Tyreen city-ship that circumnavigated the Orb in 2590YL.

Bledwyn, Aileen (Nion): Ship's prefect, surgeon [Oaken Blue]

Blue: slang for aelg with strong Meer ancestry, usually blue skinned.

Bluestrike: magical discharge from Eurthani weapons.

Borcht: humyn dish from east Amethia, a type of pickle beet and sour cream salad.

Bornald, Fanai: (Capt) Sea Mother [Ta Jaro]

Boudai, Tigh: Gael name for the public house the Cup and Pearl

Boudicci: publican of the Cup and Pearl, or Tígh Boudaí

Bracs: trousers of heavy linen or hemp cloth worn for heavy work and recreation. Based on a Cambrian garment *bracci*. Usually brown or black in the Federation, stripped or plaid in Cambria.

Brandubh: chess-like Cambrian board game of skill.

Bratt, Hilla: Strikemaster [Starshard]

Brawlyn, Elush: (Lt) deck officer [Oaken Blue]

Braz, Tellon: Striker [Tidebreaker]

Bright Plains, The: lands settled by the Sulani after migrating from the forest.

Bronuede, Dagmar Ni: Cambari owner of the only print shop in Tyrum; wife of Manweth Lanash (o Bronuede)

Bronuede, Dagmath Bronuede: (Lt) Strikemaster [Oaken Blue]

Bronwen "Bron" merch Cerran: Cambari/Prithi mercenary, volunteer[Tidebreaker].

Brother: euphemism for a homosexual male. Often a target of fetish obsessed women, but not considered a threat to society.

Cambari: Aelg of Cambrian humyn ancestry, usually weak in active essence.

Cambria: territory in the north west of the Mother Continent occupied by humyn tribes.

Carn: Lancer from Falls Gate

Castan: Crewmaster's mate [Tidebreaker]

Castelyn: a ship companion [Tidebreaker]

Cataclysm, The: extinction level event about 25,000 years ago caused by the Dying Star.

Cathan: Maritime humyn city on the north coast of Nomclar. Under the Sultan's rule.

Cathead: on a ship, a timber protruding from the top side of the hull used to raise and lower the anchor

City-Ship: aqua driven ships built originally for ocean exploration, used as warships when needed.

Coal: always means charcoal

Coit: technical word for sexual intercourse in elfyn languages. Not offensive.

Coiting: to coit

Col: Colm mac Fionnbarra ó Síoran

Colm "Col" mac Fionnbarra ó Síoran: Cambari Gael scholar/warrior. Lover of Pearl Sharol. Sulanized form: Colm Nisheeran ó Bharr. Note "Ni Síoran" has been fossilized, like women with the surname "Macdonald."

Colmar: Gael tourist, cousin of Fearghan mac Briggia

Command: government body that manages all the Federation Armed Forces

Consort: a married man.

Coraco-Aniadan: Sula elfyn song to wake the dead at dawn.

Coratta: mysterious Eurthani dream messenger.

Crèche, The: complex in an institution that includes a crèche and other amenities, especially in a military base.

Crèche: a place in an estate house or town block where children below school age are managed while mothers work.

Crewboy: man serving in the Tyreen or Federation navy, usually in the junior ranks; also, generally any male deck hand

Crewgirl: woman serving in the Tyreen or Federation navy, usually in the junior ranks; also, generally any female deck hand

Crewmaster(Boatswain): manages crew on a ship

Crownland: Startolthia

Cup and Pearl, The: public house catering to Cambrian culture.

Curach: Cambrian boat, usually with a hide over a frame

Daiyasu: King Consort to Her Humble Majesty

Dame: ruling matriarch of an estate, usually the grandmother or great grandmother of the present generation. But she may abdicate and retire, either appointing a daughter or sister. If not, management of the estate might fall to a vote among eligible mothers.

Dameryn: young Sula noblewoman in service to the Exiles palace

Danshor, Hanmet(L): cavalier, close friend of Elderyn Farthal.

Darav Ormaz Damaski: The Sultan of Sharitan

Dawn Country, The: old name for the wild, explored lands in the northeast, near the Altan range.

Day Sea, The: also The East West Day Sea; largest ocean of Eurath. Because of the placement of land masses, the Day-Sea, at it's widest, is almost 2/3 the circumference of the Orb.

Desmet, Olesh: (Lt) Strike captain [Tidebreaker]

Diar: Gael druid living near Dunvan

Disincration: powerful essence operation that temporarily removes essential elements from an object, resulting in complete collapse.

Djinn: fire spirits in humyn legend. Also used as a slur for elfyn or elf magic.

Djinn, Port Of: Jaret Harbor.

Door, The: the place in dreaming through where a soul's consciousness passes after death.

Doyera: Blue, diver [Tidebreaker]

Drake: an alluring, attractive man.

Dreamchanger: doppelganger, particularly by a dreaming predatory soul.

Dreamchildren: elfyn conceived by two souls trysting in dreams, with no physical contact. Such souls are known to be essence powerful.

Drothmey: Ensign [Black Seal]

Druai: See Eurthani

Druzanthia: ancient name for Eurthantal

Dunvan: Dún Bhéal (fortress at the mouth) largest city in Cambria

Dwen: Dwenifee.

Dwenhilish: dialect of elfyn used by Dwen.

Dwenifee: Elfyn with active wood-essence. There are three main tribes: Oak, Ash and Red. Oak Dwen tend to be "tannin complected", with light tan to dark skin and variegated blond, red, brown or black hair, an effect called "roan". Ash Dwen have pale silver gray to gray skin, and long fine ash to black hair. Red Dwen have a red-tan hue and thick black hair. All Dwen have green eyes.

Dwenoshire, Ta: the forest nation to the north of the Sulani Federation.

Dying Star, The: meteor or small asteroid that caused the Cataclysm , See also, Grimstar.

Edryn, Cauld: Master Navigator [Oaken Blue].

Effa: term of respect for a man in Sulanilish.

Eirok: Luserani

Eladryshorn, Loethryn: Admiral in the Her Shining Majesty Fleet during the Age of Light.

Eladwol, Borthyn: (LtC) copilot [Tidebreaker]

Elam: Sulanilish and Hiltekash word for "thank you".

Elf: informal word for an individual, usually female, though plural can be for mixed company. Used like "guy" in Modern English.

Elfborn: aelg

Elfling: common way non-Aelgyn Thyn address elfyn.

Elfyn: dominant Aelgyn race in the Orb. Elfyn are physically distinguished by accented ears and eyebrows, greater strength and speed, and average 6 ft/2m. tall. They are androgynous to humyn eyes; elfyn rely more on amphermones than dress and customs to seek mates; individual elfyn identity is primarily based on essence not gender or skin hue; these are considered "roles for a life". Elfyn essence vigor makes them immune to most disease resulting in slow aging and long life. Elfyn are genetically telepathic but only a small segment of the population develops this skill for practical use. It is difficult for an elfyn to pass off a lie even with each other, and nearly impossible for elfyn to be deceived by humyn. Elfyn also can travel in dreams as if in waking. This might be a side effect of native telepathy, but some humyn are known to dreamwalk so scholarship is uncertain.

Ellushia The Starry Blessed: myth; Daughter of Jaro of the Dawn by Lun. Credited with building the first civilization of mothers on the Bright Plains.

Emha: term of respect for a woman in Sulanilish.

Er: history/myth: ancient elfyn city destroyed by the Cataclysm.

Erhilish: oldest known language of the elfyn people. Few samples survive.

Eshela Yal Makhaul: (corp) marine [Tidebreaker]

Essence: technical word for magic, magical force.

Estate: the buildings, properties and concerns run by a family, descended from, and inherited through, the female line. A basic institution of Sula culture, estates are the largest contributors to the economy.

Etheric Metal: legend? Essence concentrated metallic liquid or vapor used in Er to create planetary magical works. It's making is lost to scholarship and some dispute it's existence outside of legend.

Ethynsul: West Province of the Sulani Federation.

Eurath: myth; Mother-God of the planetary Orb all life depends on. Also elfyn word for the planetary Orb.

Eurthan: Eurthani

Eurthani: Elfyn who can manipulate stone and metal. In appearance they have skin tones in all the colors of the earth, from alabaster white to onyx black. North Shindi tend to be darker than Deep Druai. Hair varies as wildly as skin hue, black, gray, brassy and white, and tends to have a metallic shimmer compared to other elfyn. Eyes are red, yellow, amber, green or blue and always glow from active earth-essence.

Eurthanilish: indigenous Eurthani language. Has been replace by Druzan, an argot based on Eurthanilish.

Eurthantal: the subterranean lands of the Orb.

Eurthantian Empire, The: Eurthan theocratic expansionist state ruled by Our Holy Avatar.

Eurthantian: of Eurthantal.

Evarain, Saphin: (Lt) deck officer [Oaken Blue]

Eyrie: Luserani community or settlement on mountain cliffs

Fadwen, Aflelett:(RO) woodweaver [Tidebreaker]

Faithbourn: Blue, male diver [Tidebreaker]

Falls Gate Keep: the garrison near Falls Gate.

Falls Gate: township on the border of the Sulani Federation and Dwensohire.

Fanswar: a send off ceremony in Tyrum for ships going on important voyages. Also, an informal send off for any sea journey.

Farni: crewboy managing male volunteers, [Tidebreaker]

Farthal, Elderyn(Eld)(L): cavalier in the Federation Host, Lancer.

Farthal, Shedann: son of Elderyn Farthal.

Farthal, Traith: daughter of Elderyn Farthal.

Fati: informal word children address their mother's married consort involved in their upbringing. May or may be their sire.

Fay: marginalized cultural group who live in Eurthantal. Descendants of Athlantian elfyn pressed into slavery millennia ago, mostly of Dwen ancestry. Most fay have pale white skin very similar to a human from northern Cambria and blue or green eyes. Eurthani ancestry gives many of them white hair; those with more recent Eurthan blood have eyes that glow with active earth-essence.

Feargal: Gael tourist

Fearghan: Fearghan mac Briggia, Gael tourist

Felkan: the planetary Orb Saturn. Named after Felkeni.

Felkeni: Goddi of fate, fortune and luck consorted with the Mother-God Myngar.

Felkinoc: clay votive stone made by ancient settlers of the Bright Plains, usually impressed with the astalyn. Considered lucky.

Fenras ó Síoran: uncle of Colm mac Fionnbarra ó Síoran

Fionnal mac Fionnbarra: sire of Colm mac Fionnbarra ó Síoran

Fiorseth: dappled white and gray cavalry horse assigned to Elderyn Farthal.

Firelance: farm and crafting tool using sulessence, similar to an army lance, but not as powerful.

First Fire: elfyn puberty, around the 8th decade.

Fish: slang for Blue aelg. Can be a slur.

Flintstar: Flintsun

Flintsun: stylized heraldic sun on the Federation flag.

Flout: metal or leather cone holding a rider's ponytail on the top of her head, perched like an erect horse's tail. A distinctive cavalry military fashion. Vaguely resembles an inverted funnel. Also worn by Tyreen marines.

Fluorescence: sulessence discharge in a Sula aura.

Flyer: Luserani, especially one using a wing for travel. See WING

Freya Merch Mathweni: Cambari/ Prithi mercenary, volunteer[Tide-breaker]

Gaels, Gael: humyn tribe in Cambria similar to the ancient Irish . Also, language of the same, represented by modern Irish (Gaeilge).

Gains: popular trick taking card game played with a deck of 98 cards: 5 suits of 14 cards, plus 28 trump cards. The suits are darts, orbs, lunats, rubies and clovers. The trump picture cards are sometimes used by superstitious men in fortunetelling.

Gallens-Farthal: Full name and title of the Farthal estate but not used in modern times.

Gallens: Ancestral stream of Gallens- Farthal.

Gallowglass: Gael mercenary.

Galyn, Loran: (LtC) copilot [Tidebreaker]

Garden of Lun, Garden: night parties run by Temples of Lun for people to meet and tryst anonymously.

Gashora: large cosmopolitan city on the south coast of the Federation.

Gashoreen: of Gashora, also a resident.

Gate Step: village near Falls Gate Keep.

Gathelyn, Roselyni "Rosen": (Capt) Sea Father [Tidebreaker]

Gathelyn, Therald Gathelyn: Tyreen council auditor. Sea Father Rosen's mother

Gathelyn, Trezmen: Rosen's sister

GaTHu: Thyn-wolf from Dwenoshire, close friend of Tentynlar Aldwyn

Gelenethwait, Salin: (Capt) Sea Mother [The Lunat]

Gerindis, Nan: (Lt) deck officer [Oaken Blue]

Glendwol, Loran: (Lt) deck officer, orlop [Tidebreaker]

Glenfar, Ta: young magi [Tidebreaker]

Glethlyn, Becan:(1st Lt) Copilot [Tidebreaker]

Glimmer: a cosmetic made of finely ground solstone and pigment.

God Storm, The: hurricane event in 999 YL that devastated the west coast of the Sulani nation.

Goddi: myth; a male deity, usually consorted with a Mother-God.

Gold: slang for aelg of strong Sul descent or with Sula features. Also used by Dwen and Yino for any Sula.

Grimstar: Dying Star

Grimsteel(Grim): a crystalline black metal with green and blue inclusions composed primarily of meteoric iron exposed to an essence source in the distant past. In the Athlantal found scatted on high mountains and plains. Also found in the deep ocean near the Cambrian Basin and the probable impact zone of the Dying Star. In Eurthantal it is much more abundant.

Gryphon: essence powerful Thyn living east of the Altans. Reportedly have the heads and wings of black eagles with a powerful lion-like body.

Guardlock(s): bound hair to either side of the face in Sula fashion, particularly in the trilock style.

Hadi az Daria: Hadi of the Sea. SEE, Parviz, Hadi

Hadrin: (Sgt) cavalier in charge of the Marshal's escort

Haj: hooded shoulder cape worn by Brownie professional women

Hak: elfyn word for nonsense, crap, or excrement. Mildly offensive.

Hal Suldan: Sula winter solstice festival. Second biggest Federation holiday.

Haldwynshor: a Dwen city.

Halgyn: Surname of the monarchy in exile. SEE: Her Humble Majesty

Hallault: Former wooed of Rosen Gathelyn

Hanno: Cathan sailor.

Haranshor: valet to Her Humble Majesty

Hastol: decorative crown-like headdress worn by Sula men based on the Dwen yastol.

Haulet, Remard (yal Rooth): Blue (LtC) copilot [Tidebreaker]

Heefa, Ti: King consort

Hefamia, Ta: the Sunqueen, currently stylized as Her Humble Majesty.

Helanault: Captain of the Tyreen City Guard

Helix: military slang for an officer.

Helper: informal, from: house helper. Consort of the house, usually married.

Her Humble Majesty(HHM): The Sunqueen, currently Sesilmyn Argreev Falcinin Hoeth Orvanae Halgyn. Though the monarchy does not rule, they are still the head of state and enjoy celebrity throughout the nation.

Heron, Ta: magi Ship's Adept [Black Seal]

Hethlion, Ta: Aeon magi [Tidebreaker]

Hiltekash: trade language based on Sulanilish, with elements of Dwenhilish, Aelgyn dialects, and Gael and Shari loanwords.

Himli: Cathan sailor.

Holastine, Tharn: also Ta Tharn. Scholar, was a victor in the Sularun during her youth.

Hood: slang for a self-centered, obnoxious woman.

Host, The: the assembled forces of an army.

Hothyn: Sulanilish for "dragon".

Hound: deputy of the Hound's Master.

Hound's Master: equivalent to a sheriff in rural lots.

House-girl: female servant working under a butler. Duties include serving at meals, and tending to the needs of the mothers of a house, residence or estate.

Humyn: Aelgyn closely related to Elfyn but less strong physically and mentally, and with low essence vigor. While humyn have no active essence, individuals have been known to develop passive essence becoming shamyn, druids and holy women/men among their peoples. Such individuals often can dreamwalk. But having a lifespan of barely a century, few humyn master these skills in time to accomplish much with them. Due to low essence vigor humyn are susceptible to a variety of disease. Care should be taken with livestock around unknown humyn tribes.

Hybernat: Shari word for barbarian tribes in the distant northwestern lands of gloom.

Indri: Shari woman of Indus ancestry, close to Komar Zan.

Indus: humyn tribes or nations east of Sharitan, near the south of the Altan range. Physically and culturally resemble Indians from the Vedic Period.

Isenatti: Prithi tribe in east Cambria

Jaffa: indentured Shari oardriver.

Jansenwol, Jonan: eldest daughter of the admiral

Jansenwol, Farthan: daughter of the admiral

Jansenwol, Gemal: daughter of the admiral

Jansenwol, Jonsaymanor "Jonsay": (Adm) admiral of the Tyreen fleet. [Oaken Blue]

Jansenwol, Oni: adolescent son of the admiral

Jansenwol, Tergani: (Ta Tergani) consort of the admiral. Trained magi.

Jaret Harbor: Sula merchant harbor near Jareth. Called the Port of Djinn by locals.

Jareth: coastal township in Sharitan.

Jaro of the Dawn: Hero of the Elfyn people. In Sula myth she is the semi divine daughter of Sul, born at dawn to live among the mothers of the Orb to guide and inspire them. Also, the constellation Ophiuchus.

Jarroth, Tocyn: (En) ensign and student pilot [Tidebreaker]

Jasmenal, Sonan: Master Sailor and Navigator. Also a trained pilot. [Tidebreaker]

Jeddah: bay along coastal Sharitan, near Jareth.

Jolarund:(CaptP) officer [Oaken Blue]

Jonat, Jandin: (Capt) Sea Mother [The Sprite]

Kabir, Lamia: Shari woman, mother of Hadi az Daria.

Kalendi: man employed as cleaning knave for naval officer's apartments.

Kalhoon: Blue, diver

Keeper: informal name for a married man of a woman's house. Also can be a man hired to run domestic staff or manage child of the house. In an estate, a keeper is also a younger, lower ranking consort.

Kettle, The: kitchen in an institution, especially an army mess.

Kettle: a kitchen.

Kettleboard: planter beds for growing salad greens on voyages.

Kirtle-shirt, kirtle: shift worn by Sula men, usually ankle length and warn under a robe of contrasting colors.

Knave: male servant.

Kohl: black cosmetic pigment around the eyes.

Komar Zan: admiral of the Sharitani fleet.

Korah: a Thyn-raven

Kraken: general term for large squid or cephalopods.

Kurus: hist. Humyn general who served under King Maccadan in ancient Sharitan. Led first and only attempt to invade the Sulani Federation.

Laifmyr: (myth?) The first Sea Queen's brother who died during the Cataclysm.

Lanash, Manweth: (Capt) also Lanash o Bronuede. Sea Father. Married to Dagmar Ni Bronuede [The Starshard]

Landsbridge: unincorporated suburb of the coastal island city Tyrum.

Lant: refined urine used as a cleaning agent

Lanthorn: lantern used at sea with a hollow horn for a candle

Laysaid: dominant form of football in the Sulani Federation.

Leaf-felt: a Dwen fabric, flexible if the wearer has wood-essence.

Ledowyn: a politician.

Lekatol: Luserani flyer

Lethglean: city on the south coast of the Federation.

Light Impressions: a type of photography.

Linastola: Meridian traveler who visited Jaret Harbor.

Literalist: a person who holds theist views and beliefs, that the Mother-Gods of the Court of Heaven are real persons. Also may still hold on to discredited ideas and superstitions.

lithog

Lomastal: Howl's Peak, a hill near Gashora with ancient standing stones.

Long Winter, The: ice age triggered by the Cataclysm.

Longship: Nord vessel

Lor: honorific of the matriarch of feudal ruling estates.

Lorthensul: myth: physician of the Court of Heaven.

Lot War: an emergency vote where qualified mothers and men are volunteered by being allotted by the majority, whether they want to serve in government or not.

Lot: an area of land set aside for productive use and development, particularly agriculture. Can refer to the territory of a feudal lor. Also, a vote or the act of casting a vote.

Lun: a beautiful but aloof, high maintenance man.

Lun: myth: Goddi of the Moon, passion, dreams and magic.

Lunat: crescent moon symbol. Also a suit in a deck of playing cards.

Luserani: Elfyn who use wind-essence and kites to fly. Also called Eirok. Not frequently seen away from the mountains, but known to be thin and tall, with feather-like hair and hawk-yellow eyes.

Maccadan: Ancient humyn king who ruled over the Fertile Basin in much of what is modern Sharitan.

Madgath: friend of Fenras o Síoran

Madwol, Tethini: (LtC) copilot [Oaken Blue]

Maer: Mother-God of the Sea and Oceans. Matron deity of the Meerfee.

Maer: the planetary Orb, Neptune. Seen by the elfyn naked eye, only formally recognized as an orb in the last couple thousand years.

Maeve: daughter of Boudicci

Magi: order of wizards founded by Sunqueen Selastimor the Great to speak to the Court of Heaven. In the modern nation they are an empirical institution of magical research, teaching and discovery.

Magiath,Yeren: (Capt) Sea Mother [The Water Bull]

Maleen: Meer floating island.

Malori: former wooed of Pearl Sharol

Maral Mendasc: Falls Gate

Marked: slang for Cambari aelg, due to their abundant tattooing

Masculate: describing a mother dressing or acting in a way considered more appropriate for a male, especially if seen as frivolous or weak.

Mathrisash: Emissary of the Meer Conclave

Mathynwol, Ordryn: Ship's Prefect [Tidebreaker]

Matrician: describing a woman with a serious, authoritative aspect.

Meer Conclave: collective governing body of the Meer nation

Meerfee, Meer: elfyn with water-essence. Known to have dolphin gray skin and webbed hands and feet. All have blue eyes without tear ducts.

They are excellent singers and use echolocation. Like cetaceans, they can hold their breath for long periods. Most live in or near the ocean.

Meerhilish: Meer dialect of elfyn.

Meloshok, Ta: city near the mountain of the same name. Capitol of the Sulani Federation.

Meloshok: mountain in the center of the Sulani federation rich in solstone deposits.

Merideen: resident of Meridian

Merock: Blue, diver, volunteer [Tidebreaker]

Mert, Hocta: (LtC) copilot [Tidebreaker]

Metee: elfyn for small child. Also, term of affection.

Mistalryn: Sula professional troubadour

Mite: slang for small child, usually affectionate.

Moonchildren: elfyn conceived in dreams only with the thought and will of the mother. Often very essence powerful. They are technically magical clones.

Mordmhol, Ledranal: Captain of the navel guard on the Tidebreaker

Morthian: Tyreen Admiral, retired

Mother Culture: matrilineal and matrifocal cultures of the elfyn peoples and their nations founded by mothers and managed to prioritize mother's needs and the welfare of their children. Men, while sometimes marginalized in the public sphere, are not second-class citizens as all men are some mother's son. The exception is the Eurthantian Empire, a true matriarchy where a man has no rights separate from his mother or wife.

Mother Host: an organized block of the Federation Army Host.

Mother Tree, The: history/legend; the legendary cedar that elfyn races sheltered in to survive the Long Winter. Historically, a forest of great cedars, probably on the north and west slopes of the Altan range.

Murdan, Ta: a magi, Aeon.

Myngar: myth: Mother-God of abundance, prosperity and industry.

Myngarth: south and central province in the Federation where most grain is grown. Named after Myngar.

Mynge: the planetary orb Jupiter. Named after Myngar.

Nabi Cuanaiya, also, Nabi Cwanaiya. Sulanilish: no worries, no problem.-

Navi: See Hoethnav Roelyn

Neh: informal. Used like "nah".

Nenivey: Eurthani priest

Nesthet, Corma: (Lt) deck officer [Black Seal]

Nethers: privates, genitals.

Nit: slang for a foolish, annoying person.

Nomclar: land in the South Straits.

Nord/Nords: humyn in the territory to the far north and west of the Federation. Resemble ancient Norse.

Obscura: type of camera used to make light impressions

Oleth: Dwen archer.

Oracle Isle: Island to the west of the Federation. Last landed community before the East West Day Sea.

Orb and Rays: script developed by poets during the Age of Light.

Orb, The: the planet Eurath.

Orb: a planet. Also, a suit in playing cards.

Orenath, Doren: Midship [Tidebreaker]

Orlop: deck below the waterline of a ship

Orukyn: Neanderthal humyn.

Otherside: The Afterlife, what is beyond the Door. Can also refer to the land of true dreams.

Othmar, Talin: Ship's Prefect [Black Seal]

Othyn: dragonkind, word for dragon in the older elfyn languages. Dragons are the most powerful essence users living in the Orb. They are also the largest beings of any kind in the Orb: forest dragons average 200 feet from nose to tail; flying dragons, if standing perched on the ground, would stand at least a 100 feet high. The origin of dragons is unclear though it is known a flock of Thyngalu (flying dragons) manifested during the Cataclysm. Thyndwendesh (forest dragons) may predate the Cataclysm. There are also ocean and lava dwelling dragons. Black dragons that breath fire like Ramoth only exist in legend or dreams.

Our Avatar: also Our Holy Avatar: ruler of the Eurthantian Empire. See Avatar.

Pakut: cream liqueur made by Shindi.

Pangeal, Ta: "The Net of Time". Usually refers to all known reality. Also used to describe the known world of Eurath.

Par: elfyn word for "two".

Paragothyn: icy plains north of the Mother Continent where dragons nest.

Parviz Chabahar: Stepfather of Hadi.

Parviz, Hadi (az Daria): young Shari man seeking his father.

Payeen: myth: Sul's second child, Mother-God of wind, speed and messengers. Also called, "Quick". Matron deity of the Luserani. Also, elfyn name for the planetary orb Mercury.

Pearl Sharol: Sharol-Hauktee-Yal. Essence powerful Blue diver with very humyn figure.

Petty dragons: dinosaurs.

Picti: a humyn tribe in Cambria similar to the Picts.

Princar: title of daughter of a Queen or ruler of an ancient city-state

Prithi: a humyn tribe in Cambria, similar to the ancient Britons.

Quay Shepherd: manger of a dock.

Queen: a gold plated coin, basic denomination of currency in the Sulani Federation.

Queen's Capitol: most common script and print font in the modern Federation.

Queen's roads: network of major roadways throughout the Federation, paved with white stone or ash-lime pavers. Date from the time of the Sun-queens.

Quickening, The: the Sularun.

Quol: Month in Sula calender, roughly late May, early June.

Raffins: rambunctious near-do-wells, often adolescent girls.

Rakki: Shari archer.

Ramlachi: "Eclipse". Myth male hero and War-king. Consorted with Amer.

Ramoth: myth: legendary Black Dragon in many myths, usually with a relationship with Selis of the Fold. Also, the constellation Draco.

Rau Jethar, Ta: "Hornblower"; ceremonial parley role in the Tyreen Navy.

Rays of the Field: Also, Rays. A type of cuneiform, Rays were an early script of the Bright Plains used where pottery culture developed.

Red Kraken, The: early aqua keeled ship that drove off longship raiders.

Regular host: enlisted soldiers.

Reverie: unique to Elfyn, the ability to have visions of the future. Always true, but rarely complete, or even relevant, and dangerous to try to control.

Rhion gath Meervan: Sea Mother of the Black Ramothyn

Rhondalyn: Dwen volunteer[Black Seal]

Ringling: ring formed of wood or vine given by a Dwen woman to a man she favors causally. A Sula imitation in gold, silver or glass used like an engagement ring.

River Script: First widely adopted written script used in the Bright Plains.

Roan: In Dwen, describes the variegated shading of Oak Dwen hair. Typical colors, from crown to ends, are: red-brown, brown-black, blond-brown. The crown color is always lighter than the ends.

Roanteth, Maeven: (Capt) Sea Mother [The Sunchaser]

Roel, Camryn: (Lt) officer in Federation army host

Roelyn, Hoethnav: sulessence powerful Gold woman suspected of being full Sula, volunteer[Tidebreaker]

Ronali: Dwen knave serving in the Admiral's household

Rondaleth, Bornad: (Lt) deck officer [Tidebreaker]

ronel, Ta

Rootcord: Dwen vine used for belting garments.

Rootings: tentacle like extensions on the hull of a vessel, usually made of woodyvine.

Ruanai: Meer fisher working on Oracle Isle

Ruger: a type of rugby.

Rut: an unreliable, shiftless, or promiscuous man held in low esteem. Offensive; can be mildly obscene in context.

Sadol: circle of odd numbered menhirs used for long distance dream and audio communication. This elfyn technology has been imitated by humyn cultures without, of course, any functionality.

Samath: Gold, male volunteer [Tidebreaker]

Samhain: Cambrian New Year

Sandryn, Carvus: (LtC) copilot [Tidebreaker]

Sassy Spark: plucky, spirited youth

Savalis, Moradrin: (En) Brownie, ship's secretary [Tidebreaker]

Sea Mother: a captain pilot of a Tyreen city-ship (Sea Father is the male equivalent). Sea Mother is a unique Tyreen institution. Only in the Tyreen navy is the captain and the main pilot the same individual. Pilots of aqua driven vessels were traditionally seen to be an extension of the vessel and given the greatest authority over their management.

Sea Queen: unofficial symbol and seal of the city Tyrum.

Seadrinker: vine used to desalinate seawater.

Seahome: collection of large islands in the southern seas Meerfee use as a base.

Seand inion Morgu: Cambrian/Albini. Volunteer. [Tidebreaker]

Sel: myth: Selis of the Fold.

Selan:(LtC) copilot [Tidebreaker]

Selastimor the Great, Queen: Sunqueen who lived about 12,000 years ago at the height of the monarchy during the Age of Light. Larger than life figure credited with building the Queen's road, founding the postal system, and defensive works. Founder of the Order of Magi.

Seldan, Braun: (1st LtC) Co-pilot [Black Seal]

Selenath, Lenoran "Lenor": young Gold Sea Mother [The Fortunate]

Selimor, Colma (Uí Rosa): (Lt) Lower deck officer [Tidebreaker]

Selis of the Fold, Also Sel: myth/history In myth Selis is the foster-mother of young Jaro. She can shape shift into a dragon or is a dragon who shape shifts into a wizard. Selis is known to be based on a historic person but anything beyond dream impressions have been lost to history as she lived long before the Cataclysm or the founding of Er. Understood to be the greatest wizard that ever lived. *The Seat of Sel* = the constellation Cassiopeia.

Selkie: informal, Meer. Also seal women in Cambrian folktales

Sellisyn, Galen: Boatswain Crewmaster [Tidebreaker]

Sephus

Sernalash, Azar: Strikemaster, Brownie with strong sulessence [Tidebreaker]

Sesilmyn "Sesil": See Her Humble Majesty

Sevitah, Anglyn: (Cpt) Captain of the Federation Patrol Fleet Frigate, The Crane.

Shamyn: humyns with passive essence who can travel in true dreams.

Sharethan, Remard: Sea Mother [Meer King]

Sharitan: arid humyn country to the south of the Federation border.

Sharitani: inhabitants of Sharitan, including surrounding tribes subjugated by the Sultan. Resemble ancient Persians.

Sharkhook: Blue, diver, volunteer [Tidebreaker]

Sharmain: valley to the east of the Altan mountains

Sharol-Hauktee-Yal: Pearl Sharol

Shedann: son of Elderyn Farthal

Shindi: marginalized Eurthani cultural group who live in the Athlantal, high in the Altan range. Trade and interact frequently with Dwen.

Ship's Adept: Senior magi on a ship, usually a master adept.

Ship's Prefect: senior healer on a ship.

Sídh Mór: Gael word for Sulani elfyn

Sídh: Cambrian Gael word for fairies in their native myths. Also used for Elfyn.

Sire: biological father.

Sissy: a disparaging term for a homosexual woman. Mildly offensive.

Sister: a close female friend, buddy, chum. Can be short for War-sister. Also a euphemism for homosexual women, especially when plural.

Sithinas, Dwool: (LtC) Brownie, copilot [Tidebreaker]

Skerries, The: Cambrian islands managed as Sulani territories to keep the peace at sea.

Skyflower: blue daisy native to the Ethynsul coast

Sleath, Lusaid (yal): (Capt) Sea Mother [Helix Bow]

Slet: a slovenly man of questionable morals. Rude, but not obscene.

Snails: slang for Tyreen city guard because of their shell shaped helmets

Sol Suldan: Sula summer solstice festival. The biggest holiday celebration in the Federation.

Solcannon: a tube of solstone mounted to strike enemy forces with sun-strike.

Solglass: glass mixed or embedded with solstone powder. Commonly used for windows and skylights to extend daylight.

Solshar: elfyn name for the planetary orb Venus.

Solshari: "Bright": myth: the first child of Sul. Originally a girl, "Solshar", Solshar become masculinized to "Solshari" as the culture changed. Solshar was the Mother-God of light, hope and joy. Her role in myth was replaced by the hero, Jaro of the Dawn. Solshari is a Son of Sul, and the avatar of all masculine virtues in Sula society: beauty, modesty, grace and hospitality.

Solstone: a type of essence imbued sunstone, solstone is a pale gold, usu-ally translucent, feldspar. Found in many places the largest deposits are around and near the mountain Meloshok and the Shard Hills. Ancient Sula settlers discovered they could use solstone to extend their natural sulessence. The basis of modern Sula magical technology.

South Straits: tropical sea lanes to the south of Azhinazu and north of Nom-clar.

Sparkwit: used like "nitwit".

Spined Eel: myth: massive demonic, snake-like creature with poisonous spikes that threatened to devour the Orb. Killed by Jaro.

Sprite: elfyn child between the age of 3 and 30.

Spritehood: a developmental age after toddler-hood unique to elfyn, starting around 4 years. Elfyn acquire motor skills about the same time as humyn children, but continue to improve and take longer to develop higher mental functions and essence control unique to the race. Sprites are full of energy and may know many words but don't have a mastery of language until about 30. Most use a types of sign language; mothers rely on dreams and mind links to communicate with their children during this time.

Spriteling: sprite

Startolthia (Star-tolthia = Crownland): North and central province in the Federation. Ancient seat of the Sunqueen.

Staties: (STAT-eez) upper-class, schoolgirl slang for relatives of an estate

Strike crew: crew assigned to maintain and use solcannons and lances

Strikemaster: officer in charge of solcannon maintenance and strike crew.

Sul: the Mother-God of the Sun, matron deity of the Sulani nation.

Sula Bríd: elfyn inspired monastic communities in Cambria.

Sulamar: "Sun and Sea". Tyreen prayer, praise or cheer to the Mother-gods Sul and Maer.

Sulani/Sula: Elfyn with sulessence, the dominant ethnic group in the Sulani Federation. A typical Sula has warm, pale skin of a hue similar to a human from the north and east of the Asian continent, but with actual yellow overtones. This hue is called "Gold". Individuals can range from yellow tan to bronze, but people of strong Sula ancestry never tan; sunlight is a tonic to Sula and they are not harmed by it. They can't even be blinded, though looking too long at the sun will overwhelm a Sula's essence and produce temporary blindness. Sula eyes are shade of yellow, amber or gold, and their hair varies from white blond to dark, brassy gold.

Sulanilish: elfyn dialect of the Sulani.

Sularun, The: The Quickening a competition among youths to represent the nation at the festival in the capitol during Sol Suldan. Held once every twenty years.

Sulessence: technical word for the magical manipulation of heat and light, particularly from the sun.

Sulforce: measure of sulessence in artifacts.

Sultan, The: the ruler of Sharitan. The Sultan's government is understood to be a patriarchal caliphate.

Sunbake: baking using sunlight.

Sunblessed: food freshly cooking in sunlight. Also, water set out in sunlight.

Sunlance: military fire lance using sulessence.

Sunqueen(s): Ancient Sulani Monarchy. Founded the Commonwealth of Mothers after the fall of the feudal lors. They ruled for about 10,000 years until abdicating 6,000 years ago. Descendants, stylized as Her Humble Majesty(HHM), are still the head of state in the modern Federation.

Sunstrike: discharge from military fire lances or solcannons channeling concentration heat and light from the sun.

Sunwands: sulessence toys

Ta: definite article of most elfyn dialects. Also used to designate noteworthy persons combined with their birth name. In the past the monarch was always addressed as Ta (Her name); likely the origin of custom with magi. Sulanilish has a masculine form, "Ti", but it is not used as an honorific in the modern nation, with the exception of the King Consort. Male magi are called "Ta".

Taffelan, Nanyesh: Dwen/Brownie volunteer [Tidebreaker]

Tafl: Cambrian board game

Tagathtal, Ta: The Federation: informal name for the Sulani nations. Full name: Erdro Sulani Tagathtal -Western Sulani Federation

Tahmery, The: ancient mother culture in the region of modern Tamask. Known for it's lush gardens.

Tal-al-Amlot: port city in Sharitan.

Tal-hiK-naw: Thyn-raven

Tamask: capitol of Sharitan.

Tamidwyn, helan

Tamithryn, Mellasan: (Lt) strike captain [Tidebreaker]

Tanartham: Blue, Quay shepherd

Tantilaan, Egalsh(Gen): Field Marshal of the Federation Army.

Tantilaan,Tinyan: consort of the Field Marshal.

Taq: small round cap, worn by Brownies and Healers

Taren, Ta: magi, Ship's Adept Master Tarenol Ganith, [Tidebreaker]

Tarnoc: a coastal city in the Ethynsul province.

Tathum: ceremonial rod of foxglove twined in a helix of two serpents, the wand of Lorthensul. Also a symbol of the Temple.

Telshorn: Sula man who owns the public house in Jaret Harbor.

Temple, the: institution of healers in the modern Federation. Also, a hospital run by the same.

tenaiya

Tenes-Cambri: Subcultural group, usually Tenes who have allied with other tribes, but can also refer to elfborn.

Tenes: a humyn tribe living on the borders of Cambria and Dwenoshire. Similar to the ancient La Téne Culture.

Ter: elfyn word for "three".

Tergani (Ta): former betrothed of Egalsh Tantilaan. The most essence powerful man to graduate from the magi universities in centuries, but does not work as a wizard. Lives in Tyrum. See: Jansenwol, Tergani.

Tharn, Ta: See Holastine, Tharn

Theedween: myth: son of Eurath, Goddi of the Forest, patron deity of the Dwenifee.

Thrund: myth, Goddi of caves, vaults and passages. Called the Drummer in early myths. Consorted with Eurath. Also, tentative name for a planetary orb speculated by magi to have a path beyond Maer.

Thyn: scholarship: category of living beings with intelligence and language. Includes Aelgyn, Othyn(dragonkind), and animal counterparts with elfyn intelligence. Not all animals have Thyn; the most common are: ravens, wolves, elk, otters and whales.

Thynamar: Dragons of the Seas.

Thyndwendesh: Dragons of the Forest.

Thyngalu: Dragons of the Air. Can "breathe" lightening.

ToKeh: A Thyn-raven.

Torc: thick neck ring of twisted wire worn by Cambrian tribes.

Torshad: a rude parrot, pet of Lenoran Selenath.

Tosslon, Solet:(Capt) Sea Mother [The Leviathan]

Touch of Lun: a woman with amphermones so strong she can physically arouse compatible souls. Can be mistaken for love with the young or inexperienced. Can not compel someone to coit, but is very hard to resist in the woman's presence.

Traith: daughter of Elderyn Farthal.

Traveler: a type of sandwich on a long roll of cut bread, usually making a good sized meal. Can also refer to Yino.

Tree: slang for Dwen.

Treeriders: Dwen who use a tree for locomotion.

Treerunner: a Dwen messenger or scout.

Treesilk: fabric manufactured in Dwenoshire made from wood waste. Similar to rayon.

Tresmadore, Bornath: Tamnath's aunt

Tresmadore, Talinault: daughter of Tamnath Tresmadore

Tresmadore, Tamnath 'Tam':(Com) Sea Mother and Fleet Commodore [The Black Seal]

Tri-oar: trireme style ship used by the Sharitan Navy

Triad: the smallest usable sadol of three stones. Also, an Eurthan weapon.

Tricklers: informal; taking an interest in gambling and wagers.

Tricolor: flag of Tyrum, blue, green and white, though usually white is at the top.

Trilocks: common Sula hair style of dividing the hair into three parts: sides and back. The back may hang loose while the guardlocks are bound in thong, ribbons or clips. Worn by women and men.

Tuiric: horse assigned to Lancer Hanmet Danshor.

Twilight, The: legend?: descendants of the survivors of Er who live in dreams. From dream observations, their skin shined white, like starlight(not at all like northern humyn), and their hair and eyes can be any color of the rainbow. It is uncertain if they have physical forms or are essence powerful spirits lingering after the Cataclysm.

Twining: Dwen tool and ornamentation of twisted wood around their ankles and legs that assist with walking through trees. Can be used for protection.

Tynlar: Tentynlar Aldwyn

Tyreen: of Tyrum, also a resident.

Tyrum: (from tyrumeave, tyreameave = the three horns) coastal island city in the south Ethynsul known shipbuilding.

Uncle, dowager: older adult unmarried son of a woman in an estate. Has rank over Uncles married into the house.

Uncle, estate: a man with authority of the domestic estate matters due to marrying into an estate.

Unders: underwear

Vardashi: Shari word for elfyn.

Varga: Nord word for Thyn-wolf

Varsadmer: City-Ship

Vineflower: name of Shedann Farthal's favorite toy, a Dwen tree doll.

Vinings: Dwen decorative accent of living vines, worn on the arms like bracelets. Can be used defensively.

Vision: a brief premonition of danger. Unlike Reverie, is not fixed or inevitable. A Vision may also be an illusion for entertainment.

Voice, The: the speaker for Parliament.

Voice: political representatives in Parliament.

Wahoon yal Nomney: diving school herder [Black Seal]

War-king: a man skilled in fighting and martial arts.

Wasps: Federation elite cavalry.

Waudans: tribal humyns who inhabit the Azhinazu jungle.

Welansha, Yulen:(Capt) Sea Mother [The Dragon]

Weshet-ah-heem: large maleen city

Wildling(s): common word for Yino, not exactly offensive, but many consider disrespectful.

Wing: Luserani magical artifact used for flight. Made of the bones of birds and dragons.

Wolast, Ta: magi [Black Seal]

Woodweaver: officer in charge of all deck, hull and sail repairs, especially involving wood-essence. Usually Dwen.

Yalinsinmar: Previous Emissary of the Meer Conclave

Yastol: traditional Dwen crown of leaves headdress used to regulate wood-essence.

Yino: the least offensive name for the traveller culture known as "Wildlings". From, A'Yinomehey = The Bereft of the Forest. Displaced from their land after the God Storm.

YL: Year of Lots. Beginning of the modern Sulani calender. "Lots" refer to the first government of mothers allotted by vote after the abdication of the Sunqueen.

Illustrations

TOPS

Details of a Tyreen City-ship by Deck

Aftcastle

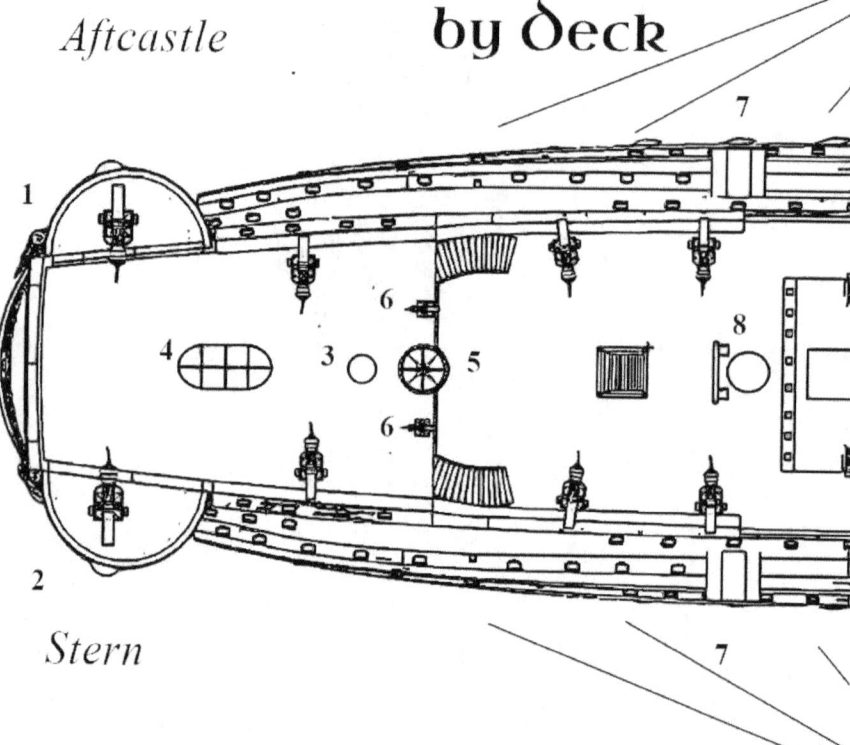

Stern

10 Cargo port entry
11 Skidbeams(boats not shown)
12 Bell tower
13 Fore mast
14 Solcannon
15 Cathead
16 Anchor
17 Observation
18 Bowsprit

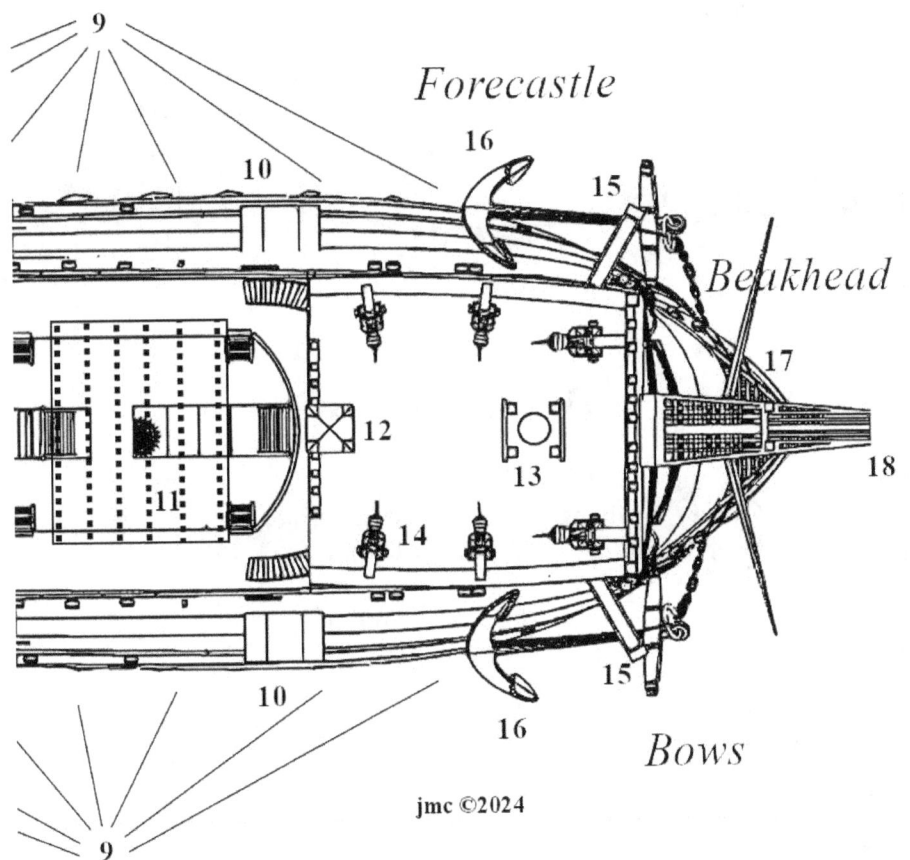

Forecastle

Beakhead

Bows

jmc ©2024

Quarterdeck

1 Captain's cabin
2 Gallery
3 Pilot's mess
4 Master's cabin
5 Secretary's cabin
6 Wheel
7 Cage pillar

8 Magi berth
9 Ship sadol
10 Ship Adept's cabin
11 Study/scriptorium
12 Dream chamber
13 Magi gallery

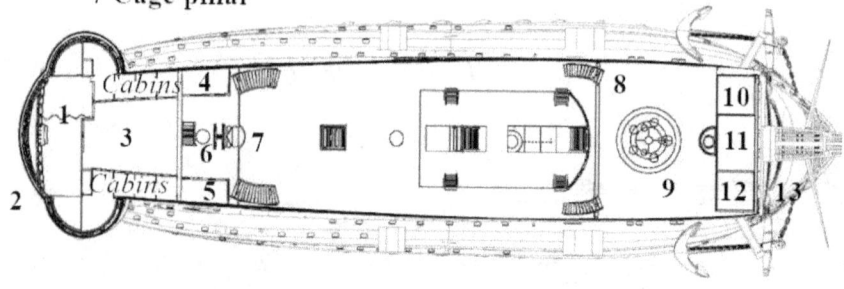

Upper Deck

1 Officer's gallery
2 Wardroom
3 Heart chamber
4 Toilet
5 Baths

6 Crew Mess
7 Galley
8 Stores
9 Galley compost

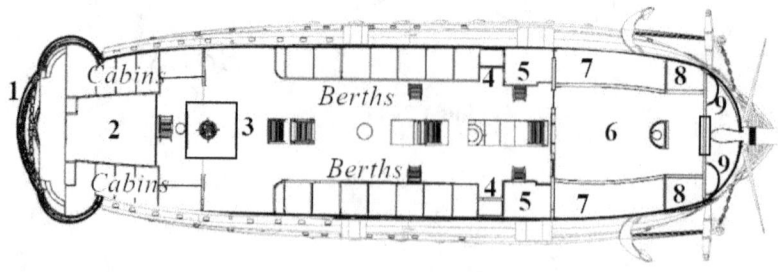

jmc ©2024

Middle Deck

1 Gallery
2 Ranks Officer/Midship mess
3 Toilet
4 Jeer capstan
5 Port entry
6 Fore capstan
7 Cargo port entry
8 Commisary
9 Stove/forge
10 Chain capstan

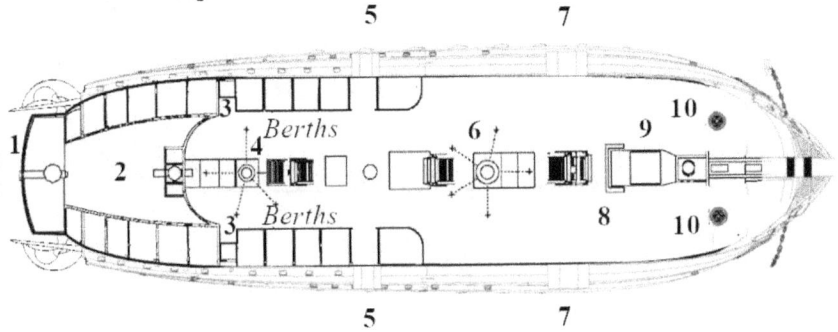

Lower Deck

1 Tiller
2 Toilet/washing room
3 Lower jeer capstan
4 Lower fore capstan
5 Drilling/work area
6 Chain windlass
7 Manger

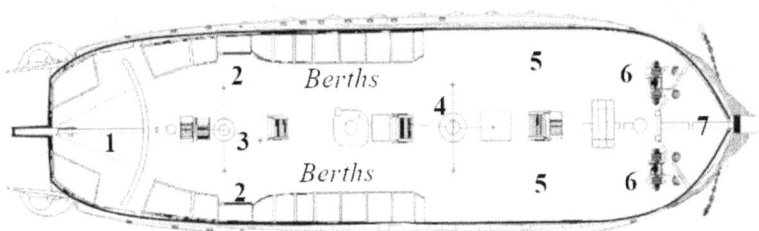

jmc ©2024

575

Orlop Deck

1 Steward/food supplies
2 Spirits and lant
3 Dry goods
4 Purser's cabin
5 Stores
6 Armory, Guard/Marines
7 Marine berth
8 Ship's Prefect cabin
9 Healing supplies
10 Healers

11 Lamp/light supplies
12 Pump room
13 Cockpit
14 Sail room
15 Cable tier
16 Crewmaster's cabin
17 Woodweaver's cabin
18 Weaver's walk
19 Top of chain hold

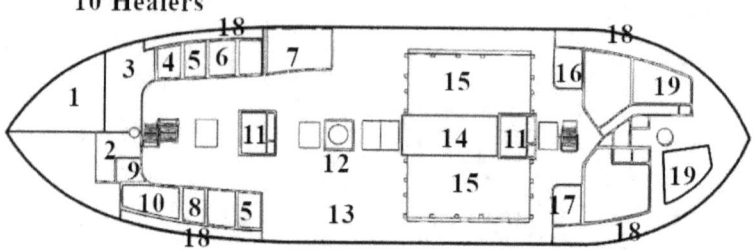

Hold

1 Cradle
2 Diver's berth
3 Diving supplies/ drink vines
4 Water
5 Well
6 Arrow locker

7 Store room
8 Armory
9 Chain hold

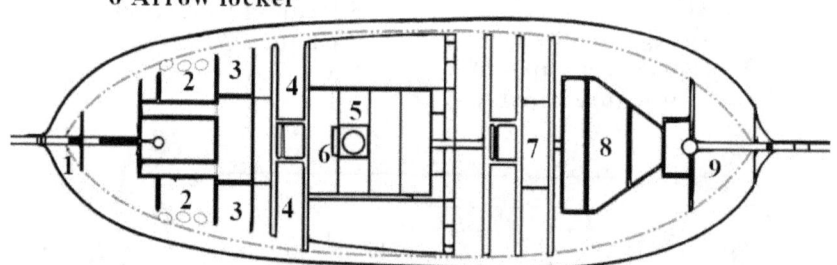

jmc ©2024

Tyreen Naval Insignia

Admiral
Commodore
Fleet Commander
Captain
Lieutenant Copilot
Lieutenant
Ensign
Midship

jmc ©2024

577

Solcannon

jmc ©2024

Shari Scorpion Warship

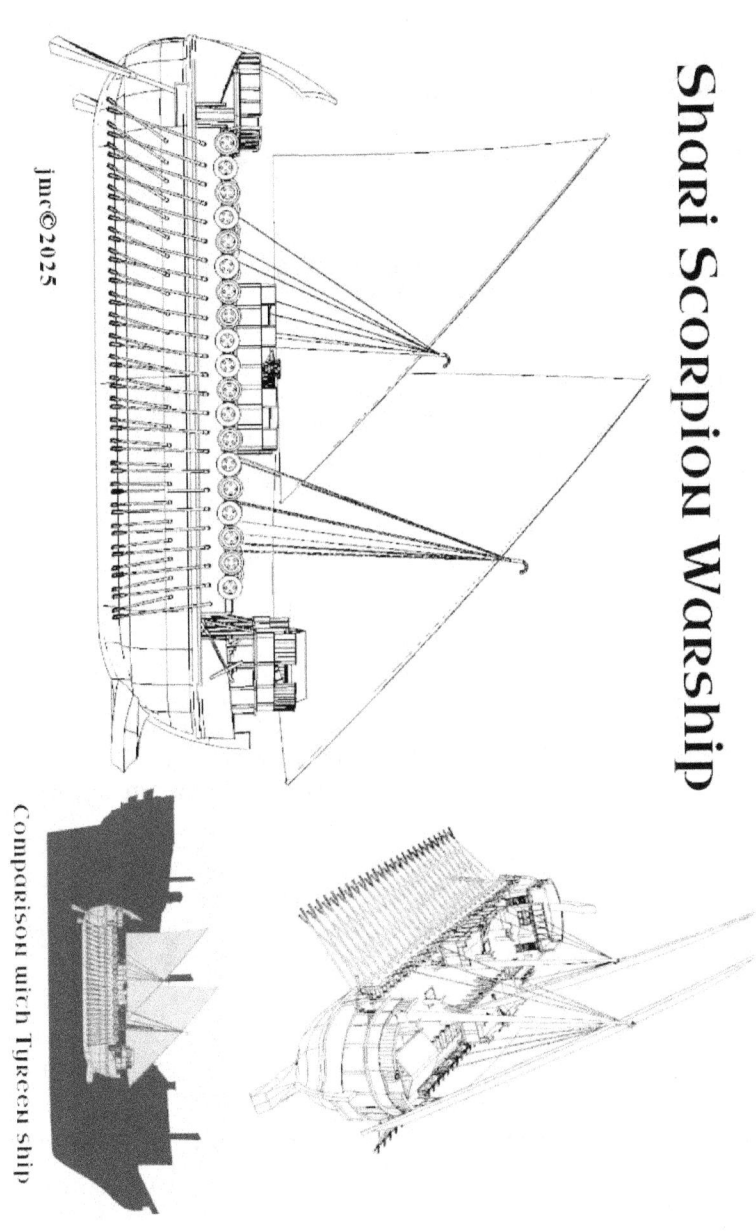

jmc©2025

Comparison with Tyreen ship

A Select Time-line of Historical Events

BL: Before the War of Lots. Historical reckoning before the founding of the Sulani Federation.
YL: Year of Lots. Historical reckoning after the War of Lots.
AL: Age of Light. Reckoning from the beginning of the first Sunqueen's rule to the abdication of Her Shining Majesty Daris Orvanae Halgyn.

20,000 BL~		The Cataclysm: large meteor strikes the Orb about 24,000-26,000 years ago.
15,000 BL~		Migration from the shelter of the Mother Tree.
14,500 BL~		Bright Plains settled, agriculture developed and discovery of solstone deposits in the Ta Meloshok mountain hills. Pottery and glass culture flourish with the use of solstone.
14,000 BL		Metalwork and smelting begin. The Elfyn Bronze Age.
11,500 BL		Rise of feudal lors and struggles to control solstone mines and placers.
11,300 BL		Iron replaces bronze as feudal Lors seek military dominance.
10,050 BL		The first steel made by resistance sympathetic wizard smiths in Ta Wenthia(Meridian); the secret of manufacture is kept for decades.
9800~ BL	Year 1 of the Age of Light	Final rebellion and overthrow of the Lors; the mothers of the nation are united under Elushian Trynador Halgyn who becomes the first Sunqueen. Solstone is declared a resource owned collectively by mothers and men of the Sula nation.
9791 BL	9 AL	Land allotment reforms. Mills, looms and various shop industries bring security and prosperity to the nation for the first time in hundreds of years.
6000 BL~		Humyn in Sharmain Valley develop primitive agriculture about 10,000 years ago.
5,120 BL –	4680 AL –	Rule of Sunqueen Selastimor the Great. Age of explo-

4,730 BL	5510 AL	ration and public works; Queen's roads built and national postal system founded. Order of Magi founded. Grimsteel first used to strengthen steel edges.
4000 BL – 3000 BL		Migration of humyn from high Altan pastoral steppes, through the Sulani Realm and Ta Dwenoshire. Those peaceful are allowed to pass unhindered; those who act maliciously are culled. These tribes eventually settle in the far west and north of the continent in what is now Cambria and include the modern tribes of Gaels, Prithi, Tenes and Nords. The history of the journey through elfyn lands are the basis of humyn folklore about elves and fairies. South and east of the Sulani Realm, in the Sharitan flats, the agricultural settlements grow that will be the future city of Tamask.
224BL	10000 AL	HSM Daris Orvanae Halgyn is forced to banish her twin after an attempted coup. Her sister's followers pillage several Dwen settlements as they travel, leading to the Outrage of the Forest.
200-? BL		In Eurthantal: Fall of the High Queen of Avigon.
103 BL		In Eurthantal: The Epiphany of the Empire of Eurthantal and rise of Our Avatar Emporator who founds a religious matriarchal cult under the claim she is the incarnation of the One True Mother God.
5 BL	10219 AL The last year of the Age of Light	Unable to find her sister's band to bring to justice, Daris abdicates and goes into self imposed exile, her house eventually settling on the island Tyrumaeve. Descendants of the Sunqueen's dynasty remain head of state but the honorific is changed from Her Shining Majesty (HSM) to Her Humble Majesty(HHM).
0		The War of Lots. With the fall of monarchy rule, an emergency voting or allotment to manage affairs is instituted: mothers and men of the commons are bidden to volunteer those souls they consider to be worthy to guide the nation through the unstable times and build a new government of mothers. Being alloted to rule in government in an emergency is considered a duty not to be shirked; many "winners" of the vote are resentful and one woman is jailed for attempting to flee it.

19 YL		The Midwife Government of six mothers and one man lay down the foundations of the Federation of Mothers.
192 YL		Pharon, ruler of the North Azhins, consolidates Tamask into a city state, the Tahmory. A lush culture of building and gardens flourishes until wars with competing humyn territories start desertification.
999 YL		The God Storm: Lightning sparked forest fires decimate the Ethynsul hills driving the Dwen population out. Opportunistic Sula landowners expand their properties under the pretext that without trees, the territory is no longer part of Ta Dwenoshire. The Voice and Parliament suggest mediation to both parties but don't intervene while the Dwen are evicted. Some travel north to Dwenoshire, but most try to regrow and squat only to be driven out and forced into a nomadic traveller lifestyle. They become the Yino, commonly called Wildlings.
1000 YL		First Sultan conquers Tamask, then unifies the lands Lin and Alon into the humyn nation Sharitan. Many Shari flee north to Federation lands.
1201 YL		The Burning: Plague strikes the western continent sea board. In the city Gashora, Shari humyn are scapegoated and flee, many killed as their boats are burned by hateful Sula in the Federation Patrol. Survivors reach Tyrumaeve, now called Tyrum, and are given sanctuary by Her Humble Majesty.
1201-1295 YL		The Barrier to the Forest is made by the Dwen nation in response to The Burning. 1251 diplomacy reestablished but forest remains closed.
1203 YL		Battle of the Blue Fields: Last alliance between elfyn and Thyn horses against the Sultan of Sharitan's invasion. Solstone cannons scorch a quarter of the humyn army in the first minute of engagement. Soon the humyn are routed and driven out or killed. No ruler of Sharitan has attempted a land invasion of Federation lands since.
1257 YL		Sultan's dynasty falls. Rise of Zorastar class that revere elfyn wisdom. 300 years of peace in the region follows.
1542 YL		Rise of second Sultan dynasty in Sharitan.

2153 YL		After expanding Sharitan territories, a mix of disaster, war and famine lead to the fall of the second dynasty and the loss of the nation. Lin and Alon war and the region is unstable for hundreds of years after.
2201 YL		Grim edged steel perfected in the Shard Hills, adding strength to the carbon wave process.
2510 YL		Piracy in NW Cambria becomes an unacceptable nuisance, causing Parliament to create laws declaring the sea lanes a Federation protectorate. Territories and humyn tribes affected are to be governed and midwifed to civilized standards. First roads in Cambria built.
2531 YL		Recognition of Tyrum as a Federation city, with maintenance to build aqua driven ships under the command of the Admiralty.
2590 YL		The Black Ramothyn circumnavigates the Orb.
4680 YL		A new Sultan rises in Sharitan, reuniting the nation under a religious patriarchal cult of the Eversky. The Sharitan Empire grows steadily for the next few centuries, mostly east and south.
4922 YL		First Light Impression images developed.
5000 YL		Invention and spread of the modern printing press.
6016 YL		Eurthantal: Our Avatar's government makes plans to expand the frontier, a popular distraction for the pious.
Koigeal 29th		Battle of Gate Step
Quol 7th		Military duel between Lt. Roel and L. Farthal. Farthal is the victor.
13th		The passing of Aeon magi Ta Murdan.
		Dispatches report a planned attack at sea from the humyn nation Sharitan. Volunteers are requested to join the Federation Marshal's guard as she travels to oversee the Admiralty in Tyrum.
15th		Lancer Elderyn Farthal leaves Falls Gate Keep with the Marshal's escort.
16th		Luserani flyer Lekatol arrives in Tyrum

In Victory or the Otherside